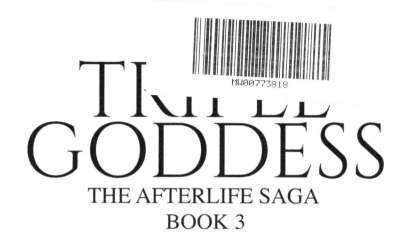

# TRIPLE GODDESS

## THE AFTERLIFE SAGA

### BOOK 3

# STEPHANIE HUDSON

*The Triple Goddess*
*The Afterlife Saga #3*
Copyright © 2020 Stephanie Hudson
Published by Hudson Indie Ink
www.hudsonindieink.com

The Triple Goddess/Stephanie Hudson – 2nd ed.
ISBN-13 - 978-1-913769-20-8

*I would like to dedicate this book to my great uncle, Sapper Joseph H Close of Royal Engineers Corps, who gave his life for his country at Arnhem in September, 1944.*

*"The time was now and with this war men will fight, Holding themselves strong and gifting the Country with all their might"*

### 'This is my Time'

*In the distance I heard the call,*
*The enemy's coming, get down all,*
*And slowly I move, my mind going numb,*
*But my limbs are quick and my body not dumb.*

*I duck, I dive and I reach for cover*
*The men must be following, I think as I recover,*
*I take a minute amongst the fighting,*
*To wish myself back in the barracks sat down writing.*

*I think what I would say to all whom I love,*
*To all I hold dear and far from the bombs above,*
*But to wish myself anywhere but here's not enough,*
*For I am a soldier above and beyond all of the rough.*

*So through all the smoke, bullets and raining debris,*
*I think of my family and brothers of three,*
*My two sisters at home waiting to hear,*
*Anxiously worrying and praying for the all clear.*

*But as I stand here now hearing the cries of others,*
*I know I won't be coming home or seeing my brothers,*
*But what would I say and ask of them all,*
*Please look at my death as a man unable to let his Country fall.*

*"For all the courageous men and women who serve their country,*
*May their sacrifice help to bring Peace and Freedom to the world in*
*which we live"*

# WARNING!

This book contains explicit sexual content, some graphic language and a highly addictive Alpha Male.

This book has been written by a UK Author with a mad sense of humour. Which means the following story contains a mixture of Northern English slang, dialect, regional colloquialisms and other quirky spellings that have been intentionally included to make the story and dialogue more realistic for modern-day characters.

Please note that for your convenience language translations have been added to optimise the readers enjoyment throughout the story.

Also meaning…

No Googling is required ;)

Also, please remember that this part of a 12 book saga, which means you are in for a long and rocky ride. So, put the kettle on, brew a cup, grab a stash of snacks and enjoy!

Thanks for reading x

## CHAPTER 1
# FLIGHT OF FEARS

M y new life was born in the sky high above the world, riding along waves of a calm atmosphere where clouds were the only sight to see and now...well, it only seemed fitting that my death would begin the same way.

It may seem a tad dramatic but when sat opposite Death himself, it was hard to see any other outcome. I had been in the plane for hours now without any shining heroic attempt of a rescue being made and my hopes for such had plummeted along with all other ideas of surviving.

The silvery head of hair that kept catching the sun's rays flashed in my peripheral vision and was becoming harder to ignore. Who would have thought that Death would have had kind and handsome features? He reminded me of some typical ageing businessman who had a big white house, complete with picket fence, golden Labrador and a loyal wife baking cookies in a country style kitchen. Someone who went fishing in a small boat on the lake at weekends with his son before coming home with the catch of the day to cook on a grill for the family feast.

"As quaint and perfectly idyllic as that picture portrays I do, however, hate boats and get quite seasick." My head whipped up to see the man himself staring at me with a soft expression and his head cocked to one side as though studying me for more visions on what I believed would have suited this man more than that of the gruesome truth.

"How did you see that?" I asked, opening my mouth for the first time since leaving the airstrip in Portland.

"Ah well, although it is clear, my dear, that you possess a most extraordinary mind, it is quite easily accessible when such turmoil and despair enters one's state of thought. I find you like an open book, only one I wouldn't wish to read...no, no, far too depressing." He closed his eyes and shook his head as if to emphasise this point.

"Well, please excuse my manners, how terrible of me to be thinking things as depressing as my death and never seeing the man I love again when I should what...be thinking of happy little unicorns racing over golden hills under rainbow covered blue skies...? How inconsiderate of me!" I said, laced with sarcasm. I was sure somewhere deep down I should have been cowering in fear from my plane journey with Death, but for some reason I just couldn't find the point, let alone the energy.

"Oh, my dear, please do call me by my name, Death sounds so very dreary." At this my mouth actually fell open cartoon style.

"My name is Carrick, young one and I don't see where you get this notion of your end being so near."

"Are you joking?" I almost found myself screaming or laughing hysterically, either one I think would have been acceptable conduct for such a conversation.

"Where I am taking you is not to your grave but most likely to your destiny." At this I snorted.

"I don't think so, you're taking me to Lucius, right?" He nodded at my question.

"Then you are escorting me to my end just like any other poor soul you encounter."

"And what makes you so sure?" I kept expecting Mr Death Carrick to keep losing his cool but for someone who was in charge of taking life, I was very surprised at how chilled out a guy he was.

"Well, the last time I saw Lucius we didn't exactly play checkers and sip iced tea!" At this he laughed heartily, throwing his head back making the sun dance in his silver streaks, almost like a halo.

"Well let me be the one to assure you, your life is not on my books and Lucius will need you quite alive for him to accomplish his plan."

"And that being?" I raised my hand and made little circles as if this might help to prompt him to elaborate.

"Oh no, my young one, it is not for me to say but I will go as far as to promise you this, for if the Gods wish your safe return to their instrumental son Dominic Draven, then no Vampire King and his growing army will prevent such an action from taking place."

"Then what on earth would he want with me? I mean it's not like he can defeat the Gods, then why even bother trying?" This conversation was draining my mental ability to stay calm. I mean, here I was ripped away from my life, with the only notion that my death was all that was left to follow, filling my every thought and the man in front of me telling me what...? That I'm not on his bloody books! Like life and death was just another number for an accountant to consider. I bet tax season was a riot for this guy.

"These are questions beyond my pay grade, so to speak. But have no fear, if Lucius wanted you dead he would have commissioned meto do so." I couldn't believe that at this he actually smiled at me as though this was a comforting thought. I shook my head at him in disbelief.

I took his silence for what it was, nothing more to be said on the matter, but one thing was for sure, I was secretly shitting myself for what was to come next. If there was one man in this world who scared me more than my past psycho stalker Morgan then that was the Vampire King, Lucius. Weeks of endless nightmares mixed with a very gruesome crescendo, which I foolishly allowed myself to think was the end of my torment, was to be a constant reminder of Draven's arch nemesis.

However, every attempt to get to me had been crushed by Draven's protective nature...that was up until now. No, no, now I was on my way to become a puppet in the man's attempts at getting back at my boyfriend. Oh, of course it would have helped my situation if I had been forewarned what it was exactly that the two had been feuding over all these years. All I knew was that Lucius wasn't the King's first name or life for that matter. He began his existence as one of Jesus' disciples and his name was what the common world knew as the meaning of betrayal.

Judas.

The very mention of this name can be used to hurt or dismiss the one that has wronged us in some way. History has taught us many valuable lessons in life but not all are to be believed in the ways in which they are written. As a huge history buff, I was used to relying on the evidence, but after being thrown into the supernatural world of the Dravens I soon learned that everything has its place in the world and its importance for those who rule our lives yet can't be seen.

Judas played such a part, being the important role of wrongly accused conspirator in Jesus' death. Draven described it best once, in which the memory of a great man outlives that great man. Jesus asked one of his most faithful followers to help him accomplish his wishes and that of his Holy Father. Of course, word of Judas' compliance and not his betrayal never found its way to the other disciples as it should have done. Nothing could have prevented what came next in the way of his most brutal death, but the renouncing of his faith by dying, sun cracked lips was what altered his afterlife by the hands of a very different god.

Bitterness carried into his next life for all things that were once his strengths, his life and his worshipping faith, now lost in a hateful vengeance for the Gods themselves for what he believed was his betrayal. In a way, although difficult, I felt sorry for him all things considered. He started his life a man as any other, only to let the all-consuming hate twist and grow with the power within him. After all, he and Draven had once been friends and coexisted, often working together but now, well that was another matter entirely and one I knew very little about. For some reason Draven not only neglected to tell me any details of these events but outright refused. So here I was now, with only Death for company by the name of Carrick and a stomach that felt like it had been pumped with lead.

Carrick kept noticing the way I would wipe my sweaty palms on my jeans but thankfully refrained from commenting. I think if he would have told me not to worry again I would have pulled some hair out and thrown it at him in a full out hissy fit. He might think that no harm would come to me but he didn't remember in detail the last nightmare Lucius bestowed on me and the everlasting mark of the most painful experience of my life. Think flesh melting from bone and molten lava replacing the blood in my veins and you would have some small concept of why such an event remained firmly embedded in the darkest corner of my brain. And that was only a dream! Now of course, I was to meet the man and to think of what hell he could put me through, how much could my body endure and how far would he take his new instrument of revenge? I wondered what state my body and my mind would be in if I was ever to make it back to the arms of my Dark Knight.

A shell of myself, was all my thoughts could conjure.

"That is quite enough, my dear!" Carrick spoke, bringing my mind back to the present.

"You will be a mere shell before I even get you to my employer if you carry on with this despair." I merely shrugged my shoulders and said,

"I already am, without Draven."

"Ah young love, or for Draven a lifetime in waiting, how sad it is to have lost you now after only a short time." I couldn't believe he actually looked sad for my situation. His eyes met ones of disbelief and then turned cold in a heartbeat.

"I am not without feelings, young one and I can only sympathise to your future but if you think now is bad then you have very little idea of what is in store for one that is chosen. He cannot save you from your fate nor can he prevent it from playing out, like the dawn brings the light and the dusk brings the night, for a son of the Gods knows this. But you are not only young and human but also ignorant of the ways of our world and that does you no favours." I actually wanted to say "Well durr!" but refrained.

"So, if you're not without feelings and can sympathise then why not let me go?" Okay it was a long shot but what did I have to lose?

"I am afraid your safety on getting you to Lucius is all I can provide. Once my blood is given in bond then my life also is in the hands of my employer. If I was to fail, then my life would be given in return for the life I am commissioned." This was said so matter of fact I snorted.

"But nice try," he said, laughing to himself.

"So, what you're trying to say is that I should just give up, is that it? Just resign myself to the inevitable, is that what you would do Carrick, just lay down and give up?" I was getting angry now and worked up, to the point that my hands made their way into fists and my nails penetrated the skin on my palms.

"Not at all dear one, my you are feisty indeed, much suited to a King such as Draven. I merely stated that given the inner strength you surely possess, you should rise above fear and never lose faith in the extraordinary gifts you have been blessed with. After all, they will save your soul more than once I am sure of it. Keep your mind locked firmly shut to those who wish to control it and you will find you hold more power than even that of the man you so deeply love. Heed my advice, young one and take it with you if nothing else of our time together." At this I lost all my anger like a deflating balloon in the hands of a child. I had nothing else to lose but a lifetime of understanding to gain. It seemed to me that the advice of this man was the most important I was ever to receive in my life and I was not arrogant or stubborn enough not to see it for what it was...a warning.

So, with this in mind, I did what I knew was the only thing in my power to do, I blocked my mind off to the world. I built not only walls keeping out any intruders but a mental fortress. I spent what felt like a great deal of time picturing my mind as some priceless artefact that needed castle walls ten feet thick and when that didn't feel enough I would place the most important emotions inside a locked vault made of pure titanium, this was where Draven would be safe and nothing else mattered.

"Ah peace at last, you have done well dear one, your mind is nothing but a blank and to one of my kind that is quite rare indeed." At this I actually found myself smiling. It felt a bit like getting praise from a teacher or a pat on the head from your father for cleaning your room.

"A drink to celebrate," he said, motioning a stewardess with his hand, who I had quite forgotten was even on the same plane. She was like every other flight attendant I had seen, dressed in a tight navy-blue suit with a blood red neckerchief tied firmly in place around the slim column of her swan like neck. Hair pulled back into a twisted roll held there by what could have been magic for all I knew as not a clip or grip could be seen. And to top off the generic similarities, a killer smile covered in thick glossy red lipstick to match her perfectly manicured nails.

I felt like doing anything but celebrating but as the tray was placed before me after Carrick had helped himself, I felt somewhat compelled to accept his hospitality. After all, better to be on the good side of the devil you know than the devil you don't. I took the champagne flute, the lower half of which was in the design of a metal spine and the glass held by the ribcage, I shuddered at the thought of how I had seen Carrick in his true form as a master of death.

It was hard to think that the man sat so casually in front of me now, had the ability to strike fear into the most courageous man at just one second of insight to how he truly looked. Death, you imagine to be cloaked in black from head to foot, long staff held in the icy grip of a fleshless hand, with most of the horrors thankfully hidden. But some think what is concealed is more frightening than knowing, that one's imagination is scarier than the truth the eyes see...

They would be wrong.

Carrick... a walking torture that you prayed wouldn't be taking you to a place where he had once walked and been subjected to the horrors that had resulted in his ghoulish appearance. For what could have caused half his body to start decaying before the rest I do not know, nor do I ever wish to, but I will never forget the taste of bile that rose upon seeing it. Half a black cloak, hooded to hide his face only instead looked more like an oily second skin of burnt plastic. It had moulded to a powerful frame of solid shoulders, down to bulging biceps and hands that could crush skulls with very little effort. But that's where the flesh ended, and a bloodied skeleton continued. How only a twisted spine could hold so much without added muscle and tissue I couldn't fathom but the truth remained, and his immense power was a testament to the fact. He had brought the mighty Ragnar, my Viking protector, to his knees, something I didn't think possible. And in order to save his life I had given myself to Carrick as a willing soul for him to take far, far away from the one man who owned that soul.

Dominic Draven.

As my mind had wandered to only hours ago I saw that we seemed to be descending through the cloud bank. My heart instantly raised a couple of notches at the thought that my journey was coming to an end, to be handed over to the one person I didn't want to ever meet.

"Are we landing?"

"Shortly yes, but do not get yourself in a flurry, try and relax, I assure you the champagne is the best of the region, you should try it." He nodded to the glass that remained untouched and in a tight death grip, from my thoughts.

I looked down at the golden liquid and saw a sad reflection staring back, so without further prompting I gulped it down to the last drop. Carrick at least looked satisfied and turned back to the window to watch our descent. Meanwhile, as if being on standby, the stewardess came hurrying past to collect our empty glasses and returned back to remain unseen somewhere on the plane.

My grip, now without my glass, had turned to the thick leather armrests that held my body snug to the lazy boy style chair. If not for the circumstances that brought me to my first encounter of the luxury of a private jet, then I would be enjoying this flight. However, no matter how comfortable my butt was, I couldn't help trying to will the ground to get smaller instead of bigger. The patches of urban jungle were getting closer until soon the tiny insects running along strips of grey were seen to be cars on motorways, making their way in life.

That's when my vision started to blur slightly, as if a heavy night of drinking was finally catching up with me.

I could see the sun in the distance getting lower and dusk fast approaching. My body was torn between wanting to run for the door and throw myself out and being rooted to the seat. I didn't want the next part of this nightmare to play out and there was nothing more terrifying than knowing what waited for me at the end of my destination. Carrick was scary enough, but I would rather provoke his wrath than meet Lucius in the living flesh any day of the week. So, I mentally prepared myself for the landing of a lifetime. As soon as the plane stopped I would bolt for the door and hoped...no, no, more like prayed that I would make it to freedom.

I think Carrick took my tightly closed eyes for one of fear as the plane's wheels hit the tarmac. Of course, thanks to the solid walls I had built, my mind was no longer accessible, and my thoughts were far from the plane hitting land. I was gearing myself up until my blood pumped at a greater speed thanks to the adrenaline now coursing its way around my body like an unstoppable river. Just a little bit longer and then there was a chance, just a small chance, that I could make it...I had to.

The plane made its stop outside a hanger pretty much like the one it left, and I gathered they didn't want to draw too much attention to the fact that they were kidnapping to Customs. The question "Do you have anything to declare?" sprang to mind.

I was close to bouncing in my seat trying to choose the right moment and hoping that Carrick didn't get up before me. These things were racing around in my mind when the sound of the door opening made my final decision for me. Without a second thought I jumped out of my seat and raced down in between seats like the one I had just vacated. I saw my chance and didn't hold back as my legs pushed me to the only freedom I could see. I was surprised at the speed I seemed to travel, as with one turn of my head I saw that Carrick hadn't even made it out of his seat by the time I reached the door. I turned back and soon realised why.

The door was fully open, and a figure stood in its opening preventing all chance of escape. My eyes tried to fully understand the trick they were playing. Surely this couldn't be real...it just couldn't be.

I was losing my mind, or was this some mind control, a cruel game, anything but the truth that now faced me. This person was my friend, not an enemy...how did this happen? When had my friends turned against me?

"Hello Keira." The voice that had greeted me so many times before didn't sound right with the picture in front of me.

"It...it... can't be!" I finally managed to get out as tears streamed down my flushed cheeks. I turned around now understanding why Carrick hadn't even bothered to try and stop me, he never needed to. He actually looked sorry for me until then I saw the nod he gave the betrayer behind me. That's when things started to get numb. Like my brain was shutting itself down from shock but when my legs started to cave I knew the horrible truth...

I had been drugged.

Hands grabbed me and pulled me securely so that I wouldn't fall and I couldn't help but shout out at the contact,

"HOW COULD YOU?"

"I'm sorry, but there was no other way." That voice, the voice of a friend, was the last I heard before a sickening blackness took me over leaving me feeling cold, frozen to the bone with a bitterness so deep I could drown in it.

Trust was a clever thing, one that accrued so blindly that it didn't take thinking about, that was until you discovered the reason for every bad thing that had happened the last few months now had a name...

*Traitor.*

## CHAPTER 2
# DEATH OF A FRIENDSHIP

I woke to the sound of voices deep in conversation and if I wasn't mistaken my name was the subject choice. It felt like I had a hangover without the happy memories flooding back from the night before. I remembered feeling like this a few times before and it was a strange thing to admit that it had been far too many times that I had been drugged against my will. Hell, it was becoming a monthly occurrence.

I decided to go along with what I usually did in these circumstances and that was to remain limp and play dead. I opened my eyes into slits and turned my head slightly to free both ears. I could pick up a few things this way, one being where I was lay. The combination of leather against my skin and the slight rocking motion didn't take an intellectual genius to realise that I was lay spread out on a car seat. Also, the gentle hum of an engine could be heard as an undercurrent to the conversation taking place in front of me. The second was the people that were mentioning my name so frequently. Of course, there was Mr Death himself, Carrick and I had to confirm my fears one last time by opening my eyes,

Yep there sat my friend...

*Karmun.*

They both sat in the seat in front of me with only the backs of their heads on view. Carrick's silver head looked a dark grey with the lack of sunlight, only flashing lighter when the orange glow of street lamps hit the window. Of course, there was no mistaking the glossy black hair that flowed like a silken sheet down the shoulders of Afterlife's barman.

I wanted to cry. I had to bite my lip to prevent it. Karmun was my friend and all this time he had been a traitor to not only me but to his King. Nothing made sense, why and how flooded my mind but I knew I needed to concentrate if I was to find out any answers to the never-ending stream of questions.

"What will happen to the girl?" I heard Karmun's deep accented voice ask.

"It is a little late for that now, don't you think?" Carrick sounded amused. I had to agree with his statement.

"I had very little choice in the matter and you know it. I have fulfilled my side of the bargain and I am more than ready to receive your end of the deal."

"My end? Don't you mean your own?" He asked in earnest. At this Karmun just shrugged.

"It is all just a means to an end, whichever way you look at it."

"You care for this girl, I think?" Once again Carrick sounded amused by his statement.

"I don't want her to suffer during the time until the King can reclaim her, and I know not of any plans that Lucius holds for her." I could see that Karmun was about to turn around, so I slammed my eyes shut and tried to steady my beating heart. It was only when I heard him shift back around that I continued my spying.

"She has been through a lot and does not deserve what is happening now."

"Are you trying to cleanse your soul, because you know I'm not the right man for that!" Carrick snapped.

"I care little for what becomes of my soul! And the only soul I care about will soon be safe once again. Speaking of which, when will we get there, Keira will not stay under for long until she will need another dose and she is more than a little wilful." Karmun let out a sigh as this was all very taxing on his nerves and for that I had a huge urge to just smack him upside the head.

"Yes, so I have seen. It will not be long until you are reunited with your precious one, but the girl's journey is far from over."

"Where will you take her?" At this I could almost hear one of Carrick's eyebrows raise.

"What, you think I would have time to get that information to anyone before the inevitable?" Karmun laughed deep within his throat, a sound I had heard many a time.

"True, with the deal made I doubt there would be much harm. She is to go to Germany where Lucius awaits her most eagerly." I tried not to shudder at this thought.

"So, it's true what they say...the Vampire King has remained strong in his quest with the Nazi's beliefs?" At this my ears pinged up like a dog on smelling an intruder. Nazis... What on earth did they have to do with a Vampire King? All I knew was the rumours that Hitler had had a huge following in the supernatural and occult but an alliance, was it possible?

"I know little of Lucius' plans nor do I want to, my only reasons for being here are the same as yours, although granted, our ends differ greatly." I heard Karmun snort before giving his response.

"That they do but answer me this, what will you do when Draven catches up with you? Surely you won't expect him to let you live beyond minutes of such an encounter?" Karmun said in a very smug tone, which I couldn't help agreeing with.

"Do I look worried? Even one such as he would not dare to take a Death Dealer from this realm."

"You can't be that sure, can you? Not even when you took from him his Chosen One, the Electus? She is the key and something is coming that only she will unlock but let me guess...you care little for the prophecy or the balance which the King keeps. If that is the case my friend then my fate I welcome, yours I would not!" At this Carrick lost all his cool exterior and let loose a primal snarl. His hand whipped out so quickly I jumped back but thankfully the noise I made was drowned out by Karmun's gasp of terror.

Carrick's hand had encircled Karmun's throat and he was squeezing the life out of him with very little effort. The deadly grip changed between that of the flesh of a man and the blood dripping bone of Death itself, Death at its core, Death in its truest nature. I could hear the joints cracking as he flexed, like wood splitting on a roaring fire and I couldn't help the shudder that crept up my skin like insects crawling up my veins.

"You will remember your place, Kokabiel! You may be ready to die but do not forget that I care little for your last wishes and your windpipe feels a little brittle in my grasp, like a soul of the dammed. Almost too easy to take and send to an awaiting damnation of my choice. What do you say now?" Carrick hadn't lost an ounce of

13

composure during this threatening speech, but the words sent more fear into me than that of a roaring lion. His eerie calm was of such dominance that there was no doubt this dude was a big player in the supernatural game of fate and I was almost sorry to think about what that fate had in store for my traitorous friend Karmun.

He took Karmun's spluttering for submission and released his throat with an audible snap making Karmun cry out in pain as now one bone looked too close to the skin and protruded at an awkward angle. I had to try extremely hard not to gag out loud as I turned away from the gruesome sight. When the acid left my mouth, I turned to find Karmun's head was missing and soon realised he had bent his body to cradle his head in his hands near his lap. He was sobbing words in a different language and Carrick looked out of the window as though he was alone in the world.

It took a while for Karmun to calm enough to sit back up and acknowledge his mistake. I guess it was a big no, no to threaten a soul collector. That or he had hit a major sore spot when mentioning Draven's reaction to my kidnapping and considering what happened the last time that attempt was made, I didn't doubt Karmun's words of warning. But obviously Carrick didn't appear to be worried, which brought on the mental picture of that day at the warehouse. What if Carrick had been there? Would Draven have ripped open the van, saw Carrick and said "Oh, didn't know it was you... sorry, you just go ahead!" I didn't think so somehow!

This once again brought my thoughts back to Draven. What would he be doing now? Going crazy with worry and an anger that would equal Mount Vesuvius' eruption I could imagine. Did he have a plan? And most importantly when would he put that plan into effect?

I riddled my mind full of questions like this for what seemed like an age. It was only when the SUV began to slow down that I finally broke away from my quiet meltdown. What now? Make another break for it...'cause I have to say, that didn't fare so well for me last time.

"Is he here?" Karmun spoke for the first time since Carrick's violent stand on respect and he sounded gruff and sore. Like a cold, flu, tonsillitis and bronchitis all rolled into one.

"Have no fear Kokabiel, I keep my promises, despite my urges." He said the word 'urges' in a demonic voice that could rattle the bones of the fiercest warriors. Me, well I was no warrior and the flinch my body made was testament to that, but I did have one over on most people...this wasn't the first time I'd heard a demon's voice.

"Are you ready to do what was discussed?" Karmun asked in a sombre voice that I had never heard from him before.

"But of course, it is after all, what I was created to do. And did you really think you both could just go back to the way it was before?" Carrick snorted after his last statement.

"Of course not! The King no doubt knows of my betrayal and after the warehouse attempt was made his spies were far too close to discovering the truth. They knew her drinks were being spiked but I doubt he realised just how long it had been happening." After Karmun said this I had to bite my lip from crying out in anger! All this time I had been blindly trusting him as a friend when really God only knows how many times he had betrayed that trust. I felt stupid and utterly naive when thinking back to all those times we had laughed together but most of all, the strongest emotion was hurt.

"I am curious, when was it you were first commissioned by Lucius?"

"When Constantine was taken from me, before the girl even arrived at Afterlife." I remembered Karmun speaking of this Constantine before and I also remembered the sad and desperate look on his face as he spoke of him. Now it was becoming clearer but the next question on the tip of my brain was asked by Carrick.

"And how did Lucius know the girl would even be found? From what I know of the Chosen One it was prophesied that she was always the one to find, not be found?" For the first time Carrick looked truly interested and Karmun just shrugged.

"It is of little matter and I do not have the answers either way, but the fact remains that Lucius knew of the girl before the Dravens ever did. I believe his plan only ever had one flaw."

"Which was?" I almost asked this at the same time as Carrick but thankfully realised I wasn't part of this conversation, just the choice of topic!

"He didn't count on not being able to control her," Karmun confessed.

"And that's where you came in no doubt," Carrick replied dryly. The car had now stopped completely, and I wondered what they were waiting for? I had to resist the urge to sit up and see where we were but once again stopped myself. There was no harm in letting them believe I was still under the drugs.

"At first, I was only there to see, to make sure the Electus and the King continued along the path of their fate but it soon became apparent that the girl's natural power was being triggered by the King's ever growing presence. Lucius was losing his control and needed my unique gifts to help control the girl." Karmun looked frustrated and dragged a hand down his face. He didn't keep his gaze away from his side of the window as if he was waiting for someone...which I guessed he was.

"Yes, I saw his form of control, it was surprising indeed to find his only control lay within her dreams. She is powerful, there is no question to it and the walls around her mind are indestructible when needs be, I convinced her to keep these walls in place if she is to survive in our world." At this Karmun finally turned his head from the window to stare at Carrick in shock.

"You did...? But why?"

"And why not? I am not immune to the prophecy and just because I chose not to take a greater part in it, it is not without some interaction and if I can ease some of the injustice that is being bestowed upon an innocent girl then I am not so much of the cold-hearted bastard that you take me for."

"What makes you think she is ever going to be strong enough to do what is really expected of her? After all, she couldn't prevent my powers when used on her." Once again, I wanted to bitch slap him for the arrogant tone in his voice when saying this.

"Ah yes, the power of persuasion is a gift indeed and one I hear you excel at. I gathered it was your intervention that prevented the girl from speaking to Draven about all that was going on in her mind. Let me guess, you let her convince herself that her fears were unfounded and not worth mentioning to the man she loves?"

"Well, if you are unable to control a mind to do what you want, then try and lead her into convincing herself instead, after all, she cannot fight her own mind." Carrick actually looked like he admired Karmun's technique of mind control. I however looked disgusted! It actually all just fell into place. All those times when I couldn't convince myself to tell Draven what had been going on. Why I felt the need to lock those thoughts away and never let him see what had been happening under his nose all this time. I felt sick! I felt as though I had betrayed my heart, body and soul. Like my mind had lost its way and decided to turn against me.

"You used her own power against her. I can see now why Lucius used you."

"Yes, well it is over now. He will now have what he wants, and I will soon be whole again. Everyone gets what they want apart from the girl, whose fate, for the first time, is left uncertain." At this point Karmun turned around to look at me and I just managed to close my eyes in time.

"Keira, open your eyes, there is no reason to pretend, I know you are awake." Karmun called my bluff and I decided not to call his, so I opened my eyes and tried to sit up. My mind felt clouded when put in the upright position and I swayed slightly.

"Take it easy," Karmun said gently.

"Piss off asshole." I said calmly giving him my best evil eye.

"Okay, I deserve that." He said turning back around before opening his side door. The door slid back to reveal where we were, and I was surprised to see that we were in what looked like an underground car park. Strip lighting flickered above as though it only just had enough power to function. The walls were a mixture of dirt covered, ageing cement and X-rated graffiti that spoke volumes to which part of any city we were in. I could almost guarantee that if I left this concrete maze I would find barely dressed women on street corners and dark alleys full of junkies shooting up poison into their veins. Given the circumstances and the streets they were living on, I could hardly blame them for trying to see the world they lived in differently, even if just for one false minute.

Carrick made a motion with his head towards the open door for me to move from the back seat and get out of this black people carrier. When I didn't move he sighed and snapped out something I couldn't understand to Karmun.

"Saada tüdruk!" ('Get the girl' in Estonian) Once Carrick had spoken I found Karmun pulling the seat forward giving me room to get out. I decided not to fight and just get out peacefully. I didn't know when I would get my next opportunity to run, so I wanted to save my energy for battles I could win. As soon as I had my feet firmly on the ground my whole body hummed with anticipation, ready to fire my limbs into action. Okay, so I wasn't utterly convinced I would get away and outrun a Demon or an Angel but every fibre in my body was screaming that I had to at least try. All I needed was to get away long enough to find somewhere to hide and then wait for Draven to find me. It was a nice dream and one could only hope, so that was precisely what I did. I kept myself pumped and ready to go at any moment.

"Why aren't they here?" Karmun asked, clearly getting upset.

"Patience, Angel." Carrick said, taking out a mobile phone from his beige suit jacket after loosening his blood red tie. He flipped it open, pressed a button and then snapped,

"Speak to me!" In clipped tones. He nodded once before closing it again and depositing it back in his pocket.

"They will be here in but a moment." At this Karmun's shoulders relaxed considerably. However, mine took their place and tensed until my neck ached. Of course, it didn't help when another black SUV came into view. What was it with bad guys, did they have a specialist car dealership they all went to or did they just walk in and ask for something dark, threatening and with enough boot space for a body, to kidnap young mortal girls!

Like the one I had been in, the windows were all blacked out and when it stopped opposite us I couldn't help but move a few steps back. The doors opened and Karmun made a dramatic cry as a body was pushed out and thrown to the ground. He had been tied with his hands behind his back and it was clear he had been beaten many times as his face held a mixture of bruises, some almost healed and others fresh and angry looking. Karmun ran over to him and took his bruised mottled face in both hands.

"Gods, what have they done to you?" He wept as the other man was just coming round from his punch drunk slumber.

"K..Kar?" The man mumbled.

"Yes, it's me... it's me, I'm here now." Karmun was sobbing and holding his friend's beaten face to his own as both their foreheads met. It was such a touching moment I didn't realise that I too was shedding my own tears. It was quite clear that not only was this man Constantine but he was also Karmun's captured lover. So, this was why Karmun had done what he had...he didn't have a bloody choice! They had taken someone he loved away and tortured him until Karmun had all other options taken from him. Could I blame him anymore...? I looked deep but couldn't find the hate there that I had felt not so long ago. What wouldn't we do in life for our loved ones? Where was the line we wouldn't cross because looking at the scene in front of me, I think that line had been whipped away and replaced with a silver lining of hope. Tunnel vision and a mission to keep going until nothing else stood between these two and I could not find any blame in my soul to hold onto, so when men dressed in black got out and tore the two apart I couldn't help but cry harder for them.

"LET THEM GO!" I screamed moving forward towards them both with all past fear lost in my anger. Everyone stopped dead and turned to stare at me, including the two damned lovers. Carrick grabbed me back by my jacket and I twisted to try and get free.

"Calm yourself, young one." He whispered in my ear before nodding towards the thugs in black. They let Karmun and Constantine go and like magnets to metal they sprung forward into each other's arms.

"Tell me, oh God tell me that isn't her!" Constantine said in a desperate voice that matched desperate eyes staring my way. Karmun just nodded and hung his head in shame.

"NO, NO, NO! Kar what have you done?" He was shaking his head back and to and I could see the colours of red, purple and blue blurring on his face.

"I had no choice." Karmun spoke in low cast words that were only just audible.

"Had no choice! We always have a choice and we both lived by the prophecy for a reason! We took an oath to our King and it was always going to be life binding. Oh Karmun, what have you done?" He said hanging his head as though he couldn't look at him any longer.

"Your life means more to me than any prophecy and I am not going to apologise for that!" Karmun sounded adamant in this statement but Constantine just silently shook his head. Karmun let the silence invade the underground space for minutes more before helping Constantine back to his feet. He led him over to where Carrick and I still stood waiting for this tragic scene to play out. It was now, as he came closer, that I could make out more than just his bloodied features.

A breath caught in my throat as I couldn't believe how young he looked. Surely this person standing in front of me couldn't have been more than sixteen! He wasn't at all manly, being too cute and baby faced to be classed as a man but so much more of a boy. His soft brown eyes looked like brown sugar, which were framed by curled lashes with tips that touched his femininely shaped eyebrows. His pale milky skin put mine to shame being almost translucent and was such a contrast to Karmun's mocha toned skin. It was like yin and yang, the differences were startling. Even with their hair, where Karmun's was as straight as a pin and black as night, Constantine's was almost white and cut very close to his skull. His clothes were dirty and torn beyond repair, but I could imagine they were once fashionable when new. He had even lost a shoe and my heart melted into a pity puddle at just the sight of this boy that looked far more broken than what he portrayed. I couldn't help the tear that slipped down my cheek at the thought of what had been done to him, what he had been through since he had been taken. I knew what it was like to be a prisoner and I'm not talking the cushy kind where you get three square meals a day and can go out and breathe the fresh air. I am talking about torture both in body and soul. Torture so deep that it seeps into your blood and invades not only your every nerve but every thought, every single one, to a point that you crave only the unthinkable...

Death.

I wondered if Constantine had been this way. What a morbid thought that I just couldn't hold back.

"What did you do to him?" I asked before I bit my lip. I expected Carrick to answer me in his usual unmoved manner, but it was Constantine himself that approached me.

"Do not cry for me Electus, I have enough to be sorry about without adding to my old bones." At this I couldn't hide my shock and disbelief.

"Trust me child, I am older than I look," he said whilst catching an escaping tear. His lip was torn and the cut spread to a painful point as he gave me an endearing smile. A single drop of blood fell from the split that reminded me of a bloodied tear and a few of his teeth were missing, but this didn't take away from his beauty by any means.

"I am sorry for what is happening to you and I tried to help you, but it just wasn't enough, at the time I wasn't strong enough." He looked behind him towards Karmun and Carrick just scoffed at this, which was ignored on all fronts.

"That was you that night?" Karmun asked, slightly baffled. Well he wasn't the only one.

"Help me how?" I added to the questioning.

"Yes, it was me and despite the beatings that followed that action, it was all to be in vain."

"What do you mean?" I asked.

"The night that the warning appeared on your window was with the blood of the guilty." He turned to face Karmun now with a face full of disappointment.

"I saw what you did, how you controlled her protector, the Viking. How you used your own blood to write the Vampire King's message. How you let him use you like a puppet on his arm. I had to do something, beating or no beating, I had to try and counteract what you had done. I never thought it would get this far, that you would go this far. If only my message would have gotten through enough to alert the King." He was shaking his head and for the second time Karmun looked away from his lover in shame. Meanwhile I was going through that awful night like a flicker book of horrors. I remembered seeing the words that I naively thought were red paint at the time, words that spelled out my doomed fate that weeks later came true. But I also remembered the words that Constantine was talking about. After running back to my car to get my keys, I found the earlier threat gone and replaced with sound advice,

Tell Draven…. Everything.

Now that I thought back to it I could remember every time that I had battled with myself. I tried so hard sometimes to find enough inside that would have made me tell Draven, but it never came and now I knew why. Every drink served, every little voice in my head that screamed doubt and even the phone call my sister received saying how Draven didn't want to see me after our argument. It was all down to Karmun.

Did Draven know?

"I think that is enough confessions, don't you? Time is getting on and coming to an end for you both. Say goodbye Keira." Carrick said and motioned for someone to take me away. Just as I was about to move away Carrick's hand circled above my elbow and held me in place. Karmun finally looked to me and I noticed his eyes glistening. He approached me, and Carrick's grasp tightened.

"Keira I...Please..." He struggled with the words and I shook my head about to tell him he didn't need to say anything. I understood now. I saw it all the second his eyes met those of his love. What wouldn't I do for Draven or what wouldn't any of us do for a loved one, a sister, a husband or more importantly, a child. No, I couldn't hate this man. I couldn't even find it in myself to blame him.

"Karmun there's no need. I understand." I said trying to hold back the tears.

"You are a pure soul Keira and along with that comes a strong heart. You will survive because you are a fighter and more importantly you are chosen by the Gods themselves. I am just sorry that I wasn't strong enough for you but mostly..." He came closer to me and lifted one of my hands in his, making Carrick's grip grow painful. He lifted it to his lips and before kissing my knuckles he whispered,

"...I am just plain sorry." Then he gave me one last glimpse of the old Karmun I knew and loved by giving me his usual easy-going grin. Then he was gone. He had turned his back on me in a silent goodbye and I couldn't help but cry.

Then, pulling out of my inner turmoil, I watched a man dressed in black combat gear walk around from the van and flick a cigarette to the ground causing little orange sparks to bounce from the cement. He was like every other bad guy extra from all action flick that I had ever seen. He was tall, rippled with muscles and wore a scowl to match the hard lines of his face. He grabbed me none too gently and walked me over towards the SUV that Constantine had been pushed out of. I tried to dig in my heels at one point, but the man just growled at me like a dog. While I was being half dragged away I looked back to see Karmun and Constantine turn to face each other and hold onto each other's arms in half an embrace.

"Get in and shut up, girly!" The brute said in a gruff voice that had obviously been smoking his body weight in nicotine daily. I did as I was told without taking my eyes off the two men who were now getting on their knees without breaking their hold. Carrick stood slightly back as though waiting for something. I was practically pushed into the van and the door slammed shut sealing me in. Yet I still couldn't take my eyes off the two men. They looked like they were whispering to each other and then they closed the distance and met each other half way to seal their lips in what looked like a departing kiss. A single tear slipped free from my right eye and I let it travel the length of my cheek without wiping it away. I wanted to shed tears, I wanted to let my emotion free as did the lovers who quite clearly were about to meet their fate.

They broke away but remained close enough to touch their foreheads to one another. They both closed their eyes and even from here I could see the last words spoken,

'I love you'.

Then without warning Carrick pulled a spear from behind his tall frame and when he swung it round in front of his body the world around him changed. For about three metres around them all the concrete turned to crumbling ash, the walls bubbled black tar and melted into mounds of steaming lava. The ground shook and on the few cars that had them, their alarms started to voice their protests.

Some of the older models that couldn't take the pressure had their windows shatter and their tyres burst. I couldn't decide where to put my hands as the urge to place them both over my ears and over my mouth to prevent the scream was confusing.

Carrick stood there in all his Hell wielding wrath and became the Soul Collector whom I had seen fight Ragnar. His hood hung over to hide his face but the cloak did nothing to hide the rest. His fleshy bones held the weight I knew not how, but bulky arms that still had meat on swung the spear high above ready to strike. I felt the pain shoot up my arms as I hit the window with side on fists.

"NO!" I screamed as I pounded and pounded hoping to stop the work of Hell's henchman, but when the room let out a flash of blinding red light I blinked a few times in time to see the staff being driven into the two bodies still entwined in a lover's embrace. The staff pierced both hearts and not one sound was made by either of them. Their faces still locked in peace, not one shred of shock or pain touched their features unlike mine which wore a mask of horror. I screamed out and hit the window until it vibrated beneath my sore fists.

Then something began to happen. From the floor upwards, the ash covered their legs and worked its way up their bodies until covering them completely, like statues in a mausoleum. Their skin became the same shade of pale grey and their eyes turned into wet ice. Once the very last tip of their hair was covered, Carrick, still gripping the spear, pulled back his arm in an exaggerated manner and spun round, turning his back which caused the spear to leave the lovers' bodies.

Carrick then turned the spear round in his hand at such a speed it was hard to see properly, like a propeller on a helicopter and then, with a blur, it was gone. The change began as the sight of ash and bubbling fire started to turn to stone and fade away into dust. He walked back around the locked stone bodies and with each step his body changed back to the businessman in a plain beige suit. First the legs appeared from under a smoky cloak and then human tissue started to wrap around each bare bone until it formed solid muscle that went from bloody red to fleshy pink and then finally to a pale skin tone. It looked as though imaginary hands were wrapping flesh coloured ribbon around each bone and I don't know why but some sick twisted version of a maypole came to mind.

The last thing to disappear was his hood before showing me the most gruesome face. I gasped and scrambled backwards on the seat to get away. His face was elongated, with yellowing skin that stretched across high cheek bones like burning plastic. His eyes were huge and missing eyelids as it was obvious that they had once been cut away with a very blunt object. His lips were also absent with only blackened teeth that were longer and thinner than regular teeth. His hair was reduced to thin straggly bits that were long and growing only from the base of his skull, leaving most of his wrinkly head bare. But this was nothing compared to his soulless eyes. They pierced my spirit and it felt as though it had shattered into a million shards, like delicate pieces of a stained-glass window hanging high up in a church tower. They burned yellow and when he blinked the pupils folded in on themselves causing his eyeballs to bleed when opened. I badly wanted to vomit but thankfully I withheld it long enough for the rest of the transformation to take effect.

When he opened the side door I was cowering as far away as I could get, and Carrick looked unaffected by my reaction. He shouted something I didn't understand and got in to sit next to me before slamming the door home. I jumped at the sound and let out a pathetic little yelp. I so wanted to be brave and strong and all the things that Karmun had said to me, but I couldn't find it. I was shaking and kept fisting my hands to try and control myself. Two of the men got in the front and soon we were on the move again.

I glanced back one last time at the statues still locked together wondering what would become of them now, when my question was answered.

Their bodies started to waver in an impossible wind that seemed trapped indoors somehow. As the wind got stronger it whipped and licked around their stone skin and kept taking pieces away with it.

As it grew so did the pieces until eventually as we turned a corner, I saw the last of their faces get taken away and I could only hope.

*To a better place.*

# CHAPTER 3

# HENCHMEN

I didn't know how much time passed before my nerves calmed enough to take in what was happening around me. It could have been minutes, or it could have been hours, although hours seemed unlikely. It was as though time had stood still and no longer mattered. My mind kept returning to the fading statue of love and how symbolic it was to my situation. Every mile that was placed in between me and Draven was like a Hell's wedge driving through us inch by inch. I tried not to think about it that way, but my nerves were shot to pieces and normally, right about now, Draven would be the one convincing me that it was foolish to think such things...but where was he now? What was he doing...was he trying to find me?

At that point I actually found myself slapping my palm to my head. I was being ridiculous! Of course, he was trying to find me and I needed to keep that faith if I was to survive this.

Carrick had raised his eyes at me when I hit myself and if he was thinking that I had truly lost it this time, he kept quiet on the matter. I resigned myself to looking out of the window and taking his lead by keeping quiet. I had nothing to say anyway, nothing that wouldn't be followed by screaming profanities at him. I saw a city's lights flashing as we went speeding past but what city I couldn't tell you. It was an upsetting feeling, not knowing where you were in the world and it had only ever happened to me once before. But that dark place I was staying far away from.

The traffic wasn't busy for a city, so I gathered it was late in the evening or early in the morning. Had I lost a day already? It started to rain heavily and soon my vision of the outside world was lost to little streams of water running down the tinted window. That's when I couldn't stand it any longer.

"How long?" I asked in a dead voice I didn't recognise as my own.

"What, are you getting tired of my company already? That does not fare well for my ego." He said with a humour that I wanted to smack out of him with a shovel! A shovel because why use two tools when one would suffice, after all, I would need to get rid of the body and I didn't fancy dirt I couldn't get out of my nails for a week! Okay, I knew with these thoughts it was a clear sign I was losing it but I still smiled at the murderous thoughts, one he took for other reasons.

"Ah, a smile at last."

"One you don't understand I assure you. Do you really think my situation would bring on smiley faces and giggles? Hell, what do think this is to me, a fucking party?" I swore for the first time in ages and man it felt damn good! I think in situations like this I would start making it a habit. That brought on another smile, one I didn't feel like hiding. Carrick joined me and followed it with a rumbling laugh.

"I am indeed going to miss your feistiness, Electus."

"My name is Keira!" I stated with a sharp tongue of disgust. I didn't give two hoots and damnation about any bloody prophesy right about now! To hell with the fate and destiny crap, I just wanted to be boring, plain old Keira who the only thing about her that was quirky was the crazy Demon sight thing. I didn't want to be what they were saying. I just wanted to have Draven without knowing why. Without feeling like all the choices were taken away from us both and even if I had been some troglodyte, buck toothed, hillbilly mutant with major hygiene issues that Draven would have no other option than to be with me. I wanted it to be for me and for me alone. No other reason. That was why I was starting to get sick to death of this 'Electus' shit and was exchanging curiosity with self-loathing.

"That it is, forgive me. I forget what it must be like..."

"Don't! Don't you dare try and sympathise with me, Carrick! I don't need your patronising tones or your Goddamn pity party. You don't know anything about me, so don't go pretending you do... to what gain exactly...to try and put me at ease? I just learnt my good friend betrayed me from the moment I met him and then watched as he and his lover turned to ash at your hands, so don't you dare sympathise with a twenty three year old human girl that you have nothing, not one shred in common with! JUST DON'T!" I screamed at him. To give him credit he didn't get angry or even look out of place. He just nodded his head and turned away from me to leave me panting out of frustration.

Once I had calmed, I relaxed my shoulders and slumped in my seat.

"Feeling better?" He asked without looking at me.

"Yes, that felt surprisingly good," I admitted.

"Glad I could help...in any way." He added with an unmistakable smirk curling his lips.

"Sorry," I said in a quiet voice.

"Are you?"

"Not really but it was rude of me." Okay, never thought I would live in a world where apologising for being rude to the Soul Collector was the norm.

"Fair enough," he said with a slight nod of his head.

"We are nearing our destination." He stated, and I looked out into the rainy night.

"Where are we?"

"It is not important as to where we are but more important as to where you are going." Oh no, now I wanted to panic.

"Me? As in...me alone?" I don't know why but the thought that Carrick was just going to drop me off somewhere without him had my palms sweating. I mean, I know I should have been dying to get away from him but into the hands of someone else...I don't think so! Better the devil you know than the one you don't.

"Don't you go worrying that pretty little head of yours, no one will hurt you, they have had their orders, just as I've had mine." I didn't find this reassuring.

We had left the city streets behind and were travelling down a large motorway, but I couldn't make out any of the signs. I did however notice we seemed to be taking an exit off onto a ring road and it was hard to miss the large building in front of us that had a tall control tower at its centre. Oh goodie, another airport!

"Another plane?"

"Another plane." He replied. I was hoping he would have given me a bit more, but he seemed reluctant to explain so I continued,

"And will I be on my own on this flight or will you be joining me?"

"I am afraid this is where you and I part ways, but you will not be alone." Nope, didn't think so. I mean what could I have done anyway...parachuted my escape, I was brave, not suicidal!

We drove away from the public entrances and I gathered that we weren't going to be flying the conventional, public transport way. Oh no, it was another private Jet! It didn't take us long before the smaller planes came into view and one had all the lights on, the stairs were down and there was a long black limo parked close by it. Now it seemed my bravery had fled and taken its vacation time as I was close to peeing my pants and I wasn't ashamed to admit it.

We pulled up alongside the limo and my heart rate started playing a heavy metal beat in my chest. Please, oh please don't let it be Lucius in that car! Carrick looked at me as if he was expecting me to run but considering the doors were locked and there was about a mile of empty concrete desert surrounding me, where the hell was I to go?

"Time to say goodbye, my young one," he said before opening his side door. He unfolded his body and I noticed another body doing the same from the limo. A pale hand motioned for me to follow and after a quick thought I didn't really want to be seen being dragged out, so I put on a very fake brave face and got out. The freezing air slammed into me making my body shudder. I now wished I had dressed in a snow suit not a pair of jeans, long sleeved t-shirt and my usual black jacket. I should have added gloves a scarf, snow boots and a bloody sleeping bag with arm and leg holes!

I raised my hood for more than just protection from the cutting wind and held it there as I moved to stand next to Carrick. Well, at least the rain had stopped I thought with a shrug. As far as silver linings went it wasn't a very bright one. Three people exited the Limo and if I thought I would see yet again more typical thug henchmen then I was oh so wrong.

The three of them all stood in a line and it made me want to release a nervous giggle. The accountant geek, the tiny punk rocker girl and the badass biker that looked as if his favourite look was Spike from Buffy! I would never have put these three together in a million years. But here they were, and it was painfully obvious as to why.

"Carrick." The nerd nodded in acknowledgement when he approached. He had a stern voice that really didn't mix with his appearance.

*"Abaddon."* Carrick nodded back but I couldn't miss the waver in his voice or the single bead of sweat that travel the full length of his face. Was I missing something?

28

"Play nice baby." The tiny little girl said while coming up to the nerd and planting herself in front of him so that she was now nearer to us both. She was one of the cutest girls I had ever seen and also the most diverse. She had a mass of green hair that was electric blue at the tips which she wore piled high on her head, held there by a large skeleton hand clip that had painted red finger nails. This looked so out of place with her outfit. It looked as if she had got it out of a summer wardrobe, clearly getting the seasons wrong. The tiniest cut off jeans made into the shortest of shorts with the pockets hanging down past the hem. She combined this look with a kid's Thundercats T-shirt with the sleeves cut off, one of which showed her extensive sleeve tattoo that I couldn't make out because of the lack of light. I gathered though that she was a fan of the popular 80's kid's cartoon but whether it went with the black and white striped stockings I wasn't so sure. One of which kept falling down into her black cowboy boots which had spiked metal tips that looked painful if ever on the receiving end.

"Hey Toots, I gather you're the girly that we're here to pick up for the boss." She said smiling like we were BFF's. Her nose and lip ring flashed in the car's headlights and I could see my own freaked out reflection in her aviator sunglasses. She looked like a cartoon character!

"Enough of this friendly shit, get her on the plane, Pip!" The badass biker dude snapped. Yep, he was really living up to his image. The nerd scowled next to him not saying anything but then again it didn't look like he had to 'cause the biker turned his head away in submission. Seriously? A big muscled meathead with arms large enough to strain the leather concealing them and he's almost cowering at a geeky, glasses and tweed wearing nerd who looked like he was used to getting asked about tax returns! Strange.

"Come on then, Toots. Laters, soul dude!" She said trying to take my arm. Carrick's hand came to my arm and pulled me back.

"Aren't you forgetting something?" Carrick said in a casual tone.

"Ooops, my bad! Honeybee, where did I put that thingy again?" She asked over her shoulder after checking her empty pockets. The 'honeybee' aka nerdy man who stood close by nodded to her chest and she smiled before dramatically slapping her forehead.

"Of course, Jesus Christ, Holy Mother of the Earth and shit, I would lose my pocket money if it wasn't for my hubby!" She said, and I wondered if she took note of my gaping mouth. Did she just say that nerd was her hubby? I think I was close to choking on my own tongue!

I could not imagine two people so far apart, a bit like the President of the United States or Prince William dating the chavvy Chantelle that worked at our local chippy back in Liverpool.

She pulled her top out and stuffed one hand down it, all the while screwing up her face in concentration.

"Voila! There's the sucker!" She said smiling at me as she lifted a vial on the end of a very long thick chain. How she'd had problems finding it was beyond me. She waved it in front of Carrick like a pendulum and as he went to grab it she pulled it out of reach making it seem like he had just been naughty.

"I don't think so handsome!" She said, making the nerd growl possessively. She smiled.

"The girl first, Caveman!" She said showing us her perfect teeth, although her fangs seemed longer than most. She tapped her steel boot on the ground to indicate she was waiting. Meanwhile, I couldn't take my eyes off the swaying red liquid that was sloshing around in the miniature bottle with a wax coated top. I didn't need many guesses as to what the liquid was.

"But of course," he said smoothly before letting my arm go.

"Over this way Toots, time to join the Dark Side." She said lifting her glasses and winking at me. She had the most incredible green eyes that were the colour of lush grass and they had a bright blue ring around the iris that bled out like rippling water. There was also something more. They were kind and held a hint of childlike innocence to them, they also made her look about twelve and way past her bedtime.

I moved to her side as there was little else I could do. She tossed the vial Carrick's way and he caught it with little effort. He then raised it to his mouth and I watched in surprise when one fang extended down and pierced the top. He then tossed it back like a shot and threw the bottle to the ground. It didn't smash but when he nodded his goodbye in my direction he turned and stood on it causing it to shatter under his foot.

"Dramatic, much!" The girl called Pip commented.

"I hope you feel better now that you have your soul back!" She shouted at him when he was getting back in the car that brought us here.

"Pip!" The nerd warned, and she smiled at me before turning to face her unlikely husband.

"What? I hope he does." She said unconvincingly.

"Yeah right," he grumbled back.

"Right, let's get this show on the road...or is it in the air, you know cause we're flying?" She asked as she walked up to the other two.

"Come on Toots, keep up," she said to me as I seemed to be rooted to the spot. She gave me a look and then shrugged her shoulders before walking over to her husband who was waiting for her. They both nodded a silent order and walked away.

Where were the fierce evil henchmen I had been expecting? Oh wait, there he was. The biker dude walked straight up to me and grabbed my arm, nearly wrenching it out of its socket.

"Oww, hey... ease up asshole!" I shouted up at him as anger quickly replaced any fear at the feeling of pain he was inflicting. He growled down at me and after being with Draven the sound had little effect! But it did make him grip me harder which bit into the skin above my elbow. This made me turn quickly and I surprised him enough to be able to knee him in the man dangly parts! This worked as he released me to cover his bits in pain. I guess being hit in the privates is a universal pain no matter what the hell you are...Demon, Angel, human or fan of Tina Turner you are gonna go down if kicked hard enough! I decided not to wait around for him to retaliate and turned to run from him.

Okay, so the good news was that I'd hurt him but I didn't really take into consideration his supernatural speed! He grabbed my ankle and pulled causing me to hit the floor like shit off a shovel. My chin hit the ground and I bit my lips making me spit blood from my mouth. He dragged me back and lifted me by my neck. It felt like my bones would break and I was starting to lose all the air from my lungs. I was choking as he lifted me to his eye level. The sick bastard liked what he saw and grinned displaying a mouthful of wicked teeth. He licked his lips before bringing my choking face closer to his before he licked the full length of my face, playing special attention to my chin and lips that were bleeding.

His breath stank of chewing tobacco and now my blood. It stained his fangs black and red which made his sadistic smile all the more frightening. I gripped at his hands, trying in vain to pry them away from my neck, using every last ounce of strength I had left. That's when I heard the shouting.

"Klaus, you stupid son of a Bitch bear! Get your hands off of her NOW!" The girl called Pip screamed. That's when he just dropped me to the ground and I landed like I didn't have any legs attached. It hurt when I landed but it was nothing compared to the burning in my throat when trying to take in lungs full of air.

"She tried to escape!" He said folding his arms.

"So you thought you would kill her! Genius Klaus, Lucius would love that...'cause that's what he wants, you know...another dead body! You dumb fuck!" She said sarcastically standing up to the biker like he wasn't two foot higher than her. He growled at her and she just smiled.

"I wouldn't do that if I were you," an icy voice said from the steps of the plane. Pip looked over her shoulder to her geeky husband and blew a kiss before turning back to the biker named Klaus.

"And I really wouldn't if I was you, he can get a little grouchy...if I let him...you understand my meaning of course?" She said with utter confidence and to my surprise the biker actually found his boots in submission. She skipped back to her husband (yes actually skipped!) And I was trying to get to my feet.

"Get up!" He snapped.

"Trying, Dickhead!" I said under my breath, which of course he heard making him growl again. He lifted me up under my bruised arm and even though he had just nearly killed me, my fighting instinct didn't leave me, if anything it just burned brighter. Once I was upright I couldn't stop what happened next. It was a bit like saying something before it went through that naturally inbuilt filter. Well this thought kicked the filter to the side and slid right out in the form of me doing something disgusting. I spat my bloody saliva at him which landed half on his cheek and half on his leather jacket which from the looks he gave me, he didn't appreciate.

His eyes flashed deadly red before things went bad. He flung his other hand back and backhanded me, letting his grasp on my arm go, so that my body could fly through the air before finding the ground for the second time in minutes. The pain simultaneously exploded in both my cheek and the side of my head that had collided with the concrete.

This is where my world blurred, and the dark world found me.

*I just hoped that I was still breathing when I got there.*

# CHAPTER 4
# WHERE IS MY HERO?

I opened my eyes to a scene I wasn't expecting. I was lying on a bed I knew well, in a house I classed as home. I was back! How the hell did that happen? I sat up from staring at the ceiling for all of five minutes just wondering what on earth had happened. Had I been rescued?

I looked around the room and saw it still held the changes that Hilary had made while she had been staying here. I searched the room before looking down at myself, yep, I was in one piece and still wearing the clothes I'd had on. Surely if I had dreamt I had been kidnapped then I wouldn't have gone to bed in my clothes...would I? It was still dark in the room, with only the moon casting any light. I looked at the clock at the side of my bed and noticed it was three in the morning but as I turned back round I noticed I wasn't alone. A figure was stood over by my desk, hunched over something. He was by the side that was deep in shadow, but I knew it was a man from the sheer size of shoulders.

"Hello," I whispered timidly but the figure didn't move. Then he started to shudder as though he couldn't contain his emotion. Heavy breathing mixed with the dark chill that filled the room. I looked back to the window and only just realised the window was wide open and it was snowing heavily outside. I tried to pull the covers over me, but they didn't move. My hands connected as I could feel the material beneath my fingers, but the bedding didn't move an inch, neither did it show the pressure my hands created.

What was happening? Was I...*dead?*

The man turned around and I gasped.

It was Draven.

However, he didn't look at me, instead he just stood there looking numb. His face came into view and he looked like a different Draven. Handsome all the same but more lost, more...broken. He had no spark in his deep black eyes and the frown I was used to seeing was now replaced with a harsh scowl. Hard lines marred his beautiful face to the point of it being painful to look at. I wanted to run to him, to hold him and tell him I was here, everything was fine, but I was frozen in a disbelieving moment that this couldn't be real and if that were the truth, I didn't want to move in case I ruined it or lost it.

He had something in his hand and he walked to the door to leave. That's when I couldn't stand to watch him walking away from me, so I got up and followed him. I lost sight of him and quietly panicked while I stumbled down the dark, narrow staircase. I checked downstairs but there was no sign of him, so I headed back up to the first floor.

I found him in the room I had been using while Hilary had been staying in my room. He was sat on the bed facing the window with his back to me, with my pillow on his lap and he bent his head down to take a long inhale of the fabric. I saw him shudder again, the material of his tight t-shirt rippled with his movements and then he let out an almighty roar at the ceiling and ripped my pillow apart causing feathers to scatter and float around the room. He then cradled his head in his hands with his elbows rested on his knees. He started to shake, and I took a cautious step forward.

"Draven?" I whispered but it was fruitless. He didn't respond and that's when it finally hit me, and I knew that I wasn't really here. Draven was...I wasn't.

I couldn't stop the tears then and cried along with Draven. His were soundless and although I couldn't see him, I knew he was crying, which caused a sob to get stuck in my throat.

"Draven, please!" I pleaded but it was no use, if he couldn't see me then he couldn't hear me, but I couldn't help it.

"It's all my fault, it's all my fault." I repeated over and over and then stopped when he spoke,

"It's all my fault, Keira." He whispered, and my heart broke into too many pieces to hold.

"No, no it isn't!" I answered in vain. He started shaking his head like we were in sync with each other's dream but to be honest I wasn't quite sure what this was. Was he really here and I wasn't or were we both dreaming? A noise answered my question. His phone started to ring, and I saw him whip it out of his pocket and answer it in a blur.

"Speak to me!" He demanded, all traces of sadness gone, only to be replaced with a burning, raw power that screamed one pissed off male!

"THAT IS NOT GOOD ENOUGH!" He roared out and I heard the metal frame of my bed crunch under his fist. I took a step back and hit the wall with my outspread palms. Good God he was scary in rage!

"She needs to be found and she needs to be found yesterday! This is the only thing happening in the world, do you understand me? DO I MAKE MYSELF CLEAR?" He screamed out again and this time the house shook! I opened my eyes to find myself crouched in a protective ball and my hands over my ears. I had never seen Draven this angry before...I mean, sure, I had seen his raging fits over Morgan, Sammael and even that guy who threw me to ground in his club but this...this was something else...this was something I had never seen before,

This was desperation.

"I want her found and I want all the people involved to die at my hands!" This last part was said in his demonic voice and it was unlike any other. I found myself shaking at being the cause and if only he could just turn around and see me it might help, I could give him some clue.

"Is he awake yet?" Draven asked, and I took a wild stab in the dark that he was talking about Ragnar. I worried for my giant protector and hoped he was alright.

"Good, I will be there shortly." He waited for a moment listening to the side of the conversation I couldn't hear.

"Don't worry about that! He can destroy the whole building for all I care, I will calm his rage soon enough, but Ragnar has the answers I need so nobody speaks with him but me, understood?" He listened to one short word and then crushed the phone in his hand as a way of disconnecting. It made me wonder how many phones he had been through this way since I had been taken?

Draven brushed the crushed phone's dust from his hands and stood. He went over to the window and picked up something that had been leaning against the wall. He lifted it to the window and the moonlight caught the canvas I had painted when Draven and I had fallen out. I had forgotten about it until now and I watched him very gently run a fingertip along the heart that was in the middle of a forest.

It had been symbolic at the time and now it seemed it was once again. He put it under his arm and turned around to face me. I scrambled to my feet quickly and watched as he picked up another canvas that he had placed on my bed. This time it was one that I had given him but he had left in my room. I think he'd used it as an excuse to come around at some point 'cause when I mentioned it to him once, he smiled a secret smile and didn't elaborate on the gesture.

Well, now he added it to the other and placed them both together under his arm. I watched him walk towards me and approach the door. Once again, I watched him leave and followed him back up to my room. He walked straight over to my window and I knew he was getting ready to leave this house. I couldn't stand the idea and ran to him to grab his arm as he bent his frame through my window. But I was too late, he had jumped down to the ground and was clearly getting ready to fly off into the night.

"Draven...Draven...DRAVEN!" I screamed this last one out and finally he looked up at me in pure shock. He stood frozen and I wasn't sure at first if he could see me, so I looked down at myself and noticed now my body had started to fade. Like some parts of me were becoming glass or more like shimmering water.

"Keira?" He asked as though it was his turn to be in this dream. I looked up one last time to see utter joy be replaced by pure fear.

"KEIRA!" He shouted as I held a hand up to my face to watch it fade away like the rest of me.

"No, no, not yet! NOT YET!" I shouted back at no one, but I couldn't stop it, not me, not Draven, not even the Gods, nothing could stop it as I faded into the night like an unheard whisper.

The last thing I saw was the man I loved, his face crumbling into complete misery and it broke my heart for the second time that night.

"You know he's going to kill you, don't you?" Said a voice I didn't recognise at first. I heard a muffled noise that reminded me of a snort of disbelief. I felt groggy and my head hurt like a son of bitch when I moved. No scrap that, everything hurt! All one side of my body ached and when I licked my lips it stung and left a metallic taste on my tongue. It also felt like I had taken up the habit of chewing on sandpaper before swallowing the entire packet. Oh dear, this was so not good.

"She is just some human snack to him!" A rough voice said in return, but it was met with musical laughter. I couldn't help but shudder at the thought of Lucius feasting on me, which brought on a flood of images I didn't want but couldn't get rid of. His imposing height and his predatory gaze sizing me up like I was some innocent gazelle sipping water from a spring, then that dangerously handsome face with perfect shaped lips that would utter deadly words in the softest voice. If Draven was the fire, then Lucius would have been the ice and both elements were more than willing to burn me when touched. I had no idea what Lucius had in store for me but considering what had happened in my last dream of him I doubt it was to have cream tea, ask if I knew the Queen and talk about the benefits of being English!

"Seriously, did you get dropped on your head when you took your vessel, or did he already have his brain dribbling out of his nose?" I recognised the voice as being the pint sized strange tattooed girl that looked as though she had just been thrown out of school.

"Keep talking, you little shit and I will show you what my brain tells my fists to do!" The voice responded with a growl. The girl called Pip started laughing and another man's voice spoke with frost lacing every word.

"Disrespect my wife again...go on, *please, give me one more reason!"* This last threat was made in a demonic voice so deep it actually made the plane shake with a violent turbulence so powerful that I rolled off the seat I was lying on and hit the floor like a sack of spuds! I first screamed and then let out an umf sound as my bruised side hit the carpet. I looked up to see all three heads had turned to look down the aisle at me sprawled on the floor like I was there doing snow angels.

The girl Pip came running over to me to help me to my feet.

"Whoopsy," she said as she hauled me up with a surprising strength. When I was stood up I was looking down at her, which hardly ever happened considering I was only five foot and three inches.

"Thanks," I said quietly. I mean I didn't want to be rude as she had seemed to stick up for me and was being nice by helping me up but I did need to keep in mind she was also helping with the whole kidnapping deal, Umm...rock and...weird hard place!

"No worries, I'm Pip," she said offering me a hand that had a huge candy flower shaped ring on it and a tattoo of the name ADAM written across her knuckles with hearts and flowers around the swirly writing in reds and pinks. Her hands were tiny and delicate, but her fingernails had been shaped into wicked points. Unless they grew that way naturally I didn't know but I doubted the tiny painted snowman on each of them were. Everything about her screamed the word 'crazy' but she was so cute and adorable that you couldn't help but instantly like her. RJ would just love this little gothic pixie!

Now she had lost her sunglasses I could see the roundness of soft baby features, cheeks that had some curved lift and were tinted pink at the top. Soft saucer eyes that were framed with thick black lashes. Electric green eye shadow that was a perfect match to her eye colour. She had huge dimples even when she didn't grin like a cat in an ice cream factory and a lip ring with a yellow ball in the middle with a tiny smiley face on it.

"And you're Keira!" She announced proudly like she would win a teddy for getting it right. I just nodded, 'cause let's face it, what else do you say or do when faced with that obvious statement.

"Well, Mr Grumpy Pants over there is Klaus." She paused and held her hand up to her mouth to whisper to me the next part,

"But between you and me, I don't think he's gonna make the next squad." She then mouthed the words "He's gonna get cut." And then she made a slitting throat action that I found more than a little creepy.

"If ya know what I mean." She whispered before carrying on with introductions like I was at some party, not a mile in the air being kidnapped by Demons.

"Now that gorgeous, nerdy looking dude who looks to be far too good with numbers and shit, is the team captain, the only man that matters, the sex god of any state, the love of my..." He coughed out loud and shifted in his seat, looking both amused and uncomfortable.

"Squeak honey, get on with it," he said with a smile that transformed his face into a GQ model and made nerdy fashionable. He wore black rimmed, square glasses that sat on a straight nose which matched his angular face. With high cheek bones and a pointed chin, he looked more like a professor of astrophysics than your typical kidnapper. He even wore a grey tweed jacket over a very sophisticated navy sweater with a white and navy check shirt underneath. This was finished with a navy tie done up to the top button. The only shred of casual was the stonewashed jeans, but even these were finished with highly polished black dress shoes. This was definitely a man you would not have put with the miss-matched colour queen stood in front of me with her hands behind her back swaying like a naughty child.

"Sorry nerdy," she said, sticking her pierced tongue out at him. Yep, another piercing, how many did she have anyway? There was a ring in her nose, one in her lip, tongue and too many in her ears to count. At this rate I would bet big blue she had one in her belly button and I adored my truck!

"This heated marshmallow of lovely sweet gooeyness is..." He coughed again and tried to look stern but she just spun around and continued grinning.

"...is Adam." I think at this point I was too shell shocked to do anymore than nod once more.

"You look like shit. You don't say much do you? Are you shy, 'cause you know what they about say people don't you, they're right animals in bed! Grrr, so which animal are you?" She railroaded me with a mouth that moved a mile a minute.

"Squeak, give the poor girl a chance to speak and I'm sure she will." Adam said with not an ounce of malice or reprimand in his smooth voice. He kind of reminded me of that actor Ed Norton. Slim built but with an air of something stronger hiding behind the cool facade. It was like a hidden warning of immense power that made you respect this man and you didn't fully understand why.

"Poor? Poor, you're poor? Oh you poor thing, ha get it? We're not poor, I would hate to be poor..." She paused and once again placed her hand in front of her mouth to whisper the next bit.

"I have a habit of buying things I like." Well that made sense I thought sarcastically.

"And I like lots of things." She giggled

"Lucius is rich though, like a friggin' Sultan! But seriously, you look like shit!" She said again making me wince which hurt a lot more than it should have.

"You should go clean up in the loo, lav, toilet, privy or little Keira room, as I'm sure as shit you will feel better then. Klaus really did a number on your face. You were really pretty before he made half of it purple...He is such an asshole, did I mention he's getting cut?" She finally took a breath and pointed to the back of the plane making a little motion with one hooked finger to indicate the door on the left. I smiled again and whispered a small "thanks" before nearly running to the bathroom just to get away. My God she was something else!

After almost tripping up on my way there I could still hear Pip's voice as she was saying,

"Wasn't she pretty, Lucius is not going to be happy you did that to her face."

I took the last few steps quicker and shut the door before I could hear anything else. The light flickered on and off once before finding the power to stay on. The bright light illuminated the small space enough to make my eyes squint. When I opened my eyes I really wished I hadn't. I was more than a mess and Pip had been right, it was anything but pretty. Not that I ever relied on my looks for anything but this was something else!

I leaned in closer to the mirror and winced as I poked at the fist sized bruise that covered my right eye and most of my cheek. It was both an angry red and purple with a lump that had formed on my cheekbone and my right eye refused to open all the way. It hurt no matter what expression was on my face which made my lips go tight with pain. Of course, the cut on my lip would just split more and blood would ooze out, dripping down my chin. I would have thought by now that it would have scabbed over but I guess I must have been biting my lip in my dream. That thought brought me back to Draven and I wondered what he would make of my face if he could see me now. Seething would be a word I would no doubt use.

I couldn't help but frown when I started to pick at the dried blood that had crusted over my right nostril and all the way down my face to my neck. Thankfully, I noticed that my nose hadn't been broken and all the damage was stuff that would easily heal with time. However it didn't stop me from shaking my head at myself. This wouldn't have happened if I had just played it safe and done as I was told. It had turned out a painful lesson to learn and there was now only one thing to take from this. I. Had. To. Survive.

There were no other options left. I was not getting away and there was no use getting myself killed for it. I knew Draven would come for me, there was no question in my mind that he would but the one question was time? How long would I have to be subjected to Lucius' world before Draven pulled me back out again and more importantly...would I still be breathing when he did?

I had to believe that Lucius wanted me alive and to remain so for however long it took him to get what he wanted from Draven. It had occurred to me on the plane with Carrick. He was adamant that Lucius wanted me not only alive but unharmed. Why? What would it matter? My only answer was that I was leverage, plain and simple. Lucius wanted something, and Draven wanted me.

My hand fell forward suddenly in heart stopping fear as a new thought slammed into me with the force of a stampeding horde. What was it that Lucius wanted? And what if it was something Draven couldn't give him. My life was hanging in a dangerous balance and I was praying it would tip in my favour, but knowing what I knew of Lucius, then the thing he would be asking for could most likely change the fate of the world!

Would Draven be willing? But more importantly...

*Would I?*

# CHAPTER 5

# TRANSFUSION

Afeter spending far too long in the toilet trying to clean my face the best I could, all the while wincing in tender pain, I exited the tiny cubicle and was about to take a seat as far away from the rest of them as I could. There was one especially that I didn't have any burning need to ever be near again. The biker bastard!

He turned my way and looked almost gleeful at the sight of what he had done.

"Come sit with us Toots, he will behave himself...I won't let him touch you." She said kindly. Klaus just growled low in his throat before saying,

"Don't count on it." At this she turned to face him and after placing each hand between the seats she leaned down close to his ear.

"Play nice or I will have to kick you out of the playpen and I don't know about you, but to me, it looks a long way down." She made a whistling sound and motioned with one of her hands a nose dive before hitting an imaginary ground, then making a booming sound before clapping her hands in front of his face making him jump. He didn't say a word after that.

I couldn't help a smug little smile from showingbusiness before getting a handle on it. After all there was no reason to add fuel to the fire...not when we were a mile up anyway. Nowhere to run to on a plane!

She turned back round to me and nodded to a seat opposite her and her husband. At this Klaus stood up and stormed off to the front of the plane.

"Ah don't mind Mr Pissy Pants down there, he's just sour 'cause he's gonna die soon...drink?" She said like talking about someone being murdered was so the norm for her that it required toasting to.

"Umm...water please," I said in a timid voice I hardly recognised anymore. It was the same voice I used to reserve for the early Draven days.

"Well aren't you polite, considering we kidnapped you and all...isn't she polite honey?" She asked turning to Adam who was busy reading the Financial Times. He answered without moving his face from the page he was reading.

"Certainly is love." She smiled at his answer and plonked herself down with a little jump. She swung her legs around to hang over the plush armrest and faced me fully.

"Soooo...tell us about yourself, Toots." She asked cocking her head to one side.

"Squeak," Adam said in warning.

"What! I'm bored and we still have ages to go yet and you're boring and won't screw me when we're this high up...'cause you're all weird about heights and stuff...for a demon you know he's a bit wussy with certain stuff, and you know the big man can't come out to play this high up." She finally took a breath and I looked over to Adam who was smiling with flat out amusement. Me, well I was just confused as hell. Who was the big man...his penis? I shook that thought out of my head quickly and couldn't help but laugh when he stuck his tongue out at her. She blew a raspberry back.

"Besides, I think her walking out of the toilet to us at it like bunnies would have been a little much, don't you think dear?" He asked in a dry tone and it was obvious what his honey little wife had been up to when I was absent.

"Bunnies...? You're more like a horse, honey!" She said with a wink and he gave her a cheeky grin back before straightening his paper to indicate the conversation about the size of his penis was over.

"So, back to my questions, what's it like be the Chosen One?" She asked boldly while clicking her fingers to an air steward who appeared from behind a curtain. He came forward and she snapped out her order in another language.

"Umm..." Was all the reply I had for her.

"I mean, it must be so cool knowing how important you are and that none of my kind can feed from you, that must make you stronger. I've tried to feed from you but couldn't, not only that but you haven't been very happy since I've met you and fear tastes nasty...sour to me anyway...you don't say much, do you?" No and I doubted I ever would around her!

"Squeak, remember what we talked about. Remember what doc said at group?" Adam reminded her, and she just giggled like a naughty toddler. I could imagine that Adam had his hands full with this cute little pixie.

"Yeeesss of course I remember, I just sometimes choose to ignore it. I go to a therapy group for talking too much, it's held by a harpy called Sheila and she says that as an Imp, I have issues with size and find a bigger voice makes up for insecurities I don't even have, silly dugong...I mean why would I with a husband like him that I can control." She steamrolled without taking a breath.

"Dogong...Imp?" I said the two words that confused me the most.

"Dogong? The dugong is a large marine mammal which, together with the manatee, is one of four living species of the order Sirenia. Sireniais commonly referred to as sea cows... get it...silly seacow?" She reeled off all this information that would have made David Attenborough proud. I bet she loved watching Blue Planet!

"And Imp?" I reminded her.

"Well that's me, I'm the Imp and a very important Imp at that! You don't know much do you and you do a funny little wrinkle thing with your nose when you're confused." I could feel myself doing it and let my face relax feeling self-conscious. She fished around in her pockets looking for something when Adam cleared his throat. He held out an expensive looking smartphone without looking up.

"Ah, there it is...you sneaky little bugger...if you have been on my Facebook again me and you are having words!" She said as she started tapping away on the small screen with her pointed nails. She looked up and said over her phone,

"He changes my password and messages all my male friends telling them to fuck off." At this I looked over to Adam who turned his head to wink at me. I couldn't help but smile back.

"Righty, here we go." She cleared her throat and read out a description in a posh voice that didn't suit her look.

"An imp is a mythological Being similar to a fairy or demon, frequently described in folklore and superstition. The word may perhaps derive from the term ympe', (Which it's not by the way)" She interrupted before carrying on.

"'Used to denote a young grafted tree. Originating from Germanic

45

folklore, the imp was a small lesser demon'. (Which they so are NOT!)" She shouted out.

"Squeak, blood pressure!" Adam reminded her and now that he mentioned it, she had gone quite red in the face.

"But have you heard this shit! I am not a 'lesser' Demon! I could beat the crap out of everyone I know...well, with your help that is, but still."

"I know darling, of course we could, please continue, I like to hear your voice," he stated seriously and at this she instantly calmed enough to carry on.

"Ah, finally some sense. It now says 'It should also be noted that demons in Germanic legends were not necessarily always evil. Imps were often mischievous rather than evil or harmful, and in some regions they were portrayed as attendants of the Gods'. Now that is better! I got that straight from Wikipedia by the way. Some of it's true, like that last bit. But I am by no means a 'lesser Demon'. If anything I am more, 'cause I have a berserker." She whispered this last part but Adam had heard and snapped his head round to glare at his wife.

"Pipper Winifred Ambrogetti!" Adam said her full name sternly.

"Uh oh, now I'm in trouble, he always means to spank me when I say something I shouldn't, what he doesn't yet realise is that I love a good spanking." She said again behind her hand, which I was soon discovering was a little quirky habit of hers.

"Oh trust me sweetheart, I know." He said before once more, getting back to his paper. If there was one image I didn't want in my head, it was this little Imp being placed over Adam's knee and being smacked on the backside, while screaming with pleasure! Too late I thought trying to pry it out with the help of closing my eyes and shaking my head. I heard Pip laughing.

"Ambrogetti means immortal you know." She stated randomly. I found myself nodding, even though I didn't know that.

The steward came back with our drinks and when I took a sip and coughed at the burning in my throat, she came over to me and started to pat me on the back gently.

"Not a whisky fan eh? I thought when you said water you meant with your whisky, oh well never mind, drink up, it will help with the pain." She said kindly after moving a stray bit of hair out of my face.

"Thanks," I said.

"You know that's the eighth word you have said to me, tenth if you include 'Umm'. Is that a word? Is that a word, Sugarbake?" She first asked me and then her husband, 'Sugarbake'.

"I don't think so, Sugarcake" He said emphasising the word 'cake'.

"Cake, bake, what's the difference, they're both sweet to lick, eat, bite... devour." She said the last few words husky with desire and I wondered what I was going to do with myself when these two would soon be at it. I didn't think it would be long before that would happen with the sight of Pip licking her lips and him groaning behind his paper.

"Behave Pip!" He said and now she was the one groaning but for a different reason.

"No fair! Alright but you so owe me when we get off this plane Nerd Boy! And it's my rules!"

"Pip, I'm not doing Mexico all over again, we were stuck like that for two days and you giggled the whole time."

"Fine, but we're doing the cruise ship and no buts!" She interrupted him before he could protest, and I could happily say that I had no clue what they were talking about.

"Do you like 80's cartoons?" She asked me, completely changing the subject ...unless she was going to bring up sex being dressed as Minnie mouse!

"Umm, yeah I guess."

"There's that word again 'Umm' I'm gonna have to submit that one this year to Merriam-Webster's Open Dictionary. Few years back it was 'fugly' which means fucking ugly, well it's in there now, 'cause of me." She said looking extremely happy with herself.

"Nerdy was so proud." She said thumbing over her shoulder at him.

"Sure was babe," he said sarcastically which she either didn't pick up on or she ignored.

"Oh damn, it is on there." She said after playing with her phone for a bit.

"So which is your fav?"

"Sorry?"

"Cartoon, which is your fav?"

"Oh, umm..." She smiled again when I made my trademark noise but didn't comment.

"She-Ra." At this she made me jump as she clapped her hands.

"YES! Me too, well I prefer He-man, cause he's like, well fit and all, apart from that hair, God that was bad, looked like a ginger monk with that bob. That hair style wasn't popular EVER! Just very gay and not in a cool, good looking way...don't you agree?"

"I do and have always thought that myself." I told her honestly which brought a beaming smile to her heart shaped lips.

"See Adam, I knew we would get on and you said for me to cool, to rein it in and give her space, we're like best friends already! Aren't we Keira...? Tell him you like me, and we're cool and shit." I couldn't help the genuine smile at the idea of being kidnapped by someone who also wanted to be my friend. Adam gave me a thankful smile and winked at his wife.

"Ah, but did you know they were actually brother and sister, She-Ra and He-man that is? I think She-Ra kicks ass and in those heels, well I love those heels, I have a She-Ra costume at home...don't I?"

"That you do." Adam answered and raised his eyebrows like a memory came to mind and the look that followed made me blush.

"And a Bumblebee costume." The image I got was adorable until she continued,

"Not the bug, the Transformer. I love Bumblebee and Optimus Prime, I cried when he died in the movie, did you cry...wait have you seen the cartoon movie?" I shook my head and she gave me a look of horror.

"Oh my you need to, it explains so much in life. It's like my bible, that and the Carebears movie, those two combined will blow your mind...it's some deep shit." She said with such certainty that I couldn't help but laugh out loud.

"There you go, you're laughing now. She finds me funny, Nerdy." She said over her shoulder.

"Well you're a funny girl, sweetheart," Adam said before she got up and bounced over to him landing in his lap. He made an 'Umff' sound and he tried to wrestle the ruined newspaper from under her body. She wrapped her arms around his neck and poked him repeatedly with her little nose, all the while saying "peck, peck" over and over again. He laughed while trying to restrain her. The sound of a mobile phone ringing brought an end to the play fighting and Adam was trying to smooth his hair back while Pip answered the phone with a singing voice.

"Hello, hellooo." Adam pushed his glasses back up his nose and tried to re-straighten his paper to no effect.

"Okay boss, we still have the girly." She said sweetly and although I couldn't hear the voice on the other end I knew who it belonged to and that was enough to form the beads of sweat that broke out across my skin.

"She is fine...I even made her laugh." She said, clearly feeling good about this fact, I on the other hand, was wondering why he would even ask after my welfare?

"Sure thing, boss man," she said handing over the phone to the outstretched hand of her husband.

"I am here, My Lord" He said, getting down to business and losing all past playfulness, replacing it with a powerful man of authority.

"No, as we mentioned before, he has not been allowed near the girl and awaits your judgment alone." I knew they were talking about Klaus and he knew it too if the look of terror was anything to go by.

"He would not get far, my Lord." So, Lucius thought he would make a run for it, well, now he had two flight risks on his hands, 'cause I couldn't guarantee I wouldn't bolt if given half the chance, no matter how nice my captors had been. At this Klaus turned back around and slumped in his seat. I would like to have said that I felt sorry for him, but I couldn't find it in me, thanks to the pain every movement my bruised body made. When I was in the toilet splashing water on my face I had lifted up my t-shirt to find all my left side was bruised and scratched by the impact of the tarmac. It hurt slightly to breathe in deeply and I just hoped that I hadn't cracked a rib. There was also a bump that had formed under my hairline on my right side from my head hitting the ground which was probably what knocked me out. I have to say that I think as far as being knocked unconscious, I was beginning to think I preferred being drugged.

"We will see you in Munich soon. I have arranged for a car to take us straight to Transfusion." He said with the smoothest poker face I had ever seen, even though he now had a little horny minx that was straddling him in his seat and was pulling his tie from underneath his sweater. She then tickled his nose with the tip. He grabbed her wrists and she giggled.

"My Lord, if you could control her, I would be indebted to you, as you know I never can." He said dryly making Pip pout. Of course, it looked endearing and adorable. He put the phone to his shoulder and bent his head to keep it there.

"Yes, there is no doubt in my mind that Carrick knows to disappear for a while." He said as he used one hand to grab both Pip's wrists and bend them behind her back, as she was trying to undress him now. With the other hand he picked up the tie she had discarded on the table in front of him and he used it to wrap around her wrists until tight. She continued to giggle, bouncing up and down on his lap which made him groan a few times. All the while he spoke without a hint of distraction in his voice but only his face gave away his growing arousal when he would bite his lip and look strained whenever she would grind herself against him.

He finished tying her hands behind her back and gripped the column of her neck to hold her still. Every time she wriggled he would tighten his hold until she gave in and remained still. He leaned his head down to her face and kissed her nose soundlessly, she snapped her lips and teeth back at him in return, now clearly sulking. He just smiled at his victory.

"He is bound to you my Lord, whether or not he has his blood back, he knows this, but I have had some of my men keep watch on the Otherlands just in case." He nodded once and finished the phone call with a simple,

"My Lord".

"No fair! You always use your strength." Pip moaned, and Adam just pretended to snap back.

"Well if I were you, I wouldn't give me the means to tie you up my love. Besides if you didn't like it, my little Imp, then you would have stopped me...if you had tried...hard enough." He said this last part strained as she rolled her hips, grinding herself against his manhood with a curl on her lips.

"Talking about hard things," she said giving him yet another roll of her hips making him growl. I felt as if I was watching a live sex show or a porn movie I couldn't get away from. I wanted to turn away, but it was difficult trying not to watch. I found these two fascinating. They were so unashamed of their obvious love that it was heart wrenching to watch. It made me ache for Draven in a way like never before. Did we look like that in front of people? Could they taste the sexual attraction in the supercharged air around us? The way we always had to touch, to feel one another or we would fade away. It was like my dream when I had tried so hard to touch him, but I couldn't move, why couldn't I have moved towards him or touched him?

"Not now kitten, you have a friend to play with." He said like she actually was the age she looked. She looked up to see me staring and my cheeks went hot with a deep blush at being caught. She just smiled and jumped off his lap and snapped the tie, freeing herself.

"Hey, I liked that tie little Miss."

"I know, it was your punishment for not giving me what I want." She held the tie in her hands and looked down at it with concentration. I watched as it started to move around in her cupped hands like it was some kind of material snake wrapping around itself. When it finished moving it ended up as a neat navy bow with long bits hanging down. She lifted it to her head and tied it on the top of her head like snow white. It matched her lush green hair and brought out the blue flecks in her startling green eyes.

"Mine now." She said as she came back to plonk down in her seat.

The rest of the journey was the strangest flight I had ever taken. Not only was it filled with terrifying thoughts of what would happen to me once we landed but mainly the depressing thoughts about the worry that Draven must be going through and what I wouldn't give to be in his arms right now. To wake up with him calling my name back to sanity, cradled in his strong secure arms, holding me and telling me how everything was okay now, that I was safe, and he wouldn't let anyone get to me...wouldn't let anyone take me away from him...

But it had happened, and it was all my fault.

I wanted to cry, I wanted to scream and run and hit and shout the F word at the skies but no, what was I doing, sat here watching the bloody Transformer cartoon movie on Pip's tiny phone screen. I have to say even I got a little teary when Optimus Prime died!

I had no idea how long I had been gone for now, as all nights were merging into days I had no idea the name of. I was well fed and watered on the flight and Pip had insisted that someone get us some popcorn when we stopped to refuel. As we watched the movie, which half the time she was close to sitting on my lap, I would sometimes find Adam watching me without once making a comment about the way his wife took to me. The wife that had no concept of personal space, that was for sure and every time she played with my hair, I don't think she noticed my body go ridged.

She kept saying that even though I was their prisoner, there was no reason we couldn't have fun together. I had to smile at this. I think I could have picked worse kidnappers, although getting hit by a Demon was an experience I wanted to avoid if I could help it. I suppose Pip and her quirky ways did prevent me from spending hours curled up in a puddle of self misery. It was hard to do when having a brighter than life firecracker jumping around and asking everything there was to know about my personal life. Everything from my first time having sex to having a twenty-minute conversation about a goldfish I had once when I was six. She couldn't understand why on earth I would call it Goldy and not Fred. She liked the name Fred, only for a girl not a boy…weird… much?

When the plane landed Adam got ready to walk off the plane with Klaus. It was clear he didn't trust him not to try and run, so he stuck to him like glitter to a Christmas card. Of course, Pip stuck to me the same. There were two black SUV's waiting for us and Pip jumped in the front of one and said,

"Shotgun!" I envied her enthusiasm as I dragged my feet to the back seat. I got in and only when not moving did I again notice the bitter cold. I didn't know how Pip hadn't frozen to death but after asking her this question she simply said,

"It's hot in Hell!" Without a pin thread of amusement.

I had never been to Germany before and with it once again being dark I didn't think I was going to see much of it. It felt like I was living in a permanent state of darkness. The only light had been whilst flying over here but Pip had promptly walked around and pulled down all the blinds telling me how she didn't like the light. Even when we refuelled I wasn't allowed to get off the plane. So here I was, yet again, staring out into the night of yet another city. At least this time I knew where we were, unlike the city we had first travelled to and the city we refuelled at. I didn't see any sense in keeping me in the dark about these things, it's not as if I could get a secret message to Draven…what did they think, that I had some homing pigeon stuffed down my pants!

As we made our way into the city Pip stayed unusually quiet, which was fine by me as it was the first chance I got to actually take in what was happening around me. What did I know so far? I was in Munich and I was on my way to Lucius' club called Transfusion. I just hoped we stayed in the city as it would be easier for me, given the chance, to escape. You could quite easily lose yourself in a big city. I decided the best course of action was to play the good little prisoner and hope that they got lax in their guard, then I would make my move. I would run like the Meatloaf album and hide until I could contact Draven. Okay, so as far as plans went it wasn't a master one by any stretch of the imagination, but I just couldn't lie down and die! I had to survive this! No other option was allowed to exist.

I don't know how long I was in my own bubble of escape but when we started to get closer to an amazing building that was lit up by an orange glow from the street lighting I couldn't help but stare up in awe. It gave it an unearthly presence, glowing in the mist of the onyx black sky. It was a huge building that stamped such a presence in the city, like some castle someone had dropped down from heaven or a gothic palace that had pushed its way from Hell and broke through the human world's surface, yeah, that was more fitting.

We drove more slowly now as there were people everywhere, walking around the building, taking pictures or weighted down with Christmas shopping. I realised it couldn't be much later than nine o'clock. I heard the automatic locks switch on and I jumped at the sound. I looked to Pip as she turned around to give me wink.

"That building is amazing." I said not being able to help the nagging need to know more about it. It came from both the historian and artist in me, as it was by far one of the most incredible buildings I had ever seen.

"NeuesRathaus, the new town hall." She said as she too took in its splendour. It had too many windows to count, hell it looked like it could be hundreds, all different sizes. On the walls the stone blocks were carved to look like one continuous rock sculpture that formed a building. There were arches all entwined with gargoyles and inter-laced with fancy stone balustrades carved into intricate patterns that made it look like tree branches frozen in time. The hexagon turrets were given stone guards carved onto elegant plinths. All held swords in their hands that went up to two thirds of their body. Even though the gargoyles were in some parts eroded by weather it didn't take away their features. Faces of mischief were holding their fingers to their mouths to entice passersby with untold secrets. Offset to one side was the imposing clock tower that seemed to reach out to the skies with its many spires, like hands trying to claw their way into Heaven.

"The bay of the tower contains statues of the first four Bavarian Kings," stated Pip as she pointed to the centre of the tower which indeed held a cut out section that housed different statues.

"The third one along was an asshole." She added as if she was talking about an annoying neighbour with a yappy dog she once had. I had to shake my head to mentally clear the image of Pip being at court in a long dress bitching about royalty.

"See the dragon?" She said pointing to one of the corner bits closer to the ground.

"Lucius made them add that and the terrified humans that are trying to get away...he laughs whenever we drive by," she said with a shrug of her shoulders, like it was a mystery she had never solved.

I was pretty sure we weren't allowed to be driving right passed the building, but no-one stopped us or got in our way. Even after we drove round an enormous Christmas tree did anyone even bat an eye. It was as if no-one even saw us.

After weaving in and out of narrow streets we headed further out of the busier part of the city and instead of happy late-night shoppers we had people dressed with one thing on their mind...sex. It was a nightlife I had forgotten since leaving Europe and moving to a remote town in the mountains. I wasn't in Kansas anymore and Toto had been replaced by a green haired Imp named Pip!

"Here we are!" Pip announced with way too much enthusiasm than what my queasy stomach could cope with. It felt like your usual butterflies had been replaced with ones made of metal and they were rock banging in my stomach.

We had pulled up outside a five story building made of black brick and thick smoky grey stonework carved around the windows and doors. It was angled so that the front door was on the corner and each way it went out to the sides for ten sets of windows all reaching up to the top. All windows seemed to be blacked out and held wrought iron artwork at the top of each stone arch. The bottom windows held huge metal flowers that wilted down like they had died long ago. These were lamps that deflected red light from the black windows causing a freaky glow onto the street level below. I looked up and saw the top windows all had thick, lush looking curtains in blood red velvet.

Around the door, a metal vine as thick as my wrist came from the ground and spread out and up the wall, surrounding the opening. It curled outwards to the second and third floor piercing the brick with bloody spikes the size of rugby balls. Above the door the red and black metal words were designed in elegant calligraphy spelling out the name,

### 'Transfusion'

A single drop of blood dripped down the elongated F in the middle of the word and it made my spine tingle. The car had stopped right outside the door and the line of people waiting in the cold, barely dressed, looked at us as if they were expecting someone famous was about to step out of the car. The two doormen stood like unstoppable forces in the night, one held a clipboard and eyed the next clubber waiting to get in with scepticism. He checked his clipboard and then shook his head, pointing to the back of the line. I wished at that moment I was that girl and I would be refused admittance too, but as the door to our SUV opened, reality hit me, and I knew that was just a pipe dream.

Pip stood waiting for me and when I hesitated, she said,

"Come on Toots, you're not getting any younger." I made an umff sound as I shuffled across the seat and out into the chilling night. I could see both Adam and Klaus stood there, and Klaus looked a little pale. Pip just looked excited and looked up whispering the word, "home" before gently grabbing my arm and pulling me with her. Adam and Klaus went in first and Pip nearly had to drag me up the steps because I couldn't help my heels from digging in.

"Keira, please don't cause a scene, it would look odd, don't you think, if someone my size just slung you over my shoulder and skipped in... and I totally would you know...I love skipping." She said in that sing song voice of hers. She reminded me of what I imagined a forest nymph would look like, only instead of luring people into the water drowning them while listening to a pretty little sing song, she would lure people into a deadly wood, where creatures lurked ready and waiting to pick and lick your bones dry. Okay, I know my imagination was doing overtime right about now but when you've spent as many years as I have seeing things that even the brothers Grimm got wrong, well then these images were kind of hotwired into my brain with very little required to bring them out to play.

We walked through the doors and Pip winked at each of the muscle clad doormen with a flamboyant flick of her hair. Each winked back and Adam, who was in front of us growled, making the doormen wince back and eyes find their feet. I wondered not only how he had known about the wink but also what it was about Adam that had everyone cowering. All except for Pip that was. I mean, to look at him he would be the least scary one out of the lot but I knew in this supernatural game, it wasn't what vessel you wore it was what was inside the vessel that counted. I reminded myself to keep my mental guards up at all times, especially around Adam.

I followed Pip up a staircase and noticed all along the walls were paintings of dead artists. As in, famous artists that had their dead bodies painted in the styles they were famous for. There was Salvador Dali being smothered with melting clocks and little clockwork pieces sticking out of his eyes and piercing his skin. There was also Van Gogh on the floor bleeding into a bed of dying sunflowers with one made of metal protruding out of his chest. I walked on and shivered seeing one of Andy Warhol's severed head half sticking out of a Campbell soup can, which put a whole new swing on tomato soup! There were others, about ten in total, all with two things in common...Death and the fact that they were creepy as hell!

The stairs were high polished dark wood with a plush red carpet border. The hand rails matched the wrought iron theme outside and when the staircase opened up wider at the top, I could see it ran throughout the whole club. The heavy dance music was some sort of mixture between rock, rap and techno beat. There was the main stage on this level in a curved half-moon shape with great metal columns reaching the roof, with a dance floor on the lower floor below us. We had entered a wraparound balcony wide enough to drive a bus down and the floor from the stairs continued around the room. There were numerous metal staircases leading both below and above as the club was on many levels. We walked to the right and as I got closer to the twisted metal railings I looked down at hundreds of dancing bodies all jumping and moving as one. They sang in a different language to the band's main singer and when he started screaming out the next set of lyrics the crowd went wild and crazy. There was a set of metal stairs that looked more suited to a warehouse building and that's when I noticed the mix of old world elegance and harsh industrial grunge that made up the clubs interior.

I noted where the band was, at the opposite side to us and the staircase that was packed with bodies so that the band could be seen better, situated next to the stage below and above. The strobe lights lit below like some sci-fi horror flick in both flashes of green and laser lines of blue. There was a bar set off to one side but most of it was hidden under the balcony we were on.

"Keep up Toots, some people here bite." She said as she snapped her jaw twice to mimic the action. As if I needed to be any more freaked out, I thought sarcastically.

We followed the two men in front and I could see they were taking us up to the next level. These stairs had a thick black carpet with the same red border and the handrails were now high polished brass with twisted soot black iron. It kind of reminded me of an evil force trying to destroy the nicer, posh parts of this place. The walls up here had classic wallpaper with thick, black velvet swirls on a deep red background colour, whereas downstairs the walls were a mixture of dark brick and brushed steel sheets with pentagrams hammered into them. Blue strip lighting was situated under the fixed furniture and gave the floor a glossy water look as it reflected off the high gloss marble.

My head was everywhere, taking everything in as quickly as I could. I thought nowhere on earth could match Afterlife on the wow factor, but this was just as incredible. What was it with supernatural Lords anyway? They all seemed to own an alternative club and they all tried to outdo each other on a grand scale.

At the bottom of these stairs another two colossal guards stood like an impending doom waiting to crush skulls and disembowel at the first sight of trouble. Adam waited and held Klaus back with one hand placed at his chest. Even though Klaus was clearly much bigger he didn't struggle or even move from under the less threatening hand. Pip skipped past blowing Adam a kiss and took my hand in hers to lead me upstairs. When I passed the guards, they growled down at me and I hurried up the next few steps so that Pip's arms didn't extend behind her as much.

At the top, the next level was just as impressive as the rest of the décor but in a completely different way. Up here was clearly meant for one thing...playing!

The walls were a mix with box lighting that held dancing girls behind, causing shadow dancers to play with the mind. One minute they didn't look real as arms, legs and fingers would grow longer and thinner. There were seven in total, all with different colour lighting and a very different shadow behind. There were all sizes ranging from a size six to a size twenty plus. Curves of all sizes and hair both long, touching the back of the knees, to buzz cuts with large curved Mohicans. All the girls had one thing in common and it made me blush as I walked past the wall of bodies, they were all clearly naked.

The next section had swags of material in lush reds, burnt oranges and fire yellows hanging from the walls, some of which hid different sections to make more private areas where people were obviously doing more than sipping fine wine and talking about the weather. I wasn't looking where I was going and nearly walked into a half-naked girl on a swing mid-motion. It was a half-moon curl of clear plastic that had little diamonds sparkling around the edge, this matched her nipples which were encrusted with gems. After muttering a brief apology Pip laughed at my burning face,

"Come on Slick, games to play...I just love jumping on the pogo sticks," she said clapping at herself and I heard Adam behind me chuckle. This was when I turned around to find I was being closely followed by Adam and Klaus. He nodded to me and I turned to see where I was going so that I wouldn't run into any other horny people. I felt like I was running the gauntlet only instead of getting out of the way from big metal balls filled with spikes and tree trunks slamming me into a thinner version of myself I was trying to avoid skin and sin hanging from the walls and ceilings. Literally there were half naked bodies draped over some form of surface, whether it was furniture or chains coming from the beams above that were cuffed to wrists and ankles. The room was filled with people that were all enjoying some form of entertainment. Tables were set about the room keeping a clear path which we walked down, but I couldn't help where my eyes drifted to. One man lay naked on a long table and was surrounded by both men and women licking both cream and was that...blood off his body? His hands were tied above his head attached to a metal ring on the floor. He didn't look like he was there against his will.

Another table had a small Asian women sat cross-legged in the centre and was smoking from a long pipe the length of my arm. She would then blow out the smoke into different long tailed smoke creatures that would attack each other, and the surrounding guests would lay down money as if placing bets. I watched as one destroyed the other by ripping off a smoking head with non-existent talons. This club made Afterlife look like Disneyland, while this would be a theme park from the 'Nightmare before Christmas'!

We rounded a corner and now along the wall were five person length cages that also held half naked girls. They were surrounded by little round tables which sat one person each. The girls were dancing enthusiastically trying everything in their power to entice the people at the tables, all men apart from one very butch female Goth. It soon became clear that all the girls were human, unlike most in this part of the club. One of the girls had even written 'Come play with me' in black marker on her stomach, either that or it was a tattoo...You would never know in a place like this. Another of the girls had 'Bite me' with an arrow pointing to her neck and when she spun round it had the words 'I told you I tasted good' written down her spine. I shuddered as one of the men walked up to that girl and fed what looked like a note into a slot by the door. The cage swung open and the excited girl sprang free into the tall man whose arms shot out to catch her. He hauled her over his strong looking shoulder and walked past me with a quick glance combined with a handsome wink, before disappearing behind one of the curtained areas.

When I finally tore my eyes away, I was finally seeing my horror in the flesh. I looked to where Pip was running to, like an excited puppy seeing its owner. The VIP had widened into a larger part of the upstairs which jutted out over the floors below. The huge metal columns that were attached to the stage came up to this section and in between the steel was thick glass frosted at the bottom in a tribal pattern which reminded me of a design a pub regular at home had tattooed all up one arm. We seemed to be directly above the stage and you could see the dance floor two floors down.

I scanned back to the wider space and saw it was taken up by a massive rounded couch that could have easily sat ten people. It was plush black velvet with blood red piping around the edges. The base was thick dark oak carved into dragon's feet and the talons were actually embedded into the wooden floorboards. It was both feminine and masculine, with its mix of comfy, soft looking material that curved into a plump backing that you could sink into and the striking red that lay next to the haunting black and dark cut wood that framed the whole piece. However, although the piece was beautiful in every way, it was crystal clear this was an unmistakable throne for the man who sat in the middle amongst his subjects.

A fear so deep crept up my spine and kept going until my forehead broke out in a panicked sweat. I stopped dead in my tracks and couldn't physically go any further. It was as if my shoes had been replaced by dead weights and moving would actually tear my legs from my feet. I still had my hood up and I wanted to pull it all the way down over my face so that I could hide like a child, using the theory that if you can't see them they can't see you.

This was fear.

This was my destination, and this could be my end.

*This was Lucius.*

# CHAPTER 6
# BRINGING A KNIFE TO A GUNFIGHT

I was transported back to every image I had ever had of Lucius. Every memory that he had burned to my brain, whether I liked it or not, flooded every one of my senses and it all combined into one thought process...RUN!

But I had nowhere to run to, nowhere to hide in a room full of God and the Devil only knew what. It didn't just feel like I had been thrown to the wolves but into a pit full of lions, tigers, sharks, crocodiles, cobras, scorpions and even a few box jellyfish thrown in for good measure! Basically, anything that would maim, poison and devour.

I felt a slight push behind me and jumped, giving Adam a wide eyed Bambi look that was like watching as a truck was about plough into me. He gave me a frown before nodding to where Pip had trotted off to. I had no choice than to follow them all into that pit and I just prayed that none of them thought of me as dinner!

I swallowed the frightened lump in my throat and put on my big girl boots that I have to tell you were getting a little worn around the edges. I walked further round and when it got too much I was gripped above the elbow and gently forced to walk to the front of the curved couch that had a great view of the whole club around all floors. It kind of reminded me of being at the theatre in one of those box seats that gives you the best view of the stage and everything below. I went to see Midsummer Night's Dream once and now it seemed I was in the front row for Midwinter's Nightmare and now sat casually in front of me in the centre of the massive gothic couch was the sadistic play's star.

Lucius.`

Now I really was about to wet myself. No big girl panties in sight!

This devastatingly handsome creature in front of me had caused me the most pain in all my life and that was only the 'him' from my dreams, now he was here sat in front of me, in the flesh and every bit as, if not more, scary as I imagined.

Once he saw me standing there he let go of the back of the girl's neck he had a possessive hold on and pushed her further away as though he was finished with a snack. I couldn't help the small gasp that escaped when I saw the half-dressed girl turn to shift away and moved a hand to the side of her neck where blood dripped down from two puncture marks. I felt my nose wrinkle in disgust and thought… umm what do you know, Pip was right, I do wrinkle my nose sometimes.

Lucius took note of my reaction and one side of his mouth curled in a brief sign of amusement. He leaned over to Pip who was now sat crossed legged next to him holding her knees swaying. He whispered something to her and she nodded in answer. While this was going on I had time to observe the man who had been the pinpoint of misery for me for months.

He looked even more terrifying in person than he did in my dreams and I wondered if this was down to my subconscious knowing he wasn't ever really there. But now…well that was so horrifyingly real. This wasn't like some gorgeous evil baddie you found yourself attracted to in the movies or just some shadow of the darkness your mind conjured up. No this was real, and it hurt to even look at him. He was the King of all my nightmares and by the look on his painfully handsome face he damn well knew it! It didn't matter if he could no longer reach inside my mind and pull my dancing strings, he didn't need that kind of control over me anymore…no he had an entirely different level of control and it included a very physical matter in the palm of one strong pale hand.

He looked so powerful sat there dressed all in black with a casual air, he didn't have to even remotely try. He was hard and cruel all wrapped and entwined into one simple entity. His flesh and bones made from fear and the blood of others running deep in his veins fuelling his hunger for dominance and power over others. Draven told me once that Lucius was the only one who could change a demon or angel into a vampire, giving them the chance to enhance the powers they already had. Then they automatically became his child of the night. He could control anyone, whether they had been turned or not. He had even been known to control Draven at one point, but I knew very little of that story, only that the one time it happened was the reason the war between them started in the first place. I was the only one he couldn't control and from the look he gave me as he stood, he knew it. I wondered if it gave him as much of a bitter aftertaste as it seemed to, given the way he stalked towards me. He reminded me of some sleek jungle cat eyeing up his dinner. Well at least I was nice and tender for him after the beating Klaus gave me.

His long legs were encased in dark leather and he was one of the few men I had seen to be able to pull off this look without being a biker. His slim waist was the start of the V shape that was his upper body. His chest spanned out into muscular pecks and wide shoulders that would fit my folded frame with room to spare. I couldn't see his arms but knew the power that lay beneath the black material that made up the shirt concealing his impressive torso. I couldn't help but work my way up his body from his black army style boots to his stern chiselled face. He had cut his hair since my dreams and now instead of reaching down to the start of his spine it was side parted into a messy cut of choppy sand coloured strands that he pushed back from his face before reaching me. The last detail my vision took in was his incredible eyes. They were like grey ice with blue flecks coming from his pupil. They were ringed with black and were almond shaped giving him an exotic essence. Long thick lashes the shade of coal matched the natural black around his eyes, giving a gothic angel vibe. One honey coloured eyebrow rose at my scrutinising gaze.

"What, surprised to see me without a tan?" He said in a voice so deep it felt like it could cut into my skin, crawl there and stay buried forever.

"That was a clever parlour trick, my little Keira girl, but was nothing more than a minor annoyance." He made the last few steps up to me and I dropped my head so that my hood covered all of my face back into the shadows I had been hiding in. He leaned down to face level and given his imposing height he had to bend his head fully. I could feel his breath brush the skin I was trying desperately to keep concealed from his touch.

"I warned you all those times." He whispered like a secret caress. I felt a determined thumb under my chin and it pushed my head up with little resistance. What could I do, he was an unstoppable force of nature without even trying. My palms felt sticky with a thick layer of sweat and my nails cut into my skin thanks to tortured fists. My head was raised so far back that I was looking up into his stunning eyes. My hood fell back, and he stepped into me causing my face to come into view thanks to a spotlight on the ceiling. His eyes changed in slow motion, like watching someone injecting red liquid into the centre causing it to mix into the murky waters that were his eyes, before consuming them in blood and hatred.

He pushed me back and at first I forgot about the glass barrier and thought I would go over the side into the dancing crowd below. I was being held by one grip on my shoulder and one at my waist. He flexed his hand at the point of impact and saved me from slamming into the glass with too much force. He got down into my face and his lips snapped twice at me making me unable to look away from the fangs elongating down his bottom lip.

"MINE!" He both hissed and shouted. It was laced with venom from the pits he once came from. I closed my eyes so tight the tears I didn't know had formed squeezed from behind my closed lids. He scared the living shit out of me and I couldn't help but shake in his hold. He tightened this hold momentarily before running his thumb in little circles down by my side. I think it was meant as a soothing gesture which confused me more than my brain could compute.

"Step forward the one who dared touch what belongs to me!" He was livid, so much so that he looked as though he was trying to control his body into listening to the command not to shake in fury. Klaus stepped forward looking like he was very close to soiling himself. He stood against a wall to the right of us and it was at this point that I finally found my pity.

Lucius didn't look at him as he already knew who had done this to me. No, Lucius didn't take his eyes from my face for even a second. He was studying me in depth and when I tried to look down he shook his head and held my chin firm. This close, my heart pounded to an uncontrollable beat of fear and shamefully… arousal. I didn't want to be attracted to this creature of the damned, but it was so hard knowing his past and what one mistake made him into. It was a combination of all the dreams where he had been soft and gentle but with an undercurrent of raw energy that coursed through a body of betrayal. Right now, he was both.

He gently examined my head, turning it one way and another to get a closer look at my bruised eye and the lump that had grown in my hairline. His gaze dropped to my lips and I couldn't help but bite the bottom one. He released his hold on my chin and my waist to use both hands to touch my face. Each side was cupped by a hand that spanned the length of my head. He let one slide down to the column of my tender throat to find it bruised from when Klaus had held me there. His lips curled in a sneer and his fangs were still stained red from his earlier feed. His thumb slid across my bottom lip to prevent my teeth from finding a place there and he pressed in a little deeper until I felt the sting. He had my blood from the open slit on the pad of his thumb. He raised it to his lips and just before I thought he was going to taste me he raised it higher to his nose and inhaled deeply.

"Mmm, suavissimo peccatum" ('The sweetest sin' in Latin) the words flowed from within somewhere deep beneath a petrifying surface, but I had no clue as to their meaning.

"I gave you an easy command to follow and you failed me, Klaus." Lucius said in a flat deadpan tone. He was still looking at me and I refused to meet his sharp eyes.

"She is only human, my Lord." Klaus stated, and a flash of a spark came back to me and I whispered,

"No shit, Sherlock!" Of course, being close enough to crawl into my skin Lucius heard me. Was that a smirk I saw flash once before a scowl took its place?

"Yes, but she is *my human.*" I tried to take a step back but remembered I was flush against the glass. So, I opted for the welcome of a shiver to tremble along my skin.

"But my Lord…"

"BUT NOTHING!" Lucius roared making every sound on this floor cease with his demonic outburst. His eyes had flashed a deeper red giving the appearance of black blood seeping from the deepest of wounds. Once again, I shut my eyes and was close to repeating over and over "There's no place like home, there's no place like home". Mind you, if Dorothy had come here instead of Oz then I think she would have picked up one of those happy little yellow bricks and bashed her brains in with the bloody thing! This was a whole new level of crazy and I was the sanity that was smack bang in the middle of it.

One of Lucius' hands finally left my body and went behind his back. That was when I noticed the thin black straps that blended into his shirt that went under each arm.

"Hold out your hand Klaus!" Lucius ordered, and Klaus looked to where his hand was going to and all the colour drained from his face. I always wondered where all the extra blood went to?

"But Master…" Oh yeah, he was so close to begging. It was so pitiful to watch that I looked down and shook my head in the sickness of it all. I had weight in my stomach that told me something bad was about to happen and I was not going to want to witness it.

"Dignity or force?" Lucius said and after digging deep Klaus found his balls and raised his hand to the level of his face.

Before a whisper could be breathed in, Lucius' hand had produced a large blade that curved slightly at the end, getting wider on one side before coming to a deadly point. The knife sailed through the air with an audible whistle before pining Klaus' hand to the wall. It had hit him dead centre in the palm and blood squirted in a spray around the ornate blade's handle that was soon dripping red and the only thing left of the weapon showing.

Klaus screamed out at the impact and the whole floor was now being given a new form of entertainment and they clearly loved it! One small girl was even being hoisted onto a man's shoulders so that she could see better over the growing crowd. It felt like when a fight breaks out on the school playground only there wasn't a single chant or whispered word. The air was charged with an impending death on the cards and I naively thought this was the only punishment he would get, however the next command out of Lucius was one that sent me to a new depth of terror.

"Take the knife, slit your throat and die quickly." He said, and I moved my head to the side to hide this self-mutilation from view.

"No, you will watch this, my Keira girl!" He grabbed my chin and forced my head back round to face the gruesome show. I closed my eyes just as Klaus pulled the knife from his hand and placed it at his throat without hesitation.

"Wait!" Lucius said, and my breath left me in a revealed whoosh. "I want your reason for death to watch." He stated, and my heart plummeted. He couldn't be serious? I opened my eyes to see that he was…like a heart attack!

"You will watch this or a mortal will die every second your eyes are closed." My eyes snapped open the second he finished his whispered sentence in my ear.

"Good girl, now time to enjoy the show." He said in such a calm voice it made it downright sick which was a feeling I couldn't keep hidden.

"You're sick!" I said as I turned my head with no other choice than to watch as Klaus raised the knife he had clutched in one hand back to his throat. I looked into the eyes that knew he was going to die at his own hand and was no longer in his control. His pupils dilated and flashed red before he dragged the blade across his neck. Blood went everywhere at the force of his cut. I swallowed over and over trying to force the food and bile that threatened to come up, back down where it should be. All the time Lucius hadn't taken his eyes off my face. It was like he was soaking up my emotions and feeding off me like I was a Goddamn happy meal! I knew he couldn't but the looks he was burning me with made me more than a bit wary.

Meanwhile the spluttering sound of one dying Klaus was getting too much for my sanity I was trying desperately to cling onto. When it finally got me to a point that made me turn to the side away from Lucius and start retching he made a little snort at my behaviour.

"Very well." He said and I shot up despite feeling sick and woozy.

"No, no, please don't kill anyone...I'm sorry I thought it was over....I'll watch, bloody hell I'll watch!" I said in a tumble of words, utterly terrified that he would turn his sadistic wrath on any poor mortal that was out for nothing more than a good night. He turned to me and placed a hand out on my forearm to steady me from swaying I felt that dizzy. He frowned and turned his head to the slumped body of Klaus that was still fighting for his life. I watched as Lucius rolled his eyes as if this was all very taxing on his time. He went to his belt and flipped open a hidden leather flap pulling from it a small blade that resembled a thick nail file.

"Not quick enough," he said as he threw the little knife which landed perfectly in Klaus' heart, without taking one look in the direction in which he threw the knife. I watched in sick fascination as the blade started to glow into poker red before Klaus' body was set alight and then crumbled into ash just as quickly. This all happened in seconds and soon all that was left of Klaus was a dark stain on the wooden floor.

"Ruto, knife!" A figure came from behind the shadows like he had bent the darkness to his will. He seemed to have come from nowhere. He floated over to the non-existent remains of Klaus and I saw a pale hand swipe across the black stain on the floor a few times before the charred area the size of a paella dish started to turn into liquid wood. It was fascinating to watch as something so natural as wood became supernatural, as if this Ruto was opening a portal beneath his hand.

Then I made a pathetic little noise as a hand that was dripping in blood barely visible on his black wrinkled skin came from the watery hole. In its grasp was the knife that Lucius had thrown the first time. Ruto took the blade and before the hand could retreat back to the depths from which it came, Ruto spun quickly and severed the hand. A great howl resulted, that and another hand shot out quickly to retrieve the vital part he had lost. The portal closed quickly once that hand disappeared to where I shuddered to think, and the crowd lost interest after that, going back to their prior entertainment.

The shadow that was named Ruto appeared in front of us in seconds since retrieving the knife and I couldn't believe the face I was looking at. There was only one way to describe Ruto and that was a teenage punk. He couldn't be more than thirteen or fourteen years old and although tall for his age, his face screamed adolescent. He was slim and undeveloped with baby smooth skin on a baby face. Although he was scowling, it was hard not to see the cute face he was masking with indifference. His hair hung longer at the front than the spikes at the back and covered one eye. He had bright turquoise eyes that shone with an experience he shouldn't yet have. There was something in his manner that screamed this kid was not just smart but he was smarter than most of the people that surrounded him. I don't know exactly what told me that but the look he gave made me feel that I was so far beneath his intellect that I was the child here, not this boy who looked more like some skater misfit.

He was wearing skinny grey jeans that tucked into his cherry red Doc Martins at the ankle. They had skulls painted on the boot tips over the metal spikes that would hurt like holy hell if ever used them to kick someone. He had on three belts, each different and only one that looked as if it was doing its job. One plain red that was thinner than the rest, one black and white squares and the one actually hooked into belt loops was black with silver spikes. This matched not only his shoes but also the numerous leather straps coating his wrists. If I could take a guess I would say he had a thing for spikes, that and guitars if his t-shirt was anything to go by, which featured two crossed guitars, one made of metal and the other lit on fire. This look was finished with a tight leather jacket that hugged his slim build like an expensive black glove. He was so achingly beautiful it was painful to look at him, despite his evil glare and his 'I don't give a damn' vibe!

With him and Pip combined it looked more like school had broken out for a Demon holiday! What was next, I would turn a corner and there would be twenty demon Girl Guides all selling poisonous cookies. It wouldn't have surprised me if Lucius had a classroom full of henchmen all with adorable plump cheeks and fangs sharp enough to slice through skin like a knife through soft cheese.

Ruto gave me one last scowl before handing Lucius the knife. He then sank back into the shadows as though it was his special place. I looked down at the knife and saw the handle that looked like carved black bone. The blade itself was red but this wasn't just down to the blood that covered most of it. No, now that I could see it outside of a body, it was clear that the blade was made of red glass with a steel edge that gave it the extra sharp tip. He looked down at it and frowned.

"You should always keep your weapons clean," he said and took the last step which eliminated any space between us. I backed up once again into the glass wall and he looked me up and down as if he was looking for something I had no clue as to what.

"You'll do!" He said before bending his frame to lean down and wipe the blade across my leg, transferring the blood from his blade onto my jeans.

"Eww" I said once again wrinkling my nose in disgust. He actually chuckled at the noise I made before flipping the switch back into Demon Lord mode.

"Take the girl upstairs to my private suite, she needs cleaning up!" He stated wrinkling his own nose at me as though I smelled like a footballer's feet. I couldn't help but glare at him for the insult. Okay, so it was true, I probably did stink after not being able to shower for days and being manhandled since New England.

Pip bounced over to me with way too much enthusiasm for the show that just took place but then again that was probably the reason for it. She had been sat on Adam's lap since I had been escorted to Lucius. Adam had gone over to where Pip sat and lifted her crossed legged and placed her in his lap, as though that was the only place he wanted her. What I wouldn't do for the lover that owned me to do that right now. For Draven to march right in here, kick major demon butt and pick me up like the Goddamn hero he was and whisk me away into the German night. Only that thought was hit with a bat of reality and dripping in disappointment.

Draven wasn't coming.

"Come on Toots, let's get you clean, sparkly, glittering, shiny and smelling like candy floss." My stomach filled with lead for the second time. Please Lord no.

"Pip...No sparks, no glitter and nothing shiny." Lucius said after stopping her gently. She looked like he had just stomped on her favourite Tonka toy and the wheels had come rolling off. Then her eyes lit up as she asked,

"And candy floss?" He looked as though he was giving it some thought, and I had to resist rolling my eyes.

"She smells sweet enough," he said shocking me at the sincerity of that statement. Did Lucius just give me a compliment? It didn't look like anything but what it sounded. I was left dumbfounded as Pip took my hand to pull me away.

We started to walk around the opposite side from where we came in and it was busier this side thanks to the better view of the band playing. There were people huddled tightly to the banister that curved round and went down the staircase which looked like it had been taken from a deserted warehouse. That's when the idea hit me and only gave me seconds to think it through. If this went wrong, I could face plummeting into the dancing crowd below, giving a whole new meaning to crowd surfing. Pip only had a loose hold on my wrist and with one sharp yank I was fairly certain I could get free. I saw where she was taking me and the staircase that led to Lucius' place of R and R. There was no way I wanted to be anywhere near that! His idea of rest and relaxation was most likely a BSDM club in a dungeon with blood on tap! I think I will pass thanks.

I had to time this just right as the crowd near the stairs down was the busiest part and the two bouncers that stood there had their hands full preventing anyone from below getting in the VIP, as it was clear that's what this level was. We were just weaving in and out and round a girl that had been let in when I decided it was now or never. I yanked hard taking Pip off guard and felt a slight guilt using our new friendship to my advantage but using that trust was a fleeting moment in the background of importance to what I was doing. I pushed past two girls dancing by the rail and gripped it with both hands. I took one breath and...

Jumped.

It felt like a lifetime until I landed even though it was no more than a terrifying second. I landed on the stairs that curved under where I had jumped which meant I got past the two guards that were surrounded by gothic girls all jumping to the beat. I didn't even try to find Pip in the crowd as all I needed to do now was make it past the stairs full of bodies. I had jumped into the only space and half landed on someone who started shouting at me, swearing no doubt in German. I pushed past everyone leaving a trail of pissed off people in my wake. Then as it curved passed the stage area I decided why the hell not, it worked the first time.

I held the rail and heaved off it again to land on the stage. I fell forward and landed on one knee that felt like it burst. I looked down to see the ripped denim and blood coming from the skin beneath. I waited for the pain, but it never came and I put this down to the incredible burst of adrenaline that coursed around my body like Draven's demonic blood. It pushed me forward like someone had shot a gun and I was running for my life, which was probably true 'cause if Lucius got hold of me now I didn't think I would just get sent to my room without supper.

The band carried on despite the fact that a girl had just dropped down from nowhere and was making her way through the members like some crazed fan. The song they played sounded more like it belonged in a Bond movie but it went well with the chase. I managed to jump over some cables as I passed the drummer and a guy on base. The jump down to the next level looked too high but then I noticed some stairs further back which I made a beeline for. I gathered this was where the band went when they finished their set. I jumped down them taking three steps at a time as I went. I almost lost my balance once more but righted myself as I rounded a corner onto the bottom floor. Thankfully most people were around the stage and on the dance floor, so I manoeuvred around the club with little more than a few shoves here and there.

I saw the bar and ran towards it with the notion that if it was anything like every other bar I knew then it had access to a door that led out to the back alley. I ran over and dipped down before the bartender knew what hit him. I ducked under the side opening and ran to a door I could see behind him. I left him shouting at me in German and when he made a grab for me he dropped the bottle he was holding. Something that smelled like vodka splashed up my jeans, but I didn't stop, not for a heartbeat. I found myself in a dingy looking corridor and walked past an open door that led to an office. I saw the door at the end that had the word 'Ausgang' painted on it. Man, oh man I hoped that meant exit in German. I pushed myself even further and it was only now that the throbbing in my knee started but I couldn't stop for anything. I threw myself at the door and thanked my lucky stars when it opened. Even better it opened into fresh air. There were stairs that went up to street level and I scrambled up them in my haste, scratching my hand on a piece of jagged metal. I bit my lip and winced at the sting. When I looked up I was in a dark alley with nothing but two huge bins that reminded me of the dumpsters outside Afterlife. On the three sides I had a fence to my left with no door, a brick wall facing me and my only way out to my right. I could see the cars whizzing past on the road and knew it was time to run again.

I started to run toward the road watching the space around me getting brighter thanks to the street lamps when suddenly a black limo appeared blocking off my exit.

"SHIT!" I shouted before turning back and giving the fence a shot. My foot lost traction and I skidded as I turned quickly trying to make the distance between me and the car grow. I made it to the other side and bounced back slightly from the force of my body hitting the fence. I looked up and thankfully the top wasn't covered in barbed wire, so I gripped it in two places and was just about to haul myself up when I felt thundering from behind me. I didn't want to look, knew that I shouldn't. But still I looked. I saw the bins shaking violently like they had some monster trapped inside. Okay time to go!

I whipped back round and took a firmer hold pulling up my weight. I felt my muscles strain and thought with dry amusement that they wouldn't feel this way if I had gone to the gym sometime! I dug my foot into the holes but when the metal by my hands started to get hot and then burn to the point of pain I had no other option than to let go. I dropped to the ground, but thankfully landed on my feet this time. I just had time to look up when I heard metal being scraped across concrete. I saw the sparks before I realised what they were coming off. One of the huge bins was coming right at me with the speed of a moving car in fifth gear. It was going to crush me and I was trapped in a corner. There was nothing I could do but wait for impact.

It was wrong what they said about your life flashing before your eyes, actually it was utter bullshit, not unless you had a zombie walking slowly towards you that gave you ten minutes to think about it. There was only enough time to do what every other human would do in my situation and that was to cower into a small ball and wait for death by rubbish. Not the most poetic death but very few ever get to choose.

The noise hit me before the pain ever did. The bin had come flying at me with enough force to cause sparks, but it had crashed into the wall leaving me enough space in the corner without being touched. I let out the breath I had been holding in long enough to almost kill me instead and stood up on shaky legs. I was about to climb out of this little smelly hole when I saw something travelling at a great speed from the sky. My heart leapt at the thought that it could be Draven!

It looked as if someone had jumped from the roof and I felt the landing without seeing it. I was just about to heave up when the lid to the bin flew backwards caging me in. I landed back against the wall and slid down till my butt touched the ground. I now had a little roof to my hole and all my dreams of it being Draven here to rescue me were squashed into a black pulp of rot!

I had my head rested on my knees and my hands covering my head in a pathetic attempt at a protective cocoon. I only raised my head when I heard the bin had stopped moving backwards, scraping its wheels across the ground like nails on a chalk board. I first saw the black scorch marks on either side of me, that the sparks had created and saw my captor stood there with his arms folded across his chest. He looked so powerful I found tears well in my eyes at the fear that the figure in the dark created. I remembered that same imposing figure being in my room one night, which had turned out to be the most painful experience of my life. I still had nightmares about it and now my nightmare stood there in the muscle and flesh ready to hurt me once again.

I looked up as the tears slipped down my dirty cheeks and saw two red eyes glowing in the mist that had come from nowhere. It was as though his essence was so evil it changed nature itself forming a cold visible air around his form like it was drawing off his power. Was he feeding the evil aura or was he feeding from it?

I didn't really care, just so long as he wasn't feeding from…

*Well, from me.*

## CHAPTER 7

# NO ESCAPING YOUR FEAR

"That wasn't playing nice, little Keira girl!" Lucius' voice penetrated the darkness and his eyes lost their red glow. I was hoping that would mean that he was getting control over his rage. My escape had failed and now it was time to pay the price...problem was, I didn't yet know what I was buying into, so I was in the dark on the payment type.

"Stand!" He said that one word so covered in authority it became something new the way he said it. It became a threat. I did as I was ordered and got up to stand on shaky legs making me look like a baby fawn.

"Where are you bleeding?" He asked as his face appeared out of the shadows. I jumped back but he just grabbed my arm to steady me.

"I asked you a question!" He stated, and I found myself becoming mute. What would he do if I told him, chow down? He squeezed my flesh that he had his large hand attached to and I yelped before I found my voice.

"M..my knee." On seeing my compliance one side of his mouth crept up in a smirk.

"Does it hurt?" He asked and I nodded my head to indicate yes, not being able to give him the satisfaction of words.

"Good. Come with me and if you try anything else, you do remember what I can do with my knife, don't you Keira girl?" I gulped, and he took that as my answer. He tightened his hold until the point of pain and dragged me from my corner. He walked me down the alley towards the car, cutting the distance at a greater speed than I could keep up with, so I ended up being dragged behind him. Also, my knee was throbbing, and I stumbled a few times which he stopped by hauling me back to my feet before I would fall down fully.

"Please…slowdown…I can't walk that fast." I said, trying in vain to pull my arm free.

"So, first you try to run from me and now you want my pity." At these words he unknowingly flipped the switch to release the fighter in me.

"I don't want your stinking pity!" I yanked my arm free even though it hurt and would no doubt be leaving one hell of a bruise. I stood facing him with my arms crossed over my chest and when he turned his body round in slow motion it felt a little like I would imagine a bull fighter felt.

But I didn't run. I was done running. There was nowhere left for me to run to.

He cocked his head to one side as if he was trying to figure me out, as though no other human in this world had stood up to him before and he looked, well, he looked amused.

"And if pity is all you're gonna get, what then?" He asked showing me a cockiness that I was surprised I'd had to wait until now to come out to play. I couldn't help my reaction to his question and although it was one that was likely to get me killed, it happened before that thought had time to fully process. I slapped him so hard across the face that my palm stung so badly it felt like I had burnt it. I held in my shock of both the action and the pain but really I wanted to cower back to my corner like a kicked puppy.

He face had whipped to the side from the impact and I could see the mark I had left on his pale face like a child's red hand painting. He turned his head back slowly and I wanted to cringe at the deadly look his eyes inflicted. His hand flashed out and had grabbed my wrist and yanked me to his chest in one swift moment that left me breathless. He snarled at me but wouldn't let me move from him like I tried to do.

He lifted my hand to his lips and opened his mouth to let his fangs lengthen down past his bottom lip, I watched as they kept growing until nearly past his chin. What was he, a sabre-toothed tiger in a past life? I watched in horror as he looked as though he was about to take a chunk out of me.

"Don't," I whimpered but it just made him smile. He lifted his free hand to his face, joined his three fingers bent to his thumb, leaving one up that he held to his lips and said,

"Ssshh" He then used that hand to hold my forearm to keep me from pulling away. With my hand captured in a way that made all of my fingers splay out with the pressure he applied to both the front and back of my hand, he raised my middle finger to his lips and took the whole length of it into his mouth. He sucked it in and pulled it back out. I thought that was it but I screamed when he placed it at the end of one fang and applied enough pressure to pierce the skin. Blood pooled and dripped down my finger which he then put back in his mouth.

His eyes rolled back in his head in what looked like extreme pleasure before turning into a different shade altogether. They changed into the colour of the sun! I had never seen anything like it before in my life. His eyes became alight with fire, like he was staring into flames where there were none. They were utterly beautiful and unlike any eyes I had seen. They were Hellfire eyes. And then they were gone. His body had gone ridged and for the life of me he had acted like he had just found sexual release.

"Fuck!" He said through gritted teeth and one look told me to get far away from him now before he wanted more than just a sample. I tried to tug back but he refused to give me even an inch. However, the fear he found in my eyes made something in his soften. He let my finger slide from his lips and lowered my hand without letting go.

"What are you?" He asked in a voice so soft that it was almost like liquid sliding across my skin leaving goosebumps in its path.

"I...I...don't know what you mean." I said trying once again to back away from this man who was all predator. He was back to being that jungle cat, only now it looked as though someone had just teased him with a slice of raw sirloin and he was coming for the whole joint.

"Please...don't." I said placing my other hand on his chest to stop him from taking another taste, which seemed to shake him from his blood lust. He let my hand go and I pulled away from him to get some distance between us.

"If you strike me again I will do more than bite you." He leaned down to get eye level with me and said words I dared not doubt,

"I will bite your hand off!" His eyes flashed red at the thought and he turned to walk to the Limo that was waiting for us.

"Get in the fucking car!" He snapped.

Once situated in the limo I tried to get as far away from Lucius as possible but with all his other minions in there waiting for us I had only one space left for me. Lucius put a possessive hand on my thigh when I tried to create as much space as possible, even if it meant being plastered against the window but this was the third time he had stopped me now and when he tightened his hold on my leg he said,

"Don't!" I froze at the growl he put behind that order and decided to just give up. I hated him so much it actually seemed to leave a bitter taste in my mouth. I looked over towards Pip but when she caught me looking she just stuck her tongue out at me and I didn't need any guesses as to why she was upset with me. Well, that was the quickest BFF relationship I had ever had.

"Is the bird ready?" Lucius asked Adam.

"She is being refuelled as we speak, my Lord" Pip huffed at this and Lucius raised an eyebrow.

"I didn't want to go to the lake house yet." She said like a spoilt child.

"Squeak!" Adam said in a tone full of soft reprimand.

"Well, I thought we were at least going to get one night at the club, we don't even have a playroom at Königssee!"

"Behave Pip. I apologise my Lord." Adam said nodding at Lucius who just looked amused at Pip's behaviour either that or he was just used to it. Pip huffed once more before sticking her bottom lip out to sulk in silence.

"What of the bartender?" Lucius asked Adam, which made me stiffen my spine in anger.

"Karmun," I whispered looking out of the window.

"Excuse me?" Lucius snapped like I wasn't permitted to speak.

"His name is...was Karmun." I found tears starting to well when thinking of the friend that had no other choice than to betray me for the man he loved and it was all Lucius' doing. He turned to look at me and I looked away before I let the tears fall and give him the satisfaction.

"Ah, I see he did his job perfectly in building trust. He met the end he wanted as payment then?"

"Payment?" I said horrified, wiping away a stray tear angrily with my sleeve.

"YES payment! He chose the outcome of his actions." He said with his voice on a razor's edge.

"What a steaming pile of shit!" I said shocking everyone in the vehicle. Pip looked delighted, Adam looked cautious and the boy Lucius called Ruto looked downright murderous and snarled at my outburst. Despite everyone's reactions I couldn't help but carry on.

"Oh, okay, so kidnapping his lover, forcing him to betray both his friend and his King and then giving him the option of death or umm… let me think…DEATH! Something you class as payment…Give me a br.." Lucius' hand snaked out and grabbed me by the throat squeezing the words unfinished. He pulled me closer to him until our noses almost touched.

"Listen up, Keira girl and listen good, because the next time I explain this to you, you will find yourself on the ground begging at my feet! I do not care for the opinions of some lowly human on matters in which they have no concept! This Karmun chose his fate and yes, death was his payment for him and his lover. Befriending you was his JOB! One he executed perfectly considering your reaction to his death." He snapped out every word and I couldn't help but wonder if my opinions meant so little to him then why was he explaining himself like he was. When he didn't see the fear he expected he tightened his hold painfully but still allowed for the air to fill my lungs. He was happy when my eyes at least showed discomfort before continuing.

"Death is too good for some people, but Karmun did his job and did it well enough that I allowed his wishes to be carried out. You do not understand enough of our world to know where they went and I have no intentions of teaching a child! You will behave and show me some GODDAMN RESPECT!" He lost his icy cool and screamed the last two words at me making me close my eyes in pain. Then he pulled my face to his mouth and licked my tears away. I was frozen in the fear at what this man could actually do to me. One minute he was showing me the very meaning of the word hostility and then the next he was kissing away my tears and rubbing soothing circles around where his thumb and fingers had gripped me in a vice.

"Do I make myself clear, pet?" He whispered into my forehead and I nodded, too scared to be the cause of his outrage again.

"Good girl," he said softly, smoothing back my hair before letting my head go. I tried to retreat back to my window but he shook his head at me to indicate I stay at his side, close enough for my leg to be flush against his solid thigh.

We drove for about fifteen minutes before I noticed signs for a place called Klinikum Bogenhausen. Once we made a few turns here and there I saw something that caused my skin to sweat. Sat there lit up with red floodlights was a sleek black helicopter. Oh no, no and hell no!

I think everyone in the car could suddenly feel my fear thicken the air and Pip smiled before saying a comical little,

STEPHANIE HUDSON

"Uh oh, me thinks someone doesn't like to fly." She said and nodded to me when Lucius was looking at her. The colour must have drained from my face and I looked down to my lap to see I had twisted a bit of my jacket round and round in my fist until the corner looked like I was trying to make a fajita. Lucius looked at me and rolled his eyes before saying,

"Humans!"

I decided to swallow the stream of insults I had ready to go and continued with the dread I had going on. It was one thing flying in a plane that you could kid yourself into believing it was just a nice room with a view. The same went for the few times Draven had flown with me in his arms, keeping me safe and flooding my open fearful mind with wave after wave of reassurance. But this, this was a death trap with a propeller!

The limo was pulling round and my heartbeat felt like someone was playing African drums in my chest cavity. It seemed ironically unfunny that I would end up with a boyfriend that had wings when I was terrified of heights, surely that spoke volumes on my mental health!

I jumped at the sound of the door opening and as Lucius got out I was very close to breaking my one rule…begging. His hand came down expecting mine in return, but I had sat on my hands and couldn't move. I heard an exasperated noise and then a stern voice that held no argument.

"You have no time left before you put your hand in mine and get your arse out here before I come in there and drag you out by all that lovely hair you have hidden. It would be a shame to rip it all out, don't you think?" I didn't need asking twice! I slapped my hand in his with more force than necessary, thanks to my anger. Was that a chuckle? He pulled with the same amount of force and I practically fell out of the car or would have if Lucius hadn't grabbed my upper body and hauled me to my feet.

I landed into his body and when my face pressed against his chest the first contact was ice cold then turned incredibly warm. It was like someone had flicked on a heat blanket he had on under his clothes and I couldn't understand it. I looked up slowly before he let me go and if his startled look was anything to go by, he didn't understand it either!

"οήλιος" ('The Sun') He had closed his eyes while speaking a word that sounded Greek. Then, as I inhaled it must have brought him back to himself and he let me go. Did he even realise that his arms had

80

wound round my torso in a protective manner? I stepped back to put some space between us and he frowned once before turning his back to me.

"Gelmek" ('Come' in Turkish) He used two fingers over his shoulder to indicate that I follow him. I decided not to look at the black beast of modern man that sat waiting for us to get into its metal belly and instead I looked at my captor's strong looking back. For a man of his size he really was quite graceful in the way he moved, gliding, his long legs cutting distances into nothing as his tall frame reached the helicopter. I watched as he bent his tall frame ducking his head slightly as the helicopter's propellers whipped round at such a speed that it became a circular blur in the air above the roof. It reminded me of an engine powered panther, sleek, beautiful, fast and so deadly. It even purred as the propellers made a whirring sound that filled me with dread thick enough that I felt sticky.

I hadn't realised I had stopped dead while watching him walk away still feeling confused about the look he had given me, until Pip bumped hips with me chuckling in her sing song way.

"Yep, master's got a fine ass. Come on Toots, time's a'wasting!" She said entwining her fingers with mine and walking to where Lucius was waiting. She swung both our arms out like you would see two young girls doing in the playground holding hands.

"I'm not angry at you anymore, so back to being best buds okay?" I was shocked at her statement after seeing her giving me evils in the limo but then thinking back I had seen Adam whispering to her and her nodding at what he was telling her. After that she had smiled and resumed back to playing with his hands in what looked like trying to make shadow puppets with them. I could have sworn I'd seen a duck, bird, dog and...a wolf eating a man? I didn't think I was going to remember that one for my new little niece or nephew.

Oh God, that was when it hit me! What on earth was my family going to think? I was supposed to be there now introducing them to Draven and getting last minute Christmas shopping with my mum and Libby. What had they been told, were they worrying about me not being there or would Draven have come up with a believable excuse for me missing the holidays?

My mind reeled in thoughts that were miles away with my family, when I didn't even realise I was being lifted into the helicopter by Adam until I was being positioned in the seat opposite Lucius. This caused my breaking heart to freeze over with an icy glaze of fear. The door slammed shut and my panic started to rise.

"I can't do this!" I said in a voice I didn't recognise as being my own. I was frantically looking around for my escape route. Pip was sat next to me and Adam opposite her. I gathered Ruto bravely sat up front with the death trap's pilot.

"It's okay Toots, this baby is an Agusta A109 and only goes 165 miles an hour and is powered by two Allison Model 250-C20R-1 turboshaft engines. She could out manoeuvre a humming bird and their wings beat at 80 times per second. Besides, master would be mighty pissed if this thing crashed, that would be 6 million plus down the shitter. Oh but it won't, that is if the fuel line doesn't…"

"Pipper!" Adam warned but it was too late as my last shred of bravery drove away sat in the limo.

"Did I say too much again?" She asked innocently and took one look at my green face and said,

"Ooops…maybe I should call Sheila when we land?"

"I already made the appointment," Adam said trying to do her seatbelts for her but with her bouncing up and down he was having a hard time doing so. I saw Lucius shake his head at the sight of both of them. Meanwhile, I was just plain shaking. I grabbed the belts but couldn't seem to grip them enough to put them in the right bits. I think I even heard Lucius roll his eyes and I jumped when I felt hands take the belts from me.

"Relax," he said so softly it was as if it had come from someone else. He gripped my wrists and placed them down on my lap, but he didn't release them until he felt my pulse beating an erratic tune beneath my skin. He frowned and let them go as I screamed out when the sound of the engine changed. I felt like meat would feel before being put in the blender, or juicer as I looked more like the sad lemon sat here with a sour look of trepidation on my face. As we started to lift off my hand flew out and grabbed onto the first thing I could find which turned out to be Lucius. I grabbed onto his shirt like it was a life preserver. It fisted in my hands causing the material near his biceps to tighten. Wow, someone worked out, his arms were friggin' huge! Okay, focus Keira, death trap remember!

"I think she's gonna puke, Luc!" Pip said to Lucius using a nickname that sounded strange given that she had been calling him Master and my Lord.

"Oh, for the love of death, come here little one!" He said, clearly exasperated. He took me by the waist and hoisted me up and as I screamed he sat back down in his own seat with me now on his lap. I squirmed and wriggled trying to get away but every time I got closer to the window I would nearly end up on Adam's knee. Lucius cursed and tightened his hold before lifting me as though I weighed nothing more than a paper bag full of feathers. He turned me to face the other way so that I seemed further away from the window.

Adam took my space next to Pip to allow more space for my kicking legs.

"Ssshh, be still, calm yourself. NOW!" He growled the command in his demon voice and the helicopter actually shook making me freeze and I gripped onto the arm that he had anchored around my waist. It was my best death grip.

"P..please, d..don't do t..that again," I stuttered. His arms tightened, and his other hand smoothed back the shorter bits of my hair that had tried to cover my eyes.

"Then don't make me!" His harsh voice didn't mix with the caring way he handled my shaking body.

"B..but, I'm scared, I..I can't help it," I said feeling so weak and pathetic that it brought tears to my eyes. He shook his head and his hair rested forward, so before he made a comment he pushed it all back with one hand.

"Incredible. Humans are such irrational creatures. So here you sit, a small space filled with demons that could tear you limb from limb as easy as pulling wings off a butterfly and you're scared of the helicopter crashing, which has a less than 2 percent chance...tell me Keira girl, what do you think the percentage is of a vampire sucking a human dry?" I gulped and bit my lip which sent a sharp sting to the area. I licked my lips before the blood dripped down from the split. Lucius didn't miss the action.

"Want to find out?" He said cocking his head to catch my eyes that were trying to dodge his. He laughed when I silently shook my head in quick succession.

"Then I suggest you get that habit under control before I take it up myself, your lips look too good with that colour upon them." His thumb had brushed across them while saying this and taken the excess blood away. He looked like he was going to suck my blood off his thumb but thought better of it. He wiped it on my jeans instead and I just hoped it wasn't going to become a habit as it was the second time he had stained my clothes with blood, well at least this time it was my own, I thought darkly.

The helicopter shuddered, and something beeped twice.

"Oh God!" I shouted before covering my head with my hands. Lucius growled far too close to my ear. He so was not helping in trying to get my fear under control by doing that. I felt myself being lifted and every muscle tensed.

"What are you doing?"

"Straddle me!" He ordered as he shifted my weight to face him.

"No!" I said trying to get away, but he gripped the back of my neck forcefully and dragged me to his face so that our noses met.

"Yes!" He positioned my legs and I had no other option than to go where he put me. He was like Draven, just too damn strong! How was I ever going to fight when forces like these faced me?

"Just try and relax." Was he joking?

"I remember the last time we were in a similar position and you asked me to do the same thing...look where that got me!" I snapped remembering back to the nightmare that resulted in me coming far too close to death. The bastard actually chuckled!

"Well if I do recall, you were trying to kill me."

"And if I recall you were there to try and take control of my mind, so excuse me if I tried to warm you up a little." At this comment he laughed out loud and my body shook under him. When he smiled it lit up his entire face reaching every part. His eyes actually glowed and the lines around them softened his usual scowling face. Pip and Adam exchanged a look I couldn't determine but I was pretty sure it started out as shock.

"A little warm, Keira, you set me on fire."

"Yeah and I was the one who got burned...go figure!" I said with enough sarcasm that my mother would have been ashamed. Wait a minute, these people had kidnapped me, forget about being ashamed, hell, she would have taken up cheerleading if she could see my feistiness now.

"Well next time, I suggest you don't play with fire and do as you're told." He warned but let's face it, he might be the big and tough Vampire King but he didn't know the first thing about me and my inability to follow orders! Then the helicopter made another of its many noises and my irrational fear took over making me grab back onto Lucius like a baby monkey! I couldn't believe that I was using a man I utterly loathed as a base for staying safe. What the hell was I doing? My brain answered that question and mentally bitch slapped me for acting like some little Stockholm Syndrome victim. And forget what I was doing, what was he doing? I was his prisoner and he had me sat on his lap while we played 'who had the wittiest comeback'!

"I told you to relax but if you insist." I pulled back from hiding myself in his chest to glare at him. I would have slapped him again if his last warning hadn't flashed up and I was rather fond of the idea of keeping both of my hands intact.

"I'm not sat here for your entertainment!" I snapped out.

"No, for that you would be naked and bound. However, I'm not into innocents, I like my meat with a little more bite!" He snapped back, only he used his teeth at my face making me fall backwards. His arm snaked out too quickly to let me fall and he pulled me back. I couldn't help but try and get away from his handsome face that was doing strange things to my mind. I made my hundredth mistake for the week and turned my head towards the window. At least it was night time but still, seeing the city's lights so far below had my heart pumping at full speed. My chest felt like I imagined it would if Leivic had given me a bear hug! I couldn't seem to drag enough air into my lungs and I grabbed my throat with both hands as if that would help. I couldn't tear my eyes away from the window and my imagination kept playing tricks on me...I was sure the ground was getting closer...it was, wasn't it!

"No, no...we're going down...Oh NO!" I screamed trying to get off Lucius like this would help my situation.

"Foolish girl! Look at me! Keira. Look. At. Me. Now!" His voice brought me to a level where I could think past the panic but when my face didn't turn quick enough Lucius grabbed my chin and forced me to look at him. When I tried to get away from his hold he grasped me roughly by the neck and his hand felt far too big for the column. His other hand seized my twisted hair and held it in a tight fist. He then pulled my head back to make my neck stretch out under his palm.

"Enough! If you cannot be trusted to keep your eyes from that window and keep your fear in check then I will take the option from you! If you look at anything other than my face I will hurt you...do you understand?" I couldn't focus on answering him as my fear of flying had quickly been replaced by the sight of one very pissed off Vampire who was currently controlling my head like a ventriloquist's dummy.

"Keira, do you understand? Answer me, pet." He eased his hold on my hair and I nodded with his assistance.

"Good girl, now tell me what you're studying?"

"What?" I said stunned at his question. He tugged on my hair and tightened his hold on my neck.

"Let me explain, so that there is no confusion, the next time I require a sensible response. I am going to ask you questions and you, in turn are going to?"

"Ooooh, I know this one! Answer them! It's answer them, right?" Pip said, like she was so close to getting that A on the non-existent pop quiz. I actually wanted to laugh at the look on Lucius' face. He didn't answer but shot a look her way.

"But I was right, wasn't I?" I could hear her whisper to Adam, but when I tried to look round Lucius' steely gaze blazed back at me, his hold preventing any other movement than the one he wanted.

"You sure was love," Adam responded quietly and then everything went back to just me and Lucius, including his stupid questions.

"Right, now that we're clear, let's try that again, should we?" He said before repeating his earlier question. I really wanted to tell him where he could stick his damn questions, but I didn't fancy bald patches in my hair so with gritted teeth I answered him.

"History, Spanish and English Literature."

"See that wasn't so difficult, was it?" His smug smile confirmed he was enjoying his control.

"And you paint." It was more of a statement than a question, although his look told me he still expected my answer.

"I do...did, sometimes." He raised one of his dark honey eyebrows that were a slash across the top of his eye making his eyes seem fiercer, deadlier looking. His face only seemed to ever soften when he laughed and I doubted I would witness that emotion very often.

"I saw paintings in both the rooms you stayed in, so try not to lie to me, it would not be wise." Another warning. Should I be making notes?

"Fine! Yes, I paint but not very often anymore."

"Ah, of course, not since Morgan I gather." His answer took me not only by surprise but took every other thought away. Like someone had thrown me into a hole in a frozen lake, no other sense came to me other than feeling cold...so, so cold. He must have seen it in my eyes because he started to make a soothing motion with his thumb that went up and down the full length of my neck he still had trapped.

"I don't want to talk about that!" I said feeling a burning anger that did nothing to help defrost the bitter memory of what that name still did to me.

"No, I can imagine that you don't." What, how and when did he find out about my past? I didn't ask…I couldn't ask.

"Don't worry pet, I won't make you talk about it. I'm cruel, punishing and heartless but not sadistic." He stated, and I couldn't imagine him getting very far with that description on a dating site! I wanted to laugh at the idea of what it would read…

'Vampire King, kills for fun, collects knives as a hobby and commands his vampire army as his job but likes to spend nights having long walks along the beach with his latest victim before sinking his fangs into them for a midnight snack. If you're a tasty AB negative then call on 0800- murder but don't forget to leave a message on voice mail if ringing in the day!'

The crazy thing was that in this day and age he would probably have received thousands of calls trying to set up a date. If only they knew the truth when reading and watching all these vamp romances, that the truth would terrify them into running for their lives not getting naked, flicking their hair back and practicing their gyrating!

"What did you think of the art work at the club?" His questions were throwing me off guard and I hated that he was trying to have a normal conversation with me…I mean, I was sat straddling his bloody lap for Christ's sake and I'm not even going into the solid package I could feel down there. Nope, not doing it!

The Helicopter had another vibration and we tilted to one side. I yelped pitifully and was too afraid to feel ashamed of myself.

"Focus, Keira girl!" He let go of my hair finally but wrapped it firmly around my back coming to rest his hand at my side with a sure grip. I closed my eyes tightly and tried to hear his words and was strangely taking comfort in his secure hold on me. I put it all down to being up in the air when I could die any minute…No, No, don't think about it, or about how many things that could go wrong…like if these vibrations worked one of the thousands of pieces that held this machine together loose…NO, stop it Keira!

"I can see you fighting yourself girl, let go and listen to my voice. I want you to open your eyes and look at me. Do it now!" I did as he asked after letting out a squeak of pain as his fingers pressed into my fleshy side.

"Good. Now you are going to listen to me. We are just turning. You should know that I have put far too much time and effort into obtaining you and I am not going to give you up until I fulfil my goal. That includes helicopter crashes, which this one isn't going to do. Now concentrate on answering my questions. It isn't a request."

He continued to ask non-important questions about me, which included art I liked, books I read and even places I would like to visit. I answered every question like an obedient little submissive and all the while I wanted to hit, punch and scratch every time he pried another slice of my personality out of me. Why did he want to know these things? Why would he care about simple things that a human girl enjoyed in life? I could have understood if he had asked about Draven or things that went on at the club, not that I should be complaining but it was still baffling.

After just over an hour we were coming into land and that's when all my previous panic seemed tame.

"I can't, I can't...I ..please, I can't do..." Lucius gave me a shake but I was far too gone no matter the amount of pain he inflicted this time it wouldn't work, nothing would! Going up was bad enough but it was the coming down that really sent me over the edge. White hot unstoppable fright, panic and horror all rolled together causing an actual pain to flare in my chest. I felt like I was suffocating on my fear and nothing, nothing in this world could...

"STOP!" Lucius shouted before taking my head with both hands and merging his lips with mine. He took hold of me and forced his way into a deep all-consuming kiss. I couldn't think and the helicopter we were in vanished, it actually started to erode as though it had been left for thousands of years and someone had played the footage back on fast forward. The wind blew away at the metal and machine leaving us sat together kissing as the earth's elements took my fear away. When there was nothing left of the helicopter I saw the blinding sun high in the bluest of skies. The wind blew my hair around my face but Lucius' kiss deepened before I could pull back. He ran his hands up gently pushing all the hair from my forehead. The kiss was burning and I tried too hard not to like it, not to find any pleasure there in his tender touch, I tried... but...

I failed.

He dominated my movements and I caught myself responding to

his power. He explored every last bit of me and did it over and over again. I noticed my hands had turned into fists in his shirt as though holding him to me instead of pushing him away. Then without understanding why, my hand crept up to his shoulders and kept travelling up his neck to his head. It was as if my hands weren't my own when one grabbed a handful of his silken strands and the other scraped my nails down his back. He groaned in pleasure and his hands left my face to rap around my torso in an unbreakable hold. He pulled me so close I couldn't breathe and when he knew it, he left my lips to trail kisses down my neck. He found where my pulse beat the fastest and sucked my flesh into his mouth, making little nips at me without piercing the skin. It was driving me crazy and I found my hips were making circular motions of their own accord.

I felt something bump under us and tried to pull back but his hands fisted on my jacket and he moaned into my neck.

"My little Keira girl," he whispered when I tried to free myself. The fog in my mind was starting to clear and I shook my head to rid myself of the dream. Where was I? As soon as that question formed, the field vanished along with the summer's day. I opened my eyes to find the helicopter wasn't ancient dust a million miles away but was a very real, solid reality. But more importantly a very real, solid Vampire King was under me sporting one hell of an erection!

Oh no, no, no, what had I just done…I had kissed Lucius and worse still,

*I had enjoyed it.*

# CHAPTER 8

# REACHING OUT TO LOVERS LOST

OH MY GOD! I had just been kissed until my toes had curled and I had kissed him back! What was I doing? I felt like crying but my shock was still too fresh for the tears to follow. I fell backwards and Lucius let me. I landed on the floor below him and his face told me I wasn't the only one in shock. Why was he shocked, he's the one who kissed me?

"Phew, now that was hot, hot and hot! Adam did you see how hot that was?" Pip said causing the real heat to find my cheeks. I looked her way and she winked at me, giving me the thumbs up. I looked away to hide my shame which is when I noticed we weren't moving and were firmly on the ground. I looked back to Lucius and just caught sight of his Hellfire eyes flash before resuming to darkened grey. I couldn't tell what he was thinking but I knew one thing, whatever had just happened was not what he had expected. Without one word he flicked a latch on the door and opened it to get out without a backward glance. I had no clue what to think so I didn't. I was just too glad to get out of this bloody thing and finally have my feet on the ground.

"So, it was good for you too, yep?" Pip said as she helped steady my wobbly legs.

"It's from the flight," I said keeping my voice tight. The only thing was that I wasn't sure I could trust in the answer I had given her.

After the horrendous flight, I found myself yet again in another vehicle and driving away towards some Lake house that Lucius owned. Well one thing was for sure, I didn't think I was going meet Keanu Reeves and Sandra Bullock there that was unless they were really demons. That would have put a whole other perspective on the Matrix!

This time round I found myself sat next to Pip and Lucius couldn't have sat further away from me if he had tried. I wasn't complaining and if kissing me had been that bad then maybe if I flashed him he'd let me go! Ha, I actually made a snorting sound at this thought.

"Oh, how adorable was that? You snorted! Like a cute, little pig, like Babe...only I preferred him in the city, its cleaner than the farm and I only like getting dirty when I mud wrestle and only with Adam, he can't pin me down when I'm all slippery and I finally get to win, do you eat bacon?" I didn't know what to respond to first, the fact that I was getting referred to as a pig, that she liked to mud wrestle with Adam or that she wanted to know my thoughts on bacon! This girl was just intense... WOW wasn't she just!

"Love, remember breathing," Adam said dryly.

"I do, I do," she whined. He leant over to her and lifted her with ease onto his lap. I got the impression that he didn't like her being anywhere else than stuck to him. She let out a little sigh of contentment.

"I meant other people, sweetheart," he said nuzzling into her neck making her squeak. I decided it was far too painful to watch anymore and turned away to look out of the window. As I turned around I saw Lucius staring at me with his hand half on his cheek and chin. He looked as though he was studying my facial expression. I turned from everyone towards the limo driver determined to remain this way for the rest of the drive.

"We have news, my Lord." I woke up to a new timid voice I didn't recognise. At first I didn't know where I was but when I looked down at myself I knew it was happening again. I was a shimmering, translucent form of myself this time but my heart still leapt at the man in front of me. Draven was in a study I had only been in once and it seemed like a lifetime ago. He was sat at a desk the size of a bed and there wasn't a space not covered in paper. Charts, maps and ancient text on ripped pages from books that looked older than the written word.

Draven looked like a mere shell of the man I knew so well. He was so dark and frightening he was hardly recognisable as my lover. His deep-set eyes looked formidable in his quest to find me.

"Speak!" He snapped with a deadly intent so fierce that two glass vases shattered on the mantle of an enormous fireplace. No one batted an eyelid and when I looked about the room I saw why. It wasn't just a mess but it was close to being destroyed! Chairs lay in splinters with the cushions that were once attached to them now charred black remains. Around the room there were multiple holes in the stone walls that looked the same size as Draven's fist. Stone dust lay underneath from the crumbling aftermath. There was smashed glass and pottery in most corners and it was anyone's guess what form they used to be. In fact, the only thing in the room to survive seemed to be the desk and chair as they were the only things in use.

"My Lord, the waitress Rue received a message a while ago, but it was in code, she has only now discovered what it means and who it is from." At this Draven brought his fist down on the desk causing the papers to rise and fall but thankfully he refrained from destroying it.

"Bring her to me NOW!" He ordered and both I and the poor messenger jumped. I had seen Draven angry before but this...this was something else!

"Yes, my Lord, she is with Lady Sophia and Lord Vincent as we speak." He flinched as if waiting for his master's wrath and habit of breaking things soon to include bones...mainly his.

"Good, get them in here!" He said standing and folding his arms in waiting.

"Yes My L..."

"GO!" Draven's interruption caused flakes of stone to float down from the ceiling. I looked up to see it had started to crack in places. If Draven kept up this fury then pretty soon he would end up standing in a pile of expensive rubble.

I wanted to run to him but couldn't move from the long couch I sat in. It too hadn't managed to escape Draven's thunderous temper but at least it was in one piece if not a little sharp and splintery around the edges. The thick teal velvet was split around the rounded arms and the stuffing was coming out like fluffy white clouds of flesh bursting from material skin.

Draven was wearing ripped jeans that weren't done for fashion purposes and a black t-shirt that strained every time he tensed his fists, which was often. The action caused a rippling effect to travel up his forearms and then hit his biceps so that little rips left his sleeves with slits showing skin underneath. He reminded me of the purple Hulk trying to contain that other side of him. His hair was a disarray of black strands that didn't know where they should be and his jaw was shadowed in days old stubble. He looked like a fierce warrior ready to do battle and in a way I guess he was.

Vincent walked through the door, which was held there by only one hinge. He looked around the room and silently shook his head. He also looked like he hadn't slept in a month, only his stubble was blonde and his eyes, instead of their usual crystal blue, were now a deep navy. There were also lines of worry on his face where usually there were none.

Sophia followed him and also took note of the room but instead of following her brother's silence she did comment.

"Bad time for redecorating don't you think, brother?" At this Draven growled so low and deep, I half expected him to break out in fur and start howling at the moon. However Sophia didn't look scared but she did hold up her hands in peace.

"Down boy, just saying."

"Stop Sophia, don't fuel his rage, not this time!" Vincent snapped and for him it was unusual to lose his cool. Normally Vincent was the meaning of icy reserve. Not that he was unfeeling in anyway, just an Angel who never let his feathers get ruffled.

"But where's the fun in that?" She asked sweetly as they walked over to where I was sat. I quickly moved out of their way before they sat on me. Whether I was a ghost like figure or not, nobody liked to be sat on!

"Enough! Where is Rue?" Draven responded with his raging authority.

"I'm here, my Lord," Rue said from the doorway. For the first time since I had met her she looked terrified. I didn't blame her facing Draven like this. Intimidating didn't even cover his left pinkie finger let alone the full man that was close to shaking, he was that angry.

"Come!" He ordered and she nearly tripped over herself as she hurried closer to him. A few words could describe Rue and that was little, skater style and blind. She never let her burnt eyes become a problem though as she had aided sight in the tattoos of eyes she had etched into the palms on her hands. She had ink black spiky hair that was shaved on one side. She wore knee length camouflage combats and army boots to match, to this she added a black t-shirt that was tight to her large breasts with a red heart shaped grenade and the band name 'Greenday' written underneath.

"You have news?" Draven asked looking down at Rue, who was

even smaller than me. She nodded and took a large gulp that looked as if she was trying to swallow a gobstopper.

"Then out with it!" Draven snapped making me frown. I knew he was angry and hurting but there was no need to make everyone miserable because of me.

"Mmy Lo…Lord," She coughed before she continued as if trying to find some courage to carry on.

"Over the last few days I started to receive a string of emails that were all broken cryptic files. I thought it was someone trying to hack my computer and I couldn't open the files or delete them. Then the last email I received was a code and a list of instructions to open the files. Once I did, I found…" Rue hesitated but it was long enough to make Draven's bones click when he tensed.

"Speak! What was in the files?"

"Everything my Lord. I..I think they came from Karmun."

"Dom, I have seen the files she speaks of and she is right, Karmun's disappearance has everything to do with Keira's kidnapping. It is as we thought and the files he sent prove he was the traitor all along. The blood oath somehow got broken, I don't know how but…"

"Carrick!" Draven said the name dripping with venom and topped with dark revenge.

"Dom, do you really think a soul collector would…?"

"He is the only one powerful enough to collect Karmun's soul which was tied to me by oath. It was foolish to believe that those ties could not be broken and that the traitor was not one of my own. Carrick had Karmun's soul ever since Constantine left."

"Taken, my Lord." Rue spoke in whisper.

"Speak up!" Draven shouted and Vincent went to stand by Rue and place his hand gently on her shoulder. Thank god for Vincent and his kindness because no one was going to get anything remotely like that from Draven for a while.

"It's alright Rue, tell us what you know," Vincent encouraged kindly.

"Constantine was my friend and before he left he confessed to me that he thought he was being followed, but whenever he mentioned his fears to Karmun he just convinced him that it was nothing." She looked down and started to fidget with the drawstring at her waist band.

"Continue child," Vincent said holding up a hand to prevent Draven's angry response.

"The night he left I got a text message saying that he was right. At the time I thought nothing of it because he had been telling me that he was thinking of getting away for a while. I thought he meant that he had done the right thing. Whenever Karmun was asked about where he was, he always said that they had parted ways and it seemed too painful for him to explain further."

"But?!" Draven couldn't help himself or his demanding tone.

"But when I received the emails I knew the truth, that Constantine had been right in his fears and Karmun did what he felt he must to save him." At this Draven erupted into purple flames that were blazing white at his skin and black at the ends. His wings burst from him and spanned the large room with barely space to spare. Oh yeah, he was mad!

Poor Rue threw herself to the ground and knelt at his feet.

"Forgive me my Lord," she whispered and I wanted to slap Draven for scaring the poor girl half to death.

"DOM STOP!" Vincent said in his own outrage.

"Your actions help no one, especially not Keira. Just try to control yourself and think, damn it!" Draven looked to Vincent and his words seemed to calm the beast that was consuming his mind. He took a few deep breaths and the flames died down along with the rest of his demon side. The only one that looked amused was Sophia, damn naughty little demon!

"Rue, you may leave us now, you have done well. Take some time off and tell no one of what you know." Vincent said as he helped her to the door.

"Yes, but of course my Lord," she replied, looking relieved to have made it out of there alive.

Once she left, Vincent tried again to control the situation.

"Dom, you are going to have to get a hold of yourself if you are to have any sense left in finding her. You need to focus. You are connected in such a way that only you can help her."

"Yeah, so get your angry head out of your ass and get that head back in the game, bitch!" Sophia said making me choke on a breath I think I was taking?

"Thank you, Sophia, helpful as always," Vincent said in a dry tone he only reserved for Sophia's benefit.

"Vin, enough with the sugar frosting, what our dear brother needs is an ice cold splash of reality. Dom, you know Keira, the little minx is more than even you can handle, and she is stronger than most Demons

I know. She will not put up with shit and when that shit hits the fan she will come out swinging." I found myself grinning and shaking my head in a little big-headed nod of approval. Did she really think all that stuff?

"She is right, if not a little blunt, but right none the less. Keira is strong and besides gaining your powers a little more each day, Lucius will not hurt her, what he needs from her is far too important to him to let anyone else do the same." Umm hold up, back up and slow down... what was that about me gaining more of Draven's power?

I walked over to Draven and waved my hand in front of his face.

Nothing. Zip. Nada! I even started jumping up and down but my floating body just kind of moved at a slower speed and didn't have the same effect, not that anyone could see me anyway! Man, this was so utterly frustrating! I was finally getting some answers now I couldn't get them to explain fully. I was also torn between trying to throw myself into Draven's arms and kissing him on every available space and slapping him for keeping these things from me!

"Explain what was in the files." Draven said as his only response to his siblings trying to talk sense into him. Vincent let out an exasperated sigh and continued,

"The files all indicate the same thing but the last one sent was from a mobile device, most likely his phone."

"Vincent, I fear my patience is snapping, please get on with it!"

"They're in Germany, Dom and I doubt we need any guesses to why or where."

"So, he took her to his home in Königssee and now we know what he wants in return," Draven said shaking his head.

"Shit!" Sophia said getting up to stand. She walked over to her brother and looked so tiny next to both her brothers' tall frames.

"But Dom, you know you can't... don't you?" Draven turned his back and walked over to the open balcony that spanned the length of two sides of the room. He looked out into the night and took a deep breath.

"Bring Ragnar to me when he wakes from the sleep I put him in. His rage should be under control by then enough to explain things."

"Dom?" Vincent said in question and my heart felt like lead. I knew what this was about, and I had an idea at what his answer would be. I just prayed that I was wrong. My survival depended on it.

"Brother, you do realise that you can't give him what he asks for in return for Keira. Tell me you know this and are not even considering it!" Vincent was sounding a bit panicked now, coming to stand by his brother. I looked at Draven's back and saw his shoulders tense before dropping in defeat.

"I know Vincent." He said dropping his head and I couldn't prevent my reaction.

I screamed.

I dropped to my knees and when my body made contact with the floor I changed into myself for a second before I switched back to the ghost. I kept wavering between the two like someone had pictures of me on a flicker book or a projector on an old screen.

"Keira?" I looked up at the sound of Draven saying my name in wonder. I saw all three faces staring at me in jaw dropping shock.

"You can see me?" I asked feeling stupid. Draven took a cautious step forward as if he was worried that I might disappear, which was more than likely what was going to happen.

"It can't be, it's not possible is it? Dom, is this what you were telling us about, is this how it happened before?" Vincent whispered as if also afraid he would pop some kind of spell.

"Yes. Keira, is it really you? Speak to me." He said so softy it broke my heart to hear that level of desperation in his voice, he sounded like he would soon break into pieces.

"I'm scared if I do I will fade away like last time." Draven let out the breath he was holding on hearing my voice.

"Gods! Keira tell me, are you alright, what happened to you…why are…" He came towards me but I held up my hand to stop him and saw for myself how it continued to glimmer.

"Don't touch me, I don't know how long it will last and I don't want to leave. Draven I can't go, I don't…" I started to cry and he flew to his knees just in front of me. He held fisted hands at his sides like it was taking every ounce of will he owned to keep them from touching me.

"Don't cry, please sweetheart, don't cry. You have to be brave alright…I will come for you, I promise but you need to be brave."

"I don't know if I can, I..I.." I was trying to control the overload of emotions, but it was hard and the flickering of my body started to become more erratic.

"Keira listen to me, we know where you are but you have to trust me, I will come for you."

"But how, you can't, you said…"

"I. Will. Come. For. You. Do you trust me?" He said each word in a way that looked both painful and absolute.

"Yes," I said and he closed his eyes briefly in relief.

"You are so brave, I am so, so proud of you but I need you to be brave for a while longer, can you do that?" I lowered my head, knowing what needed to be done, it just wasn't easy telling someone what they wanted to hear, but I said,

"Yes, I can do that." Draven's eyes misted slightly before he shook his head.

"Good girl."

"How is this happening, what does this mean?" I asked motioning down at myself.

"I don't know exactly but I think it has something to do with our strong connection. Keira? Keira no, hold on to it, Keira, NO!, KEIRA HOLD ON!"

"Draven?" I looked down and realised what he was seeing. I was fading and looked up to see him lunge for me screaming out,

"Keira! Be brave! ...I..lov…"

"I love you!" Were the last words spoken and an almighty roar in the darkness echoed through the night as I bolted upright.

"Bad dream?" Pip asked. She was sat at the end of a bed which I just so happened to be lying in. The room was filled with a twilight glow from the sun already saying goodbye to the day. I was getting really confused about which day it was.

"Where am I?" I asked with a croaky voice that was the result of lots of sleep and no liquid.

"The lake house of course. Do you like your room? Mine's down the hall but Adam is still asleep, well he's still tied to the bed and he was asleep when I left him. He'll be cranky, but he will get over it. He hates waking up and not knowing where I am, you should see him when I play hide and little Bo Peep."

"Little Bo Peep?" I had to ask.

"Yeah, I dress as little Bo Peep or little Bo Pip as Adam calls me. Anyway, I then go hide and he has to find me, then we have sex wherever he finds me. Have you never played it?" I coughed my surprise and felt my throat get drier.

"N…umm… nope," I said through the coughing.

"It's fun, you should try it but not with Adam! I would have to hurt you and I don't want to do that 'cause I like you, you're funny and I don't have many girlfriends, they say I'm annoying and then Adam growls at them and then they shut up and I laugh. But you like me

don't you? Adam says you do. He can tell. So do you like your room?"
I smiled as it was hard not to with Pip sat at the bottom of my bed
dressed in Thundercats pyjamas with My Little Pony slippers and a
badge that said, 'Flip the bird with Angrybirds'. I mean, her green hair
was even in high pigtails. She was so bloody adorable that you
couldn't help but like her.

"Okay, firstly no, I haven't played that game and definitely would
not with Adam! Secondly, I think you're funny as well and think
anyone that doesn't like you is just plain stupid. Thirdly, yes Adam is
right, I do like you, even though you helped kidnap me. And last of all
I don't know about my room 'cause I have just woken up and haven't
really had chance to take it all in yet." She had the biggest smile I
think I ever saw on a person so small and didn't have time to brace
myself when she threw herself at me.

"Yey! A friend and you're a girl! I'm so excited, this is going to be
so much fun, you'll see. I won't let anyone pick on you and Adam
likes you, he thinks that you're nice to me and he likes anyone who's
nice to me. He gets a bit over protective you know and he…" A
massive roar echoed down the hall and shook the door to my room.

"Ooops, gotta go, sounds like my hubby is awake and a little riled
up, better go and calm the beast." She winked at me as she jumped
from my bed onto all fours before straightening, shouting as she went,

"Coming, Tiger!" I think my mouth was still hanging down when
she popped her head back round and skidded by my door.

"Oh, I was supposed to tell you some things." She winced when
another roar sounded, and I must have looked terrified 'cause she said,

"Don't worry about him, he gets fussy if I'm not with him for a
while." I was in utter shock that those sounds were coming from the
same man that I had seen wearing glasses and reading about the stock
exchange! She scratched her head in a comical way that pulled one
pigtail down further than the other.

"Ah, that was it. The bathroom is through that door over there.
That door there is a closet or is it a wardrobe? Umm? Oh well, the
balcony is open and you're not locked in or anything, but I wouldn't
go walking around at night on your own. You're allowed to go
anywhere that's not locked, which is obvious, 'cause how would you
get there if it was locked." She smacked herself and another roar
sounded all the time getting louder and it started to frighten the
Bejesus out of me.

"I'M COMING! Jeez, needy…much! Okay what else did Lucius

say…oh that's it, he will expect you there tonight, in the great hall and he expects you to be dressed for the occasion, his exact words were… show some skin. Okay, gotta go 'cause I think I just heard him break one side of his chains and damn him those were made from expensive Tungsten!" At that she shouted,

"See you tonight," from down the hall where snarls, growls and howls had been added to the immense roars that were actually shaking the walls. Then it all went silent and just when I thought that was it, moans of a different type started up, that and…meows, then was that…? Oh no…spanking! I quickly ran to the door and slammed it shut.

I swear every time I woke up around Pip it was like tripping on acid or something! It was hard to think of anything, but Pip's erratic behaviour and I was desperate to try and understand what was happening every time I went to sleep. It was as though I was being transported back to what Draven was doing at the same time I was asleep. But what did it all mean and why was it happening? He asked me to stay brave and that was the only thing that I could do for him and myself. He told me he was coming for me and I had to believe in his words. He would find a way and I trusted that man with my life, so this was the time to put that trust to the test. They said that Lucius wouldn't hurt me and so far, all I had had from Lucius we're threats of pain that hadn't been delivered and something else, something so out of character that it confused the hell out of me and that was kindness.

I wasn't a fool and after little thought I knew what he was trying to do in the helicopter, which he had in fact succeeded with unconventional tactics but nevertheless he had done a wonderful job in distracting me from my fear. At the time I was pissed, angry and ready to use his body as a scratching post but now I had time to think about it, why did he even care enough to take it to the next level and kiss me? And more importantly what had happened when he had? Where had we gone?

I found myself leant up against the door twenty minutes later still going over questions that I had no answers to. I let out a frustrated,

"Arrg!" And pushed from the door and turned, barging into a solid frame.

"Is there a problem, my little Keira girl?" A formidable voice asked, causing me to think one thing,

*Umm yeah, you could say that again!*

101

# CHAPTER 9
# THE LAKE HOUSE

L ucius stood there and folded his arms across his chest after I had bounced back from him. His gaze travelled down the length of my body and I almost felt like every layer of clothing I had on was melting away with such a heated intensity I couldn't help but look down. Someone had taken my jacket off and my top clung to me like a second skin. The cool air in the room had made my chest look as though I was hiding a couple of pencil erasers down my top. I flashed my head up and crossed my arms over my chest which made Lucius' mouth quirk up on one side.

"Is there a reason you're here trying to penetrate me with a death-ray look?" 'Death-ray look'? How stupid of a line was that! Think Keira before speaking, I cursed myself. Of course, he found it amusing...smug bastard!

"Umm, 'death-ray look', now that is a new one. But have no fear pet, if I was trying to penetrate you, it wouldn't be with my looks." I actually gulped as I turned away to hide a heated blush. Why did he have to look at me that way?

He laughed out loud as I walked away from him towards the bed. I grabbed the grey throw off the end of my new bed and wrapped it around me.

"You think covering yourself will change that statement?" I jumped at the sound of his voice at my ear but before I could move away from him his hands circled around my neck from behind.

"No flight little bird. Still. Calm." He said in a golden voice like maple syrup. It dripped down my spine and caressed every nerve on its travels. He made little soothing circles with his thumbs at the point where my spinal column started just under my hairline.

"I..I'm cold," I said weakly just praying my legs didn't give out and let me crumple to his feet.

"Is it cold in here?" He said not even trying to keep the mockery from his tone. I shivered right on cue and heard his silent laughter vibrate from him.

"I like the colour of your skin when it's cold. So pale. A frozen doll ready to be painted on. The perfect canvas for the colour red, don't you think?" I frowned at the image he delivered, and the memory of my arms covered in blood hit me like a battering wave making me sway. Of course, Lucius had me in his hold so I couldn't fall but the picture of blood so dark it looked like congealed black ink oozing from my white skin, torn at the wrists made me shiver. I looked down and was thankful I still had on my gloves under my long-sleeved top. Lucius must have noticed where my focus leaned towards because I felt his breath at my neck before he spoke.

"Let me see them!" This snapped me out of his sticky web of confusion and distraction so that I could take back control. I tugged myself out of his hold taking him off guard long enough to create distance between us.

"What do you want from me?" I snapped without facing him, pulling the cover around me tighter as if it would protect me somehow.

"Everything!" The word echoed around the room and I whirled around to find I was now alone. Heat surged through the room and I heard crackling coming from the middle of the room.

Lucius had vanished and left flames in his place.

The water felt good pounding the last hours away from my skin. After my encounters with Mr Cryptic himself I walked around my room and took in my new surroundings before taking a shower. Like the bathroom I was stood in, the bedroom was nothing like I expected it to be. Given Lucius' nature I expected blood red walls, black furniture and maybe a pile of skulls in one corner. What I got was ultra modern, urban chic that looked straight out of a catalogue advertising first class hotels.

My room was split into sections; a bed, living space with even a small kitchenette and a bathroom bigger than my bedroom back home. There was a walk-in wardrobe that held clothes I had no intention of ever wearing, including what looked like fetish wear in every colour! Umm that was a big no, no. My bed was a queen size made from white painted wood with four twisted trees, one at each corner. All the bark was stripped and they looked like pieces of driftwood sanded smooth. The top branches had gold filigree painted around them where they disappeared into the ceiling. The bed was a work of art. It was then complemented with soft greys, faint silver and light gold with the materials that covered it.

The bed faced a glass wall that led out onto a decked balcony that even had a set of two black wicker chairs and a square table with a glass top. The view outside I had yet to see as it was as black outside as if I had been in a hole underground. The walls were white washed with only a single painting in the whole room. It was a painting of a tiny one storey house with a small glow from one window. It was situated on a mountain top with a raging sea below that was trying to reach it with giant waves fuelled by the storm. It looked like a dire situation to be in for the image behind the window and at that point, I felt that we had a lot in common.

Half of the room was sectioned off by a stone wall holding a glass fireplace which could be seen from all sides of the room. Thanks to Lucius the room was toasty warm and still held a roaring fire. The other side of this wall was the living space that had a rectangular three seater settee and looked more fashionable than comfy. There were two single chairs to match in a white material accessorised with black and silver cushions. The three seater had a throw along the back to match the cushions. On the wall the seating was positioned round, was a huge flat screen TV that was twice the size of Frank's back home.

The flooring throughout was light, beech wood boards that stopped at the bathroom where black slate took over. The bathroom was sleek lines of carved marble and glass. There was a beautiful free standing black bath with white cast iron dragon style legs. There was a separate room with toilet and bidet. The sinks were square slabs of stone that had been left natural and rough. They sat on top of a black slab of thick wood that also had white cast iron legs in the same design as the tub.

The shower I stood in had had me thinking twice before getting in. It was the focal point of the room and was strangely positioned in the centre with clear glass walls. It looked more like a clear cage that was made to put bodies on show rather than be used to get clean. I spent more time watching the door than what I was putting on my skin. I think I ended up using shampoo on my body and body wash on my hair. Thankfully though, no-one had come in while I was in there and I think it was only when I had finished and stood at the sinks that I finally was able to breathe naturally.

I looked at myself in the mirrored wall and noticed my damaged body was already starting to show signs of healing. It was as if it had happened over a week ago not a day. The bursting around my eye had changed from blue and purple to an insipid green colour. The split on my lip had gone altogether along with any marks that had been around my neck like some sadistic necklace. My ribs still ached when I stretched in a certain way but the bruising there had gone down as well. What did they give me?

After towelling myself dry and wrapping my hair up in one lush fluffy towel I wrapped a dry one around my body and walked back into the main room to find I had a guest.

Pip was back and wearing a lot less than the last time I saw her. She had on a pair of pants that looked like they were made of latex and I could not even begin to imagine how she got the skin tight material on her legs. She had a white studded belt the same thickness as the length of her hand. It pulled in her tiny waist and rested over more delicate areas. The only other item added to this outfit was an emerald green leopard print scarf that was draped around her neck and barely covered her little breasts. Her green hair was done up on the very top of her head in one massive twisted curl and then hung down on one side in sea green waves with electric blue tips. At the start of the giant curl was a pretty bow that matched her scarf. Her makeup was just as outrageous as her clothes, or lack of. She had blue feather eyelashes with longer purple ones at the sides. I wondered if they annoyed her as much as they looked like they would with keep tickling her eyebrows.

Her eyelids had a thick line in blue that flicked out at the end and on her left eye she had a black scroll pattern around the edge and down her cheek. In between her lips she was sucking on a blue lollypop that she popped out of her mouth to wave at me.

"Hey girlfriend, I'm your date tonight or am I an escort and Lucius is your date…? Ooops, I can't remember that bit but I'm here to help you get ready and take you down. But you're nowhere near ready… this isn't good. Master doesn't like to be kept waiting…God that sounded so clichéd didn't it? Master doesn't like to be kept waiting!" She said this last part in a deep, spooky voice that sounded like she was trying to imitate Frankenstein.

"Anyway, you need to get your cute little heinie ready and I'm just the Imp to help. Besides, Lucius gave me some rules for how he wants you to look, sooo…just think of me as your 'STYLE ENFORCER'. Hehe, this is going to be so much fun!" She said, and I laughed at the way her voice got all deep and she stood like a superhero with legs apart and hands on hips when she said, 'Style Enforcer' and I tried not to notice her flashing a boob at me when she did it. Then it hit me and alarm took the place of amusement.

She was going to help me get ready? Oh no, this was so not good!

"I'm not wearing this!" I said walking out of the wardrobe that had a load of nightmares hanging up like Goth ghosts!

"Toots!" Pip said jumping up from the couch and she hit mute on the remote. I glanced at the screen and noticed another cartoon.

"Err…Dangermouse…really?" She looked back at the screen and then back at me.

"Not a fan, eh? Anyway, I watch it mainly for Penfold." I snorted out my laugh, was she serious…? Ooops from the looks of things, yes she was.

"You know Penfold is the real hero don't you?"

"Ummm, I thought that was Dangermouse." Now it was her turn to snort.

"Oh hell no! Ernest Penfold may just be a humble little hamster, but he's the one that had to put up with the cocky little mouse's shit! One day he will get the credit he deserves. You're wearing it, come on, time to go." She moved to grab my hand, but I stepped back.

"Okay, let's try this again, in terms you will understand. I am Penfold and I am telling the mouse NO!" I said folding my arms in determination. Pip smiled a grin so big her piercings flashed silver from the reflection of the fire. From what she was wearing or not wearing, I could now get a good look at her extensive tattoos. I realised that the sleeve she had covering one arm also travelled down the same side of her torso. It was beautiful and the artist in me recognised the masterpiece. It was the sea, the earth and the sky. Each section looked as though it had been painted on. The sky on her forearm had stormy clouds of purple and grey with a V shape of tiny birds flying past. Then there was a thick black ring that created a band of ancient text and riddles of symbols I didn't even try to understand. Her upper arm was the earth and started at the other side of the band. It was the forest with lush greens of all shades, mints, limes, teals and olives, all of which entwined together in perfect swirls. Then there was another band, thicker this time that curled around her shoulder and snaked off under her ribs. The last stage was the ocean. It came up from her waist in great waves that burst into white foam and spray out to her bones. It reached the black band and as she turned I could see a ship getting swallowed by the dangerous dark waters. It reminded me too much like the only painting in my room and I had a feeling I would find out why all this seemed relevant.

I realised as she lifted her hands in the air dramatically that the whole tattoo made up one long picture from the deepest depths to the highest possible place left.

"Am I the mouse?" She asked me pulling my attention back from the beauty of such painted skin.

"No, Lucius is the mouse, you're Agent 57!" Her face beamed at me like I was her new worshipped hero!

"You do watch it! Okay, Okay, you are like the coolest friend ever, I knew the Electus wouldn't be some boring ass twit that thinks her shit don't stink…You're actually cool and you like cartoons and you think that I am Agent 57! I think I love you." She said with a frighteningly serious face.

"I don't do girls, sorry!" I said weakly not wanting to offend her.

"Me neither, but for you Toots, I would way make an exception. But the man I own, known as Adam, would be mad and he is a bit over the top possessive, so I think we should just be friends 'cause he might lose it and then rip you apart or something. But I still love you. And by the way, you are so wearing that!" I looked down and shivered at what my body was covered in.

I turned to face the glass walls that covered two sides of the room and saw an entirely different me looking back. I found myself wearing a dress made of black lace so fine that it showed most of my skin underneath. I had on a black lacy underwear set that I was also instructed to put on and you could see every one of my curves as it pushed my breasts together like they were old friends getting re-acquainted. The dress was cut across my shoulders but I might as well have been just in my bra and knickers for the good it did me. It went down to my feet and was cut up in four slits to the tops of my legs. My feet were also encased in black lace in the form of ankle boots that looked like a tube of the material had been cut at the front and then peeled back like skin from fruit. They were lined with plush red velvet that was so soft I didn't even notice the high pointed heel or the way my feet were forced into the unnatural position only comfortable for ballerinas. The stiff red curls around my ankle were the only flashes of colour. That was unless you could count my blush that matched them.

I couldn't even be comfortable that the dress had full length sleeves reaching down to my knuckles as the black lace was a pattern so big that there were too many parts that ended up being sheer see through. My scars were only slightly covered in a black gauze and the pattern of black roses with curved deadly looking thorns was the thickest in the places I didn't need to hide. Like at my cuffs which flared out over my hands not my wrists, or like the strip across my collar bone not my ample cleavage. Even on my legs the pattern only got thicker at the bottom and faded as it got higher up my legs. My most private parts were left on show under a black sheen.

"Look Pip, if you're really my friend and you care about me then you have to know that if I walk out of here looking this naked then you are going to have a hyperventilating mess on your hands. I have a major issue showing not only lots of skin but skin in certain places…if you know what I mean." At this she looked down to the V of my legs and I shook my head, not even showing that part of me was as bad as showing my scars off to the world! No matter how much I had looked I didn't find one pair of gloves in the whole room and the ones I had been wearing had somehow vanished along with the rest of my clothes.

"Okay look, I have an idea. Lucius only said you have to wear the dress but he didn't say we couldn't add to it." I smiled at where her mind was leading to, that was until she came out of the wardrobe carrying a thick black leather corset that had more laces than a boot camp!

When she had finished I was feeling a little better with what she had done. I now had on a tight leather corset that tied at the back all the way down to the curve of my behind. The front also went down in a V shape that hid my lacy briefs well. The only thing that felt more on show was my bust thanks to the corset now setting them up like a shelf under my chin, although pushing them higher to the thicker pattern managed to hide them a little better. She had done my hair in a strange knotted plait with lengths of black ribbon that gave a startling contrast to the gold in my hair. This was positioned to one side and the ribbons curled down past the point that had been wound around the end of the plait to keep it in place.

She had also done my make-up and every time I fidgeted she would pull down on my plait like the rope from a bell tower. As long as she didn't get it in her head to start swinging from it like an overzealous monk doing his own interpretation of rock music! I don't think my hair would survive without a year's worth of split ends.

I ended up looking like a doe eyed pet as the dark shadowing made my eyes look huge. The smoky effect made my eye colour stand out as being stormier grey than blue and combined with my pale skin, made them look like a glass window keeping out the raging storm behind them. My lips matched the red velvet on my shoes and soon the flush of my cheeks whenever anyone would see me. But no matter how I looked I couldn't keep my worried eyes from finding my scars that seemed to stand out even more under the thin veil of black mist.

"Ah here we are, I think these will do." She said holding up some thick satin ribbon in long strips.

"I took these off another outfit I found in there. Hold out your arms." I fisted my hands twice before stretching my fingers out in a nervous manner.

"Come on little Tot, I have seen far worse in my years…hell, I have done much worse so gimme gimme," she said holding out her hands ready to restrain my wrists. I closed my eyes before handing over my past for someone other than Draven to see.

She moved the long sleeves up over my elbow and started to tie the ribbon into a knot at the top then she wound the thick ribbon around and around my arm until she got two ends the same length at the wrist. She tied a pretty bow tight so it wouldn't move and did exactly the same with my other arm. I looked down at her handy work and when I saw my arms completely covered in black satin I looked up and must have given her a beaming smile. She smiled sweetly back but I couldn't help pulling her shoulders to me in a heart-warming embrace. She laughed and hugged me back.

"Thank you Pip," I whispered, and she patted my back.

"Oh, you're welcome Toots, I had fun dressing a real doll. Come, we are running late and Lucius gets antsy." I flinched at the name and she dropped her smile.

"He won't hurt you, you know that right? He… well he…ah hell Toots, he likes you okay, even if he is a dick douche bag about it! Don't be afraid, okay…I will take care of you." I nodded my head and started to follow her out when I realised something about Pip and couldn't help but ask because all the time she was wrapping my arms up like gothic bandages she never once asked about them and morbid curiosity got the better of me.

"Pip…don't you want to know what happened?" She stopped dead by the door and turned so slowly I thought I might have offended her in some way.

"I know why already, Keira." She paused as if to confide something more and this time didn't look at me when she said,

*"It's one of the reasons I respect you so much."*

# CHAPTER 10
# MASTER FOR MY SINS.

P ip led me down a series of hallways that were all carved cold stone that dripped with damp in some places. All the while I could hear a faint rushing of water that sounded as though I was on the other side of a waterfall. However, in some areas it got so loud that I couldn't hear Pip when she spoke. Whenever I started to lag behind she would grab my hand and pull me along like the doll she had called me. I bumped into her when she stopped abruptly. I saw that we had turned a corner and through a small arch way that lead to an open balcony. That's when I gasped.

The great hall was exactly as it sounded…One great big almighty hall! It was as if someone had converted a church into a Goth club! The walls were covered in rippling red material that was well over twenty five feet high. They were lit up by lights at the bottom angled upwards and this made the silky material shimmer like liquid causing it to resemble blood coating the walls. The whole thing added a warm yet freaky red glow to the room. Oh yes, this place was definitely freaky alright! The room was a strange mix of old world elegance and a sadist's palace, actually the more I thought about it maybe I was more right with that last one, given who this place belonged to. There were two staircases that went down from the balcony we were stood on into the centre of the room.

"Before we go down I forgot to do something, here," she said as she lifted the edge of my sleeve up to one side of my face. She flattened the flowered section along my eye and cheek. I looked down at her open palm and saw a little pile of fine black powder that shimmered with added silver glitter.

"Close your eyes!" I did as I was told and then flinched a little as she shocked me by blowing over the place where she had placed the lace. She peeled it off my skin carefully and then I heard her clap her hands.

"There! What a beautiful doll you are for Master to play with. Come on 'cause he's also pissed off." Before I could comment she was pulling me down one of the staircases.

I tried to steady myself on the elaborate railings of twisted black iron that was made to look like metal flames coming from each step. I had to be careful though as the smooth railing was cut short with added spikes that penetrated up as the tips of the higher flames stabbed through the top. They looked razor sharp.

I took in my surroundings as I nearly stumbled. I felt like Alice, who fell down into a rabbit hole, only my journey was a delirious drugged trip, death ride that landed me smack bang in the middle of Goth Wonderland! I couldn't take everything in and I felt my skin crawl in both pleasure and disgust.

There was a huge raised stage facing the staircase we were making our way down and it reminded me more like something from an old theatre. Great black curtains framed either side of where the band was playing very heavy rock. The lead singer screamed his words into a standing mic that was one long skeleton arm and the fleshless hand clutched the mic. The singer wore only a pair of leather trousers with a studded belt. Bare feet and a bare torso, which was mostly covered in tattoos of demons ripping into his own flesh, was glistening with sweat thanks to his exuberance.

Around the stage were swags of the same black material as the curtains, with up-lighter lamps in between causing eerie shadows to cast on each band member. From up higher I could make out the layout of the room easier and it looked like the more important beings were raised higher all along the right side of the room which was raised on a dais. Their exclusive area was a half-moon shaped seating area with a larger section in the middle which was clearly where their King sat waiting for us. The rest of the room was split between seating areas, dance floor and disturbingly, what looked like a dungeon style play area. I tried not to look but seeing people in dog size cages spinning from the long chains that were attached firmly from the ceiling beams, I couldn't help but look horrified.

However, they didn't look in pain and even though hands played with them from all angles they looked more turned on than anything. Then there was a group of girls all tied to arched, high back chairs with men at their feet licking their way up, some higher than others making me jump when one girl screamed in orgasm when the man starting feeding from her breast. Pip laughed at me over her shoulder.

"Not your kind of shindig, eh?" She commented as we passed a couple of Cyber Goths. The girl was sat obediently at her master's feet on a short chain leash attached to a brown leather collar. The other end was wrapped around her owner's fist a few times and his other hand stroked the top of her head affectionately like a cat he owned. Both were wearing masks over their mouths, vented on either side. I had seen a few Cyber Goths at Afterlife but these were certainly extreme and never were any of them bound with their hands behind their back like she was. They had matching brown leather outfits that looked something straight out of Conan the Barbarian, that was if you added latex spikes, furry knee high boots and space goggles.

"Umm, that would be a no," I whispered, scared that I would get overheard and cause any type of scene. In a place like this I just wanted to scurry away and hide until all these people became a distant memory. But as we made our way closer to the dais I couldn't help the shocked expression that had taken up residence on my face. All the while I could feel eyes burning into me, analysing every movement I made, every shift in expression being scrutinised with cool eyes that frosted my every nerve. I was in two minds that were slowly tearing me apart. One, that wanted to feel safe and secure in the sea of demons I sailed on and Lucius was the port to which I was headed and the other, the one trying in vain to think rationally…well, that one wanted me to run like hellhounds were chasing me and Lucius was the one who had released them!

But thanks to this place and Pip by my side all decisions had been taken from me and I had no other choice but to follow the twisted path that crumbled under each step I made. I looked down at my feet to try and find some courage in my dwindling reserve and bumped into someone because I was too busy concentrating on which of my worries to file away where and knew before I looked up I was just about to add to the pile of worries. But when I did finally look at the eyes facing me I didn't know if I had anywhere deep enough to put his face!

White eyes with only a black ring around the iris to match the tiny black dot that was his pupil glared down at me. He was tall and I mean tall, being at least six foot eight, I felt like a child looking up. His hair was like fine metal wire that waved up from his forehead giving him the appearance that his head was elongated which added to his high cheek bones and deep-set eyes that screamed with natural authority. He had the bridge of his nose pierced with a metal bar to match the metal balls shown from the centre of his lip and either side of his chin. The same wiry hair that covered his head also covered half of his face in a trim grey beard that came down into a long point. His body was a thick rectangle of muscle with limbs long and hard due to his height. And I thought Ragnar was intimidating, this guy would be the one to give Ragnar an equal fighting chance for sure.

"Caspian, what a gentleman you are coming to escort us to Lucius, you big lug you." Pip said after placing her tiny hand on his arm, one that was covered in candy jewellery already with chunks missing. He looked down at her hand and shrugged her off like an annoying bug before speaking.

"You are late with my Master's toy, little girl!" He said in a heavy accented voice that sounded as though he had a tongue made from splintered wood. At first, I didn't realise he was referring to me...I was the toy, oh goodie! What dangerous fun could I get myself into this time, I wondered with dark humour.

Pip just nodded and refrained from commenting which wasn't like her...was it? It made me wonder who this guy was? He went to grab my arm with one spade sized hand when, thank god, Pip intervened. Which was lucky 'cause I think I would have lost control of my bladder for a short time!

"I wouldn't Caspian, I don't think after what he did to Klaus that he wants another man touching her. Oh did you not hear yet...it was quite entertaining, he taught him some fun games with his knife, you know how Master likes playing with knives, almost as much as he likes his play things untouched by others, so drop your fucking hand unless you wish to lose it! Come Toots, time to play dolly!" She reached past him for my hand and I had never felt anything as comforting since being the centre of this nightmare. Of course, then I caught sight of who she expected me to play 'dolly' with and my heart thought I was running a marathon again.

I felt the giant named Caspian behind me as my footsteps wavered slightly thanks to the rumble of vibrations his own footsteps created. Thankfully, Pip didn't let me go until we walked up the steps to her 'Master's' area. I looked around and noticed that Pip and a few others seemed to be the only part of this space that added any colour as everything raised on this large platform was black. The large seating arrangement was black velvet on a burnt black wooden frame that was so distressed looking I wondered how it held up any weight let alone six people. There was a huge round table that was low to the floor made from what looked like polished petrified wood with a black centre. Drinks in glasses of all shapes and sizes scattered the surface along with ashtrays and lines of white powder on mirrored tops, that even to my naive ways, looked like cocaine.

I looked up to see Adam and Ruto sat either side of their Lord and Adam seemed to visually relax when he saw Pip bouncing towards him. His shoulders had lowered from being tensed and the light in his eyes returned from their dark brooding anger. That was one man who loved his wife unconditionally, without restraint and whole heartedly. If you asked me it was bordering on obsession as it seemed he couldn't be without her touch for more than an hour before the signs of strain could be so visibly seen. It made that hollow pain in my chest rise when I thought about what Draven was doing right now? I wanted to run back to my room, hide away and find somewhere to sleep until he could get to me. Just the thought that my sleep was the key for us to be together made me never want to wake up again.

A girl's yelp brought me back round from my fantasy and I saw a girl rise from her knees at Lucius' feet. She turned again and got slapped on her bare bottom by Lucius to get moving. She was naked apart from the tattooed arms and tiny red thong that only consisted of a red triangle that hardly did the job of covering her womanhood. She had layered bubble-gum blue hair with red cat's ears sticking out and heart shaped red tattooed nipples with tassels attached to rings that had pierced through each one. She actually sounded like a bell when she walked past and I looked behind me to find the cause to be a tail of bells coming from her cheeks. I blushed, looked away and tried not to think about what they were attached to!

"You're late, Pip!" Lucius snapped in her direction as she jumped into the space next to Adam and another man that I would do well to stay clear of.

"Yep, we are, but what can I say...we're girls, Master and I wanted to make your dolly pretty for you." Lucius hadn't looked at me until she said this and then his eyes flew to lock with mine before taking his leisurely time to scan every inch of me making me feel like some naked exhibit in a glass case.

"Oh that you did pet, that you did indeed. Come here little doll!" He ordered in a deep gravelly tone that made me shiver. I took a step back out of pure primal reaction, the way prey can't help but want to run from the predator and Lucius was without a doubt, all predator. He looked like some dark commanding warrior in his black leather trousers that were loose and wide legged but pulled tighter at his trim waist, held by a thick belt. They looked like martial arts pants and I noticed a dagger's end glinting in the low light, protruding from its scabbard which hung low on one leg from another belt around his waist.

"NOW!" He stood as he shouted this and held out his hand ready for me to place myself at his mercy. I noted Caspian still at my back and knew I had no other choice but to walk around the table and put my hand in his. I noticed the muscles tense in his upper body, tightening the black t-shirt to a point where it looked close to ripping apart over large biceps. His torso was crisscrossed with leather straps and belts which looked to hold more weapons but they must have been on his back as only his dagger could be seen from the front. His arms also had black strips wound around his hands like a street fighter and thick leather cuffs that stretched up his forearms tied with four buckles, two of which looked strained as they travelled further up his muscular arm. He looked pumped and ready for the fight, one I couldn't see coming.

I finally braved finding his eyes and the corners were black near his nose giving him the look of a sinister ruler surveying his horror filled kingdom. When I was near enough I stretched my arm out as far as it would go still keeping an arm's length between us. I placed my shaky hand in his leather strapped one and like a snake he struck! He tightened his grip on my hand and yanked me into his chest and captured my body in arms so clad with muscles it felt like I had been placed in a tight stone crate. He flipped me round to face the crowd and with one arm around my waist the other went up to stroke my confined hair before fisting the plait. He lent his head down to my ear so only I would hear his words.

"You look oh so beautiful my little Keira girl, I knew your body was made to wear black lace." He ran his hand over the top of my thigh and up my corseted side causing heat to invade my cheeks until I couldn't look out into the crowd any longer. I held my eyes shut and fisted my hands until my nails dug into my palms.

"Although I'm not sure I approve of the corset." At this my eyes flew open and I tried to turn around but his grip tightened and he growled low in his throat.

"Be still or I will rip it off!" He threatened. I froze, and I heard a huff of humour from him.

"Ah, so I now know how to get you to comply, good to know." I took in a deep breath and my mind starting drowning with dread... what would he do?

"Kneel!" What! He wanted me to what! I tensed in his hold and he laughed.

"Do you know why I love black lace Keira?" He asked in that seductive tone of his and when combined with his breath on my neck it did strange things to my insides. I shook my head in answer.

"No? Then let me enlighten you." He moved behind me and repositioned his arms so that they encircled me and now he had both his hands at the front of my stomach. He flattened his palms on the corset and smoothed his hands up and over my breasts. He then reached the lace that covered my cleavage and gripped the tight material with both hands before pulling suddenly, causing a tear down my breasts. I jumped and looked down to see the lace torn and hung down on either side of the corset allowing my heaving chest to be seen.

"It tears easily. Now kneel, before I give you another demonstration and bare all to see!" I didn't need a second to think about it as my legs bent. There were plump cushions around the base of his seat from where the last slave had sat adoringly at his feet. I felt humiliated and my adrenaline was pumping around my body waiting for me to attack, run or breakdown. I couldn't help but look up and see his massive frame towering over me and in that moment, he looked like an Olympus God stating his claim. Of course, the next thing that happened proved that image to be more true than not!

With a possessive hand lay on top of my head he waited for the room to go silent and when I saw his eyes mist into a violent red I knew he was controlling the room. I sucked in a breath when every last person in the hall went quiet and didn't so much as breathe too deeply from fear of making themselves known. Their fear was for a different reason to mine. They didn't want to incur his wrath and me...

well I had just witnessed one man's control over two hundred people in seconds.

That scared the shit out of me!

"This girl here is Keira, say hi Keira," he said looking down at me but when I didn't do anything he bent down and tilted my head back arching my neck as far as it would go.

"Speak little doll," he whispered, and I held back the urge to spit at him. He cocked his head to one side as if trying to read where my thoughts ran but before he got anything I nodded to indicate my compliance.

"Hello," I said bitterly not talking my lethal glare from his face. He laughed once and straightened up saying,

"Good girl," before addressing the room once more.

"Keira here is a beautiful little morsel that I know will tempt many of you but Keira here is MINE!" He screamed the last word making everyone flinch back, even Caspian who had tree trunks for arms!

"If anyone so much as looks at her in a way I do not like, well then, Keira here will watch you die! It's that simple but please... continue, enjoy your evening." He finished breaking the spell he had held over everyone. Pip was the only one who dared chuckle.

"Oh my Luc, you really know how to get a party started!" She giggled and Adam frowned and then plucked her right out of her seat and onto his lap to restrain her. He snarled when he saw her scarf shift to flash her chest.

"Why do you push me, Squeak?" He asked shaking his head. She winked down at me before turning on the puppy eyes at her husband.

"What's wrong hubby bubba, don't you like my outfit?" She twirled a green and blue lock round her finger innocently and from the looks of things Adam wasn't buying it for one second. He decided not to respond but instead he pulled the scarf from her shoulders and whipped it out and around her breasts before anyone got a look. He pulled it tight against her skin and tied it round her back so it now became a tube top that was deep enough so only a thin line of skin showed above her trousers.

"Hey! No fair!" She complained and was about to untie the back when Adam grabbed her arms and held them behind her back. He then used the ends of the scarf to tie her arms to her back.

"Hush!" He snapped and she smiled at his anger but gave in and snuggled closer into his chest. She looked like she was having way too much fun playing this game.

"Shame you're not wearing a scarf yourself." Lucius' voice so close to my ear made me jump. He sounded way too amused when he saw me shiver.

The night dragged on and my legs were starting to cramp, being sat in the same position for so long. I was only allowed to be sat in between his legs on the cushions by his feet. I had tried to move away a few times, but he just silently repositioned me back using force and I would find myself with no other choice than to sit like a pet leaning back against the base of his chair.

Like this the only thing left for me was time and it gave me plenty to study the place in great detail but the more I took in, the more freaked out I made myself. For starters the two other people around the same seated area were just as strange looking as the rest but at least Adam and Pip seemed friendly enough towards me. I looked towards Adam and the man sat next to him. He didn't say one word to anyone and only nodded when spoken to. He was clearly of native American Indian decent, with toffee coloured skin, almond shaped eyes and long silky black raven hair that went straight down in two half's reaching his naked stomach. He wore maroon coloured material round his legs that looked to be wrapped loosely and tied at his waist. Almost like a skirt with the middle tucked up between his legs.

His chest was bare apart from the strange metal wire that wound around his body in random ways. This was all over his upper half and even down his arms where it got thicker at the wrists and neck area. I couldn't understand it as it was like someone had bound him in silver wire without actually restraining him. I found little sense to it but knowing this place I didn't want to find out the full reasoning behind it anyway.

"Hakan, say hello to Toots." Pip said, as I was caught staring at him. He turned to face me and nodded down at me. He had his arms crossed and he too was a beefy male, but it was the painted black mask he wore across his eyes that made him look like the Lone Ranger. It was just a straight black strip, but it made the whites of his eyes stand to attention along with the veins that bulged just beneath the skin.

"Do you like his tattoo? I call him Dennis." I laughed at Pip's comment and couldn't help it from the look he gave her glancing sideways without moving his head.

"It doesn't look much like a Dennis." I said before thinking about my 'mute for the night' rule I had given myself. At this Hakan's mouth twitched in what looked like amusement and he nodded his head at me for the second time. Well, he didn't need to thank me for speaking up on his behalf, it was pretty clear that the big tattoo of a wolf howling at the moon didn't look at all like it would be called Dennis! But I mentally thanked Pip for trying to make me laugh. I would see her sometimes wink at me or pull a funny face trying to make me smile. Of course, she was still bound but Adam attended to her just fine, with drinks and even sharing a cigarette.

"Drink!" An order was barked at me when a bottle of beer got lowered in front of my face. I hadn't looked up at Lucius once since his little expressive scene in front of the crowd and he hadn't spoken to me, however I could feel his eyes on me the whole time.

I shook my head but this wasn't good enough for him. I felt his breath before I knew he had moved.

"It wasn't a request. Now stop being a stubborn ass and drink!" He called me an ass!? Why, of all the nerve! I grabbed the bottle and chugged the whole lot before slamming it down on the table.

"Happy!" I snapped feeling my temper rise. He laughed at my behaviour and before I knew what was happening he leaned down and gripped me by the waist, picking me up as though I weighed nothing and placed me in between his legs on his seat that was roomy enough for us both. Of course, like this, I had to be far too close to him that I couldn't disguise what it did to my body. Although I was happy to have moved as my legs were cramping up.

"I am now!" He growled down my ear and then wrapped my long plait around his fist to hold me secure. I instantly felt like that girl I had passed, only I was minus the collar!

I stiffened my spine and every muscle was high on alert as his free hand started to make soothing circles along the slit in my skirt. He left goosebumps where his cold hand touched my thigh and he moved the fabric further to one side to continue, baring my leg completely.

"Please...don't" I said weakly, losing all the earlier fight and anger.

"Ssshh, relax!" He demanded in a hushed tone and with his hand gripping my hair in an unbreakable hold he pulled me back ever so slowly until my back was flush with his chest.

"There, that's better. Keira you are so tense, why?"

"Why? Are you joking?" I said stunned at the audacity of this man, King or not! Again, with that deep baritone laugh that sent shivers through me for reasons I didn't want to think about.

"I could bite you if you want to experience a real reason for being tense, although I'm thinking it would be more intense than anything else." He seductively whispered this last part and the word 'intense' lingered as did his lips at my neck when he said it. Of course, this didn't help me relax at all and he was finding some sick fascination with my reactions to him. I tried in vain to pull away, but he held me firm and said a defined,

"Don't!" But at least this made him let go of my leg. I refused to look at him again and I definitely didn't relax like he ordered me to. No, instead I took in more of my surroundings just to get my mind away from my hopeless situation. A Vampire King at my back holding my hair like I was on a Goddamn leash, like some bloody pet of his! I was beyond angry, I was bloody fuming.

"I need the toilet." I informed him in clipped tones.

"Is that so?" The smug bastard said.

"Yes that's so, but feel free to let me piss all over you and cock my leg up on your leg like the dog you're treating me as!" At this he growled like that dog and I tried to keep my spine stiff under the noise I caused from him.

"Liessa, take the girl!" He barked his order at the only other woman sat up here who was next to Ruto.

A beautiful brunette looked up from Caspian's neck that she had been sucking on, which made it clear they were an item, well at least for tonight. She nodded and Caspian released the firm hand he had on one of her breasts. Man, was anybody here not thinking about sex! Was there something in the water?

She stood and held out a hand for me to take. I took a moment to admire her black satin fingerless gloves, wishing I had my own pair. She really was a beauty but more a refined radiance with pearly skin tones brought out more by dark brown hair that had flashes of the most unusual colour of light peach running through it. She had it coiled up with tiny plaits entwined with something else I couldn't see in this light but it looked like some kind of tubes of rubber looped through in different places. She had peach tinted eyes, a colour that I had never seen before and it was brought out more by the blush she wore on her high elegant cheek bones. Her cherry red lipstick wasn't even smudged even after the six hickeys she had kindly given Caspian. I shuddered at the thought.

I took her hand and was more than thankful to be getting away from Lucius, even if it was only for a short time. I felt I could breathe properly for the first time in hours as I walked away from him, but then a strong hand shackled my wrist and I was pulled back.

"Don't be too long little doll, you would hate for me to miss you." He warned running a knuckle down my cheek. I refused to meet his gaze knowing without looking the burning I would find there. He let me go and I nearly stumbled to get away. I still heard him laughing as I disappeared into the crowd.

We didn't have any problems getting to the restroom as thanks to Lucius' dire announcement earlier, threatening every one's lives if they so much as looked at me wrong, can do wonders getting around in crowded places. Anyone would have thought I was Moses the way people scrambled out of my way like a freight train was coming.

I stayed on Liessa's heels as I didn't think Lucius would take kindly to an excuse of 'I got lost' so I hurried along trying to keep up with her long legs. She was at least six foot and had a slim athletic body. She reminded me of a dark swan, long neck and ever so graceful in her stride. Well, if she was the swan then I was the flapping goose that squawked after her asking her to please slow down as I nearly stumbled for the second time. Heels really weren't made for power walking in clubs!

Thankfully, she took my short legs into consideration and slowed down as we neared an archway. She had to duck under it where I felt a teeny bit smug that I didn't have to. We walked into a beautiful luxurious bathroom that had huge black velvet fleur de lis on a deep gold background on every wall. The sinks were gold leaf bowls with highly polished, fancy old fashioned taps. The mirrors were all gilded gold frames that were elaborate tree designs. The floor was like black glass with a black chaise longue in the middle with fancy gold moulding around the edges.

"My husband doesn't like you. He says that you will cause trouble for our Lord and Caspian doesn't like anyone that can cause waves." She said, going to stand in front of the mirror while she leaned in and checked her makeup. What was I supposed to say to that!

"Sorry, I guess," I said lamely not really meaning one word of it. She turned to face me and smiled.

"Please don't be, I am grateful for this." I frowned not understanding where this was going.

"Why?" I was almost scared to ask.

"Because, tonight I am in for a treat and will for the remaining time you are here. My husband delivers the best sex life when he is angry and frustrated and considering I cannot anger him, you will do so nicely, so for that I thank you for annoying him." I think my mouth actually dropped open at her statement.

"Umm…you're welcome." I said bewildered, which made her smile down at me again.

"Oh how I do hope you are here for a long time." She winked at me before opening one of the stalls which was a hint for me to hurry up and get peeing!

Once I had finished with my business I stepped up to the mirror and saw for the first time what Pip had done with the lace at my face. It was beautiful and gave me a mysterious air as the black pattern shimmered in the form of a rose along my face. I looked down and frowned at my pushed up cleavage showing thanks to Lucius' rough treatment of my dress. I looked like I had been ravished by a wild beast trying to get to the goods. No wonder he had wanted me sat at his feet, from up there he'd been awarded an eye full all night and thanks to the corset they looked even bigger, like they were begging to come out and play.

I looked over to Liessa while I washed my hands, making sure not to get the ribbon wet and noticed what the rubber was in her hair.

"Squid?!" I shouted before I could engage a filter to stop me blurting out whatever I think. But come on…she actually had squid tentacles in her hair! Thankfully she laughed at my outburst.

"Oh how I do love humans. I am an aquatic shifter Demon and I favour ink as a deception." She lifted her white silk blouse from the tight pencil skirt she was wearing. She reminded me of a school teacher but the marks on her body quickly squashed that image. The skin on her stomach was different shades of peaches and cream and that does sound yummy until you take into account the hundreds of little suckers that were married across her skin in diagonal lines. She touched one with her fingers and I was in utter amazement when one started to ooze thick black liquid. She caught it between her fingers and rubbed them together before washing it away in the sink.

"It can be quite poisonous if I choose and as you can imagine, I don't get hugged often." She laughed at her own joke and smoothed her hair back in one place where it had come loose. I now realised that the tentacles on her head were part of her, not put there freely. My eyes opened wide and I had to shake my head to try and process what I had learnt from this woman, who had just shown me she was half squid. I just didn't know if my night could get any damn weirder but hey, I guess there was still time!

We walked back out into the crowd and apart from seeing one girl dressed in black duct tape and nothing else, two men dressed in leather bondage gear going at it on a couch and a young girl wearing a dress that looked straight out of 'Gone with the Wind' complete with hat bigger than a serving platter, I still didn't find anything weirder than what Liessa had shown me in the bathroom. But as I got closer to Lucius I saw a tall man with his back to us. He was wearing a long black jacket down to his feet and his black hair curled around his neck at the collar. His powerful looking shoulders dominated the jacket and a memory hit me like a fist to the gut.

There had been flowers, grass and a forest surrounding every side. There had been a breeze that didn't reach my skin and a jutted stone that caused me to trip at the feet of a stranger. The feet of a handsome man. The feet of a living God.

Feet that belonged to a King.

*Draven.*

# CHAPTER II

# A COLD HARD SLAP OF REALITY

Draven? It couldn't be, could it? My heart had started to beat uncontrollably at the sight before me. Draven stood with his back to us as we approached but was facing Lucius with his arms folded. That's when I heard his formidable voice.

"Where is she, Lucius?" He demanded and everyone flinched but Lucius.

Oh my god! He had come for me, he said he would but now he was here my heart soared. He was here and now I was going home! I found my legs moving without thought and I was running to him. Running to my home.

"Draven!" I shouted over and over causing him to turn.

"Keira? Keira. No!" He said but it was too late. I threw myself into him and instead of landing into the arms of the man I loved I fell through him! I felt my body shake as I passed through his body and landed hard into another body. Hakan had caught me before I ended up part of the furniture and spun me round into Lucius' arms before I even had chance to take a breath. I was still shaking my head trying to understand what had happened when I heard Draven's voice again.

"Let her GO!" Draven was furious beyond words and when I could finally focus again I felt Lucius' grip on me tighten across my body that was locked to his chest. I looked at Draven and couldn't understand what had happened? He looked like the whole and solid Draven I knew every hard line of, but why?

"Come now Dom, do you really hope to threaten me when you are nothing but a projection? You always were so hot headed and I see time hasn't granted you with the power of patience."

"And you are the Being to lecture me on such matters?" Draven snarled out his words and Lucius growled back.

"As a matter of fact, I am just the Being to do such. Do NOT presume to know me any more my old friend, it would be unwise given your current predicament and remember what of yours I hold in my arms!" At this he looked down at me and his lips gently touched my neck making me wince.

"Lucius!" Draven warned but it was useless. Lucius had me and Draven could only be left to cruelly watch. He looked on with tight emotions playing across his handsome face, trying so hard to portray the man of power he was. All dressed in black like the man who held me, with that long jacket reaching his feet, it took me back to the times before, one of which I had thought he had been my captor. How I wished that to be true once again. His black hair was pushed back giving his eyes a more penetrating stare, a hard glint that flashed with every contact Lucius made with my skin. It looked as though he was calculating his revenge even now, taking note and stock of all the charges stacking up against him. Oh yes, Draven wanted to punish him, but knew he would have to wait. Bide his time until judgment could be declared, and punishment could be received.

"Oh yes Dom, I have been patient indeed." He ran the back of his hand down my neck that he had arched to one side with his hand fisting my hair once again. I didn't leave Draven's eyes as this all played out and the pain I saw there, matched my own.

"I have waited so long for this day, so long for her to come. It's refreshing finally finding something that can make you crumble, a man without weakness, to watch him fall. Tell me Dominic, how does it feel to be so helpless for the first time in your existence?" He asked bitterly and Draven, for the first time looked...defeated.

"Is this all you wish to see Luc, to watch a King fall to his knees at the feet of another King, because know that my pride means nothing compared to what you hold in your arms. I will gladly..." Lucius didn't let Draven get to his knees because his voice turned harsh, losing all the icy reserve.

"You know what it is I want Draven, what you stole from me is the only reason I stole from you. When my property is returned then so shall yours but until then know this, I will have fun playing with our little Keira here." He said, his voice smoothing out like you would the creases in a bedspread. One minute he was hard, cold and the next caressing me with his words like he covered my thoughts in fog so that I couldn't see my doubts.

"If you do anything to her, you will pay Lucius and then it will be time for me to play!" I shivered at what Draven's idea of 'playing' involved.

"Ha, threats coming from a man I can control. Tell me something, for I am curious, what did it feel like that day? To finally discover someone more powerful than you, making you do something you couldn't control as you yourself have done to so many in the past. Was it…liberating?" He laughed where Draven only frowned and tightened his arms across his chest.

"What I would find liberating, is me and you, just one on one, no powers, no games and no gimmicks, henchmen or council…Just you and me, Luc." The deadly intent in Draven's eyes scared me to the bone. I actually felt a tiny shudder from behind me which didn't match Lucius' laughter.

"What just like men Dom? But we're not men!" Lucius spat out.

"This world is coming to an end and will you still believe in your precious balance when the sky falls around you and all that you love?" Lucius' bitter laughter continued, and Draven just shook his head.

"What happened to you, Luc?"

"I woke up! And now it is time for you to do the same! Give me the Spear of Longinus, King and you shall have your Queen returned. You have ten days to comply or she will witness an Afterlife you can't control!" All dark laughter now gone, his anger flowed so freely causing me, for the first time, to take my eyes from Draven and close them in fear. I had ten days. Just ten days.

"You will not touch her?" Draven demanded to know.

"Oh I would not say that, after all she is such a tasty little thing, you did such a good job in changing her." He said running a fingertip down my neck and across my collar bone.

"Changing me?" I couldn't help but ask. I was so confused, what did he mean?

"Ahh, she doesn't know what it is you have done to her…tricky Dom, very tricky!" Lucius was now quickly back to being amused.

"Lucius!" Draven warned but this only added to his amusement.

"Do you want to know why it is you taste…oh so good!" He said making me wince after he had paused for effect and then dug a nail into my skin that was still pulled taut at the neck. I shook my head but didn't get far as his hand tightened, making Draven growl ferociously.

"Lucius I am telling you NO!"

"Did you hear that pretty little Keira, he's telling me no! He doesn't want me telling you the truth, he doesn't want me to tell you what he has done to you." I was still trying to shake my head but couldn't due to his hold.

"Draven?" I whispered.

"Yes Draven, tell her. Please share with her what she has become at you're doing." This time he let me shake my head, this was wrong, he was wrong...Draven wouldn't do anything to me...would he? I couldn't take my eyes from Draven and knew something was wrong.

"Fine, not going to spill any little secrets, eh Dom, then allow me to use your own words for people like her...what was it I heard you say once...Half breed...ABOMINATION!" He shouted the last word and I thought my legs would dissolve to the floor below my feet. It was a lie! Half breed? No, no it was all a mind game! Only I looked up at Draven and when I saw it in his eyes I knew the truth...

It wasn't a lie.

"You see Keira, there is a reason our kind shouldn't infiltrate the human form with our sexual needs. Your lover should know about this, considering it was one of his own rules! Isn't that so Dom?" Lucius looked above my head but Draven's eyes didn't leave my own, but this time I was too hurt to find the comfort in them.

"Enough, Lucius!" Draven demanded but Lucius was having way too much fun to stop now and I needed answers.

"No! I want to hear the rest." I said straightening my spine and everyone looked shocked.

"Ah but of course you do my little Keira girl and you shall. See, Draven here has been very selfish indeed, trying to change you into what he wanted."

"What do you mean?" I asked looking at Draven, wanting my answer from him.

"Keira I..."

"He has been changing your DNA Keira, making you one of us. You won't die and you will never grow old. You're stronger than most humans and you don't even know it. See, your lover there has been pumping you full of his magic seed and growing a new you inside of that perfect pale skin of yours. One that will be forced to watch all those around you die, the people you love will perish while you stay beautiful forever, all thanks to your new…"

"Lucius don't, no more, you have done enough!" Draven was getting desperate to stop the next words out of Lucius' mouth, but I had to know, Draven wouldn't tell me, I knew that with clear certainty now.

"Go on," I whispered, lowering my head unable to look at him anymore.

"No Keira, don't you see, this is what he wants!" I still turned my head away and couldn't look at him. I felt sick knowing he was right, that this was what Lucius had wanted but I needed to know the truth!

"You want to know why, why it is you taste so fucking sweet! Demon blood Keira. The Demon blood yours is changing into!" He licked my neck from bottom to top before letting go of me completely letting me crumple to the floor.

"NO!" I screamed and fell to my knees hoping this was all just a bad dream! He didn't, it wasn't true! Draven wouldn't have done that to me…would he?

"Tell me it isn't true…Tell me it's all lies, Draven," I whispered looking up now feeling like a broken doll. But his eyes told me the truth…Draven had been slowly changing me all this time. Every time we had made love had just been another step he took in turning me. How could he?

"How could you?" I didn't realise I had spoken aloud until I heard him growl.

"I had every right!" He stated firmly straightening his back.

"You are mine and you are the 'Chosen'. FINAL! You accepted your fate long ago Keira, now is the time to deal with it. I do not have to explain myself further!" Where was the man that I knew? In his place was a King that commanded me along with every other person. Was I just another step for him to take? Another Being to live a life he chooses, and for what reason? I am the 'Chosen One', like he said 'I accepted my fate' but when did I do that exactly? Living forever wasn't what I chose! He didn't even give me a bloody chance! I wanted to lash out but I couldn't find the strength as my body remained frozen in shock. How could he have done this to me?

"I think I made my point. Bring me the Spear, Draven or you will find yourself with a very different Keira when it's time to retrieve her. I believe a lot can happen in ten days. Some things can leave a bitter taste in your mouth, my friend and I think you can see for yourself the evidence before you." Lucius said calmly and I knew I was that 'evidence' he was talking about.

"Keira, look at me." Draven's voice instructed softly. I raised my head slowly and saw a flash of regret in his eyes before they turned hard.

"Remember what we talked about? Remember what I asked of you?" I knew he was referring to when he asked me to be brave and all I could find in myself to do was nod, he did the same. I could feel something in the air that resembled a chilled heat. Like having flu and being so cold but still having the sweat travelling down your skin from burning heat. It flickered and I knew what was coming.

"Draven!...I..I.." I shouted before stumbling on my words but he gave me a slight smile of reassurance.

"I know Keira, as do I." And with that he was gone. He had disappeared in such a way that made me doubt he had ever been here. He knew what I was going to say and he kept our emotions private as they should be. I almost felt as if we were the only two people in the room displaying our love in that silent way. It was true. That no matter what Draven had done, how much it still hurt, I couldn't lie, to him or to myself.

I loved him and thankfully he still knew it.

After that I was escorted back to my room and Adam finally had to release Pip to do so. Neither of us spoke and I was thankful for this. My mind was in utter turmoil. I couldn't understand what it all meant but I knew one thing, no matter how much I loved Draven I felt...betrayed.

I noticed the way Pip kept rolling her shoulders, but she would smile every time she did it, probably thinking back to the way Adam kept playing with her ass and kept getting her worked up when he thought no one was looking but it was a little bit hard to be discreet when I was sat on the floor facing them and Pip purring like a cat being stroked. Adam would just nuzzle her neck and bite down when she got too loud. I could say that I had felt uncomfortable, but I felt too numb for any other feeling than self-pity.

"You really do love him don't you?" Pip asked, once we were back in my room and to be honest I didn't recall most of the journey.

"Yes." I said going to the window to look out into a night I couldn't control. I felt like a lost soul wandering the graveyard still confused about where to go and what to do next?

"And you're pissed at him." She stated making me nod at her reflection.

"Why?" Her question caught me off guard.

"Why?" I repeated.

"Yeah, I mean so there is some stuff he didn't tell you but does it suck so bad to be like me? To be one of us?" She looked sad, no not just sad but…oh God… Insulted!

"Pip, I mean no offense when I say this, but you really don't understand." I turned and found her down turned lip and I felt like I had just back handed a child.

"What, because you think like everyone else does…?'Oh there goes Pip, little stupid Pip!' I'm not stupid! Adam doesn't think I'm stupid!" She stated proudly.

"Of course he doesn't." I stated back.

"Why should he, when you're not?" I added before she could fly off the handle again.

"But if you think that, then why do you think that I wouldn't un…" I stopped her with my hand and spoke the truth,

"Because Pip, You're not human."

"Oh!"

"Just imagine how you would feel if you found out Adam had been changing you every time you made love, how would you feel?" Her eyes opened wide and then she smiled as a thought hit.

"Like a tiger? Or like a…"

"Human!" I said and she winced. Yep, she was getting the idea.

"Eww, no offense." She said screwing up her face, making her cute little nose wrinkle.

"None taken, it's how I feel about becoming one of you." I said shrugging my shoulders.

"But now you get the message right, what would you do to Adam?" I asked.

"Tear his balls off and make earrings out of them, of course after I had pierced his ears to make the bastard wear them himself! Okay, so I see your point, you want the King's balls!" I coughed at the image she painted, and she laughed at my face, one of horror I can imagine. I was also shocked she had referred to Draven as King.

"You think of Draven as your King?"

"Of course, why shouldn't I? He is after all everyone's King."

"But I thought…" Ok, so I was now completely confused.

"Ah, you thought just because Lucius is also King that we would only recognise him as our Lord. He, he you are funny." She giggled at me before taking a bite out of her last candy ring.

"Draven has always been King, it's all my kind has ever known. But we chose to follow Lucius, follow his cause and call him Master. But I will admit you're a lucky girly, Draven is a total hottie, microwave style!" I laughed when her eyebrows wagged at me.

"Yes he is!" I said quickly, thinking back to my Dark Knight standing there with guilt hidden in his depths. That brought me right back to the reason behind that guilt and I bit my lip in frustration

"You're still upset, aren't you? I could call Sheila for you. She's my therapist." I gave her a little half smile and walked in the direction of the walk in wardrobe.

"Didn't you say she was a harpy?" She nodded and came over to one of the couches to plonk herself down in it.

"I think I'll pass thanks."

"Cool beans, she isn't that good anyway but she makes amazing hash cakes, I always bring some back for Adam and then make him beg me for one…it's become a bit of a ritual after my sessions, the only reason I still go actually, I love begging sex and Adam does this thing with his tongue that…"

"LA LA LA, not listening Pip!" She laughed at the sight of me holding my hands over my ears as I walked through the door. I could still her laughing when I was trying to find something that didn't scream SEX to wear to bed. Man, were there no normal clothes in here? I was close to asking Pip for some cartoon PJ's as I was stripping away my corset.

"What's Lucius' deal anyway…this thing he asked from Draven?" I bent over trying to take off one shoe and jumped around before it came off. Then I leaned down and flicked up my other leg to do the same.

"Pip?" I called out but was met with silence, which was very un-Pip like.

"Lucius is thinking of calling the deal off and just taking what's in front of him." That didn't sound like Pip!

I pulled my shoe off and had the urge to throw it at him as I held on to the pointed heel with a death grip. His voice sounded both amused and aroused. That's when it hit me that this dress was see through and I had just taken off my corset. My cheeks suddenly felt steamy as I had been bent over when I had first heard his voice, so there was no chance of him not seeing my near naked behind.

"You have a lovely ass Keira, like a ripe peach!" He said so close to my ear I gasped and turned quickly, too quickly in fact that I wobbled sideways. His hand snaked out and grabbed my forearm to help steady me. I looked up and up as he was so tall and even more so now I didn't have the added height. I took a step back but his hand wouldn't allow the space.

"What are you doing here?" It was a bit lame but I didn't know what else to say. He looked me up and down taking his time to stare freely at my underwear before coming back up to look me in the face.

"You're not confident in your skin, are you Keira? Although I must say, this blush does suit you." I think he only said these things to get me to blush more, of course it worked.

"What? Come to spill more family secrets?" I snapped and yanked out of his hold. I stepped back and crossed my arms over my chest to try and hide at least some of my body from his heated glare.

"What would you like to know, I can see that Draven doesn't treat you as an equal." He was different here than he was in the Great Hall. Here, it was like talking to him back in the helicopter, annoying but still not fearful of what he would do to me, although the predatory look did worry me somewhat.

"Don't! Don't you dare do that!" He raised his arms out in a 'whatever could you mean' type action.

"I know what you're playing at, you're trying to turn me against him, but it won't work"

"I wouldn't dream of it, you loyal little puppy. But I can tell a one-sided relationship when I see one." At this I actually laughed. What? Lucius giving me relationship advice...ooh goodie! What was next, Jeremy Kyle supernatural style?

"And what would you know of relationships?" I laughed when I said it making him frown.

"I'm not celibate doll, and do love a good fu..."

"Yes, well I don't need to hear about it thanks." I said turning around to try again in finding something with more material than a handkerchief!

"Mmm, peaches."

"Sorry?" I said over my shoulder to see him by the door leaning with his side on its frame with one foot crossing the other.

"Didn't say a word. Is there something in particular you're looking for?"

"Yeah, something other than a dishcloth would be nice. Who

picked all this stuff?" I said trying to find anything that would work in covering some skin.

"Pip." He said and I laughed surprising myself. Was I laughing with Lucius, the same man that was towering above me and making me kneel at his feet? God what was wrong with me!

"Figures," I said under my breath.

"Here," his voice said over my shoulder, making me flinch again. I looked to the side and saw a black T-shirt in one strong pale hand. I turned and wished I hadn't. Lucius had taken his T-shirt off which left me close to panting. Lucius was all man and then some. And I hated to admit that I could barely tear my eyes away from all his muscles. Lucius was a slimmer build to Draven and where his physique looked more packing bulk with shoulders that were built to throw around tree trunks, Lucius had the body of a fighter. Defined eight pack on a long stomach that you could have ran a finger along each ridge. Strong pecks that were flat but solid, unlike some body builders that look like they had a pair of hard breasts. His shoulders and arms looked made to swing a battle axe around an arena in ancient Rome. All of this showcased under a midnight moon skin that seemed to shimmer, it was so pale.

I took the T-shirt and turned away from him mumbling a barely audible thanks. It seemed painful to look any longer. I didn't want him being nice to me, I didn't want anything from him, least of all his kindness. I shook my head at the differences once again and how quickly the bastard, who had humiliated me not long ago, stood here now with what…a peace offering in the form of a shirt?

"That's a lot of thinking, even for someone so small." I frowned at him and wanted to kick his shin for the smirk he gave me. Good, I needed a little fire back in my veins!

"Why are you being nice to me?" I decided to cut the crap and lay my cards on the table.

"I wasn't aware I wasn't ever being nice." He smiled and it just made me want to kick him higher, preferably in a more painful spot.

"Make all your friends sit at your feet do you, control their movements by gripping the hair, threatening to bite them and order them to do anything you want…I could go on?" I said trying to get past but his arm on the wall blocked my escape.

"Let's get something straight sugar, I'm not your friend, never gonna be. I. Am. Your. Jailor. And if you feel better me being a bastard then I'm not opposed to that. But just so you know, down there, in my realm, I am King and I have to make clear who is in charge or you'd get eaten alive! So what's it gonna be, Peach?" I frowned but now I thought about it I got a better sense of why he had made such a display and when I walked to the toilet I didn't even get anyone looking my way, not like some of the snarls I had received when Pip and I had first entered. Could it be possible that Lucius had been putting on more of an act?

"So it was for my protection?" He shrugged his shoulders.

"Nothing I do is an act sweetheart but letting myself get heavy handed will do more good than not in a place like that, despite what you may think, doesn't even come into play. As for allowing your rescuing Knight to say his piece...well, if he doesn't come up with the goods then me and you are gonna get a lot better acquainted."

"I don't think so, I would never let you touch me that way!" I shouted but he just laughed.

"Don't be so sure pet, I may be cold to touch but we have time yet and I have a feeling that kisses from you would take us both to a warm place...oh wait, I know they do!" He winked at me and I huffed in frustration while pushing past him. I stormed into the bathroom and slammed the door on Lucius and his amused chuckle. I locked it and almost started ripping the dress in a hurry to get the damn thing off. I had thrown the T-shirt to the sinks in my temper and now stood over them, shaking in anger, half naked apart from my black lace underwear. My chest heaved as I grabbed Lucius' shirt, hating that it was the only thing for me to wear. I hated even more that it smelled of him. Man, wood and musk. I almost wished it smelled of sticky sweat, dirt and dried blood, but no such luck!

I pulled it over my head and was thankful that Lucius was such a large male as it came to just above my knees like a large nightie. I started to undo my hair, not being too gentle about it and ran my fingers through it in a feeble attempt to get out the knots. I left the ribbon on the side to use later.

"There must be a toothbrush around here somewhere," I said out loud close to praying for one as it felt like spuds would soon start growing.

"Try the panel in the wall, there is a cabinet behind there hidden." I screamed a little yelp and spun round to face Lucius watching me, sat on the side of the tub.

"How did you ...What are you...?"

137

"Door and Demon, remember?" He said, answering my unfinished questions. I closed my eyes and took a deep breath.

"Don't you know the meaning of privacy?"

"Oh, I know the meaning well enough, never thought of it as a rule though…but please carry on, don't let me stop you." He said holding out his palm and that combined with the smarmy grin, I wanted to scream again. In the end I just huffed. It was rather that or either a string of profanities that once I started I didn't think I would have been able to stop.

I found the cabinet and after minutes of struggling, a hand came from behind me and pushed it in the right place for it to click open. By the time I turned he had returned to his seat on the tub. I think I actually growled. But that mood left me when I spotted what was in the small cupboard, hidden away like treasure. There was a hair brush, complete with bobbles and clips, tampons, face crème and wash. And there buried at the back was a new toothbrush in a packet and toothpaste. I pulled out the two packets and laughed when I saw my toothbrush.

"Let me guess, Pip was in charge of Keira supply shopping?" I said to Lucius and he raised an eyebrow.

"Or do you have a fondness for pink Power Rangers?" I laughed when his eyebrows turned slanted into a frown. I laughed again ripping the pink figure with a brush on the end from its wrapper.

Lucius and I didn't speak again but he didn't leave and by the time I had washed the makeup off my face, brushed my hair and finished my teeth I was getting worried why he was still in my room.

"Do you find something fascinating about watching a human girl get ready for bed or do you just have some messed up hobbies?" I asked turning around but again with the sneaking up on me and making me jump, because there he was again right in front of me. I stepped back and bumped my lower back into the sink's worktop.

"No, my hobbies are more of the… active variety." I gulped down that image and tried to shift away when he started feeling the material of his shirt by my shoulder. He rubbed the fabric between his thumb and forefinger, all the while not taking his eyes off me.

"Why did you kiss me back?" His question took me back and I shook my head slightly trying to make sense of his question.

"I…I…didn't."

"Oh, but I know you did Keira, I was there remember. Now answer me!" He demanded and just like that, Master Lucius was back.

"I…I don't know," I whispered.

"Not good enough! Tell me now!" He shouted making me flinch back but all the while he never stopped feeling his shirt on my shoulder. I looked to see what he was doing and why, but he snapped at me again,

"Look at me Keira, nowhere else." I immediately did as I was told and hated that I did it.

"Good girl, now tell me why?"

"If I do, will you finally leave?" He slowly nodded his head and that predatory gaze was back looking as if he was getting ready to strike again.

"I was scared and I, well… I wanted to feel safe." I must have blushed beetroot at admitting that because he smiled, bearing one of his fangs where his lips curled slightly higher on one side.

"And you thought of me as being a safe choice. That's like the rabbit kissing the wolf!"

"More like the wolf kissing the rabbit, you kissed me." Even to my own ears I sounded like a whiney child in the playground.

"Umm, I remember it well."

"I answered your question." I said arching back as he seemed to be getting closer.

"So you did." He was still smiling.

"So, are you going to leave now?" I was close to panting.

"And why would I do that?" He paused and got real close until his breath fanned my neck and his lips made contact with my skin.

He sent a deep shiver down my back and then it came to rest at my earlobe where his lips had found home. Then his next words chilled me to the bone.

*"It's my room, Keira!"*

# CHAPTER 12
# RIBBONS AND SUNSHINE

"What do you mean this is your room?" I said nervously.

"Don't look so worried pet, I'm not in the habit of forcing young morsels to my bed, besides, you're not my type!" He said pushing himself off the counter and crossing his arms over his chest.

"Why? Because I have an IQ and a pulse?" I said, wondering why I was even pushing him in the first place. He laughed and then shook his head as though I wasn't doing myself any favours in proving that IQ.

"Why is it humans insist the rules of being a Vampire means we're dead creatures without a pulse! It fascinates me how humans class themselves as being so evolved yet bring a supernatural legend into play and they become mindless idiots." He said turning around and walking straight out of the door. I couldn't believe I found myself going after him.

"Man, you do have a high opinion of yourself!" I couldn't help saying.

"Do I? Must be what being me does to you. Answer me this, if I didn't have a pulse then how would all that thick delicious blood I consume get around my body, I think even you're smart enough to know I would need a beating heart for that one, no matter how heartless you consider me to be." He said, coming to stand by the balcony door opposite the bed. Okay, so when it was said like that then yeah, it did sound pretty stupid.

"Oh but garlic, now that's a real killer, what would I do without breath mints!" I could see him rolling his eyes in his reflection on the glass and hoped he didn't miss my scowl.

"I didn't say anything about garlic. Tell me more about turning a human!" I blurted out the question even before I thought about it and when I saw his grin I knew I had made a mistake.

"Never mind, I don't want to know" I said quickly, turning away to hide my blush.

"You can't lie for shit! I know you have a million and one questions rolling round in that pretty little head of yours, ones I can guarantee your Dark Knight won't answer."

"Stop calling him that!" I snapped, making him laugh. I hated the way he tried to degrade Draven but considering what he said about him not telling me, well that I couldn't deny. How long had Draven and I been making love? How many times, how many opportunities did he have to tell me? Not one tiny little 'Oh by the way, I don't want you to die or get old, so I have been slipping in a little something extra, hope you don't mind' .

When I thought back to all those times something referred to death or ageing and Draven's reactions to it, I now understood why. It made me feel as though Draven should have come with a warning sticker attached to his side, 'Side effects may vary'.

"Do you want to know things or not, it's your choice I will not make the offer again?" I could feel Lucius trying to hold in his smile as he knew he had me, hook, line and sinker! I walked over to the bed and slumped down defeated. I felt like I was now the one betraying Draven by getting another to explain things to me but what else could I do, I had been left in the dark long enough and where had it gotten me?

"Yes, I want to know."

"Of course you do," he said softly, making me want to throw one of the many fancy pillows at his head and shout 'Stop being nice to me!' It was messing with my head when he did that, like running on a playing field where someone kept changing the game.

"Ask away!" He said seating himself in one of the chairs by the corner of the room. He stretched out his long legs and didn't seem to care that he was still half naked. I brought myself up fully onto the bed and pulled the throw at the end over my folded legs, hiding my modesty.

"What is a half breed?"

"Let me ask you first, what do you know about the human essence?" He held his chin and lent his elbow on his knee while he stared at me intently, waiting for my answer.

"You're talking about feeding from the emotions of humans, aren't you?"

"It's nice to know you're not completely ignorant of our ways." I made a huff sound which he chose to ignore.

"The human essence is what we feed on, this is done in different ways but for the majority, through strong human emotions. Vampires, for example, feed straight from the source. Why buy your meat in packets when you could slaughter the cow yourself, that's what I say?" He laughed when he saw me shudder at that image. Lucius slaughtering anything would be terrifying enough to need therapy for a very long time and I should know.

"Vampires therefore, get the essence for power from not just human blood but any blood. If I was to feed from a Demon say, or an Angel, depending where my tastes lie, then I would consume their essence and with that, their power. Not enough to cause permanent damage but enough to weaken them for a short while." Looking into his eyes it hit me, like someone planting a vision and it was a painful one at that.

"Oh my God! You fed from Draven didn't you? That's how you grew strong enough to control him, why you had never done so before and it's the reason you're no longer friends! It all makes sense now." I was shaking my head fitting all the puzzle pieces together when his clapping brought my head up.

"Very good Keira, what a clever little human you are, but there is a lot about that day you do not know and I have no intention of telling you."

"It's how you knew isn't it?" I asked, ignoring his last comment.

"About my blood being changed by Draven? You could taste it in me." His eyes seemed to get darker for a second before flashing red at the memory.

"Yes I could, that and more. You want to know what you have become Keira, then I will tell you." He leaned forward after rolling his neck muscles and stared at me like I was an utter mystery.

"You, my dear, have been changed into the only Being of this earth to possess a powerful mix of Demon, Angel and human blood." When he said it I sat back against the headboard and Lucius got to his feet to come and stand by one of the four tree posts.

"So you see, you are his little unique gift from the Gods and one he intends to keep whether you wish it or not! You are mistaken if you ever thought that you possessed choices with a man like Draven. You are a puppet, a toy to amuse a King and more importantly, a means to an end for the Gods to carry on such power. You will learn your fate soon enough, whether you accept it is irrelevant. Choices are never given to those chosen by the Gods." He said bitterly and remembering his past I gathered he was something of an expert on those matters.

"You would know, wouldn't you?" I said before thinking. He growled and lunged for me. I found myself flat on my back with a two hundred and fifty pound Vampire on top of me. He held his weight easily with one arm and with the other ran fingers down my cheek, neck and side. He was breathing fast and so was I but for a very different reason as I doubted his was due to fear.

"Draven's been telling little stories has he?" He continued down my side with his hand and I stifled a moan when his hand grabbed a fist full of his T-shirt to yank up my leg.

"Curious about me were you, Keira Girl?"

"I…I…" I couldn't seem to get words formed and out of my lips thanks to what he was doing to me. I could feel cold fingers caress circles on my thigh.

"You…You?" He mocked as his hand got higher, near the very top of my hip.

"Your name…" I whispered and he lowered his head, turning his ear my way to hear me.

"Yes?" He whispered back and I knew the next word out of my mouth would cause a reaction from him, hopefully one that wouldn't get me killed and that would put a stop to his hand from getting any further. I could feel it inching across and so close to my core that I tensed. It was now or never, and never meant the unthinkable. I couldn't let myself give up my body, a body that belonged to Draven. So I opened my mouth and let out his fears, one word, one name,

"Judas," I whispered so slightly I wasn't sure I had even said it, but when Lucius snarled at me between the deadly fangs, I knew he had heard. His fangs got longer before crashing down on my neck making me scream. My arms came up and tried to push him away but he grabbed both my wrists and hissed,

"Be still!" At me, causing me to give up the fight. He gripped his teeth at my flesh but thankfully hadn't yet bitten down. He sucked my skin into his mouth and I felt his fangs ready to tear into me at any moment. I did as I was told and remained still as any sudden movements would no doubt cause blood loss.

He stayed there sucking at my neck but never drawing any blood for what seemed like paralyzing hours but when he pulled back there was surprisingly no blood on his lips and my neck just felt numb. His eyes burrowed into mine and I wanted to look at anything but his angry glare. He must have heard every mad beat of my heart because when he leaned down once more and dragged the points of his fangs across my skin it raced faster, causing him to smile on my neck.

"Ssshh, little rabbit, I'm not going to eat you, not tonight anyway, but…" He released my wrists and pushed all his weight up so that he hovered over me.

"If I ever hear that name come from your sweet lips again, then I will make it so it is the last thing ever heard from them." To make his point he snapped his jaws at me coming so close to the lips he was talking about that I thought he was going to bite them now. I flinched back and he smiled as his fangs retracted to the normal size. I was panting in fear and my rising breasts kept brushing along his bare chest.

"Have I made myself clear, Keira Girl?" I could only find myself with the faint ability to nod and now instead of blind white hot anger he was back to being amused. He lent down one last time and put his lips to my forehead for a gentle kiss. He must have tasted the little beads of sweat there because he proceeded to lick and kiss each one away. I was so shocked at how one minute a raging beast hung over me like a guillotine and then the next he was so gentle it was building up as being pleasurable.

After I lay immobilised under the ministrations of Lucius he finally finished with my skin and eased himself off me. He moved back to his chair at a speed too fast for my eyes to register.

"So, where were we before you brought something sour into a sweet mix?" I shook my head being too afraid to say anything that might set him off again.

"Ah I know, I was about to tell you about Cambions and Nephilims." He rubbed his jaw that was starting to show day old stubble. I pulled myself up slowly, the way you would move around a dangerous animal that's unpredictable.

"I wouldn't have fear Keira, I doubt you will make the same

mistake twice and I believe I am quite calm… for now anyway." He held his thumb under his chin and one curled forefinger over his mouth while he lounged back in the chair with his elbow on the armrest. He looked perfectly at ease, the complete opposite to me, I could imagine.

"For someone usually so fiery in nature, I find it unnerving having you watch me with those big frightened eyes, saying not a word. I wish for you to speak." That last part was demanded and his hand left his face momentarily to motion me to do as he asked with his palm out and his fingers together folded in his outstretched hand. I remained silent.

"What, nothing to say, no burning questions about your royal lover?" He smirked at what he had named Draven and I had no doubt he was trying to get a rise out of me.

"You just want me to bite." I said turning to look the other way.

"Umm, now there's a thought." He laughed when I shot him daggers.

"Better. It's no fun sparring on your own. Now, do you want me to continue or not?" I hated the smile he gave me when I nodded. I felt like I was giving in and just fuelling an already inflated ego. I just hoped one day soon a certain somebody's fist was going to make it pop and then he would see me smile!

"Thinking happy thoughts Keira, tell me… am I naked?" He asked behind his hand like it was a secret.

"No but you'd like it, there's violence!" I said sarcastically. He fell back and clapped laughing.

"Ha! There she is, our little firecracker is back! Good, now you can be done being a damn girly girl and get your head back in the game!" I didn't give him the satisfaction of responding and he actually looked a little disappointed. Good!

"A Cambion and Nephilim is what we call a product of our kind crossing over and tasting the forbidden fruit, when we change from being just Demons and Angels into Incubus or Succubus."

"I don't understand," I said.

"Of course you don't, I doubt you know what they are, considering Draven likes to keep his pretty little doll in a glass cage, highly polished with ignorant bliss. An Incubus is a male supernatural that takes a human to his bed. A Succubus is the female version, both of which are punishable by death. Although I doubt Draven is about to do

146

the honours and throw himself down on the sword." He said waiting for my response.

"I'm sure Draven's only reason for keeping things from me is that he means to protect me." I said, trying to put the belief behind my words.

"Yes, from himself. Don't kid yourself little girl, he wanted you and he took you. Hey, not that I'm blaming him but don't be naive enough to think all his intentions are so honourable."

"I find it hard to see how you two were ever friends," I said choosing to ignore his last statement.

"I think you will find we're not that different, you for example."

"What about me?" I asked shaking my head, not seeing where he was going with this.

"Well, we both wanted something and we just took it, snatched you away without a care for what was best for you. Tell me, does he still keep that hot piece of ass called Aurora around his table?" He studied my reactions and smiled when he saw the pain flash across my features.

"I will take that for a yes. Can't say I blame him, after all, I hear humans can't hack our sexual appetite for long."

"Enough!" I shouted and slammed my fist on the bed in anger. He was doing this on purpose and I hated the insecurities he was planting in my head. What was he doing now, was he with her? Was she giving him fake comfort while I was no longer there? I stormed off the bed and paced the room clenching my fists, all the while Lucius was sat taking in my anger, dripping in smug satisfaction.

"I know what you're doing but it won't work!"

"Is this what you call not working?" He asked causing me to pause and that's when I lost it, I lurched myself at him like an angry cat that had just been thrown in the pond. I couldn't hold it back. I was lost in rage and everything that I had felt the last few days snapped me, broke me and all that remained was a mindless aftermath consisting of nails, girly slaps and hair pulling. Yes, I was actually trying to pull his hair!

He grabbed my wrists to control me and started shaking me gently calling my name.

"Keira! Keira stop. Just stop!" I was panting again but this time fear didn't even register. I was far too angry. Angry at Lucius, angry at Morgan, angry at myself and even more to the point, I was angry at Draven! Lucius had taken me for his own gain. Morgan had taken me and had made me weak. Myself, well I made bad decisions that had resulted in letting me get taken, both times. And Draven? I was so blindly angry at Draven for lying to me. For not trusting me enough to tell me the truth about what he was doing to me. All these things had merged into one and erupted into a meltdown.

"Let go of me!" I whispered once I had calmed and Lucius just gripped me harder.

"Are you calm?" He said looking down at me with a strange emotion I had not yet seen in his eyes before...was that... concern?

"Do I seem calm to you?" I said in a dead tone.

"Okay, so I will admit I went too far, but didn't it feel good to get all that anger out?" I actually laughed.

"Oh so you did this purely for my benefit, to help with my rage Doc Phil?" I said sarcastically, causing one eyebrow to rise.

"I can't deny I didn't get a kick out of it. An angry female is a big turn on." He said smiling and I laughed again.

"I thought you said I wasn't your type." I regretted it as soon as I said it but it was too late to retract it and Lucius only showed a moment of surprise before giving me his intimate answer. He lowered his head and when I tried to lower mine he tipped it back up to meet his eyes with his grip on my chin firm and determined.

"Oh there's time yet and I find myself warming to pretty little dolls with unruly tempers and bad attitudes." He winked at me and I blushed looking down to play with the edges of the ribbon that was still wound round my arms in unconventional gloves. Lucius' gaze travelled down and when he took one in his hand I pulled away.

"Show me them!" He said and I gasped stepping back.

"No...why would you...no!" I said more firmly.

"Keira." He warned as he took a step towards me. I took another two back and felt like I was being stalked.

"Keira!" He said again only this time in a more masterful tone. I looked over my shoulder to make sure I wasn't going to run into anything as I backed up further.

"I said no!" I tried for forceful, but my voice wobbled too much to achieve that.

"Fine, it's your choice." He said and for a moment I thought he was going to give in as he stopped coming closer. I still backed up another step and his eyes widened.

"Keira lookout," he said calmly, nodding at something behind me. I momentarily turned to see what I was about to walk into when I felt his body crash into mine and wrap his arms around me from behind. I screamed and tried to get from his hold, but he just repositioned himself so that my arms were held crossed over my chest with his hands holding them there. It felt like a solid wall of muscle behind me with his chest plastered to my back.

"Keira, as much as I love the feel of your cute little ass pressing against certain areas of my anatomy, I fear that I would embarrass both of us if you continued much longer, so please be still." After feeling the evidence for it myself I instantly did as I was told.

"Good kitten, now stay still." He moved one of my arms behind my back and wedged it between our bodies so that he could free up both hands. He then went for my other arm and held it out straight in front of me. His arms were so long that he had no problems with his movements in carrying out his task.

"Please, don't do this, I don't show…"

"Ssshh pet, I am not going to hurt you but I am curious." I held my breath and closed my eyes tight, for the feel of him unravelling my past like some sick Christmas present had me fighting to take in air.

"Just breathe, I'm not hurting you." He reassured me once again but this was a different type of pain. I felt the air touch my skin and for some reason it always felt colder on the actual scars themselves. I looked down and the ribbon passed through his fingers and floated to the ground in slow motion, like under water, my mind didn't want to catch up to the reality I was living in.

"Well would you look at that." He said in a caressing voice, no mockery, no humour and absolutely no pity. I sucked in a deep, needed breath and closed my eyes once again as he ran his cool fingers along each line, taking his time and extra care on the thicker deeper scars, the damaging ones. The real killers.

"Did it hurt Keira?" I swallowed hard and nodded.

"Speak!" He said turning me around to face him.

"Say the words," he asked again holding my arm and slowly bringing it up to his lips.

"Yes," I said, a single tear falling down my cheek, one he watched with deep fascination.

"But you carried on?" I was about to nod when he tilted his head to silently warn me into speaking.

"Yes." He kissed a scar after he nodded.

"And you bled a lot?" I don't know why he kept asking me questions but after each one he would kiss a different scar, making it all feel strangely erotic.

149

"Yes." Again another kiss.

"And when he got caught, did it feel good?"

"Yes." Another kiss.

"Real pain cuts to the bone and stays fused there long after the scars fade. But to know real pleasure only comes from knowing true pain. And these look like they hurt a lot Keira, do you know what that means?" I shook my head.

"Speak." Again with the order to say the word.

"No." No kiss this time.

"Tell me Keira, did it feel good…?" His lips hovered over my last scar as he paused and his grip got so tight it was verging on pain. His eyes never left mine and I felt beyond trapped by them, I felt… enslaved.

"To watch him die?" He waited, lips so close to touching my skin that little bumps broke out, thanks to his cold breath. He waited and… he waited.

I looked back to that night. I saw his face falling further away from my own, so far down that it felt like I would never see it hit the bottom and I never did. But I knew. I knew he had died and what did I feel, even as I thought I was also dying. What did I feel? It was there, the answer so easily found, it scared me to death. I turned my face higher up and looked him dead straight in the eye and answered,

"Yes!" His eyes flashed to blood and if I thought that he was going to kiss my last scar then I was wrong. He pulled me roughly to him and captured my lips before I could blink. He crushed himself to me and took control of my body. The room filled with a powerful blinding light the second our lips met, as though the sun was crashing down through the sky like a meteorite. He clung to me as though I was going to disappear and kissed me until I felt like I was drowning. I had nowhere to go and he wouldn't let me think, just feel. It was like holding on to a sinking ship instead of grabbing the first lifejacket and jumping from a doomed fate. Lucius was the ship and I was the fool, letting him kill me.

Why was I letting him kill me?

He pulled back and broke the spell, plunging us back into the room we had started off in. I looked at my hands on his body and felt heat where there was normally only cold. I couldn't understand why I had been holding onto him in the first place? I dropped my hands in surprise and stepped back. He still had his eyes closed and he looked like a wild animal fighting for control. His chest rose up and fell, as if he couldn't drag enough air into his lungs. His hair fell forward as he lowered his head, every muscle tensed and fists clenched by his sides, so tight his knuckles went an even paler shade of white, like the bones could be seen through the skin.

"Lucius?" I whispered his name like I was committing a crime. I gulped when his head snapped up and the red in his eyes burned as if I was looking at the Devil himself. I must have reacted because the icy grey bled back into his eyes and soon I was looking at a controlled Lucius once again.

He kept his lips in a tight line and forced his gaze from me as he leaned down to pick something up from the floor. I watched him rise and run the black ribbon through his hand as he straightened fully. I thought he was going to hand it to me but instead he turned his back to me and walked towards the door. He turned once to give me one last look that felt as though it could penetrate every single wall I had ever built to shield my fragile mind.

"Sleep well Keira and thank you for your gift." He said raising the ribbon to his lips to kiss before he disappeared out through the door.

Somehow, I didn't think he was talking about the ribbon or baring my arms to him. My mind flickered back to that kiss and my knees hit the floor. What had he done to me? Why hadn't I fought him harder? I loved Draven! I wanted Draven! I felt like screaming to myself. I rocked my body back and forth while I held my shameful head in my arms. I was pathetic! I needed to fight and I needed to get back to Draven. He was going to save me. I had to believe in that!

I looked down at my hands and saw tears drip down onto my palms and as I held out my arms, one white, one black with the ribbon still entwined, I thought about what Lucius had done to me. He had taken a piece of me with him and it was a lot more than a strip of black ribbon. He had taken my secrets and instead of showing me pity for those secrets revealed he had given me something in return, something more. He had given me reasons for pain and forced me to see a dark truth. It had felt good knowing that someone who had hurt me, suffered and it scared me that I didn't find shame in those thoughts. What did that make me?

I picked myself up and walked to the bed. I tore off Lucius' T-shirt because I couldn't stand sleeping wrapped in his scent. I stripped out of my underwear and didn't care that I was naked or that the lights were still on. I just didn't care about these simple things. My mind was too busy, too consumed with stronger emotions that involved two men.

What one man gave me and what one man took away. The love Draven gave me and the love that Lucius took away, but what did he give me instead? My mind flashed back to that kiss and I had my answer,

*Lucius gave me the sun.*

# CHAPTER 13
# GUILTY ANSWERS

I woke to a blinding sun and for a moment it took me back to a guilty kiss. I sat up and saw the day coming through the wall of glass and it felt as though I could finally breathe for the first time in days. It felt like a lifetime ago since I had last seen daylight. I stretched my arms out and three things hit me. The most important was that I hadn't visited Draven in my dreams this time and I had to put my fist to my mouth to stop from crying out. Why? Why hadn't I seen him in my dreams, when I needed to the most?

The second thing was that both my arms were now bare and the lights to the room had been turned off. Had someone come back into my room last night? I looked down and saw the answer was the third thing for me to notice. I had been left a gift.

I picked up a roll of material that had been tied together with long black satin ribbon. I pulled on the bow causing a pair of long gloves to unravel down the bed and a dried red rose head fell from the material. I picked it up to examine it and it looked like it had been picked this morning from a deep frost. It had been carefully wrapped up in the palm part of the glove and rolled up ready for me to find, but why?

The gloves were made from the softest black knitted cashmere and were fingerless. I pulled them on and couldn't help the sigh of bliss that escaped. Gloves really were my comfort blanket and I felt far too exposed without them. The head doctors I had seen had tried to get me past this dependence, saying that I needed to face my past without the aid of mental crutches. I simply disagreed.

I also noticed that Lucius' T-shirt had been put back on the bed, folded and ready for me to put back on. I didn't know how I felt about the obvious fact that Lucius had been back in my room when I was asleep. Was that why my dreams hadn't taken me to Draven?

I got out of bed after putting the oversized black T-shirt back on and went in search of some much needed food. I went into the little kitchenette and nearly cried when all I could find in the cupboard was coffee! Yuck! Well at least there was some bread and a toaster. I made myself some toast and found a little fridge that was hidden in a cabinet. I dreaded to think what Lucius would have kept in there when this was his room. And why was I even in here or had he been joking about that? Man, he was so infuriating.

Once finished I settled down on one of the couches and ate my toast and drank some juice I found in the fridge. Well, at least they hadn't forgotten that I was human with basic human needs. I was half expecting to have found bags of blood in the fridge like some mini blood bank. Once I had finished I went into the bathroom and tried not to think about the last time I was in here with Lucius watching my every move like some perverted hawk. For these reasons I had the quickest shower and like before, couldn't take my eyes from the bathroom door. Why have a clear glass shower in the centre of the room like some kind of entertainment pod! Next time I think I would choose the bathtub, at least I could use bubbles to hide under.

After taking care of bathroom business I soon found myself stood in the walk-in wardrobe staring at my bleak choices. I looked from one end that was more plastic than fabric and then to the other end that screamed gothic fairy tale. Long dresses, hooded cloaks and corsets galore but not one single pair of jeans in sight, just row after row of lace, velvet, silk and satin waiting for me to choose. It felt like I was in some medieval play no one told me about.

In the end I found myself grabbing a hanger and trying to not to think about it too much. It was as if someone was playing some weird joke on me trying to fool me into believing I had woken up in the wrong time and any minute now a person was going to burst in the room dressed as a court jester and shout 'surprise!'

I couldn't put it off any longer, as I had been stood wrapped in my towel for about twenty minutes staring at material. I pulled the masses of material over my head and twisted it until the skirt fell past my bra and to the floor. It was made from thick black brocade patterned with large black roses that were a shade darker. The skirt was beautiful and hung from my hips in heavy waves. It was one of those dresses that even though you're not a little girl anymore, it still made you want to twirl around and made you feel like a princess. It was a medieval style that was tight on my chest and had a Celtic pattern embroidered in brushed gold and copper around the edges. It had the same design in a thicker belt that came around the waist then hung low at the front before cascading down to the floor. The sleeves were tight at the tops of my arms but came down into a bell shape at the wrists allowing me room to put my gloves back on. They had large cuffs in the same gold embroidery that came past my knuckles but I still felt safer having my gloves on encasing my scars in comfort.

The back pulled tighter with some hard work trying to pull the crossed straps that tied low to my back, this pulled the top tighter to fit perfectly. I tied them the best I could with a bit of twisting but managed it in the end. The back also had a large hood attached with a black lining that matched the part of the dress that wrapped around my shoulders, not quite covering them. As far as fancy dress went I couldn't have been happier but everyday captive…I wasn't convinced. One thing was for sure, I was going to be having words with Pip!

I decided to tie my hair in a loose plait to hang down my back as I didn't see a hair dryer and didn't want to wear it wet to my head in its usual twist. Well, at least I looked the part with long hair and when I caught my reflection in the mirror before leaving the wardrobe I laughed at myself, I looked more like an extra from Lord of the Rings!

I walked over to the window opposite the bed and gasped at the view I saw in front of me. It was breathtaking. I tugged down on the handle and was surprised when I found it opened, I had half expected it to be locked. The cold air whipped at my skin and started blowing material behind me like the train on a wedding dress. I was faced with mountains of white snow and frosted trees standing to attention on every side. It was a perfect winter wonderland and so picturesque it reminded me of an old fashioned Christmas card.

The lake house was not the name I would have used to describe what I was now living in. It was a bloody castle, set into a mountain side and when I looked down after taking a few deep breaths for courage I saw the lake frozen around the mountain walls. It looked like grey coloured glass as it reflected the harsh landscape that surrounded it. I had to step back as my nerves got the better of me seeing that the drop was a sheer cliff face straight down to the frozen water at least a hundred and fifty feet to certain death. I actually laughed when I recalled Pip telling me that I could go anywhere I wanted. Ha, no wonder, even if I did find my way outside I wouldn't last five minutes. I was on the side of a bloody mountain for God sake!

I looked from one side to the other and from what I could see the building was made from dark grey stone that looked well weathered, as though it had been standing here for as long as the mountain itself. It was hard to see where one stopped and the other began as the walls were the same colour as the rock. Like the mountain had cracked open over a thousand years ago and the towers had burst from under the Earth's mantle like some demonic palace fit for a…well a Vampire King!

I slumped down in the chair and brought my knees up to my chest to hug myself. It really was a hopeless situation to be in and if I didn't trust that Draven would keep his word than I would have been tempted to just give up that last shred of hope I was clinging on to.

"You look depressed." I shot up and grabbed at my erratic heart!

"Jesus!" I said making Pip laugh.

"Nope, try again…someone less beardy this time." She jumped in the opposite chair and she made me feel cold even looking at her. As usual Pip's eclectic taste was astounding. She had a baseball style top that was white with black sleeves and it had a disturbing picture on the front of a devil killing a fashion model with flames on either side of the catwalk, the words underneath in gothic writing said 'The Devil kills Prada'. To this she added a pretty floral patch skirt that flared out around her bare legs and ankle length, bright green wellies with little black frogs. There were literally no words to describe Pip's dress sense, which brought me to the next question I asked.

"Pip, can I just ask?"

"Umm?" She said looking at her pointy painted nails, each one having a different flag on them.

"Why on earth did you fill my wardrobe with medieval fetish wear?" She stopped picking at Japan and looked me up and down.

"Don't you like it? That dress looks good on you and I managed to wash all the blood out of that one. Okay so I admit it, Master gave me a job to do and I got a little caught up with other things but Adam bought me this pink bouncy castle for my birthday and I always wanted to have sex on one and Adam does this thing where he lifts my leg and…"

"LA, LA, LA, Not listening to that bit Pip, so you can put your leg back down!" She smiled from under her inner thigh. Boy was she flexible and Adam was one lucky boy. Okay, now all I had was pink bouncy castles and Pip and Adam working their way through the Kama Sutra on it popping around my head like pornographic cartoon bubbles. Then another thing she'd said made its way back and I hoped, I really, really hoped I had misheard her.

"What do you mean by 'washed the blood out'?" She laughed nervously.

"Oh that… oh that was nothing, just a big misunderstanding really, I mean they thought I was a witch, stupid bastards didn't even know what an Imp was. But the river washed most of the blood away when they tried to drown me in that dunking chair thing, well that was after they stabbed me first to see if my blood was black and to see if I would try to call the Devil to see if he would come and save me." She turned very serious and pointed to her top before whispering,

"He is a very busy man, even in Hell they have paperwork you know. So anyway, I patched up the bit at the side and now it's like new, but I guess now you want a new dress don't ya?" I automatically looked to my side and noticed a tiny little patch where the material didn't match up with the other roses. Oh my… she wasn't kidding!

"This used to be your dress?" I had to ask just to be ultra clear.

"Yep."

"And I'm wearing it because….?" I raised my eyebrows at her and motioned with my hand for an answer.

"Pink bouncy castle…remember?" I shook my head and thought that even Dan Brown wouldn't be able to crack Pip's code!

"Please explain." I said feeling a headache coming on.

"Lucius put me in charge of buying you clothes, but I ran out of time because…"

"The pink bouncy castle," I finished for her.

"Yes, see now you're getting it." She actually clapped her hands making her Japan nail to chip off completely. She grabbed the piece mid-air and simply gave it a lick and stuck it back down.

"I thought I could kill two bears with one axe. Adam had been on at me for a couple of decades to sort through my growing wardrobe… I'm a bit of a pack chipmunk and hate throwing things away. They were the two eras that I didn't want to keep."

"So I got them?" It was horribly starting to make sense.

"You did, you lucky girl, you!" She leaned over and pinched my cheek and wiggled it like you would a child. I laughed because it was just too crazy to be anything but funny.

"Couldn't you just do what other people do when they want to get rid of all their crap and sell it on ebay?" I asked but she shook her head.

"Adam won't let me near a computer again since what happened to Lucy." I was scared to ask but nope, curiosity won.

"And who was Lucy?"

"My computer and let's just say…she didn't make it. Drink?" She got up and skipped into the room but was back before I even got up. She held a bottle of clear liquid that had a picture of an apple and pear above the name 'Obstwasser' on the label. She had one shot glass in her hand and another hanging from around her neck on a thick silver chain. Where did that even come from?

"Isn't it still morning?"

"I think so, at least that what Mickey Mouse told me it was on my clock. Don't worry, Adam's busy. So what will it be, 'little britches' or 'big girl pants'?" It took me a minute to decipher yet another Pip code and realised she meant the size of the shot.

"Big girl pants," I said and she gave me a beaming smile as she handed over a shot glass filled to the brim. I waited for her to fill hers and we raised our glasses.

"PROSIT!" Pip shouted and I gathered it meant 'cheers' in German. We knocked it back and I felt it burn before the flavour registered. Pip gave me a goofy grin before refilling my glass back up with Schnapps. We shot it back and this time it didn't burn as much.

"So does this mean I can convince you to get me some clothes I can actually wear?"

"You're wearing that one and besides, it looks good on you. You have bigger tiddly winkers than me so it's a bit tight on the top half but still…Va,va, voom!" She then threw her head back and howled in a comical fashion.

"But if you would feel more comfortable, I didn't much like renaissance, now those bastards were heavy and don't get me started on the bone breaking corsets!" She said creating a choking motion with her hands before refilling up our glasses.

"Not selling it to me here, Pip!" I said sarcastically tapping my glass to hers that still hung from the chain and slinging another one back. Of course, she filled mine back up.

"So tell me, was this room really Lucius'?" I asked after forcing down another shot. Pip raised her eyebrows and gave me an evil grin.

"Diggin' the Master, yeh?" She said waggling her eyebrows as she usually did.

"No!" I said spilling some of the liquid to the tiled floor as she was refilling yet another glass.

"Shame...mmm two Kings, one bed, sounded a bit fun to me but hey, whatever floats your cruise ship! Anyway, I think he was just pulling your boobies with that one. He doesn't like the daylight and this room has too much of that going on. Me, well I sympathise, being a night Imp myself I don't much like the daylight but here it's not so sucky. It's the mountains, they don't let too much sun in this part but Lucius has a huge, huge, huge part of the caves as his quarters." She said after showing me just how huge, huge, huge, with her hands. I couldn't help but giggle and maybe it was a little down to the many shots that were still being poured my way.

"Caves?" I asked.

"Oh yeah...man there is oodles of caves in this place. It was built in to the mountain in such a way that most don't even know it's here. All but Lucius' guests of course...well more like subjects, as all those faces in the great hall, Lucius turned. The only ones there that haven't been turned is his council and you met all them. Liessa likes you by the way and she told me to tell you thanks." She winked and I knew what the thanks was for, although I really couldn't say I did anything.

"So everyone in that room was..."

"Sooo not human! Nope you're the only one here with that title and everyone is so jealous that you're my friend and Adam told me to make sure I keep you safe, so 'ere I be me matey', keeping you safe, although we need rum if we're gonna be pirates. But I don't have any so schnapps it is." She said all this while giving me pirate's themed salutes which again made me giggle until her words started to filter through my schnapps' flooded mind.

"So let me get this straight...all the people in the great hall are turned Angels and Demons that are now Vampires and the only ones not are you, Adam, Ruto, Hakan, Liessa and the big dude that hates me, that I can't remember the name of...oh and me?"

"Caspian, and don't worry about him, he hates everyone when he first meets them, and he is like so overly protective of my Lord it's not even funny, although I do extract the mickey, but then get spanked by Adam and then we do this thing that makes my..."

"LA,LA,LA Pip! Please spare me the 'sex freak on'." Another shot and I carried on.

"So these caves, is that the way we came in here?" Again with another shot.

159

"Yep, this place is full of them but don't worry about getting lost 'cause the doors that stay locked are the ones that go deep into the mountain and further into Lucius' domain. I know I will have to give you a tour of the place soon but not today as I will have to get back to Adam soon before he gets out of his…oops nearly let that one out of the big bag." She got this little sheepish look on her face like she was soon to be in big, big trouble and being Pip, I didn't doubt it!

"So tell me about the King, do you love him and want his baby love child, 'cause I love babies…not to eat or anything!" Her question took me back and I instantly felt that pang in my chest that ached just being without him and talking about it made it more real. I think she saw my face contort in pain because she filled up my shot glass again.

"I do…I love him so much it hurts and I feel I am going to go crazy if I don't see him again soon. He's…he's not just someone I love, he's someone I need…you know what I mean?" I asked feeling as if my words were getting stuck, choking on thick emotion. She simply nodded.

"I know and I am sorry. I couldn't be without my Adam and I would hate to see what would happen to the world if he was without me! Now that was a scary thought!" I didn't fully understand what she meant and it made me wonder who the hell this Adam dude was in the supernatural world?

"So you will feel better once you see the King more often?" I didn't really understand the question but nodded yes making her start tapping her nail against her lips…I think it was Canada.

"I think I can borrow some from the Moon but she will get pissy, so maybe Forester will help out, either one will do but I will see if I can do my best." She smiled but I think my head must've been getting far too fuzzy thanks to the schnapps 'cause I couldn't understand a word that she just said…Moon, Forester?

"Ooo…k!" I said but when she tried to fill my glass again I placed my hand over the top. I could drink a lot but with the bottle close to empty I think the slow buzz that was creeping across my brain was ringing the bell on that limit meter.

A great roar echoed in the distance and Pip turned pale.

"Wow, that was quicker this time. Men, eh?" She said picking up the bottle and finishing the lot.

We both jumped at the sound of my door being torn open and Adam stormed in looking far less conservative than usual. His grey sweat pants had been put on back to front and his T-shirt looked ripped at the seams but was still holding it together in some places. There were big damp patches under his arms and along his chest. Had he been working out? There was one thing though, he looked utterly wild and Pip, well Pip just looked excited!

He stormed through the room to the balcony and shot daggers at Pip.

"Squeak, you have been bad!" He said in a deep rumbling voice that I didn't recognise as belonging to him.

"Please excuse me Keira, Pipper here is needed," he said calmly and then bent his body and practically threw her over his shoulder making her giggle. He turned and nodded to me before he walked out of the door into the room.

"See ya tonight Toots, oh and have a good sleep." She said but stopped speaking when Adam smacked her on the bottom making her squeal. I heard the start of her reprimand as they walked away.

"Think you could lock me up in that cage again little wifey? I think it's time for a little pay back and I know my favourite kind!" I heard another smack and a cry out as they went down the hallway.

I shook my head and tried to focus on what just happened. Did she really lock her husband up in a cage? Knowing what I knew about Pip then yeah, I could easily have believed it.

I was quite glad to finally have the alone time as when Pip had suddenly asked me about Draven I had used all my power not to cry. I couldn't even begin to explain to her how much I missed him but not just him, it was everything in my Afterlife. It was my sister and Frank. It was RJ and Jack. The thought of Sophia made me want to be as strong as she would be. The thought of Vincent made my chest hurt, an ache that had me closing my eyes to try and squash down the pain. And of course, at the very top of the misery was Draven. Dominic Draven.

I couldn't stop the tears that started to stream down my cold cheeks. I lifted my knees up to my chest and repositioned all the flowing material around the chair I sat in feeling not only cold but frozen. It was as if someone had emptied everything that filled my soul and drenched, soaked and saturated me in the icy water below. I don't think I had ever felt so cold in all my life and it wasn't down to the winter weather. I wanted Draven so badly I didn't think it would ever stop hurting.

I looked out to the harsh snowy terrain and found myself frowning at it, like it was mocking me somehow. I wanted to scream at its beauty for being part of my prison. It didn't have the right to be beautiful! It didn't have any right, damn it!

"I HATE YOU!" I screamed until my lungs hurt and my hate echoed around the mountains for the unseen world to hear. I got up and went closer to the glass surround not caring about the height anymore. I was far too angry for fear. It felt like my veins were burning and being powered by fire and brimstone. I felt hot all of a sudden, like I could start shooting flames from my hands. God I was so angry!

"DID YOU HEAR ME? I HATE YOU!" I screamed again and threw my shot glass over the edge, stupidly trying to hit the mountain side opposite me. Then something unbelievable happened that I could not explain. The little glass flew like it was shot out of a gun and amazingly hit the side of the mountain I had been aiming for. It exploded on impact but it didn't just smash, it boomed and caused a rock slide that fell down into the icy lake below. It broke into the water and another piece the size of a car fell into the water causing an enormous splash. It was as though I had just gone at the mountain with a rocket launcher!

What the hell was in that drink? And how did I just throw something that must be at least a thousand feet away across the lake? Did I just imagine that?

My hands gripped at the metal railing that sat on top of the glass panels. I felt like I could crush it if I tried and when I heard the metal groan I let go and took a step back. What was happening to me? I looked down at my hands and noticed my veins looked more noticeable on my pale skin. Was that just because I was cold?

"Aaah!" I shouted out as pain rushed to my head and chest simultaneously. I backed up holding my head and closing my eyes to the pain. I backed into the door and felt for the handle with my free hand.

"Ahhhhhh!" I shouted again as another pain travelled down my arms and back up again. It felt as though my heart was on fire and pumping the flames to my arteries feeding my body with scorching pain. I fell on the floor and got twisted in the dress as I gripped at my body. I needed to do something, I needed to breathe and call somebody. I took a deep breath and another as my anger was soon snuffed out by fear.

Then bang! The pain left my body like someone had flipped a switch and I was left as though it had never occurred. My muscles relaxed where they had been coiled in tension only seconds before and I fell flat on my back by the bed, left feeling only exhaustion. I closed my eyes, took a breath.

And that's all it took for me to pass out. One breath.

I opened my eyes to the faint feeling of being lifted and a gentle murmur of voices. I could then feel myself being lowered onto something soft which even in my fogged mind I could recognise it as being a bed. I tried to think back to what had happened but couldn't find the memory. I couldn't even manage to open my eyes fully, but the little slits under my lids showed bright light. It felt like my head was too heavy and was I drunk?

"Wha... di...yo...do...her...look at...Pip" I could make out more broken words than full ones but was that Adam's voice?

"Sh...seemed...fi...or...left her. Will...sh...okay?" That was Pip's musical voice wasn't it, well that made sense if Adam was here but why were they here, what had happened?

"I hope s...or my Lor...not goi...happy." What was wrong with my head, why couldn't I focus properly?

"Pip, let h...slee...needs th...rest." I felt someone lean over me and then start to play with my hair. It felt like little fingers were unravelling the plait and brushing through the damp waves.

"There sh...prett...fo...the Kin..." I felt a slight kiss bestowed on my cheek and a whispered word I couldn't understand in my ear before something sprinkled across my skin making it tingle. I still couldn't seem to move and just as I started to try I felt my body fall deeper into a dark place as though someone had removed the bed and opened up a chasm under me. I was falling faster and faster until my mind couldn't keep up and so, it gave up. And I let the darkness take me to a place that swamped my senses as if I was coming up for air after being forced under the water for a small eternity. I gasped and bolted upright the second my lungs filled with cold air. I opened my eyes and looked around to see where the darkness had brought me and the shock caught in my throat as if I was trying to get the drowning water up and out of my system.

I looked on in amazement trying to take in the scene and everything else around me. But it was when my eyes came across the figure looming close by that captured every ounce of my attention. I looked him up and down trying to judge if he was really here, if I was really here? How had this happened?

There were too many questions and not enough time to think about the answers. So I didn't. I just stopped thinking and focused on the man in front of me.

And then he said my name and I shuddered at the sound of such a beautiful voice.

"Keira?" Such a bewitching voice, so majestic and alluring, with such a strength that one wouldn't dare question it… ever. But most of all,

The voice of an Angel.

*"Vincent?"*

# CHAPTER 14
# VINCENT'S LEAP OF FAITH

"Vincent, is that really you?" I asked so timidly that I wasn't sure he would even hear me ask. He raised a perfectly sculptured eyebrow before gracing me with one of the biggest smiles I had ever seen on him.

"Keira!" He then ran at me from across the room but I scrabbled away on the bed I was on and put up my hands desperately.

"Stop!" He did as my shout ordered and then looked at me with something close to hurt.

"Keira what's wrong, why don't you want me touching you?" He frowned down at me and yes, he was hurt. That look felt like I had just swallowed a fist. Didn't he know what happened when anyone touched me like this?

"I don't want to go Vincent, I can't leave… not yet, please don't make me go…please." I was shaking my head as the raw emotions took over. I hated feeling so weak, but right at this moment, knowing I couldn't connect in the way I really wanted to was slowly killing me. So the tears came and I lowered my head in my hands trying to hide my weakness.

"Keira….Keira listen to me, I would never make you go. I. Don't. Want. You. To. Go." He said each word with such certainty and layered so thick with his own emotion that big fat tears came following the others.

"Keira, look at me!" I shook my head still cradled in my hands. I think I was sat on his bed as I remember seeing it once, of course it had been filled with beauties draped over his naked form but I still remembered his bed. Its frame was floor level, it was round and everything was white. And I was now sat on the edge of it crying like a child.

"Keira look at me now!" He demanded sternly and hearing such authority from Vincent was unusual to say the least. I sniffed a few times and looked up to find him looking so tall even with him knelt in front of me. His hand came out so slowly making me flinch back. He frowned and tilted his head to one side.

"Keira, do you trust me?" His question sounded so euphoric, like the words themselves could caress me. Could flow over my skin and wrap me in a warmth I needed so badly. But just being here was enough and I was terrified that one touch from Vincent would send me hurtling back down the rabbit hole and down there, waiting for me, was the King of no Hearts.

But Vincent had asked me if I trusted him and I couldn't lie, not to him.

"Yes," I said looking up into his incredible topaz eyes that shone with the same emotions that reflected my own.

"Good because...Gods I missed you!" Vincent said as though something in him broke. Something snapped and the words came out in a rush of hard solid truth. Then he grabbed me and yanked my whole body into his, crushing me to his chest. I gasped at the contact but then his skin started to glow and I was quickly engulfed in an intoxicating haze of bliss. The emotions that conquered my mind were such a heady mix of reassurance, hope, safety and comfort that I melted into his strong hold and let go of every other feeling other than the one he was supplying me with.

I felt one hand hold my head to his chest, stroking my hair and the other was wrapped around my waist, where he made soothing circles with his fingers.

"Ssshh, you're safe here, no one will hurt you Keira...I won't let anyone hurt you." He spoke into my hair and then leaned back to kiss my forehead. I looked up at him and when he brought both hands to my face to capture my tears with his thumbs it was only then that I realised I was still crying.

"How is this possible Vincent? Every time Draven touches..." He held a finger to my lips to stop me from carrying on the sentence.

"I am an Angel Keira, I can touch anything so pure, even when you are like this, even when it's just your soul sent to us." I started

166

shaking my head but then it clicked and I felt as if the next words were torn from me.

"Draven can't...because...he's half...Demon?" Vincent looked truly sorry in that moment but he nodded.

"I'm sorry Keira, but your body is still where they are keeping you. This form is your soul and that part belongs to us, not just to Dom, but Sophia and me too. That's why you come back to us, although I suspect you have help because it is unheard of for a human to do this without some aid." He looked at me a moment and then his eyes got brighter for a second and he gave me this look as though an idea had just come to him.

"Ah...of course!" He said smiling and shaking his head at the same time, all the while never taking his hands from me.

"What? What is it?"

"She is a sneaky little thing, your new friend...naughty little Imp!" He laughed and I pulled back further which I don't think he liked but he allowed.

"Who, Pip?" He nodded while he laughed.

"She's the one doing this?"

"If I know Pip like I do, then it is her without a doubt. Think back, was you with her when it happened the first time?" He asked brushing the back of his hand down my cheek.

"I was on the plane," I answered thinking back.

"And the second time?" He asked already knowing the answer to be something simpler.

"I woke and she was sat on my bed."

"Of course she was!" He laughed again and stood in one fluid motion from being on his knees.

"Come Keira, I think there is someone you will want to see and I bet my wings he will want to see you."

"Draven!" I said in a breath and grabbed his extended hand for him to heave me up. I started to feel almost giddy at the idea of seeing Draven again and then the depressing thought seeped in and I knew that I couldn't yet touch him. But at least I could drink in my fill of him, which was better than nothing. My mind whirled at the thought that me being here like this was all down to Pip. I wanted to give her the biggest hug ever and tell how much it all meant to me.

I looked at Vincent as he turned his back and saw him shrug on a dark brown leather jacket which was a military, combat style that zipped up to the collar. There were also zips up the forearms but both were left undone like the front. When he turned around I noticed he also wore a faded white T-shirt that had the word 'Triumph' Logo at the top that looked well worn. It looked quite retro and I remembered seeing the T-shirt somewhere before.

"Steve McQueen!" I blurted out and Vincent shot me a bad boy grin that was both sexy and typical of a Draven boy. I remembered my Uncle, Hilary's dad, had a poster of Steve McQueen on a motorcycle in his garage.

"The very same, sweetheart!" He said still smiling as he took my hand in his and started pulling me from his room. Which made me wonder...why I had ended up in Vincent's room to start with?

Vincent led me down a corridor that I vaguely remembered from the night I had come here, thanks to Lucius and his unforgettable touch. But then when we walked past the door that I knew led to Draven's room I pulled back on the hand that was entwined with mine.

"Where are we going?" I asked feeling suddenly nervous.

"I thought you trusted me, Keira?" His voice was honey dripping seductively over my cold skin and I found I could only nod. What was it about the Draven brothers that had you doing anything they wished of you. It wasn't just their voice, it was everything, every tiny little supernatural molecule they possessed had you jumping to whatever beat they set. It was their sheer strength. Their inbuilt authority and their never-ending power to use at will. And I was hooked like a junkie. I wanted it all and felt like I was losing a part of myself the longer I was kept from them. That's what it was, I had finally found a word to describe what being around the Dravens was...it was, grade A, uncut and premium kind,

Addiction.

It felt like we had been walking through various hallways, tunnels and open archways for hours when in reality it was probably only fifteen minutes. I was so anxious to see Draven I was terrified that I was going to fade away before I even got there. I clung onto Vincent like he was the only thing anchoring me to this place and in a way I gathered he was. He didn't seem to mind that, even though my hand was in his, my other hand gripped onto his jacket by his elbow until my knuckles were bone white.

We finally got to a large spiral staircase that seemed to go down so far that I would have been able to hear the Devil himself laughing from the bottom. I leant over the top and looked down the open middle section.

"Wow, you can't even see the bottom, tell me we don't have to go down all those steps," I said still looking down.

"You don't," he said with a slight hint of amusement in his answer and before I could look around at him I felt my body being swept up, making me squeal.

"Wh...What are you...?" I asked, having a very bad feeling about this. He lifted me to his chest and seemed to test my weight with one arm under my knees and the other around my body.

"God's Keira, have they even been feeding you?!" He sounded angry which was unusual in itself hearing it from Vincent. I didn't have chance to answer him as he growled low and I jumped a little in his rock solid embrace. Then he walked us to the edge and every muscle in my body tensed before I started to squirm like a fish on the floor of a boat.

"Vincent! No...please tell me you're not going to do what I think you're going to...right...Please tell me you're not!"

"Ssshh Keira, just relax. I've got you now." He turned his back to the edge of the brick staircase and for one wonderful moment I thought I had it all wrong and he was just waiting for something. What I didn't realise until it was too late was that, yes, he was waiting for something, he was waiting for me to take a deep breath before he twisted his body quickly and sat on the edge with his legs and me dangling over the middle section of the spiral.

"Take another one Keira!" Was he joking! I froze in his arms because moving might mean he'd drop me and my fear of heights wouldn't permit any other thought than...Oh Shit!

"Take a deep breath now, Keira." He said sternly and I did as I was told.

"Good girl!" He said and then... he jumped!

I felt the air whoosh up around us like we were in a wind tunnel. The speed was immense, and I turned my frightened face into his chest. I opened my eyes for only a second and saw the word 'Triumph' rippling like it had been thrown into the restless waters. All the material from my dress was flapping around us like a useless parachute and I quickly closed my eyes dreading the inevitable impact.

Then BOOM! Vincent had landed, taking all the impact and only the sound echoing through the tunnels that lay ahead was the only indication that we had even landed. I wasn't even jostled but that didn't mean to say I didn't have shaky legs as he set me down. He held me firm by the arms until he thought I was okay and when I thought he would let me go, he spoke,

"Wait!" He commanded softly and I froze under his spell. His hands left my arms but went to my waist and started feeling my sides, holding them and moving up and around. What was he doing? It was as if he was looking for something but this dress didn't exactly have any pockets!

He started shaking his head and I felt the heat invade my cheeks. He tipped my chin up to look at him and being over six foot I had to tilt it all the way back just to meet his eyes.

"You need to demand they feed you more Keira. This is NOT acceptable!" He actually shouted out the word 'not' and I flinched. Remind me never to piss off Vincent if this was only a glimpse of the fiery anger that lay buried deeply under the layers of angelic innocence. He flinched when his hands felt my protruding ribs and he fisted the loose material by my side.

"We're lucky Dom can't touch you 'cause if he felt how much weight you had lost then it would only fuel his rage and I doubt we would have any of his men left." He released me and I stood back. I held my arms around myself feeling colder now without his touch.

"What do you mean?" I asked, but instead of answering me he held his hand out for me to take. I did and only when his fingers held my hand secure did he speak.

"You will see." At this I shuddered. Draven's rage was something never to be taken lightly and right now, it wasn't the Draven I wanted to meet.

I put that thought behind me and continued following Vincent through the underground tunnels that led only Angels and Demons knew where. I felt like an intruder whenever coming down here. Not that it had been more than that one time but still, it even felt like the stonework itself didn't like me and I couldn't help but hug myself a little tighter around the middle.

"Penny for your thoughts!" Vincent's voice was that craving honey tone again and when his hand tightened a little on mine I couldn't help but smile up at him.

"I was just thinking that it doesn't feel right, me being down here." He gave me a reassuring smile and tugged me closer to him to wrap an arm around my shoulders. There he tucked me under his arm and I found myself nestled into his side.

"Keira, that could not be further from the truth. You feel uneasy because you're the first human these old walls have ever seen. There are a lot of souls that find this to be their place of rest, so no doubt you can feel their leftover energy. But never fear your position among us." He turned his head over mine and I could have sworn he had just kissed me there.

"What do you mean...my position?"

"Keira, do you doubt us or even the Gods themselves? You know what you are to us." He seemed to be teasing and also reprimanding at the same time.

"You mean about me being this Chosen One...don't you?" I couldn't help but frown at the term everyone had classed me as.

"This Chosen One? The Chosen One, you mean."

"Vincent please understand, I am just me...just Keira. Someone who's terrified of heights, drinks way too much tea and barely has anything but shades of black in her wardrobe. What makes everyone think that I even have it in me to be this...this Chosen One? I don't even like spiders and freak out even if I get a ten year old web on me." He laughed heartily and spun to face me so quick I had to blink a few times.

"What did you expect the Chosen One to be Keira, Xena warrior princess?" He asked laughing again and I couldn't help but smile back, I also elbowed him in the ribs.

"Hey! Cut that out Xena."

"Don't you dare start calling me that! Anyway, what's an Angel like you doing watching that cheesy show...fancy a bit of what Xena's dishing out do ya?" I said teasing and I went to punch him playfully in the stomach. His hand whipped out and grabbed my wrist before I could make contact. He pulled it to him and placed it low on his back which forced my body to take a step into him. I looked up and noticed a new mischievous grin that I hadn't seen on him before. He lowered his head to my ear and I felt the rush of blood to the surface when his breath fanned out and over the tender skin by my neck.

"Nah, I prefer blondes!" He whispered and when I met his eyes he winked at me. I gulped down the lump and the time we kissed erupted into my mind's eye. I must have blushed like I had spent far too long on the sunbeds 'cause he laughed at the sight of my cheeks.

"Cool it down sugar, I promise to behave." He ran all four fingertips down my cheek before kissing me there. He then dropped his hand to mine and took it in his strong hold. He turned and my other hand had to let go of the material of his t-shirt I had surprisingly clung onto.

We didn't speak again until the end of an arched hallway brought us out to a huge open space. As we walked past the open arch I jumped at the sound of a voice at my ear,

"Ssshh..." The willowy voice spoke and Vincent pulled me nearer to his side.

"Don't worry, it is only the watchers...look!" He pointed to the side of the arch we passed through and as the room lit up with flaming torches I could then make out the two stone figures of cloaked women on either side. They faced each other and had their grey fingers positioned at their lips. They were very, very creepy and if they weren't bad enough I turned to take in the room we had just entered.

There were arched recesses around the walls, each with its own female form either side in a different position. Stone enticements were all positioned seductively holding an offering of some kind. One held a bowl full of fruit that also held her cold naked breasts in. Another played a very long flute-like instrument, although I had never seen one the length of your average person. Two others each had their bodies half covered with gold coins and the orangey yellow shone brightly against the dull dead grey.

As I walked further into the room I heard stone moving against stone behind me and when I turned the two cloaked figures by the door had moved into a new position and no longer had their cloaks covering their breasts. They also now had their head thrown up to the ceiling and looked to be silently howling.

"They moved, Vincent they just moved!" I said twice but he just shrugged his shoulders and continued onwards.

We passed a number of provocative statues that made up the base of the pillars in the vast room. It looked almost like a cavern with huge tree size arched pillars each with three naked figures stretched up with their arms outstretched to the ceiling and then when we were walking past one I noticed the reason for their positions, they were chained this way. It was only when inspecting each one again I noticed they all were chained in some way, like frozen sex slaves.

At the end of the room stood two of the biggest pillars I had seen down here so far. They must have been at least ten foot wide and made of thick stone blocks that were a reddish colour, almost like oversized bricks. Past these was a door to match their size made from dark wooden panels that were crisscrossed and held in place by thick black iron strips all with shiny metal studs hammered along the centre in a line. It looked truly impenetrable and completely intimidating. Only a fool would try and attempt to get in through these doors without a personal welcome.

"So you really don't believe you belong here?" Vincent said causing that question to echo around the room and reach all the rock carved ears of at least thirty women. What did he expect me to say, of course I didn't feel like I belonged in this fairy tale dungeon. Even as I thought it he was looking me up and down and I followed his line of sight. Okay so maybe in this dress then, yeah I did kind of fit the part but in reality…

"Give me your hand, Keira." I did as I was told even before I thought about what I was doing. It was one of the gifts the Dravens all possessed, utter compliance without even thinking about it!

He led me over to an opening by the door and the hole in the stone reminded me of something out of Indiana Jones and the Temple of Doom. I tried to pull back when he proceeded to place my hand in the dark opening but with one arched eyebrow and a look that made me feel like a scolded child I was doing his bidding.

"When you feel a piece of metal shaped like a handle bar then grab it and hold on with your palm flat against it." I did as I was instructed and felt for the cold bar and as soon as I located it I gripped on tight.

"What now?"

"Now, you hold on tight and we wait for the door to recognise you as being one of us." I whipped my head round to face him,

"What do you mea…Arrh!" I shouted but then screamed as the metal pricked me again. I yanked my hand away and saw five little pin pricks on the tips of my fingers. I sucked the blood off and scowled at Vincent.

"Next time I think I'll let you open the door!" I said, frowning down at my hand. I heard Vincent laugh before taking my hand in his. He kissed each of my digits and didn't take his eyes from me the whole time. I noticed more of my blood smeared along his lips with every kiss.

"You were very brave and I think I made my point." He nodded behind me and I saw the iron strips being released on one side and swing down one by one in a synchronized motion. When the door had released of all its metal locks, which now hung motionless by the sides the door, it parted and opened for us to enter.

"I did that?"

"Your blood did. So you see Keira, you are more like us than you may think." I flinched at remembering why that might be.

"Thanks to Draven, is what you really mean." I said stopping him in his tracks just before the door. The bright light coming from behind him haloed around his figure making him appear ever more the Angel he was.

"Ahh, so you are angry with him?" I shook my head and really wished I could see his face but with the light coming from the opening it put all his features in shadow.

"Not angry but hey, how do you know what happened, did he tell you? Does he think I'm angry at him?"

"And why wouldn't you be? I knew keeping the importance of your immortality from you was unwise. He and I disagreed." I hated the idea of them arguing over anything, let alone it being a conflict about me, but when he said the word immortality it caused little bumps to break out over my body.

"Why didn't he tell me?"

"The truth…?" I nodded, not knowing if I actually wanted to hear the grim truth.

"He didn't think it was your choice to make. You belong to him. You're his and he is yours. He simply did not see any reason against making it for longer than one lifetime. Do you?"

"I...I… would have at least like to be asked, given a choice. Those still belong to me you know!" I said with a bit of a bite.

"And that is precisely what I told him. You are right, your choices still belong to you, but well, Draven is hot headed and has ruled everyone he has ever met, that is until you came along, so cut him some slack, he is still learning, Keira." He didn't say this with anything but love for his brother and caring concern which I couldn't disagree with. He was only trying to help, which made the flirty attention he showed me sometimes make his words all the more confusing as to why he would act the way he does around me. I mentally shrugged my shoulders and decided not to look too much into it.

We walked into the room and I had to close my eyes and was thankful for Vincent's guidance as I was momentarily blinded. I think we rounded a corner and stepped into another room because now a noise could be heard that sounded like swords clashing together.

"Great, now he's at it with Takeshi!" Vincent said with exasperation. I blinked a few times and my vision slowly came back to me which awarded me a sight enough to make any woman swoon. We stepped up to a balcony that wrapped around the room below. It was obvious what it was used for even without the evidence in the form of two very male figures fighting in the middle. It was a training room and all the walls were covered top to bottom with weapons of every style.

There were daggers and swords of different sizes splayed out in a deadly dome against one wall and in between each blade was a throwing star. Another wall had metal rings attached which held an arrangement of spears, all different lengths and different styles. Some with red hair hanging from the blades that looked African. Others where the blades were a wavy design at the end of poles covered in some animal hide. These also ranged in various sizes.

Then there were the more practical weapons that were arranged all along different stands on the floor that were better suited to training. Wooden staffs that at least wouldn't take off limbs with the flick of a wrist, all stood waiting to be used. Of course the danger wasn't lacking in this section, as there were always the numerous sets of samurai swords that went up in three sizes. They seemed to be the most popular choice as the whole of the training room had a Japanese feel. With the bamboo flooring and cream coloured walls decorated with what I could only imagine to be Japanese symbols on the tapestries. These were in long red strips that hung ceiling to floor in between each section of weaponry displayed.

The more exotic looking weapons were displayed on the largest wall behind the fighters and opposite to where we stood above. I shuddered at the thought of ever seeing any being used on the human body and the irreparable damage they would do. There were axes, clubs and maces, all looking more deadly than the rest, always one bigger, sharper and with more spikes. Even sickles hung there, that looked more for agricultural uses. Blades of so many shapes and sizes, made from a wide array of materials, looked so pristine that they could have come straight from the hands that made them. The collection was vast and no doubt expensive as there was more than one piece that looked made of solid gold, encrusted with sparkling gems and diamond tipped.

And there, in the middle of such destructive instruments stood the man, who not only owned the room, but every being in it. The crowd sat around the edges of the matted area which took up most of the room and watched as two men circled each other holding the longest and most deadly Samurai swords I had ever seen, firmly in their grasp. Two hands held onto the grip part of the sword that was long enough to accommodate both fists. Both held their weapons at different angles, Takeshi in protective stance with his blade shielding his body from a blow to come, while Draven just looked as though he was getting ready for the kill with his blade held in front of him. I was no expert but from the looks of both men they looked as if they had been doing this since the first samurai sword was even created.

I looked down at the man who loved me and in that second saw an equal part of him that could so easily hate. A terrifying thought, when faced with Draven as a man. A horrifying thought when faced with Draven as a demon. But facing both Dravens wielding a blade...

*That left me shaking.*

# CHAPTER 15

# ANGELS, DEMONS AND THE BLADES IN BETWEEN

I think at that point my mouth had actually stopped working and wouldn't stop from hanging open staring at the most delicious male specimen on the planet. Draven stood with his legs slightly apart wearing only a pair of black, very wide trousers that looked to be authentic martial art, fighting gear and he had crimson coloured strapping wound tightly around his hands that crisscrossed through his fingers, completely covering his fists, stopping at the wrists. And that was it.

Draven's naked torso looked so pumped and primed full of muscles I ached to trace my fingertips across every one and that, combined with a thin sheen of sweat, made him look like the ultimate fighting god! His arms tensed as he gripped the sword tighter and the action caused a ripple of muscles to flex. He had his hair tied back from his face in a thick leather thong making his cheek bones look more defined giving him a harsh, sterner look of a man ready to do some damage. He looked so hard, so strong and so unbreakable I felt sorry for his opponent.

"What's that he's wearing?" I asked in a croaky voice not being able to take my eyes off Draven's powerful form.

"It's called a Hakama which is traditional wear in Samurai fighting but whatever you do, don't tell him it looks like a skirt." He laughed to himself and I could see where it would look like a long black skirt if Draven's legs hadn't been parted.

"旧友準備ができて？" ('Ready old friend?' In Japanese) Takeshi

asked in a smooth elegant voice that held no fear. They circled once more when Draven's eyes started to glow before he spoke.

"持っていけ" ('Bring it!' in Japanese) And then it started.

Draven ran at Takeshi and as their swords connected I jumped. Takeshi had deflected his blow and bent in half at the pressure Draven put on his blade. Then he flipped his body over and the force pushed Draven back. Takeshi spun in the air twice before landing on his feet. He swiped the floor with his sword before bringing it back up and around in the air over his head in a large arc before bringing it down full force at Draven.

Draven deflected it with a loud clash and spun round on one foot before attacking Takeshi's back but another clash of steel saved him from injury. I couldn't help but flinch with the sound every time the blades connected and should really have closed my eyes but it seemed like an impossible task when Draven was dominating a room.

They both spun again and it looked more like a well synchronized dance than the deadly game they were both playing. The room was silent although there was at least fifty people all sat round waiting for their turn. I could even see a few bloody faces already, where they had met with Draven's fury. Then my eyes spotted Zagan's pale form slumped over slightly, with Sophia at his side looking mighty hacked off at her brother. No wonder, as I could see from here the trickle of blood that was a stark contrast to his snowy albino skin.

Then an almighty clash brought me back to the fight. Draven stood to, his hips twisted and his sword down by his leg with the blade pointing at the floor by his foot, he stood looking ready for Takeshi's next move. He nodded his head and Draven's blade twisted with the slight flick of his wrist which caused the reflection of the light to momentarily blind Takeshi. Draven took advantage of his dirty trick and went at Takeshi's head, blade raised high but Takeshi dropped his body to near splits and raised his sword over his head to protect himself against the oncoming blow. They stayed in this position fighting each other's strength when Takeshi couldn't take any more and dropped down further spinning to get away from Draven. He jumped back up using only his back muscles in a flip.

That's when things turned supernatural. Takeshi brought his blade to his lips and licked the length leaving a blue flame in the wake of his tongue. Draven took another stance, legs far apart and sword held in front of him with the blade pointing to the ceiling.

"そうなんですか？" ('Is that so?") Draven said, raising an eyebrow at his opponent.

"時のニーズはわが主なければなりませんか" ('When needs must my Lord') Takeshi said before bowing his head in deep respect. Draven gave a short nod back and spoke in what I imagined was perfect Japanese.

"非常によく、古いマスター" ('Very well old Master) then he let go of the sword's grip and held it with only one secure hand. He rolled his neck in a wide arch and the click of his spine seemed to echo in the silent room. I watched on in amazement as his back muscles tensed and I could then see the faint purple coming out in his veins as it travelled its way down his arm that held the sword. It seemed to get brighter the further down it went and by the time it reached his hand it was glowing in angry pulses through his skin, until suddenly it erupted into flames and his hand started to fuse itself to the blade in what looked like cooled lava. I took a startled step back but felt Vincent behind me keeping me from going anywhere.

"It won't be long now." He whispered in my ear as they started once again circling each other.

"Doesn't he know I'm here?" I whispered back.

"No, he can't feel your presence like this, nor can my sister." He didn't need to explain. I knew the reasons why and they were the same ones as to why he couldn't touch me.

"Watch!" Vincent said nodding over my shoulder back at the two fighters that now each held a flaming Samurai in hand. Takeshi's grip tightened while Draven didn't even need to grip as it had now become a part of him. I swallowed hard and watched in horror as Draven once again ran at Takeshi who was swinging his sword in a figure of eight pattern in front of Draven, causing my eyes to blur from the effect. It was both a beautiful light show and a death defining move…and Draven was running straight at it with sword in one hand. I almost couldn't look.

However, just before getting too close to the flying blade, Draven leapt into the air and spun to land behind Takeshi's back, once there he kicked him sending Takeshi flying forward. Takeshi righted himself before he fell and came charging at Draven, flames held high. They both hit the weapons together and the fire in both joined and sparked with each other, both feeding from different sources of power.

Takeshi swung his blade around in a full circle just missing Draven by a hair's breadth as he doubled over backwards, arching his body in a painful looking way. Draven then pushed himself back upright with one arm and took a sidestep to catch Takeshi on the arm with the end. It left a slice in his arm but he didn't even flinch. Blood ran down his embroidered training wear but because it was black it could only be seen because it looked wet from the tear in his sleeve. He threw up his sword and caught it with the other hand preparing to fight with that one instead.

Things got unbelievably faster and it became difficult to keep up and with one quick turn Draven had the upper hand and with his free hand pulled Takeshi by the shirt and brought his head down on his face in a dirty looking head butt. Takeshi's nose exploded and he staggered back. He shook his head and spat the blood from his mouth to the clean floor leaving a shocking spray of crimson. Takeshi tilted his head and Draven gave him a deadly smile.

"Needs must my friend!" He said to Takeshi, causing him to smile in return. They both nodded and this time Takeshi ran at Draven with everything he had, having lost some of that cool exterior. Draven waited until the last second before turning to the side, catching Takeshi by the wrist and with a quick and ruthless snap, his hand dropped the blade. Takeshi didn't cry out or even hold his broken hand, no he just came at Draven as his other hand started to transform into long and deadly talons like a giant bird of prey. But before he could take a swipe at Draven he kicked up Takeshi's fallen blade from the floor caught it in his free hand and put the two flaming blades to the floor behind him. He then threw his body weight backwards and kicked both his legs out at the same time that landed so hard in the centre of Takeshi's chest you could hear his ribs cracking.

It catapulted Takeshi backward and he landed hard in the centre of the mats. Draven then ran at him full pelt and jumped in the air bringing both his blade up ready to impale down on Takeshi. I couldn't stop my eruption when I screamed,

"DRAVEN NO!" But I was too late. I closed my eyes on impact but when I opened them again I saw that there were two swords sticking from the mats, one either side of Takeshi's head, neither one had touched him.

Draven was kneeling down on one knee over a very still Takeshi with his head looking down. The hair that had come loose from its leather tie fell forward covering his face from view. He started to raise his head slowly looking up and as soon as our eyes met his flashed purple before I saw my name being whispered on his lips. Everyone else in the room was also looking up at me and Vincent.

Without taking his eyes off mine he let go of Takeshi's sword that was still embedded in the floor and said in a voice loud enough so all the room could hear,

"Remember old Master, to lose your weapon means to lose your head! Everyone is dismissed! GO!" He addressed the room and after they all jumped at his shouted command, they all filed out of the doors underneath the balcony we were stood on. I couldn't help but feel sorry for the ones that needed aid to walk and limped out.

Draven then started to back up and made his sword detach from his fused fist letting it drop to the floor, all the time not letting his gaze unlock from mine. I wondered why he was still backing away from us until he reached the end and started to run back our way. He reached where Takeshi was trying to get on his feet and launched himself in the air. I yelped when his hands grabbed the railing and it shook on impact. Then he flung his body over the side and landed on his feet in front of us and once again I found my jaw had gone slack at the sight of him.

"Keira…" He said my name like he had waited a thousand years to say it and when he took a step closer I also took a step towards him but then caught my action and retreated making him raise an eyebrow.

"I can't touch you." The words left my mouth before I thought about them and he lowered his head in response. I could see his fists clench by his sides and it looked as though he wanted to rip something open with his bare hands.

"No, you can't," he said softly, which was a contrast to the muscles that bunched up as he tensed his entire body.

"Leave us, brother!" He didn't even look Vincent's way when he said this and I suddenly felt wary. What if I disappeared when he left?

"No, Vincent wait…I…" I turned to face him and he smiled back at me but had backed further away from us.

"It's alright Keira, you won't go anywhere, not yet. Dom, do me a favour and get hold of your rage before you frighten her, she's been through enough!" Draven growled low in his throat but nodded in Vincent's direction.

"Vincent, I wanted to say…"

"You're welcome, Keira." He said before I could thank him and gave me a wink before he jumped off the balcony. I watched wide eyed as Vincent landed silently on one knee beside Takeshi and helped him to his feet. He placed his one good arm behind his neck and led him to where the others had left.

"Oh, and next time brother, do try and leave some of our men a little less broken, it was only supposed to be training exercise not an excuse to dish out your famous wrath!" Vincent said before disappearing and the only response from Draven was an impassive grunt.

"It's nice to see you're handling this well!" I said not knowing what else to say.

"Don't joke Keira, not now." He replied pushing all his hair back with two huge hands, which I knew to be a frustrated sign from Draven.

"If I don't joke then I will cry. Why did you lie to me, Draven?" I asked before I lost my nerve.

"I did not lie to you, Keira," he stated calmly, which considering what I had just seen him do was surprising.

"Ah, so you're going to go about this on a technicality, fine then, I will rephrase the question. Why didn't you tell me, Draven?" At this he frowned.

"I think I prefer you joking." He said dryly before walking over to a large bench that was made from wicker and bamboo. He sat down on one side that left enough room for me without the possibility of touching by mistake, although that thought was enough to weaken my control and burst into tears. I wanted so badly to touch him, to run into his arms and place my lips to his.

"Sit down Keira… please." He added the please as an afterthought, not a word I could imagine had been said by him since I was taken. I sat down next to him keeping that distance in mind and hating every millimetre of it!

"Was it from the first time we…we made love?" I asked almost losing my voice for a second.

"Yes, and if you're expecting an apology then you will wait a long time."

"Yes and well, thanks to you, I now have a long time." I replied sharply before continuing on.

"It was still my choice Draven, whether you disagree or not." At this he almost lost his temper. His head snapped up and his eyes looked black and dangerous.

"That's where you're wrong, Keira. You belong to me and that makes it my choice. What did you want me to say, Keira? Did you want me to stop and tell you what being with me would make you become. The one thing you had feared since being a child. No, I couldn't have done that, not at that time." He looked away from me and I wondered what he saw in his distant mind.

"So when, Draven? When all of a sudden I started to wonder why I didn't need wrinkle cream? When all my friends around me started suffering from arthritis and broken hips?" I asked sarcastically.

"This is not about age Keira, or what you look like. You are beautiful now, Gods Keira, you are so damn beautiful it hurts to look at you and know I can't touch you because of who I am or who I am not." He said bitterly looking off towards the direction Vincent had left and it broke my heart that he knew Vincent could touch me where he could not.

"But you would still be beautiful to me at any age. As for watching those you love die, then that is a part of life for everyone not just immortals."

"But I wouldn't be able to be around them Draven, that's my point, I won't be able to grow old with my sister and complain about 'kids today' and 'the price of milk'. I would have to leave everyone I love a long time before any of that because they would wonder why I never got old. I love you Draven and I know I will come to terms with it all at some point but that doesn't make it any easier." At this he gave me such a heart-warming smile it made me want to kiss him so badly it was hurting inside my chest.

"Ah well, that's where the good bit comes into it. Do you really think I would rip you away from all those you love? I could never do that to you Keira and I refuse to ever see that type of pain in your eyes." I frowned at him and shook my head not understanding what he meant.

"I don't under..."

"I would make it so that you appeared the right age to all who see you. You would never have to leave your past life, your human life behind. I would not be so cruel to the only one I love, Keira." On hearing this I almost did cry out but this time it was in happiness. He must have seen my eyes widen with this new information and he turned and had to stop mid-motion from grabbing me to him.

"You would do that, you can do that...really?" I was shocked and his eyes softened at my realization that I wouldn't have to give up everyone I loved.

"Yes, I can do that and will do that for you. I would do anything for you Keira and as soon as I get you back to me I will prove it." I shook my head at him.

"Draven, you never have to prove anything to me but do me a favour, next time try and give me a little more credit. You can't keep things from me because you think it's for my own good. It ends up back firing." I could tell he really didn't like me telling him how to do things and I remembered Vincent's words, he really was new to this dating a human thing and for someone who spent so many lifetimes commanding everyone around them, then having someone on an equal level was going to take time to adjust.

"Does this mean I get to keep you?"

"Does this mean you're giving me a choice?" I replied trying to keep the huge smirk from my face but doing a lousy job at it.

"No, it just means I will have to remember to placate you next time. You're already mine, that is why your soul is here and when your body is here too then I will really show you what it means to belong to me." He said this dripping with erotic promise.

"I wish I could touch you," I said not even bothering to try and keep the sadness from my voice, there would be no point as I would fail anyway.

"I know my Angel, but you have to trust me, I will come for you." He tried to keep the hard tone from his voice when he said this last part and I had to remember how hard this all must be on him.

"I know and I do but last night…"

"You thought I was really there." I nodded and he looked up at the ceiling as though he was looking for the right words.

"I cannot enter that place without permission from Lucius. That's why he took you there and it's why only my projection could be seen, he granted my request to see him, that and he knew that I would want proof you were alright." He gritted his teeth when describing last night and it was strange to hear for the first time that he couldn't command everyone. There was a place that Draven couldn't go and there was a person in this world he couldn't control and it wasn't just me.

"What are we going to do?" It seemed like a helpless case but Draven's hands turned into fists making the red material that covered them strain against his strength.

"You are not going to do anything but wait. Don't try and run Keira, I cannot do what I am about to do if I worry about you getting hurt."

"Why, what are you planning?" I asked, not liking the sound of this.

"You don't need to worry about that but you said that you trusted me and now is the time to prove it, can you do that?"

"Yes but…"

"Can you do that for me, Keira?" He asked again in a sterner tone that broke no argument.

"Yes," I said quietly and once again he went to touch me but had to stop himself. He closed his eyes and said,

"Good girl."

"Tell me at least that they are treating you well, I know Lucius well and I hope that his little display of dominance was just for my benefit, tell me he doesn't treat you that way every time Keira, please tell me that much at least. I don't think I could contain my rage if it was any other way." He seemed to be close to begging for me to put his fears to rest and now I had to choose between a lie that would give comfort and a truth that would bring pain. I now understood why Draven had kept things from me and knew that from now on I couldn't question his logic, no matter the price. If there were some things he didn't tell me then it must mean that he was trying to protect me, just like the next words out of my mouth would protect him.

"I hardly see him and even when I do, he doesn't treat me that way." I hoped he would take the waver in my voice as being over emotional and not the lies that they were. He nodded and when I heard him exhale the breath he had been holding I knew he had trusted my words. I felt like shit! I hated lying to him but now knew what it felt like to be on the wrong side of information you couldn't share.

"Gods Keira, I miss you!" His declaration had me blinking frantically to keep the tears at bay.

"I miss you too, I just wish…" I raised my hand to his face without touching him and he closed his eyes.

"I know sweetheart. Soon, I give you my word." I could see the effort it took for him to keep calm but I couldn't get a handle on my emotions like him at this moment. I stood up and walked away and then turned to face him.

"Why is he doing this? God, I hate him! I have done nothing to anyone and yet here I am, not even whole and I feel so helpless, I want to do something, I want to help!" I shouted and all the time Draven sat leaning his elbows on his knees with his fingers interlocked like you would if you were praying. His eyes took all of me in over his hands as he waited for me to calm. I stood staring at him, panting from my outburst thinking how goddamn sexy he looked. His shoulders and biceps looked big enough to crush a bear and his formidable eyes calculating, holding me in his sight like he would never let me go. Draven was a dark Angel and a demonic King that wanted something he couldn't touch, that was the look he gave me….it was hunger… building hunger and I stood as his feast.

He stood slowly and walked towards me like a predator would stalk something he wanted to sink his fangs into. I couldn't help but back up until the wall met my back.

"Draven?" I said his name but he didn't seem to be listening to me as he came closer.

"You know you can't touch me…don't you?" I got out but the obvious arousal was clear in my voice. He raised an eyebrow and soon a corner of his lips curled up in a devilish smirk.

"Is that so? Then I will just have to find other means." I frowned but shook my head at him. Whatever he was thinking was too risky and I wasn't ready to leave yet, I was never going to be ready.

"No?" He said before quickly making the distance between us disappear. I flinched back but he didn't touch me. I looked up at him and we were so close I could almost taste him through his addictive scent. I just wanted to lick his neck and taste the salty skin there. I only came up to his chest and when his hands rested either side of my head it became my perfect cage, one I would be more than happy if someone threw away the key. He leaned down and I was too scared to move in case we accidently made contact.

"Did you say no to me, Keira?" His hand moved from the wall and went to my waist without touching the material.

"This is a beautiful dress Keira, but I think I prefer the body underneath…In fact…" He let the sentence linger as his eyes flashed purple

"I know it is!" And then his body erupted into his demon form. Power pulsated through every pore and I could see it travelling around his body under every inch of skin showing. His face was now cast in shadow, thanks to his great wing span that had broken free from his back. His feathers ruffled slightly before he folded them back into each other.

"Draven what… are you doing?" I whispered and he smiled.

"Letting my Angel flow!" And with that he let the purple be taken over by a bluish glow and his dark grey wings turned a few shades lighter. He closed his eyes and tensed as though he was concentrating hard on controlling this inner part of him. His eyes flashed open and became a beautiful shade of deep indigo that I had never seen on him before. His hand still hovered over my side and when I let out a gasp at the feeling that shot through me he smiled.

"Was that you?" I asked shocked that I could feel a part of him.

"Maybe, let's try it again and find out should we?" I looked down and saw his hand coming up my side but without making full contact. I could still feel as if his fingertips were brushing across my skin. I couldn't help the moan that passed my lips. They got higher and when he reached the top of my ribs he changed direction. He started to skim across under my heaving chest and my breath caught when he went higher. The delicate feeling of being touched so softly, by someone so strong, was intoxicating, so much so that my lids felt heavy and my breathing became laboured. It wasn't exactly like Draven's touch but something woven together by magic and man. His hand moulded over my curves and my reaction made him growl. I looked down to see my nipples had pebbled and the pleasure of it happening shot straight down to my core.

It felt as if his power was dancing on my skin and bouncing back to his in some electric imbalance. Then his hand moved lower and I had to bite my lip to stop from crying out. Draven was touching me in the only way he could, and the anticipation of this moment felt like I could release myself in pleasure if he only asked it of me. But lower his hand went and when he reached that point in between my legs my head went back against the wall, my eyes closed, and my mouth fell open in a silent scream. His touch hit my core like a dam breaking, my walls cracked and all the emotions that had been locked up came flooding out with extreme pleasure. I screamed out, not being able to contain it. I think I heard Draven do the same but with my own screams still ringing in my ears it was hard to tell. I continued to ride the waves of my release against his supernatural touch and it was heavenly.

I must have been panting because Draven put his forehead close to mine and said,

"Ssshh, just breathe sweetness." I could only nod my response.

"But what about you...you didn't..." I finally managed to ask but when I looked up at him I saw him raise his eyebrows and smile.

"Didn't I?" He looked down and yep there was a definite wet patch on his trousers.

"How, I didn't even touch you?" I asked a bit bewildered.

"I find pleasure in most things when it comes to you Keira and you finding yours is definitely one of them. Did I tell you that I missed you?" I laughed and I nodded my head.

"Yes I think you did." This was what I needed and yet I knew it would only make things harder when I woke up in my body and found myself cold and alone but I couldn't help but need this. After all...I was an addict.

"Keira?" I looked up at him saying my name and when I saw the utter misery there, I knew what was about to happen.

"Time to wake up, Toots!" I heard a little voice whisper in my ear.

"NO! Not yet, I want to stay!" I shouted and Draven frowned.

"Keira, what can you hear?"

"It's Pip, she's trying to wake me up." Draven howled in rage. His wings flew out and he hammered his fist into the wall making me jump sideways.

"NO, YOU CAN'T HAVE HER BACK!" He roared in his demonic voice losing all the Angel in him. The flames erupted around his body and he went beyond the point of no return. He made a desperate grab for me as I started to flicker between the two places, between body and soul. His hand went straight through me and the walls started to shake with the second roar that tore from lips twisted in fury.

"Draven!" I screamed.

"Keira NO! Come back, come back to me!" I could still hear him shouting for me as it echoed around the room I'd come back to. I cried out at the loss and felt nothing for the body I had gained. I would rather have lived in a world as a bodiless soul just so long as I could remain by Draven's side!

It felt like my heart was made of glass and seeing the pain on Draven's face had just shattered it causing the splinters to puncture every vital organ I had. He had looked so lost, so broken and so forsaken in his blinding rage that I started sobbing and didn't even flinch when I felt Pip's arms go around me and pull my body into hers. She started rocking me back and forth, rubbing my back in soothing strokes.

"Ssshh, I know, I am sorry but I couldn't hold it much longer, I'm sorry my friend...I'm so sorry!" Her words rolled right over me without sticking as I cried out my loss.

"Draven, Draven....Draven! I want you back...I want...I..." I stuttered on my words and tried to drag in a much needed breath as the sobs were rattled out of me.

"He can hear you Keira but be quick, I can't hold on!" I looked back at Pip and saw she too had tears in her eyes. I sucked in a quick breath and said the only words that ever mattered.

*"I Love You Dominic…"*

# CHAPTER 16
# A STEP TOO FAR

After I was brought back it took me a while to get over leaving Draven for the fourth time since New England. I felt mentally drained and poor Pip had to be the one to help me through it. I had cried like a child and Pip had been an unlikely mother figure dressed in bright blue and pink shell suit trousers, straight out of the late 80's and a tank top with actual shells attached to it. Bright pink sequins kept sparkling from her straps and whenever she hugged me I could feel the hard breasts that were covered by two clam shells, spray painted silver. I wondered if she and Lady Gaga shopped at the same places.

I don't know how much time passed while on my 'sobathon' but after Pip had made sure I wasn't about to throw myself over the balcony she left when Adam's usual growling could be heard from down the corridor, although she had assured me this time she hadn't tied, chained or locked him to anything.

When the sun had started to set I got up, found something to eat and had a shower, this time not caring about the door or being on display in the glass cubicle. I leant my forehead on the glass, closed my eyes and let the water take away my tears. I kept seeing Draven's face, the heartbreak etched into his perfect features that I just wanted to kiss away. I remembered the blind panic in his voice, one that was normally so in control, so powered by dominance that it never wavered. Not until I had been taken.

After all my tears had been spent I got out of the water before my skin started to fall right off my bones from being so wrinkly. I decided it was time to just man up and take this shit with a clear head. I would do nobody any favours if I became a blubbering idiot at every turn and if I was this 'Chosen One' that everyone kept sprouting on about, then I needed to start acting like the Gods had really chosen me for a good reason and without giving them chance to start regretting it. The last thing I wanted was to be replaced by some chick that wielded a sword like some Austrian shot putter with a gold medal and a man eating philosophy!

With this in mind I walked straight into my wardrobe and picked out something that would at least give me a sense of power. I pulled down a dress that made me swallow hard but before I could chicken out I loosened the ties and put it over my head. After pulling it all tight, pulling on a pair of spider web tights and some knee high boots, that thankfully were only a little bit too big for me, I grabbed the bag of makeup that Pip had left me from last time and walked into the bathroom.

Once I was all finished I hardly recognised the angry person staring back at me. Forget the old whimpering Keira who looked like some lost princess, no, tonight I was going to walk into that hall with some balls, Goth style!

I grabbed the only pair of gloves I had thanks to Lucius and was glad they were black, so they would match anything I wore, which included this dangerous dress. The top half was corseted taffeta, thick and secure against my skin and it pulled tight at the front with thick laced ribbon crossed over through black metal hoops. The material was an iridescent deep red that looked purple in the places that hit the light and went down to mid-thigh. The back however went lower but the under skirt was made from layers and layers of black satin that gave the bottom half body. It flared out but all of the front section had been pulled up to the top of my thighs and tied there with the same lace ribbon on the corset. It felt a bit like a curtained window for my legs to be seen underneath and thanks to my tights and boots I didn't feel quite so naked and on display. Although there was nothing I could do about the amount of skin being shown thanks to ample cleavage.

I decided just to leave my hair down and left the waves to dry naturally thanks to the lack of a hairdryer. I threw my head forward letting my hair hang down in front of me and gave it a ruffle at the roots. I then threw my head back and my hair whipped over hitting the lower part of my waist. With it still slightly damp it was a dark golden colour and the top part of my dress reflected off each strand, turning it a strawberry blonde tone. As for my makeup, I had gone for thick black around the eyes that gave me a pissed off look that matched my mood. My pale skin was the perfect background for my bold lips that I had painted a dark red that almost made them look like they were bleeding. I nodded to myself, took a deep breath and walked to the door where the night awaited me.

Pip had told me that she would make sure that tonight I was left alone, that I didn't need to come down to the great hall. What she really meant was that I could hide away like the frightened little human everyone took me for! Well I wasn't about to let that happen. No, I needed to show my enemies that I wasn't someone to be underestimated and hiding away in my room crying over a situation I had no control over wasn't the way to achieve that. It was time to wake up to this world and use the motto 'that if you can't beat them then join them' and find out their weaknesses while you're at it!

I gave myself this little speech until I reached the main staircase and when the full room of turned Vamp Demons and Angel bad ass beings came into view I gulped down my fear. I took a deep breath.

"You can do this!" I whispered out loud to myself and walked down the stairs remembering about the sharp spikes that came up through the railing. I tried to look as confident as I could and although every molecule in my body told me to turn around and run far away, I held my head high and looked at everyone who gave me a glare with utter indifference. I gathered, thanks to the parting of people as I walked through the crowd, that Lucius' threat still held its weight, as not one person got in my way when I walked towards the dais. The music pounded a heavy beat that I could feel from the floor travel up my legs and with every step my hair came more forward and ended up becoming split in two parts, one either side of my breasts. One lesbian couple dressed in rubber hissed at me and the shortest one snarled out the word,

"Electus" as I walked past. My eyes stayed in front but my hand whipped up and I gave her the one finger salute. That's when my eyes met with the dark Vamp King himself and I held in a smirk at the shock I saw in him, seeing me here.

One point to human and Vamp King zero!

I continued and with every step his eyes drank me in but his posture didn't change from its relaxed state. He was sat with legs slightly spread apart with one elbow holding all his weight on his knee. His hand held by his chin and one finger covered his lips, lips that held a secret smile. I tried not to let this look get to me but I think even he could detect the increase of my heart rate. It was just something about the guy that had you gulping at just the sight of him and that's taking away from the fact of how powerful he was. I think if he had just been walking down the street he would not only be turning heads but it would be the whole stopping traffic, a stream of girls trailing behind him kind of thing. He was painfully handsome, which just annoyed me even more, that someone so evil could be so sexually attractive. I wish I could say that I was not affected but I would have been lying.

By the time I made the few steps onto the dais my heart was pounding and all my bravery was a mere shell of what it had been. One bloody look and the man had you undone! He actually made you feel as though you were standing there naked the way his eyes drank you in and undressed you of every layer.

"Keira." He said my name as though it was the beginnings of a spell. He stood and I froze on automatic pilot. He cocked his head slightly at my behaviour and a devilish smile curled his lips. He was wearing worn grey denim that had rips in the knees and a black fitted top that had long sleeves pushed up to reveal muscled forearms. The top had a big roll neck that zipped at the side which was pulled down to show a white t-shirt underneath. It was the most casual I had seen him looking and I was surprised considering almost every night at Afterlife Draven would wear a suit. I gathered Lucius didn't play by the same rules. Hell, he probably killed a guy with that rule book before chucking it out of the window, guy and all!

"Come here!" He demanded losing his smile momentarily. I found my feet moving me forward before I even gave it the thought process. As soon as I got within distance his hand snaked out and grabbed me by the waist pulling me roughly to his chest. I let out a startled umff.

"Well Pip, considering that she wasn't well enough to come down, I think from looking at the beauty in my arms you were quite mistaken." I tried to turn to look at Pip but Lucius growled,

"Eyes on me!" I stiffened in his unbreakable hold and wondered what the hell I was thinking in the first place by coming down here. If I was trying to regain some power by not showing fear to my enemies, one look at Lucius and all those hopes unravelled like sand down a sink hole.

I felt fingertips trail down my cheek and when they reached my chin he gripped it and forced me to look up at him.

"Mistaken indeed, you look good enough to eat but wait...there's something missing." His lips formed a knowing grin and when he saw me gulp down a swallow I heard him chuckle. He still had hold of my chin and started setting my head to one side to lean down to my ear. He didn't say anything for the moment and I felt his breath linger at my neck.

"Yes, good enough to eat, bite and to suck. Mmm, I could quite easily lick you wet and then back dry again." He hummed in my ear and then took a long leisurely lick to my neck causing me to shiver. I felt the heat invade my cheeks at the crude image he portrayed and only when I felt his knuckles on my cheek did I realise my eyes had closed.

"Ah, there it is, that's what was missing on that porcelain skin of yours." He laughed when my blush must have deepened at his words. Then suddenly he spun me round to face the crowd and pulled me down by the waist to sit with him. And when I say sit with him I don't mean at his knees like last time. No, this time I found myself sat in between his legs, with my back held firmly against his chest. His arm locked tightly around my waist while the other hand brushed all my hair to one side so the skin on my neck was exposed. Normally I wouldn't have batted an eyelid at my neck being so exposed but when you clearly had a horny Vampire at your back that had just been talking to you like you were an appetiser, then that changed matters.

"I see you found my gift," Lucius stated, lifting up one of my arms with his free hand. I noticed the dark leather cuff tied around his thick wrist when he picked up my arm to study it. I tried to pull it away not liking the feeling of anyone touching me there.

"Ssshh Sugar, I'm not hurting you," He whispered in my ear at my obvious discomfort and I don't know why, but his words calmed me. He waited for me to relax and only moved again once he felt the tension leave my back muscles.

"Good girl." He said softly and even though I couldn't see him I felt him smile on my neck. Why was he being so nice! It was so confusing, I felt like a ping pong ball being batted to good, back to evil, then back to good again. I was starting to feel dizzy and the only anchor I had was Lucius' arm around me, keeping me secure from sinking in a sea of demonic chaos.

I felt one of Lucius' fingers curl under the top of my gloves and felt him slide one in to look for the closest scar. My breathing picked up and instincts kicked in as I tried to pull away from him. I didn't get far as it felt like being on one of those rollercoaster rides with the seat restraints that wouldn't let you go until the ride was over. I just wished that this ride was over. Hell, I wished I'd never come to this nightmare theme park!

"Come now, Keira am I hurting you?" He said in my ear but I was still trying to pry my arm from his hold.

"Answer me!" He said sternly.

"N...no but…"

"Then be still and show me how brave you are." His words weren't mocking but the opposite, they were comforting. In the end I took a deep breath and let him continue without resistance. I mean it's not like he hadn't seen them before so what was the point. He wasn't pulling my gloves down to expose them to the room but just feeling for them under the glove. He went back to the ones nearer my inner elbow and ran his fingertip over it as gently as a moth's wing.

"Did you like my gift, Keira?" His question took me off guard enough to disarm me. I felt his arm jog me into responding.

"Yes," came out in a shaky voice that housed not one ounce of the confidence I was feeling earlier.

"I wanted to encase painful memories in the softest material." He said finding the next scar down and running a smooth, cold finger over it.

"Why?" I couldn't help but ask.

"Contrary to what you believe I do actually like you, little human." His confession astounded me but not enough to prevent the snorted retort.

"What, as a snack?!" I commented sarcastically.

"Is that an invitation?" He asked and even though it was laced with humour I still shuddered in his arms.

"No, I didn't think so. Don't worry Keira, I am well fed." He said before he clicked his finger behind me. I turned to see a waitress come over to us with a drink ready for him. It looked like a bottle of lager and the label read 'Krombacher dark'. The cap was still on and he hugged me closer so that he could hold the bottle with the hand he had around my waist. With his free hand I watched in horror as his thumb nail started to grow into a stone talon. I tried to move but the only response to my pointless struggles was him chuckling once, before he used the rock hard talon to flick off the cap. After that he took a long swig of his beer and tapped his talon on the side of the dark bottle. I could only breathe when it started to go back to normal and he put the bottle in front of me for me to take.

"Drink!" He ordered but when I shook my head to refuse this wasn't good enough for him.

"Keira, drink now!" I rolled my eyes that he couldn't see and took the bottle from him. I took a long swig only realising now that my throat had been dry and the lager was thirst quenching. The flavour was unlike any lager I had tried before, with its subtle chocolate hints that mixed with caramel and the end tang of bitterness. It was different from my usual Corona but still not unpleasant.

He nudged me to take another drink before taking it back off me. I didn't understand his behaviour and why he wanted to share his drink but after passing it to me at regular intervals I realised that he meant to continue.

As the night went on I seemed to relax against Lucius without realising it until his arm no longer needed to hold me to him in a secure hold. No, I was now leaning against him by free will and it scared me as to why?

I took in the room and as usual it held no end of weird and creepy things to watch. The red glow from lights directed onto the material that hung down the walls gave the room an eerie background for all its guests, who looked to be doing a lot more than just drinking. One woman was in the middle of a group of men in leathers, and was being painted with different coloured paint, laughing heartily as they used the different colours to designate which pieces of her body they had claimed. One of which had already started to lick it off her blue breasts. I looked away quickly and shuddered when one other couple roared out their climax. Lucius started laughing behind me.

"Innocence smells so fucking sweet, you make me want to drool." He growled in my ear and his hands spanned my ribcage pulling me further back. I was shocked at the feel of his arousal straining to be freed at my back.

"Don't!" I whispered looking down to where his hands remained. He growled again but amazingly he let me go and didn't make a comment.

"I'd like to take Toots outside tomorrow." Pip announced from her usual place on Adam's lap. Tonight's attire consisted of a red and black tartan tutu with matching converse shoes that were laced with red ribbon instead of shoes laces. The side of the rubber had black writing that said 'I will be your 80's bitch' on one side and the words

'And play with your Pac-Man' on the other. I couldn't help but smile looking at Pip and even full of tattoos and piercings she still looked cute as a kindergartener with her red hoodie that had Elmo from Sesame street with the words 'Tickle me' under Elmo's happy smile. She even had her hair in high green pigtails that Adam kept wrapping around his hand to try and control her from bouncing all over the place.

"I can see no problem with that." Lucius surprised me by saying and then handed me some more of his beer, which he wouldn't take back until he thought that I'd had enough. At that moment a beauty walked past who had a gorgeous shade of red curls that were piled high on her head. She smiled at Lucius and licked her lips seductively, but I was shocked when he snarled at her before snapping his teeth in an aggressive manner. It was such a strange reaction to a girl that was obviously trying to get him to bed but he acted like it was an insult and the girl scampered off in a hurry looking terrified. I was left confused at his behaviour and even more so when his arm went across my front and his hand went to hold the column of my neck to find the rhythm of my beating heart. His fingers remained still at my pulse point while his thumb stroked up and down the length of my neck in a controlled manner.

"What are you...?"

"Hush now, the feel of your pulse calms me." Was his only response to his strange reaction towards the girl's 'come on'.

"Where will you take her?" His question came after about twenty minutes of silence from Pip's idea to take me anywhere.

"My Lord?" Pip asked, coming up for air from locking lips with Adam.

"Take her to the silent garden, not the forest Pip, understand?" Pip lowered her head in a show of respect for her Master's wishes and I couldn't say I would have argued given the authority he put behind the command. I looked to Pip for reassurance that this was a good idea but she just winked at me before going back to Adam's waiting lips.

"Dress warm tomorrow, the winters here can be harsh and the cold cutting for human skin." He said in my ear, still touching my neck and bare shoulders.

"I think I will find that difficult considering my wardrobe choices." I said under my breath which he heard.

"Explain!" Given his order, I wished I'd kept my big mouth shut.

"I…I just mean…umm, I'm sure I will find something." I quickly added not wanting to get Pip into trouble.

"I will make sure you have something suitable." He said looking down at me over my shoulder.

"I wouldn't like you looking like this without my presence. It is too much of a temptation for my kind."

"You mean I look like a dressed roast turkey ready for Christmas dinner!" I said crossing my arms over my chest.

"I'm not food you know!" I added with a huff.

"There are other things I would take from you other than sustenance my little Keira girl, but tasting would definitely be on the menu." I closed my eyes and tried to get us kissing out of my head. Of course, I failed.

"I need to go to the bathroom!" I blurted out making him laugh at how it was obvious he affected me. He let me go by holding out his arms to his sides and I got up too quickly nearly falling back into him. Man could I appear any weaker! He gave me a bad boy smirk that made me want to slap his face. He took a long swig of his beer never taking his eyes from me. I moved away and he nodded to Liessa but I quickly added,

"I think I'm good on my own this time." Lucius took in my flustered state and nodded for Liessa to sit back down. I was surprised I was allowed to leave on my own but considering how everyone in this room obviously feared their Lord then I didn't think I was going to encounter too many problems.

I made my way through the crowd like I was spitting venom, as everyone backed away from the scary little human. Once in the toilets I leant on the counter to try and compose myself.

"Don't have a bloody melt down, Keira!" I said out loud looking at myself in the mirror. Thankfully I was alone in here, not that I cared if any of Lucius' freaks thought I was weird talking to myself but being on my own definitely helped. What exactly was Lucius playing at? One minute I didn't think I could hate him anymore than I did and the next he was turning me to mush with his flirtations that were showing me a different side of him. That what he said about the scars of my past being wrapped in soft material was a sweetness I couldn't comprehend coming from him. Was he doing this for a reason? Was he hoping to turn me against Draven?

There were too many questions swarming my mind making it hard to do simple tasks like having a pee. I was just glad I realised that my skirt was stuck in my knickers before I walked back out there and showed every Tom, Dick and Demon my pale bottom.

Once outside the bathroom I was getting ready to walk back to Lucius when I heard a voice that I had only the pleasure from my dreams.

"Draven?" I whispered putting my head down to hide the fact that I was speaking.

"Keira, come to me!" It was Draven but where, how? I looked around and noticed a low archway to the left of the stage. I heard his voice again and it sounded like it was coming from in there. Was this the plan he had spoken about? Did he need me to follow his voice to safety? There were too many questions to just stand here wondering what to do. I found myself storming that way without another thought about right or wrong. I knew if Lucius caught me I was in big trouble, but what was the worst he could do, he couldn't kill me that was for sure. After all, you couldn't bargain with a dead body!

I made it through the stone arch without one person stopping me and once there I had to stop and take a breath that I had been holding in.

"Keira come now, follow my voice." I heard from down the dark passageway. I took one last look at the great hall and when I didn't see anyone coming this way I decided to listen to what Draven was telling me. I started to run down the dark passage and just when I thought I was going to run out of light, torches hooked on the wall by massive hoops lit up by themselves. I jumped at first but then found comfort in the sound of wood crackling.

"Keira, come on my Keira." Draven said in an echoed call that had me moving again. The passage looked made from rough stone blocks that built up into a low arch. The smell of damp and smoke that came from the torches filled my nostrils and my skin started to sweat but not out of being warm. I hugged my arms around my stomach but kept going. Why didn't I like this plan?

"Don't be afraid Keira, I've come to take you home." Draven spoke as if sensing my fear. It was enough to keep me walking until I came to a cross section that opened up into three different options. It was left, right or straight ahead.

"Draven?" I said whispering, hoping he would hear me.

"Straight ahead, Keira!" Draven said and I followed blindly through the lit tunnel. Every time I came to a section that was too dark another set of torches would spark into life and every time I would flinch away as if I would get burned being too close.

After a little while walking without an end in sight I came to another section only now the choices weren't just left or right but now up or down. For some reason I really hoped the next instruction from Draven was up but of course I wasn't surprised when his stern voice said,

"Down here, I'm down here!" I closed my eyes and wiped my sweaty palms on my dress before doing as instructed.

"Okay, I can do this." I said as I took the first steps.

"Draven, tell me you're really here?" I said feeling the fear creep along my skin the further I went down. It felt as though I was walking into the belly of the mountain and I could feel the trickle down my spine as a result of my fear.

"Trust me Keira, this is the only way out." It was so hard doing anything other than trust in that voice and my continuation was proof of that fact. The staircase started to curve round and then continued on straight down once again. I wondered how far it went down and hoped it wasn't much further.

"I thought you couldn't come here?" I asked after not hearing his voice for a while and each passing minute getting a sinking feeling in the pit of my stomach.

"I found a way but you must hurry or they will find you." This didn't sound like the Draven I knew. He wouldn't put me in danger, would he? I stopped and looked back to the way I'd come. I could still find my way back couldn't I?

"Keira, why don't you trust me? I would never let anyone hurt you, come with me." His words penetrated my doubts and the last of my cautious walls crumbled.

After the next turn in the stairway I could see a door and I let out a breath of relief. I didn't know how much longer I would have lasted. The door was ajar and after a few heavy whole body pushes I managed to get it open enough for me to slip through. The room opened up into a huge space and the torches in this room had bright green flames. It reflected off the stone and created an eerie glow from every space. The floor couldn't be seen with the heavy fog coming from nowhere that didn't make sense. The ceiling was at least thirty foot high and arched over in decorative stone work. It was carved into a sea monster taking apart a ship in stormy seas. And in the middle of the sea were two whirlpools that were actual holes in the ceiling. They matched perfectly the holes in the floor being the mirror opposite and were about the size of a Mini Coupe. I wondered what they were for as the ones on the floor were edged with silvery bricks that looked wet and reminded me of two wells. The room also smelt damp but more so in here than the passageways.

I got a bad feeling about this and kept to the walls to avoid the wells. I kept looking at the ceiling, expecting something to happen.

"Draven?" I whispered, quickly wishing I had never come down here.

"Just walk to the other side of the grate and you'll find the exit. I promise." I looked to where Draven spoke about and saw the other side of the room had a door and on the floor was a metal grated section, the width of the room and went from the second well to the wall by the door. There was no way around it and to get to the door I had no other choice but to cross it. I decided just to get it over with before I chickened out and I made a run for it.

The door was made from heavy wood and had a small arched window that had three bars in the middle. I pushed and tried to turn the thick ring handle that hung down on one side.

"Why won't you open you stupid thing!" I said pushing and twisting as hard as I could.

"It's locked!" I shouted but didn't get an answer.

"Draven?" I said fearing the worst. I started to hear something move, like stone grating against stone but it was coming from above. I closed my eyes and shook my head fearing what I was about to see. I looked up and forced my lids back to take in the cause of the noise. What I saw was my fears come real. The sea monster was moving round on the ceiling and when one tentacle unwrapped from around the well it smashed down onto the carved stone ship breaking it in two. The room then started to shake and the stone ceiling started to crumble and come raining down in patches.

"DRAVEN!" I screamed as the sound of immense pressure on the stonework could be heard. I felt like something was coming and I turned and started to pound on the door with my fists.

"DRAVEN!" I shouted again but he had left me. Had I not made it in time? I turned again as the noise got louder and then drops of water started to rain down in the cracks that had appeared. I had a really bad feeling about what the noise was and when I saw the holes in the ceiling start to move round, each turn getting faster I knew it was close.

"LUCIUS!" I screamed the only other name that I had any chance at being saved.

Then it came.

The water erupted from the walls and came crashing down into the wells on the floor. I plastered my back onto the door and just as I thought the room was going to flood causing my definite drowning, the water seemed to flow straight down into the holes in the floor and nowhere else. I took a relieved breath that I wasn't going to die and this depressing room wasn't about to become my watery tomb.

The spray from the water soaked my dress to my skin like an extra wet layer and I decided to try the door one last time before heading back. I turned round and screamed louder than I ever had before. The face that had appeared in the window was the root of all my fear. It was what nightmares were bred from and I was staring into the face of Hell. You could have wrapped all the faces that haunted my darkest dreams, Morgan, Sammael, Gorgan Leeches and every Demon face I had ever seen before and it still would not have amounted to the face that was staring at me right now. I couldn't stop screaming.

It had more of an oval shaped head where the skin had been pulled tight across the jagged bones underneath. The eyes were the size and shape of tablespoons but were black and hollow, soulless eyes that had thick serrated skin around them, almost as if they had been gouged out. There was no nose, just a horrifying mouth that took up three quarters of the face. Long pins about six inches in length spanned from one side of the face to the other and there were around forty of them all splaying over the open grin. Behind them was a split face of razor pointed teeth for three rows one after the other that reminded me of a shark after tearing into a limb as there was an endless amount of blood dripping down from the mouth, if you could call it that. I would have said it was more like a weapon than a facial attribute. The hair line was a ripped scalp peeling away from the forehead like demonic fruit.

I started to back away but the floor beneath me started to move and when I looked down I saw the metal grate that I was stood on started to disappear into the rock. I was too late to try and jump across and had nowhere to go. I had no other choice than to grab onto the bars in the window near the face. I think it started to laugh and ended up spitting blood at me in a spray. I swallowed down the bile that rose over and over but at the last few feet of grating I turned my head to the side to throw up. I gripped on tighter as my last space of footing was disappearing and didn't think as far as what I would do after it was gone completely.

I looked down as my toes held on, leaving just enough space from the metal. I slipped a few times but regained my footing, scraping my boots along the rock step below the door. The face got nearer and I was torn between plunging to my death and being snapped at by this Demon. I looked down one last time and back up again to find the face was at my hands and I screamed again.

"TIME TO DIE NOW!" It said in its demonic voice that vibrated the walls before it turned its head to the side and opened it huge mouth. I didn't even have time to let go to get away, as it plunged six inch bloody pins into my fingers spearing straight through to the other side.

I screamed in agony and let go of the bars, falling backwards to my death, wishing that hadn't been the last face I saw before I died.

*But it was.*

# CHAPTER 17
# AN UNLIKELY SAVIOUR

I was starting to get used to relating my death to falling into a dark abyss but landing had never happened before.

Until now.

I crashed on my back into water and let my limbs float in front of me. My hair danced around me in slow motion and I saw the blood coming from my fingers like red ribbons before mixing with the dark water. It took me a moment to react to the fact that this was not my death but my survival. I started to grab at the water, the way one does in a panic and realised I wasn't that far from the top. I broke the surface and took in deep mouthfuls of air trying to fill my lungs over and over.

Once my body began to respond to the intake of air I took in my surroundings. It looked like I was in a cave under the room I had just fallen from and I could hear the water fall from above. I tried to get my bearings and find a way out of the water but it was quite dark with the only light being the green glow from above. Thankfully it reflected off the water and lit the cave to a degree. I looked around and saw the water was vast and went off into different bits of the cave but to one side looked like a miniature beach that sloped upwards from the water. It looked as if I would have to drag myself out which was going to be difficult given the pain in my hands. Fortunately, I think the cold had numbed them, as all I could feel was a throbbing every time they moved.

I used my arms, trying not to move my fingers, in big circles pulling the water towards me and I started to make progress. I tried to be as quiet as I could and I just prayed that the demon that obviously wanted me dead wouldn't come back. I moved slowly but was getting closer to the embankment. I couldn't help but go a little faster at the thought of getting out of this freezing water and hoped that I would before I broke all my teeth from them chattering so violently. I was not in a good way but I was breathing and that's all that mattered for the moment.

I came closer to the side and my feet finally started to find something underneath them but they kept slipping on what I presumed was mud. I kicked one foot in as hard as I could underwater and launched myself at the side. I managed to get part of my body out of the water but couldn't help the scream from erupting as my fingers grabbed onto the earth. I could see the blood spurt from them onto the sand but when my fingers sank into the embankment I realised that it wasn't sand at all, it was more like...like soap? It was a white clay like substance but was foamy between my bloody fingers and far too slippery to hold on to for long. I bit through the pain and tried to pull myself up but I wasn't getting enough grip.

Then my situation got worse as the walls started to shake and the water vibrated in little waves that splashed onto the strange cave floor. I heard something behind me, a chanting coming from above and then the waves started to get bigger. My fear spiked until it wasn't just down to the cold that caused my shaking. I battled with the fear and tried in pure desperation to get out of the water. I looked up and saw an opening in the rock that could have been a way out, if only I could get there. I yelped again at the pain I was putting my hands through but my survival took over and flooded my body with lifesaving adrenaline. I had to get out.

I heard another noise behind me like something was rising out of the water and I stupidly looked behind me to locate the source. A body started to rise out near one of the rocks which was a tiny island in the water and it looked like a burnt skeleton with pieces of flesh hanging off in big sections like flaps of muscle that had been sliced. It climbed out onto the rock using all four disgusting limb bones that cracked with each movement creating a horrifying echo in the cave. I couldn't help but heave to one side but from being sick already I had nothing left. Upon hearing me its head snapped up and its face added to my sickness. It had flesh melting down its skull like some invisible force was pulling it downwards, stretching the tissue across the holes where eyes, nose and mouth should have been. It made a clicking noise like a giant cricket and still down on all fours it turned its head to look at me like a man sized Praying Mantis.

I had to move! I had to get to the exit or there was no making it out of here alive. I cried out again at the pain of trying to dig my way out. I clawed at the clay but it just slipped and squelched through my fingers like it really was mashed up soap. My whole body was getting covered with the stuff as I thrashed around in a panic. I turned round still trying to pull myself out when the creature started hammering its bony fists into the rock it was stood on. I couldn't understand what it was doing but I didn't care, I just needed to get the hell out of here!

"Oh come on!" I said in frustration when my foot slipped and I went further down the slope. The white thick clay stuff started to move under me, pulsating and forming bubbles that got so big when they popped it splashed my face, neck and bare shoulders. But I couldn't let go, my only hope was that opening, if I went back into the water I was never getting out of here. I knew that and that thing knew it as well. I got one more good footing and bent my knees to then throw my body upwards. I made better progress and for a minute thought I really was going to make it. Most of my body was covered in thick white foam that felt heavy like cement.

But then something happened. I looked down and started to make out thousands of little red veins in the ground and the mud started to pulsate and vibrate harder around me. It was as if the mud was alive and soon I found myself feeling it penetrate my skin like it was slowly sucking the life right out of me. My arms could no longer support my body and I fell, face forward with my elbows sticking straight up in the air. My legs had stopped moving half in the water and slowly started to drift like two dead floats.

I didn't just feel cold but I started to feel…hollow. I opened an eye to see the veins growing bigger and it was as though my body was fuelling them and they were travelling back to the creature with my essence. But how? I thought no one could feed from me. Well they sure got that one wrong, didn't they, I thought sarcastically. I know it was hardly the time, considering I was lay in this shit hole about to die but it was too heartbreaking to think that Draven's voice had led me to my death. My only hope was that no one would ever find me down here as this lifeless shell. I would never want Draven to know how I had died, it was too painful to even think about.

I turned my head to the side and let the mud slap against my face without care. I had tried to escape, I had gone down fighting and I had lost the battle, my only hope was now that with my death, Draven would win the war. Lucius was never getting his hands on this Spear they spoke about. Was this the reason for what was happening now? Was I always meant to die, and this was the Gods' great plan for me? Well if it was…man didn't that suck!

"D…Drav…en…I…love you" I said out loud letting that be the last words my lips spoke before I let my Afterlife take hold. A single tear rolled down over the clay on my cheek that I could feel hardening and it fell onto the ground. In that second the brightest light erupted from my tear and I heard the creature howl. I then saw two black army boots step into the ground near my head and the clay turned black under the person's feet.

"I knew you would be trouble." A male voice said without emotion. I felt two hands grab for me and I slid along the bank as I was being pulled from the water. I got yanked upright and was too shocked to speak. My saviour wasn't a man but just a teenage boy.

Ruto pulled me towards a boulder and set me against it.

"Stay there girly!" He said in a dark tone that I wasn't going to argue with. He then turned back to face the creature and I saw something I wouldn't have taken Ruto to be. He was an Angel.

Great wings erupted from his back but instead of them being fully developed with thick feathers, only the bones unfolded from under his skin slowly bending until they had fully emerged. I could see everything now as torches by the exit had been lit and the orange glow reflected from the red stone of the cave.

His torso was bare and he wore only black jeans that rested low on his hips showing white boxer briefs at the top. He had black swirled tattoos that formed daggers pointing down his back and the handles became the section where his wings came from. I saw him crack his neck this way and that before I saw silvery energy come from his trousers up his back. It was as if he was drawing his energy from the ground and as it travelled along his skin it all found its destination at the point his wings began. I watched as it started to leave his body and light up the bones of his wings before it erupted outwards, forming what looked like metal shards of all different sizes that were triangular in shape. Thousands started coming from the network of bones that reminded me of the skeleton of a giant bird. They made a tinging sound as wave after wave of metal grew outwards until the last bone was full. I looked in awe as now a full set of metal wings could be seen, like shiny steel feathers that looked deadly sharp and filled a large space in the cave.

The creature made a deafening, high pitched wail as it threw its head up at the cave's ceiling. Then it focused back on Ruto as if getting ready to attack. But it never came, it never got the chance as Ruto stretched out his wings and when the metal ruffled out, some of the shards left the others and shot at the creature in a quick fire. The deadly metal spikes all made their target and soon the creature looked like a gruesome pin cushion. It howled one more time, only now it was clearly in pain as the metal started to drive its way further into the bones of the fleshy skeleton. Light then exploded from the points of impact and soon the creature started to crumble to the water that had kept me captive.

"Well, don't you look a mess?" I turned to find Ruto staring at me with arms folded like I was some naughty child that need reprimanding for playing in the mud! I wanted to say 'Well Durr' but decided that wouldn't be the wisest move, besides I didn't think I even had the energy to speak.

I watched as the metal wings started to fold in on themselves and soon I was left in the cave with a teenage punk that looked mighty pissed off.

"Can you walk?" I pushed myself up from the boulder but my legs refused to support me and I sacked it to the floor.

"I guess that's a no." I heard him say as I felt myself being lifted from the floor. I felt like a bag of bones as I was slung over his shoulder and for a slender teenage boy he was remarkable strong.

"Shit woman, your covered in this crap! I'm glad I took off my favourite shirt now. Man, you stink!" He complained and I couldn't help but start laughing. I think the stress had finally seeped and turned me crazy, either that or I was just so damned happy not to be some dead Northerner decomposing in some Hell hole with Mr Clicky Bones for company.

"Ah, so it begins!" He said, not sounding like the adolescent he looked.

"Whhht... yy...oumeeeeen?" I couldn't get my voice to work. It was like I was drunk. My speech was slurring and whenever I closed my eyes my mind would feel like someone had replaced my brain with fog.

"It's the mud you're caked in. Once it's washed off you should be fine, although I'm surprised you hung on as long as you did." He said shrugging me further on his shoulder.

"Whha...t wwasssss...it?" I asked hoping Ruto spoke slur, drunk and crazy.

"What was it?" He repeated for me as he ducked into an opening and pushed a door with his hip on the other side to where I lay limply over his narrow shoulder. I felt like a huge wet fish and when I opened my eyes they would only just focus on my new grey dreadlocks that hung down like fossilised snakes.

"It was an offspring of a Demon named Asag, which was long ago banished leaving his children of the mountains just waiting to be summoned. But the question is, by whom?" Well if he was expecting me to know then he was going to be disappointed. Of course knowing my new track record for collecting people who didn't like me, then Christ that could be a long suspect line-up. Thankfully dating Draven far outweighed all the murder attempts and death threats.

He didn't say anything and I was glad as I don't think I could have replied anyway. We continued down an endless amount of passageways and tunnels that weren't exactly heated so of course I couldn't stop my body from rattling with shivers. Ruto didn't seem to mind or if he did, he didn't comment. I think I must have even fallen asleep at some point because the next thing I knew I was being placed down on the floor and Ruto started talking but it became clear it wasn't directed at me.

"I have found her my Lord." I looked up and could just make out through a hazy blur that Ruto was holding something to his ear. It didn't take Sherlock to know that he was talking on the phone to Lucius but as to where I was, then Yeah, I'm sure Sherlock would have been real handy. I could only imagine that this was what the world must look like for people who wear glasses and then have them taken off them.

"She was in the room under the well locks before someone must have opened the grating. I found her in the cave below being attacked." Even from down here I could hear the roaring on the other end of the phone. I gathered that was the sound of one very pissed Vamp King. Ruto didn't even bat an eye at his Master's outburst, but just replied,

"Yes, my Lord," and hung up the phone.

I must have passed out again because the next voice waking me up belonged to Lucius and I felt bigger, stronger hands lifting me.

"Explain now!" Lucius snapped and I cringed in his hold. What did he want me to say? I think it was more than obvious that I was trying to escape but then Ruto spoke and I realised his demand was directed at him not me.

"Asag Nachkommen meines Herrn" ('Asag offspring my lord' in German) I felt Lucius stiffen where he had hold of me when Ruto was speaking in what I presumed to be perfect German.

"Summoned?" Lucius asked and Ruto must have nodded 'yes', as I didn't hear him answer.

"And I gather, as you have not brought me back a severed head, that you do not know by whom?" Lucius' voice was like acid that could eat through metal, he sounded so furious.

"No my Lord, but I am going back into the caves to see if I can pick up on an aura or a summoning signature."

"Good, take Liessa with you and see if she can pick anything up in the rock pools. Report back to me when I am finished here. Go!" Lucius' voice didn't waver even though it was clear the emotions coming from him were thick with controlled rage and I found myself more fearful than I did when I thought I was going to drown and become some skeleton man's flesh smoothie.

"Keira, can you hear me?" The question came through as strained but also from a man who was clearly concerned.

"Y…yy…esss," I stuttered and opened my eyes but the blurred surroundings still hadn't cleared, so I still had no clue as to where I was.

"I am going to get you undressed and submerge you in water, so don't panic when you go under." I felt his hands go to my dress and I tried to pull away.

"Nnn…nnno!" I couldn't stop shaking and my voice was proof of this.

"Keira, listen to me now! If I don't get this stuff off you then you will only get weaker still. Now shut up and let me take care of this. Take care of you." I felt his hand cup my cheek for a second before I heard the thick material of my dress tear right down the middle. I sucked in a breath as I felt the sides being pulled back like a door to showcase my naked body. I felt his large hands span my hips and then a deep breath that for once didn't come from me, before I felt my underwear coming away along with my ruined tights. He must have already taken my boots off because the only thing I felt on my skin was thick, crusty mud and the cold air.

"Take a deep breath when I say," Lucius said gently when picking me up and walking with me in his arms. I could feel the warm steam and hear the sound of running water, but it wasn't from the shower.

"Now!" He said and as soon as I did as instructed I felt myself being lowered into water. He pushed my head down and I didn't like the feeling of being held there by his hand on top of my head. I felt his other hand over my body like he was trying to remove the mud but when I started to thrash around he let me up.

"Take another breath!" Was all he said and because I had to take one after being under there he decided that he could push me back down. I started thrashing again but he knew how long I could stay under without running out of air so he held me in the water with ease as he continued to wash the mud out of my hair. Finally after three more times he let me stay out.

"Stop trying to drown me!" I shouted as I coughed and spluttered up water. Lucius growled at me and grabbed my head back by my hair without actually hurting me.

"Do as you're told before I do decide to drown you!" He snarled down at me and I froze. Now I didn't have as much of that stuff on me I started to feel better, things became clearer and the fog started to disperse. I could now see my surroundings and it looked like I was in an ancient bath house straight from Roman times. The space was a large room that gleamed with pale sand coloured marble that had veins of rust red running through it. This matched the rough rock walls in colour but was the polar opposite in texture. In the middle of the room was a round pool that was raised from the floor about seven feet but had steps all the way around it. The pool was made from the same marble and had six great pillars that went up about fifteen feet to the ceiling. There they moulded into beautiful carved works of art that made them look like the tops of trees mixed with grape vines and berried fruit.

Lucius had me positioned by the edge of the pool with my head arched backwards out of the water. He sat further down the steps given his height, so that he could tend to me at the right level. He looked over me and I saw him eye my strained neck for a moment before popping my head back under. Once he released me I came up and moved to the other end so he couldn't get to me. I hid my body as best as I could but considering moments ago he had his hands all over me I didn't know what the point was.

He raised an eyebrow and crooked his finger at me to come back.

"No!" I said utterly refusing.

"No? Really Keira, you don't want to play this game with me." His threat sounded very real but without the full force of anger behind it I thought it better to take the chance rather than be dunked over and over again.

"I'm sure I can get myself clean," I stated stubbornly.

"Actually, no you can't." He said before doing something that if I had been a cartoon, my eyes would have been popping out of my head in some unbelievable way. He stood up and putting both hands over his head to his back he pulled his top off and threw it to the side.

"Stop!" I shouted when he went to unbuckle his belt and started undoing his jeans.

"Too late," he said pulling everything off, including kicking one shoe with one foot and doing the same with the other. I turned quickly after seeing him flash his nakedness at me and there was one part of his anatomy I didn't want to focus on. Okay, so too late but I didn't want to stare at the large member that could have rightly had its own postcode. I shook my head as if that would help but by doing so I was too preoccupied to notice he had already gotten into the pool with me until his hands found my shoulders. I jumped making him chuckle.

"Now stay still and let me do this properly." He spoke in my ear sending a shiver down my naked spine at the sound of how deep his voice had turned.

"I…" I had to clear my throat before I could continue.

"I told you that I could do it." The words didn't come out half as determined as I planned for them to.

"And I told you that no, you can't." I tried to move from under his hold but his fingers bit down on my shoulders just before the point of pain.

"You see this isn't just mud, not anymore. It's been tainted and the longer it's on your skin it will keep you too weak. Human hands can't remove it as their touch just makes it spread and therefore it grows and only gains more power."

"What is it?" I asked taking a quivering breath as his hands washed my back in big gentle circles. He then went back to the top of my shoulders and started massaging my knot of muscles.

"Relax Keira, don't tense up so. Nothing will harm you. Not even me." He whispered this last part in my ear and kissed the sensitive skin under my lobe. As he returned back to his task he answered my question.

"The creature that attacked you was summoned from deep within the mountain. An offspring of the Demon Asag and one that feeds from sickness, but first the victim must be close to a large body of water then it transforms the earth to this." He had scooped up a bit that must have been stuck to my lower back and then held it out in front of me. He rubbed it between his thumb and fingers while he continued.

"It's how it forms a connection between you and it. Then it proceeds to suck the goodness out of you, your health and it leaves you with a sickness that if left on long enough will eventually kill you, leaving it stronger and you very much dead. It could also make you start seeing things that aren't there or feeling things that it wants you to. It is a drug Keira, like a hallucinogenic. Do you understand?" He asked softly and I found I could only nod.

"Good, then turn around." At this instruction I think my knees would have given out if Lucius hadn't been holding me around the waist with both hands. I wanted to say no, I wanted to turn around and push him back with both hands but I knew if what he was saying was true then I had no other choice than to do what he said. I tried to think of it as just like going to see the doctor for an exam but as soon as I turned around to face him that thought flew away and left me like a flock of frightened birds.

I was at least thankful that the water came up to just below my collar bone but it left Lucius with most of his upper body bare and the sight of his pale smooth skin over hard muscle, he looked almost godly and ethereal in the reflective surrounds of the water and marble. I couldn't raise my face and felt my cheeks burn at being so close and, very, very naked together.

"Eyes on me, sweetheart." He said raising my head up with a firm grip on my chin and I couldn't help but hold my breath as if waiting for a kiss I didn't want to happen. I didn't know if I could have handled that right now, not with him being here like this with me, helping me, soothing me like a gentle knight does to the fair maiden. Okay, stop now...No fairy tale analogies, no thinking about the steamy setting and definitely no thinking about being naked!

"Ha, you look like you're trying not to chew on something sour. Just relax will you or you'll start to make me nervous!" He teased and I actually smiled and dropped my shoulders from their uncomfortable hold.

He started to run his thumbs across my cheek and the side of my nose and when I saw the thick paste on his pad I knew what he was trying to do. Once finished with my face he then started down my neck and when he started to go lower I sucked in a breath making him freeze.

"I realise you are not this type of girl Keira, but I can assume you have been touched before or has Draven joined the Sainthood and is keeping his prize wrapped until the wedding day." He said sarcastically and I scowled at him.

"If I was you and want to continue then I wouldn't mention Draven again!" I said feeling disgusted with myself that I was allowing this to happen, even if I didn't have any other choice and my health wasn't on the cards.

"I could restrain you if that would make things easier on you," he replied with a bad boy grin only ever seen on the Devil inside.

"I think I will pass, thank you very much." I said folding my arms in front of my chest which he stopped me from doing at the last minute. He pulled my arms outstretched to the side and leaned down to my face so that only inches were between us.

"Oh don't thank me yet my little Keira girl, I haven't even got started!" And with that said for me to gulp over, the arms he held in a secure grip he started to put behind my back. He transferred both my wrists in one hand and with the other tried to smooth out the worry frown on my forehead.

"Ssshh, I am just making things easier for you," he said, voice like drizzled cream over strawberries which was probably how my cheeks looked right about now, creamy pale skin flushed with a berry blush. And then his hand lowered and no matter how many comforting words were said I tensed every muscle in my body like iron girders. His hand curved over my left breast and then over to my right taking the mud away with each gentle swipe. It was almost hypnotic the way he moved, so precise and careful, almost like he was handling a fragile, priceless antiquity. I closed my eyes and held my bottom lip firmly in between my teeth to stop the moan that was bubbling up. With my eyes closed and my breathing heavy I felt his hand moving further down the dangerous path along my stomach making slow, lazy circles as he went.

"Please!" The word was released before I could stop it. I felt his head lower down to mine in response and his lips spoke over mine.

"Tell me. Speak the words and tell me what you want?" I felt every word whisper its way across every nerve and travel straight down to my core. I didn't realise that his other hand had let me go and now both hands wrapped around my body holding me close but obviously not close enough for him.

"Tell me!" He said pulling my lower half into his frame with both hands holding a cheek full, kneading the rounded flesh with strong experienced fingers, until I could feel every hardened ridge of his toned body. And I mean every single inch.

"I…I…" I couldn't speak for the sensations flooding my body's responses with confusion. It felt like my skin was on fire and my insides would self-combust. I could feel my own pulse in my neck and wrists, and it felt like my blood was being pumped around my body just for Lucius' need alone.

"You?" Lucius spoke over my lips before dragging the bottom one from my teeth and into his mouth to take a long, hard suck. This time I couldn't prevent the moan from escaping. He groaned at my response and just before he took the action further a blind flash of realisation hit me and I knew I couldn't do this.

"I can't do this!" I said now speaking over his lips and I felt them smile as he rested his forehead to mine.

"No…but I can!" This was my only warning before he fisted his hand in my hair, tilted my head back and crushed his lips to mine in a heart stopping kiss. The moment he turned my head to the side, licked the seam of my mouth and dipped inside to deepen our connection the whole room erupted in daylight so bright I had to close my eyes. It was like someone had just dumped us on a Caribbean beach at the hottest part of the day. Lucius groaned louder before taking the kiss to another level of passion and I felt his hands glide down my body and hold on to me like he would lose himself without my skin touching his. I could feel every part of him and his manhood rested heavy against my stomach just waiting for the green light.

My mind felt fogged again like it had back in the cave but this time it had added a sex induced craving that caused my hands to hold onto Lucius as if he pulled away I would only pull him back again. I couldn't stop this, my body was screaming out for it in the worst way. When his lips left mine I nearly cried out at the loss but then I felt his lips trail sweet kiss after kiss along my neck and I threw my head back and the word,

"Yes!" Came out in a whimper.

"Say it again!" Lucius said not only commanding my body with skilful hands but also my mind, my whole being and my sinful soul.

So I gave it to him.

"YES." I said growling out my demand at his lips then grabbed two handfuls of hair to pull him and locked his lips to mine. This caused the sun to get even brighter and he grabbed my backside roughly in his hands. The growl in my open mouth was the only warning I got before he gripped tighter and picked me up to then step into my body eliminating any space between our nakedness. He wrapped my legs around his waist and walked us backwards to the edge of the pool.

"Tell me you want this," he groaned out between gritted teeth, like he was trying to hold back but was losing it. I looked up at him and seeing the sunlight drenching his skin in a luminous glow I wondered if I had ever seen anything as beautiful before. I couldn't find the words as every erotic point on my body and the bits in between had never wanted anything so badly. All I could do was nod and in that he found his green light.

He thrust up into me with the raw power of a Vampire king and ignited me like kindling. I screamed my release in a howl of pleasure that only one movement caused. Lucius pushed my torso backwards so that I was bent over the ledge with my breasts laid out like a welcome home mat. With one firm hand on my backside and the other covering my breast in a possessive hold, he unleashed his passion and blew me into a different world.

I could feel the tight coil of orgasm growing tighter in my belly with every hard thrust into my most secret place as he used my body without restraint. I was his to use. My body no longer my own but given over freely to a pure male savage. His movements were such as I had never known, no soft gentle words of love, no careful caress, just a powering need so basic that it was the only reason man survived for so long.

The love of sex.

The need of sex.

For Lucius' sex.

"Keira!" The manly roar of my name undid me as with one last delicious plunge we came together in a blinding furiousness that had me whimpering at the after spasms that wracked my body.

*Then I opened my eyes and the world crumbled.*

# CHAPTER 18
# AN INNOCENT MISTAKE

When I opened my eyes I could not understand what had just happened. One minute I was writhing in ecstasy and the next I was wrapped up in what looked like thick bedding in the arms of Lucius, being carried through a wide hallway where various artwork covered the smooth walls.

"What just happened?" I asked after taking in my surroundings.

"Well, with the moaning of my name coming from your bitten but kissable lips, my best guess... we were having sex." He couldn't wipe the smirk from his face and I didn't know who I wanted to beat to a bloody pulp more, me or him! How could I have done that! What was wrong with me, I loved Draven and I would never have done a thing like that! It was now official,

I hated myself!

Lucius started laughing and even though I knew I was still naked under the covers I was wrapped in I didn't care, I still started to struggle to get out of his hold.

"Shut up! This isn't funny! We had sex and now I have lost everything!" I was close to tears knowing I would have to tell Draven but God, what would he say? I was the worst girlfriend in the history of the human race and I wanted to take it all back with every fibre in my body!

"I thought as much," he said smugly.

"What do you mean by that?!" I snapped at him but he just shifted his hold and hoisted me further up against his chest.

"As hot as it sounded Keira, I don't think even your wild

219

imagination could live up to the real thing. Besides… I don't think you could handle me." He whispered the last part down my bare shoulder. But wait! What did he just say?

"We didn't have sex?!" I asked praying like I never had before.

"Now she gets it." He said with exasperation.

"No Keira, we didn't have sex. I prefer my partner to be responsive at the very least, not comatose, I may be a Vampire but I'm not into Necrophilia." A huge whoosh of pent up aggression left my body and was refilled by massive amounts of relief, complete and utter relief. One thought.

Thank you God!

"What happened?" I asked after I had taken the time to process that I hadn't cheated on the man I loved from some over sexed Vamp juice.

"I explained that if I didn't get all the mud off you that the effects would eventually get to you. I can only imagine that you got yourself too excited in my naked presence and started hallucinating, which is what I told you would happen." He was being way too smug but his teasing was actually making me feel better about all this. Let's put it this way, I would rather Lucius knowing I was having hot, steamy, watery sex with him in my mind and come thinking it was real, than waking up finding out that we had in fact had hot, steamy, watery sex and I had come full stop. Nope I would take embarrassment over that fact any day of the week!

"Man, can anyone say EGO much!" I teased back making him laugh.

"So was it as you expected it would be or more…no doubt much, much more." He said so full of humour that it was like flirting with a long-time friend about a drunken one night stand that we never had. I laughed and took the game to the next level. A cruel level.

"Actually, it was really disappointing. And much, much less, if you know what I mean." I said shaking my little finger at him so he got the hint. He stopped dead in the hallway and burst out laughing. He then leaned down to my bare shoulder and held the skin there with his teeth making me shiver.

"You will pay for that comment, not now but one of these days my little Keira girl." I laughed at him because I was trying to hide how his heated words got to me and plunged me straight back into the dream of the places those smirking lips had been.

"So what really happened, because I gather I am now clean." My cheeks heated even more at the thought of me still being naked around him.

"You passed out when I asked you to turn around. But don't worry sweetheart, I continued to get you clean. Oh and Keira…" He paused, leaned down and whispered in my ear like a lover's kiss,

"I was very, very thorough."

We continued on through the honeycomb of tunnels, passageways and hallways until we reached familiar ground and I knew where we were. One more turn around the corner and we would be at my room. I don't know how the supernatural did it? But nevertheless here he was, he'd been carrying me for the last twenty minutes at least and not even a sweat. Lucius looked strong, hell he was strong, no doubt about it but other than Draven it was still a shock to witness that strength. With Draven it was more of a natural thing, you took one look at him and didn't expect anything less. He looked like the man that could crush, devastate and pulverise any enemy too stupid enough to get close to him but Lucius was more a silent but deadly weapon. It wasn't as obvious to his power but it was there and I gathered it had lain dormant for all those years until his refusal to stand by Draven's side any longer. No, for now they stood opposite each other having, what was told, an equal power but why?

I couldn't stop from wondering what had happened? What could have been so earth shattering that made them turn against each other? What could possibly have shook the world and turned it on its axis to make one side become two?

My questions disappeared when I felt myself being placed back on the bed. It dipped as Lucius sat at my side and I couldn't speak when he lifted his hand to gently brush some hair from my cheek. He tucked it behind my head which is when I realised he must have brushed my hair because now it was hanging down my side in a wet plait. I don't know why the idea of Lucius doing that made goosebumps break out over my skin. I had to know.

"Did you…umm, have any help?" He raised one eyebrow and then gave me a bad ass grin that made him look even more painfully handsome.

"Nope, it was all me and all my pleasure." He winked at me and trailed his fingertips across my collarbone.

"You're cold!" He frowned quickly and then pulled the covers around me before adding the throw at the bottom of the bed. Lucius was tucking me in?! Okay now I had seen everything, first the Vamp

King can plait hair and then instead of stripping a girl naked he covers one up because they're cold.

"You need rest," he said cupping my cheek in his palm and then ran his thumb over my bottom lip making me close my eyes and shudder.

He moved and I couldn't help what I did next. My hand shot out to grab him and his wrist was so thick my thumb and fingers wouldn't even meet.

"Lucius wait, I…I don't want to be alone." One look at my face and he knew why.

"I will not let anyone hurt you again Keira, you have nothing to fear!" He said but then he turned his head and looked for something deeper.

"But you still do." He commented on my fear that was still fresh and obviously written all over my face.

"Very well," he said with no mockery, no lack of respect just a knowing. He moved off the bed and before I reached out for him again he walked around the other side and lay down next to me, turning me on my side to spoon my body against his. There was no sexual tension. No skin on skin contact. Just a solid presence that felt strong and secure at my back. He laid his arm around my middle and pulled me until my body was snug against his and moved my head so that it lay rested on his upper arm. I was taken aback by how smooth his skin was but there was no mistaking the hardness of pure man underneath.

"I will stay with you until you fall asleep, so you can rest without fear." His voice soothed me into believing his every word. I don't know what was happening, but this Vampire King Lucius was not the person I saw when he was like this. No, it was not the Vampire but a man, a man wrongly accused named Judas.

"Thank you," I said giving in to the feeling of heavy lids.

"Rest well, little Keira girl." I opened my tired eyes to see his pale hand in the moonlight that came through the balcony doors. It was held open as if waiting for something to fill it, so before even thinking about the action I put my hand in his and entwined my small fingers with his, only now seeing that my fingers had been bandaged with strips of tape. Why didn't I feel the pain? How did I ever forget that had happened? He must have felt my reaction to seeing the night's events creep back like some deathly spider spinning a web of nightmares ready for me to live through. He gripped me tighter and spoke in my hair.

"Ssshh, I am here, I am here." He said softly. Too softly for a Vampire King.

"Lucius?"

"Yes Keira?"

"Thank you for saving me, with Ruto." His hand lifted to my face, brushed back my hair and whispered on my cheek,

"You're welcome my Keira." The last thing I felt before the darkness took me was Lucius' hand holding my hand tighter and whispering beautiful words into my hair.

Ones I will never understand.

I felt the body next to me stir and the fingers I still held untangle themselves from mine. I kept my breathing even and remained still as Lucius started to remove himself from my side. I kept my eyes shut tight but could tell that he bent over me and when his knuckles travelled my cheek to my neck I had to hold in a shivered reaction. He then pulled up the covers higher as if he had only been touching me to judge whether or not I was cold. He proceeded to tuck me in and before leaving he leaned closer to my side, kissing below my ear.

"לישוןפחדקקלובלי, הילדההיפהשלי" ('Sleep easy and without fear, my beautiful girl' In Hebrew) Lucius whispered in my ear before kissing my temple.

And then he was gone.

I opened my eyes and saw the light from the winter moon still filling the room with bluish warmth and I was just happy that it wasn't the pitch black nothingness that my nightmares were summoned from.

I slowly sat up and looked around the room but froze mid-stretch. No, it couldn't be…could it? I pulled myself closer and my heart leapt at the sight before me.

"Ava?" I said her name and the huge bird ruffled her feathers looking quite aggravated. I got up from the bed ready to run to the balcony where she was sat on the railing when I saw the flash of purple in her eyes.

Oh God no! It wasn't just Ava sat here watching me but Draven sat watching us! I raced to the window but I was too late. He had seen me and Lucius together and that had been enough. I just managed to open the door and Ava turned her head before taking off into the night, taking Draven's possession with her.

"Draven!" I screamed but it was no use. He was already hurt.

*And I was the one who had hurt him.*

## CHAPTER 19
# SILENCE IN THE GARDEN

After waking up and seeing Ava at my window I couldn't remember what happened after that, but I woke up in a bed that I didn't recall getting back into. Was it a dream? Everything inside me wished it was so, but what if it wasn't? That thought had tears springing to life before I could try and push them away.

I wrapped the covers around me making me look like a caterpillar as I took little steps into the bathroom. I looked at my face in the mirror and quickly looked away feeling disgust. I felt like a traitor. Or at least I felt that Draven would see it that way. Me, a traitor? Well I felt as if I had a new contender for worse night of my life and last night with Lucius was done purely from desperately needing comfort. It wasn't an excuse but a truth, a hard fact of the matter that resulted in something that looked so much more than it was.

Surely Draven had to have trust in me more than that… right? Well I bloody hoped so but I needed to know. I had to see for myself and I knew just the right Imp for the job.

"You rang my noggin?" Pip said from the doorway while I was on the loo, luckily though I was in the right place for wetting myself!

"Pip, Jesus! Do you ever knock?!" I shouted at her but she just shrugged her little shoulders making her ridiculously large earrings sway. I think they were of Jack the Pumpkin King wearing a Santa hat and wait, were they really flashing? Knowing Pip, then yes they were and it wasn't just my tired mind. I don't think I would have been surprised at this point if they started dancing the two step to 'Getting Jiggy With It' by Will Smith!

"Nice earrings!" I said once I finished my morning routine, all the while being watched by a silent Pip.

"You like them? Adam got them for me for our anniversary, these and a new swing for our bedroom." She said doing a swinging motion as if I needed help with the concept but then again, knowing Pip it was doubtful it would just be a happy child's playground pastime. Yep, she winked at me and confirmed it was a sex swing.

"What, not a chocolates and diamonds kinda girl?" I asked making her smile with blue lips that matched the tips of her hair.

"Chocolate is for drizzling on certain body parts and as for diamonds, well look closer to good ole Jack." She walked closer and shook her head which created little rainbows from the large diamonds that were Jack's eyes. No wonder his thin long limbs wanted to dance, he not only had flashing lights on his Christmas hat but blinding rocks for eyes…the little dude was loaded!

"Nice!" I didn't know what else to say but I really did wonder where on earth he would find a gift like that, the 'tacky meets top notch' store?

"Well I think so. You know you can't go out like that, don't you?" She looked me up and down causing me to burst out laughing. I was still wrapped up in the covers and the look on her face told me she was serious.

"You don't like the outfit?" I teased making her wrinkle her cute little nose.

"Not really, it doesn't do a lot for your figure that's for sure, plus Lucius had some other clothes bought for you, they're in the wardrobe and they're a mountain amount bigger and better than that ugly thing, you look like a grub with a pretty head and…"

"Pip stop. I am teasing you, this is just the bed covers, not a dress!" I said stopping her before she went on a tandem of crazy reasons why this was not the best thing to wear. Mind you, given what she was wearing I think my choice was more practical…didn't she ever feel the cold? Along with the jewellery choice of 'crazy', to these she added faded denim short dungarees that had bleeding butterflies on the pockets, pop art tights that had too many colours to mention in the comic book style pictures and the T-shirt was something else completely! It was yet another 80's cartoon but with a Pip twist.

It was sunny yellow with a picture of three of the Care Bears and if

I remembered my bears correctly there was pink 'Cheer Bear' with a rainbow, 'Friendship Bear' with flowers and 'Funshine' Bear with a sun. The words below said 'Without a Care 'Bear' in the world'.

I laughed until she turned around and I saw the back. All three bears were still there but looking a little worse for wear, now all being zombies. One had half his face ripped off and was eating his own bear intestines, another had his eye hanging from its socket and instead of the sun on his belly he had the word 'Fukshine' in bloody writing. And the last was giving you the finger with one hand and the other held a bottle of beer.

It was one hell of a T-shirt.

I followed her out and saw that the only practical part of her outfit which was suitable for going outside in this weather was her over the knee wellies that had Pick and Mix print on them. It looked a bit like two rainbows had sex and Pip was born!

"So where are we going today?" I asked feeling a bit excited about the idea of getting out of this stronghold and getting into the fresh air.

"To the Silent Garden or did Lucius say to take you to the forest?" I remembered the warning she'd received from Lucius and after last night's horrific events I decided I really didn't need any more near death experiences.

"He said no forest, Pip," I said walking past her to get into the wardrobe that I was praying contained some 'normal' clothes. I picked up an expensive looking package that had the name 'William Rast' and I gathered that was the designer. I opened it up and nearly wept with joy at seeing a pair of jeans. I ripped my way into the other bags being far too excited about seeing real clothes for the first time in days. I found a long sleeved top that had those trusty thumb holes by a French designer that I couldn't pronounce and the last box had a designers name imprinted with gold lettering that had me gulping.

It had a round Greek coin design and in the middle was the picture of the mythological beast Medusa. Underneath was the word 'Versace'. After staring at it for a while, Pip made a tutting sound which brought me back around to the now. I opened it and inside was the most beautiful red coat that I was sure had been made by the Heavens. I lifted it, noting its thick material and heavy weight.

"Ooooh, me likes!" Pip said confirming that she wasn't the one who chose it. Looking at all her colours I was happy about this.

After a quick shower I got dressed, making Pip wait for me in the living room, although I was pretty sure she would have kept me company in the bathroom if I had let her. I noticed in the shower that the bandages from my fingers had gone and the only evidence that the Demon had bitten me were the tiny little red dots that looked like week old scars.

Once dressed, I felt comfortable for the first time since leaving my sister's house. The jeans were made from the softest denim that fit my legs as though they had been made with a plaster cast of my lower half, they were that perfect. The top was also so soft to my skin, being made from fine cotton. But it was the jacket that made me feel as if I was being wrapped in an expensive cloud. It was a deep red cashmere fitted jacket that went down past the knees and flared out like a rippling skirt whenever I moved. It reminded me more of a dress it was so gorgeous and well fitted. The top curved over my chest with tailored panels and the neck was a long floppy scarf that tied into a loose big bow that made the outfit look cute. And the best bit…it was deliciously warm.

Pip threw a little bag that had red cashmere gloves to match that weren't full length but thanks to my top I didn't need them to. I popped them on. After also finding some new lace up boots and sorting out my hair in its usual twist, I was ready for the outside world.

The outside world was unlike one I had ever seen before. It was like some horror version of a winter wonderland. It would have been a great view to put on a gothic Christmas card!

After listening to half an hour of Pip talking non-stop about everything and every cartoon in between, we had finally just walked through the last door after managing a turret full of spiral steps. It made me realise what my New Year's resolution was going to be and it involved the word 'GYM'.

I had followed Pip who didn't ever look like she would lose her breath, even after hundreds of steps. If anything, it had looked as if I was holding her up most of the time. She would run round and round and then be sat on one of the steps waiting for me and still chatting away like I had heard every word. I hadn't found the extra breath to tell her I didn't know what she was going on about.

We had just come through the top and I looked back at the turret and saw a large jutted piece of the mountain that had been smoothed into a rounded shaped on the door side. The cliff face didn't look anything other than mountain and I now realised why no humans would ever know what was hidden here. It truly was an underground castle.

I looked around and instead of seeing all the snowy tops of rolling mountains all I got was white. Everywhere was thick with fog and it felt as if I was so close to the heavens I half expected to see the Pearly Gates. It was clear we were on top of the mountain and it had been flattened out for outside space. I had watched Pip skip along on the snow covered ground that was lay out between the stone walls like a celebrity white blanket.

It opened up into a huge circular area also covered in a thick layer of snow. Around the edge was a crumbling arched wall that showed the foggy distance from the framed stone ruins. The top of the wall was a twisted tree root that was grey and looked long ago dead. It was the thickness of my body and must have travelled a circumference of about half a football field. Next to the stone walls were cut hedges that spiralled inwards until it met with the paved stone slabs that could only be seen in patches thanks to someone's foot prints.

In the middle of the whole garden was an enormous dead tree that was devoid of bark and was a funny shape, like some colossal giant had come along and tried to twist it free from the ground. What was even stranger than its position in the garden was the fact it was the only thing around that wasn't layered with snow and it was the first tree I had ever seen that had a hollow at the base big enough for at least six people to sit inside all at once. It was like a natural made teepee tent.

The further we went down into the garden, the more I started to see inside the tree which was set up like a Gothic tea party. Pip clapped her hands twice and ran down the steps to stand next to her work and said,

"Voila!" As she held both her arms out wide and tilted her body to the side like someone welcoming you to a freak show circus.

"Do you like it?" She asked me proudly, motioning for me to enter. The space was so big that I only just needed to duck under, unlike Pip who was small enough to walk inside. We both sat down opposite each other and when Pip crossed her legs I did the same.

I looked around in awe at my crazy surroundings.

"Did you do all this?" I asked staring at the inside of a tree that had been transformed into an outside tea room with a twist.

"I did and I even made the bunting with some old clothes." She was referring to the triangles of leather, flowered brocade, latex and black and red embroidered velvet all connected together with thick, white satin ribbon that hung all around the inside of the tree walls.

"It all looks great but what's the occasion?" I asked looking at all the craziness between us, spread out like some Halloween party feast.

"I just thought that you might like some girl time. I have always wanted to do this and never had anyone to invite and dolls and bears don't gossip, now that Barbie is a right slut! Did you know that you can get dominatrix Barbie, I have two of those and slave Ken or is it Blaine? I tell ya I can't keep up with that girl! I think you have had a rough couple of days and needed to relax." I couldn't help the beaming smile that broke out across my face thanks to Pip's effort in helping me relax, that and hearing how she thought Barbie was a slut!

"Well, I appreciate it and I am starving." I said looking down at all the themed food. There were finger sandwiches all piled high on three tier cake stands made from black glass and had acrylic skeleton spines through the middle that met the skull at the top which were the handles. There was another stand that had legs like the wicked witch that Dorothy's house landed on. This one had meats, cheeses, crackers and chutneys in little black caldrons.

The last stand was a tall black wired bird cage which held a two tiered cake that was iced purple with a black cobweb draped around the bottom tier. The second tier had dripping red calligraphy around the sides whereas the finishing touch was the edible top hat that was complete with part of a head, covered in what looked like raspberry sauce to represent blood. Well I hoped it was raspberry sauce anyway! The cake had a butcher's knife sticking out of the top hat to one side and with the glint coming off the blade I doubted very much it was edible and if it was, then let's just say that Pip would be going first.

Of course, no tea party would be complete without the tea set and here we had three. One was a very tall pot with matching cream and sugar pots all in black and white stripes. This one went the best with our outside surroundings as the only colour seen in this wonderland was inside this tree. Even the sky was ghostly white.

Another set was also white but the tea cups were painted to look like they had been handled by a slasher movie victim with bloody handprints and drops of blood. Without the red paint the set would have been cute, with a dumpy little tea pot and a fat little jug for milk. However, each had the appearance that the contents were filled with blood and overflowing down the sides and out of the spouts.

The last set was very cool in a creepy it's great for Halloween, type of way. It was a set that was made to look like it was straight out of Victor Frankenstein's lab. The tea pot was made from green glass and looked like some lab equipment that was being used in an experiment. There was writing on the front of the squat glass container that said 'Arsenic' on a fake aged label. The matching set included a beaker for the milk that said 'Toxic' in the same design and a test tube in a metal holder that had the poison symbol on the front, this wasn't far from the truth as my mother would agree because it contained sugar, which we all know rots kid's teeth…it's still tasty though!

Pip handed me a dark blue and white chintzy china cup and saucer only instead of me using for actual tea it was already filled with a cupcake. It had navy blue frosting swirled high with a black candy heart sticking out of the side. With this she handed me a black napkin folded up with a red ribbon and held together with a black waxed seal with the letter P.

"Wow, you really went to town Pip!" I commented taking off my gloves before I reached for a tea spoon to eat my cake with and would you blow me down, they were also part of the gothic theme, being both black and having the face of a skull. I mean bloody hell, where did she even get all this stuff from anyway…ebay?! I bet there was a sale on at Goth 'R' Us!

"Yeah, you think this is cool, you should see what I do for Adam's birthday, last year it was a Rocky Horror Show theme and Adam looked so cute in a costume." I nearly snorted my blue frosting at this image!

"Makes me wonder what Lucius wore?" Why did I just ask that?! And what was I doing thinking about Lucius anyway and after the train wreck last night had turned into!

"Oh but of course he had to be 'Rocky Horror' you know, the blonde God created by the crazy Doc and Lucius does have the beef to pack out those gold shorts." Okay, so this time I started to choke on that bloody frosting!

"No way!" I said after drinking something that definitely wasn't tea.

"And why not, Lucius does have a sense of humour and when you look that good naked, I don't suppose he got any complaints." She winked at me and I was just shocked to hear that one, the great Vamp King would dress up at all and two…he had a sense of humour?

"Let me guess, you went as Columbia?" I said just picturing her as a little, blue haired Dr. Frank-N-Furter groupie.

"Yep and I even had the gold glitter top hat and everything! And if I recall, Liessa was Magenta, Ruto was Riff Raff and Liessa even made Caspian dress up as Eddie which he only did 'cause he got to wear leathers! If you had been there you would have made a great Janet." I giggled as I imagined them all sat round dressed as these characters. It was just too weird to picture without laughing.

"And I don't need to tell you what the birthday boy was, although he refused the first outfit he wore in the movie. He finally agreed to the one where Dr. Frank-N-Furter wears the green surgeon's gown but he had to be naked underneath, those were my rules!"

"Why am I not surprised?" I said making her smile before licking the frosting off her own cupcake that was almost the same colour as her lips.

"You know this was a perfect idea and I have been gagging for a cup of tea for what seems like forever." I said reaching for another tea pot when Pip started giggling.

"It's not one of those parties...sorry?" I frowned at what she could mean.

"I don't get it? What other types are there?" I was almost too scared to ask.

"Umm...the ones with no tea, just lots of yummy scrummy alcohol."

"PIP! You do remember what happened the last time you made me drink, right?"

"Yeah and if I recall you went travelling supersonic style, brain waves floating across space and shit and the outcome was one fine assed living God named Draven, who could no doubt not only could kick Superman's spandex ass but the whole X-men crew along with him, so what d'ya say, fancy a drink Janet?" During this little speech she had been filling one of the many crazy tea cups with an 'Imp' only knows what. She gave it a little shake in my direction without spilling a drop.

"You're bad...you know that, right?" I said taking the cup from dainty hands taking note of the choice of nails today, each one painted a different fruit. Strawberry was my favourite.

"Bad to bone, honey bee!" She said, taking her own cup and chinking it to mine.

After a while I was stunned at all the things we had talked about and I was even able to get a few things about Draven off my chest. I kind of forgot the supernatural being thing and although there was no getting away from the quirkiness (Not that I would want to) it was kind of like having a chat with a good friend, like RJ or even with my sister Libby. Those thoughts caused me to be quiet for a few minutes as the lump in my throat formed from how much I missed them all.

Luckily Pip was busy concocting our new mix of cocktails. I soon found out that all the tea pots and their matching 'milk' jugs all held different forms of alcohol and mixers, so we had silly fun experimenting.

"Sooo, you have heard all about me but what about you? I mean you're a married Imp who's sat at Lucius' table every night...what's that like?" I asked trying not to let the drink get to me but man, the Imp mixed a mean cocktail!

"Well, it sure didn't start out as my career choice I will tell ya but Adam is Lucius' Lieutenant so it kinda comes with the marriage. Like buy one and get an Imp for free. It's a bit risky for others to be around Adam without me being there...let's just say he gets...cranky." I frowned at this. How could she just stop at that rubic cube!

"Okay, you're gonna have to give me more than that Squeak, you're killin' me here." I said calling her the nickname she told me to use and I thought it fit her so well. She had a musical, high pitched voice and reminded me of some colourful but crazy fairy. I bet if I let go of my mental walls I would see cute little iridescent wings and adorable pointy ears. I was almost tempted.

She laughed as she opened up the bird cage to get to the massive cake. The thing opened on a double door hinge and she gripped the large knife and I kid you not, she did a comical Karate chop, even adding,

"Hi-ya!" She then placed a wedge on a black plate and handed it to me.

"It's red!" I said referring to the sponge inside, that was a beautiful rich colour.

"No, it's red velvet and you should try it, it's a yummy mummy!" She said taking the whole wedge and trying to cram it in her mouth sideways. I took her advice and gave it a bite and then I was making noises that should only be reserved for the bedroom. It was good. It was my new friend. And it made me want more.

"I knew you would like it, Vincent said you have a sweet tooth." Wait...what!

"What do you mean...you've spoken to Vincent?" My heart started hammering in my chest at the sound of his name. Then the immediate image of being in his arms and him holding me to him in a protective way had me close to making the same noises I had made eating the cake.

"Oh, no I guess I didn't tell you but I heard from Vincent and he asked me to make sure you were getting enough food, which I realised that no, you weren't, so I did this and filled your fridge with sweet stuff. You even have some candy canes under your pillow...you know in case you wake up needing to suck on something sweet." She winked at me and I nearly spat red cake everywhere. She then had me in a fit of giggles and passed me another cup filled with I didn't even want to guess. It tasted good though.

"Well thank you, I appreciate it."

"Wow you are easy to please, you're happy that we're feeding you?!" She burst out laughing and started piling another plate with sandwiches for me. That, combined with the cake, cheese and crackers, fruit and lots of blue frosting, and I was fit to burst!

"Honestly, I think you deserve a gold star for the feeding human game," I said leaning back and unbuttoning my coat.

"Goodie, so does this mean the next time you see Vincent you will tell him that...he scares me!" I bolted upright at this.

"What do you mean 'he scares you'? Vincent is harmless!" And lovely and sweet and oh, don't even go there!

"Ha! You really don't know the Dravens like the rest of us do. They are rulers for a reason and Vincent is the only Commander of the King's armies. He has legions upon legions like no other from the Heavens and rules his men with a fair but iron fist. He also happens to be the only one that has ever knocked Lucius on his ass in the ring, although Dominic has never fought him." I must have had my mouth open for every word she said. Vincent, a Commander of Heaven's armies? Now that was crazy. To me he was just Vincent, quiet and reserved but as sweet as the Angel he looked...Wow...just wow!

"You sure do know a lot about them?" I said hoping for even more information. It was like Pip had now become my dealer and this junkie needed another Draven fix and bad. So if info was all I could get, then that would have to cut it.

"Well I did used to live with them all. I was on the Council along with Adam and Ruto. I miss Sophia." She said looking down in her tea cup looking sad.

"Okay, so let me work this out...up until Lucius and Draven started this feud you all were on Draven's Council?"

"That's what I'm saying. But since then we had to split, we made our choices and all had to pick a rollercoaster. Adam picked Lucius because of his loyalty to him so I followed but I do miss my friends." I felt so bad for her I nearly got up just to give her a hug but she started concocting again so I hung back.

"You can't see them?" I asked.

"The whole 'side against side' kinda puts a stop to that and Adam would never leave Lucius."

"Why not, if you wanted to then…" She started to shake her head before I could finish.

"No, Adam can't be left without me, that would be…dangerous." She shuddered and this had me wondering what the hell it was about Adam anyway?

"I don't understand?"

"I know and for that you would have to know my story and how it was Lucius that saved both of us."

"He did… but how?" Pip gave me a little smile and her little tongue swept out and licked at her lip ring.

"You ready for story time, Toots?" She said and when I nodded she clapped her hands and said something that gave me the shivers,

"Time for some stronger drinks, I think."

*Oh, this was going to be so bad.*

CHAPTER 20

# NUMBER OF THE BEAST

"Okay, so here I was, with this right Asshole boyfriend when the shit hit the fan and I got sent down for his crime. I mean, how was I supposed to know what would happen after putting a couple of rats from China on a ship to London. The bastard told me they were lucky rats and that he wanted me to have lucky pets for our new home in England. I mean sounds harmless right but noooo, the rats wouldn't listen to a regular Demon, only a stupid ass Imp that asked them nicely to survive the journey and come home with their new mummy. I mean the beating he gave me when I asked if this was a good idea should have been a clue but he was a good looking mother foo so I did what he said and maybe, just maybe, might have caused a little epidemic that might have caused a few deaths." She took a sip of her drink and looked over the cup's brim with guilty eyes.

"He beat you! Okay wait...what date was this and how many deaths are we talking about?"

"Umm I think it was sixteen and a small number, maybe three, yeah the year was 1603 because that was the first time I bought a capotain...ooo, I think I still have it somewhere."

"A capotain?" I knew this story would eventually get off track.

"Oh yeah we don't have them anymore, well it was this tall-crowned, narrow-brimmed hat, usually black but I had a purple one and it went perfect with this lace..."

"Pip, focus. How many people did it..." I paused as it slowly started to seep in. That date and my history loving brain started to fit the cogs in the right place, when it finally started to turn again I knew the horrifying answer.

"Wait! You are not telling me…oh please don't be telling me…You caused the Black Death to come to London?!" At this she cringed.

"Umm…kind of," she said taking another sip as she kept her guilty eyes still in place.

"PIP! Bloody hell Squeak that caused over 40, 000 deaths!"

"38, 472 deaths actually but one of those had a bad heart anyway so he doesn't count."

"Oh shit, so what happened?" I had opted for gulping my drink now as opposed to Pip's sipping hers.

"Ah, well see the 'powers that be' didn't think too kindly on my circumstances and it went to trial but I…um…kind of…didn't show up."

"What! You didn't show, why not?" She popped a sugar frosted berry in her mouth and shrugged her shoulders like this was nothing.

"What can I say, I was busy hunting."

"Hunting? Like fox and hound type of stuff?" At this she laughed, but then started to choke on her second berry. I was about to help when she simply put a fist to her chest and hit it hard with the flat palm of her other hand like she had done this type of thing before. She cleared her throat before continuing.

"Fuck no! I love those little guys and hate the bastards that hunt them! Have you not seen their cute bushy little tails?"

"Then I don't get it, what were you…?"

"I was hunting the asshole of course! I knew I was getting sent down without his sorry carcass to give them but what do you know, he thought it was a great time to disappear and took a vacation." She gritted her teeth at the memory and it was the first time seeing Pip angry at someone. Even when she had talked to Klaus she had still done so in a joking, 'you're gonna die soon', kinda way.

"So where did he go?"

"Shit I don't know, Aruba for all I knew but the point is as I was hunting him, they were hunting me and I know I'm only little but I'm not invisible!"

"So I gather they found you?" I asked hating the idea that poor little Pip was being hunted over something she wasn't fully responsible for doing.

"Oh man did they find me! And the Fires of Hell don't really mix with a little Shadow Imp like me"

"Shadow Imp?" I asked needing some explanation on this.

"Well you get lots of different types of us, like my friend Forester, he's an Imp of..."

"Let me guess, the forest?" I said making her look at me with confusion.

"No, why should he be? Oh you mean the name, no Tooty Toots, that's just his name. No, he's the Imp of the Lost. He can take his power from the confused but instead of leaving a Being weak it will give them strength to see through the confusion...which is win, win if you ask me. But me...well, what can I say, I can manipulate the shadows and one's mind is full to the coffee brim of shadows." She said raising her eyebrow as if waiting for my next question.

"I don't understand Pip, so you're gonna have to help me out with this one...people have shadows in their minds?"

"But of course they do, or where else would all the new info go, Dudette? But I can fill those shadows with whatever info I like or I can simply take them away. Okay, put another way, let's say I shaved all your gorgeous locks off with a meat cleaver and with not only all your hair missing but a few missing pieces of scalp as well, now that would be a shitty hair style wouldn't it?"

"Focus Pip!" I said and she laughed at my screwed up face, thanks to the vivid picture she just described.

"Well anyway, I could take out that memory and make it into a shadow, another empty space ready to be filled, so in other words I could rather leave it blank, so you would wake up thinking you always had a scalp that resembled a butchers block or I could plant the image of that butcher doing it to you, not me. You wouldn't remember me." She said with a blue lipped grin.

"That is one scary thought Pip." I couldn't help but feel a chill at the idea of someone playing scrabble with my brain.

"I know right, but lucky for most I like to feed from happy emotions so I prefer letting people feel like they have won the lottery or something...ooo, but one guy I made him think he always wanted to be ballerina and then wouldn't you know, he got accepted as lead in Coppelia, you know the ballet? Well anyway, when he thought he got accepted he started doing pivots round his living room. The funniest part was... and you're gonna love this... he was a hairy fat trucker from Minnesota!" We both gave each other a look and burst out laughing until tears appeared in my eyes.

"Anyway, I got my thrill and left him thinking he got laid by a supermodel, so another win, win."

"So where does making my soul visit Draven come into it?" I couldn't stop myself from asking after I took a sugar berry that she offered from a skull bowl that opened at the jaw, where a berry was waiting for me to pick.

"Ah…well now, that's a tricky one and usually I need added juice but I can also detach a soul…all the shadows if you like, and pin point it all to one location, without the need for a body. It not easy and I'm a little beat after it, you know…the longer you're gone but it's still do-able if the receiver is strong."

"Okay, explain that bit…the receiver?"

"It's like this, if I had a puppy and I went on holiday, I would have to leave it with someone to take care of it, you know someone responsible, someone I know that would care for it…like if I left it with some homeless guy that couldn't even feed himself and thought one of his own arms was a snake, he was that jacked up, then it would no doubt end up one dead dodo…right?" I nodded but she could see I was still a little hazy on the edgy details.

"Right well, it's the same with a soul. I couldn't leave it with just anyone or it would try and run away, like a puppy trying to find its way home." Ah, it was starting to click.

"I'm the puppy?"

"You're the puppy Toots and may I say, what a cutie you are but I doubt you had chance to go at any Draven bones if ya know what I mean?" She waggled her eyebrows at me and I rolled my eyes at her joke.

"I don't know about a Shadow Imp, more like a Nympho Imp!" She winked and I threw a sandwich at her making her flick frosting at me. We both giggled like drunken teenagers before composing ourselves.

"So, Draven is your puppy carer?" I asked and she nodded, making all her hair shake in loose waves.

"Sure is Honey Bee, although his brother has got some serious juices flowing for the Tootinator! I think he must have been thinking about you hard girlfriend 'cause your soul shot straight to him last time! Methinks you have yourself some big, tough as nine inch nails, army commander, Angel admirer in Vincent." I made a snorted gurgled laugh while Pip smiled a cunning and mischievous little smile.

"I don't think so," I said with burning cheeks.

"Oh my god, Toots! You didn't tell me you had glasses, what happened to them, did they smash them when Klaus hit you?" She then added, to her amusement, by pretending to have lost her own glasses and was patting the ground like they were around somewhere.

"Ha,ha, I'm serious Pip."

"Yeah, me too because you must be blind not to know Vincent's wayo mucho got the hot sauce for some little Electus chica." I shook my head which she copied.

"He has not and we're now going to drop that non-existent subject and focus on what happened to you." On saying this she made a cat noise and scratched her nails in the air.

"Okay, fine by me Angel hottie ass, no need to get prissy!" She said slapping out at me with a non-existent handbag before carrying on. I just laughed.

"Right where were we before you found out Vincent's in love with you?"

"PIP!" I reprimanded but the Demon in her just smiled.

"Okay, okay, got the memo, received the telegraph and am reading the writing on the wall, so totally got ya. Right well, I think I was at the point where they hunted me down to drag my Impie butt back to the Mountain of Fire and Brimstone." She thumbed the ground and I swallowed hard.

"What! Tell me you didn't get sent to Hell…did you?"

"Sure did Kiddy Winkle." She nodded while checking out a watermelon on her nail, then she licked it as if it was a watermelon.

"For how long?" I asked, hating the idea that my little friend had been sent to Hell as punishment.

"About a year." I let out the breath I was holding until she carried on.

"That's about the equivalent to a hundred of your human years."

"What! You were there for a hundred years? Oh Pip." I said shaking my head and being close to tears at the idea.

"Hey, in the end it turned out as a good thing, being punished ending up being not so bad. I was lucky really 'cause at first they wanted me to be food for a bunch of crappy Hellhounds but in the end they needed a snack to keep Abaddon happy." At this she kissed her tattooed knuckles on the hand that spelled out 'Adam'.

"So did Adam save you?" At this she burst out laughing until tears appeared.

"Oh my, you are a funny Toots. No he didn't save me from Abaddon, he is Abaddon."

"Okay, now I'm really confused, he wanted to eat you and how is it that this Abad...something or other, is Adam?"

"Okay, here's the thing, first you have to understand what Abaddon is. See, Lucifer needed to beef up his armies right, so he decided to try and create the 'The Great Beast' from the twisted souls of lost warriors and such that had been trapped in the seventh circle."

"Seventh circle...as in Hell... as in Dante's Inferno?" I interrupted.

"Yeah well good old Dante boyo was a Demono and got drunk one night trying to write something of a stage act and ended up just writing the truth...idiot! But anyway 'The Divine Comedy' which is his work on explaining the 9 Circles of Hell is quite accurate. The seventh is Violence, and even then, there are bloody different rings to it. Like that matters, if it was me I would just throw the whole shitty lot in a room and let them fight it out! But no, Lucifer doesn't think that the outer ring of petty violence against people and property would get on well with the middle ring of sad souled suicides. And well, the inner ring bastards don't respect anything, not even the Gods, that's where most of the warriors are." I think she decided to mix another drink as a chance to give me a minute to process and bloody hell did I need it, no pun intended.

"Right, so Lucifer snapped on his experimenting gloves and merged selected souls in the flaming river of Phlegethon and tried to create 'the Mighty Beast' he called Abaddon, which means 'Destruction' in Hebrew by the way."

"Okay, destruction, got it...so what happened next?" I felt like a child being told horror stories around a camp fire. Okay, so there was no fire but we were outside.

"Where was I... ah yeah there. So, Lucifer was trying to make this mighty beast but shit kept going wrong, right. I mean they kept dying being either too weak or way too strong that they would just rip themselves apart with a rage far too great to be contained. So it got recommend, ever so delicately..." She leaned forward and added behind a hand,

"Lucifer can be a tad bit touchy but it was the King Asmodeus of the second circle that offered to try and add some lustful souls to the mix. His idea was that lust can make any creature desire, which could give a sweet big ass Abaddon a reason to live through the rage. So after the 616th try the only Abaddon was born from the souls of the damned. Not a smidgen of fairy dust in sight." No and it didn't sound like it. Man, this stuff was heavy and I knew from the way she stretched out her slim, little legs that she was getting comfy and ready for the rest of the tale.

"And it really fries my noodle when people think the number of the beast is 666, 'cause they would be so wrong. It's clear as day in the Revelation in the 66th vol. of the Oxyrhynchus series has the number of the Beast as 616, but no, everyone wanted to make it look even but you know the fluffy little white rabbit sometimes just ain't that white, you know what I mean?" I nodded but to tell the truth, no... I really didn't know what she meant but when did I ever?

"So trying to get things straight once more, you're telling me that Abaddon, who is also Adam, and also Hell's destroyer, which is Lucifer's personal army's beefy pet, is made from the souls of pissed off men?"

"And a few lusty ones," she added nodding.

"And a few lusty ones, is also the reason every being knows that 666 is the number referred to the Devil?" I raised my eyebrows in waiting.

"Pretty much, but of course the number's wrong and it doesn't actually refer to the big boss man downstairs but to my big boss man upstairs." She leaned back and looked like the Lion that found himself in a raining meat storm!

"Alright, now you have to explain how that relationship happened 'cause I take it he didn't eat you?" She gave a naughty wink and I knew we had very different ideas about that whole 'eating you' comment!

"Ah, now this is the best bit. But first you have to picture this point in my life. I had just been sent down and even though I received a warm welcome it wasn't the kind you would want! All those toothy bastards laughing their high pitched squeals and making bets at how long I would last before I became spit roast Pip. Ha, well I had the last laugh on that one, shit heads!" She said glugging back her drink before just grabbing the striped milk jug and chugging it down. I think that one contained straight Vodka.

"Abaddon was well known for his burning rage but number 616 managed at least to stay alive, but he was way too unpredictable on the battle fields to be used. The big lug didn't think he had any masters and I guess if no one can destroy you or control you, then you're a servant to no-one." She finished the Vodka and threw the jug over her shoulder. It smashed and when I jumped she mouthed the word 'sorry' at me. I don't know why she had turned a bit serious but I guess the rest of the story was going to enlighten me.

"Right, well they now had a problem on their hands, one that Lucifer couldn't even handle, so what did they do? The bastards threw him in his own caved realm of Hell and locked him there with a few meat headed guardians and I use the word guardians in the loosest sense of the word...like non-existent, like a cow pretending to be a pissing Reindeer I mean, can you see that, a bunch of cows pulling Santa?! Hell no, right!" She grabbed another jug and started with this one when it hit me what was wrong with her.

"You felt sorry for him?" I asked quietly.

"I loved that big beasty bastard before they even dangled me in there like a slab of beef in a noose!"

"You did?"

"Hell yeah, I mean they just locked him up Toots! They just created him and left him with a few play things and scraps. They made him and they were just waiting for the day we would die!" She was getting really angry now and I started to see her fingertips turn black and her skin become cloudy. I scooted round and I placed a hand on her arm and when she responded with shock at my touch it was as though she had only just realised I was still there.

"It's okay Pip, I understand. Nobody likes to think of someone they love ever being hurt or wronged, but it's okay now, he's got you." This last part must have sunk in and she raised her eyes from where I touched her, showing me the watery green from unshed tears.

She nodded to indicate she understood and I decided to help her continue.

"Now, tell me the good part." At this she gave me a beaming smile and I knew the old Pip was back.

"Well first off I slipped my noose and turned around and gave the fleshy bastards the one fingered salute. Then I lost my nerve a bit when the mountains started to shake. I'm talking about one scary dude when mad and when I first met him he was always angry and why shouldn't he be? It's not like he had ever been shown any kindness or had any other reason not to be a rage monster...right?" I nodded not wanting to interrupt her flow.

"So he came out of his cave, all hulk like, muscle guns blazing, looking for his fresh snack and what he got was bony little me. He

244

looked so disappointed!" She laughed at what I presumed was the memory of his face.

"I guess it's like going to a famous steak house readying yourself for a big juicy porterhouse and the waiter turning round and telling you they're all out of meat so try this stick of celery instead! At first he just seemed to look at me as if trying to find the meat."

"What did you do?"

"Well I was close to crapping my little girl panties that's what and when he picked me up by a leg then I think I did actually wee wee a bit. But then something weird happened." Out of all the things that could have happened I really didn't expect the next bit.

"What happened?" I asked totally engrossed.

"I giggled."

"What!"

"Yeah I know right, here I am being held like King Kong's got hold of me and I started giggling. But I just couldn't help it, I mean I am really ticklish, just saying the word makes me smile, like now, so I thought well if I'm gonna die then I would do it laughing, so once I started I couldn't stop. But he didn't gobble me up or more like start picking his teeth like I was a handy size tooth pick, no he just looked at me like he was seeing something for the first time, which I now know that he was." She was grinning and it was infectious.

"I bet the meat heads stopped laughing." I loved Karma.

"You bet your didgeridoo they did. For the first time ever he was entertained. He set me back on the ground and waited to see what I would do next. So I started jumping around, making silly noises and singing to him. As time went on I even think I started to make him laugh, which kinda sounds like if a mountain could cough and grunt then that was Abaddon. It even caused landslides."

"I bet." I didn't really know what else to say but I knew one thing, I don't think I was ever going to look at Adam in the same way ever again.

"It eventually got that way where he started looking after me, feeding me, keeping me warm and safe. Once they knew I wasn't going to be eaten anytime soon they made a big mistake and tried to take me off him...that didn't go down too well and his rage ended up causing the 1667 Shamakhi earthquake that killed about 80,000 people. Needless to say they didn't try doing that again in a hurry." I shook my head at her words and just the thought of how Adam seemed to react when Pip was not around, which made me wonder...where was he now?

"But it was cool, we became friends and it soon became clear that he loved me. It took a while for him to get used to having to care for me and he wasn't all too gentle to begin with let me tell ya! One time I was dancing for him and he flicked me to get me to do it again, he ended up flinging me across the space of an air field! Boy, then was I angry, I don't think I talked to him or entertained him for a week, but that was the only way he would learn and after some rock throwing, from my part, he learned to treat me with care."

"I can't even picture it Pip, what was it like?"

"Well it was pretty damn cool when nobody would mess with ya, Lucifer himself even paid me a visit. That was funny. He came over all big and powerful, you know these demanding 'I'm the man, woman so kneel kind of shit heads'. Well he tried that bullshit with me and wanted me to control the beast. I told him straight." Was she serious? Oh yeah, she was serious alright and she was damn proud of herself.

"Good on you."

"Damn straight, down the tunnel and out the other side...of course it didn't really go my way too much. See Lucifer wanted his battle tool and he wanted him controlled, which he now couldn't do without me. Me! A little, nothing Shadow Imp who was used to being the one that was being controlled and I now I found myself holding the key to the supernatural world's greatest threat and strongest Demon. Ha, well that, Honey Bee, was like winning the Demon Lotto, give me those two fat ladies cause I was singing and dancing. Not only was I in love big time, but the big fella loved me back!"

"So Lucifer had to back off?"

"Ah shit no!" Okay I had now lost count of how many times Pip had said shit, crap or the bull variety.

"The sneaky bastard sent me packing." Oh and there was 'bastard' too. Pip could quite easily make a builder blush.

"What do you mean packing?"

"Well, he said sentence revoked so it was ta ta Pipper, so get your ass out of Hell and don't come back." She saw my shock and laughed.

"I know right, talk about sucking on the crapolia pipe, but don't worry too much because the poo hit the propeller then."

"What happened?" I leaned forward needing to hear the end of this story. It was better than any episode of Corrie, Eastenders, Jeremy

Kyle, Judge Judy and even good old Jerry Springer! Okay, so I didn't watch most of those programmes but I knew the drama involved.

"Abaddon missed me and he made it very, very clear. I think Lucifer planned to use me to control him but after I left Abaddon lost all control and started to destroy everything in sight, they couldn't hold him, he just kept growing with his rage and nothing could stop him but me. Lucifer came to me and told me if I didn't find him a host strong enough to hold him then the underworld really would go under."

"Why couldn't they send you back, you know, to be with him?"

"Because Lucifer had already given me my pardon and you can't go back to Hell unless you do the crime and I wouldn't do that again, besides I wanted him out and I knew if I found him the right host, then we could be together without chance of him being used again. That's when I met Lucius." I was surprised when his name came into it and I don't know why every time I heard his name a blush would creep across my skin and find home for a while. Pip gave me an 'I know what you're thinking' kind of look but decided to bite her blue lips instead.

"Right, well you know you're gonna have to carry on with that one." I said after I didn't think she would continue. She bent forwards and looked up to the sky.

"I guess we still have mucho timeo," she said, running one pointed nail down to tap on her chin, I think this time it was a pineapple.

"Any who, Lucius met with me, knowing I needed help finding a host but this time it was going to be different, this time it wasn't just an empty vessel with no soul, naha, this time the host had to be willing to become the beast." My mouth made an 'o' as I took in what she was saying.

"Can that be done? And why? Wouldn't that have killed him or would he have to have died?"

"Whoa, slow down there Kicky Magoo, all will be revealed. Man, I feel like a professor at college 'Supernatural tech'. Okay, so where was I before you boarded train runaway questions....?"

"Ha, ha, come on Pip, I'm dying over here. You were at the point about a human host, soul and all." She snapped her fingers at me and said,

"YES!" as she was still pointing her clicked fingers at me.

"Well, see the thing is, I needed to be with this guy, like every day for the rest of my long, universe type long existence, so I had to like the guy right?"

"Makes sense." I said and she nodded enthusiastically.

"Sure does sister, so I went hunting and hunting of the best kind and with Lucius' help he could make it so that the human host had a better chance at surviving the transition."

"How?"

"He was going to make his human side a Vamp before the Beast took the host."

"Whoa whoa whoa, okay slow down a sec, He was going to turn a human...but I thought he couldn't do that...Draven said..."

"Yeah, yeah Draven said that Vamp's can't turn humans and he is right 'a' roonie but that's only because they can't survive it. However..." She held up her hand palm in my face to stop my next question. Can't say I blamed her, it must have been frustrating having someone keep interrupting and asking questions, but I just couldn't help it.

"...for the host in question, my hubby pie cream cake, would have to die anyway for the beast to accept the host but this way when the beast took hold, his body was stronger as a Vamp or he would have been ripped to shreds in the process. Vamps heal pretty damn quickly and it was touch and go for a while but they merged quite nicely. I think so anyway."

"So Adam is both a Vampire and this beast?" It was too much to even comprehend the power that Adam held.

"He is and being another child of Lucius he is utterly faithful to him, which brings us back to sides and why there was no real choice to make. The Vamp in Adam's human side has his loyalty to Lucius and the beast Abaddon in him has his loyalty to me and only me and considering I hold the kick ass side with my heart, nobody's gonna mess with the little Imp girl! Boo yeah!" She slapped her hand out to mine in a girly high five and we laughed together, all the time my mind was going through its processing cycle.

We were just getting up to leave when another question came to me.

"Wait, but how did Lucius know you needed help?"

"Draven told him to find me." At this, I stopped her with a hand on her tattooed arm when hearing the one name in the world that meant the most to me.

"Draven?"

"Yeah, it was by his order."

"Why though, did he know you?" I asked hoping for a 'yes' and I could then squeeze every last drop of information from her time with him. Was he with anyone at that time?

"Nope!" Well, there went my info but then she carried on and the next thing she told me I could never have thought possible.

"But he was ordered to help Abaddon in finding a host." What, someone could order Draven? I found it hard to believe.

"Ordered, by who...Lucifer?" She laughed at me gently, like I was missing something huge. She patted my hand which was still gripping onto her arm.

"No, not Lucifer but by Asmodeus, King of the 2nd Circle of Lust." Oh, okay, so who was this guy? But before I could ask, she shot me a knowing grin before dropping an Atom bomb.

*"King Asmodeus is... Draven's father!"*

# CHAPTER 21

# THE REBIRTH OF ADAM FITZWILLIAM

We had made our way back to my room and I could have been walking through swarms of fire ants and I wouldn't have noticed the burning on my legs for where my mind was. His Dad? Was it possible? Well of course it was, I mean he had to come from somewhere and he did tell me about him and his siblings being a product of an Angel and Demon naughty get together, so why was I finding it so difficult to comprehend. I think it was probably down to the fact that now I knew of at least one man that had a say in Draven's life and no-one likes to piss off their Daddy!

I burst out laughing at my next thought and Pip eyed me from the side as if I'd finally lost it. I just couldn't help my reaction, I mean I was dating an offspring of the King of Lust! How perfect was that! And no bloody wonder he was such a God in the bedroom and Oh was I such a devoted believer...Amen to that! Of course, the thought of him knowing I had slept in Lucius' arms sobered me up quite quickly. I was just hoping that's all he thought.

Back in my room Pip finally couldn't stand my silence, except for that one burst of crazy laughter.

"Okay Missy Toot, what did I say this time?" She had her hands on her hips and it just made her look even more adorable.

"It's just when you mentioned Draven's father, it took me by surprise that's all and I never did get to hear how you finally met Adam." This was another thing I really wanted to know. It was like the story wasn't yet complete without this last part of the puzzle put in its place.

STEPHANIE HUDSON

"Well now, that I can remedy only in a really cool mumbo jumbo, 'Pipper knows best' kind of way! Come over here Sugar Pants and sit down!" I laughed at her name choice and walked over to the living space in the middle of the room that was more of an apartment in size.

"Righty ho, this might feel a teensy bit weird but considering it's you I'm talking to I can imagine it will be just a walk in a theme park for ya." Okay, now I was sat here with an Imp positioning herself over me, telling me something she is about to do is going to be weird, I wasn't so sure the puzzle needed that last piece.

"Relax Chicarica, everything will be A okay, you'll see and man will you see, and if you don't just love that dress I'm wearing then I might not bring you back...only joking...sheesh you make one little cosmic joke and you tense up like a nun in porno! I do know what I'm doing you know!"

"And what is that exactly, apart from strangling me like we're about to make out?" She laughed and then slapped her hands on either side of my head making me jump.

"My darling Toots, what I'm about to do is so much cooler than making out and it's what I do best."

"Which is?" She leaned in so that her nose was only an inch from mine and said words that caused me to want to panic,

"I'm filling in shadows."

I was just about to start my impression of a buckaroo game when my vision filled with a different world.

Opening your eyes to the fact you have quite obviously just been catapulted into history is both fascinating and disturbing. One minute I was sat in my room with an Imp sat on my lap and the next I am staring at what I can only assume was a 17th century London street. The dark fog gave very little colour to the murky streets and it was startling to see such a contrast of classes. These days you can rarely tell one class of people from the next when on a high street shopping. Of course, it's different if you saw one person going into Gucci and another into Primark, that is an obvious difference but this...well this went from dirty brown wool clothes made from necessity to the finest brocade dresses purely for showing ones wealth.

I looked down and saw myself as I was, but as people passed I knew I was not part of this history or taken in by the eyes that now belonged to the earth on Holy ground. I was nothing here but an observer and what I was there to observe was an older child in an elegant dress walking out into what I presumed was a road for

252

carriages, although there was very little to suggest it other than the runaway carriage heading for the doomed girl.

On instinct I screamed out and went running to the girl's aid but I was beaten there by a gentleman who had launched himself at the girl's middle and tackled her to the ground, saving her life by a second and an inch. I watched the out of control carriage round a corner with the sound of wood splitting and horses in distress. What was left was a man that lay on top of a female form and when I got closer I gasped.

It wasn't an older child but a very small woman and it wasn't just any woman but none other than Pip from a very different time. She looked so unlike the Pip I knew it was like finding a cookie trail in the woods. Each piece painted a picture…her little nose and lips void of metal, her perfect cherry curls that even with today's hair dyes was hard to achieve. All piled neatly on top of her head and half hidden under a delicate little velvet hat. With her hair colouring and those remarkable green eyes, the shade of the deepest forests of the hidden world, she looked unearthly.

For these reasons I wasn't surprised that the man on top of her was stunned motionless. He just stared down at her, captivated by her exquisite beauty before he could even find words and the words he did eventually find were not what I was expecting.

"Turtle Dove," he whispered and Pip beamed up at him before the social expectancy won over the situation.

"Excuse me, Sir?" She said and if I ever doubted it was Pip that lay under the man, then her well known sing song voice cleared up any doubt. The man seemed to shake himself out of his surreal trance and raised himself up to try and regain some decency to the scene that everyone was staring at.

"Madame, please forgive me, are you well?" The man said offering her his hand and when Pip placed a gloved hand in his he helped her rise. It was now that I could see that the man was actually a very different Adam. So this was how they met, he saved her life, or so he thought.

"I am quite well Sir, I assure you, thanks to you of course. I am greatly indebted to you." Adam actually blushed but it remained hidden as he bowed in front of her.

"Not at all my Lady, my happiness lies in knowing you are well and unharmed in this matter but… where is your escort?" He looked round and found no one stepping in to claim Pip and nor would he.

"I am afraid you find me quite alone, Sir. I have lost my way and along with it my escort." Sneaky little Imp. It was at this moment that I had not a shred of doubt that she had orchestrated this whole thing.

"Your husband must not be so lax in his duties, my Lady and I feel, as a gentleman, I must have his name to rectify this matter and inform him at once, for a Lady of your great beauty is not safe alone, least of all on the streets of town." Adam sounded really upset at the idea and Pip...well Pip just looked thrilled and was looking at Adam as if she had waited all her life to find him, which I knew to be true.

"I have no husband, Sir for in which to beseech." On hearing this Adam's head snapped back to Pip and looked down at her with nothing short of hope.

"A Fiancé then?" Adam asked, losing all subtlety.

"Alas no, Sir." Again his hope seemed to soar higher.

"Not even betrothed?" His last question and only one answer away from what was sure to be a marriage proposal, he came across as that eager.

"No Sir!" She said and wait...was that a blush...on Pip?! Adam also took note of her skin and acted stunned at the sight. He even raised his hand but caught himself last minute and held back from touching her. It looked painful.

"In that case, please allow me to escort you home, my Lady." He held out his arm for her to rest her hand upon and the way he said 'my lady' felt thick with untamed possession. Oh yes, there was no doubt that he wanted her.

"May I be so bold as to enquire after your name, My Lady?" I heard him ask and Pip smiled up at him with eyes that were slowly undressing him, I think I heard him gulp from where I stood.

"Certainly Sir, I am Miss Winifred Ambrogetti and you Sir, pray, what would you have me call you?" She said then licked her lips making it impossible for poor Adam to do anything but stare.

"Umm...oh, Yes...forgive me, what was your question?" Pip laughed once, knowing exactly where his thoughts had headed and the little minx sucked on her bottom lip once more causing his breath to stutter. I laughed knowing no one would hear me and I shook my head,

"Poor bastard, you didn't have a chance did you?" I said out loud.

"Your name, Sir?" Pip said after letting her lip go with a pop.

"Ah but of course, how rude of me. I am Mr Adam Fitzwilliam of Westenbury at your service Miss Winifred." They walked off together arm in arm as soul mates reunited and I smiled as I heard Adam saying,

"Ambrogetti? That is the most unusual name."

"It's Greek, Sir and I believe it means 'Immortal'." I didn't see his reaction as they both had their backs to me but if it was anything like mine then he would no doubt be catching flies. Her name meant Immortal in Greek! Couldn't really get more fitting than that!

They just went out of sight and I thought that was the end when I was then plunged into another part of history. All I was missing was the Doc, a Delorean and Marty Mcfly's red body warmer!

This time I was inside a stately town house, that I could be sure of. With its high moulded ceilings and rich furnishing it wasn't a hard guess that whoever owned this house was a very rich man. I was stood in a grand hallway and could make out some people speaking in the room to the right but just before I went in to investigate I heard the voices get louder to indicate someone was coming this way.

"Mrs Fitzwilliam, Mr Fitzwilliam it was a pleasure, but we must now take our leave, good day to you both." Wait was that...no, it couldn't be...Lucius?

"No, no please don't trouble yourselves, we know the way and will let ourselves out. Miss Winifred if you please." There was no mistaking Lucius' deep voice strum though the spacious room and I watched as Pip came through the door followed by Lucius, with Adam in the background looking after Pip like a lost puppy.

Lucius closed the door behind them both and seeing Lucius in his elegant 17th century dress was a jaw dropper. I would have liked to have said it was funny to see a man dressed in a poncey long coat, curly black wig and frilly cravat but on Lucius it even managed to make him handsome and commandingly manly.

His rich burgundy coat hung past his knees along with a waistcoat that was a contrasting gold to the embroidery of his lapels and larger upturned cuffs. The ruffled long sleeves of his white shirt remained seen at his hands and this matched his tied cravat. He even carried a hat with a wide brim, folded at one side with a large black feather attached. He reminded me of a musketeer, especially with a sword hanger worn across one shoulder that, if I remembered my grandfather's history in the weapons he used to collect, was called a baldric. It had been my mother's side of Grandparents that lived in Cornwall, who I had received my love of history from, having a library full of books from the Ancient Pyramids of Egypt to the world's greatest conquerors and looking at Lucius dressed like this, it was easy to see him as one.

His boots tapped across the marble flooring and Pip walked by his side in such a beautiful mint green dress that corseted at the back with elbow-length cuffed sleeves over a chemise with lace flounces at the elbow, opera-length gloves, and pearls on her ears and neck. Her gorgeous red hair was in curls over her temple with longer curls hanging down on her shoulders. She was stunning and the two figures together looked a perfect combination of beauty and wealth.

"I anticipate problems little Imp." Lucius said without looking at Pip.

"My Lord?" She said cocking her head to one side and Lucius stopped and looked back at the closed door. Pip followed his gaze and a smile that went deeper than being merely mischievous spread out on her porcelain perfect face.

"Ah…the mother. She did make it quite clear didn't she and I think the comment she made about sin wasn't directed at just me?" At this Lucius looked down at her and I could see his fangs catch in the candlelight off the candelabra.

"Then she has more sense than I gave the old crone credit for. Take heed of my warning little Demon, she will try and take him from you," he said quietly.

"Have no fear my Lord, if she does, then he is not the man I was searching for." She looked sad even saying it but I understood what she meant. She needed a strong character of heart and mind to be able to take on what Pip had described about Abaddon earlier.

"Agreed but do not forget the power needed that the comet brings. You have until November 14th and that is but a month away." This was the last thing said before the butler appeared with a cloak for Pip and then he opened the door for them both to walk out into the evening.

I waited for this vision to end but it didn't and just left me more confused, what was all that about a comet? I decided since I was still here I would try and get in the room that Adam was still in but how was I supposed to open doors without a body…? Man this whole projection thing was beyond me. In the end I didn't need to as the door swung open with a bit too much force to be done unintentionally.

"Adam, you are not to see Miss Ambrogetti again, do I make myself clear?" A shrewish voice spoke from around the corner, where I couldn't see. It sounded high pitched and old. Lucius was right, she even sounded like an old crone.

"But mother…"

"No buts Adam, it does not become you. The girl does not hold the adequate birth rights and is not of high enough nobility for our family. No, you will marry cousin Mary as your father and I discussed."

"Yes Mother!" Adam said lowering his head in defeat. It looked like Lucius was right, the mother was going to be a problem. I was just about to slip past him and take a look at this mother for myself when the candlelights started to flicker and when I blinked I realised I was yet again at another place in time.

This time it was bright sunshine, so I doubted very much that I would be seeing Lucius at this point. I looked around and saw we were in a park and wasn't surprised to see Pip in full dress with layer upon layer of exquisite material. She was walking towards a man with his eyes focused elsewhere and Pip walked straight into him, knowing full well she would bump directly into her target. Adam's arms shot out and held onto Pip before she could fall back and she placed her hands on his chest as he pulled her nearer. It looked like pure instinct and once he took in the situation he stepped back but his eyes spoke volumes. He wanted her and the torment was as clear as this part of history's cold winter day.

"Miss Winifred, I beg of your forgiveness, I was not looking where I was headed and therefore the fault is mine."

"Mr Fitzwilliam, you are far too hard upon yourself, I fear my mind was elsewhere also and I find it strange that it walked me straight into the path of the root of those thoughts." He looked stunned.

"You were thinking of me, my Lady?"

"Always." She said lowering her eyes and then raising them again causing Adam to gasp.

They stood staring at each other and it was quite obvious that Adam didn't know how to respond in the right manner to Pip's confession.

"Will you take a turn with me, Mr Fitzwilliam?" Adam looked around like he was half expecting his bloody mother to be hiding in the hedged borders.

"It would be my pleasure, Miss Winifred." He offered her his arm and she took it gladly. I felt like the shittiest spy in the world walking beside them on clear day not even trying to hide myself. I think I could have started dancing the funky chicken in front of them without anyone batting an eyelid. The thought made me smile but it didn't fully stop me from feeling like an intruder.

"Do you come to Green Park often and without an escort, I might add?" Adam asked her and she gave him one of her trade mark musical giggles.

"Are you worried about me, Sir?"

"Yes. I think your Uncle should be more careful with your safety." Ah, so Lucius was masquerading as her uncle, well that made sense I guessed.

"Have no fear dear Fitzwilliam, I have a loyal foot servant who keeps watch for me but has the good sense as to when he is really needed."

"Very good then." He seemed relieved and I thought it was sweet how protective he was over her. Oh yeah…he had it bad!

"Did you know it was Charles II, who made the bulk of this land into a Royal Park it is known today, being that of upper St James's Park. He had it designed, laying out the park's main walks and he even had built an icehouse here to supply him with ice for cooling drinks in summer. Have you seen it?" Adam sounded nervous and I think he was rambling on, desperate to keep his eyes from her ample cleavage, thanks to one hell of a corseted dress.

"An ice house? I can imagine given this weather it to be full indeed." He laughed and seemed to relax a little. He was dressed in the same style as Lucius, only with the addition of another coat, styled like a cape with slits for the arms.

"Tell me, do you enjoy the playhouse?" Adam asked her after a thoughtful minute.

"I do Sir."

"Have you yet seen Nathaniel Lee's Theodosius at Dorset Garden?"

"I can't say I have but I would very much like to." He smiled down at her and I saw him cover the small gloved hand on his arm with his own.

"I thought you might, given the origins of the play."

"Given by God." Pip replied thoughtfully, tapping one finger to her lip.

"My lady?" Adam looked confused and they both stopped walking to face each other. I could see Pip's breath in the frosty day as she answered him in cryptic tones.

"Yes, it is quite fitting, don't you think?"

"I am afraid I do not follow my lady." Pip seemed to scan her mind for the start of the conversation and when she found the missing piece her eyes lit up.

"Theodosius, it is Greek and it means 'Given by God', which makes it a perfect play to watch together as our time is given by the Gods is it not?"

"Perfectly put my dear." He lifted a hand up to his mouth and kissed the back without taking his eyes from her for a second. It was so touching to witness the coming together of two souls that, in this case, really were meant for each other.

They started walking again after that but I didn't follow. I didn't need to intrude on their stolen time together anymore. But I had to laugh as the last question I heard from Pip.

"Pray tell me, does Mrs Fitzwilliam like the theatre?"

"No, my mother does not approve and therefore is never seen at the playhouse." Pip next comment made me smile as I started to fade from the park.

"Perfect" she said.

Next, I appeared to be back in Adam's home but this time I seemed to be centre stage to witness the disagreement between Adam and the old crone. Only now Adam seemed to have grown a pair as he wasn't just laying down and saying 'Yes mother', oh no…now he was fighting for his love.

"I will not allow you to speak of Miss Ambrogetti in such a manner!"

"Miss Ambrogetti, what manner of name is that! Adam she is a foreigner for a start but there is something more." I saw a woman rise from the high winged chair that was hiding her form. She had a face like a chewed up mussel. She had wrinkle upon wrinkle and it was amazing that she was still alive given the amount of white paste on her face that I think they classed as make up. Wasn't that crap white lead paint? Well it wasn't working in making her look more youthful that was for sure and with that permanent scowl she reminded me of a pit bull with a clothes hanger wedged in its mouth. I guessed Adam got his good looks from his father.

"Oh, not this again mother!"

"I am telling you my child, that girl has the Devil in her!" Adam threw up his hands in a dramatic fashion and I started choking on a swallow at what she had guessed. Maybe she was a witch, she looked the part that's for sure!

Adam walked over to a decanter of wine and poured himself a hearty glass and chugged it in one, much to his mother's horror.

"This is ridiculous!" He said to himself and filled the glass again.

"Look what she is doing to you? She has already turned you to drink."

"No mother, you have!" He shouted at her and I wanted to start doing cartwheels and cheerleading cheers for him. Okay, a little over the top but Pip would approve.

"I am going to marry Winifred Ambrogetti with or without your blessing."

"No you will not! I forbid it, your alliance would be a disgrace to the Fitzwilliam name!" Adam turned round to face his mother and his usual calm was now replaced with certain rage.

"Then you can keep it! I am in love with her!" He shouted out, arms outstretched at his sides, as if it had just freed his soul and he was rejoicing in its glory.

"Pfft, love means nothing in your duty to your family. This is your heritage Adam and you throw it aside for this folly."

"So my happiness in life is not in question?" He confronted his mother once again and even I wanted to call her a bitch.

"Love is just a word and we, that are of Nobility, rise above the sins of the flesh." Yeah, maybe if you were married to this ugly old trout, I wanted to add in Adam's defence.

"You think Love is to be classed thus as 'sins of the flesh', you say Love is a sin of men, then if that be rightly so you can condemn me with your judgement as you see fit but you will not stop me from marrying Miss Winifred!" He crossed his arms over his chest but his mother just gave him a creepy smile that was right up there with the demon that bit my hands and made me fall.

"If you think I will condone your disgrace you are mistaken, I will see you cut off, penniless and in a poor house before I allow my second heir to marry a Devil's whore!" At this Adam was furious and threw his glass down making his mother jump at the smashing of glass.

"You dare talk about my future wife with such disdain and contempt!"

"I do, and I will! I am ashamed of you and you cannot be at a loss as to know why! She has poisoned your mind with her evil." Adam had quite obviously had enough and turned his back to his mother. She may be as finely dressed as a lady but a lady she was not!

"And with this evil, Mother, what should we do as great nobility?" He asked sarcastically. His mother took a deep breath as if she had reached to him on some level, ignoring the bite of his sarcasm.

"We search deep inside ourselves and we tear that evil out." She said but it was in vain as Adam gave her one last look and made his way to the door. He opened it and stood staring out into the hallway before making his last decision known. He turned slowly and looked at his mother for what seemed like the last time.

"Then tear deeper mother for you will never release me of this feeling you call evil, the very same feeling I call love. You would do better to kill me first for as long as there is breath in my body I will be with Miss Winifred!"

"Death would be better for you if it would rid you of the sinful girl that infects your soul like the plague!" I gasped at the sound of a mother wishing death on her child.

"You're mistaken Mother, death would only rid me of you and this name you find all life is worth living for, but death would not rid me of the love I feel for this girl, who you deem a spawn of Hell, whether it be truth or falsehood, I just simply could not care, for our love knows no bounds and that, my dear Mother, includes you! So I say goodbye Mother, I shall take my leave of you for the last time." And with that beautiful parting speech he left and walked away without looking back, even when the witch starting shouting after him. I closed my eyes at the old woman's rantings about nobility and when her voiced finally died, I knew I was at my last place. I don't know how I knew what was next but it felt like the end of my journey.

Opening my eyes granted me a view of the worst part of London. The smell was so bad I felt myself gagging and I wondered if you could be sick in your projected form?

Human excrement scattered the streets like paper rubbish after a festival and festering in that filth was London's lowest class. The word poor was not low enough to cut it when describing these people. They were dying and they just didn't know it yet because they weren't used to any other conditions. I could imagine the last time some of these people were clean was the day of their birth.

I found the injustice of it too startling for words. There were so many rich people living each day without knowing what hard labour even meant and yet there they sat, feasting fat and happy, while their fellow human beings were starving on the streets or having to sell their bodies just to feed a child, who would no doubt die from drinking dirty water the following year.

I knew that places in the world still suffered like this in my time and I was not naive enough that I didn't know about it, but at least millions of pounds were raised for charities like this every year and in our own streets of London, there was at least places to go for those who deemed it necessary to live on the streets. But this was something else and society today would never have allowed this in their streets. Here, people wallowing in their own filth, littered the streets, not newspapers, sweet wrappers and cigarette butts.

After gagging again watching a man stagger down the mud path to then stumble and throw up what little he had in his belly over himself I hurried away. I had wished that my last part had not ended on such a foul sight. Walking quickly past some building slums I saw three people engaged in the carnal, raw sex that looked more animal instinct than the passionate act it could be. This was sickening.

Finally, I came to a section that opened out near the docks and even at night it was a busy place to be. But at least the air was fresher here and I found myself taking in lungs full of the stuff over and over. It was only now that I could feel my nausea clear and when I heard laughter coming from an open door I turned to see an Inn on the corner where people emerged. I was starting to wonder what this vision was supposed to show me until I heard Pip's voice in the dark streets.

I walked back towards the Inn but it was coming from around the back. I continued further into the alley way and after stepping round a passed out drunk and a young boy picking his pocket I saw Pip.

"NO! Stop it!" I screamed but no one could hear me as I called for help. Pip was being manhandled by three big guys and they were all trying to get a piece of her. She didn't even struggle and she lifted her head as if waiting for something. I looked towards the ally way entrance and when a figure came walking past I spun round when Pip started to cry out for help.

"No! Get off me! Help!" She screamed and I looked back the way I came and saw the figure had run back.

"Winifred?" Adam shouted and when he ran down the alley Pip and the three guys came into view he stopped dead.

"Adam...? Oh Adam, please help me!" She was struggling with the three men and without hesitation he ran to her aid completely outmatched and unarmed. He threw himself into the man nearest and tackled him to the ground. Punch after punch was thrown and soon Adam's face was a mass of red bloody hits. This was no doubt the first fight he had ever been in and my heart went out to him when the two men picked him up and held him by his arms.

"Oh God!" I said seeing his slumped body sagging between the two thugs. The bigger one that had hold of Pip turned and punched Adam in the gut, making him double over onto the floor. All three laughed as Adam coughed up blood. They picked him up again and held him for the bigger guy again.

"So ye thinks of spoiling me bit of fun do ye by taking me whore for thyself?" Adam's head lifted and something in him shifted and his eyes turned cold. He was staring death in the face but he didn't seem to care anymore, the determination in his face said one thing...save the girl or die trying. Adam spat out blood at his face and then pulled one of the men holding him to his face and head butted him causing his nose to explode. The other man stumbled with the weight of being pulled down and all three crashed to the floor.

Adam fisted his hands and with the first taste of rage in his life he hammered away at the other man that had held him, while the one with the broken nose held his face bellowing in pain before passing out. Adam then left punching him and grabbed his head by his hair and smashed it into the ground...once was all it took.

He got to his feet shaking with rage but keeping a tight enough rein on it to assess the situation. The bigger man had pulled out a dirty blade and held it to Pip's throat.

"Let my woman go." Adam said in a calm voice and it sounded like a different person. As though Adam had been replaced by someone who showed no fear and knew he was at death's door, waiting for entrance granted but before he went, he had one thing left to do, he had to save the one he loved. I looked down and saw he was bleeding heavily from his side but he didn't even try to stop the blood, his fists were held tight to his side, waiting to strike. He must have been stabbed in the scuffle and when I looked down at the life he had taken I saw a bloody knife in his hand. I looked back to Adam and knew he was running on pure adrenaline, it was the only explanation to why he was still standing.

"Adam don't...just go while you still can." Pip said, tears streaming down her face and I wondered why she didn't do something? I mean she could take this guy, she was a demon Imp for Christ's sake!

"I'm afraid I can't do that my love." He said without taking his eyes off the man holding Pip.

"Adam please, I want you to live, my life isn't worth you dying over...you don't know who I am." She said quietly, and more tears fell down her beautiful face and onto the blade that threatened to take that life from her.

"I don't care if you were born in the fires of Hell and were made of the damned souls down there, I LOVE YOU!" He shouted making even the big man flinch. Even though Adam was slight and much smaller than the man holding Pip, at this point he was much scarier, emitting raw energy and power as if the beast below could sense his time was near.

"But you will die!" Pip said in such a heart-breaking voice I could feel tears flow down my own face.

"Yes… but today I die a man, a man saving the woman he loves, today…*I die for you.*" He said his voice thick with emotion and looked down seeing his own blood drain from his body and hit the streets made from the mud of the earth. He looked back up, seeing his love one last time before making his move at the thug but he was too late.

"Good, it's about bloody time!" Pip said with happiness flooding her veins. She took hold of the man holding her and snapped his neck as though his bones were made from biscuits. She let him go and he fell to the ground, joining the shit beneath him to rot as a rapist's body deserved. She smoothed her dress down and straightened her little hat that had become askew and stepped over the dead body into a stunned Adam.

"You love me?" She said but Adam couldn't tear his eyes away from the body lying on the floor as if trying to process the last few minutes. Pip touched his face and moved it to one side so that his eyes had nothing to meet but hers.

"You love me?" She asked again.

"Yes!" He answered without pause this time.

"You trust me?" He nodded his head and that's when I noticed another dark figure walking this way. Pip didn't look bothered at the intrusion but kept her focus on Adam's face. She pushed his hair back from his face as he had lost his wig long ago in the fight. His hair was still kept long but now had the addition of drying blood to its lighter shade.

"Yes." He said again, all the time his eyes locked with hers. She carefully wiped the blood away from his lips and placed her own to them in a passionate embrace. It took Adam a moment but he returned her passion in a heated frenzy and I knew I was witnessing their first kiss. They cared little for the carnage at their feet, of the blood they both stood in. It was the most symbolic moment in their lives and I felt privileged to witness it. Fresh new tears ran down my face and when their lips finally parted I swallowed the hard lump as I knew before Adam what was surely about to happen.

Pip cupped his face with both hands and pulled his face down to her level.

"And do you love me enough to die for me?" Adam took a staggered breath and then with silence in the streets and a lifetime hanging in the air, everything stopped…the world froze in place for a few seconds as if this one moment would change history, not just for two people but for the fate of the world…

Adam looked up just as the night sky was lit up by a mighty comet dancing across the vast dark space. Pip followed his gaze and then heard him answer.

"Yes, I would die for you." As soon as the words left his mouth the dark figure behind closed the distance of the alley way in less than a second and grabbed him by the throat to then plunge deadly fangs into his taut neck. He didn't even try to fight as Lucius sucked the last shred of life that had been hanging on to him. Pip remained looking up at the comet and without turning to look at her love being sucked dry she said,

"The time is now Abaddon, the time is now to take your place in the world and be with us…to be with me." I looked up to see the comet had gotten brighter still and the tail looked as though made from the stars of others joining it, making it longer and longer. It was one of the most incredible things I had ever witnessed.

"Now, Lucius!" Pip said placing her hand on Adam's chest as if sensing his fading heartbeat. Lucius pulled his fangs away but kept Adam held up with one arm wrapped around his middle. Adam's face was slumped forward and he already looked so lifeless. Pip pulled up one of Lucius' coat sleeves and he placed his jaw around his wrist and tore into himself with a ferocious growl of half man, half beast. He bit straight through the sleeve of his laced white shirt and the blood soaked the material in seconds. Pip ripped the material away and placed Lucius' wrist first to Adam's wound and let the blood mix. Pip then let Lucius move it away when she had gathered some up in her palm and both at the same time, with the gathered blood she placed it over the stabbed area and let Lucius place his bleeding wrist to Adam's mouth.

"Drink child and become one of us, drink for the woman you

love." Lucius said with such passion it made it beautiful instead of horrifying.

Adam started to drink and Pip encouraged him, cooing soothing words in a foreign tongue.

When the first signs of death came to Adam I gasped out, not understanding what was going on. Why did he have to die and why here in the filth of the city?

"It's time Imp, he will not be powerful enough to contain the beast if you do not help him, reach into his mind and hold the beast steady until his wounds heal. If you let him loose then we all die, along with all of London." Lucius didn't even sound worried as he spoke of such destruction as if he was reading the bloody newspaper!

"He will listen to me have no fear about that, my Lord." They had laid Adam down as Pip straddled his torso and held her hands to his forehead. She leaned down and whispered words of love to Adam before closing her eyes to concentrate.

"He comes now." She said speaking through a demonic version of herself. I saw her twitch and then she shot a look at Lucius.

"You might want to hold him my Lord, this is not going to be pretty." Lucius knelt down and held him down by placing his knees on Adam's shoulders. Pip then locked her legs over Adam's thighs and they both braced themselves.

"Abaddon, follow my voice, I'm here waiting for you. Lucifer will show you the way, follow the bright sky up. Come on big brute," she said lovingly.

"That's it, you've found me, you found me at last." She said again and then Adam's piercing screams of agony ripped through the night like one of Hell's demons was tearing him apart. He thrashed around like a fish that was trying to avoid being stepped on. Lucius even looked like he was struggling to hold him as his body became a mass of muscle to try and add to the strength needed. His clothes ripped at the sides and on his arms where pale strong skin could be seen but it still didn't seem enough to hold Adam.

Then I watched on in horror as Adam's skin started to split as if something was trying to tear its way out of him. Adam screamed over and over and I almost prayed for death to take him just to release him from the excruciating pain being inflicted.

"No, listen to me Abaddon, this is you new host, take him, take care of him and we can be together. NO! Take care of him!" Pip shouted at his forehead as though communicating with the beast inside.

"LISTEN TO ME!" She screamed when another great slash appeared across Adam's torso seeping out in a line of crimson in the white linen shirt.

"I love you both and now you are to become one, take care of my love for me and you will get my love in return," she said more softly this time. After a minute Adam's body started to calm from thrashing in the mud and both Lucius and Pip were soon showing signs of the battle nearly lost. Mud splattered each of their faces and blood ran in little rivulets away from Adam's body.

"Wake up to your new life my love, wake up to your new birth." Pip said, her lips against his forehead before moving down to kiss him on the lips. At the first touch of her lips to his he gulped in his first breath and sat up knocking Lucius to the ground as though his strength had been nothing. He grabbed Pip before she fell backwards and it was a motion so fast it was nearly lost to the eye.

"Turtle Dove?" He asked, voice raw and used from screaming.

"Yes Adam, I am here...I will always be here." She said her voice thick with emotion.

"I feel...different...stronger, by the Gods I feel strong! I feel...like something is there...something great is waiting inside of me." He sounded both in awe and scared shitless.

"I know... I know you do but you have to control it. You are the beast now, you have both become one with each other and it is under your command...you have to listen to me Adam...you have to be strong enough to contain it, he is keeping you safe but you have to do the same for him."

"I know... I can feel him there. He's...he's talking to me, can you hear him?" Pip looked up at him through thick eyelashes and for a minute she looked fearful.

"No, I can't hear him anymore, but you can and now you must command him to stay there until you are ready."

"Ready for what?" Pip looked away as if ready for a backlash of betrayal for what she had done. He gripped her chin and turned her face to his.

"Winifred, you must tell me," he said so softly it broke my heart to hear so much love coating those words.

"Ready for the beast to arise," she murmured as tears released down her cheeks taking the dirt away with it, leaving lines of white down her skin.

"Then we have much to do to ready ourselves, for I find myself looking forward to the day." At this Pip looked at him with the spark flaming back in the green depths of her eyes. He grabbed her by the neck roughly and pulled her lips to his for the deepest kiss I had ever seen two people exchange. I thought if Lucius hadn't cleared his throat then they would have done it there and then in the mud and amongst the evidence of Adam's death and re-birth.

Adam laughed heartily and got up still holding onto Pip. He looked towards Lucius and bowed his head to show his deepest respect.

"You are my father!" Adam stated and Lucius nodded once.

"Then you will lay witness to our marriage and make my world complete. I want this day to mark the beginning in all ways." Pip jumped up excitedly and Adam caught her in his arms and I watched on as all three walked away from this disgusting alleyway which had given birth to the most powerful being on earth.

*Adam the Abaddon, beast number 616.*

# CHAPTER 22

# AN UNEXPECTED DEMON

"Open up sleeping beauty." Pip's voice penetrated the fog of visions that had played out like a historical movie on fast forward. I opened my eyes to find Pip smiling down at me and wiping the tears from my cheeks.

"Were you crying for me, Toots?" She asked with a mixture of being touched and amused.

"Maybe," I said after clearing my throat.

"Aww shucks Toots, aren't you a sweetie?" She winked at me as she removed herself from my lap.

"That was…"

"Sublime?"

"Intense." I corrected trying to get up but I wobbled before falling back in my chair.

"I would stay put if I were you Champ, I showed you a lot and used a lot of juice…man I'm whipped." Pip slumped down in the chair opposite dramatically.

"You mean wiped?"

"Ahh, potato, tomato, onion either one really." She said and now she mentioned it she did look a little worn out.

"I can't believe that's how you met…it was incredible, you know… to witness it as if I was really there."

"I'm glad you enjoyed, I know I did." She winked and I laughed at her cheeky ways.

"So you found Adam and orchestrated the whole thing?" I asked her but she wasn't the one to reply.

"She certainly did and played me like a fiddle, didn't you my little Turtle Dove?" Adam's easy voice came from behind me and I nearly jumped a mile.

"You're back!" She said and jumped up, obviously not as out of energy as I had thought. I watched as she threw herself into his arms and the way he caught her took me back to the alleyway.

"That I am love and I see you have been telling tales of woe and heartache."

"Yeah, but it has a happy ending so shut up and kiss me!" She demanded and I looked away to give them their moment.

"What did you bring me back, Brutus?" He laughed and I turned round to see him flick her nose before letting her slide down his body.

"Greedy little Imp," he complained half-heartedly and then produced a gift bag from behind his back. Her eyes got wider and then she started tearing into the bag.

"Foam love hearts and jelly rings, I love these! Oh, you're good Adam baby but aren't you missing something?" He smiled at her and then started to back away with his palms up in surrender as she slowly stalked towards him.

"Demanding Squeak, well fine then have your own way, they're in our room waiting for something of mine to fill them, so I suggest you get a head start little heart of mine...ready, set...run!" At this Pip jumped up with delight and ran from the room in excitement. I didn't even want to ask what was waiting for her but when I realised I was left in the room with the most powerful creature to walk the earth, then that sobered my thoughts.

"I wanted to thank you." He spoke the last words I thought I would ever had heard from Adam. I mean for starters what would he ever need to thank me for?

"You make Pip happy and there is nothing on this planet that means more to me than that sentiment." He said as if hearing my thoughts and I found a lump form in my throat.

"I love Pip!" Was all I managed to say but the reaction of his smile made me smile too.

"Good answer. Then we have something in common. Pip must love you back to show you something so precious to us both but don't be perplexed Keira, I trust my girl with not only this life but also my first. My past is hers to do with as she pleases."

"You really don't mind what she showed me?" I asked feeling

vulnerable. As if I didn't receive his blessing regardless of what Pip thought, I would still feel bad.

"On the contrary, I am happy she did. It means she loves another and therefore so do I. You will always have my protection Keira, whether you require it or not." He nodded his head in respect and walked to the door ready to leave but I needed to tell him one more thing.

"Adam."

"Yes Keira."

"You said the right thing to your mother. It was wrong of her to think death would be better for you."

"No Keira, she was right, death was a better choice for me...just not in the way she thought. Before Winifred, I lived only ready to die but after...well... I finally died ready to live." He winked at me and then disappeared down the hallway to entertain his wonderful wife.

I spent the rest of the day just lounging around, pretty bored with only my many thoughts to keep me occupied. My mind was a whirlwind of information. I had learnt so much today that it was hard to keep it to just one thought at a time. Talking with Pip had offered me more insight to Draven's world than he ever allowed me to see. I knew why Draven thought it best to keep things from me the way he did, but in doing so it kept me in the dark from the things that I really needed to know. Sometimes being kept within the safety net of my own world didn't do me any favours when, like now against my will, I had been put in a situation where knowing more about my enemies would have come in damn useful! But even that was becoming clouded and confusing. Take Pip and Adam for example, did I really see them as my enemies...no way. For starters I couldn't deny that I loved that crazy little Imp and my tears in seeing her past had been for a friend. And Adam, well he had just confirmed that I had his protection always, so that surely classed him as an ally.

When I thought about it even Ruto had saved my life and Liessa had been nothing but nice to me. This would have been so much easier if my captors had all lived up to the Demon reputation but of course since meeting Draven that meant I now knew that being a Demon didn't necessarily mean you were evil or 'bad to the bone' as Pip would put it.

And then there was Lucius, the main protagonist in this picture. Well so far, apart from being a dominant SOB he hadn't hurt me in any way and seemed to be growing on me the longer I was here. Don't get me wrong, I still hated that he was the reason I wasn't with Draven and I still hadn't forgiven him for enduring the worst pain of my life thanks to his inflicting dreams. But even then, I had tried to burn him into a crispy critter. Man, this was so confusing! Why couldn't I just hate these people and get on with it!

I decided to take a relaxing bath and try and get my brain to slow down on the bitter thoughts. I just wanted to go home and I had to remember that these people were still holding me prisoner, no matter how friendly they all were. I just had to keep reminding myself of this fact.

Once in the hot bath with the scent of jasmine oil and bubbles made from honey and vanilla bath cream, I let my mind go and relaxed my tense shoulders. I closed my eyes and dunked my head back letting the soft water cover me from head to toe. When I pulled back up I took in a deep breath and felt so much better. This was what I had needed, to relax, to unwind and chill out. To have the tension massaged out of my shoulders by big, strong hands...wait, what!

I shot up but those strong hands kept me down with a slight pressure.

"What...? How?" It didn't make much sense but all I received was an assured,

"Ssshh, relax." Lips said at my ear and the last thing I wanted to do was relax with Lucius sat behind me while I was lay naked in this bath.

"Get off me!" I said sternly but he just laughed.

"So tense Keira, I thought mortal girls liked to be pampered by men." He teased me before leaning down to leisurely lick some bubbles off my bare shoulder. Thankfully the bubbles hid my modesty but didn't stop his wandering hands.

"If you go any further down I will take a line from your book and bite you!" I said as threatening as I could manage with the feeling his hands created. I was outraged but I was also still a woman with a handsome man touching me. He just chuckled at my threat but my warning must have worked on some level because he kept his hands on my shoulders.

"As you say pet, but at least let me help get some of the tension from your body."

"Please don't!" I whispered but as he moved his hands in circles I couldn't take back the moan that escaped. Damn him!

"That didn't sound very convincing." He said thick with humour, the smug bastard!

"Did you have a nice day with my loyal little Imp?" With the combination of his comfortingly smooth voice and his expert fingers, I was soon finding my muscles couldn't keep up the pretence that what he was doing wasn't working.

"You're asking about my day?" I said answering his question with a question.

"And why not or is it because you're trying desperately to go back to hating me." My body gave me away that he had guessed spot on.

"Ah, so I am right." Once again, I confirmed this by my body going ridged under his hands.

"I don't understand why you would be nice to me, I am still a prisoner right?" At least ten percent of me thought he might say no, I wasn't. Of course, a hundred percent of me wanted him to say it, however it still didn't make it so.

"No, my little Keira girl, you are not free to go, however I see no reason not to make your stay here...an enjoyable one." He said this last bit with his lips touching against my ear like a lover's whisper. I shivered and he laughed again. He then gave my shoulders a quick squeeze and I felt him heave himself up.

"I think my job here is done. I came to tell you to come down to the Great Hall later this evening, as there is someone that you know with something to show us." I was looking up at him and I must have been frowning because he gently tried to smooth the line it caused with his thumb. He then ran the back of his hand down my cheek and left before saying another word.

All the air left me in a whoosh and I let myself slide down under the bubbles to submerge my whole body in water to try and drown some sense into it. I wish I didn't react to his touch! It was like my body was battling with my thoughts. In my mind I was clear as I was in my heart, I wanted Draven and only him but my body...well that was a betraying little hussy that needed to be stopped!

Feeling intrigued as to who could be here I felt almost giddy. Could it be Draven? Could it be time for me to finally leave this place, man I really hoped so! I counted back and realised I had been here for six days and Draven only had four left to come for me...But how? I know Draven said he had a plan but really, I didn't see how he would get me back if he didn't bring this spear to Lucius and from the

273

urgency in Vincent's voice that time, I knew he couldn't ever just hand it over. So what was his plan?

These were the questions that plagued me for the entire time it took me to get ready. This time I didn't have any problems getting dressed as I just didn't really care about what I was wearing. It had no relevance to my situation, so I just grabbed a dress and put it on.

It was another black lace dress but this time it had a soft under layer that didn't show all my skin through the pattern. I had shaved my legs in the bath along with other area's that needed attention and the result was the heavenly feel of material against my smooth skin, I just loved that feeling and even the lace felt soft.

The rest of the dress was full length, falling to the floor and trailing slightly behind me in a train. It flared out with more layers of fabric around the knee and the under dress only hid my torso and the top of my thighs. Around the waist it had a wide taffeta burgundy sash that tied at the side and hung low at the hip. The sleeves came past my hands and draped down in a large V shape but at the wrist had woven ribbon to match the sash that tied into a pretty bow.

Even the neck came up to collarbone, hiding what the red satin balcony bra did to my cleavage. There wasn't one plain set of underwear in any of the drawers... no it just looked as if Pip had just robbed an Ann Summers' store! Well at least not all the knickers were thongs, I thought rolling my eyes as I grabbed the matching pair of hipster briefs with red satin frilled edging.

I knotted my hair into a loose bun at the side and tied it with some matching ribbon I found on the hanger to the dress. I looked in the mirror and thought it all looked quite Spanish in style. All I needed now was a matador to escort me down to the Great Hall and I would be set to fight one big headed bull called Lucius.

However, Pip would have to do and she was definitely not dressed like a matador! She bounced in wearing a dark brown leather jacket with a high folder collar that went half way up her head. The bottom part of the jacket was made with four split panels, the longest being at the back in a straight rectangle. The side ones were thinner and curved back but the front was slashed across so one full leg could be seen where the other was hidden.

The chunky metal clasps that held it closed followed the slash up the body diagonally, finishing at the shoulder and a belt made in the same scroll pattern as the clasps hung low on her little hips. The sleeves continued the style and flared out at the wrists but the split that went up to her elbow was also held closed thanks to smaller clasps. And this was all she wore, this and a pair of tights that had a bear's footprints leading up her leg with the words 'follow me' on the side. I couldn't help but grin.

"You like my jacket!" It wasn't a question but more of a statement.

"I do, it's very gladiator meets Pip, not sure it goes with the shoes though." She held out her foot to the side and showed off her unique high heels that were covered in lolly pops and had a foamed cupcake on top of her toes with baby blue frosting and yellow stars. The stiletto heel was even made to look like the stick from the candyfloss backs that created a pink fluffy cloud of sugar up her ankle. They looked so yummy that I was close to dropping on all fours and licking her feet for a sugar rush.

"Oh these, don't you just love them? If you move the candy floss you can see they tie with strawberry laces." She said proudly.

"I bet they're hard to tie." I said putting on my own black heels and grabbing a pair of gloves that had replaced the ruined ones, thanks to some demonic mud.

"Yeah, especially when you have a husband trying to nip at your feet the whole time." She said shaking her head.

I laughed at the picture she created as we made our way out of the room.

"So, do you have any idea who is here to see me?" She looked puzzled by my question.

"Lucius didn't tell you?" I asked thinking it was odd.

"Nope, but I was a little busy this afternoon." She giggled at her memory and I really hoped she wasn't going to share, as knowing Pip it was bound to be something sexual and utterly shocking and it was hard enough seeing Lucius but having sex on the brain while doing so was not a good idea.

"But wait…" I just thought of something important, making her stop before we got to the balcony.

"How was it that Adam was up in the daylight, I thought he was a Vampire?"

"Oh that, he not's like your conventional Vamp. He doesn't like direct sunlight much but it wouldn't harm him like the others. Thanks to Abaddon he doesn't have any weaknesses like that…well except maybe one, teeny tiny one."

"Which is?" I prompted.

"Me."

"You?" She nodded and then carried on walking.

"Hang on, what do you mean, you?"

"Well he can't be without me for very long or the beast gets worried and you don't want to make Abaddon worry. He's a little touchy since the last time I was taken away from him. It's the only time Adam can't contain the beast and he takes over…Adam's very good at containing his rage but I am afraid this little wifey is his only weakness…do you like dancing, there will be dancing tonight and Lucius is a great dancer, have you done salsa before or the waltz or even Zumba, I do that on the Xbox but man what a workout!" Finally, she took a breath! I think if she hadn't been a supernatural being she would have passed out now from lack of oxygen!

"No to all dance related questions. So are you not worried when you're away from him, like today?"

"Nah, he can feel me, we're connected you see. I mean he gets a little grumpy if I'm not with him for too long but it's more like if someone hurt me or took me…man then the shit would really hit the washing machine!" I even shuddered at the thought and I hadn't even seen his beast side yet and needless to say I wasn't ever hoping too.

"Washing machine?"

"Yeah, that would be disastrous, you like to wash your clothes in a machine that's been covered in shit…nope, me neither?" She shuddered making me smile.

We walked down the steps and the Great Hall looked a little different than the last time I saw it. The various sections and seating areas had been moved to the edges creating a large space for people to dance in the centre and where Lucius' people usually wore different style of Goth and fetish wear, not tonight they didn't. It looked like I had just walked into a science fiction convention with a Victorian twist.

"Pip, what is all this?" I turned to her and looking at her jacket style I realised that she fitted in with the rest, well, apart from the shoes that was.

"This, my darling, is Steampunk at its best. We make a night of it every year. Have you never seen it before?" Pip looked almost giddy and I could see why as we made our way through the weird and wonderful. The whole room had been transformed into 19th century London revolution meets wild west saloon. The layers and layers of material that once covered the walls now found their place in piles on the floor and the strong stone walls had been decorated with hundreds of cogs, wheels, gears, propellers and various engine parts.

Another wall held empty ornate picture frames with springs and pistons in between. The one opposite had old posters advertising the steam engine and old maps in a random fashion, all of which were covered in giant clockwork pieces in different styles, shapes and metals. Large iron potbellied braziers sat together in different sizes with tall chimneys that were rather pretty twisted iron work at the top or very rustic spikes that reminded me of a crude king's crown.

Nearly everyone wore leather of some description but this was mixed with gowns, corsets, and petticoats for the women. The men mixed their leather with suits complete with waistcoats, long jackets, top hats or military style garments. This wouldn't have been too shocking but it was their accessories that I found the strangest factor. It was like a fantasy film set had been raided. There were men with old brass telescopes being used to look up female skirts that had so many layers they danced around their body in ruffles. Women who held oil lamps on curled sticks higher than themselves and most people either wore a metal gas mask or old explorer goggles. One guy we passed looked like a Steampunk version of President Lincoln, with the wild beard and tallest top hat I had ever seen.

"Come on Tooty Bean, you can openly gawk at everyone when we get to Lucius." I hurried to catch up and before I could tell her that I wasn't gawking at people, which was a lie, I saw Lucius.

My breath caught on a gasp at just the sight of him. He looked painfully handsome in his black tailored Victorian suit encasing strong, long legs that lounged out causally in front of him, with high polished army boots crossed over each other on the low table. His long tailored jacket fit his wide shoulders like a glove and he left this unbuttoned to show his tight fitted striped waistcoat underneath. He also wore a tight knotted black tie that he wore over his white shirt collar. This look was all finished with a black top hat that had a pair of copper goggles resting on the rim and a pair of black leather gloves that still managed to show the strength of his hands under the thick material. His face looked etched from steel and cool demanding eyes saw me through dark blue tinted round glasses that reminded me of Gary Oldman in the movie Bram Stoker's Dracula.

My mouth actually dropped open.

"He's a handsome man isn't he?" I heard the question asked in my ear by a voice that sent an acute level of fear down my spine and one that was very much warranted, considering our past encounter.

"Did you miss me...?" The voice got closer still and when I tried to move forward, hands with nails like talons dug into the lace, close to ripping it. Lips came at my ear from behind and called me the name that brought a flood of memories back...

Back to a night I almost died.

*"Parasite".*

# CHAPTER 23
# MURDERER IN THE ROOM

N ails dug into me and this time there was no Draven standing in the side lines ready to rescue me.

"Layla!" The name came from me like trying to talk after swallowing thick black oil.

"If you say anything to Lucius about what happened then I will gut you, do you understand me, Vermin? If you utter one word then I know where you sleep and the next time…" She leaned in closer and for a second I thought she was going to bite off my ear.

"…I will get you in the heart!" She said so fiercely that I could feel the spit like venom hit my neck from her words. I yanked out of her hold and turned to face her with white hot rage burning my veins but when taking in her appearance it was hard not to give way to fear. She was taller than me so it didn't help that I had to look up at her. She had dressed in the same style as everyone else, looking far too feminine for the murdering bitch she was. Wearing a short leather bolero with a high neck, little puffy sleeves and fastened with two leather straps that went across the collarbone. To this she added a white laced corset with a frilly top that was gathered together with a pictured brooch of a Victorian woman's silhouette.

On her lower half was a saloon girl style skirt that was short at the front and gathered at the back where it bunched up and flared out to the floor. The skirt showed the top of her tights and very close to showing something more indecent, however most of her legs were covered with her over the knee boots that must have added five inches to her height. But these were small inconsequential factors compared to the horror painted on her evil face. She grinned at me and it made it worse as the patterned skull painted there made it seem like her lips were splitting.

I remember seeing the style in a festival in Spain once. It was the Day of the Dead and stalls were selling painted clay skulls in bright colours. Some had flowers and multi-coloured swirls around the eyes, others had brightly painted teeth and different shapes on top of the skull. These had all been pretty but what stood in front of me was not. It was an ugly face of evil painted up in white with black flowers covering the entirety of both eyes and a black Ace of Spades symbol painted on her nose. Blood red thorns curved round her high cheek bones and a yellowed claw crawled down her forehead. Her lips were decorated as if they had been sewn shut with metallic paint and the memory of Sammael's lips came horrifyingly to mind. She looked sickening.

"Go on, run... I dare you!" She said showing her teeth and giving way to her murderous thoughts. Every fibre in my body was screaming at me to do just that. As if the most basic level of evolution was telling me I was in danger from a predator and I needed to find safer ground. I didn't want to give her the satisfaction but it was hard battling with my pride and my need for survival.

In the end the choice was taken from me.

"My Keira girl, come to me!" Lucius' voice broke through the hate clogging the air and my attention went back to the handsome man waiting for me, but not before I noticed the slight flinch of Layla. Well, wasn't that interesting?

I walked over to Lucius and just as I was about to sit down next to Pip, Lucius made a 'tsk' sound and I looked up to see him motion me with two fingers encased in leather. What was it about a man that wore black leather gloves, apart from screaming 'violent crime' there was also something sexual about it, dominating and powerful.

I walked over to him and he moved his legs from resting on the low table. He then pointed in between his legs after giving me space to sit where he wanted me. I think I actually groaned in response, making him laugh.

"Please don't do this again," I whispered looking at him through his glasses that rested on his nose without the aid of arms attached to the frame. He gave me a bad boy grin and motioned for the band to start back up with a regal wave of his hand.

"Sit down my pet." He said in a way that brooked no argument. I sighed, giving in and sitting down in between his legs as I had done the night before. And like the night before his arm snaked around my waist and pulled me closer to him in a secure hold but unlike the rest of the nights here, one pair of eyes watched us through a thick veil of hatred.

"Layla my child, welcome home." At this I stiffened in Lucius' hold and I knew he noticed because his hands started making comforting circles at my side, thankfully though he didn't draw attention to it.

Layla lowered her head in submission and then raised her eyes to his and said,

"My Master, it is good to be back." Every word from her mouth actually felt like someone had taken a cheese grater to my spine.

"I believe you became acquainted with Layla at Afterlife Keira, is it not good seeing a friendly face?" Lucius asked as though he was playing a game of guess the emotion. This time I tried not to react but it was difficult being so close to him and knowing he could feel every slight move I made.

"We didn't really speak." I said not doing a great job of acting through my disgust.

"Really? This surprises me as Layla spoke of you both becoming good friends." Now this shocked me. It felt like I was definitely missing something here.

"Oh I am sure Keira is just guarding her shock at seeing her good friend here my Lord, we were thick as thieves together in Dominic Draven's club." At this Lucius was the one to tense his body.

"You will NOT disrespect your King again! I have told you before and I tire of repeating your offense. You have no right to call him as such, he is your King and you will remember your place!" I couldn't help my mouth from dropping open in shock. Lucius wanted Layla to show respect to Draven by calling him King? I couldn't understand it?

"Yes my Lord, forgive me but I would have thought that after taking your place as our…"

"Enough! You WILL know your place Lahash! Now kneel for your forgiveness!" He ordered and I could say for once I was happy Lucius was being a bossy bastard.

She got to her knees and crawled closer to us both but as I flinched back Lucius felt my reaction and stopped her with one foot at her shoulder.

"Please Master, forgive me, I am your servant and have but missed you deeply." I looked up to Lucius and saw him frowning. I don't know why but my hand went to his hand at my side and started making my own soothing circles on his hand. He looked down at me and gave me a slight smile for the kind gesture. I blushed and looked away, but my eyes found the lethal look from Layla staring at our not so secret exchange. I then looked directly to my left as I heard a growl coming from Pip. It looked as if I wasn't the only one was getting the 'I want to rip your head off' vibe from Layla. Of course, by the time Lucius looked back her way she was smiling at me sweetly.

"You're forgiven, take back your seat, Layla." She lowered her head and did as she was told, and I heard Pip snigger.

I felt a hand cup the back of my neck and Lucius' lips found my ear.

"What would you like to drink, pet?" I noticed anytime Lucius touched me Layla's eyes would bore into us both and I wondered where her hatred grew from. I put down her attack on me to be from jealously at being with Draven, so what was she seeing now? Was I reminding her of when I was with Draven, when I was sat here like this? I used to remember her working at the Afterlife before she tried to kill me. I would catch her staring at Draven like some lost puppy looking for her Master to come back and claim her. I never asked but some part of me knew she had been with Draven on a sexual level. She made it so obvious whenever serving him at the top table, doing everything but throw herself at his feet naked begging for him to take her. I don't think she ever realised anyone was even watching her, so when she attacked me I knew the reasons.

I felt the hand at my neck tighten slightly to bring me back from my thoughts.

"Wine, please." I said and was soon passed a black glass goblet with little Clockwork pieces that made up the base and stem. I was glad it wasn't red wine when I tasted it as I had always found it too heavy a drink. Lucius laughed when he saw me gulping back.

"Needed that did you?" He said with his usual teasing.

"It might have something to do with the company," I said dryly.

"And I understand you're not speaking about the Vampire at your back are you?" He whispered so only I could hear. It wasn't hard to figure that out the way every time she spoke I would cringe. I just shrugged my shoulders not wanting to play with my life any more than I already was. I could see her eyes always on us and here in the arms of Lucius I felt absurdly safe but when I was back in my room, alone in the night knowing Layla lay in waiting to finish the job, then I felt far from safe.

"Come, I know of a way to make you relax, come and dance with me." He said taking my drink after removing his glasses to put in his top pocket and then standing behind me. He pulled me up with him and I twisted in his arms to face him.

"You don't know me very well if you think dancing will help me relax." I whispered in desperate tones. Swaying to music in the middle of a busy club was one thing but actually dancing real steps with a partner was quite another.

One side of his perfect lips curled up and he took my hand in his.

"I can imagine you to be a graceful swan on the floor if only you had the right leader." I frowned at the double meaning and had no choice than to let him 'lead' me to the dance floor.

"Danse Macabre!" Lucius shouted and the crowd lowered to the floor in a gracious bow to their Master. My already flushed cheeks burned scarlet at being the focus of so many people and now I was expected to dance in front of them! Oh No…this was bad, very, very bad!

I looked to the stage and saw the main singer holding his elaborate pipe smoking as he stepped up to the mic that was crawling in tiny motorised insects and he casually flicked one from the top which smashed onto the floor in a scatter of tiny cogs, nuts and bolts. He was wearing a pair of black and dark red striped leather trousers with a long tailed waistcoat in cherry red to match. His under shirt was beige and one arm was completely mechanical. It made him look like half robot and every time he moved it steam would whistle from a tube connected to a few pipes.

The other band members consisted of a pretty blonde playing a huge metal piano, a man dressed all in military gear, with exaggerated shiny guns hanging from his hip playing the base. There was also a man that reminded me of Captain Jack Sparrow with long black hair, beard to match and an exposed tattooed sleeve on lead guitar. The other man was holding a cog encrusted violin at the ready, whose face was completely covered in a gold metal mask that looked to help him breathe in clean air only the goggles for his eyes glowed a burning orange. The last member of the band was a stunning girl with plum coloured locks of barrel curls that were secured up under a plume of feathers and she was dressed as a saloon working girl with a leather pirate twist. She walked to the lead singer and took his pipe from him before handing him his red accordion with metal ends that matched his robotic arm.

As the violin started Lucius grabbed one hand and placed another low to my back.

"Place your other hand to my arm, Keira girl." I did as I was told and Lucius smirked down at me when he saw me gulp at the feel of solid bicep beneath my hand.

"Just let me lead you and I promise not to do so astray." He winked at me and then the music started from the plucking Violin intro and then after the dark sound being orchestrated it started and unfortunately with that, so did the dance. He nodded his head low to me and began to move me in step with the music.

With his arms securing the way my body moved it was hard to do anything but move in the direction he wanted me. Even my feet seemed to glide effortlessly across the floor in perfect sync with his steps. His grip was strong and assuring as we spun around and when he let go of my back I found myself spinning out to the crowd with my hand still in his and before I could utter a protest I was being reeled back into his arms. It felt both terrifying and exhilarating at the same time. It made me feel like I could actually dance and even though I knew deep down it was all thanks to Lucius, I still couldn't help feeling the thrill from it.

We came to a slower part and suddenly Lucius' hand travelled lower to an indecent area and pulled me forcefully into his body. My breath hitched as his head lowered to mine and I now realised we had stopped moving and were no longer the only ones on the dance floor. We were surrounded with couples all doing the same steps like birds in formation, all knowing each other's moves and spins.

There was only us two that had stopped in the centre of a wall of flesh and Lucius' eyes looked at me with such a fever, the colour in them turned from steel grey to hot amber burning like the sun. I knew if I continued to look I would get burned but I couldn't help being captured in such a gaze. I had to look. I had to see the man inside like no other had done. And he let me. He opened up and I gazed into a man's soul that had been scorned by faith.

"You should not look at me like that, Keira." His face changed and his eyes became eclipsed by the moon, but the fire could be seen around the edges. His soul wasn't left in the dark yet.

"Like what?"

"Like you would look upon a man." He said when his hand came up to touch my face. The leather was soft against my lips and I couldn't stop my reaction to his touch. My tongue crept out and wet my lips causing Lucius to groan.

"Do that again and it will be the end of my control!" He said tightening his hold on me as if anchoring me to his body would stop me from disappearing. I lowered my eyes to his chest for a moment to take control of my stuttering heart.

"Do you like this music?" He asked as he started moving us both to an easy sway.

"It is different," I answered honestly, considering it was the first time I had heard a rock version of a classical piece.

"It is called 'Dansa de la Mort' in Catalan or as it is more well known as 'Danse Macabre' in French meaning 'Dance of Death'. Of course there have been many variations of this piece but I believe this to be my preferred choice. Steampunk is quite unique and this band is one of Pip's favourites." I could be wrong but it sounded a bit like Lucius was trying to make conversation and in doing so getting his lust under control, I decided it best to help him.

"Dance of Death, that sounds happy." I said sarcastically making him laugh and at once the tension left his tall frame.

"But this is you we're talking about so I doubt I would have seen you doing the rumba." Again he laughed and backed away a little to allow more space between us.

"I can do the rumba if you like but I must be honest, I fear for my feet." I raised my eyes to him in silent reprimand and he laughed again. It was so easy being with Lucius like this, it almost felt like spending time with a friend but then his hand would take a possessive hold of me and plunge me back into remembering my place in this picture. Also the shiver that wracked my skin whenever our skin connected was a sobering reminder of what my body thought about his touch and there wasn't anything friendly about it.

"So this Dance of Death, is that what it means?" I asked trying to get my tempting dance partner back where he belonged, in the far corners of my mind.

"With you as a partner then it's quite possible." He joked and I pulled back from him and tried to storm off but he just pulled me back to him laughing.

"I jest sweetheart, you're doing fine." He said in my ear after brushing some loose hair from the side of my neck and back to the side the bun was tied by the ribbon.

"It means, to put us at death we will be at the same level. The 'Danse Macabre' considers death summoning representatives from all walks of life, to dance their way to the grave, to embrace death no matter their title being either Pope, Emperor, King, Child, or Labourer," he said taking my hand in his again to continue a much slower version of the dance we had just done.

"Tell me, you reprimanded Layla earlier because you said she didn't show Draven respect...I don't..."

"Understand? No I don't suppose you would. I may not follow my King but I will never forget that he still is just that...My King." I shook my head still not understanding.

"But you took me, you went against him and I don't understand why you would still feel that way?" I couldn't help my questions but I felt like I needed to know and then get to the root of the biggest question of all...what had happened between these two that had caused a single lifetime of events?

"Consider this then Keira, I have spent most of my life walking beside Dominic Draven as my King and I don't suppose I will ever be able to see him as anything under that title but do not mistake my respect, it is merely for a man I used to consider as friend."

"And now?" I asked and for a second his jaw hardened and his frown created a fierce scowl.

"Now he is the man standing in my way to a goal that is my right. You see, my little porcelain doll, your lover and dark King stole something that belonged to me and now...I want it back!" He snapped out at me and I knew he was getting riled up by my questions but I couldn't stop now, not when I was so close.

"And you don't care what you use to get it?" I couldn't keep the bitterness out of my reply and his hand tightened on my hand to the point of pain before he eased.

"No I do not. He stole from me and I stole from him. You are a tool Keira, a pawn in this game Dominic and I play, nothing more." His words cut me like icicle shards and I yanked out of his hold. I almost stumbled but caught my footing enough to straighten up and face him. My face must have said it all because for one shred of a second I thought I saw guilt, but then it was hidden under a mask of indifference.

"Oh, I would consider myself more than a pawn, Lucius!" I said trying to use my anger to overtake the urge to give in to my misery.

"Ah, you fancy yourself a queen on the board naturally." He mocked, making it so much worse but I kept going.

"That's your mistake to make not mine, I do not consider myself a queen at any point but I do consider myself a player, one next in line to kick the shit out of you!" I shouted making a few people turn to us and gasp. I didn't care, I turned ready to storm off when I was grabbed from behind and spun so quickly it made more than my body spin. Before I could utter a single protest I found burning hot lips crushed to mine in such a powerful embrace I couldn't breathe. My mind tried to function, to find the will it needed to push him away. I moved my hands and pushed at his chest but it did me little good. Lucius shackled my wrists and forced my hands behind my back.

The whole room hushed but the beautiful solo of the violin continued on, creating a dream like quality to the night. His mouth took complete possession of mine and he licked at the seam urging me to allow his to deepen it further. I opened my mouth a little and that was all it took for him to take the kiss further. The light dimmed and the candles flickered for all but me and Lucius. No, for we were alone in the world, just myself the captive and Lucius my captor connected and merging as one under a blazing sun. The heat encircled our bodies like water crashing into the shore and I could almost hear the waves of my heart beating wildly in my chest. That sun felt like something holy was touching us and only when he pulled away did the empty darkness engulf the room. Yet the violin played on. Lucius let go of my hands but I couldn't move. He cupped my face and tilted my head down to lay a kiss on my forehead which caused the candle to relight as if that little gesture used sparks from the sun's energy.

"Electiunamlucis." ('Chosen one of light' in Latin) Before I could ask him what he meant he continued,

"You're most definitely a queen Keira, whether you wish to believe it or not." I frowned at him but he chose to ignore my anger and he signalled to his people to continue dancing.

"Now you are going to tell me what your problem with Layla is," he said surprising me out of any other thoughts.

"I…I…" I didn't know how to answer that one. Surely if I told him that Layla had tried to kill me he would make her leave…wouldn't he? But then again he had just told me I meant nothing but a means to an end, so what if he let the cat play with the mouse, would he care? I just couldn't chance it so I shrugged my shoulders and said nothing.

"Keira, I am not blind, did she do something to you?" At that moment the person in question came up to us and tapped me on the shoulder causing my skin to crawl and an urge held back to spit at her feet!

"May I cut in?" She asked and before Lucius said his answer I stepped away before his grip on me tightened and I said,

"Sure, I need a drink anyway." I walked away hearing my name being whispered from Lucius but I didn't look back, I just kept going until I reached Pip. She was my life saver in the cluster F-word storm. I sat down next to her and she put her arms round me for a much needed hug.

"Thanks." I said into her leather clad shoulder.

"You look like you needed it," she said softly.

"You also look like you need this." She passed me a cup of something that smelled like a mix of paint thinner and toilet duck, which was perfect 'cause it burned like hell all the way down and took my mind off the poisonous Layla and King of the jerks!

"So I take your need for enough alcohol to knock out a Barghest is due to your wanting to join the 'I want to behead the bitch' club?"

"Barghest?" I asked first because I was at a loss on that one.

"A legendary monstrous black dog with huge teeth and claws and hung like a friggin donkey! So you wanna join, 'cause you know I am like, the president of that club?" She asked looking at her nails that were now painted like miniature Star Wars characters and she was playing with one of the storm troopers on her thumb and didn't little Hans Solo just look adorable.

"Pip, I need you to do something for me…" I pulled her closer and even Adam looked concerned.

"You can't tell Lucius but please, promise me you won't leave me alone with her." She stared into my eyes and when she must have realised my very real fear then she just nodded and turned to Adam to whisper something in his ear.

I tried not look at Lucius dancing with Layla but when Pip started talking to Adam it was near impossible not to. They looked like bloody Torvill and Dean minus the ice! I doubted I looked that graceful in his arms and even though he said he was joking about my dancing skills I knew there was more truth in his teasing than not.

He had just spun her round and dipped her so that her head arched back and her long blonde hair reached the floor but instead of looking down at her his eyes looked past the evil beauty in his arms and directly at me. I couldn't help the blush that look generated, his eyes even flashed amber, hot like the glowing coals in the braziers that were dotted around the room.

Layla looked up to wonder at her Master's pause but then her gaze followed his and found mine. I looked away then, trying to escape her filthy look and turned towards a friendly one in Pip.

"She doesn't like you much, does she?" Pip said but before I could comment Adam spoke,

"What did she do to you?" He asked in a calm tone but the leather on his gloves groaned as he tightened his fists. He too was dressed in this Steampunk fashion, with a black shirt under a dark red leather waistcoat and black pinstriped trousers. He also wore a pinstriped tie that folded into a cravat style held in place with a clockwork pin. His sleeves had been rolled up his forearms and his black gloves tied up to his elbows with rust coloured cord.

To finish his outfit he had on his head a pair of goggles that reminded me of something an optician would use to check your eyesight, highly polished copper on one side and two different sized lenses on top of each other on the other side which was held together with the same dark red leather of his waistcoat. He looked quite dashing, like an explorer about to jump in his air balloon and find the treasures of the new world.

"Keira, come here!" Lucius' voice saved me from having to answer Adam's question but when he pointed to my usual place in between his legs it changed from being saved to needing to be saved once again. I started to shake my head but his dangerous growl stopped me and I gave up, moving to do his bidding.

As usual when I got within range he made a grab for me and pulled me the rest of the way. I managed not to look at Layla, who I could feel trying to burn holes in my head with her heated gaze. I was just lucky she didn't have such gifts or I would be Swiss cheese by now.

"You know, I would have thought little Pipper, that you would have told our guest about dressing appropriately for our Steampunk night, how do you think we will rectify this problem?" He asked full of ease, all traces of our earlier fight gone.

"Umm…I don't quite know my Lord, do you have any ideas?" She asked mischievously.

"As a matter of fact I think I do. Turn to face me my little doll." I wasn't in the mood to play these games but the look on Pip's face was sheer delight. I started to turn and Layla looked as though she wanted to rip the cogs off the wall and batter me to death with them. Well, the

STEPHANIE HUDSON

feeling was definitely mutual. In fact there was one that looked very sharp and full of spikes that would have done very nicely.

"My Lord, you know I have something of great importance yet to show you," Layla said trying in desperation to get his attention away from me but it didn't work. Lucius held up his hand to halt her from removing an item from a leather case sat at her side.

"All in good time, first I want to play and without interruptions!" The last word was certainly said in warning and Layla looked too shocked for words.

Lucius turned me further until I had one of my knees bent and leaning against inside his thigh. He placed a fingertip under my chin and applied a little pressure to raise it up to his face. He smiled down at me and then took off his hat to place it to the side on my head. It had to be on its side or it would have been too big for me. He then leaned back to examine me, making me blush. He tapped his chin and mouth with his finger.

"Umm, it is missing something more," he said to himself and then he raised his brows, when it came to him. He pushed his hair back and then removed his glasses from his pocket and placed them on my nose until they pinched enough to stay put without hurting. The smile he gave me now was one that warmed my insides and shot pure untamed hunger through to my core, one that needed to be stopped using ice water and a good stub to the toe!

In true Lucius style, which he was making a habit of, he ran his knuckles down my cheek in a caress.

"Before there was beauty and now I have added 'adorable' to the mix." I bit my lip, embarrassed at his complement.

"And that blush only makes it more so," he whispered onto the skin on my heated cheek before kissing it lightly.

After that the night went on in a lighter mood and Lucius dragged me up to dance again but I was happy that Pip and Adam joined us. It was a faster number and more upbeat, though I still managed thanks to Lucius holding me and taking the lead from start to finish. I even found myself laughing whenever I would step on Lucius' feet and he would then spin me round and under his arm in retaliation. I actually found myself having fun and when sat down I would be making conversation with Pip and even Liessa on the rare occasion that she wasn't entertaining her huge husband, Caspian. Hakan, as usual, remained sat in silence only to nod occasionally to certain songs played.

Of course I knew the easiness of the evening wouldn't keep with Layla in the room. After her third attempt she finally got her wish and was given time to tell Lucius of her important news.

"As I said earlier my Lord, I now believe your plans have to change." Lucius was just taking back his drink that he was sharing with me.

"What is it of which you speak Layla, I do not have time for your petty theories." At this she frowned but when Lucius faced her she bowed her head to hide such a look.

"I do not think of this as a theory but as a fact and I have evidence my Lord."

"Evidence to what?" Lucius snapped.

"Evidence to suggest that the King no longer wants your prisoner to bargain with." I shot up out of his hold and stood over her shaking.

"You liar!" I was so outraged I couldn't control my hands from fisting so hard my nails dug into my palms, yet I didn't feel any pain.

"I have proof!" She said with a smug smile that I wanted to turn into a twist of pain.

"Keira, sit down!" I couldn't stop shaking, even as Lucius guided me back to his seat.

"Show us!" He said through gritted teeth.

"Yes my Lord." She tried to conceal her glee but it was difficult when she couldn't stop showing her teeth, she was so happy! She unzipped a leather case and took out an electronic tablet. After touching it with her fingers it powered to life and started to play a video clip.

After less than a minute I screamed so loud it felt like the sound would crack my head open.

"NO! It's a lie, it didn't happen! She lies, Draven wouldn't do that to me! NO, NO, NO!" I screamed and even as Lucius tried to contain me, I was like a frightened bird, flapping my wings, desperate for escape.

"I do not lie! This was filmed yesterday." Layla said trying to appear insulted but this was just kerosene to an uncontrollable forest fire!

"NO! That...it's...no, it cannot be true! I refuse to believe it!" I was shaking my head over and over.

"Keira...aren't those the paintings I saw in your room?" Lucius asked so softly it just added to the hurt. Of course I had already seen the paintings Draven had taken from my room. The ones I painted for him.

The very ones that were now over the bed where he was making love to Aurora.

*The ones he saw, when he broke my heart.*

## CHAPTER 24
# EVIDENCE, DECEPTION AND HEARTACHE

I think I actually felt the exact moment when my heart shattered. It was as though my mind was waging war, logic against emotion. One side I was convincing myself it wasn't possible, that no way could it be true. Draven would never have done that to me! The other side was going back to the night he had surely seen me in Lucius' arms through Ava's sight. What had he thought? Did he really believe I would have done that to him, so what was this now, retaliation or worse, did he really still have feelings for Aurora and was mad enough with me to act upon those feelings?

I wanted to scream again! I couldn't stand not knowing the truth. I knew this could just be a ploy by Layla to get me to back off Draven but how? Was the footage even real?

This was how my mind operated since that vision entered my mind and it started to consume me, slowly beginning to bury me alive, with each bit of earth shovelled on another question adding to the pile until I felt suffocated.

"Pip, take Keira back to her room and stay with her. Layla, I will speak to you alone." Lucius' commanding voice brought me back to the fact that I wasn't alone and I was staring down at my lap trying to work through my emotions, which was not something I wanted an audience for.

I felt Pip touch my arm gently and I looked up at her through a veil of liquid where I tried not to shed my tears.

"Come on Toots, let's go somewhere private and have ourselves a girly chat." She said so softly it was a voice I had never heard from

293

Pip before. I did as I was told and walked away from everyone, but I was not far when I heard Lucius snap,

"Layla, come with me to the courtyard, we need a chat you and I!" His voice was like ice and I was happy I was not the one on the receiving end of his cold displeasure, although I had obviously been there before, but not like this…this sounded deadly.

Pip and I made our way upstairs and once out of sight I pulled her back by the arm and spun her to face me.

"Pip, I need you to do something for me."

"Anything my friend," she said without hesitation.

"You may not be saying that when you know what it is," I warned but before she could reply I carried on in a hurry,

"I need you to go and spy on Lucius and Layla, I need to know what's being said." She started shaking her head and was about to argue but wouldn't let her.

"Please Pip, you're the only one that can do it, I need to know or I will go insane!"

"Toots I…I.."

"Please, oh God Pip please. This is my life Pip, and I need to know what's happening to it." Pip closed her eyes and took a deep breath.

"Hell's bells and monkey balls! Fine, I will do it but if I get caught then I am blaming you for taking away my sanity!" I pulled her to me for a crushing hug and she made an 'umff' sound before patting me on the back.

"Right, I'd better go quickly then but I will be back, go straight to your room and do not leave, you got it?" I nodded my yes in a frantic way just to get her to get going. She shook her head as though I was the biggest pain in her behind and I guess at the moment she was right.

I couldn't breathe until I saw her figure disappear around the corner and then I turned and walked back to my room. By the time I got there my hope levels had reached fever pitch. I was praying that Pip was going to come back here after discovering Layla's deceit. Would she tell Lucius the truth, could he detect her lies or would she try and fool him as she had tried to do with me.

After time to think I knew it was lies. She had somehow fabricated the whole evidence to try and give Lucius the excuse to get rid of me and then no doubt Layla would continue to get rid of me, in a 'never coming back' kinda way.

I don't know how many times I had paced the length of the room but when Pip finally did come back I collapsed on the bed with relief. I would have felt terrible if she had been caught and I should never have put that pressure on her but now she was back I couldn't bring myself to regret it.

"Okay Kitten, you owe me big styley."

"You weren't caught?" I asked as she came to plonk herself down on the bed next to me.

"Oh please...me? Are you insane? I would never get caught and just so you know, this Imp right here is friggin' awesome!" She said the word like a surfer dude and added a victory fist pump.

"Okay, so are we ready for using some more Pip juice?"

"Wait, I thought you would just tell me what went on, you know like gossip, only true." She grinned at me and pushed at my shoulders.

"Now where's the fun in that little Toot? Now lie back and relax, this won't hurt a smidgen."

"Ooh goodie!" I said sarcastically making her laugh as she straddled me again.

"Pip have you got something to tell me, only this is the second time today you have climbed on top of me." She winked down at me and shifted her jacket to one side in a dramatic fashion.

"Sorry Toots, you just don't have the right equipment for me but you do have a lovely bottom." I laughed, even though it was harder with the extra weight on my solar plexus. She unclipped my glasses and threw the hat behind her, items that I completely forgot I was still wearing.

"Okay, so you've played this game before, close your eyes and just relax, well as much as you can with a kick ass Imp sat on you." I smiled and opened an eye to look at her but she just flicked my nose to tell me off. I waited and was about to let her know it wasn't working like last time but then I was plunged into moments not long past.

"Explain yourself Layla and make no mistake, if I find lies then there will be consequences!" Lucius said leaning against the waist high stone balustrades. His stance was one of ease but his facial features told a different story...he was royally pissed. The winter night was lit by an almost full moon and it made Lucius' pale skin look as luminescent as the marble floor that gleamed like liquid.

"I tell the truth, the King has taken another to his bed and therefore he must believe a mistake has been made. She must not be the Chosen." Lucius actually growled at her and looked more terrifying than the heads of beasts that were situated either side of the balcony's square design. It was a large open space void of any plant life or furniture. From what I could see it was made from a part of the mountain that jutted out from the rest. I looked down from where I stood and saw it was a sheer drop to the frozen lake below. I felt my stomach churn at the height.

"Not possible, she is the Electus!" Lucius said and I saw a brief flash of pain in Layla's eyes.

"You know this for sure, my Lord?"

"You doubt your Master? Yes, I know this for sure. I have not been planning this from her seventh year on a mere whim!" He snapped making me slap my hands to my mouth in shock. Since my seventh year? No, that couldn't possibly mean what I thought it meant…could it?

"I do not doubt your trusted beliefs my Lord, but if Dom…the King doesn't believe then he will not swap the girl for the spear and that makes having her here a liability." At this Lucius nearly roared.

"Does your jealously know no bounds Layla, or is your memory of being slighted never at any point ready to fade?" At this she looked away.

"I come to you with this information because of what was asked of me. It was you my Lord who had me work closely with the King and become your eyes on the inside."

"And I didn't hear you complaining at the time. We both got what we wanted, some of us what we needed." I don't know why I felt surprised at hearing that Layla was a spy and it was obvious her gain came from being around Draven and fuelling her obsession. But for Lucius to go to such lengths, I couldn't help but know I was missing huge chunks of the puzzle.

"Yes, I'm glad you think so, my Lord." Layla said bitterly.

"Remember your place, Lahash!" Lucius warned and she lowered her head in defeat.

"How did you obtain this evidence?" He folded his arms and in his suit he looked nothing short of masterful.

"Afterlife is full of secret passages that I learnt of in my time there, I simply gained access and found one that led me to the King's chambers. I took the footage on my phone when I saw him and his former lover in the act. I knew this would change things." She said, trying so hard to keep her happiness of the fact in check. Lucius dragged his hand down his face in a show of stress and held his hand to the lower part of his face taking in this new information.

"This changes nothing. He will still come for the girl, I feel it."

"But my Lord…"

"Enough! The girl will stay here until I choose otherwise. If Dominic has lost his head to his manhood then it is unlikely to be anything more than a carnal need in the girl's absence." At that point I wanted to take off my heels and haul them at his head! A carnal need in my absence! What the hell was that? A polite way of talking about blue balls and how men couldn't possibly do without for a bloody week!

"With respect my Lord I think you are wrong, I think the girl should be given to Malphas sooner than you planned." This time I gasped before I could stop the noise but this was the past and this conversation had already taken place. I wasn't going to be noticed even if I jumped in front of Layla and while flipping her the bird and poking her up her nose with my finger, while kicking her in the shin, while smacking her round the head a few dozen times, while….well you get the picture.

"There is never any respect telling your Master that you think they are wrong Layla." He said with controlled rage. She saw the blood in his eyes and quickly dropped to her knees in front of him.

"Please my Lord, it is only my worry and loyalty for you that compels me to say these things." She had grovelled over to him and with her head hanging down staring at his feet, I snorted in disgust. He took a sharp grip on her chin making her wince at his painful grip. He forced her head all the way up and he lowered his head to get in her face.

"Tell me, why were you no longer allowed to work at the King's table?" He raised an eyebrow before she spoke and yanked her head further to his face making her moan in pain.

"And do NOT lie to me, Lahash!" With the word 'not' he sounded all predator.

"It is as I said my Lord, the King started to grow suspicious of all his staff and was looking into interrogating everyone, he was going to have his seeker, Takeshi looking into memories and only Karmun wasn't vulnerable to his powers." She spilled it out desperately.

"Then tell me, why is it that the girl flinches at just the sight of you?" He still wouldn't release her face, even when she tried to look away which from where I was standing looked painful to do.

"Answer me!" He seethed.

"I think she must have been jealous, my Lord. She never made an effort with her appearance and looked down at all others for doing so."

On hearing this he raised her body from the ground with just his hand on her chin. She made a strangled gargle at her rough treatment but Lucius was too far gone in his fury. When her feet came within reach of the floor she scrabbled to find footing, in order to take the weight from her face and throat. He tore her hand away from his hand that she tried desperately to get him to move. He pulled her just an inch away from his face.

"So you are telling me vanity is the reason she fears you? Fucking vanity!" He screamed in her face and even I flinched back. Then he dropped her and back handed her so fiercely she landed hard on the far side of the balcony.

"You LIE!" He roared, eyes transformed into two crimson suns burning into the woman that lay at his mercy.

"I saw your handy work on her body, Lahash! I didn't know who had inflicted her hidden scar on her side but the touch of our kind can still be seen. I wondered at the time but it only became clear when I saw Keira holding her side in a memorable pain when I danced with you. I saw it in her eyes." He moved over her and I thought for a moment he was going to kill her. I saw his fingers at his sides change and curl into lengthy claws that looked too eager to strike, twitching in waiting.

"You have seen her body?" Was all she said and it came out like a plea for it not to be true.

"I have been with her naked, Lahash and the vain creature you portray, she is not! I touched the evidence of your jealousy and even in sleep she flinches. I should tear your heart out but you are simply not worth my time!" At this she shot up and even though her lips had been busted open to the point a large section of it was now a bloody open flap hanging down, she didn't seem to care.

"She is an abomination to our kind! I would have done the world a favour taking her life, as she in return has taken the one thing that meant anything in mine!" Lucius pulled his arm back wide as if to hit her again but stopped. She held her ground and said,

"Do it my Lord! It would be fitting by your hand." She spoke with a sorrow I didn't believe she possessed and Lucius instead of following through with his action he lowered his clawed hand.

"Death is not deserved by you, so I will opt for a much harsher punishment. I banish you as my child and take from you the gift I bestowed."

"NO! You can't! I would rather die than have that part of me taken away. You can't do this to me over a pathetic human! I am a child of Vampire and you cannot ever take that from me!" She said bravely but Lucius merely laughed at her, a hurtful and malicious sound.

"Maybe not at this moment in time but when I banish you for the rest of your years on this plane then your power will degrade the longer you're apart from me. As your maker I have this right and it will be so that from the next moon cycle you will burn in the sun if you set foot in my presence again! Now go and salvage what is left of your pitiful life, for your power will start to die and with that, your host." Lucius turned to leave and she spat at the floor where he was stood. Lucius barely gave her a glance but then she wasn't quite finished.

"You have grown weak and pathetic over a lesser being, a human parasite that is nothing more than a cockroach to this earth! I spit at your weakness and laugh when the time comes for you to hand the girl over to Malphas as was your deal. And what do you think he has in store for the precious Electus. Do you suppose he plans to dance with her and woo her into a trust that was never meant to stem from both sides. He plans to gut her, my Lord and when he does I will rejoice and my only regret is that my hand will not be able to touch the torn flesh which I could inflict. That I am not there to see the life drain from her shell, in which I could then bathe in her blood! SHE. WILL. DIE!" She screamed out this last part in such a rage that she flew at Lucius like a banshee, but it was a wasted energy. Lucius simply lifted his hand and she dropped to the ground and started to writhe in agony on the floor. She screamed over and over and clawed at her own skin as though it was too painful to wear. I saw it ripple like thousands of bulging bugs infested in her flesh and were eating her insides.

Lucius got down low and rested his arm on his bent knee to speak through her pain.

"I never intended to let Malphas have her Layla, he was only ever just another instrument to utilize. Keira is mine now and you...you will perish long before she ever does!" These were Lucius' last words to her and she screamed out, through excruciating pain or through cavernous loss, I didn't know but she continued screaming as she had received both.

My vision faded with the evidence of her torment vibrating in my mind. I opened my eyes to Pip and now I knew what she did, there was none of the usual humour in her features. She got off me and I sat up slowly, still trying to understand the depth of the deep shit I was in. I had learnt more in those ten minutes than I had in the entire time I had been here.

"So let me get this straight, first it was Lucius that had not only sent Karmun to spy but Layla as well?" I wasn't even looking at Pip when I asked her. I was just staring into a nothingness that seemed to sum up my situation.

"Yes he did."

"And he planned all along to double cross Draven and give me to this Malphas, like a fucking playing card?" I said so full of anger it felt too thick to swallow.

"Yes, he was." She said gingerly.

"Was?"

"Yeah he was, but not anymore. I think there is something you should know." I held up my hand to stop her.

"If you're about to tell me he changed his mind thanks to some divine intervention, I think I am going to throw up! At this point Pip, I can't see myself as anything other than what he told me I was. I am a bloody pawn, I always have been and just because he doesn't want his pawn dead doesn't mean diddley shit to me!" I said bitterly. I knew I was taking my anger out on Pip by being snappy and I felt guilty about it, so I tried to get a hold of my resentment and think logically.

"I'm sorry Pip, I shouldn't be taking it out on you." She waved me off and started pacing back and forth looking more agitated than I was.

"Oh, never mind all that Toots, we have bigger problems here."

"Like what?"

"Like when Lucius has to tell Malphas that the deal is off! That is one dude that A – does not take kindly to the word 'No' and B- he is one scary and powerful son of a beehive!" Oh goodie…another powerful supernatural being that wanted me in pain or to hold me against my will, Christ was there a bloody club or something!

"I met him once and he spoke about me being the Chosen One but back then I knew nothing about it really…I suppose not a lot has changed on that front, I still don't know what the hell I am supposed to do, I mean I don't even know what it means…or what I am…or…"

"Okay, okay slow down there Jessie."

"Jessie?" I asked thinking this question should have been lower down on my need to know list.

"You know, from Toy Story, geez Toots don't you ever watch the flat screen?"

"Yeah me and Draven sit down and watch America's next top model every week!"

"Really?" She said obviously getting excited by the idea but with one look at my face it told her I was being sarcastic.

"I'm sorry Pip but in between being attacked, drugged, kidnapped and finals at college then I haven't really had much time for telly." I said with slumped shoulders.

"And sex, there's always time for sex and I can imagine with a boy toy like Draven there is little need for Buzz and the gang…Draven supplies woody I can bet!" She said waggling her eyebrows and I actually couldn't hold in the laugh but then the thought of Draven and sex had me catapulted right back to the video footage of my boyfriend and Aurora.

"Pip, I need to know if what happened with Draven and Aurora was true. You need to send me to him before I go completely crazy." She looked away at the door for a second as if she could hear someone coming.

"I will see what I can do Toots, but not tonight, I have to recharge and besides, you have company." I was just about to ask her what she meant when Lucius stormed through the door looking masterful as usual.

"Leave us little Imp!" He ordered sternly and Pip stood up quickly and squared her shoulders before giving him a salute. She turned and winked at me and then left the room…skipping.

Lucius walked further in the room and stalked his way to the living space. He went up to the kitchenette and grabbed a spirit bottle from a cupboard, one I didn't recognise as it was German, and filled a glass. He knocked it back and grabbed another glass in between his fingers to carry them both and the bottle, back to the coffee table. Lucius hadn't yet said a word and I just watched him from the bed too afraid to move due to his obvious rage. And after seeing it in full throttle mode on Layla, I didn't fancy getting the tail end.

He took off his tailored jacket and flung it to the three seater sofa. He was no longer wearing gloves as he hadn't been in my vision and this brought me back to seeing him with claws so large that he would have made a wild jungle cat scatter. I gulped back the lump at the sight of broad shoulders under his shirt and his fitted dark striped waistcoat that hugged nicely at the waist. He had rolled up his sleeves so that muscled forearms could be seen and when he sat down he leaned back in the single chair before taking off his tie and unbuttoning his shirt to where the waistcoat tied. I wanted to say 'Make yourself comfortable why don't you!' But thanks to the intense mix of steel grey and ice blue eyes drinking in my every movement I decided my sarcastic mouth was better under lock and key.

"Come here, Keira!" He said motioning with two fingers held together. I really didn't want to but it had been said as an order not a request. I got up and walked very slowly to the seat opposite his, all the while it felt like I was being sized up as a meal. I suppressed a giggle at the thought of him seeing me as one of those cartoon cooked chickens like Wile e Coyote does in The Road Runner, only in my image I was still wearing a black dress. Surely thinking this meant I was losing my sanity!

"I want you to tell me what Layla did to you." He said and then after giving me a minute to collect my thoughts he nodded to my side which I didn't realise I was holding in a protective manner. He had been right, I must have been touching my side like this subconsciously when I was looking at Layla.

"I will start for you, should I?" He said and I couldn't find my voice around him at the moment, not when he was like this. His look would have given me chills at how cold his mannerisms seemed, if it wasn't for his heated gaze every time his eyes lingered on my body. And if his manhood was anything to go by then I would say with certainty that for this Vamp, rage and lust went hand in hand.

"Layla was working the club at my order, but at least that much you have no doubt gathered for yourself?" I nodded when he paused.

"Her mission was simple, befriend you and report to me on your progress."

"Progress?" I questioned. He actually looked uncomfortable for a moment but it only showed in his expressive eyes, his body gave nothing away.

"I was waiting for Draven to yield his restraints and take you as his." I frowned at the thought of being played, the second my foot stepped off the plane.

"How did you even know I was ever going to meet him?"

"It is of little matter how I knew." I think the noise that came out of me was an actual growl and a clear sign that I was spending far too much time around aggravating, pig headed men!

"To you maybe, but to me…well, I am very interested." I crossed my arms over my chest and Lucius frowned at me.

"Later I may tell you, but for now I want to know about your painful exchange with Layla."

"What does it matter now, you sent her to spy and she must have interpreted that as to stab. She always seemed a bit warped." I added dryly and I couldn't help but notice Lucius' hand twitch when I said the word 'stab'.

"My intent was never to hurt you Keira, it was only ever to…"

"Use me!" I finished for him, making his eyes flash red and his fists clench in a show of emotion. He had to wait until he could take back his ragged control before leaning back and resting his elbow on the arm of the chair. He held the lower part of his face in his hand and tapped his index finger on his cheek.

"You are right. As I made clear earlier, you were a pawn, a tool and a means to get what I need." I was about to butt in with my own feelings on the matter when he held up his other hand for me to stop. When I remained silent he continued and placed his free hand back on his thigh and I couldn't help but follow his fingers as they tapped on the firm muscle that they found there.

"However, at no point did I ever want any harm to come to you, those were my orders Keira."

"Funny then that it was you who also broke them." At this he shocked me and laughed.

"Yes and I do recall you were trying to give me a tan, I think we're even." He looked better smiling and for the first time that he walked in the room I found my shoulders relaxed.

"I think you started it," I said trying not to grin.

"Yes and as you can see, I finished it. You are here now, under my…"

"Rule!" Again I interrupted which I was happy to note seemed to be pissing him off.

"Care! And would you please stop putting words in my mouth, it's very…"

"Amusing," I said not even trying to hold back the grin. Even when he growled at me I found myself closer to laughing than flinching.

"Annoying!" I don't know why but I had the biggest urge to fling myself at him and start tickling him just to get him to start laughing. When Lucius laughed his whole face transformed into a man full of life and sexy ease. But then with the flick of a switch he could turn into a glacier, frozen and without feelings.

"Me? Never!" I said and this time he did smile.

"Caspian is right, you are trouble." He said, the teasing Lucius was clearly back.

"Oh and you're a saint are you?" I said before I could think of his past but instead of blowing up he merely shrugged his shoulders and shocked me by saying,

"No, a Disciple but that is beside the point. While you are here you are in my care. I am not ignorant of the prophecy."

"No, but I am!" I snapped. I was sick of everyone knowing my path in life and expecting me to just live what people knew and I didn't.

"And that is no doubt for the best, trust me on that my little Keira girl."

"Trust a Vampire, who haunted my dreams and then kidnapped me to hold me ransom for some bloody relic...yeah, yeah, I will trust you."

"Other than that one time and holding you against your will, have I hurt you?" I wanted to scream at him about making the deal with Malphas but that would have got Pip in trouble.

"Not yet no," I said begrudgingly. He laughed and I looked up from staring at my folded arms.

"What?"

"I find you look utterly adorable when you sulk." I grunted at his teasing and when I gave him a glare, he tried to mask his smile under his hand.

"I have to say I am surprised," he said as another thought popped in his head.

"I hate to ask, but why?"

"Because when I came in here I was expecting female hysterics."

"And why would that be?" I asked and grabbed the bottle and spare glass considering it was obviously meant for me. I also decided not to be a bitch and poured him one as well. He nodded his thanks and shot it back as he waited before answering me.

"Well given what you just saw Draven doing in your absence, I think you're handling it rather well." I flinched as though I'd been stung but I put on a facade of indifference and said with confidence,

"That's easy, I don't believe it's true." His reaction put a dint in my beliefs as he looked sorry for me, eyes creased at the sides, full of pity. An emotion I utterly loathed. This made me down my drink in one and thankfully Lucius didn't start laughing at me when I started coughing at the burn it created.

"You have that much faith in a King surrounded by beauties when his lover is out of his reach?" He said without a thread of the smug arrogance that I would have expected.

"Well you don't see me banging every Vamp with man bits!" I snapped.

"I would rip them to shreds, so it is a good thing." He said frowning. I ignored his confusing statement and continued,

"So you don't have faith in him then?" This question wasn't supposed to make me sound as vulnerable as it did.

"I know the man well but I must confess, I have never seen the King in love. But I don't see a motive behind Layla's actions. She stabbed you so I have no doubt that Draven had sentenced her to be disposed of. I am actually surprised he waited but then he is a man of honour and is ingrained with a sense of duty."

"You mean giving her a trial?" He nodded and refilled my glass.

"Although I hear Sammael didn't fare so well."

"Well, he was trying to kill him at the time." I added, taking a sip this time as I didn't fancy a raw throat for the night.

"Yes, so I heard. A fight I would have enjoyed watching."

"I'm not going to ask which side you would have been rooting for." I commented, making him raise an eyebrow and hide his smirk behind his tapping fingers.

"You seem to know a lot about when I first arrived, which brings me back to what I really want to know."

"Which is?" His fingers left his face and motioned me to ask.

"I want to know how long you have known about me and how you knew I would find Draven." I asked and he hesitated about what to tell me. At one point it looked as if he would end our conversation altogether and just leave but he must have thought better of it because he leaned back again and started to swirl the amber liquid around his glass.

"I have known of your existence since you were seven." I wasn't so shocked at this thanks to what I'd heard in his exchange with Layla on the balcony.

"And how did you know that?"

"The gypsy you saw that day in the fairground was somebody loyal to me." This did shock me. Lucius had been involved with the day that changed my life forever.

"So she told you, not Draven." I stated the obvious.

"I went to great lengths to keep you a secret."

"How so?"

"I sent the gypsy back to you on your seventh birthday and told her to hide you from all of our kind until fate brought you to Draven. Unfortunately it caused the reverse effect for you and gave you the sight of our kind." I couldn't believe what I was hearing.

"So finally I have someone to blame for making my childhood Hell on Earth!" I shouted wishing that all those bloody supernatural beings would just have left me the hell alone!

"No, I was the reason you survived it!" He shouted back leaning forward like he was ready to spring for me.

"Oh come on! How much damage could a seven year old do?"

"You have no idea, do you?" I rolled my eyes and threw my hands in the air in exasperation.

"Obviously not!"

"Okay sugar, then let me lay it out for you, nice and simple. No Chosen One, then no prophecy, no prophecy then no more living! Get it?" I shook my head in denial. What was he talking about?

"What do you mean no more living?" I asked, my voice now down a few octaves.

"Just as it sounds little girl, no you then no us...what...? Am I not being blunt enough? Try this... if you don't live then nobody does!" No, he was wrong...this...I, this wasn't right... he wasn't right...was he?

When I couldn't stop shaking my head his frown smoothed out and his tone became lighter, softer and more soothing.

"I told you Keira, it is better that you don't know."

"I can't believe it, you're wrong...this isn't right...I cannot...how can I be responsible for whether or not your kind lives or dies?" He looked down as I waited for his answer but I couldn't stand it.

"Just tell me!" I felt myself breaking, crumbling into a pit of dangerous knowledge that I could drown in. His eyes flashed up at me but his motions were calm and something in his gaze looked too much like regret and compassion mixed as one.

"You're mistaken Keira, I was not talking about just my kind."

"I...don't understand, what did you mean?" I had a sinking feeling in my belly like I had swallowed a snake and it was coiling tighter and tighter inside me.

"I talk about Judgement Day Keira, about the end of days." I shot out of my chair like someone had just lit it on fire! NO, NO, NO! This was not true, this could not be possible.

"You're wrong!" I almost screamed at him.

"I am not wrong Keira, you are chosen in this prophecy."

"And what on earth am I supposed to do?" I could barely think, let alone speak, however the heart breaking question was asked and when I heard his answer my legs crumbled beneath me and I fell to the floor in a hopeless pile. But his answer came again, whispered in my ear as he held me close,

*"You will prevent the end of the world!"*

# CHAPTER 25
# DON'T LET IT BE TRUE

"Sshh, little one, do not stir and do not fret." A whispered voice penetrated my shadowed mind and I felt like a frightened fawn running through a sinking forest. Then I was right there. The forest was real and I was no longer a skittish creature but a human girl running for my life along with everyone else. Trees came crashing down towards me and I was tripping over myself to get clear from their path. Then what I saw was the earth opening up and the edge of the clearing disappearing like it was falling over the edge of the world.

It was as if some mighty hand of a God was dragging the surface of the planet towards him and nothing could run fast enough to get away from the end. I couldn't understand why, what had I done wrong, what had caused this to happen? Then I felt it and I doubled over in pain. Like my insides had been stabbed from the inside out. I looked down at myself in the mist of endless destruction and saw my life heading the same way. My stomach had been slashed open and I had failed. My death had brought this Hell to Earth and I fell to my knees in horrendous defeat.

As soon as my knees touched the ground the world went up in flames the height of the few trees still remaining upright, but it was no good now as the blaze engulfed them.

It took away everything but me. I still remained untouched but waiting no less to die from my mortal wounds. The falling world behind me was getting closer and closer as the tremors increased, causing my bones to rattle. I raised my head up at the red sky that mirrored all of that below it and screamed,

309

"WHY?" And then my reply was more than I could take. It was the sound of a baby's screaming all around me.

That is what finished me off as I finally died.

I sat bolt upright and my body was wracked with soundless sobs. Immediately arms wound around me and covered me in a safe haven. I found a shoulder and never wanted to move. The male scent engulfed me and wrapped around every inch of skin that still trembled. "Ssshh sweetheart, it won't happen. It was just a dream." Lucius' words sunk in and when I was finally able to breathe without dragging in the air in gasps I pulled back. At first I didn't think he was going to let me but after another minute of holding me to him he let me go enough to stare into his soulful eyes. I couldn't stop my hand from reaching up to his face and cupping the side in my palm. He surprised me by closing his eyes and leaning into it.

"You know what I dreamt?" I asked, my voice hoarse from the sore throat.

"Yes." His answer was simple but his shuddered reaction spoke volumes. It was obvious the regret he felt in telling me of my fate. He still kept his eyes closed and in turn I still kept my hand to his face. We remained like this for a while, each drawing from it the comfort we both needed. Like two statues under the moonlight that filtered through the glass windows. In this moment, if any other was to witness our position they would think of us as nothing short of lovers, captured in a symbolic embrace.

I still wore my dress and all at once it felt constricting against my hot, sticky skin. Lucius still wore his trousers but nothing else and like this, his skin matched the moon's glow. He was perfect, as though every last bit of him was sculpted by an artist of the Gods, carved into white marble that gleamed in this dark room. I didn't even try to prevent my hand from moving from his face down his neck. My fingers curled round his shoulder, not surprised at the strength it found there. With a mind of its own it moved down further still and the tranquillity of both his body and the room was making my every movement scream out.

He still kept his eyes closed and the long, thick eyelashes created little shadows under his lower lashes. I heard him suck in a jagged breath when my hand continued its forbidden journey downwards. I felt the hard contours of his chest and then lower still on the firm lines that marked out the strength in his hardened abs. I traced each line with a butterfly touch and when getting down to the lowest set of his six pack his hand bolted out and seized my wrist from further movement. His eyes flashed open and for a few moments our locked stare was the only communication that was needed.

"There will be a point of no return between us Keira, but that point is not today," he said through husky tones. Then he did something so out of character I froze. He leaned down and when I saw his hands come up to frame my face I thought at first he was going to kiss me and if that had happened I knew no power would have made me stop him and no power would have made him stop me. But he didn't. Instead he just lent his forehead to mine and held my face to his.

"Why did you have to make me feel again, Keira?" He asked me and the large lump I swallowed could be heard clearly in the silence. I didn't know what to say…Hell, I didn't know what to think? What did he even mean by that?

I was just getting ready to try and find some words, any words that would slice through this confusing moment that had stopped time. Anything to get it to start up again, as it felt as if I was locked to him and just one word from me would break his private prison.

"I…"

"No Keira, don't speak…don't speak the words, not now…not ever." He whispered into my skin and his thumb caressed my lips, getting ready to apply pressure if I didn't take heed of his warning.

"I want you to close your eyes, can you do that for me, Keira girl?" I found myself nodding without thought.

"Good girl!" He leaned to my ear and his whispered praise filled me with warmth. I did as I was asked and then felt his hands at my shoulders pushing me back with ease. I knew it was foolish but I trusted him. I trusted not the Vampire above me but the man trapped beneath the evidence of God's punishment.

I felt his presence held over me waiting for I didn't know what but if any more time passed he would soon find me trembling.

"Luc…Lucius?" I couldn't say his name without the waver in my voice. He didn't reply to my unspoken question but he knew his answer and at the sound of my dress being ripped open I found his reason. I shrieked out and tried to move but found the sheet quickly covering me, calming my racing heart. I never once opened my eyes and now more than ever I didn't want to.

"I want you to be comfortable in sleep pet. Your body was overheating under the lace, from your nightmare." He said softly and he was right. The sheet cooled my skin and felt amazing.

"Turn over." He directed me with his hands on top of the material, rolling me onto my stomach. I tried to breathe normally but when I felt his hand snake under the covers I tensed and dragged in a heavy breath.

"I promise I'm not here to take advantage of you my girl, I just want you to sleep peacefully that is all, I will not look again." I felt his hands undo my bra and slip it from my arms, all the while keeping his promise which included keeping my body hidden. I lifted my body to help him remove the satin cups from underneath me but I shuddered at the feel of his hand as it brushed the side of my breast.

"So soft!" He purred in my ear, making me shiver as he then kissed the sensitive spot there. Then I felt his weight removed from above me and travel further down to my waist. He straddled my legs, sitting back on my thighs and his hands came at me from either side, gathering up the sheet as he inched closer to my hips. I couldn't help every time that I felt his touch, flinching like being scalded, cold hands to warm skin that unbelievably created even more heat.

He hooked his thumbs into the elastic of my underwear's waistband and so, so slowly, with his palms and fingers holding the rest of my flesh, he pulled them down, feeling every part of me as he went. God, what his touch was doing to me! I felt so betrayed by the need I had growing at my core that just one touch would be all it took to have me begging to be taken. I was so utterly ashamed of myself and my wanton need that I had to bite into the pillow just to stop myself from begging to be given blissful release by Lucius and being left alone in order to achieve it by myself.

Thankfully Lucius tucked the covers securely round my body, tucking it into each curve. He pushed the loose strands from my face and kissed up my jawline and down my exposed neck only to kiss his way back up again.

"Dormir avec ma touché attardé assurer votre sécurité" ('Sleep with my lingered touch keeping you safe' In French) His foreign words were like fingertips being dragged across my sensitive breasts right down my belly and through the damp curls he would find at the junction between my thighs.

"Lucius?" I said his name but it was too late, he was gone. And I was both glad and disappointed. However the ache inside me didn't recede with his departure, if anything it started to increase and my hand went down to relieve the yearning. I turned back round to face the ceiling. I then started breathing faster as soon as my fingers made contact and when I saw Draven's hands in my thoughts it wasn't my body that he was touching.... It was Aurora's.

I cried out in pleasure as the hands changed to those of Lucius and I shamefully came hard, crying out his name in nothing short of frenzied rapture. I lay panting still with my eyes closed but when I heard another person breathing, my eyes shot open. There, in the shadows, was a male silhouette breathing just as hard as I was, watching every move I made. My hand was still at the place of pleasure when I had called out the name that brought it crashing to its height and when the figure walked forward the same name escaped my lips once more.

*"Lucius"*

# CHAPTER 26
# SHAMEFUL INHIBITIONS AND ULTIMATE BETRAYAL

I woke the next morning after one of the most mind boggling nights full of emotional roller coasters, most of which I didn't want to think about. I had learnt so much in one night but none of it had done me any good, if anything I just felt even more vulnerable than I did before. I lay on my back and found myself just staring at the ceiling trying to make some sense of the last thing that had happened. The last name on my lips I whispered again and my heart started pounding like a jack hammer.

"Lucius!" Just the name made me bolt upright with the memory of last night's mistake. I realised I was still naked and couldn't help but groan as more images of the man flooded into every corner of my mind. It was as though I could still feel his hands on me, those confident fingers gripping the material of my dress and ripping it away from my skin. I felt my cheeks get hot and I started shaking my head in shame. I had pleasured myself to the thought of Lucius touching me and I didn't know what was worse, that I felt like I had somehow betrayed Draven or that Lucius had stood there the entire time and witnessed everything.

"Oh shit!" I groaned into the covers after pulling my knees up and cradling my fragile head with my hands.

"If I'm not mistaken, I would say that sounds like regret. That or your brain itches." I groaned louder before looking up to find Pip sat on the end of my bed. I hadn't even heard her come in let alone felt her sit down next to me.

"Let's put it this way, I wish it was my brain that was itching, then

I could try and scratch away certain memories." I noted Pip's half smile and couldn't tell if it was one of understanding or tamed delight at my predicament.

"I take it things went well with Luc last night then?" When I groaned again and hid under the covers she laughed and said,

"Maybe not," and then pulled the covers off my face.

"Well there is some good news," she said ignoring my whiney moan.

"What's that?" I said with a muffled voice from my hands still covering my face.

"Venger the bitch is gone and is no more." She said winking at me and I smiled when I saw her crazy make-up that was painted over her eyelids. One was an open green eye painted like a Disney princess, impossibly wide and innocent looking. And the other, the one she had used to wink at me was another winking eye with exaggerated long lashes. Only Pip knew how to work craziness and get away with it, she still looked incredibly cute and pretty.

"Venger?" I asked not understanding who on earth she was talking about.

"Oh come on, please tell me you watched Dungeons & Dragons… you know, big bad pissed off guy, flies an even more pissed off looking black horse, one horn and wearing a very gay looking skirt, that if you ask me kinda spoils the whole bad ass dude thing but each to their own." I shook my head and thought it was too damn early and my head was too damn fragile to be deciphering Pip's wacky code.

"Please explain, Pip," I said no longer holding my head in my hands but now holding the bridge of my nose in my fingers, trying in vain to ease the pounding drum headache I had building.

"Layla!" She said the name causing my head to shoot round as I scanned the room for my arch nemesis, the murderous bitch Layla.

"Not here, man someone needs a vacation at rancho relaxo. I was referring to Layla as being the baddie from Dungeons & Dragons but you ruined that bit of genius for me, so moving swiftly on…Layla has been made to leave so ding dong…"

"The witch is dead!" I finished and she gave me a face splitting smile.

"Now you got it! I mean, she isn't dead but she might as well be, 'cause being cast out by Lucius pretty much means bad things for her from now on."

"What do you mean?" Pip leaned back on one out stretched arm behind her back on the bed and looked at her nails before answering me, this time I think they were different retro sweets...was that a coke bottle she was picking at?

"I mean sister Toots, that Layla is a Vamp no longer to be." She said this like she was reciting some Shakespeare play and waved her hand in the air like Hamlet without the skull.

"She is a Vamp?" I said in shock.

"She is and soon to be a 'was'. You see dumpling, all Vamps are made by Lucius, he is like their father but he has the power to take back his gift if he chooses, which means all amplified gifts that he created get...well uncreated. All Vamps need to be around Lucius at some point each year to maintain a part of his essence, his mumbo juice if you like. But now she has been cast aside like a wet chamois when all a car needs is a good hot wax! She will soon find herself weak and that my dear is a fate worse than damnation to one of our kind." She gave me one last look when she finished and started licking her cola bottle which had white glitter to represent the bubbles. Her pierced tongue flashed out and she ran it between her teeth, displaying the pink metal ball.

Well, what she had told me certainly gave me food for thought. I now at least understood why she had looked so distraught last night and I couldn't help that the image made me smile. I mean, she did try and kill me and would no doubt try again given half the chance.

"Okay, so are you ready for flight on Pip 'o' Vision airways?" At this my head whipped up and Pip laughed at my enthusiasm.

"Now?" I said feeling both excited and wary at what I might find.

"Go shower and change Toots and I will wait for you, unless you want to be seen naked?" She nodded to the sheet barely covering my breasts and I flushed bright pink.

"Don't worry Toots, I told ya before, you don't have the right equipment to tempt me but if my tastes ever change from muscle to moobs then I might jump you."

"Oi, you saying my breasts look like flabby man breasts?" I said trying not to smile at her obvious teasing.

"Me? Never! You have lovely breasts that look nothing like a man's extra bits but if I ever fancy dressing Adam in drag then I would so go with the size of your beasties. Now go dress, you temptress you!" I got up and flicked her little nose after wrapping my body in the sheet. I could still hear her giggling when I walked into the bathroom.

After the quickest shower I nearly fell out of the glass door to get ready quicker. I was still putting clothes on when my skin was damp and trying to get tight jeans on when water was still dripping down my hair to my legs was not the easiest task. I heard Pip call out when I slipped and managed to catch hold of the sink before falling hard on my butt.

"I'm fine!" I shouted before she came in here and found me tugging my waistband up with one hand and the other, half way sticking out of the arm of the sleeve to a soft light grey t-shirt. I looked like a failed contortionist getting dressed.

I pulled the top over my wet head and finished pulling up the jeans over the other side of my hip. I then pulled on a pair of full length leather gloves that went right up and over my elbows to my poor excuse for biceps. These were also soft and had finger holes so that half my fingers weren't covered in the black leather.

I added a chunky soft knit cardigan in cream with grey flecks that matched the t-shirt and stonewash jeans I was wearing. I brushed through the knots in my hair as best I could and tied it up without having the time to dry it fully. I couldn't find any socks so I walked back into the living space bare foot trying to ignore the cold under my feet.

"Wow that was quick!" Pip commented as I sat down opposite her in the same chair I had been in the first time I had taken a transatlantic flight on Pip Airways and what a mind trip it had been.

"You ready, Toots?" I thought about her question and answered honestly.

"No, but go for it anyway," I said taking a deep breath. I knew this was what I needed to do to find the truth but that didn't mean I was sure of the outcome. I wanted to believe it was all lies but with the image of Draven up against Aurora in the same bed where we had first shared our bodies with each other was playing in my mind like a recurring nightmare.

Pip slapped her hands to the arm rests with her elbows sticking up in the air and heaved herself up. It was only now that I really took in today's outfit as I was so used to waking up to see a living rainbow sat on my bed it was becoming less of a shock.

She now wore a see-through hooped skirt that was covered in rows of fluffy pompoms in electric, luminous colours but I was happy to see that she at least tried to cover up her female goodies with a pair of black latex hot pants. This she topped off with a bright turquoise bustier with a pretty butterfly print that pushed up her little breasts. It also had some 3D wings that looked to be made from glass like you would find in a window catching the sun. This would have been quite a normal top for Pip to wear if not for the added four inch wide ribbon in hot pink that was wound round her torso in random angles that slashed across her bare shoulders and arms only to finish hanging loosely on her wrists like large cuffs.

I was almost afraid to look down but found myself glad I did when I burst out laughing at the knee high socks that were made to look like a wonder woman costume, complete with cape. This she added wonder woman converse shoes to match... which was something she rarely ever did.

"At least I'm wearing shoes," she said pouting.

"I'm laughing because I think they're great," I said honestly, never having the guts to wear them myself personally but still admiring the diversity in the design.

"Oh, well that's alright then...Right time to say bye, bye my pretty." She said in a witchy voice before jumping on my lap like last time.

"You know you could warn me before just launching yourself at me like that."

"Oh Tootie cake, you're no fun. Good luck honey." She gave me what I could only assume was a gangster sign before slapping her hands to the side of my head and plunging me into a world six hours away.

I opened my eyes to find myself in the very familiar club Afterlife's VIP. It was dark, quiet and empty, something that only ever happened very early into the wee hours of the morning. I wondered why I would have ended up here with no one around but then I saw Sophia come storming in the room with Vincent hard on her heels. I don't know why but I decided to step further into the shadows near the bar to hear this out.

"Sophia, he will handle it, calm yourself." Vincent said in his usual soothing tone.

"I will not! Keira has been gone less than a week and this is the behaviour that is being tolerated! Why are you not as outraged as I, brother?" Sophia whipped round and folded her arms at Vincent in nothing short of an accusing manner. He just frowned and folded his own arms, making the sleeves on his long sleeved black t-shirt strain and tighten around his impressive biceps. The material moulded to his upper body like it was trying to be another layer of skin, which

319

STEPHANIE HUDSON

showcased his fine physique beautifully. This was combined with black dress trousers and it had to be said, the man sure knew how to wear clothes that created a drool worthy effect! I shook my head to get myself back in the game and remembered why I was here and from the sounds of things it might not be the happy, optimistic answers that I had hoped for.

"Because when Dom tells me he will do something, then I have no other option than to place my trust in those words as should you."

"Bullshit! This goes deeper than Dom's word! I am surprised, as you of all people should be more outraged on Keira's behalf, considering how you feel." I couldn't believe it when Vincent actually growled.

"You go too far, Sophia! Back down and just leave it be or Dom will no doubt find out about your interference and as you know, my anger compared to his is quite different."

"As you know I am not afraid of our brother's temper and besides, don't you think he has more pressing matters on his hands than my personal feelings on what he is doing?" She really looked upset and it didn't sound like the reasons were going to fare well for me. Was it possible... was Draven with her right now? Was this what Sophia meant? I felt like praying to every God in the heavens for it not to be true.

"Be careful, Sophia!" Vincent warned in a low gravelly voice that sounded threatening. Sophia looked like she was going to say more but in the end she lost all the heat of her argument and deflated into a nearby chair like a wilting flower. As usual, her appearance was flawless and her floor length dress floated around her where she sat. Surrounded in midnight coloured silk that made her hair look like it shimmered for the same reason, its softness hard matched, she looked like a queen goddess and it made me feel like praying to her instead.

"I miss her, Vincent." She said dejectedly making Vincent's scowl fade and my heart break. I wanted to pop up and shout 'I'm here' like a live jack-in-the-box but I didn't think they would like a supernatural heart attack!

Vincent walked to her chair and knelt down on one knee to get to her face level. He tilted her head up with a soft grip on her chin and wiped away a stray tear that rolled down her ivory skin.

"As do I Sophia, much more than anyone truly knows and much more than I ever should." He said and I couldn't help but shove my fist in my mouth to prevent the gasp that wanted to escape my tactless brain.

"Then if we feel like this, then Dom should be feeling it tenfold..." He nodded in agreement so she carried on.

"Then tell me why he is now in the room he shares with the girl he loves with one he never did?" This time I couldn't stop my reaction. Nothing could have stopped me.

I saw Vincent look up and take in the sight of me stood there, no longer in the shadows but now very visible, right down to my fisted hands and my body that was wracked with a disbelieving tremble. No, it couldn't be true...it just couldn't...could it?

"Keira?" Vincent said my name with the same disbelief my body was displaying and now Sophia had turned to witness it as well.

"Oh my Heavens...Keira...it's you!" She got up and for a long moment we were all frozen like actors in a play who had all forgotten the next set of words that were meant to be heard by an invisible audience. Silence...just bitter, air slicing silence.

A silence so thick it would soon crack the skin stretched across my knuckles, my fingers were fisted to my palm that tight, until finally I could no longer stand it.

"Where is he?" I asked still shaking with a rage that I foolishly still hoped unnecessary.

"Keira I don't think..." I cut Vincent off with an action I didn't even know I had done until I heard my fist bang down on the table top in front of me.

"DON'T!" The one word came out like the cracking of ice under a heavy foot, dangerous and fatal.

Vincent looked like he was debating whether to run to me and scoop me into his arms or not. In the end I took that choice away from him by turning away from them both. I found the door that would give me the answers I needed to see and found myself running towards it before either one of them acted. I was actually surprised at how fast I was running. I knew they were making chase but I was faster...faster than I had ever been in my whole life. Was this because I wasn't really here and my soul was faster than my body or was it the side effects of being with Draven. Was this what it was like being supernatural?

I started to think it was, when I could hear his voice before I ever should. So it wasn't just my speed then, it was also some other senses.

"I am not afraid of speaking my feelings Aurora, not when those feelings are of love."

"Oh, Draven." I heard Aurora say as if close to swooning.

"I am not finished my dear, as I said earlier, I do not regret our time together as it has brought us to this point but I refuse to hide the way I feel any longer. You must know of what I speak, I have presented you with enough evidence."

"The physical evidence that night was enough for me to understand your feelings my Lord. I know what you want and I can only be happy in the knowledge that I can finally give you what you want, what you need...from me." I almost crumpled to the floor when hearing this, for I had found my answer. Layla hadn't been lying and I was the fool.

I felt myself start to waver back to my body as no doubt Pip could feel my distress but I had one last thing left to do and I had to summon all my courage to follow the truth through to the bitter, twisted end. I locked my legs and placed my fading hand on the door, ignoring the desperate pleas of my name being called by Vincent and Sophia.

The door opened and there in our sacred place was the most beautiful woman I had ever known in the arms of the most beautiful man I had ever known.

They were utterly perfect together. Two flawless beings entwined in an embrace so deep and meaningful my presence wasn't even known. I couldn't even penetrate their senses enough to become another heartbeat in the room.

A heart that at that moment had started to replace a beating muscle with cold hard stone that didn't even know what it meant to beat.

A heart that Draven had stolen in a meadow of beauty and destroyed in a grand room of ugly truth. A heart he no longer wanted and a heart...

*I no longer needed.*

## CHAPTER 27
# THE STRONGHOLD OF OLD KEIRA

Pip released me and fell backwards when I screamed out in my grief. I didn't even look back as I ran into the bathroom and threw up an already empty stomach. The painful retching pulled at my stomach muscles in a pain I welcomed.

He didn't want me. Plain and simple. But how could something so plain and simple be so confusingly agonizing to comprehend. I knew I should have stuck with my instincts and trusted my insecurities the way I did around Draven but to witness the truth in my fears was too much to bear. I had wanted to be wrong! I had wanted my fears to be spun from not believing myself good enough and all those times that his arms held me so close to him had said otherwise. But it had all been lies.

And what hurt the most…I had foolishly let myself trust in the first man to take my heart and make it beat solely for him. No matter all the problems we had run into, the one thing we had was an unstoppable love that should have stood the test of all of that Heaven or Hell threw at us but in the end…

It hadn't even stood the test of time. Not even a week.

My stomach clenched again and I spat out the remains of my disgust. I then felt a little hand at my back and without a second to hold it back I threw myself into Pip's arms and broke the dam on my heartbreak. I sobbed into her bare shoulder and she softly uttered words of ease in a different language. Gone was the energetic Pip that couldn't ever hold back the avalanche of words she usually used to describe things but in its place was a friend's comforting security. And I couldn't have needed it more.

After a time, when my eyes were too sore to even close let alone produce tears, I found myself sat outside on the balcony wrapped up in a soft woollen throw. I looked out to the white world and I found myself wanting to join it. To become lost in winter's nature, one so cold that it would steal my breath and with it, the excruciating pain. I just wanted to be numb.

Pip had left me alone as I had asked, although I could tell she hadn't wanted to but what could she do…send me back for more proof on how Draven didn't need me. Didn't…didn't want me. I swallowed that thought with a thick lump of cold hard reality. Hell, I wished I was one of those girls that could find the anger in it all. Find the guy and bitch slap the hell out of him for cheating on her but there was one solid reason why I couldn't find it…

I still loved him.

And it burned me to think that I loved him enough to want him to be happy and if I wasn't enough to give him that then…well…

Well then, here I was now. Alone and forgotten.

I wanted to snap out of my pity party but I knew it would no doubt take a lifetime for that to happen, so what next? The answer was almost as painful as my situation. It was time to do what I did best and after years of knowing and living daily with real pain then faking happiness came to me like punching does to Frank Bruno.

I got up after hours of staring at mountains that didn't change, hard and unyielding like my situation. Before I could even ask myself where I was going I found my feet taking me to the path I had walked yesterday with Pip. I just needed to escape this prison that was starting to blur as home, just for a minute. I needed to find the wind, to get the clear, crisp air and feel the bitter cold against the numb state I had asked for. I needed to feel something other than this endless stream of emptiness that was being pumped around by Draven's fist that had hold of my heart like he was crushing everything that was me…out of me. I couldn't let that happen. I had things to live for, I had good friends, I had the best sister imaginable, one tied to the best brother in law I could ever wish for. And then there was the child she nurtured inside her. The life that needed protecting from a world only I knew existed inside my own world.

I had to survive and to do that I needed the hard shell that I had created, one I had left behind when meeting Draven, and would have to come back out and cocoon me in a stronghold of emotionless feelings. I could do this…couldn't I?

By the time I found my way back up to the silent garden I had convinced myself into believing I could do this. I had no other choice so I might as well suck it up and keep breathing. So Draven didn't want me anymore, yeah that fact hurt more than any open vein this time but in this case bleeding wouldn't change a thing. So what to do…carry on and try and get the hell out of here! I doubted I was much of a concern, considering Draven had his hands full. Oh God! That thought alone brought up more bile that I had to swallow back down.

Think Keira, think! I had to take back my life. There was no more relying on my dark knight to come charging the castle for his woman, no, my knight had found himself another. And this time she was a Goddess! Hell, I felt like the bloody kitchen hand locked in the tower peeling spuds, with finger nails that were never getting clean again! No, I had to become my own knight. I had to save myself and in doing so I had to leave my misery until a time when I could afford to grieve.

I walked down the steps and saw the withered tree that the last time I had sat there held a very different Keira, one full of smiles and laughter thanks to Pip. But now all I wanted to do was curl up inside it like a small wounded animal and stay that way until the frost no longer touched this part of the earth. Surely it wouldn't hurt as much by summer? But as I stepped around the tree, running my fingers along the battered trunk, they fisted as I knew the truth…it would always hurt.

I mean, do any of us ever get over our first love? Do we ever forget the way they made us feel with just one light touch or one soft word whispered in breath by our ear. Even now I was getting goosebumps just thinking about his breath on my neck, my name uttered in bliss as he gave me that part of himself that no other had given me before.

My name spoken in thorns of love.

I shook myself and wiped a stray tear that managed to spring up from my tired eyes.

"It's no longer my name but…hh…hers." God it was hard saying it out loud but for some reason it made it more real and the sooner that happened then the sooner I would come to terms with it. Moving on wasn't an option but living through it was the only way forward.

I moved away from the tree and followed the stone wall that arched up, giving me a beautiful framed picture of the mountains around us. From here you could see the lake and the natural walls that surrounded it, sheer cliff faces that dropped straight down without so much as an incline, drops that would kill given one wrong step. I don't know why but this added to its raw beauty.

I sucked in an icy breath when the wind picked up, making me grab the sides of my cardigan and pull it closer together around myself. I was grateful for the fluffy winter boots that Pip had made me put on my feet once she knew I was determined to sit out on the cold balcony. Thinking of Pip brought a pain to my chest. God how I would miss that little Imp when I left here. She was a true friend and one that I could no doubt trust but could I trust her enough to help me get out of here?

In the back of my mind the thoughts betrayed me still and said that Draven might still come for me, but I squashed that down under an imaginary boot and wiped it on a wall to leave behind me. He wasn't coming for me! That was why Sophia had been so upset... she knew, Vincent knew...and now I knew.

I startled out of my thoughts when I heard a noise to my right. I looked just in time to see something jump back into the bushes and I wondered what animal I had seen? That's when I finally had a good look around and found myself further than I should be. I turned around and saw I had passed the walls to the circular courtyard and managed to walk down some broken steps without falling. How did I do that without thinking about it or without looking where I was going?

The steps went further down and when I looked to where they might lead I saw a dead looking forest looming back at me. I followed it round and noticed that it surrounded the courtyard like an army of dead, straight soldiers all waiting to be commanded forward. Shadows could barely be seen for lack of light, one needed to be able to penetrate the tight knit of trees that held no leaves and never looked like they ever did. It was as though day never saw this part of the earth and it was forever to live in the darkness of night. No wonder it looked as though nothing lived in there, for how can you do that without the sun? Then I thought about Lucius and how I saw the light of the sun in his eyes every time he kissed me. Was this place cursed as he was? It certainly seemed so.

I turned around and began walking back when I heard another noise and this time it didn't come from any animal finding home in that dark, dead dungeon of trees keeping guard. I knew someone was behind me but it was a bit like when you were a kid and heard a noise in your room at night. You didn't want to, would have done anything not to, but no matter how long you waited you knew there was no getting around turning your light on and checking under the bed or in the wardrobe. This was that same moment, heart pounding so loud it felt your ears would pop and having to fist your hands to keep your fingers from shaking.

Turn around Keira. Do it now!

I turned and faced two cloaked figures emerging from the trees and I couldn't help but scrabble back up onto the first couple of broken steps.

"Sister Triad, come with us." A whimsical voice came from the figure on the right and with that, combined with the size of the figures, I knew they were both women. I released a breath but then Layla flashed in my mind and I knew even women weren't safe to me. I needed to be smart and not fall for anything like last time when I nearly drowned.

"What do you want?" I asked, surprising myself with the strength in my voice, one that was completely faked.

"You need to come with us Sister, we will protect you from the evils of men!" The one on the right spoke again and I almost laughed out 'Well it's a bit late for that one, love'. But thankfully I had my brain filter switched on, so remained silent. I mean, so far, they hadn't come screaming at me like some raving banshees so why press matters.

They came closer and a chill ran up my spine that had nothing to do with the weather. The one on the right was taller than the one on the left who still hadn't said a word. They were both heavily hooded and their features remained a secret, but one thing was blindingly obvious, being up here, on top of a bloody mountain, they were definitely not human. I backed up another step and this action provoked something in the one of the left.

"In the name of the Lady of the Moon and the Horned Lord of Death and Resurrection you are one of us child. A Sister of Triad and will come with us, to be one of us, to complete the cycle." The voice was croaky and broken, like someone had stomped on their larynx and it was the complete opposite to the other woman's voice.

"I'm sorry to tell you this, but there is no way I am going anywhere with you two." On hearing this they both turned to look at each other as if what I was saying was unbelievable.

"But you must child, for you are The Triple Goddess." At this I nearly laughed! I didn't think these two were operating on all cylinders if you know what I mean. Or was this Goddess thing another word for Chosen One? Because I doubted very much that was still the case considering what Draven was probably doing right now. God even now, facing these two, that thought still packed a punch in the gut!

"Look lady, I'm sorry to burst your holy bubble but I ain't no Goddess and I ain't going anywhere with you two... sorry but I don't know you." I said, my thick accent coming out with my growing nerves. There was something really off about this whole thing, an undercurrent that was trying to suck me in and using these two to do it. I could feel the magnetic pull lying there just waiting for my shields to break, ready to suck me in a trap, one I wasn't falling for again!

The one on the right whipped her hood back and revealed herself to me as though this would help. I could see her beauty from ten feet away and when I scanned down her body, that's when I noticed the large swell of her belly, one very pregnant belly. Her deep red hair was long and straight and like mine reached her waist. She had kind eyes and a glowing aura about her that said ...safe. Mother.

"You are wrong Keira, you are one of us and we are here to protect you, the Horned God has demanded your presence at the temple to get you ready for the rebirth of his Lord." Oh, okay now that she put it like that, then hell no!

"I think I will pass thanks, but you two go right ahead and say hi to his Hornyness." Okay, I know that sounded rude, but these two were really starting to grate on my last nerve. This was when I actually heard the shorter one growl. I guess she was a big groupie of the Mr Horn!

"You will learn not to be disrespectful girl and know your place!" The other whipped her hood back and I felt myself gag. Jesus that wasn't a face for radio but more like a cave to live with Gollum from Lord of the Rings! She was hideous and every cruel line told a story to that effect.

Deep lines, as though they had almost been cut there, ran from her nostrils to either side of her chin, setting the frame work for a wrinkled muzzle. White, clouded eyes were filmed over by cataracts that shone in the sun like she was lit up inside and these were the windows into a heartless soul. I knew there was evil there, under the cloaking of an old woman and even though the hump back and limping suggested she was more to be pitied than feared, I knew the truth. Her long hair hung like the rags she wore, dirty grey and knotted into tubes from years of neglect.

I started to walk backwards quicker and they in turn started to close the distance between us.

"Stay where you are!" I shouted but this just made me want to gag again when the old woman smiled showing me a set of rotting teeth that hung there by withered gums.

"You are the Maiden Goddess and you have no choice but to become one with the Triad. The Gods have cast this burden onto you, come willingly and you will not suffer," the redhead said, almost singing in delight at seeing my trembling lip. For now, they had friends that had joined them in their quest. The forest became alive with red eyes set deep into shadowy beasts that started to stalk forward on all fours. With taller front legs, they almost dragged their backs legs that remained low to the ground. Long fingers dug into the earth aiding their movements closer and the old woman started to cackle, her laugh sounding like a boiling kettle. All the while the redhead just shook her head like I was a naughty child.

"Take her!" The command was given by a voice neither one of them possessed and I saw a flash of the looming black figure in the background, deeper in the forest that was witnessing this whole scene. I turned round and ran up the remaining steps just as I heard the scream in the air by I don't know what but it caused the shadows to leave the trees and come running at me. I couldn't look back but I could feel the darkness of their souls getting closer. Like an illness you could see, it was threatening in a whole different way.

A thick fog rolled in from all around me and turned my visibility into a white blanket of nothingness. I tripped and felt something snap at my ankle which instantly took the pain from my fall. After pulling my foot underneath me I staggered forward until I regained some footing. I felt the stairs finish and finally something flat under my feet, indicating I had made it back to the courtyard. I then heard a gruff yelp which turned into a blood curding howl. As soon as my body made it past the archway that hung broken over the last step it was as if someone had snapped their fingers and the fog vanished.

I turned my head and screamed at seeing how close the shadowed beasts had come to me, only now they were shadows no longer. I fell backwards in my shock as elongated faces that were made from twisted bark in the shape of fleshless skulls stared back at me. Their long chins pointed to the ground and with mouths stretched like this it showed all seven rows of tiny teeth that were rotating like some medieval meat grinder. They had no eyes just empty spaces where a red glow pulsated in its depths and skin rough with thick gouges torn out in chunks, like some woodcutter had taken an axe to a living tree.

These were terrifying creatures but before my imagination took a dark turn and pictured being ripped apart by these things I took in what was happening. The one closest to me looked hurt and was limping backwards, which looked painful given the way its front leg twisted underneath its body like a broken branch. I looked up and noticed he wasn't the only one retreating. All the shadowed beasts were moving backwards past the two women until they became part of the forest again, where my eyes lost them.

"You should have come when you had the chance child." The old hag said pointing one stiff jointed finger at me. Before I could come back with some smart mouthed comment, the younger one spoke.

"You have angered your ruling God and soon you will see that the Vampire King will not protect you forever...for he knows what you are." This last part was spoken as a warning on the wind, for the two had retreated back like their shadowed friends and the words were spoken in eerie whispers that lingered like an echo in the air.

I scrambled back like a crab, scratching my palms on the rough ground, being too afraid to get up and turn my eyes from what was once there, petrified they might come back. What was I supposed to do now? I mean it was obvious that with the creature howling in pain that none of them could come past the arches that surrounded the courtyard, one had tried and failed if its broken limb was anything to go by. So what next...Do I just get up, dust myself off and calmly walk back to my room?

I decided that I very well could just stay like this all day so I did the only thing I could do, I got up. I dusted myself off. I walked back to my room. But once there I collapsed into a chair and continued how I had spent most of the day...I sobbed.

I must have fell sleep through exhaustion because the next thing I knew I was being woken up by something flicking at my nose. I opened one eye knowing what I would see.

"Oh goodie, you're awake," Pip said bending over me with her head turned to the side like a colourful parrot.

"Of course, and you would be too if I flicked your nose with those nails!" I commented dryly but she just laughed and looked at one painted like a liquorice allsort, blue sugar balls and all.

"You look like shit by the way and only have about fifteen minutes to make yourself look pretty." I frowned at her thinking. The Great Hall was the last place I wanted to see right now, but then I still noticed the light coming through the windows. Confusion took over my annoyance and I couldn't help but ask,

"Why?"

"Because you don't want Draven to see you like that now, do you?" On hearing this I shot up out of the seat like the chair had bit me.

"What! He's here?" I asked, heart pounding greater than when I faced those creatures only hours ago.

"Well no but... I have to send you back." Pip said, trying to hide her desperation, which made me wonder what she was up to. I folded my arms across my chest in nothing short of defiance and stood my ground, even though at that moment I really needed to both pee and rub the annoying sleep out of my eyes.

"No!" I said simply making Pip's eyes go wide.

"Ah come on Toots, don't make this hard."

"Sod that Pip, I refuse to ever go back there! I won't do it and I don't understand why you would want me to." Okay, here it was, the bit she really didn't want to tell me.

"Look, if it was left up to me then you could sit here all day and grow roots if you wanted, but it isn't up to me and now it isn't up to you." She was starting to get agitated and very un-Pip like.

"What are you talking about?" I just knew I wasn't going to like this answer.

"He wants me to send you to him...demanded actually, so you're just going to have to suck it up like a big girl and direct your anger at the man himself." I almost choked... it couldn't be...could it?

"Draven... wants to see me?"

"The King has ordered it and now knowing I am the one responsible for sending you to him in the first place, there is little I can do but obey." She slumped down in the chair and all of a sudden looked very worn out.

"I'm sorry for all of this Pip," I said coming back over to join her on the opposite couch. I finally rubbed the crust out of the corners of my eyes and rested my neck on the back of the chair looking up trying to find reasons in this room full of whys?

"It's alright Toots, not your fault you're a pain in the ass!" She said with humour glinting in lush green eyes. I smiled and threw a cushion at her head in retaliation. She caught it without looking and placed it behind her head like she needed it to help her relax.

"That might be so, but it doesn't change the fact...I can't go Pip." At this she bolted upright, no longer looking relaxed.

"Toots!" She said in warning, but I just waved her off.

"No Pip, I said before and I'm saying it again, I am not going and his Highness can't do a damn thing to make me!" I said feeling the pulse of anger swimming on the surface getting ready to emerge.

"Oh shit, please don't do this to me Toots, the King scares the Bejesus out of me and you want me to tell him...no?" She wasn't kidding, she looked terrified.

"Well, I can't do it without you sending me back and that kind of kills my point doesn't it? I'm sorry Pip, but he can order me around as much as he likes but that fact remains I am not his to order into doing anything... not anymore." I added feeling the bite of pain in my chest at the memory.

"So let me get this straight..." She stood up and held her hand out in a dramatic way about to count her fingers off with each point she was about to make.

"One, you want me to send myself back there...two, you want me to tell the King and one of the most powerful Beings on earth, that I couldn't send his Chosen One back because of what exactly?" This made me stand up and face her.

"I don't know, you could try reminding him that next time not to listen to his masterful dick! Yeah, tell him that and while you're at it tell him that I may only be a lowly human but he's a low life two timing bastard who doesn't deserve this low ranking human...oh and don't forget to mention how this 'Chosen One' un-chooses him! Yeah I think that will do it!" I said panting like a rabid dog.

"Feel better?" She asked trying to hold in her smirk. I deflated into the chair I had left, stuck out my bottom lip and shook my head saying,

"Yeah, I think I do."

"Good, but you know I'm not going to say all that...right?" Pip said sideways at me from checking another nail, I think this time it was a fruit salad wrapper.

"Why not, it was a damn good speech?"

"And to the point definitely, but never the less I like my head attached to my spine thank you very much and I hear it's very hard to have sex without an actual body, I might add." Pip said finishing with doing the actual actions for sex, which I so didn't need to see.

"Thanks for the educating sex display that I so didn't need, but my answer is still going to be no Pip. I can't see him."

"Why not? You could say all that to his face and hell…knock his block off for all I care but by the powers of Greyskull Toots, I can't go there and tell him for you." She was starting to look desperate and I felt my reserve slipping.

"Because I know if I take one look at him ever again then I don't know if I could stop myself from begging him and I have more self-respect than that. It would break the last fragments of my heart Pip, I can't do that to myself…I just… can't." At this she finally softened and thankfully by seeing how much this meant to me she caved before I did.

"Alright, but if I come back dead then I'm blaming you! Oh and if you think you have seen creepy then you have a shit load of spooky in store when I haunt your ass for the rest of your days!" I laughed a little snort at her adorable threat and with one guilty look from me she rolled her eyes and came over to kneel next to my chair.

"Alright, I am going to do this but if I do then my one condition is that you're coming with me." What! No way...she saw my face and cut me off before I even started to voice my opinions on that matter.

"He won't know you're there, Toots. You will be just in the background being a witness. You will be hidden I promise, but I am not going in there and telling the King why…that is not my place, that and like I said, I'm not bloody suicidal!"

"Aww come on, we both know Adam could take Draven." I said trying to lighten the shadows that had crept in, rimming her eyes with doubt. She raised an eyebrow in a look that said…you think so?

"Alright Toots, time to get this show on the road because Mr 'I Am Too Impatient for my Kingdom' is calling me."

"He can do that?"

"Oh Toots, don't you yet realise…?" She crawled on my lap and slapped her palms to my temple in what was becoming an everyday occurrence before finishing her statement…

*"He can do anything he wants!"*

# CHAPTER 28
# ANGRY KING

I had once again found myself whisked off to a place my body didn't follow. I opened my eyes and for a moment I held my breath in waiting for Pip's promise to present itself.

I took in my surroundings and realised I was in a room I had not seen since this whole thing began. Draven's Marble room took me back to what seemed like a lifetime ago and I guess in a way it was, for this life that I was living now was still new. Of course, the difference was that before I was living that life for Draven, now I had no need for this supernatural existence. Did that mean I could just go back to the way I was before…? Somehow, I didn't think so.

Still, seeing this room plunged me back to that day when Draven plucked me from my ordinary life and set in motion the wheels that spun me into one filled with the unimaginable. I still remember lying there on that same couch waiting for everyone to leave the room. It was just after Draven had taken me from the car park outside Afterlife. I was running from my past and ended up running into the arms that held my future. At that time I was confused by what to think of my handsome captor and now it was no better, as I was even more confused.

Why he wanted me here I couldn't understand. The person he wanted was by his side once again and with me out of the way, didn't that make things easier on him? Or was it because he felt responsible for my human life and he was now doing the responsible thing in trying to get me back to my family? Either way I was definitely confused.

For the moment the magnificence of the room just held me…Pip and a magnitude of marble statues, some bigger than your average person, like the two winged warrior Angels that stood either side of the gigantic fireplace. The room was long and immensely grand, with lush red and gold fabrics that complemented the pale marble that ran throughout the room. Marble table tops and a mix of carved Gods and Demons on plinths ran along the edges, while softer furniture was placed in certain parts, creating separate sitting areas from the main focal point of the room.

The grandest table stood there in the centre like it belonged in some royal dining room used by the world's most powerful people. Of course, this table was most likely used by the most powerful people in the world and needless to say, none of those were human. The thought of that dining experience caused a tingling in a body that wasn't fully here.

It was one of the most beautiful pieces of furniture I had ever seen and it had a red tint to the high polished wood which drew me to believe it was made from Brazilian Rosewood thanks to one I had seen before on a school trip to a manor house in the Midlands. It gleamed under the rustic wrought iron chandelier that flickered against the smooth marble that dominated the room. The other domination in the room, being that the table was large enough to hold twenty people on each side with only one end that had a seat, one that was clearly at the ready for the master of the house. All the seats, but one, were made from the same high polished wood. Two long rows of arched backed chairs that looked like gothic steeples from an imposing cathedral stood in waiting ready to be filled by Draven's elite. But at the top was nothing short of a carved marble throne that was more than fit for a King's place.

It was made from a marble I had never seen before and was the only piece in the room that was like it. It was the purest of white but veined with blood crimson running through it like that of a person. Almost like someone's skin had been turned transparent and the travelling blood could be seen flowing around the human body.

It stood taller than the rest and had two large spiral pillars that joined the wide arm rests. From where I stood I couldn't see if there was a comforting cushion on the seat but I knew the chair was more than wide enough for Draven's large frame with no doubt room to spare.

The back arched like the others but a round section had been cut out to fit the glass plate that the window behind caught in its daylight. It was one piece that was swirls of yellows, oranges and reds that were made to look as though the section contained liquid fire. In the centre a simple symbol and it was one I was very familiar with. The symbol was the same one I had lived with on my body since my birth, the same one I had received as acceptance on entering the Temple and the very symbol that to this day I still didn't understand. I had asked Draven about it but every time I had mentioned it, the subject had been brushed away as being unimportant. But every time I saw it, it was as if I could feel a pulsing at the back of my skull where it lay hidden under my hair line. Now you couldn't tell me that meant nothing!

The odd shape at the back of my neck was like a quarter moon with its back to a sideward V but this time it was different and I realised why. In the centre of the seat's glass plate it was angled differently. Now it was an A with the bottom parts flicked upwards and inside the bottom part of the A was the quarter moon fit snug with added flat side pieces. I was just about to ask Pip to test whether or not she could hear me when I heard the door open and my heart leapt at the sight.

Draven walked in dominating the room with every step and with one look at his granite features that were set in a formidable wrath, I actually took a step back. With one scan of the room his eyes narrowed and a muscle in his jaw twitched before even saying a word. He walked up to his throne and the sound of it moving back against the stone floor echoed around the room making me flinch. He hadn't touched it but it slid back by an invisible force and the King took his seat.

My heart pounded so hard it hurt and I was sure, even though it wasn't in the room with me, that it would be heard. It was just the sight of him like this and I now could fully understand why Pip hadn't wanted to be the one to tell him no. This was not a man you said that word to often and survived, that much was as clear as seeing your reflection in the high sheen of the marble that gave this room its name.

Draven was dressed all in black and it was the first time I had seen him in one of these visions back in a full suit. He unbuttoned his jacket and leaned back before resting one elbow on the solid arm rest. His deep set eyes and his black stare reflected his dark mood, causing my guilt at putting Pip through this to double. Poor Pip might have me unseen by her side, in her magic shadows but I was unlikely back up for the clear anger on Draven's face. But it was not only Draven she had to contend with, it was also Vincent, Sophia, Zagan and Takeshi who were all situated behind their master. I gulped on her behalf.

Pip started to bow graciously and Draven actually growled.

"Cut the fucking formality Imp and tell me why you're here and Keira is not!" Draven snapped out with a voice so deep it was like he had swallowed gravel. It was also the first time I had heard Draven swear in front of me this way but then again, as far as he was concerned, he wasn't in front of me.

"My great Lord, she...she would not come." Pip looked like she really didn't want to say it and the reaction she received backed up her fears. Draven roared out and banged a hammer like fist on the table and a crack travelled almost the full length, splitting the beautiful wood down the centre. Pip tried not to cringe but Draven ended up being the only one in the room that didn't react to his outburst.

"Dom, calm yourself." Vincent braved to say but he was shot down with one of Draven's hands, held up in a motion for silence. Draven then looked as though he was trying to get his dangerous emotions in check for a few still moments. He placed his hand at the place of impact and the crack that had ended just short of the table's edge started to fuse back together and it did so all the way back to Draven's large hand.

With that epic over-reaction finished Draven opened his eyes and stared at one scared Pip.

"Come closer!" His command was one I wouldn't have liked to have received right now but as Pip walked closer I did the same, keeping my word and watching her back while facing this.

"What do you mean...she would not come?" This part that was repeated by Draven came out in nothing short of a demonic growl.

"She refused to see you, my Lord." Pip stated bravely making Draven's glare darken further. Meanwhile I was utterly confused as to why he was behaving this way? It just didn't make any sense...or was I still needed for something and I had been kept in the dark all this time? Was I not only just a pawn for Lucius but one for Draven as well?

"I tried to convince her of your order my Lord, but she is, as you know, a little wilful." At this Draven looked like he would have throttled me at that moment, given half a chance.

"Wilful or not, I have ordered her to be sent to me and as you know little Imp, I am not a patient King." Pip looked at that moment like she wanted to run away and with Draven's penetrating natural dominance, I really didn't blame her.

"My Lord...I...can't...I..."

"ENOUGH! Bring her to me now, with or without her approval!" Draven was so furious I saw his eyes had changed from their usual very dark night colour to flaming purple in seconds. But this wouldn't have stopped me from what I did next. I stormed past Pip and stood myself in front of him ready for the fight.

"How dare you! You can't order me around after you cheated on me, you two timing shithead! And who the hell do you think you are talking to my friend like that? You might be a King but at the moment it's 'King of the Assholes' speaking about me like I am one of your bloody minions ready to jump on bloody command!" I screamed out but only when I had finished and not one person registered what I had said I realised I still wasn't being seen. But wait...I looked up and saw a slight smirk on Vincent's face. Could he see me? He was staring straight at me and when I looked behind me to see if there was anything there, I realised that yes...he could see me!

I looked back at him and he winked at me without anyone noticing.

"You can see me?" I couldn't help but say and when I saw the slightest nod I knew he was the only one.

"Well at least someone enjoyed my speech," I said sarcastically and again he smirked as if to say, yeah, he really did.

"But my Lord...you know I can't do that...I...I cannot bring someone unwilling, it doesn't work like that...the mind has to be open for the taking, she has to want for you to see her." Pip said emphasising the word 'want' making Draven's frown deepen until it became scary.

"And why is it you suppose she refuses?" Draven asked folding his arms across his massive chest that expanded even more when he was trying to rein in his anger.

"Oh for bloody hell's sake, do me a favour Vincent and smack your brother upside his head for me. I think he needs to get a clue!" I snapped out making Vincent trying desperately to hold in his need to grin.

"My Lord, it is not my place to say." She said lowering her head in submission.

"Make it your place, little Imp!" Draven wasn't giving an inch for her to back out of this one and my guilt tripled. Maybe I should have just been brave and not chickened out of doing this but at the time I had felt more needy than angry but at seeing this...well I felt more like punching than grovelling.

"My guess....she saw something she didn't like the last time she asked to see you." At this I saw Sophia and Vincent look sideways at each other.

"Yeah, you're damn right I did!" I shouted but when Vincent's eyes flashed to mine, Sophia noticed his tense expression. Now this was the part where things were turning even more serious. However Draven took a deep breath and closed his eyes as though this new information caused strain and tension in his handsome face. Well so it should I thought, folding my arms.

"Keira doesn't know what she saw and it is clear she does not know what is best for her. No matter what the circumstances are or how they may have changed, she will be returned to me. You will go back to your Master and tell him the negotiations have now changed. I know Keira too well, as now it is quite possible, given half the chance, she will do something stupid! Foolish girl!" He added angrily and he wasn't the only one feeling as though about to blow! I was utterly fuming!

I think Vincent saw the moment my eyes turned cold and my blood started to boil. He touched his brother's shoulder and said,

"Brother, think, you are upset and are not thinking clearly. Keira knows what she saw, as did we all." At this Draven stood so quickly the throne was tossed as though it was made from polystyrene to one side and it crashed into a sitting area like a boulder from a mountain slide. Wood splintered and pieces of a sofa, small table and a mounted vase in a glass square turned into the broken evidence of Draven's destruction.

"Dominic, NO!" Sophia shouted but it made no difference to what I was already seeing. I stood there with my mouth hanging open at the sight of Draven squaring up to his brother, one hand curled into the shirt he was wearing.

"Tell me Brother, what did you see?" Draven snarled but Vincent didn't even flinch or back away one inch.

"We saw you, my Brother...breaking her heart." Vincent said softly and then turned to look at me before continuing,

"As you still do now," he said then his eyes lowered in sadness but it was not before Draven had seen where he was looking at...or more like...who.

340

Draven turned around after letting go of his brother and looked straight at me like we were the only two people in the room.

"Keira?" He said my name in a breath and tears filled my eyes at hearing it. It was amazing how one name could hold so much emotion... defence...guilt...shame... and even love, but what did my name hold for Draven, I was too emotional to tell. Maybe all of these things, maybe none, but one thing I did read in his eyes was shock and that brought me back to my situation like a cold hard slap across the face.

"Pip, get me out of here!" I said in nothing short of a plea and Draven's eyes turned from softly holding my gaze to stormy resentment on hearing these words. I looked away before my will crumbled but one look at Pip, said she was torn.

"You will stay, Keira!" Draven's voice quickly went from amazed to authoritative in seconds but when I shouted out Pip's name it changed again.

"Keira, NO! Don't do this!" This time it was in pleading and my last response looked like it hit him the hardest.

"No Draven, I have heard enough! Just let me GO!" I shouted and just as I and Pip started to fade I heard Draven's last roar followed by a word that sent my mind, body and soul into a shuddering mess.

"NEVER!"

I collapsed back into myself and I noticed Pip do the same, only now she was panting on the floor. Tears were streaming down my cheeks and I couldn't stop my hands from shaking at the energy that still coursed under my skin like a current of supernatural electricity. I placed a shaky hand on Pip's shoulder and she flinched at the contact.

"Pip...are you alright?" I asked my friend who looked just as shaken up as I did.

"Y...yeah...I think so...I...I mean...wow, I have never, ever, ever, in all my years...but wow."

"What...what is it?" I asked not knowing whether the reason for her broken sentence was a good thing or not.

"Defied a King...HA! Toot's, I defied a King! A KING!" She shot up and started to jump around the room leaving me feeling like I had taken crazy pills! Christ, even her pompoms were flying off her skirt! I stood up trying to think of a way to calm her enough for her to explain.

"Pip? Are you sure you're alright?" I asked feeling like any minute she was going to go supernova on me and then I would find myself answering to Adam...and that was so not good.

Speaking of Adam, as if on cue, he walked in the room...well walked is putting it lightly, more like raced would be a better explanation. He even skidded when taking a corner of the room too quickly. He spotted Pip still dancing around in circles, laughing her little green locks off and I saw all the air leave him in a whoosh. Relief washed over his stern features at seeing his wife overcome with such happiness and when she noticed him finally her eyes lit up.

"Nerdy!" She called him before taking a running jump and blast-off, she was in his arms. His glasses twisted and his hair tumbled in every direction thanks to his wife's erratic little kisses that she was covering him in.

"Pipper?" He said softy but when she wouldn't stop he tried for something sterner.

"Winifred!" At this she finally stilled and she looked up at him with her hands still clutched firmly behind his neck.

"My darling wife, as much as it pleases me to see you so happy, please put me out of my misery and explain." She smiled, then readjusted his glasses for him. She jumped out of his arms and came over to stand next to me before slapping her arm round my shoulders and pulling me closer to her.

"Me and Keira defied the King." She said proudly and Adam looked like he had swallowed a bug. However, instead of going mad and screaming in what looked like a close emotion that could possibly make an appearance, he just calmly cleared his throat and pushed his glasses further up his nose.

"Please explain what you mean by that exactly." He said causing Pip to start rocking back and forth on her heels like a child hiding a secret.

"The King wanted me to send a vision of Keira back to him, but considering he's been a really bad boyfriend... Hugh Hefner style...." She felt me flinch and turned to whisper 'sorry' before carrying on.

"...then she refused, but she came to see what he had to say but you know when I do that thing...remember the bombing in Rastenburg, East Prussia. Well anyway, same deal but then lovely Keira here was just too damned angry and wanted to be seen at the end. Well, then the King goes bat shit crazy right! So when he orders me to keep Keira there we just cut and run, thus completing my epic tale of how an Imp managed to defy a King." She said this last part in a low voice, mimicking a deep manly voice that could have been a piss take on Draven.

Adam rolled his eyes before closing them as he processed the 'epic' story Pip had royally named it. I looked at Pip and she was actually chewing on her bottom lip looking nervous, awaiting Adam's approval.

"So let me get this perfectly straight, Keira, you didn't want to stay with the King...am I right?" He still hadn't opened his eyes and without looking he held up his hand to stop Pip from answering.

"No, I didn't." I answered in a way that I would have if I had been caught fighting in the playground at school and this was now the headmaster's office I was stood in.

"And he knew this?" This time he looked straight at me and seeing that gaze I could feel the power that lay dormant but waiting under his 'Everyday Joe' persona.

"Oh trust me, I made it clear!" I said, still trying to deal with my mixed feelings on the matter.

"Very well then. I see not a King ordering his subjects, but a man ordering his lover to stay when he has given her no reasons to do so. You were right in your actions. Come here my naughty little Squeak." At this she 'yipped' and ran at him full pelt. He caught her again and she started to rub herself up and down against him like a purring cat.

"Will you be alright on your own for a bit, I need to go and screw some sexy brains out but I will be back for you later...okay?" She asked as Adam was devouring her neck in a bite that looked more painful than arousing but if Pip's moans were anything to go by then looks were clearly deceiving.

"I will be fine," I said knowing the inevitable breakdown that would consume me when left alone but this time I welcomed it. Adam started to take her to the door and I remembered what I really wanted to say as I ran round the edge of the room's divider and called her name just as they went round the corner. I looked down thinking I was too late but then I saw just Pip's head pop around the door frame where Adam was still holding her. I couldn't help but laugh a little at how comical it looked.

"Yeah Toots?"

"I...I just wanted to say...Thank you. You didn't have to do that for me but you did and I just wanted you to know...I will never forget it, Winifred." The smile she gave me brought a light to my soul that had already started drowning by darkness. But this girl...this little Imp had brought me more than just an impossible friendship...she had brought me truth, a truth that had the faintest glimmer of hope surrounding it. No matter how faint that hope was, it was there all the same.

"I know you won't, just as I will never forget the way you stood up to the most powerful leader of our existence for a little Imp like me. I will never forget, my friend... Keira." She finished with a wink and I filled with warmth at hearing the first time she said my name, like I had done the same with her. She disappeared back around the corner and I heard her excited giggles until a door slammed shut down the hall.

As my friend left me, all the emotional day's events came colliding to the forefront of my mind. I collapsed onto the bed and curled my body up in a foetal position to continue once again how I had started the day...feeling confused, lost and hurt. Emotions that consumed me until my tears ran dry for the second time and in-keeping with the theme, I passed out in exhaustion. But unlike the circle I had come back to, something different happened.

"Keira!" My name was spoken by the only being I ever wanted to hand over control of my dreams to....

*Draven.*

# CHAPTER 29
# DRAVEN'S STORM

B a doom, ba doom, ba doom. The beating in my chest played to a rhythm of death as I ran for my life. Something was chasing me and from the sounds of the growls coming from close by, I wasn't just being chased…no… I was also being played with.

The forest floor bit into the skin on the bottom of my feet as I ran further and further into the unknown. Branches grabbed out at me as though they were aiding the beast's attempts at slowing me down. But I couldn't stop…I must not stop. I kept looking behind me to try and judge how close I was to being ripped apart but every time I looked back I would lose precious seconds by slowing my senses into being more careful.

My thin white dress snagged on a bush I jumped over and ripped all the way up to my thigh. Even what I was wearing was against me. I tried to process what events had brought me to this point and the only answer I received was the beast's growls as a reminder. That one word screamed through my brain, vibrating around every corner in a half man, half demonic roar….NEVER!

Draven's warning had come through in a clear cut message. He would never let me go and I was running now to find out why. Only the beast behind me didn't want me to know why….it just wanted me.

Another few steps brought me closer to the end of the forest, as I could see the night's moon shining through the patch of trees ahead. I was almost at a clearing but what lay ahead for me I didn't yet know. Would the beast stop playing with its prey and just take me for the final kill?

I could almost feel its breath on my bare legs where the skirt of my dress had been sacrificed to the forest. It was gaining on me and I could feel it thinking when was best to pounce, when best to finish what it had started and take what it wanted from my body. I could almost hear its thoughts, its pleasure in the idea of the feast it would soon be tasting. It wanted me, without one shred of a doubt but how it would take me left me quaking inside. I didn't know whether the trembling in my blood was making me run quicker or just the adrenaline that kept my body going was being powered by something greater.

"Not going to make it, little rabbit!" The voice warned through the trees in a rough whisper that echoed off the rough bark from every tree in my path. This made me push for that extra boost as the light of the clearing started to grow brighter, my escape and my sanctuary was so close I could almost feel the light touching my skin. It would save me, it would save me, I repeated over and over in my head but the beast could hear me and responded, causing the trees to shake.

"I am your sanctuary, little rabbit. I am your saviour and I am your HOME!" It shouted this last part and I felt the earth ripple beneath my feet. I looked up to see the leaves that couldn't hold on through its demand rain down around me. I swallowed down the fear and churned it into more energy directed at my survival. I was nearly there...I was nearly there...Just a bit more. I was so close ...I was...I was...

Trapped!

I watched in horror as six shadows came in line with the bluish moon lit behind them, all of which were standing there waiting for me to run straight into their trap.

Wolves. I was now trapped by six wolves. I froze as they started to fan out around me. Black and huge, being twice the size of regular wolves, they looked as though driven straight from the gates of Hell. All with long snouts that showcased row after row of bloody fangs that didn't look as though they would all fit. These were not the majestic creatures that ruled the forest and sang at the moon in howls of dominance. No, these were not even of this earth and knew nothing of its living beauty. These creatures knew only one thing and they relished in delight of it. They knew how to hunt, how to terrify and how to kill. And now...they would soon know the taste of my fear.

One coming closer still shook out its black matted pelt and its eyes started to change from clouded blue to deep vein crimson. As those eyes of death locked onto me I started to back away, knowing I was just extending the inevitable. But then something different started to happen.

The wolves behind this one started to whine and back away. It was as though they saw something that had them spooked and as they began to slowly retreat they snapped at each other in frustration. It was only when backing away further that I started to realise why. A pair of steel bands crossed over my upper body and my back hit a solid force. All the air left my lungs and the feeling of being trapped had me panicking inside. I couldn't move and the wolf that was closest was weighing up the situation. I was so close to being his kill but the beast behind me had me caught in his grasp finally and didn't want to let me go.

"Caught at last, little rabbit." The demonic voice spoke in my ear and its words didn't stop there. It travelled down my spine like caressing fingertips received from a lover. The wolf in front came closer still and growled, making its lips curl back as it bared its triple row of teeth at us. They were crisscrossed over one another and it looked as though this thing could chew its way through barbed wire if it wanted to.

However the beast at my back merely laughed deep and grounded as though the act of this Hellhound was nothing but a bit of entertainment. However the wolf didn't appreciate the lack of fear and I felt the spray from his mouth as it snapped out just missing my leg by inches. This finally got the beast's attention.

"MINE!" It roared above my head and tightened its hold of me until just before the point of pain. The beast then growled in anger and the wolf started trying to retreat like the rest of its pack. Unfortunately for it though it didn't get very far without first being punished. Its eyes started to turn deathly white and the end of its fur start to smoke as if being set on fire by an invisible flame. It rolled over and over setting the forest floor alight with its actions until one final snarl from behind me finished everything. The wolf fell to the ground and everything around it turned to white ash that the wind picked up and took along its way. The wolf remained still for a few moments and the chest against my back regained some calm for its breathing slowed.

"Be gone with you, Gytrash." On hearing this, the wolf got up and staggered off into the mist that now surrounded the clearing ahead, leaving me and the beast alone in a forest full of abandoned life.

"Why do you run from me, little rabbit? Why run when I will always catch you?" The voice started off as a Demon but finished as that of a man. That of...

Draven.

On hearing his voice my feet fell beneath me but his arms held me up like an unrelenting force. He was the beast. The one hunting me in my dreams. For I knew now what this was and had always been...a reality of my situation transformed into a dream. Draven was always there, was always going to be there and no words of mine would make it otherwise. He was never going to let me go, just as deep down I knew I would never do the same. The reality of this dream hit me and I spoke my suspicions out loud.

"You're manipulating my dreams?" I felt his head lower so his lips could be closer to my neck. I felt the contact he made there all the way to my bones and I shuddered, still with his unbreakable hold on me.

"Yes and you continued to run from those dreams, turning me into a beast when all I wanted to do was find you, to... have you." He sounded hurt but that changed with the last two words, ones said in a possessive growl that was only enhanced by the hold of his hand at the column of my neck. He wasn't hurting me but I could feel the strength in his fingertips that held me in their unyielding grip.

"But...why?" I asked feeling the words that formed under his hand and in return I felt his lips smile under my ear. The hand he had free started to wander down my waist gathering thin material as it went. I swallowed hard at the feeling of being touched by such raw power.

"Why? Explain this to me Keira...how is it that after all I have told you, after all I have confessed...." This last word rolled out of him in a hiss that told me all I needed to know about his emotions, emotions he was trying desperately to hold in check, fighting for the control that he was so utterly used to having was the hardest thing for him to give into.

"...explain to me why you run from me? Don't you yet understand how that is not an option?" I closed my eyes at the stream of confusing emotions that hit me like a thunderbolt. Why was it that he was still doing this to me? Didn't he already have who he wanted in his bed, yet his hand continued its journey south, igniting my flesh as he went.

"You...you chose another!" I stammered out and his hand fisted in the last bit of material covering my womanly core.

"No!" He growled in my ear making me tense up in his hold.

"I chose only you, my little frightened bird, one whom so

desperately wants to take flight, isn't that so…you wish to fly away from me?" Before I could answer his hand dipped the last inches until he covered my bare and waiting sex. At the first feel of contact I moaned out my "Yes" making him growl.

"Then a living cage I will keep you in!" He promised before spinning me round to face him and taking possession of my mouth. His lips commanded my own into a response and all my will to hold back broke with a resounding snap. As soon as our lips touched it was the start of something explosive and we both marvelled in it together.

I couldn't stop my hands from curling up to his shoulders to pull him impossibly closer still. I wanted him to feel my heart beating solely for him. I wanted him to feel each thud of my pulse that played to the rhythm he set just by having his hands on me. I wanted to fool myself and drown in the lost sensations that tugged at my vulnerability. I just…wanted….him.

I could feel his hands almost shaking and then they would fist holding me closer until they stopped shaking. It was as if he was trying to hold onto me, afraid that I might finally float away this time without ever coming back. I could feel every solid inch of him pressing into me and moulding me to fit his frame. Well, if this was his living cage then he could keep me here and never let me out, hell I would even swallow the key for him!

I felt the earth moving beneath us and when I tried to look he grabbed my face with both hands to keep me there. Unbelievably his kiss got deeper still and I felt myself giving in to his control with little resistance. He explored my mouth like it was the first time and my senses started to become overloaded. I was panting for air so he had no choice but to let me gain a moment of freedom.

His lips travelled across my jaw line and down my throat, nipping and sucking his way along. Without his lips on mine, I felt some of my senses coming back and when I opened my eyes I couldn't help but flinch at what I saw. Not only was Draven in his other form, causing the forest around him to glow but that forest was now slowing dying and floating away. The trees looked as though the life was being drained from them by an unknown source and each one was in a different stage of deterioration. Ones closest to us seem to be the worst off as they were turning grey with a bright white light burning in the centre. It was if they were dying from the inside out and when one burst into a cloud of ash I jumped in Draven's arms.

"Ssshh, you're safe," he whispered softly in my ear and I couldn't help myself from relaxing. No matter what was happening between us I knew that Draven would always have that effect on me...I would always feel the safety in him. And this was why I grabbed his face and pulled it to mine in my own fierce, possessive kiss.

He groaned low in his throat till it almost sounded like pain and before I could pull away to ask, he lifted me with both hands holding my cheeks and then he wrapped my legs around his waist. That was when everything around us burst all at once as the rest of the forest died away. I felt the ground's rumbling grow stronger and stronger until pieces of the earth started to fall into the clutches of Hell. I tried to be scared but Draven wouldn't let me. I clutched on tight and all the air left me in a whoosh as I felt Draven start to lean forward and as we were about to fall I called out breaking our connected lips,

"Draven!" The only response to his action I received was a confident smile. I felt my weight shift and tried to cling on tighter but when he gave me a wink it was the only notice I received before his mighty wings erupted from his back. Just before we should have hit the ground I looked back in the less than seconds I had and saw the last of the earth collapsing away leaving nothing between us and death but his wings.

He held me tight as he let us both free fall for terrifying moments before I felt the force of his moving wings pull us both backwards. I must have screamed but I was sure the sound of the destruction we were leaving behind had drowned out my despair.

"Do you think I would ever let you fall, my Keira?" Draven whispered into my hair as my face had found a secure spot in his neck to bury my fears in. He actually chuckled at my response when I shook my head quickly still not leaving my secure hold that was sure to be half strangling him.

I felt the soft pull of his wings that set a calming motion to our flight and it was a strange feeling as my eyes started to drift in a sleepy state. What would it be like to have a dream within a dream I wondered as my eyes kept creeping shut?

"We are here," Draven said in my ear after a time and I shivered in response at feeling his lips once again. As he set us down I still didn't open my eyes as now a new fear at where we would be this time found its way to my mind. I could hear his wings ruffle slightly before folding back into place and his hold on me forced my legs down to the ground. This was when I finally gave in and opened my eyes.

"What is this place?" I asked as I took in the sight before me. He released me and before he said a word he walked over to an iron fitting that was embedded into the rock of the cave wall. He lifted his hand and fire emerged in his palm before he transferred it over to the twisted torch that was the length of my arm.

"This is my place, my…secret place." I had never heard Draven sound so vulnerable before and he waited for my reaction silently. I looked around the dimly lit room that was no doubt hidden from the outside world.

This was his place. A place for solitude and personal time.

I don't know what I found more surprising, the mountain cave I now stood in that reminded me of a giant nesting place for a huge bird or that Draven even had a place of his own. I walked closer to the edge and Draven rumbled his worried warning making me smile. It wasn't a large opening, just big enough to have fit Draven through to land on the slight ledge that stuck out further than the cave. This side of the mountain was mostly hidden from anyone's view and as far as secret places went this one was as secret as they came.

The view below was engulfed in a white mist that seemed to roll along like fallen clouds making me feel like a bird's pet…or prey. I turned around and saw the room was about the size of the full downstairs of Libby and Frank's house and went further back than I could see. It looked like the shadows in the rock that were the size of people could have been doors that lead further into the mountain. But there was one aspect of the room there was no escaping and being how I craved Draven's touch, the sight of the low bed in the middle had every nerve in my being screaming out what my body wanted.

"Come here!" The soft command had me facing Draven to see if his features matched up with that command but he remained in shadows with his back to the light. He was no longer in his other form but by no means did this make him seem less deadly. He stood with his arms folded causing the material he wore to stretch painfully around his biceps, that tensed harder when I didn't move. His long legs were also encased in black and this combined with his olive skin was creating him as the figure Gods were seen as.

"Now, little rabbit!" He said, only this time in harsher tones. In this situation, I knew better than to push at the restraints that held his anger in check. I nodded once and walked slowly towards him feeling exactly like the new name he had given me. Even if this was a dream it didn't deter from how intimidating Draven was naturally.

Once I got within an arm's reach, he pounced on me like the

predator he portrayed so well. He walked into me making me back up until I fell backwards. At the last second, he grabbed my forearm and lowered me onto the bed slowly, with one hand holding all my body weight like it was no more than the pillows my head sank into.

Half his face still belonged to the shadows, but the other half made me blush. The pure carnal look of lust he showed me was heart pounding. He still stood above me as he drank in the sight of me like some helpless victim of his waiting to be devoured. His eyes trailed the full length of me up and down, again and again and the heat in my cheeks burned hotter than ever before. His eyes seemed caught in an unintentional trance I held him in and they stayed frozen at my breasts that were heaving with my laboured breaths. I couldn't stand it any longer and made a move to cover myself up when he made a growl that vibrated around the hidden room.

"Put your hands above your head!" He ordered, and I couldn't stop from shaking when I complied. However, when he took in my fearful reactions he lightened my heart by winking at me before complimenting me,

"Good Girl!" His approval seemed to shoot down to the junction of my thighs and pleasure took the place of fear.

He leaned over slightly and I thought he would move further to settle himself over me but I was wrong. He had grabbed the edges of my skirt and torn the whole dress in two without any effort used. He whipped the material from under me with the slightest of flicks and soon I was trembling from a mixture of the cold chill the night offered and the anticipation of what would come next. As I was left naked in every place for him to drink in, I watched as he stripped his body of clothes so that he was the same.

At this I had to close my eyes at the onslaught of my senses and he hadn't even touched me yet. I must have jumped a bloody mile when I finally felt his hand run lightly up my inner leg. My hands came down on impulse and my legs locked closed.

"Uh ah, back in position, little rabbit, I want to enjoy you while I have you here and that means…" He ran both hands further up and pushed my legs aside with little pressure needed.

"…taking my time." He stated roughly as he leaned the rest of his body down onto me. He took my lips in a kiss so deep it was as if he was marking me as his. And I let him like a willing sacrifice ready to throw myself onto the heated brand for just one touch. His hands curved round my sides with palms plastered as flat against my skin as he could get them.

They travelled upwards and I shuddered when they brushed the side of my breasts. But he kept going until they both curled around my arms, coming to finish at my wrists. Once there he shackled them before lifting them above my head. He then transferred one wrist to the other and held both with one large hand that had no problem with the task.

"Hey!" I said after he had unknowingly captured both my hands restraining me against his ministrations. I felt him smile against my lips before pulling himself back to look at me.

"I like you in restraints, little one," he said, smirking at my obvious disagreement. He looked down my body and he ran his knuckles over one hard nipple just begging for something hot to taste it.

"It allows me to explore without disruption," he said before taking my body's silent plea to be touched deeper into effect. His mouth captured my nipple and that hot wave of euphoria sent my body into a spasm without even being touched at my core. My back arched up, pressing myself against him as my body found its first release. Draven sucked hard as each wave hit my insides like he could feel it also and my moans soon turned to cries for him to stop.

"It's too much...I can't...I...c..." He released the flesh in his hand he had been feasting on like bountiful fruit and before I could stop him his fingers found the little bundle of nerves that was like the ignition switch to my internal bomb.

"You can and... you will." He said before setting me off again. I tried to bolt upright but his hold on me didn't waver. My middle lifted and collapsed back in on itself as I had no other option than to ride the waves again and again until I felt drained. I felt my arms being freed but I had no energy to move them from where Draven had set them. With my eyes still closed and my body still shaking from the aftermath of Draven's power over me, I felt the bed dip.

"Look at me, Keira!" I knew why he wanted me to, but something in me snapped. I couldn't do it knowing what he would see. I shook my head to indicate my answer, but he wasn't having it. I felt his solid presence waiting at my core for its chance at entry, but he waited.

"Keira!" He said my name in warning, one I wouldn't listen to. I don't know what had happened but after my release I felt ripped wide open and as a result the past came flooding in. I saw Draven like this

STEPHANIE HUDSON

only it wasn't me underneath him...it was her. I was so scared to open my eyes and see the look of a man that wanted not what was beneath him. If I opened my eyes he would see that fear trickle out of me in the form of tears.

"Look at this quivering beauty before me. This satin skin cast like a spell by the firelight. This golden mane like a cape of glory..." His hands moved with his voice, so gentle, as his words left trails in the path he followed. Hands over my stomach splayed out covering the whole space under my breasts and he leaned down to take in the scent of my hair.

"The smell of cotton flower, so natural you would not expect it to be so ingrained in your genetic makeup, but it is Keira, and that combined with the sweet musk of your recent release is testing my control..." He came closer still to my ear and bit the lobe hard enough to get a response.

"I suggest you not test that control any longer, my Keira." At this he bit down where my neck met my shoulder, eliciting a cry from me and my eyes flashed open in a surprise he counted on. At this second, he plunged deep inside of me and the walls of my sex pulsed around him in another orgasm that milked him into not moving. He waited for the last flutter and started to drive into me with a force I had never felt before.

This caused my orgasm to continue on in an endless ride of pleasure that I screamed over and over but never once did I take my eyes from Draven's. I felt locked to him like never before and when I saw his eyes flash purple I knew he was near to losing himself in me.

The sky behind him cracked and rumbled in the distance full of a thundering roar. A harder thrust lit the night with lightening in answer to his actions and the sound of rain falling in sheets to the mountain floor added to the intensity of this moment, that I wanted never to end.

I felt myself building up once more and when I was so close to coming apart beneath him once again he saw it in my eyes as they clouded with intense sensations he growled before his entire body erupted into his demon form. His wings blocked out the storm outside and the air that was moved with them extinguished the flame on the wall making the power coming from Draven's body the only driving force to provide light.

He came hard, harder than I had ever witnessed before and my last thread snapped that had been holding on to my last orgasm. He reared

354

up like one of Hell's beasts and roared into the night. I felt his hands fist and he ripped the bedding by my sides to shreds as he pumped into me, riding his own wave. I felt myself rippling down his shaft that had no intention of leaving my body yet.

The night grew still, with only the sounds of rain, the thunder in the distance from the passing storm and the sounds of two bodies gaining much needed air. The darkness didn't seem to matter to either of us and Draven's power seemed to pulsate with every breath he took until he calmed enough to let his other side fade away like the storm.

"H...How?" I managed to find my voice and with that Draven found his smile. He leaned down still embedded deep within me and hovered inches above my face. He ran his fingers across my cooling forehead and then licked the pad of his thumb tasting the saltiness his actions put there. He groaned lightly before smoothing the rest of my damp hair back.

"Don't you believe in magic?" He asked and I don't know why but his question brought a blush to my already overheated face.

"I...don't know," I answered honestly, making him raise an eyebrow at me, a feature of Draven that I was so used to I couldn't help but smile.

"That's a beautiful sight on you, my lovely one." He smiled back at me making my insides melt, insides he could still feel intimately.

"You don't strike me as a man who would hold much weight in magic, Draven." I said causing him to frown before thinking about his answer.

"I hold my weight in many things Keira, and these days, anything that will allow me to touch you. You belong to me Keira and only me...when will you accept this?" His question turned his answer into something so serious that it was like flipping a switch.

"I'm sorry Draven, it doesn't work like that." I whispered feeling the words come out of me like lead. I didn't want to say them but everything I believed in knew I had to be true to myself and speak them.

"Then tell me how you think it works Keira, because I will need more than magic on my side to make you see the truth. Tell me Keira, what do you believe in?" Draven's features had turned to granite but the hands that still caressed me could have belonged to someone else, they were so gentle.

"You can't have me without giving back, Draven and after what I have seen…I know that you don't belong to me." At this he let out a snarl that sounded back to being more beast than man. I stilled under him and his hands captured my wrists again but this time in solid restraint, more than passion. I struggled beneath him in a fruitless attempt at getting away but he was having none of it.

"Be still and hear me!" He raised his voice and the shaking of my head stopped long enough to see the regret in his eyes.

"You speak of what you have seen but not of what you have heard. Think back Keira and you will find my truth. I am yours and no one else's! I did not insist upon using forbidden powers to get this moment with you…a moment to try and regain a trust that should never have been broken in the first place!" He was close to shaking by the end of this and I felt the tears slip down my cheeks, ones he watched until out of sight.

"Let me go Draven." I said feeling the emotions building up until they could no longer be contained.

"You already know the answer to that one." He said dryly.

"And you already know why it is that trust was broken….YOU KNOW!" I screamed this last part as the emotions bubbled over and spilled out in a fiery overload. But instead of screaming back he took in my reactions and tried to find his answers silently.

"Please let me go." I whispered and he lay his forehead down on mine as if this would help his search but all he found were my indestructible walls that sealed everyone out.

"I can't." He whispered back and before I could cry, his mouth took mine in a kiss that felt like the last. He caught my sobs and turned them to moans of an inner pleasure I could never escape from. He released me long enough to speak one last time before taking my body again.

"And I will show you why." He said and like his words, his actions rang true. He took me to a new place of divine bliss and this time when he found his euphoria, he did so screaming to the Heavens that he loved me.

I found myself crying into his chest as he held me close, not understanding what this all meant? He held the back of my head to his body and cradled me like a frightened child, as I lost every last fight in me. I loved him and knew in this moment that as much I would try I would never live another day without loving him and the last words from Draven proved to be too much.

"That is why Keira. Why I can never leave you...why I will never leave you." I looked up at him through a veil of damp lashes and teary vision before his last word was said, cutting my insides like a blade he held to brand my bones with just one word...

*"Never!"*

# CHAPTER 30
# THE DEMONS THAT WANT YOU

S tanding on the balcony looking down at a sight that was fast becoming a scene I was used to, was a little unnerving. Pip was next to me as usual and she smiled at my reaction. The Great Hall had been decorated like a Gothic Grotto and given Pip's love of Jack from the 'Nightmare before Christmas' it didn't take me long to know where she had got her inspiration from. It was dark and it was beautiful…in a weird way. But mostly, it was not the type of Christmas I was used to seeing. Where you would normally find mistletoe, there were single dead flowers hung down in ribbons and all the holly had been spray painted black.

A large Christmas tree was the focal point like any room at this time of year but I had never seen one like this before. It was made from black stone and instead of twinkling lights there were actually candles burning on the solid ends of each branch dripping with wax and I was amazed to see each flame was a different eerie colour. There was a string of sparkling skulls hanging in the place of tinsel and instead of bright cheerful baubles there were ones with bloody body parts painted on Christmas paper wrapped around large balls with black laced ribbon tied in a bow at the top. Added to these were different sized glitter spider ornaments crawling over the thin stone branches.

The rest of the room carried through the same theme, with glass bowls filled with black and white candy canes in the middle of every table and instead of green lush garlands there were swags and swags of cobwebs and instead of berried filled wreaths, there were burnt twigs twisted into large circles that were decorated with flashing red lights, little bats and different sized bird skulls.

As far as crazy went, this room ticked all the right boxes! And of course it was all Pip's doing.

"Soooo, what do think Chickadee?" Pip asked nudging my shoulder. I couldn't keep the smile from my face, even after one of the craziest days of my life, this...right here...well it was like the cherry on top of a very big friggin milkshake!

"I think...Pip...you're awesome!" I said making her start bouncing up and down like the big/little kid she wasn't. For a change Pip wasn't a living colour swatch but it was still very unique and completely Pip. She wore mostly black tonight and most of her outfit actually matched, which was a first for me to witness on Pip. Black pinstripe trousers were three quarter length that showed off her calf boots that were high shine black with bright green hands that looked like a monster was trying to drag her body off somewhere by the ankles. These were in the shape of cowboy boots but the pointed tips were curled up like a pixie's.

The rest of her outfit was a ruffled black top that was slashed diagonally baring one shoulder and in the middle was a tight half corset that was also pinstriped black and white, only a section the size of a dinner plate was cut out of the middle. Instead of a different type of material, there was a picture of an x-rayed middle, complete with part ribs, spine and the beginning of a pelvis bone. This was all framed with pretty white lace and rippling black ribbon.

As far as outfits went this one definitely matched the best with the theme of the room which was no doubt why she chose it. After taking one look at Pip I was surprised I had let her pick my own outfit but thankfully she at least knew when to tone things down for other people.

I had woken from the most incredible dream that Draven had controlled, down to the bitter end. Did I really think I could have just said goodbye to Draven and think he would have just gone on without me having someone new...no, I had not. But I had never counted on him wanting both of us either. Draven had neither denied or confirmed my fears when it came to Aurora but one thing the dream gave me was an absolute answer to whether my future included Draven or not. And he had made it more than clear that he was not willing to let me go, so what next...because one thing I was clear on, was my decision not to stay in Evergreen Falls if Draven did think he could have us both.

I had opened my eyes, got up, looked at myself in the mirror and saw the very moment that the decision finalised in my mind. I was not going to be any man's doormat, even if that man was Draven, so the answer was one I was quickly getting used to…I would simply leave.

Of course by the time Pip had arrived I was just picking myself up from the sticky mess I resembled on the bathroom floor and without her knowing the full extent of my heartbreak, at the thought of leaving Draven, I had found refuge in the shower. By the time I came out I had my game face plastered on in the form of a smile, food on a plate and a dress waiting for me.

The dress was like all the others had been… beautiful, tight and forced on a body more comfortable in jeans and a T-shirt. I think in this week alone I had worn more dresses than in my entire life but even this was not getting me used to the idea of playing dress up with Pip every night. Although it must be said that Pip was indeed a genius when it came to 'Dressing the dolly' as Pip worded it and tonight was no exception.

Tonight's dress was a strapless, large patterned lace top with a very wide black satin ruffled belt that tied in a large bow at the back. The ends of which trailed down the skirt that was a black floaty material with numerous layers that flared out above the knees. A pair of strappy black heels that had white lace ties, high up the ankles was to complete the outfit. The only thing missing was a pair of gloves that I would not be seen without. Thankfully Pip once again used her expertise and did as she had on the first night in the Great Hall and wrapped thick black ribbon around my forearms until they made unlikely sleeves with bows tied at the wrists.

"So, you ready to rock, Toots?" One look at my frown said enough and didn't match my answer when saying 'yes'.

"Right, well then…let's get this showboat on the river." Pip said with a wink making me roll my eyes behind her. I walked down the stairs, again being cautious of the spiked railings that made no sense at all, for their purpose I would never know and once again I found myself spending an evening in a room full of vampires. An evening that I should be spending sat in a dark room, getting shit faced drunk and singing 'Think Twice' by Celine Dion in my horrendous singing voice. I think the lyrics to that song would definitely be playing right about now if this was a movie of my life!

As usual I followed Pip into the crowd, a crowd that were using the festivities as an excuse to play even more erotic games than they usually did. On one side of the hall there was food laid out like a breathing buffet and playing the role of serving trays were a naked man and woman spread eagled on long tables. Another section was closed off by knee high gates where two naked women were wrestling in what looked like a mixture of blood and snow with people around placing bets.

"Ooooh the TTS wrestling has already started." Pip clapped excitedly and I raised an eyebrow.

"TTS?" I asked already knowing the answer would weird me out even more than the man eating a vol au vent off a man's nipple then turning to pass it on to the next in line...using his mouth... Eww.

"Taste. Touch. Sex. The one who makes the most money gets the winner for the night"

"And the loser?" I was almost scared to ask.

"Oh, everyone else gets to play with them." I almost choked.

"But there's like twenty people around there!" I was horrified at the idea but Pip just gave me a smirk as if to say 'Naive much'.

"Yeah, and if I know that blue haired little slut like I do then she will lose on purpose!" I shot a look her way and nearly bumped into a man leading another man on a dog chain over to the sex/food conga that was happening near the bar....man what some people could do with spray cream I thought, shaking my head.

"Well, I think someone is going to be sore in the morning." I said referring to the blue haired beauty that I remembered seeing at Lucius' feet the first night. Speaking of whom, the man himself sat watching our every move like some damn hawk at his perch. Okay, so one hot looking hawk I would give him that and damn, tonight was no different.

Lucius made the smart casual look into something beyond sexy, he also made it dangerous and risky. He sat there in a pair of charcoal coloured jeans that looked tight in all the right places or for me...all the wrong ones. To this he added a black shirt open at the top and tucked into his jeans showing his gunmetal studded belt. The sleeves were rolled up his forearms showing the strength in his corded pale arms.

But it was the light grey waistcoat that was fitted tight to his large upper body that was making me gulp at the sight of him. His hair was pushed back from his face as usual which made his penetrating features stand out like an angry beacon. Sculptured cheekbones led up to a pair of deep set eyes, the colour of a storm brewing, which took in my form the way I did to him. I could see from here the twitch of a smirk playing at one corner of his mouth and I couldn't help the frown. One he full out laughed at, the bastard!

I tried not to let it show but considering the last time I had seen Lucius, it was hard not to blush the way my body always did, giving away my embarrassment. Last night I had shamefully called out his name when finding my pleasure and there was no way I could go back on that, no matter how guilty I felt. But last night the memory of seeing Draven making love to Aurora had scarred me until I needed another vision to take it away. Lucius had been that vision and as guilty as I did feel about that I couldn't find it in myself to regret it. Now, if the fantasy had been real then that would be a different story but the fact remained that when I thought I had been alone I had come apart at the thought of Lucius' hands touching me and Lucius had witnessed the whole thing!

Not good Keira...so not good!

So what to do now in that kind of situation, the only thing I could do...pretend like nothing had happened and pray like a horny nun that Lucius wouldn't mention anything about it...yeah like that was ever going to happen!

I watched Pip go bouncing up the steps to the raised seating area where Lucius and his minions sat, one nicely placed to watch over his kingdom like some King of the Pride. And at that moment Lucius reminded me of more Lion than man. His gaze was predatory as always, taking in every wary move I made and when I must have frozen he motioned me forward with two flickering fingers. I wondered at that moment if he could hear my pulse racing as my feet finally gave in to the movement he wanted them to make.

I followed Pip's steps, although not as exuberant as when she did it, but soon I was stood directly in front of Lucius as though I was awaiting criminal sentence for my actions. Then he surprised me by standing up which in turn caused me on instinct to step back. He noted my retreat and raised an eyebrow. For a moment the whole room seemed to stop and only the music from a solo pianist on stage filled the Great Hall. Then Lucius' voice cut through the silent time like his favourite weapon.

"Come here, Keira girl!" He said which was nothing short of an order, one I had no option but to obey. I bravely walked towards him around the large centre table and only came to a stop when I was directly in front of him. It felt like the first night seeing him all over

STEPHANIE HUDSON

again. Palms sweaty, heart pumping like a generator, all in reaction to not knowing what was going to happen.

Then he surprised me by looking me up and down before pulling me roughly to his chest. I let out all the air I was holding in with an umf sound and he lowered his head to my ear.

"You are stunning enough to make a beating heart shudder but you test me by making me wait for the sight. Now sit, my Keira girl!" With that he spun me around to face the crowd, one staring at us, and sat down with his arm still around my waist taking me with him. Before I could get my bearings on what had just happened, a black goblet was placed in my hands and I found myself drinking it back before the taste registered.

"Mulled wine?" I asked, but Pip was the one to answer me, making me focus her way.

"Yep, I had it made just for you, Toots." She said smiling which flashed me her lip ring in the wall of red fairy lights behind her and Adam.

"Umm...Thanks," I said giving her a shy little smile.

"You're umm welcome." She mocked, making Adam pull a curl of her hair. I smiled at him and he winked behind her at me. I then had to look away as she twisted round in his lap and started attacking his lips, which reminded me a bit like a face hugger from the Alien movie. I saw Liessa looking graceful as ever in a gorgeous ink blue dress that cut across the shoulders and came down into a pencil skirt which showcased her beautiful long legs. Legs that were resting on the lap of one pissed off looking Caspian. Man did that big dude ever look happy? Even as he lovingly ran his hands up and down Liessa's smooth looking legs he still didn't look happy...maybe she hadn't shaved for a few days, I thought cheekily.

And then there was Lucius' Kimosabe, who instead of being called Tonto was named Hakan. This was one dude who I still hadn't figured out and what was with all that wire that was twisted around him like it always belonged there? Well one thing was for sure, Lucius' council were certainly an interesting bunch of unusual suspects. Of course none were as mind bending as the man himself...Lucius.

I was surprised that instead of a confident reminder of his role last night he chose not to say a word about it. Instead the night went on as any other with the same possessive display of having me sat where he wanted and sharing his drinks with me every now and again, even though German beer and mulled wine didn't really mix, I couldn't find myself turning down his offer. It was like being taken care of and this show he put on was for my own benefit amongst this crowd. That much he had made clear on the first night and every night since.

I would have preferred to have hated Lucius, hell it would have made it so much easier but the truth was, the more time I spent around him I was beginning to understand not the Vampire that ruled all others but the man that had been there before... before the living darkness that met him every time he woke. I saw the man who felt betrayed by his faith and who had forsaken his soul as a result.

"Pip, take Keira back to her room. Now!" Lucius' command brought me out of my trance and I noticed two things in seconds. One being the room had now dropped the volume to a deathly silence and the other, every muscle at my back was now as ridged as a plank and I could practically hear Lucius' teeth grinding.

"I don't think..." Pip started to say as the crowd parted to let through a figure I'd hoped never to see again.

"I know Pip, there won't be time. It is as he planned." Lucius said in a growl and I could almost hear him weighing up the different options in his mind. But it was too late for that now, Malphas was here and one look told me everything I needed to know...

*He was here for me.*

# CHAPTER 31
# BEING TRIPLE CROSSED

Malphas was not a Being you would ever forget meeting and it took me back to the night that I had foolishly put myself in harm's way just to piss off Draven. And just like then, I felt a chill run down my spine like the long fingernails on his pale hands. He walked through the room like he owned the place and from the looks of people around him cowering away, there seemed to be some solid backing to the arrogance he wore.

As before, he was wearing a suit with some sort of half cape to the side. I wanted to say it looked corny, 1930's Dracula style but unfortunately I would have been lying. If anything it just made him look more royally powerful and judging by everyone in the room getting out of his way, they felt it too. His suit was black with a strange deep red piping around the edges. The dark clothes just made his pale features all the more startling and his piercing eyes were directed on only one person...me!

I think Lucius must have felt my reaction because his grip on my waist tightened and I was drawing safety from it like a leech. Malphas quickly noted the position I was in as he mounted the dais, clearly intent on being heard.

Two guards followed close behind him and one of them motioned to someone in the crowd who went running off like his ass was on fire...can't say I blamed him as I felt like doing the same....Hell at this point I wouldn't have been opposed to a rocket in the same place, at least that way it would have got me out of here quicker!

"Malphas." Lucius acknowledged and this brought an evil leer from his thin lips.

"Lucius." His hoarse voice had me wincing and the memory of how bloody reckless I had been on Halloween put me back in the Limo with the man who was trying to convince me how much I had meant to Draven. But now I knew why he found this so important. After all you can't be a pawn if you're not on the damn chess board!

"I would say it is a pleasure but as you know I would be lying, so time to cut through the shit…what are you doing here?" Lucius' voice took on a tone I only had heard when roaring out his dominance and a strange thrill ran through me. I guess it was the same as going to a boxing match and seeing the fighter you supported get in a good uppercut.

"Ah, as always the politician," Malphas commented sarcastically.

"I don't care for your kind's idea of politics," Lucius counteracted. Meanwhile the man in the crowd that had made a run for it, had come back with a fitting chair for Malphas to sit in, one high backed and cushioned…one word went through my head…pansy!

"Nor do you care to keep your word on certain matters." He said after taking his seat and resting his foot across his knee.

"You never had my word Malphas, at the time you just had my acceptance on your plans…plans that changed along with that acceptance. I would have thought I had made myself clear on that, but if not, then let me now." Lucius' voice had gone from authoritative to lethal in the time it took for one of Malphas' eyebrows to rise. Then I gasped when one of his guards held Malphas by the shoulder and the other guard put his hand around his throat. Malphas didn't move, not like he could even if he wanted to but one thing I did think odd, considering he had his neck in a big guard's hands, was that he didn't even look fazed by it.

"I may not be able to control you so close to the Winter Solstice, but do not underestimate me Malphas, you will not be leaving here with the girl as you no doubt planned." At Lucius saying this I felt like adding on my own 'Yeah Asshole!' but thankfully thought better of it. For starters Malphas was one scary ass pale dude, one I didn't think it wise to piss off any more than Lucius was already doing. I expected Malphas to admit defeat and leave at this point…it is what any sane person would have done considering the feral vibes coming from Lucius in an invisible steam but no, instead he simply smiled.

"I have to say, as a son of the mighty Lord below, I expected more from you and you would have gained more from my alliance as I promised." Malphas said with an ease I was surprised at, coming from a man whose throat was situated in a meaty grip.

"I have enough alliances," Lucius said now in a bored tone.

"Yes, but are any of those the alliance of Gods?"

"Malphas you should have had your lackeys do better research, then you would know that I hold little faith in the Gods!" Lucius snarled the word like it was dirty and I flinched.

"That is because you are not yet one." At this Lucius laughed but there was nothing heart-warming about it.

"And this Winter Solstice will not make you one!" Lucius spat out and at this point I thought it would have been real handy knowing what they were talking about…Supernatural Beings couldn't become Gods…could they?

"Don't be so sure!" Malphas said and as if to prove his point further he raised one hand and rubbed his thumb and forefinger together ever so gently. Then when I saw the slightest blue spark come from his fingertips and with that the two guards who still had hold of him started to freeze. And when I say freeze I don't mean by being still, I mean starting from their hands their skin started to glaze over as though liquid nitrogen had been injected into their bodies. It kept travelling up until it covered their bodies in the stuff and then in seconds it was taking over their shocked expressions.

Once the two were fully transformed into ice sculptures that had skin like glass with a smoky cloud behind it, Malphas grabbed both the hands over his shoulders and crushed those that had kept him immobile into powdery red dust. I heard the two men screaming in agony without either of their mouths moving, which added to the haunting sound.

I tried to get away from it all but Lucius held me closer to him and wrapped an arm diagonally across my chest to hold me still.

"Your weak attempt at proving your point has had no effect on my decision. The girl is mine and the deal is off! Now go before I give you a demonstration of what real power looks like…one you will not soon forget!" This was the first time I had heard Lucius' demonic voice and if I was trying to get away before now I was really panicking. It was like someone had taken all the voices people would most fear in the world and joined them all together to produce a horrifying symphony that would make you want to fling yourself out of a top floor window rather than facing its creator!

Lucius, on feeling me struggling, leant down to my ear and softly said something only I could hear.

"Ssshh little one, do not fear me for my anger is not directed at you." On hearing the protective voice float into my senses I relaxed as his words took effect.

"Ah, so I see you are still able to control her. That would have come in handy for my cause indeed but I can see you are not to be persuaded. Very well, I shall take my leave." He got up in a swift action for someone who had been looking so casually at ease in his chair, that it shocked me.

"You may keep your little pet for now Vampire, but soon the axial tilt of Earth will be perfect and then nothing will stop me from being powerful enough to take her, not you or your royal alliances." This threat rumbled from him in a hoarse hiss and Lucius growled possessively at my back.

"I will be seeing you soon my Chosen One!" Malphas promised before turning to leave. At this point the icy spell shattered and the two guards became whole again...with a little bit missing than before. Each one had lost a hand and were now cradling the unfinished limbs to their chests with the look of utter pain evident on their faces. Malphas stormed past the two and snarled the word 'Useless' at them before they followed with fear clear in their thoughts.

No one moved or said a word until it became apparent that Malphas had done an Elvis and had left the building.

"Well, that went well!" Said Pip with a smile. Adam rolled his eyes and groaned. Then I flinched in Lucius' arms when Caspian crashed his fist into the table causing the sound of splitting wood to echo.

"I say we kill the bastard!" Caspian roared and Liessa smiled at seeing her husband's rage, so she started rubbing his thigh getting closer and closer to his obvious hard on. What was it that made sex and violence go hand in hand for men and from the looks of Liessa, some women?

"No one can kill a President of Hell without first finding a replacement for his forty legions Caspian and he must be of noble blood." Lucius said as though he had given it some thought. Caspian seemed to calm slightly and Liessa sounded close to purring in his ear.

"Liessa, take your husband and give him something to direct his frustrations on, I fear Keira's cheeks will explode if you do so here!" Will explode? ...they already were!

"My pleasure," Liessa said making her husband growl with a

growing lust. As they both stood Caspian swiftly scooped Liessa up and slung her over his massive shoulder and Pip giggled. Liessa looked as red faced as me and just before leaving he bowed to Lucius still holding her in place with a firm hand on her curved behind, when she tried to move he slapped her there making her yelp.

"Be still wench!" He said like the barbarian he looked but as they walked off I could see him caress lovingly where he had slapped.

"Aww, they're so cute!" Commented Pip before turning to straddle her own husband, ready to give him the same amount of attention.

"Man, what is it with this place... do you guys put something in the water?" I said dryly, making Lucius laugh.

"We're just very sexual beings Keira and normally... we just take what we want!" Lucius whispered this last part in my ear and then bit my lobe as if to emphasise the point. My blush then turned scarlet and I looked over to Hakan as he was the only person in the room who wasn't doing anything X-rated. I don't know how he could stand it, seeing all these couples grinding against each other like animals without even a slight uncomfortable expression...if anything his expression never changed...EVER! I just could not figure that one out.

"So, are you going to explain what just happened?" I said finally after not getting any indication of an explanation. I mean, as far as Lucius knew, then I was in the dark about what Malphas wanted with me and also about the bargain they had made. It was only thanks to Pip that I had any idea what was even going on!

"Keira!" Lucius groaned in my ear, as though now was not the time, but to hell with that! I tried to turn round but he held me stiff.

"I am not having this conversation with my back to you and you nibbling on my ear, which you shouldn't be doing anyway!" I said in a huffed and over flustered way...man I sounded like a girly girl.

"Fine, there you go little one." He released his hold on me and I moved to the seat where Liessa and Caspian had been, with another huff.

"And I wish everyone would stop with this 'little one' crap! You make me sound like a bloody Umper Lumper, and being 5'3" is not that short, Pip's shorter than me and she doesn't get called anything patronising!" Okay, so as far as important rants go I knew this shouldn't have been high on my list of priorities but it was really starting to get on my goat! (I am pretty sure that is a saying) I was really starting to get sick with all this macho bullshit that I kept getting sucked into.

Lucius was trying to keep in his grin along with everyone else, all apart from Hakan that was, who I was beginning to think was a mute.

"Consider it noted, woman of normal size." Lucius said sarcastically, although his sarcasm clearly came with humour, one I tried to ignore but when Pip spoke I found myself laughing with the rest of them…again discounting Hakan.

"I dressed up as an Umper Lumper once…do you remember Adam and you were Willy Wank…" Adam wouldn't let her finish that sentence as his hand shot out to cover her mouth. He growled in her ear and then whispered something that made her blush. And wow, if it could make Pip blush, then I really didn't want to think about what that could have been.

"Okay, so back to more important issues, like, what was that all about?" I asked again directing all my attention to the man with the answers. And I was curious as to how much truth would be in his answer.

"Malphas is under a misconception of his power, that is all." WHAT! That is all? Okay, so now I knew that Lucius was going to try and worm out of this one without telling me anything but that was so not going to happen!

"That is all…oh no, that is bullshit, that's what that is! You may want to keep me in the dark here Lucius but I kinda have this little rule about my life…I like to bloody well know what is happening in it!" I shouted making him raise an eyebrow at me.

"Are you giving me an order, little Keira?" I found myself not caring about the strength in his observation but instead ignoring it completely.

"You bet your ass, Vampire!" I was almost shaking now and didn't care for the worried looks that Pip and Adam were sending my way.

"Be careful Pet, you don't want to go too far with me!" He warned but I was so beyond fearing him now it felt like arguing with a pig-headed friend.

"Oh sod you and this macho bullshit!" That's when I made my mistake, he snarled at me, showing his deadly Vampire side in the image of long fangs that gleamed with his anger.

"I will show you macho bullshit!" He raged before he lunged for me. And in half a second I found myself hauled up like a prize kill on a hunt and in Liessa's position, only on a different demon's shoulder.

"Put me down, you caveman!" I screamed but he just hauled me further up and kept my legs pinned with one unmovable arm.

"Quieten down female or I will club you over the head first!" He sounded stern but I could also hear his smile in the threat. The rest of the room erupted into cheers of excitement as Lucius walked through a room full of his people. Was this what they classed as entertainment?

I felt him sweep down and grab something from one of the chairs but I couldn't see what it was because not once did he slow down.

"Next you will be calling me Jane," I commented dryly, having resolved myself to being carried like a dead pig.

"So now I am Tarzan? Do I look like I am wearing a loin cloth to you?" He said laughing now as he was out of ear shot and making our way through a door that led out of the Great Hall. Of course this brought a vision of Lucius in that loin cloth and not only did the image fit with his behaviour, it would have also looked damn fine on him...damn him!

"Not going to answer that one yea, or are you lingering on the image?" Cocky bastard!

"Umff!" Okay, so it wasn't the best come back but with an image like that my female brain couldn't get past the man candy that had been dangled...Damn me!

I would like to have seen where we were going but with my hair acting like a wavy curtain swaying from side to side there was no point even trying. Wherever he was taking me it wasn't far and as soon as I felt the chill he put me down.

"There you go," he said, setting me on my feet and holding me until he was sure I was steady. I looked around and was surprised when I recognised it. Of course I couldn't let Lucius know that so I asked,

"Where are we?" I saw the moon was almost at its fullest and it cast a beautiful glow on the balcony I remember seeing in my vision, the one where he and Layla had spoken, the one where he had cast her out and cut her from his power for good. Well at least this place had good memories for me, I thought smugly.

"This is what we call the 'ruhigen Ort', which means 'Quiet place' in German" I snorted a little.

"Wow that's original!" I said now being the one using sarcasm. He smiled at my comment and then shocked me by zooming so close to me I almost staggered back. God Vampires were fast! I didn't even see him move, he kind of just appeared. He must have seen my shock because now he smirked making him look even more devious. Then before I could try and come back with a witty comment he whipped out a length of material that felt like velvet. It was the colour of a peacock and it felt like heaven against my skin.

He had draped it over my bare arms and shoulders in a protective manner and his kindness had every smart mouth comment fleeing my head like wasps from a hive on fire.

"Don't want you getting paler, people will start thinking I broke the rules and made you one of my Vamps." He said in his usual seductive tone that would have had ministers melting.

"B...but...you can't do that...I mean, I have been told..." He gave me a smile that caused little creases by his eyes making him look even more handsome and carefree.

"So they say!" He teased...or did he?

"So why did you bring me out here?" I needed to change the subject from one that didn't include his fangs coming anywhere near my neck.

"Because you were demanding the truth and it is easier to argue with a mortal out here without undermining my position, one you keep forgetting about." He added a bit prickly.

"Well, what can I say, apart from this mortal doesn't really give a shit!" I said folding my arms across my chest.

"Yes, I gathered that thank you. So elegantly put by the way."

"Screw you!" I shot back, feeling my blood start to boil again. What was it about this man that one minute had me wanting to throw myself at him, climb him like a cat to rub up against and the next, wanting to scratch his eyes out while I was up there?

"And also very lady like, that Draven is a lucky man!" He snapped back at me making me lose the climbing stuff and cut right to beating the crap out of him with the potted conifer in the corner!

"Arrg! You are so...so..."

"So?" He said gesturing with his arms out that I should continue.

"Arrogant!"

"It's not an insult when being called something that is commonly known and not minded."

"I haven't finished! You are a fool, a hypocrite, an asshole, a back stabbing bastard, a kidnapper , and..."

"And?" He asked looking very unaffected by all my insults so I hit him where cocky men would really be knocked of their stride.

"And a lousy kisser!" I added, changing his arrogant expression to one of shock. HA! But the next thing to happen didn't really help in my mission to wound his pride.

"Oh Yeah?!" He said getting up in my face, or at least if I was a foot taller it would have been, but even raising my head as far back as I needed, I still didn't back down!

"Yeah!" I shouted which is the second he tried to prove me wrong. He grabbed the top of my arms, pulled me roughly to him and took my lips as a prisoner of war. I tried to pull away but his hand fisted in my hair and he slanted his mouth until we fit perfectly. His mouth moved over mine in such a way that my attempts at trying to get free lessened. His kiss started to soften and he urged my lips into a response, one my traitorous body was yielding into.

As soon as I opened up momentarily he was in and had full access that he wasn't letting go of anytime soon. But as soon as his tongue met with mine the blinding light of the sun burst free like a supernova. We were somewhere on the other side of the world, in some exotic hideaway, that only the two of us were allowed to be a part of. I could feel the heat of the sun that I had not felt in so long and it didn't only warm my shell, it warmed me to the core.

I felt Lucius shaking with the thrill of it all and I realised why, this was his only opportunity to see the sun and to think of all the years that he had been denied was unimaginable. This was one of the reasons I couldn't find it in myself to pull away, why I didn't fight. Because to him, this moment was as rare as they come.

After his lips left mine he just had enough time to raise his head in wonder and bask in the sun that danced along his beautiful face which looked so alive in the sunlight. He had his eyes closed and his head up like a starved man finding his salvation. It was only when the light started to fade like the sun setting in faster motion that he opened his eyes.

"That is why I couldn't let him have you!" He said leaning his forehead to mine in silent understanding. For him his confession was a weight lifted but for me it was a grave awakening. For now everything had just fit into a place like a bloody puzzle painted with a grim picture of realisation. This was why Lucius had changed since the helicopter, since that first kiss he had slowly, everyday started to change his brutish ways with me and become more caring, more understanding and even at times reasonable. And all this time I had wanted to believe the reasons for his change were the humanity coming back to his dark soul…but that wasn't the case.

I was just being used…again.

"So that is the only reason. You make me sick!" I shouted and burst from his hold trying to get far enough away from him. I turned my back to him and clutched at one of the giant gargoyles so that he wouldn't see the tears forming.

"Keira...I..." I heard him behind me but I couldn't look at him.

"So let me get this straight. If what happens when we kiss didn't happen then it would be a bloody free for all on who gets Keira! Of course the payment would have to be good enough!" I bit out this last part, hearing him practically wince.

"No, it...it isn't as you think. Yes, I am surprised you show me the sun, it has never happened before and I would be lying if I say that hasn't changed things but ..."

"Enough! I don't want to hear it! I don't want to know how differently that would have gone in there tonight if kissing me hadn't been so...insightful!" This time I turned to face him and the look on his face did surprise me, it wasn't guilt but... hurt.

"I had never planned to give the Chosen One to him. For fuck's sake Keira, I may have my plans and I may use people to fulfil them, but I would never risk the life of the Chosen One! That was never in question and if I let him think otherwise it was for my own gain." He was pleading with me but I wasn't listening. I couldn't listen anymore. I didn't know what to believe...I just needed time. I needed to arrange these feelings of betrayal in my mind. First Karmun, then Draven and now Lucius...I just didn't think I could take anymore.

"Leave!" I said in a deadpan voice that inside was full to the brim of hurt.

"Keira you have to listen to me!" He said coming closer but I stepped back into the carved stone at my back.

"No, I really don't. You kidnapped me, took me from my home for your own gain and then to top things off you made me feel things and it was all a lie! If you didn't get your sunny rocks off every time we locked lips, then I would be in someone else's prison right now getting prepared for some bloody ritual! So do me a favour, as I think I'm due one...get lost and leave me the hell alone, 'cause I don't need Draven's bullshit, just like I don't need yours!" I shouted at him with tears streaming down my face, contradicting my rage.

I was just so sick to the death of being everyone's power tool that I felt myself splitting in two.

"Keira please..."

"Just go." I whispered turning away from him, feeling the weight of me that everyone else was holding. I felt like I was locked up in chains and only the Gods could set me free from the burden. I didn't want to be this Chosen One, I wanted to be me and not have the weight of the world hanging on my every decision...decisions I didn't know to make.

I knew the second Lucius left me I could feel it inside, like being lost in the woods without a map. See, being here, I still wasn't home but I wasn't without sight of my house. That is what it was like, having that security in sight and knowing you were close. But this... this was being blind in front of that house and Draven and Lucius had taken that sight.

I hugged the velvet to my body and shivered underneath it. I felt a chill creep over my body which was nothing to do with the winter night. Even looking at the icy lake below wasn't the cause but it still felt like my heart had landed in its icy depths but then I realised it wasn't just my heart that was soon to be down there, it was also the rest of me and the voice behind me knew it...Oh God no!

*Layla.*

# CHAPTER 32
# NEW WAYS TO DIE BY OLD MONSTERS

I would have thought by now that facing my own death would have become easier. That somehow by putting a voice to it would have given me something to focus on in a time where panic should be taking over. But panic never served anyone in a time that needed a level head in order to survive and this time I didn't think survival was going to be on the cards for me...Layla was going to make pretty damn sure of that. I mean, let's face it, just how many times can someone fail at trying to kill me?

"Layla!" I whispered as I turned to face my fate, whatever this time it might bring.

"Bitch!" She smiled at me like she was tasting her revenge and man did it look sweet to this supernatural psycho.

"You know, I really thought getting you alone was going to be harder than that, so thanks for doing all the hard work for me." She spoke like we were old friends and having her thank me for helping her to kill me had me clenching my fists in anger.

"Who said I was going to make this easy for you?" I snapped back, feeling my fingertips start to tingle from the blood flow I was holding back. At this she laughed as she stalked towards me, all the while scraping her long nails along the stone balustrade. It looked like blades being sharpened on flint with little sparks coming from the contact.

"Oh, but I really hope you don't, as where would the fun in that be but unfortunately I am rather pressed for time and you do have a habit of surviving the most unbelievable of odds." She lifted a nail for inspection, one that now looked sharper and ready to be put to use. I tried not to gulp.

"I would say I am sorry but I like living and hate you, so you see where that would be a lie." I said moving a little step back and wondering where I would go to when I ran out of balcony. Why the hell did I have to send Lucius away and how much praying would be needed in order for him to come back.

Layla noticed me look longingly at the door and shook her head laughing.

"Oh I don't think he will be coming back just yet Keira, after all, a man has his pride, one you stepped on quite nicely I might say." Of course she was right. I had sent him away and with that, my only chance at getting through another round with my personal stalker, one with a never ending murderous vendetta.

"You know, you really need a new hobby." I said trying to buy for time, although I didn't know if my smart mouth was going to be the best one for the job, it could possibly just get me killed quicker.

"Oh don't you worry, after I have disposed of you I will be taking up past things I know to be very pleasurable indeed." It didn't take much mental brain power to know of who she talked about…Draven. At this I laughed.

"And you think he will just take you back, knowing you were the one who killed me. Christ, you're more insane than I thought!" I said and for the first time she lost a bit of her cool. Her high cheekbones went higher and her eyebrows came down causing her eyes to slit in her deep scowl. Red veins seemed to dart out around her angry eyes which caused her to look even more ill on an already twisted face.

"I will have him again!" She said and I didn't know who she was trying to convince because it wasn't me. I may have reasons to doubt Draven's commitment in the bedroom but I knew I always had loyalty in other things, those that included not shacking up with those that had been responsible for my death.

"Fine then, off you go and have him! I mean what are you waiting for…? A text message asking you out on a date? I am now out of the picture and you have free range to go back to being one of the King's sluts for all I care!" I was shouting at her but was also moving back, a little shuffle at a time, which didn't really scream out my confidence.

"I don't think you quite understand here, I can never go back with you still breathing in the world, taking over his mind like the festering bacteria that you are!" As far as compliments went, this one wasn't my best I thought sarcastically still trying to edge away from her.

If I could only keep her talking until Lucius wondered where I was and what I was still doing out here. But this wasn't going to happen, as realistically I had only been out here for a measly couple of minutes without him and I didn't know how long he would give me alone. I needed to think. If I could just think of a distraction, maybe if I got her angry enough she would slip up and I could make a run for it.

"Yeah, and to think you got the boot because this festering human was preferred over you!" I said seeing her rage hitch up a notch. She shook her head and her blonde hair fell free from its up do and I tried not to gasp when I saw the tips that were dripping in blood. It looked as though she had killed someone and then bent down dangling her loose hair in the evidence.

"Oh no, I see what you are doing but I will not be rushed. I have waited too long to kill you and this time, make no mistake, I will get the job done and take my pleasure from it." She snarled and completely missed the point of me trying to piss her off. Did she really believe I was willing to give up on trying to survive this, well it was going to be her underestimation of the strength in human survival that would be her down side…I hoped.

"That might be so but I will be the one laughing my ass off in the grave 'cause there is only one place you are going to end up and I sure hope you're liked in Hell…actually, scrap that, no I don't, in fact I hope they hate you more than I do!" She smiled then and placed her hand behind her back. When she brought it back around and I saw what she now had firmly in her grasp I couldn't fake my bravado any longer, I tried to get away.

The large blade she held was the length of my arm and when she swiped out to the side it stopped my escape. It was that or become chop suey Keira, Cantonese style! The blade flashed blue in the moonlight when she flicked her wrist making me jump back again.

"Going somewhere?" She smirked and I could feel the beads of sweat roll down my skin at facing Layla with a blade in her hand yet again.

"I am so going to enjoy cutting into you. This blade is very special to me and not only does it cut through flesh like slicing rotting fruit but it was given to me by someone I live for, someone you tried to take from me, so it is ironic that it will bring forth your death, is it not?" I looked at the blade in question and felt disgusted at the idea Draven had given her this knife. I wanted to spit the bile that was making its way up from my stomach onto it, just to show her what I thought about her idea of irony!

"Oh, so it was me that made you a bloody waitress at his table then was it? Wow you're right...weren't you just the special one? Get real Layla, if you meant anything to him he wouldn't have put you to work at his table instead of being sat at it!" At this she giggled and held her hands to her mouth like a child, well it would have looked childlike if she didn't have a massive blade still in one hand that stuck out at the side of her head, pointed at the moon.

"Is that what you think? Little stupid human that you are! Completely clueless. I was made a waitress in Draven's pathetic little club as a spy. I was sent away because of you and his tragic obsession with you, one he thought I was in the way of. So now you see little bitch, why I find it is you that is the one in the way, but oh no, not for much longer." She looked longingly at her knife like they were old friends and she ran her finger down its deadly edge until blood coated it. With her finger nice and bloody she then placed it in her mouth like she was sucking chocolate cake mix from a spoon.

But wait, what had she said? I looked down while trying to process what I had just learnt...Could it be I was wrong all this time?

"You're in love with Lucius!" I spoke out loud the thoughts that had just clicked into place. I looked up when I heard her start to clap slowly, mocking the statement I just made.

"Well done, at last the bitch grows a brain!" I ignored her comment as the rest of the puzzle fit into place. All this time I had thought it had been Draven she had wanted. Every time she had spoken about 'him' I had presumed she meant Draven but it had been Lucius. I was the reason he sent her away and now I was the reason she was banished!

"So now you see why the prophecy means nothing to me and soon it will mean nothing to him!"

"You're wrong! You think my death will mean him taking you back but once he finds out what you did then he will just kill you!" Now was the time to try for reason but with her grip tightening on the blade's handle it was already a dying chance.

"Wrong again! See the prophecy also speaks of a human beyond the boundaries of death, not many know this but Lucius, as he learned in his obsession with you. But once I prove him wrong and end your life, I will finally put an end to this prophecy shit once and for all. He will realise you were not the Chosen One as he thought, that you are just another parasite, and a bug in my way is a bug needed to be crushed!" She advanced forward and I had nowhere to go but over the edge. I moved quickly out of her swinging range and knocked sideways into the gargoyle, nearly falling over the side.

"It's time to face facts Keira, if the Gods had really chosen you then where are they now? Where is your hero King! But more importantly to me, where is your heart!" She slashed out with her knife again and this time I wasn't quick enough getting out of her way. She sliced through under my left breast and on the side of my ribcage.

"Arrh" I hissed at the searing pain it caused and placed my right hand across the cut.

"Mmm, nice but not near enough." She licked the blade and tasted my blood that dripped down its length. I took this moment to try and get past her but once again she stopped me with her weapon inflicting more pain. This time she got me on the top of my thigh making me limp back and suck air through my teeth as I gritted through the agony. She was going to take me piece by bloody piece and there was nothing I could do about it. This was what she wanted, what she had been deprived of last time. Oh yes she wanted my death but not at the price of not seeing me suffer with it first.

She then went for the heart like she promised and made a slicing downwards motion which on instinct I held out my arms to protect myself. I felt the blade sink into my flesh and rip down the length of my hand and forearm, cutting not only the ribbon that covered my scars but the skin underneath them.

"ARRGGGHHH!" I screamed louder this time and for the first time Layla looked worried as she shot a look at the door. It seemed like her time was running out along with mine.

"Looks like I won't get to play as much as I wanted, so be a good girl now and hurry up with dying." Layla said coming back round to look at me only what she found was not the crumpled heap of bloody mess on the floor. I had used her moment of panic to climb up onto the balustrade and even with the great drop behind me I turned my fear of heights into one that feared death more. So I had inched my way around the great stone gargoyle and climbed into its lap making it harder for Layla to get to me.

It was hard to keep a grip of the thing with blood dripping down one palm and I kept slipping making her laugh at my attempts at hiding. With my heeled feet trying desperately to keep grip on its smooth dragon legs I gave up clinging to its neck when Layla tried to cut all my fingers off.

"You can't hide from me!" She screamed at me, forgetting her plan to keep us alone, her rage had taken over any logical thought giving way to the pure undeterred hatred. My hands slid again only before I could fall back into the icy depths I made a lifesaving grab for its open mouth, using its hand sized fangs as my anchor. I was now stood with my bottom sticking out with my body's weight holding myself to the stone beast at my feet and hands. I gritted through the pain of the torture I was putting my sliced palm through but luckily it wasn't as deep as all my other injuries. If only someone was to come now, I would have a chance, I could be saved...I could...

Just then I heard Layla let out a strangled cry and before I could think my prayers had been answered, the head of the gargoyle exploded above me, as I saw a female fist come through the stone grey powder that was its face. I just had enough time to grab its top leg that jutted out in an arch over the curved perch in which now sat its headless body.

I waited not hearing anything, filling my mind once again full of an endless stream of hopes. I didn't want to die, I wasn't ready to leave this world and with that I knew I was not ready to leave Draven. I had to hold on but my body was growing heavier with the seconds of silence that passed. Had someone come? Was she being dealt with before they looked for me?

I was just about to call out when I heard a terrifying sound, causing all hope to leave me and go crashing to the ice before my body followed. It was the sound of stone against stone and when I felt the gargoyle move I knew why. Layla was pushing the carved stone structure off its plinth hoping that I would fall with it. I saw it inch by inch as it crept closer to being too weighty to stay at its home and what would happen when gravity took over...me and it were taking a trip down to the same place, that's what!

I made one last rash decision and once again found myself hoping beyond all odds. Just before it could tip over I pushed off its legs and launched myself to the side, landing half on the stone wall that surrounded the balcony. I heard the gargoyle falling and it shook the side making me lose grip. I fell down and was now dangling by one hand with all my body weight pulling at every finger. I scrabbled for footing in the rock and managed the slightest hold on one that only my toes were dug into.

I couldn't see over the edge and the stone rail I held onto could have been made from spikes it felt that painful. But there was no relief, I couldn't pull myself up and I didn't yet want to let go. I heard the crash into the ice below me and it was like a death drum banging in my ear. Everything in me was pounding, thumping to explode and jump this sinking ship. If I just hung on I would live, if I just let go the pain would stop, if...if...but then my ifs ran out as the face of my destroyer came into view, only this time it was also a face of the not so forgotten past. A past that happened only days ago, a past set deep underground and like now, a past that tried to end me by drowning.

I screamed as the face of pure evil came over the side and took in my struggling form.

"Goodbye Keira... TIME TO DIE NOW!" She roared in her demonic voice as she repeated history and stabbed her pinned mouth into my hand like she did that time in the underground water locks. Because this was the face that I saw that night in the door's window, the same black and hollow soulless eyes, the tight skin across the jagged bones and the inescapable row after row of teeth and lethal steel pins.

I felt pain before my fingers released their life holding grip and as I fell backwards to my death the last face I saw was the monster that tried to kill me that night, the murderer Layla, that this night finally...

*Succeeded.*

# CHAPTER 33
# ICY GRAVE OR SUNNY DEATH

As I fell backwards my world seemed to change. I don't know about when people say about your life flashing before your eyes in the face of death as it didn't happen for me. But one saying certainly proved right as my body fell to its destruction it did so in slow motion.

Slow, agonising motion.

I wasn't ready, my body wasn't ready and I could only hope that Draven wasn't ready for me to die but this time, I saw no way out and it mattered little as to what I thought about my coming end. And to make matters worse, the gruesome and disgusting face of Layla in her demon form was the last face I would ever see. A demonic hatred that twisted in sick pleasure, as I travelled further to my watery grave, was my last view of the world and even though her face got smaller and smaller I could still make out the last ounce of revenge being fulfilled in her face splitting grin.

I braced myself for the solid impact of ice that would no doubt break my spine into paralysis before drowning my lungs with winter lake water but it didn't happen like that. Oh, I landed all right and my body knew it with the feeling of a thousand pins all piercing my skin at the same time but there was no ice, only water.

Freezing ice cold water.

The pain of it stole my breath at the worst time as it was one much needed to stay alive longer. I saw the cloud of white bubbles my impact caused come up around me and find the surface…a surface I couldn't reach. My body moved slowly in the black depths like it wasn't my own. It turned and twisted round and I saw the reason for my landing in water fading into the dark. The stone gargoyle was falling away to where I feared I was soon to follow. But wait, I was still alive and more importantly I was far away from the bitch with a fondness for sharp objects that she was determined to keep sticking in me. I could get out of this and might survive.

I found myself sending down a silent thank you to the headless gargoyle and decided to fight. I tried to move but at first it was like every muscle was closing down and refusing to co-operate. But then as the last of my air left my floating body I made a desperate attempt at reaching the broken ice. I raise my arms above me and dragged them back, pulling myself upward with a relentless pain that coursed through me with every move. But I didn't give up and I wanted to live damn it! I felt like I was dragging myself through sand but slowly and just before I passed out from lack of oxygen I burst through the surface.

I spluttered and coughed as I dragged in as much air as I could, but it never seemed enough. My throat burned like every mouthful was mixed with an acid cloud but soon my breaths calmed and I looked around to see myself bobbing up and down in the moonlit night.

The crashing down of the gargoyle had no doubt saved my life and it had left a mighty big hole in its wake. The ice was floating around in angular shards of different sized islands and I saw the edge of the frozen lake. I knew I wasn't out of danger yet because I knew if I didn't get out of this water soon, I would freeze to death. My teeth chattered so hard it felt as though they could punch holes through steel and the feeling in my fingertips was lost to me. I moved my arms around and started shifting the great chunks of ice out of my way when something bad started to happen.

At first I thought my eyes were deceiving me as I saw the sides getting closer and closer without me moving quick enough. What was happening now?! I stopped trying to get close to see if it was really happening and when the ice started to close in on me I cried out. The lake was re-freezing where the hole was and I looked all around as it started to speed up. How was I ever going to get out without first being frozen into an ice sculpture.

I looked back up at the mountain I had just fallen from and barely saw the well concealed balcony, actually if I hadn't just fell from it I wouldn't have known it was even there. But the balcony wasn't the only thing I saw and when I could just see the small image of a person staring down from the rocks, I knew the ice was Layla's final way of saying goodbye…indefinitely.

With the ice closing in I had two choices, one, I could be left half sticking out of the lake like some frozen ice maiden or two I could die with a little more dignity and not give her the satisfaction of seeing me at my death. So just in time I took my last gulp of air and ducked back under just as the ice joined above my head.

This was it and with one last fist banged on the ice to check it couldn't be broken I finally gave up the last of my hope. I saw my skin under the bluish night sky that managed to penetrate the thick cover above me and it looked as though I was already at death's door, knocking and just waiting for someone to answer.

My arms started to float in front of me as the weight of my body, without air, dragged me down and I saw the blood seep out in red ribbons from the slice in my arm. I was fascinated that instead of the blood mixing with the water it was like crimson oil snaking through denser liquid. It felt like I could reach out and hold it only the freezing temperatures had other ideas about me moving.

Then, just as I was floating to my final resting place I saw something I couldn't put understanding to. It was a shadow moving above the ice and I could hear the hollowed sound like someone was calling out in a storm. What was that? I saw it move closer above me and when I saw the distinct shape of two black footprints I screamed losing the last of my air. My own voice was lost, echoing in darkness and a liquid void so vast that no one would ever hear me. I watched in desperate horror as the last remaining life source left me to escape in bubbles to the surface. Then I saw a knee join the floor of the ice like someone was searching for me…well any second now they would be too late, as I could feel the lack of air finally start to shut down my thoughts.

The last thing I saw must have been a trick of my brain functions crashing as I saw a hand print lay flat next to the foot and then the blood that had left me shot towards it like nails to a magnet. The streamers of red that still hadn't mixed with the water hit the ice and landed directly on the hand print. I saw my hair float forwards like every strand wanted to join them and just as the blackness overtook me completely I felt the lake tremble around me. It vibrated through me like little shockwaves and when my hair moved aside from the undercurrent waves, I saw the cause. The hand had not only turned into two but they had also turned into fists that were pounding down on to the icy lid that was keeping me trapped.

Someone had come but they were too late...just too late. My head rolled back and my mind finally found the darkness that mirrored my surroundings. The last sense to go was my hearing as what was followed by the thick snap of cracking ice was a murmured yell that sounded like 'NO!' but it was still too late I had already gone and I wished I could say that it felt like going home but I couldn't because it felt like I was being lost...

Until I was touched by an Angel.

"Keira...Keira..." I heard someone calling my name and I shuddered as I recognised the voice,

"Draven?" I asked and heard his whispered 'yes' in my ear before I felt his lips at my neck.

"It's time to come back to me little vixen," he said against my jaw line and I opened my eyes to find myself in the familiar comforts of home. I was lay in Draven's bed and as the wood carvings above the large four posts came into focus I felt the body next to me shift. An arm shot out across my middle to prevent me from sitting up and I heard a growl.

"Stay!" The command came out hoarse and different to the whispered words that still lingered on my skin.

"Draven?" I said his name again only this time it wasn't because I was unsure of the man, but unsure as to his actions.

"I will never let you leave. NEVER. Do you understand?!" I saw his perfect features turn rigid at the idea and I didn't know what to do. Why was he being like this? What had happened? I searched through my memories for the answers and like a horror movie on fast forward it hit me all at once. The plane. The kidnapping. Lucius. Malphas...

Layla.

All were puzzle pieces that fit together to tell a grim story of my life or more like my end. So what was this? Was this my last chance at goodbye or had Draven managed to get to me in time?

"What happened?" I choked out but Draven covered my mouth with two fingers and merely shook his head at me in silent reprimand.

"Don't speak and don't ever...go." The last word sounded like it had been ripped out of him and I couldn't help the tears that escaped and trickled down onto his hand. He watched every tear make its journey and everyone that landed on his olive skin made a cracking sound that echoed in every corner of the room.

"Keira…Please, I have you now…let me keep you!" He said and even more tears came overflowing and even more cracking sounded as loud as a siren.

"Wh…what's…happening?" I whispered through my sobs and the sight of his own tear-filled eyes found mine looking like two black orbs that showed the future of nothing but despair and suffering. I saw as his face came closer to mine and as he leaned down to lay a gentle kiss on my fingers that had unconsciously entwined with his, I saw the dam break and a single tear fell from under a pillow of long thick lashes and when it landed on the top of my hand the walls of the room started to shake.

"Draven!" I shouted but he looked so absent in his own misery and I couldn't understand what was happening. I looked around the room and saw at all points it had started to crack like an immense weight was pushing it inwards, forcing everything around me to crumble.

"Draven!" Finally he looked up and what I saw made me gasp. It was Draven, the love and owner of my heart but not as I had ever seen him before. From his eyes, bled tears that streaked his face with bloody lines and when the first one landed on my hand it burned and sizzled away my skin like acid.

"Ouch!" I pulled back and saw the image of a man that was slowly exchanging upset for anger. He raised his head and the tender Draven I knew left me for one that wasn't even trying to get a hold of his rage. He grabbed my arms as I moved back and crushed me to his chest so that I couldn't move.

"NO! You will stay! Come back! Keira! Keira!" What I was hearing didn't make sense. I heard the cries of desperation from two voices but right now I couldn't see the face of either. I could smell damp earth and cold flesh but none were the man that held me. I felt my chest being crushed even tighter and knew if Draven didn't let me go that he would break me beyond even his repair.

"Let me go!" I screamed with the last bit of breath left but after that Draven wouldn't allow my chest to refill.

"NO!" Draven screamed out and the walls finally split open and water came flooding in the room moving like blue fire. I could no longer scream as his arms tightened until I could feel the pressure on my ribs increase. Jesus, he was killing me! Why was he doing this… why was he killing me?

The water filled the floor rapidly but not only that, the water was defying gravity and started to flow up the walls, over my head on the ceiling. I could only just see past the bulky muscle that was to be the cause of my death and as far as deaths go, I think dying in the arms of my lover wasn't as I thought it would be....I certainly didn't think they would be the cause. But here I was, sat on his bed, wrapped in the deadly tight grip of a Demon King that had lost all sight of the Angel half of his soul.

The lights in the room popped and burst as the water shorted out the power plunging my death into a darkness I was strangely familiar with...

Death and water.

The words were like an old friend whose name I couldn't remember.

"Keira! Come back! KEIRA!" A voice screamed my name and Draven's hold on me started to loosen but the water was coming up the bed and seeping into the covers we sat on. I looked down and saw Draven's tears of blood drop into the water like oil...like something I had seen before.

Blood that didn't mix. Blood that stood alone and became a force of its own. A life force...my life force. I had seen it, but where? The darkness had allowed me to see the blood in the water but how? I turned to face the glass doors that led onto the balcony and saw the moon's glow coming through them but the doors weren't glass, they were...ice.

ICE!

The room exploded into a dark lake and as the last of the water filled the remaining space turning my death into the memory of it. I saw Draven in front of me with his eyes closed and I screamed out his name under the water. Like before, the air left my body and I watched it bubble up to the frozen top of the lake. I looked back at Draven and panicked when I couldn't find him. I twisted and turned until I looked down and there I found him. I watched in devastation as his body lifelessly floated down to an end I couldn't see. His arms were above him and the hair, I loved nothing more than running my hands through, was waving in mock goodbye.

"Keira" My head whipped round on hearing my name in the water and I saw Lucius floating right next to me, but before I could react he hit out at me, punching me in the chest so hard I spat up a lung full of blood.

"Keira! For fuck sake Keira answer me! Damn it Keira, I am not letting you go! Do you hear me...YOU'RE NOT HAVING HER!" I

heard Lucius screaming and I turned my head to spit out the blood…
only it wasn't blood, it was…water?

"Keira?" I heard Lucius' voice but it sounded strange, it
sounded…hopeful.

I opened my eyes and was confused by my surroundings. I
coughed and more water came up, burning my throat and nostrils. I
looked down where I was hacking up onto and saw frosted earth? And
white snow with patches of grass underneath where a body's
movements had disturbed it.

"Keira!" Lucius said my name again and I felt arms coming round
me bringing me back to when Draven was crushing me. I flinched in
his hold and felt a sharp pain stab at my ribs.

"Oh shit, I hurt you. I'm sorry Keira but I didn't think you were
going to come back…I might have pushed too hard." I looked up at
him and saw a mixture of relief and regret swamp his features. In this
light, pale and with skin glistening with droplets of water he looked
like a fallen Angel, a guardian of the lake ready and waiting to save
freezing females from an early grave.

"Lu..Lu..ci..usss?" I croaked and stuttered feeling the burn even
more and he lay me back down being gentler than I had ever felt in his
touch before.

"I'm here and I am not leaving you….ever!" He added and I
shivered with his promise. It was the same promise Draven had always
made to me but what did it all mean? But more importantly…could I
get any colder?! I started to shake uncontrollably or maybe I already
was and was only now noticing.

"I need to get you warm before you get hypothermia or go into
shock. I am going to strip you, okay." It wasn't a question it was a
warning, as before I could utter a word he had ripped my dress in two
and was pulling it from my frozen skin. I then watched him remove his
own clothes with the same urgency that he had used on me and his wet
T-shirt was removed with one swift action. The material had clung to
each strong line of muscle but now the moonlight made his skin glow
white, like wet marble in one of the fountains in Rome.

"Wwwh…t…ddd…ing?" I couldn't speak from numb lips and a
shaking body.

"Ssssh, don't try to speak Keira. I am going to do what I can," he
said as he lay down on top of me and encased me in his long, thick
body that swamped me in size.

"Fuck! It's like lying on a block of ice! By the Gods your will must

393

rival those of the undead." He muttered the last part shaking his head as he laid more weight over me. He leaned on his elbows by my head and held my face in his hands. With his wet body stretched out across mine and my head locked in his hands, I felt the life coming back to my limbs and a tingling dance up my spine.

"Not enough!" He whispered as his thumb caressed my trembling lips that were no doubt a bruised blue colour. He never took his eyes off me and just before his face lowered further he winked at me before touching his lips to mine. The kiss was too light to feel at first but then he demanded more from me and before I could utter a protest he gained entrance. This is when I realised his goal.

The sun.

The light erupted and transformed this little patch of frozen plant life into a summer's day and with it, the snow melted to reveal lush green trees surrounding us, a velvet blanket of soft grass underneath and a topaz sky above. I felt the heat of the sun through the body above me and it felt divine. I raised my hands to hold his heated shoulders and he growled in my mouth before taking the kiss to a new level. With both our lips at the right angle, locked together, tasting and fighting each other for deeper possession something in me clicked. Both our bodies were not only now warm, but they were near to steaming and yet neither one of us had tried to break the kiss. If anything, we held onto each other as if this was the very last time and it was only when a single face appeared in the forefront of my mind that I managed to break the spell. Draven.

I pushed on his shoulders and after a little nip to my bottom lip he finally let me go. He held himself over me with only a hair's breadth between us touching and we both panted like the wild and untamed animals we had acted. The sun started to fade softly, putting an end to this heated joining and I saw the loss of it in Lucius' crystal eyes that were still smoky grey with lustful fever.

He ran the back of his hand down my cheek and I closed my eyes as he moved lower still until my breast peaked under his touch. I couldn't find the words to stop him as I knew in my veins that this would be the last time we touched in such a way. He had saved my life yet again, and yet again I let him take his payment in silence.

"I am glad to see you warm easily, my little Keira girl." His voice sounded deep and thick, with a thirst I couldn't allow myself to fully sate. His hand held my body captive but when I felt his grip move from my chest to stop at my side he no doubt felt and heard my relief escape in a sigh.

"Don't worry Keira girl, you're not yet mine to take but make no mistake, that one day, you will be...soon." He placed his lips gently to mine in a kiss that spoke volumes despite its feather like softness. It was meant as nothing short of a promise of things to come, that I could be certain of and the thought both terrified me and shook my core into shameless wanting.

"But in the meantime, it is best you get that naked behind indoors before I have to warm you up again." When I didn't move, I saw him raise an eyebrow and give me a cheeky grin before pushing further,

"Or maybe you like the idea of another round?" I swallowed hard and he laughed as he got from his position on top of me, which left me with a bitter blow of cold air to flow over my naked form.

"No, no, I think we should get indoors." I said quickly, making him laugh. He offered me a hand and I tried to look anywhere but at the great part of him that stood to attention, ready for what he nor I would allow.

"You know I find it amazing how one little cold human can still find the much needed blood flow to flush cheeks at her embarrassment. Well at least some places won't be getting cold anytime soon." He commented making my cheeks heat further which was made worse when his eyes drank in their naked fill of me. I covered my breasts with my hands and he found a frown his way when he made the journey to my face but the bastard just laughed again.

"Come on Rosy, time to get off this little rock." I looked around at our situation and couldn't see a way of doing that. We seemed to be on a tiny little island close to the mountain side and it was only big enough to hold five fir trees. I looked up at the rock side and couldn't tell where the castle behind it stood. Were we even close or was I further away than I thought? No wonder no-one ever saw it, it was hard to believe even for me and I had seen it first-hand. No-one in a million years would guess the amount of bodies the mountain concealed or the number of rooms that were buried deep within. As far as hideaways and secret lairs went, this one was a clear winner!

"And just how do you think...?" I was cut off as I turned round to the sight of a very different Lucius.

"Holy shit!" I said on impulse, as I was now looking at Lucius in his demon form for the first time in person and holy shit didn't even begin to cover it!

He cocked his head to one side and seemed amused with my reaction at seeing him this way…well I'm glad one of us was having a good time I thought sarcastically. There he stood like the Master of the Caves and his appearance would give new meaning to the comic hero Batman.

His pale skin was now marred with dark veins that crept in at his sides and lower stomach. Thankfully he had put his trousers back on so I didn't have to discover the differences down in that department, as I think I had enough to contend with up the other end!

Two massive horns came from his shoulder blades at the back which were the start to his unusual wings. It was like a patchwork of black charred skin that was in no particular pattern, all sewn together to create a set of bat shaped wings. Each end curled upwards at the bottom and had dagger edges that look far too deadly to touch. These weren't just a means of flight, they were a means to kill, dismember and disembowel!

They were worn and broken in places with little holes nearer the edges and each side met finger like claws that only added to the arsenal of natural made weapons. The dark grey/blue eyes had disappeared completely and I now found two red eyes staring at me, which reminded me of looking into the depths of two uncut rubies. When his gaze travelled the length of me once more they started to glow, making me take a step back.

"Come here!" The simple command had me nearly staggering. That was the last place I wanted to go but what was I to do, I was stuck on a tiny island with a Vampire and right now, he looked nothing short of one!

I saw him pick something off the ground but in the shadows of the trees I couldn't see what it was. I took another step back as he took one towards me.

"Keira!" He said my name in warning but what did he expect? This wasn't the Lucius I knew that could show kindness, no, this was the Lucius that had haunted my dreams and turned everyone into nightmares. Nightmares of burning girls and ending of worlds, nightmares of a room full of dead friends and bloody relatives. God, how could I have forgotten about those things so easily? What was wrong with me?

"Easy, Keira." He said just before I took another step back which would have proven fatal. I was now at the edge of the island and on this side the lake was still frozen. I don't know how thick the ice was but I wasn't sure I wanted to put it to the test.

"Come now, you know me and I am sure you have seen far worse." He tried to sound light hearted but in a deeper voice that belonged to this Demon side of him, it was nearly impossible to accomplish. He came closer then and my body reacted before I gave it much thought. I stepped back and heard a slight pop under my foot as I stepped onto the ice. It was a sickening sound but I was thankful that's all it was.

"I suggest you don't move, Keira!" He warned and I did as I was told. I was being foolish, deep down I knew that, but the sight of him brought back too many horrendous memories that it was hard to decipher logic from instinct.

"Ch..change back." I said, now once again starting to shiver, which was bound to happen considering I was stood at the foot of a frozen lake, naked and holding my body with both arms, not doing a very good job at trying to hide myself.

"Keira, you know I can't, not if you want us to get off this island." As his words sank in I took another step back, now placing both my feet on the ice. It made another crack that echoed along the lake and sounded like someone hitting high tension wire with a bat. He wanted to fly us both off here in that form and I couldn't even bring myself to go near him…this wasn't looking good!

My feet were so cold on the ice that I looked down just to make sure they weren't going blue and my toes hadn't yet fallen off. I was more than happy to see them in one piece but when I looked back up at Lucius he was now right in front of me and I screamed.

"AHHH!" I would have fallen backwards onto the ice but Lucius grabbed me and yanked me to his chest and back onto the solid earth.

"You little fool! I mean for Demon's sake woman, if you wanted me to kiss you again you had only ask!" He pulled me backwards and wouldn't give an inch when I tried to get away. I started shaking in his hold and he lifted my arms with ease, despite my struggles, and the thing he picked up earlier, he whipped over my head until most of my body was covered in his t-shirt. It should have been wet but thanks to our heated kiss before, it had dried out a lot more than our bodies.

I looked up at him with clear panic in my eyes and the red glow seemed to simmer down.

"I know why you're afraid of me Keira, but those things…the nightmares I gave you…I…they…Oh fuck it!" He grabbed me by the waist, lifted me up to his head height and then took off with one powerful push from bent knees. We were both launched upwards into the sky and I let out a yelp that was unheard thanks to the icy wind that lashed at our bodies.

I wanted to close my eyes but I couldn't keep from staring at his wings and the way they moved. They didn't move like Draven's mighty mass of feathers that found a smooth and gentle rhythm at catching the air, bending the elements to his will. No, these blurred in their movement, being too fast for the eye to see. But one thing I was sure about and that was the speed at which we were travelling. We made it back up the mountain in seconds and as I was being flown around the side of the cliff face I made the mistake of looking down.

"Oh Shit!" I said as I buried my head into his naked torso. I felt his chuckling through my forehead that was plastered into his neck and his grip tightened despite the humour he found in my reaction. One thing I did see before freaking out was the part of the lake that I had fallen into. Only now it looked very different to how I remembered. The massive space that must have been one third of the lake's size was now broken up into loads of icy pieces, a bit like looking down at a giant shattered window.

Lucius had done this to get me out and save my life. Not just this man, but this Demon, who carried me to safety now and I hadn't trusted him when the time came. Was I being foolish like he said or was I finally getting it? I really couldn't trust anyone in this supernatural life I was thrown into, but surely if someone continued to protect me and save me from those who wanted to harm me, then what was left to think?

These were the questions I needed answers to, but before I could find my answers, I needed to go back to history...I needed to go back to Lucius and Draven's history, one that was filled with anger, betrayal and lost friendships but weirdest of all...

*One filled with Nazi's.*

# CHAPTER 34
# PAST BURIED DEEP AND HIDDEN IN BONE

I didn't think my grip could get any tighter as we turned and when Lucius started to take us down I was practically climbing up him.

"I guess it's all flying you hate, not just helicopters?" Lucius joked as we came gently back to the earth but even though I knew we were back on safe ground, I still couldn't pry my face from his neck and my fingers from their hold.

"Hey." He said softly.

"You're safe Keira, come on now." He prompted when I didn't react and he set my feet lower, let go of my waist and tried to peel me away from his neck. I finally let go but he didn't let me step away from him. He lifted my chin up and his eyes searched deep inside making me feel even more naked than when I was just in my knickers.

He ran his fingertips down my cheek and I couldn't help but look up further and lean into his touch, one I found so comforting it was scaring me. They travelled along my jaw and over my lips that were quivering for another reason.

"Fuck, you're beautiful!" He said in a growl. I swallowed the thickness down that was a reminder of all the impossibilities standing between us but under the winter night I felt the lunar pull to a different moon…one called Lucius.

What was it about this man that had my insides doing back flips and tying in knots before landing in my belly? Was it made worse because the image of Draven with Aurora still rang true in my gut or was it just down to the scorned man buried beneath another Demon King?

399

I tried to tell myself that two wrongs didn't make it right and my attraction to Lucius was nothing compared to the combustible feelings that Draven held over me but that heat had been tainted by what I had seen. I needed to sort my head out but in order to do that I first needed to see Draven. And this time not in any dreams or half souls connecting, no, this time I had to be there, body, soul and level mind and this time I needed the truth once and for all.

But for all of this... I needed to go home.

I pulled back and his hand dropped as if he had seen for himself all the emotions playing around my mind as though on a video loop.

"Beautiful, but still a mess!" He said shaking his head at my appearance. I looked down and I had to agree with him completely. My hair hung down in wavy knotted tubes and brushed along the waist of a battered body. I felt my arm being lifted and I looked up to see Lucius looking at the slice there. It didn't look as bad without all the blood and if anything, it looked as if it was in the process of healing. More like it had been done days ago instead of hours and once again, because I didn't know all the answers, I put it down to Draven's effect on my blood. Was that why I had even survived as long as I did? And surely thinking back to the drop, would I even have survived that?

Lucius' face twisted in anger and the right name hissed from his lips,

"Layla!" I nodded and bit my lip.

"She was waiting for me on the balcony when you left." I said softly but it didn't matter how gentle the words, the reaction was the same. He let go of my arm and turned so suddenly I missed most of the action but one thing I didn't miss was the loud roar and Lucius punching his fist into a thick stone wall next to us. His hand disappeared through the hole he made and a crack appeared around all sides that travelled out in a ten foot circumference.

I had jumped back at sight of his rage in Vampire form and it was my first view of his back. His wing span was huge and spread out but where before I would have compared it to a bat, seeing it this way, I was wrong. The only thing that did resemble the creature was the stretched black skin and the ends that were finger like with deadly nailed spikes protruding from the tips. The shape was much bigger than that of the sleek wing span you find on bats.

These started at the two great horns that curled slightly and were positioned outwards from his back. They must have each been six feet long and the points at the end were like circular daggers. They were also black and the deep ridges in them made bumps along the tops that gave them the appearance of a spine.

The winged part started underneath the horns and I could see the long, thick fingers in between the skin that bent outwards and down to the ground, which gave them their distinct shape. The bottom finger curled round past the front of his body and each ended with a long curved razor claw the length of my hand.

All of this came from a thicker black spine at the centre of his back, one which was covered in a fine black fur that looked so soft I had a strange urge to touch it. I couldn't stop myself even if my brain had kicked in to the danger that lurked beneath the Demon image. I took a step forward just as Lucius was removing his hand from the wall and only then did I realise where we were.

The silent garden looked different at night and the pale stone on the floor and surrounding walls gleamed under the high moon. It cast the place in an ethereal glamour and the thick snow was like a sparkling blanket that covered every surface. But none of that held more interest to me than what my hands were stretching out to touch. I felt drawn in and before Lucius could realise what I was doing, I reached out and touched the part of him that was more animal than monster. It was like I was coming into contact with his core and the very soul of him. I couldn't understand it, but I wanted to be close, to hold onto this feeling for as long as humanly possible.

I felt him stiffen under my fingers, but I didn't care, nor did I take heed of his warning growl. The hypnotic feeling took over my senses and my fingers felt their way up and over every velvety ridge. It was like someone had covered the strongest metal in the softest material but it was all alive. I could feel it pulsing underneath my fingers like it was excited I was there, like it was responding to me in some way.

I shook my head as an image flashed through my mind as if something had just put it there. The part on his back that was looking less and less like a spine started to vibrate and the image flashed again only this time I understood it.

Lucius broke the spell too late, as I had already seen what I was never supposed to. He turned and grabbed my wrist to prevent me from going any further and his expression was clear...frustration.

"It can't be..." I said more to myself than to him but I got a reply all the same, one that was a lie.

"IT is not!" He snapped and turned to storm away but I wouldn't let it go, not after such a vision and not after the proof. I grabbed his arm back, no longer afraid of the Vampire side of him that was close to shaking in outrage.

"But I saw it!" I said and he shot me a look, first down at me and then to the part of his arm I was still gripping onto. I stupidly didn't let go.

"You saw nothing!" He shouted but I shook my head feeling so strongly about the other sight that it felt too heavenly to be wrong.

"I felt it!" I shouted back and this time instead of looking angry he just looked…well, he looked sad.

"Keira please, just let it go." For every word spoken he might as well have been on his knees for it was nothing short of begging.

"Lucius, don't ask me that, can't you just…"

"Tell you!" He snapped in for me but I shook my head.

"Trust me." I finished my own sentence the way it was meant to finish and the surprise in his face was evident. He stared at me and the colour in his eyes turned into slate.

"And why would I do that Keira, after all, your alliance is not to me." He said with bitter after tones. I stepped round his wings and came face to face with him. Up this close and in his other form, I could see the length and size of his fangs…a size that made me shudder. But I bravely placed a hand on his right wing, in between the large gap of his fingers and the skin was smoother than it looked. I saw the ends of each claw twitch and I could only hope it wasn't because they were getting ready to swipe out at me.

"Because you saved my life and therefore, you have my trust in return. And that is not a claim I wouldn't base my soul on Lucius, I give you my word." When I said this it sent a tremor through the wing I still held and my eyes darted to the lethal talons that curled round closer to me. When they twitched again I jumped closer to Lucius' bare chest and I felt a little rumble causing me to look up at him. Now instead of anger, there was a little light in his eyes that showed humour and Lucius' usual playfulness. This look told me he had done it on purpose.

"They will never hurt you, Keira." He said looking down at me and as if to prove his point he curled them further around his body until I flinched when I felt something smooth at my legs. I turned and looked down to see the longest and last finger bend so far inwards that the back of the claw brushed dangerously on my ankle.

The other side started to do the same and then the rest followed suit and bent in around me, pushing me further back into Lucius' chest. My back was flush against him and a deep thundering underneath his ribs and shoulders started to beat against the thin material of his T-shirt I was wearing. I was about to move but I felt the weight of his hands hold onto my shoulders, anchoring me in place.

The thundering continued to beat against my back and whatever the cause, it also affected Lucius' hands as they too echoed the movement on my neck and shoulders. I saw the two ends of his wings coming closer together, getting ready to meet. I shuddered under his hold and he leaned down to my ear and whispered in another language,

"Vær stille og ikke frykte meg liten en." ('Be still and do not fear me little one.' In Norwegian) I don't know what he said to me but his words soothed me all the same. He made a contented sound when I relaxed under his hands and they made their way further up my neck, still holding me close to him. I saw the bottom set of fingers come together first and the edges seemed to fuse at the seams, creating a skinned pod, made impenetrable to open by the interlocking of his claws. I watched the outside world disappear inch by inch as if someone was zipping up a sleeping bag and the sound of the locks were nailed shut with a clicking together of lengthy talons.

When they reached over my head I thought this was going to be it but then the vibrating increased at my back and I looked up and over to find the source. Lucius' great horns were twisting round in his back and moving to face his front, which brought the rest of the black skinned wings to the join up completely. The last section of night was blacked out when the horns stopped moving and locked together at their tips high above Lucius' head.

I felt hands slip down from the column of my neck, down to my shoulders. He gripped me harder in the pitch black and I couldn't even see my breath anymore in the cold... a cold that no longer touched my skin. Inside this little cocoon heat seeped back into my body and I felt like a little caterpillar waiting safely until her wings grew.

"No longer cold." Lucius spoke to me or himself, I didn't know, but his fingertips danced along the T-shirt's neck and in the dark it heightened my senses enough to have me close to panting.

"You spoke of secrets Keira, promises and trust...is this something you're prepared to offer me? Are you ready to give me this part of yourself because there will be no going back little dove. Not now, not ever." He leaned further down and whispered under my ear a gentle threat.

"I will own it and never return it. Do you understand Keira?"

When I didn't answer him he bit my lobe and held it in his teeth applying more pressure increasing the pain until I yelped.

"Say Yes Lucius!" He ordered after letting go only to take possession again to do the same.

"Ach" I moaned and he hissed, while his hands dug into the junction where my neck met my shoulders.

"Do it!" He snapped and I lowered my head in defeat.

"Yes Lucius." These words felt heavy and so wrong they warped into a right. What had I just given Lucius other than the trust I had offered? Or was I just being paranoid? If that was the case, then why did it feel like I had just passed him a piece of my soul under the table for him to play with?

"Good girl." He hummed in pleasure.

I waited for him to speak next but when I felt the rumbling in his chest I moved to step away but the deep red glow stopped me. Light started to pass through the fingers on his wings, like it was being squeezed through from behind me. It lit the small space in an eerie luminosity that burned brighter at the bone covered by skin, skin that was now made somewhat translucent by the light. It looked like what Libby and I used to do as kids, in the night under the bed covers with a powerful torch.

It was a startling colour of deep veined blood that spread out along the thinnest lines on his wings and I didn't even think before I felt them for myself. I felt him shudder under my fingertips, much like he did when touching his back.

"You know, that tickles." His voice sounded at my ear, when I hadn't even felt him move and it gave me a startled jump but he spun me around to face him just as quickly. Looking up at his face in red shadows, I could see his eyes scorching hot as he took in my expression of shock.

"You're ticklish?" I don't know why I asked him this question but it seemed to be the first thing my brain wanted to know, thanks to his comment. Thankfully this brought a smile to his face, the kind of smile that tilted up on one side, which let the view of one fang look even deadlier in the glare of the blood coloured power pulsating through his veins.

He picked up one of my hands and brought it up to his mouth, which made me bite my lip in confusion.

"I am if… Soft. Little. Beautiful. Pale. Fingers, are doing the touching." He had nipped at each fingertip with every singled out word and the pressure on my bottom lip increased. He raised an eyebrow when seeing what my teeth were doing to myself and I let my lip slip from them slowly. My action caused Lucius' eyes to flash red and he couldn't seem to take his lustful gaze from them. I cleared my throat and his stare was dragged from his point of interest. I was thankful that by the time they reached my eye level, the blood radiance had diminished from the whites of his eyes.

"So Keira, you wanted to know my secrets but first I want to know what it showed you." It was weird the way he referred to 'it' like it wasn't a part of him but I knew better thanks to the vision, so I told him as much.

"But it is a part of you." He smiled softly at me and I don't think any other look could have made me feel quite as innocent.

"No Keira, it lives within me but not until it is complete will its power be fully restored and with it, my own." My eyes widened as the vision and his words clicked together.

"That's why you want it isn't it...because...?"

"Go on...finish that sentence, Keira." His tone turned hard and once again he was gripping my shoulders, showing me to take caution but I couldn't find the strength to hold back what I knew. It all made sense now...it wasn't just a holy relic to be used to control armies like the vision had given me glimpses of. All those battle clad kings at the head of a sea of soldiers, waiting until the sight of the God's power in the hands of mere mortal men. But even then, it was all wrong.

"Power. The power of the Spear in your back is missing the tip and Draven has it...doesn't he?" Lucius nodded silently and confirmed my vision. The Holy Spear showed me a flash of history leading right back to the very day it gained its incredible power and was used to pierce the side of Jesus as he hung on the cross. As the instrument that aided in taking the life of the Son of God, the very blood that stains its blade was the most powerful part. And only two beings in the world had their piece of it. Two pieces of equal power, but together meant an unstoppable force.

When I touched Lucius' back it had communicated with me in such a way that no matter the strength of my barriers, it had been like tearing through tissue paper. I had seen its beginning start in the hands of a Roman soldier named Longinus who was ordered to make sure that Jesus was dead and unwittingly stabbed him in the side too hard. But upon removing the spear from his side the tip snapped off, still embedded in Jesus' side.

It then flipped to the heart-breaking part that was never documented. Judas wrenched the spear from its owner in rage and snapped the pole from the blades head only to then be captured himself, but this time it was by his brothers in faith. Once judged as a traitor and left to be tortured by burning sun and choking on the payment that was never truthfully received, his body was ripped open by the very spear that he had gained possession of and left embedded in his open gut.

As he was finally left alone to die, the blood of Christ mixed with his own and sent him to a very different God, one that wanted to use his powers for his own side of the balance. This was how Lucius became the Vampire King and still, to this day, that same spear never left his body.

The Holy Lance in Rome, Vienna, Echmiadzin, Antioch and even more places that I had never seen or heard of, mixed into one long stream of events of people using what they believed to be the real spear, all this time using an unknowing fake in their attempts at more power. Even with cities given as payment for its possession, it travelled the seas and passed from ruler to ruler, and all that time it belonged to only one man and now I understood why it made it rightfully so. The spear had both taken his life and granted him his new one.

"And so Draven has the other piece but wait...how did he even get it?" I asked and the mention of this was enough to get Lucius' blood pumping faster. I knew this of course because I could see it in the cage his wings had me trapped in. Lucius fury was a brighter red place to be caged in.

"A Being of his position... it's simple Keira...he took it." When I gave a quizzical stare up at him he gave me a frown back.

"What do you mean? Took it from whom?" At that he actually rolled his eyes before stating what he must have thought the obvious.

"Let me make this ever the more clear for you little Keira, he walked up to the Son of God, bent on one knee and dug his fingers into his flesh on that very same day and with Jesus' blood still warm on his hands, he simply got back up and walked away without a word...the tip of the Holy Lance in hand." At this I cried out my shock.

"NO! That's a lie...that didn't happen!" I was outraged at the thought he painted. That couldn't have happened, not Draven...not the Draven I knew.

"Is that what you believe?" Lucius said more calmly than I would have thought at being called a liar.

"Yes!" I said, holding my ground and my belief in Draven, stubbornly. But the look Lucius gave me wasn't smug and arrogant, that I could have used and turned into anger, but pity...! What was I to do with that?

"And why Keira...why would you hold that certain belief in this untruth?" He asked me far too gently for my liking. I felt the tears form and I wiped one away angrily, trying hard to stop anymore from escaping and showing a weakness in the belief he spoke of.

"That is what he told me." I said honestly but the sight of his pity increased and my dread doubled. He leaned down to me, held my face in his hands, dwarfing my size and wiped away more rebellious tears that had slipped down my cheeks, using gentle thumbs. He gave me a long look and even in this unusual light, I saw his eyes crystal over the lightest grey before he whispered the words I didn't want to believe,

*"Then Keira... he lied to you."*

# CHAPTER 35
# BEAUTY IN THE DARK

We walked down the endless spiral staircase in utter silence and only Lucius' hand that held mine in his strong grip had me believing I wasn't as alone as I felt. Everything I had just learned was still spinning round in my head, much like the way this staircase was causing havoc with my equilibrium. Draven had lied to me… again.

The thought was one I could taste like acid in my mouth. It was a bitter feeling of betrayal, one I was coming accustomed to at an increasing rate. He told me about that day and when I had asked if he had been there, he had told me no. I had been so shocked about the whole thing that I had even asked him why not. Why he didn't intervene and his answer had been simple…it was not what the Gods had wanted.

Why had he kept the truth from me? What did he ever think to gain from it? The questions for when we met again were certainly stacking up and none were going to be in his favour.

I stumbled over an uneven stone but Lucius caught me by turning quickly so that I landed in his chest as one hand still held my hand and the other carried a lit torch. He had turned back to his usual form after opening his wings like a pair of doors you were likely to find in Hell and lost that part of himself just as quickly.

"You steady?" It was the first thing he had said to me since the rooftop garden that had looked more frozen in time than in winter. I nodded once and with a quick touch of my cheek, he retook possession of my hand and led me further down.

I don't know how long we walked for but before I knew it, I was being led in another direction than the way I had come with Pip that day.

"Where are we going?" I said pulling back on his hand when it came to the junction that would lead me back to my room. And considering I was still just in his T-shirt and my knickers I was getting close to being desperate for simple comforts...like girl clothes that didn't smell like lake water and the most masculine of scents.

"I do not trust for you to be alone right now."

"Why?" I asked, wondering if he thought I would just be sat in my room, crying my eyes out, while being half submerged in a tub of ice cream and listening to songs about lonely cowboys, with a bottle of Jack in my hand!

"Because Layla has not yet been captured and I told you that I would not be leaving you alone again." Oh...okay, so I really should have given him more credit for that one. When the thought he planted about Layla came in my mind I couldn't stop the shiver that shook me once. Lucius noted my reaction and pulled me a little closer to him.

"Can I not just change first?" I said feeling like a small child in adults clothing. Lucius' T-shirt was baggy from his wide upper body muscle and long thanks to his height so it looked more like a short dress but it was still bloody freezing to walk around in.

"You can change when we get where we are headed." He said simply and tugged me to continue walking.

"And where is that exactly?"

"Questions!" I heard him mutter before he pulled me along to walk down the hallway that looked more like a rock tunnel. The walls had been smoothed down to create the path but you could still see the damp stone and the patterns of the different minerals that shone on the surface when wet.

The fire torch that Lucius still held in its metal holder, danced light along the rock and instead of just seeing the roughness of a crudely made walkway, I saw the essence of its natural beauty. I even had to stop at one part because what I saw had me locked to the spot in its utter splendour. All along this part of the wall the minerals had turned into the deepest of blues and brightest greens that swirled together in large clumps in the wall. The combination of colours reminded me of peacock feathers and when the firelight touched on them they came alive in stunning allurement.

"Kupfernickel." Lucius spoke softly in my ear as he came closer to the wall I was mesmerized at.

"What does it mean?" I asked just as softly, as though I was caught in some sort of spell. He moved to stand next to me and our sides became flush against each other, He moved the flame across the wall and the colours almost lit up like someone had switched a bulb on behind coloured glass.

"In Germany this deceptive mineral came to be known as kupfernickel, which literally means 'copper demon' but it is more widely known as Azurite and has other minerals mixed with it. Are you interested in this?" Lucius asked, and I looked up to find him staring down at me with a half-smile and wide eyes.

"I love beautiful things, I guess it's the artist in me, but I love nothing more than to paint natural beauty in its own environment." I said emphasising the word 'natural' because it was important to me. I loved capturing things in the world where they were meant to stay, yes gemstones were fabulous, all cut and polished but crack open a plain looking rock and find a small sparkling treasure inside and to me, the beauty intensified tenfold.

"Like yourself?"

"Yes...I mean...no! umm, I..." I flustered with my words as Lucius started to laugh.

"Come on, you beautiful thing, let's go before those cheeks of yours explode all over this wall and give new meaning to the 'copper demon'." He took my hand in his and pulled me along until we came to some more steps that dipped deeper down into the mountain. Man, my calves were going to be sore in the morning, I mean just how many steps can one person go down in a night?

Lucius explained as we walked, the meaning behind the nickname for the glittering mineral and how, because it resembled other minerals in simpler colour, this resulted in occasional attempts to try and smelt nickeline in the belief that it was copper ore. But these attempts always failed due to high smelting temperatures needed to reduce nickel. This part I didn't find practically very interesting as such, but it piqued my curiosity again when he told me, that for some unknown reason the supernatural were drawn to the mineral and that was how he found this place and more to the right facts of how it got its name.

"So was this place already built when you found it or...?"

"Always so many questions Keira. Here's one for you, did you drive your parents crazy as a child?" I laughed out loud which echoed down the tunnels we walked causing me to slap a hand over my mouth.

"Sorry, that laugh probably woke some people up." I said feeling guilty at the idea and now it was Lucius causing echoes with his own laughter.

"I very much doubt you will be waking our dead with that one, but Vampires no. It is not yet dawn and as you know we sleep in the day." He pushed on a door at the end of this section and it groaned along the stone floor.

"So...umm..."

"Another question, Keira?" He asked with humour clear in his tone.

"Ha Ha, yes, I know I ask a lot of questions but come on...I mean, do you really blame me? There is still so much I don't know and Draven isn't exactly forthcoming and brimming over with answers for me." He looked as though he was going to make a derogatory comment about Draven but then he held himself back, which I was thankful for. I didn't feel in the mood to start battling for Draven's side but I didn't want to hear his name being dragged in the dirt either.

"Ask your question, Keira!" He said dryly and I jumped when the door slammed shut behind us.

"Umm, oh yeah, I wanted to know about when you sleep...do you...um...like die or anything or are you just asleep like the rest of us?" At this he gave me a chilling smile which immediately had me sorry I had asked. He turned full circle and was looking down at me with one hand held high with the fire crackling next to his head. Did he not feel the burning heat?

"Ah, finally one question I do not have to answer." He said with cruel knowing in his eyes.

"Why not?" I was almost too scared to ask. His smile deepened and his face came closer to mine, casting unnerving shadows across his face thanks to the light at his side.

"Because it is one you will soon be finding out for yourself." He kissed my cheek when he heard me inhale sharply and outstretched his arm to one side to show me a heavy looking door at the far end of yet another corridor. Then he said something that sent chills to every pore on my body,

*"My bedchamber, my lady."*

# CHAPTER 36
# LUCIUS' LAIR

The door at the end was like a siren of danger screaming at me to run. Cherry red, high gloss painted doors cried out from the end of the corridor like some portal lay behind them as a gateway straight to Hell and beyond. When I didn't move I heard Lucius start to laugh before he grabbed the top of my arm and pulled me from my anxiety.

"Don't look so worried Doll, nothing is going to eat you." He said light-heartedly. But no matter his tone, I think if he had even sung it out Julie Andrew's style I would have still felt the same way about that door. It symbolised every step I didn't want to make in its direction. Red for the colour of STOP, DANGER, WARNING. You name it, it was saying it!

As we got closer I saw the heavy iron work on each side that ran three times in great swirls back in on itself from the pointed spike. One that was directed at each metal ring in the same design that worked as the door knocker in their centres. The shining black of the metal against the deep red painted wood was an unusual thing to see down here in the heart of the mountain and even more so being situated against the two stone pillars either side, that were a perfect match to the cave stone corridor.

"I…I…think I should go back…to my room…I could ask Pip, she would stay with me…I…" I was fighting with my words that only had him responding in full blown cockiness in one smile. A smile I wanted to knock off him with a back hander to the handsome face!

"Let's ask her, should we?" He said and before I could comment

413

he let the torch slide down into a thick iron ring that was fastened to the wall. The metal cylinder that still held a flame at its top, scraped down the wall and I noticed the grooves it made in the block work like it had been done before, many times over. Then I jumped back when Lucius used both hands to push on either side of the door using every muscle in his back, causing them to bunch up and tense from the weight. Those doors looked huge at ten feet tall and were made from solid wood, so I would like to have said the sight of Lucius' naked torso working his upper body strength didn't cause little flutters in my belly, but I would have been lying.

The doors swung open with a great echoing bang that was like a Japanese gong going off to indicate the master was home. The open space beyond erupted into firelight and only when I felt a little push by the hand at my lower back did I move forward. It felt more like I was entering a lion's den than just another room I hadn't seen before.

Past the doors was like stepping into a very rustic entrance to a castle and the three high arches that were directly in front of me looked as imposing as they felt. This space wasn't just fit for any old King from history, no... this was the stuff of fairytales of time and ancient stories of forgotten lands. A foyer wasn't a word to describe it but considering I didn't know what else to call this area I went with what I could only imagine. Stepping down a few steps into a large square space it didn't even grant a view of the rooms beyond the three open arches in front of me, which told me we were higher up than the main room.

I could feel Lucius at my back and his eyes taking in my reactions to where I guessed not many ventured. The flooring was made from cut marble squares set into a diamond pattern and the same marble was used in the two great sculptures that stood at either side of the archways. If their purpose was to add to the intimidation, then mission accomplished as I shuddered just looking at them.

The rest of the room was a mere background trickle compared to the great flood these two presented. The backdrop of the smooth rock walls and carved stone arches were a theatrical setting for the Demon warriors standing guard over Lucius' secret world.

Both stood larger than life deemed real and the swords they both held up high touched the top of the room. Their legs were covered in carved skirts that looked so real, if you would have touched them, you would have been surprised not to feel material at your fingertips. The wrapped coverings hung lower than their stomachs, showing the muscular V before their groins and the belts around them hung even lower, hanging down to where their feet would be.

It would have been an unusual touch also to have the flames covering up to their knees but considering the person behind me that must have commissioned them it was more than fitting. Flames continued up and were licking out at their thighs, which was also mirrored in the pattern on the floor around them, with broken pieces of marble placed in such a way, the floor looked ready to swallow us both up.

Their chests were bare and had great chunks taken from their flesh showing spiked tissue underneath, making me realise this was where the real armour was, right under the facade of what humans took at face value. These statues symbolised the real strength beneath human flesh and each shoulder blade showed the proof. No marbled smooth skin lay there but instead one large horn came from the bone that twisted up either side of their heads and the points came over their foreheads. Seeing this made me think of Ragnar and what felt like an age ago, when I had first seen him in his Demon form.

However, the masks these two wore weren't made from bone but were the only part on them to be made from a different material. The two faces had been covered with brushed gold plating and with only a pair of thin black lips and holes for eyes that weren't seen. I watched Lucius walk right up to the one on the left and was so shocked to see even at their great height, he didn't seem small.

He gripped onto the stone sword and spun the weapon one handed until the blade now pointed to the floor and the hands of the guard had twisted at an awkward angle. Then I watched as he grabbed the golden mask, pulling down slightly and then when something clicked, he opened it like a door to the face beneath. Now that it was hung down and only attached by the jawline on one side I could see the demon within.

I made a shocked noise in the back of my throat and Lucius grunted at my behaviour. But come on, could he really blame me considering the horrific face that now looked down at us both. Its face was long and slightly slanted with a large forehead that went down into a pointed chin. The face part of the statue wasn't made of marble like the rest but more like baked sand from the world's hottest and most deadly of deserts. Sun cracked, and flaky features showed high cheekbone that were almost feminine in shape, but the mouth gave me chills to the bone. Its lips had been ripped away to leave little pieces of grainy skin hanging, so delicate these pieces looked like they would crumble when touched.

But even this wasn't the most disgusting part. No it was the open mouth full of real teeth that had been set in the carving, ones belonging to numerous creatures. Triangular ones that looked as though they could have belonged to a shark ran along in the back row, where some sharper thinner ones were crossing over each other in the next line that could have come from large rodents. There were others I couldn't even begin to imagine the animal they belonged to but the most disturbing of all were the last set. These at the front looked like human teeth, only ones that had been filed into sharp little points. There looked to be hundreds of these and the thought made me close my eyes, shake my head and clench my fists.

I was just about to speak out my views on seeing human parts used in such a way when Lucius reached up and pushed something inside its mouth. The motionless eyes, which were just two empty slanted ovals, flickered from black to white light before the sound of massive rocks moving against each other had me diverting my eyes. Off to one side a doorway had appeared from behind the smooth rock wall and it was only when Lucius grabbed my arm again that I realised I had been rooted to the spot.

"All that for a door?" It was the first thought in my head and Lucius only granted me a wink as an answer. I mean, didn't these guys just use keys for Christ's sake?

I let myself be pulled past the archways and when I saw what was past them I knew why we needed the door. I was right in my earlier thoughts of being up high. My eyes were faced with a massive rock cavity which gave a whole new meaning to the word lair.

"Your bedroom is a bat cave?" I said making Lucius laugh, one that echoed up and beyond. He pulled me up a few steps until we stood between the arches in the middle. I made the mistake of letting him put me there and when I looked down I screamed at the great drop, one that went straight down onto a field of lethal stalagmites that reached up like natural made temple pillars. Of course pillars don't usually have killer tips like giant spears!

"Shit!" I tried to move backwards but Lucius was blocking my way out and snaked an arm around my waist to hold me steady.

"Easy!" He warned and I could almost feel my chest about to burst as my fear hitched higher up the notches to full blown panic.

"Let.Me.Go!" I said turning my fear into anger at being held here.

"Keira, do you really think I would drop you?" He asked in a low hum that seeped inside my skin and lay there like the sweat that was forming.

"For all I know you brought me here to get rid of me." I said not really believing the words but saying them anyway, if anything just to hear more reassurance the security his voice promised.

"Ah, but if I wanted to get rid of you little dove, then you would be nesting in your frozen grave on the floor of Königssee." I had heard them speaking the name of the lake before but coming from Lucius' whispered lips at my ear, gave new meaning to the place name. It became something dangerous and alluring at the same time, like a secret place and looking down in to the largest cave I had ever seen, being Lucius' home, it was more truth than fiction.

"So you're just trying to scare me then?"

"No. I am trying to instil trust. Do you trust that I will not let you fall...ever?" His words took on a serious edge and his arms around me tightened. I couldn't answer him with words but as the reality of it set in I nodded yes. He let out a deep sigh and whispered a praised,

"Good girl, little pet." And then he pulled me backwards with him. I didn't really give it much thought as to what all that was about but then again, I wasn't given much time until the answer started shrieking out at me. If I was terrified of the heights seconds ago then this had plunged me straight back to the balcony with Layla.

We had walked through the cave wall entrance the statue's lock had opened and now I stood in front of something that reminded me of an Indiana Jones adventure... or nightmare in my case. The cave opened into different levels, but the only way forward was a metre thick rock bridge that was a sheer drop on either side. I think I would have been braver with the sight of handrails or something, but there was nothing but empty space and the killer stalagmites stood like soldiers waiting for fresh meat to slay.

"I can't do this!" I said in nothing short of increasing panic.

"I know." Lucius said as though he had expected this reaction all along and his next action answered my earlier confusion. The reason Lucius had thought it so necessary to 'instil' my trust in him was the reason I was screaming my protests now. He had me scooped up in his arms and cradled to his bare chest as his long strides ate up the petrifying space.

"Oh shit, oh shit, oh shit, oh shit!" I said into his neck where I had buried my head and closed my eyes from the sight of possible death on either side.

"You're alright, easy now." He said and it was only then that I realised we weren't moving anymore.

"Oh God! Keep going! Don't bloody stop now….shit." I said still with my eyes fused shut and the image of us just stood in the middle of the natural bridge, swaying? Oh god why was he swaying! Was he trying to put me down!

I was about to say something stronger than shit when I felt him nuzzle at my hair and cheek.

"Keira." The way he said my name wasn't in warning more like willing me into understanding. When I just shook my head backwards and forwards, in little quick movements I felt a rumbling in his chest… was he silently laughing at me? Just before I could snap at him he gently shook me and then put his lips to my ear.

"It's safe my pet and time to put that trust to the test. Now open your eyes for me and see my world." His words felt so intimate that I trembled before doing as he asked and placed my trust in him. On opening my eyes I found myself staring at a large platform the other side from which we came and without another word Lucius placed my feet on the ground and pulled me in the direction he wanted me to follow. Like this, feeling the massive size difference between us, I felt like a rag doll being pulled along by its owner. Well I certainly looked the part, being only half dressed and having hair that looked like it had been backcombed by Sweeny Todd.

At the side of the raised platform there was an open passageway that was too dark to see in but with Lucius' unrelenting grip holding my hand, I felt submissively comfortable letting him lead me around like this. After all, I think since I had been here I had learnt time after time that I was not safe anywhere in this place on my own!

The darkness didn't last as it was only a passage to the other side. Once through, I got my first sight of Lucius' space and unbelievably, the cave looked far less threatening on this side. It was all one open space but on different levels and the walls were untamed rock of burnt oranges thanks to the glow of firelight, from the many lit torches that hung around the room. The room was warm and strangely inviting, thanks to the soft colour and lush furnishings that gave the space a luxurious manor home feeling. Even though, just looking at the jagged rock of the mountain, you couldn't easily get past that this was just a cave buried deep underground. The staircase that led down to the first level even had a beautiful intricate pattern etched into each step in swirls of interlaced symbols and had a banister made of black iron to match. Lucius walked ahead of me and the first level down was a comfortable looking living space and its plush seating wasn't empty.

"TOOTS!" Pip screamed and came racing past Lucius to get to me quicker. I nearly choked when I saw what she was wearing. She had changed from what she had on earlier into one of the most far out things I had ever seen her in and never would I have thought I would be ending this hellish night seeing Pip dressed in a light blue adult baby grow covered in stars, moons and…naked women? The outfit was zipped up at the front all the way to a big baggy roll neck that also had a baggy hood that swayed as she moved my way.

She threw her arms around me after barging Lucius out of the way and started fussing over me like a little mother hen.

"Holy shit and mother tattooed bitch, you look like you've been on the night train to Hell!" She said holding handfuls of my hair and lifting it up like she was holding dead rats.

"I very nearly did, that is… if Lucius hadn't saved me." I said quietly looking at him to see if he heard my declaration. He looked at me then and I blushed to my roots from the look he cast my way. Then as if someone had snapped their fingers he was back to being the King and ruler already dominating the room.

"I want action and revenge before the next moon ends!" He commanded his council and meanwhile Pip still fussed over me and when she pulled the large T-shirt out to the sides to see its full size she giggled, then she turned to see Lucius' back as he addressed everyone that had stood in his presence. She held out her hands to his size and then mirroring her actions did the same to my top again. I tapped her hands away at her joke and she laughed.

"Is there something funny about what I just said Imp?" Lucius' voice cut through the cave and bounced around until it came from all sides.

"Nope sir, nopedy nope nope." She said as she winked at me and skipped to Adam, who was frowning at her. When she had fully turned round I had to stop my gasp at seeing the back of this strange suit that looked to be part of the wardrobe for a porno called 'Fanny Galore does a sleepover'. All her back was bare down to base of her spine and there was a little flap over her bum that was held in place by two bunny heads.

"Ready for duty, sir!" She said saluting and waiting eagerly for instructions. I saw Lucius' bare back muscle flex as I walked around to listen to what he was planning. When he saw me he nodded once but the anger on his face was clearly trying to be kept under control.

"Hakan, you will track her down with Ruto." Hakan nodded deeply and slowly whereas Ruto, who was leaning back on a thickly studded chest, just straightened up and said,

"Fuck yeah...I hate that Vamp!" Then he flicked a blade from his side and was spinning it in his hand like some mortal combat competition he was taking part in. It was still a startling thing to watch someone who looked like a fifteen year old misfit skater dude, playing with knives instead of working on his half pipe turns.

Ruto pushed away from the waist high chest and bowed to Lucius before leaving with Hakan the same way we had come.

"Caspian, take your wife into the tunnels and see if we have a snake in our midst. If she had help, then I would like to extinguish it before it can aid her insight any longer. She knew when Keira was alone within minutes of my departure. I would very much like to know how. Find them!" With their orders received, they too nodded and made to leave. Lucius grabbed Caspian's arm and stared him down as he voiced another order.

"Bring them back alive Caspian, I want to play with them myself!" Lucius smiled at Caspian's clear disappointment and I really didn't ever want to think too much about what Lucius' idea of 'playtime' with the traitor would be.

They too left the same way and when there was now only the four of us left in the room, Lucius seemed to relax somewhat.

"Hey what about us, don't we get an assignment, do I get to kill her or at least take a chunk out the bitch?" Pip said and when Lucius held his hand up to stop her from saying more, she pouted making her lip ring stick out to one side. She still looked adorable.

"I want you to take Keira and make her more comfortable while I talk to my second in command." Pip smiled and was about to say something naughty, as it was written all over her face, but she must have thought better about it when Lucius raised one eyebrow in an intimidating glare.

"Aye, aye, Captain. Come along me matey, time to get you snug as a bug in a carpet store." She clucked out at me then snapped her teeth when I didn't react quickly enough.

"Okay, okay, I'm moving...jeez, anyone would think I nearly died tonight." I mumbled sarcastically, making her laugh, while showing me the direction I should be moving in.

Walking further round the sitting area that consisted mainly of masculine wooden furniture and a U shaped black couch, one big enough to seat at least ten people, there was a pair of steps that first went down and then up into another hidden space. This place reminded me of a stone labyrinth that had been formed naturally and its different levels were being utilised as different sections of a living space.

Right now we had walked around a huge boulder the size of a four wheel drive that acted as a divider to hide a bathroom from view.

"Wow!" I breathed out at the sight before me.

"You like?" Pip asked in a funny accent that sounded very camp and I laughed. She walked over to a hole in the wall and when her whole wrist disappeared a click sounded. I then turned to the sound of running water splashing in a little pool that had been cut out of the rock and then smoothed down. It was the same as every space in here. The walls, the counters, even a little stool in one corner alcove, everything was carved from the rock and curved until not one edge remained.

"Time to get in, Chickadee." Pip said and when I didn't move she folded her arms and tapped a foot that was part of her baby grow.

"What are you even wearing, Pip?" I said as I made my way over to the little pool that was on floor level and took up all of one corner.

"It's a onesie, what...you don't think it's cute?" She said putting her hands in the pockets at the sides and spreading out the hips to pivot round.

"I think I remember my mum saying something about buying one for Libby for Christmas or something..." My voice trailed off at the end of that sentence as I felt the deep pang hit me in the chest. My sister and Frank...My mum, dad, gran and gramps...all there waiting for me, but would I ever show up? Wait!

"Pip what date is it?" I asked in a bit of a panic.

"Umm...wait...let me think about this...how many lashes did I have yesterday..." Lashes? Oh god I really didn't want to ask.

"Ah, I had eighteen, so today is the nineteenth...yeah that's right 'cause tonight I get roses and the paddle." Paddle? Okay so now I really was burning to know but so didn't at the same time...Paddle... really? I really don't think I was going to be able to look at Adam again, like...ever!

At least I had found out the date and that it hadn't yet been Christmas. Would I ever even make it back before the year was out?

"You're still standing there Keira, and now you're looking at me like I have grown an extra head and ripped it off for you to use as a float." I shook my head at her and she giggled.

"What…too much?"

"A little, yeah." I responded. I looked down at the pool and was surprised to see steam coming from its clear waters.

"It's a natural spring but it gets filtered into the other pools, so it isn't as hot. Go on, you will love it, the minerals make your skin as though you're wearing a giant Chinchilla, although I never would, cause they're cute and roll in sand and even cuter than rats. I have to count out my lashes so that's how I remembered the date…although Adam never likes to call his numbers when I whip him, he just shouts and groans a lot and…"

"LALALALA!" I said holding my ears and shaking my head. I knew I didn't want to know. I felt Pip come up behind me and before I could stop her she whipped Lucius' t-shirt off me and with a quick tug and snap of my knickers, I was stood naked as a jaybird.

"Ah!" I shouted but she just gave me a little nudge with her elbow and I gave up trying to hide my modesty in front of this crazy little Imp. I stepped down into the water and it was so hot I pulled my foot from the water and felt it starting to itch.

"Oh go on, you big baby." I rolled my eyes and this time got two feet in and waited until I could adjust to the temperature. It seemed like this night was like an extreme lesson in battling the elements and the first course had definitely been a cold one.

I finally let myself take the plunge and dipped all the way, pulling the air through gritted teeth. However once in, the heat started to work wonders on my tight muscles and even the slices in my body, that had been Layla's parting gift, didn't hurt. I made a humming sound as the water lapped my neck, which felt heavenly and Pip made a clicking sound, making me turn to look at her.

She had plonked herself down with folded legs right by the edge of the pool and was tapping the side with her long pointed nails. I looked up to see Pip had turned serious and with her thin eyebrows pulled together, it wasn't a look I was used to seeing.

"What's wrong Pip?" I asked and she raised her head giving me view of watery wide green eyes that were shining like emeralds. Man with a look like that I was surprised if Adam was ever able to say no to this exotic beauty.

"I thought I'd lost you." Her emotional confession brought a lump to my throat. This tiny little bit of an Imp had the courage of a warrior and the heart of a puppy dog. When a tear rolled down her cheek and travelled in down the crease of her nose, I felt my own tears spring up from the sight.

"It's okay Pip...I'm ..Okay." I nearly choked with trying to keep my own emotions in check but when she flung herself at me I had to catch her in the pool. She clung to my neck like a child about to say goodbye to her mother and I found myself rubbing her bare back like any mother would.

"It's alright Pip," I whispered and even though I was naked, sat in a pool of water and holding a sobbing Imp in a onesie, I didn't feel one ounce of awkwardness at all.

That was until her husband ran in, in a panic, followed swiftly by...oh no, not again...

*Lucius*

# CHAPTER 37
# FRIENDSHIPS THAT 'TIPPED' THE BALANCE

"Pipper!" Adam's panic stricken voice brought Pip out of her sobs and she turned her head to look at her concerned husband. I don't know what this must have looked like but seeing his wife, crying on top of a naked woman in a bath, really must have been quite a mind twister. Meanwhile I was just thankful Pip was still in the position that she was, as it was the only barrier I had from two men and the sight of my nakedness. I ask you, what was it with this bloody place and me being naked?!

"Oh my dear wife, what is it that has you so upset?" I was surprised to see that at no point did Adam look at me as if I had been the one to cause his wife's tears. The faith he had in me was a beautiful thing, one I am sure was mirrored in his wife's eyes.

"She could have died!" She said in nothing short of a wail.

"Pip, I am fine...please don't get upset." I said and I saw Adam nod to me in thanks when Pip turned back round to face me. My gaze went to the other person in the room and Lucius gave me a look that I hadn't seen on him before. It was an emotion I couldn't even place but the only thing I was certain of was the exact moment it turned into heated lust; one enough to put colour on my cheeks that had nothing to do with the temperature of the water.

"Come on little squeak, I have something to put a smile on your face." On hearing this she rubbed her nose and wiped her eyes like a child before asking,

"What is it?" I had never heard her voice sound so innocent before and I had to hold back the urge to rock her like a child in my arms. To anyone else this situation would have seemed far too surreal but that very fact spoke volumes when something like this was becoming an everyday occurrence in my weird world.

"Come here and I will tell you." Adam's voice was so soothing it became a hypnotic hum of comfort, one so intense that I almost went to him. Pip turned to me and kissed me on my cheek before flinging herself backwards out of the water in a move that would have put a gymnast to shame. All the front of her was wet but this didn't seem to faze her in the slightest, unlike myself with the uninterrupted view she had just created to a very wet, naked me. I quickly shifted to the side of the pool and thankfully it was deep enough that now only my head was on show over the side. Of course, Lucius' eyes spoke differently.

Pip danced over to Adam doing a little spin before getting to his open arms.

"Now tell me." She demanded.

"We have been given our assignment, my sweetness." The smile she sent him was enough to weaken any man to his knees and Adam's audible groan was evidence that even the mighty beast, Abaddon wasn't immune to this adorable little Imp.

"Is it as I hoped?" She clapped her hands, when he nodded and then he spun her in the direction of the exit but before they left, I heard his parting comment which made me shiver,

"Time to go hunting, my love." I heard Pip's excited squeal from behind the rock. Meanwhile Lucius stood there like one of his great statue warriors…fierce and imposing.

I cleared my throat in trying to prompt an action from him but he remained frozen and his gaze on my body was unyielding.

"Umm…Lucius?" His intense stare flickered and then his eyes raked their way up to my eyes, which was when I realised that he could still see a portion of me in the clear waters.

"Yes, little dove?" He said with a smirk thick on his full lips. And was that one fang I could see showing? …Okay, so not going there!

"No offense but could you…like…bugger off?" He gave me a wicked smile and then gave me a deep nod in respect.

"As you wish." I released the breath I had been holding when he turned and left the room.

"But remember, I will be waiting for you my pet!" I shot up, making the water slosh over the floor with my movements as his voice echoed in the room as though he had been right next to me. On hearing

426

my little scream in shock, I could, in return, hear his laughter from behind the rock.

"Cocky Bastard!" I shouted back at him, which in return just got me more laughter. I groaned and went back to the task at hand.

I washed my skin with some products that I found in a little hollow in the side and I was amazed at the feel of how smooth the bare stone was on my skin as I lay there. The pool had filled from a hole in the rock with a little ledge under it that still created a miniature waterfall, as the water never stopped. I didn't know how it didn't overflow onto the floor but considering the pool was about four times as big as a normal bathtub, there could have easily been a reason I couldn't see.

I tried to concentrate on washing my hair but images of the endless night I was living, kept attacking my brain like Layla was at the controls of its projection. It was like being trapped in some creep theatre and being made to watch my death over and over. I felt exhausted and drained, not just physically but more mentally. My head had been bombarded with emotion after emotion and all being more intense than the last. I thought about the man who had saved my life out there waiting for me and my mind didn't know which feelings to pick through to fully describe the turbulence.

I did the only thing I could do and that was to painfully compare any feeling I had to ones of Draven. Even his very name had me breaking out in goosebumps. It wasn't a great surprise that thoughts of him caused this reaction, for I knew with certainty they always would. But where was he? What was he doing now? Was he with her!?

That very thought had me yanking too hard on my hair and I moved over to the waterfall to rinse the soap from it before I ended up with bald patches. I still couldn't get the image of them together from my mind, like it had been burned to my retinas and I found myself squeezing my eyes so tightly together they could have haemorrhaged. Even after all that had happened to me tonight here I was worrying about the one man I had ever loved. That spoke volumes in my book.

I finished getting myself sorted in the bath and felt like shouting up a 'Hail Mary' when I found a fluffy soft robe waiting for me to slip into. I didn't want to think how it got there when it wasn't there before and if anything, spending time here was just making me more adaptable to turning a blind eye. Hell, I was getting to be a pro at it!

After running my fingers through my hair and trying to pry the many knots apart I gave up, twisted it and I was thankful that it was long enough to put in a big knot at the base of my neck. The white towelling robe would catch all the drips that fell from it but at least it wouldn't be in my way.

I found Lucius sat in the centre of the couch back in the living space and even my bare feet weren't silent enough for him not to hear me approaching...either that or he felt my presence.

"I want everything ready for us to leave at nightfall." He said and at first I was at a loss as to what he meant but as I rounded the corner I could see a phone in his other hand. I wondered how the hell he even got reception down here. I tightened my robe closer together and when he motioned with two fingers for me to sit I walked further round to do as I was told. I flopped down like a balloon clown losing air and his frown when looking at me, had me mouthing,

"What have I done now?" He shook his head briefly before continuing on the phone, speaking a name that spiked more than just my interest.

"Things have now changed, inform Draven and if he has a problem with the way I deal with things, then he can discuss the matter with me himself!" Lucius snapped down the phone and without hearing the other end, I was in the dark as to what impact Lucius' words had. What was happening now?

"I don't give a flying fuck if he is King! I have his woman and if he ever wants to see her again, then he WILL COMPLY!" Lucius' demonic voice boomed around the cave and I nearly jumped out of my damp skin when some of the stalagmites crumbled under the force. It was incredible to think that from just a single, temper fuelled moment in time, something that took thousands of years to create was destroyed thanks to a simple phone call.

I replayed his words and was close to shaking in anger by the time he slammed the phone down on the seat next to him. It bounced four times before it stopped closer to my side. I looked down at it and thought what I wouldn't have given for a phone to be in such close contact a week ago.

"Don't start with me, Keira!" Lucius growled at me before I could expel my rant on him full force.

"You know what...?" He raised an eyebrow and bringing his face forward he said a threatening,

"What!?"

"Fuck you!" I said and got up to leave, not really knowing where I would go but I didn't need to get that far with worrying about it.

Lucius had got up from his seat and snagged me around the waist and brought me crashing down back on the sofa.

"Get off me!" I shouted, but I felt the rumbling of his laughter before I heard it. I was sideways on the seat with him pinning me in place. My hair came loose and covered the side of my face and one side of my robe was gaping open, exposing half of my chest.

"Calm down. Now!" He said sternly.

"Piss off! The only thing you are ever going to give two shits about is power! Well you wanna know something Lucius...power will never love you back!" I struggled and kicked out, catching him off guard. I heard an 'ummf' and rolled when I felt his grasp loosen. I fell onto the hard floor, making my own 'ummf' and got up quickly. The first thing I did when I stood was close my robe and push my hair back.

"You know nothing about me Keira, or of what I love!" He might as well have been spitting the words at me for there was that much venom in his voice. I shot him a look and scowled until my face was taut.

"I know enough to have faith that the only reason you saved my life tonight wasn't just down to getting what you want from Draven!"

"Then you're a fool!" It was my turn to laugh this time only there was zero humour involved.

"The only one trying to be fooled is you! Tell me Lucius, were you this bitter when you were human or has it just increased over the mounting years you were scorned?" In my head this was exactly the right thing to say but as soon as I saw the rage grow red in his eyes I quickly realised my mistake. He growled at me and then before I could turn and run, I was jumped on. I was picked up and flung over his massive shoulder like some white fluffy sack and thanks to my wet hair sticking to my face, I couldn't see where he was taking me. For all I knew he was walking us back to the stone bridge to dump my dumb ass carcass over the side.

"Lucius...I..."

"SILENCE!" He roared at me and for once, I did the smart thing and zipped up. His movements were swift and efficient, considering he had a wet lump on one side but I could feel the steady strides and graceful jumps. I didn't know where he was taking me but I could only pray it wasn't to some bottomless pit where he disposed of all his dead bodies.

Suddenly I was flung off him and yelled out as I waited for impact.

I landed on something soft and it took me a moment to realise it was a bed.

"What is it about you Keira, that has a man wanting to fuck you senseless into submission one minute and strangle the breath from your body the next?" Was he really expecting me to answer that question? Well, all he got was my mouth hanging down making a perfect O shape. I was about to speak when I got a swift spank to my exposed thigh.

"Ow!"

"Your time for words has ended. Now it is time to show you the extent of my feelings!" He said and I gulped at what he meant to do to me. I tried to move and he grabbed my wrists with both hands and shackled them in strong flesh. He pinned them out stretched above me and I tried to twist underneath him but I quickly learnt that I was going nowhere.

"Fine, go ahead and just prove me right!" I expected his rage to grow and his body to act but he shocked me by calming his gaze to one of understanding.

"In a way I feel sorry for Dom and the stubborn Chosen One the Gods picked for him! I have no intention of forcing myself on you Keira, but my feelings will be known before this sunrise." He sounded hard and his hands tensed around a pair of wrists his large hands dwarfed but his eyes spoke volumes.

"What I said got to you…didn't it?" I said pushing once again. He snarled like a wild animal at me making me flinch back.

"Would that make you a happy little human?!" His hard exterior was cracking with every syllable he said that was dripping in emotion.

"No, I said it because I was pissed off at hearing how I quickly became a tool for you to use again. It hurt me and I wanted to hurt you back…which I obviously did, but I am not cruel Lucius, I don't get pleasure from hurting people!" On hearing this, his demeanour softened and he closed his eyes before letting my wrists go. He backed away and I sat up to face him. It was the first time I got a good look at the room I was in and I couldn't stop my pulse from quickening when I saw that I was in his bedroom.

The bed was the highest point in the room and four stone columns stood around each corner like bedposts. Only when the bed swayed did I realise why. I followed the four chains up, that were each thicker than my arm, until I reached the top. Each chain was attached and bolted to the top of the pillars with massive metal hooks that were engraved in gold script. The same script spiralled down the stone lengths of each pillar and was also brushed with gold paint that was bronzed with time.

The floating frame was covered in layers of black, gold and red blankets that were thrown in disarray like a wild night of tossing and turning had caused the effect. Umm...So Lucius, mighty Vampire King never made his bed. I don't know why but the thought made me want to chuckle.

I saw him drag his hand down a tired face and finally the guilt of my words started to weigh heavily on my shoulders. I shimmied closer, making the swaying bed move and laid my hand on his bare shoulder. I wondered briefly why he hadn't yet changed into some clean clothes but then he finally looked at me, thanks to my contact.

"Explain it to me." I asked and I heard him sigh.

"And if I do, you think you would be able to understand?" The disbelief was as clear as the lake that surrounded this mountain and his tone just as cold.

"I may just be some 'little human' Lucius, but if there is one thing I know and know well...then that is pain." I said quietly and we both looked down at the evidence on my arms that, although hidden in softness, didn't hide the truth that lay underneath. I felt Lucius' hand rise to my cheek and pull a strand of hair away that clung there. He tucked it behind my ear and I finally brought my eyes up to his.

"Such strength behind these eyes that your soul glows through. Blinding. Captivating. Torturing. You may be as stubborn as a mule on a cliff side but any man would find the true meaning to foolishness to ever forget these facts." His words made me look away but before I could his fingers held my chin captive and I found myself trapped in his penetrating gaze. I didn't want to delve into that tunnel of hidden emotions that Lucius had. I could feel the air around us crackling with its electrical charge our nearness always created. I had to move past this.

"Tell me what happened to you and Draven that day." I asked and for a split second I saw his eyes flash red before returning to steely grey.

"You really want to know, because I warn you, it does not paint your lover in a kind light?" This didn't shock me. Everything I was hearing about Draven lately was painting him in a different light than what I would like, but I couldn't find it in me to let it affect my love...It couldn't even put a dent in it and that was even after seeing him in the arms of another! Can anyone scream the word...Obsessed!

"I kinda guessed as much," I said honestly and he merely nodded.

"Very well Keira, but do not say that I didn't warn you." He dropped his hand and I moved back putting space between us and when he clocked my movements one side of his mouth quirked in a quick grin.

"I was reborn into the world three days after the third day in which the Son of God rose from death. I walked my last day in the sun on a field called Akeldama or also known as the 'Field of Blood'. Once the sun began to set, my body began to change just as Lucifer had said it would. That night I became not just any Vampire, but the strongest." He said this surprisingly without one hint of the arrogance I would have expected from him.

"What do you mean?" He smiled that I asked another question, as he had learnt very early on that it was a habit of mine.

"I was born into a position of leader, an instant army at my disposal. You see until me, Vampires had been mere creatures of the night with no real strengths...just mindless parasites of the other world, with nothing to drive them but their basic need to feed. I brought them more than this....a kind of peace if you like." He waved his hand around as if he was trying to find the right words to describe it all.

"I think I get it... without leadership they were uncontrollable and once you came along you gave them purpose, strength in numbers, type of thing?" At this he laughed making me blush.

"Yes...that type of thing." He reached across and flicked my nose playfully. That was one of the things about being around Lucius...it was a bit like riding a rollercoaster blind and never knowing when the big drops were going to hit. It was a constant stream of ups and downs, angry glares and cocky smirks, playful touches and heated lust. By the time I got out of here I was going to need bloody therapy again!

I shifted on the bed at the thought and Lucius noticed my uncomfortable tension, and backed away.

"So you came along and gave them guidance, I get it, but what brought you to Draven?" I asked trying to get back on track and leave painful memories of me sat in a room being analysed by a doctor pretending to be my best friend.

"Well before I could take my new position, I was sent to the King to learn about my new life. He taught me more than about my new powers, he taught me how to fight, how to lead and the importance of keeping the balance. He was…" At this Lucius' voice faltered and I looked up into eyes full of heartache and brimming emotion. That's when the realisation hit me with the full force of the root to his emotions.

"You looked up to him?"

"You seem shocked! Of course I did. He was my mentor and in time became like a brother to me. I was his second in command Keira, his right hand man as Adam is to me." His words turned harder as his sentence continued.

"Then what happened?" I whispered, too afraid in generating a raging outburst but the need to know was too much to keep my question buried. So I went for the softer approach, in hopes of soothing him into the past instead of slapping him in the face with it.

"I was betrayed for the second time by a man I called brother!" I flinched at his harsh perception of the past.

"Tell me." I asked quietly and bit my lip as I waited. He shook his head causing his hair to fall over his hard features. Like this, even with a frown that could cause the strongest to flee, he looked so fragile to me and I couldn't stop myself from touching him. My hands tenderly curled round his shoulder and his skin heated on impact. I felt him shudder underneath me and he raised his head slowly to my gaze. The face I now looked upon wasn't the face of my captor but of a friend. A friend that had found breaking points in his life over and over again, but instead of falling to his knees and begging for the sweet release of death, he remained on his feet and took the biggest hit of all…betrayal.

His eyes spoke out to me on a deeper level and in those silent seconds I became lost in the man that Lucius was and saw that deep down that man still remained. Even if he had made it his mission to keep him locked away from the world and never to trust anyone with this side of him again. But right now, I wasn't looking at Lucius…I was looking at Judas and he didn't even know it. He had shown himself to me and his eyes were glowing with light and this time it was only with a simple touch.

"The Oracle was right…I didn't stand a chance at taming the light!" I frowned in confusion and it must have deepened when I saw one side of his mouth lift in a smirk. His eyes sparkled with mirth and he lifted my hand to his lips to kiss before placing them gently back on the bed.

"You're not going to explain that are you?"

"Not yet, no. That would be like telling you the end of a story before it has even been written."

"Yeah, right!" I said sarcastically making the bed shake with his laughter.

"Well if you want to hear this story then we are going to do it properly. Get under the covers." I think my mouth must have dropped open.

"You're not serious?" I looked for traces of the joke but there were none. Instead he folded his arms over his bare chest making the size of his strength show through tight muscles. I think I actually gulped.

"As a heart attack in Hell, yes. Now do as you're told." Okay, so bossy Lucius was back and I think even the Judas part of him would be laughing at the irritation that was written across my face. I rolled my eyes when he nodded behind me and I gave in. I got under the many layers and I think the sigh I let go of was proof enough why he was making me do this. My body was aching and felt amazing when I lay down under the soft covers, which was like getting a hug to all my body parts. It was at that point that I realised how tired I was and started to wonder what time it was.

When I was all tucked in, Lucius moved to lie next to me and I was thankful when he stayed above the covers but the position still felt far too intimate with him on his side facing me.

"So, are you ready for the rest of the story Keira, for I will warn you..."

"Let me guess...it doesn't end well?" I said interrupting him, at which, he quirked a brow at me.

"Oh no, my little Keira girl, you are wrong..." I was about to ask when he raised his fingers to my lips to stop them from moving. Then he lowered his mouth to my ear and whispered...

*"The end is yet to be written."*

CHAPTER 38
# TIP OFF

I woke up to find myself feeling refreshed after a surprisingly soundless sleep. After everything I had learnt last night I was shocked I hadn't been tossing and turning like a mad woman. I looked around having no clue as to the time but I let out a sigh of relief when I found I was at least alone.

I don't remember when I fell asleep but I do remember the soft alluring words that had got me there. Lucius had finished his story of the past and when I started getting animated at hearing everything he was saying, he started to soothe me. Hushed words whispered along my skin had taken immediate effect and it was similar to the power Draven had over me when trying to get me to sleep. So against my will, I had fallen under his spell despite the million and one questions I had, spinning my head into turmoil.

He had told me more of his friendship with Draven, which painted the full depth of his devastation on discovering his betrayal. Draven being portrayed as a mentor for Lucius was an easy thing to envisage and now I thought about it, the two Kings had a lot in common. Both believed in the balance that needed to be kept, in order for the world to continue on without destroying itself, which is where the story started.

On the 30th of September 1918, which many believed happened two days earlier, a Private by the name of Henry Tandey was on a one man mission near the French village of Marcoing. He and his fellow soldiers encountered exceptionally heavy gunfire in this area and with one thing on his mind, the slaughter began. Against all odds Private Henry Tandey single-handedly destroyed a German machine gun nest, braved enemy gunfire in bridging a huge hole that was halting British attacks and led a bayonet charge against a far larger force. He was, by all accounts, a war hero.

But this war hero had more than mere luck and skill on his side. Henry Tandey was possessed by a Demon of Death that fed from this one man killing machine that he created for his own feast. He gave him the raw power of adrenaline flooding his system until nothing could stop this dangerous mortal. Lucius spoke about this Demon with the look of sheer disgust and when I tried to press further into his name he shook his head and refused to say anything more about him.

I asked Lucius why this was even relevant to his story about Draven and with a one sided grin, he continued to explain. See, after the smoke had cleared and the sounds of gun fire had ceased to pierce the French air, a soldier appeared down the sights of Tandey's rifle. The man limped along, injured and did not even try to raise his own weapon in the second of his death. But the private did not shoot. I asked why and Lucius at that point, leaned over to smooth the deep line in between my brows with his thumb and my frown dropped at the intimate gesture.

He told me that the Demon took one look at the man and saw a glimpse of the power he could gain if he intervened in his future. He placed a hand of suggestion on Henry's shoulder and the gun lowered from the German soldier, sealing his fate and with it, the millions of lives that would find their end at the power this one man would gain. The German soldier was Lance Corporal Adolf Hitler of the 16th Bavarian Infantry Regiment.

On hearing this I gasped as the realisation took hold. This one moment in time changed the world forever and put in motion events beyond our comprehension. The Demon of Death seized this opportunity and left the Private a hero but in doing so, he gained so much more...the means for world domination.

He saw in Hitler's future that one day he would be Fuhrer but only with the right path down the supernatural rabbit hole. Of course the Demon was only too happy to be the one behind him pushing. The rest of Hitler's life was lived as a dark Demon's puppet and even Hitler himself spoke of a divine reason for his life, believing the Gods were keeping him alive for a higher purpose. He wrote about times when he would hear warnings in his head being whispered and whenever he listened, the proof of it was walking away with his life.

Years later such proof happened in the trenches, while eating dinner with his fellow men. A voice ordered him to move away and then seconds later, a flash indicated his narrow escape in death as a stray shell exploded, killing everyone in the trench but Hitler.

As a massive fan of anything that included history I found myself glued to Lucius' every word and every now and again, I felt his eyes basking in my excitement. Every time he paused, I thought he was going to stop and I had my argument ready for more but one look at my face was all it took for him to continue. He then began to tell me how the Demon needed to speed things up for the time was coming for Hitler to take power over Germany but he needed to push a little more for the supernatural beliefs in Hitler to rise before he became a man of position.

He started to whisper the name Erik Jan Hanussen, who was known at the time, as a famous hypnotist, mentalist, occultist, and astrologer. Hitler met with the man and thanks to a little mind play of the Demonic kind, using Hanussen as another puppet, he had his show complete.

Hanussen told Hitler about the means in which he would have to follow to become leader of Germany and would then lead his people into victory. He made the unbelievable prediction that within thirty days Hitler would become Chancellor of Germany, with the power of a Mandrake root and utter faith in the occult.

"Mandrake root?" I asked him in confusion and he laughed, which I can only imagine was due to the face I was pulling. He told me that the Mandrake root belonged to the nightshade family and had hallucinogenic properties, but this was not the only reason it was used in magic rituals in paganism. It is a holy root that is formed to resemble human figures for sacrifices of the soul. When I still looked confused, he described them as being like glass bottles for the souls. Souls of his kind, which could be held inside the root until another vessel became available. The thought of being trapped in one of these things had me shivering under the many toasty warm layers.

He went on to say how Hitler was convinced enough to put such faith in things and in thirty days Hanussen was proven right, sealing Hitler's obsession with the occult. The Demon now had full control over a single mortal being that could now bring forth more deaths with only a spoken whisper in the Fuhrer's ear...

Next on his list was Genocide.

When Hitler was but a boy he disliked the Jews but the dark Demon throughout the years, turned a mere discrimination into pure blinding hatred of a whole nation. For this, in a man of extreme power, was to be history changing events at its most horrific. This was more than enough to tip any balance and shift the world into another war.

These were the very reasons Lucius was sent by Draven to put an end to the supernatural interference and capture the creature to be readied for trial. Of course, by the time the Demon found out about his awaiting damnation from his King, the Demon fled leaving Hitler to still continue with his quest of eradicating the Jews and cleansing the world. He was left believing the Jews were all demon spawns and his fight against them was a holy one, doing the work sent to him by the Germanic Gods he worshiped. He believed Jesus to be the root of all evil and being the ultimate Jew himself, he was therefore the leader to such Hell on earth.

So without guidance from the Demon, he lost all faith in Hanussen when finding out about his Jewish roots and any other Mystics known in Germany. On April the 30th 1934, he ordered nearly 200 people murdered, Hanussen included, on a day known as the 'Night of the long knifes'. This was the night that led Lucius to Hitler.

With the Angel long gone, Lucius was awaiting word from Draven on how to proceed, when a conversation was overheard with one Heinrich Himmler, Hitler's right hand man, about something that would break a bond as strong as a holy brotherhood... The Spear of Destiny.

Lucius explained, that with three fake spears all in circulation throughout the years, he wasn't worried what information the Nazi leader had on the spear, that was until he overheard the mention of a powerful seer that spoke of the real spear and its missing tip, a part that contained the most power...the tip coated with the blood of Christ. He listened to Hitler give orders for the seer to be brought to him and how his plans for the tip would bring about the completion to his world domination, but for that, he needed the blood that started it all. He believed that the blood of the Jew was the ancient key to its end.

His warped mind had him believing an antidote made from the blood could be used to kill all Jewish genes from the world and his super race of German blood would become the new way of the world. Lucius cared little for Hitler's delusions but instead of complying with his orders to pursue the Demon that started it all, dubbed as the 'puppet master', he remained. He disobeyed Draven for the first time in his new life and waited for the seer to arrive in pursuit of his own destiny.

Draven was furious but none more so than Lucius, when he saw what the seer projected. The vision of Draven from a different time, ripping the tip from the dead body of Jesus Christ and walking away was, in Lucius' words, like ripping it from his own body, along with the heart it was embedded in.

I was shocked when finding that Draven had always known of Lucius' mission in trying to find the other piece of a relic that became a part of Lucius. And all this time Draven had it in his possession, keeping it from his second in command. I wondered why? Why would Draven go to such lengths to keep it from a man he considered his trusted friend? My, weren't the questions mounting up for Draven, I thought with distaste.

I finally asked about the night it all fell apart for the two friends and with a stare that looked both angry and devastated, Lucius told me about it. After giving in to the demands of his King he returned home and confronted his friend. Draven didn't deny what Lucius had learnt but did try to explain. Lucius admitted that in his rage he refused to listen and when demanding its possession, Draven's refusal sent him over the edge. After nearly two thousand years of searching for a way to make him whole, he snapped, knowing that his best friend had sat back and watched, with not only the knowledge of its whereabouts but being the very man behind the hand who held it from him.

Lucius in that moment took the devastating step in his own history and controlled the King into giving him what was rightfully his. As a man whose life was taken because of the events that day it was obvious that Lucius believed that the weapon of his death was the same weapon that would give him back that control of his destiny, one that up until now, both lives had been in another's hands. He had placed his faith in that of a man he felt betrayed and now it seemed to him that history had repeated itself.

He spoke of feeling the consuming rage that he found himself more than once wanting to end Draven's life but knowing how he couldn't do it was one of the reasons Draven let him walk away alive. Vincent had walked in just before Draven could hand over the tip and with Lucius' power only great enough to control one Draven at a time, he had to flee without the means to complete the Holy Spear.

So now here we were, both of us living in a state of limbo, but right before the most important question was seconds from leaving my lips, I was sleeping soundly with a Vampire to watch over me. The question of course was…what was going to happen next. I mean, what was left to even think about after learning something like that? Talk about being between a rock and a hard place, this was more like being in between an erupting volcano and a tsunami and the chances were they would just burn each other out was highly unlikely.

I wished I could have gone back to the days when Lucius was nothing more to me than the man that haunted my dreams but now…I would've had to have been made of stone for his story not to have touched me, but where did that leave me with Draven? I missed him beyond all reason but the longer I was away from him the more I learnt about those reasons. He was and always would be the love of my life and it felt like more than fate being with him. However, I would be lying to myself if I was going to say that my stay here hadn't changed things. For starters, what was I going to do if that video was true? Could I ever take back a man that had cheated on me, cheated on our love and our so called destiny?

I was pulled from these thoughts when I heard a thundering roar loud enough to make the walls vibrate. That didn't sound good! I jumped out of bed and tightened the robe I was still wearing, before running to find where the shouts were coming from.

Lucius' bedroom was on different levels and I had to weave my way around and down little steps that had been carved out of the cave floor. I was just surprised that running in bare feet on this surface didn't hurt as the floor was as smooth as rock could be. I eventually made my way back until the living space was in view and that's when I heard the two booming voices going at it like Alpha wolves.

I rounded the corner and passed the bathroom but a boulder was still blocking half the room from view. However it didn't matter as I would have known who the voice had come from anywhere in the world. I mean Hell, I could feel my body tingling from over here and I hadn't even seen him yet.

I tried to walk slower just to try and calm my pounding heart but my legs had other ideas. I raced down and then back up the V of steps that took me to the right level of the living space and as soon as my sight confirmed I wasn't mistaken, I let out a breath.

"WHAT DO YOU MEAN LAYLA TRIED TO KILL HER!?" Draven demanded in a demonic growl that once again destroyed thousands of years in the making as stalagmites crumbled in the distance.

"I am taking care of it!" Lucius said with a little more calm than Draven was executing.

"I remember those words once before! I demand her head, Lucius!" Draven stood with his back to me and now I was used to the effect, I could easily see that it wasn't the Draven I could touch. Even as a projection Draven made a powerful presence in the room even though it seemed Lucius held all the cards. This was amplified by the way every one of Lucius' council members flinched whenever Draven spoke, even though his presence wasn't really with them in the room.

"As do I but that is beside the point! You were informed merely as an explanation to the change of terms. The exchange will take place at Transfusion tomorrow night." Lucius spoke in such a way that it was clear to see he had been dealing with Draven for a very long time. It was like some veil had been lifted and now I could see things clearly for the first time. What must it be like for these two? For so long they were fighting side by side and now…fighting each other.

"I warn you now Lucius, if she comes back to me anything less than the perfection she is, then I will have your head and this time… I.Will.Not.Hesitate!" His threat caused a nerve to twitch in my jaw and a shiver to wrack my spine. I felt far too many emotions in that one sentence to even begin to understand. I felt like shouting out, 'if you thought I was so bloody perfect then why sleep with your ex?' but I thankfully saw the bigger picture and knew that this was probably the worst time to have done so.

"I should remind you that you are far from a position in which to threaten my actions, Dominic! I have possession of your Electus and everything you have tried in getting her back has failed! Now is the time to face facts and time for you to reap in which you sow, my friend." Lucius' voice remained steady and everyone sat around behind their master lowered their heads in respect to what he was saying. It was at that moment that I understood the full extent of their loyalty.

"Fucking royal payback! That is what this is about?!" Draven shook his head and I saw fingers rake through his black hair in frustration.

"You know what this is about my King and even the most purest of nobility steals from the sons of penniless fathers for their gain. In this case I give you a choice…which blood will you prefer on your hands Dominic, to keep the blood of the Son of God or watch the blood flow from one of their daughters?" At this Draven boomed out a screaming roar as his anger hit new levels. It was so powerful that his projection wavered, flickering back and to from the room his body was in and the one mine was in.

"I WILL KILL YOU BEFORE THAT HAPPENS!" Draven's demon promised but Lucius just merely shrugged his shoulders.

"You can try but I think you will find our little Keira isn't going to be as susceptible to your royal charms, even if you do manage to rid the world of every last Vampire! As you know better than most, that is what it will take to bring me down. Kill a King and watch a race die along with the direct blood line...now that is what I call tipping the balance...don't you think?" Lucius said smugly and I was left even more confused. Was Lucius saying that if he died then every Vamp dies with him? I looked towards Pip and Adam for a second and wondered if the look they gave each other were ones enough to confirm my prediction.

Draven growled his answer and it looked like Lucius had him stumped on that one. Even I knew that Draven couldn't destroy a whole race of creatures just to save his girlfriend.

"I demand to see her!" Draven ordered and even from back here, I could see the rise and fall of his colossal shoulders through his long black jacket. It gave him the presence of a rough modern day knight, one that exchanged shining armour for leather and biker's boots. I found myself biting my lip at just the sight of a projected back of my furious lover.

"Yes, but will she want to see you?" Lucius snarled back and I recoiled at his harsh words. Yeah sure, I had issues to discuss with Draven and answers needed before we could move forward but these were my decisions here, not his! I was just about to unleash these thoughts when Draven's rage stopped me.

"SHE BELONGS TO ME!" He screamed in his face and nothing but the tension of Lucius' jaw was his reaction to being roared at that close up. I saw Draven take a few deep breaths and it reminded me of a panting animal.

"She belongs to NO man but me! Keira knows this. Now bring me my fucking woman. NOW!" Draven's crass words hit me like a fist to the chest. I knew Draven had caveman issues and a dominant nature but this was something else...this was a man possessed!

"This isn't you," I whispered on a breath. It may have been barely uttered but it was enough for every supernatural ear to hear it clear as day. I was so stunned at hearing Draven talk about me as though I was nothing more than the piece of relic he was keeping from Lucius. What was this…was I just a tool to be used when needed?

Draven whipped round to face me and his features went through an array of emotions…relief, happiness and then my words sank in and the last emotions went quickly from guilt to anger.

"Are you hurt?" His question snapped out like a bear trap and I found myself closing my eyes against the onslaught of reactions my mind wanted me to go through. In the end I just shook my head up and down in answer.

"Keira, look at me," Draven said gently and I didn't know if I could. I didn't know if I could continue with this crushing disappointment that kept creeping in on me whenever Draven re-entered my world. I looked to Pip for comfort but Draven's voice cut through my motions.

"Do not look at them Keira! Look. At. Me!" His demand was brutal and made it all the harder to comply with. I dragged my eyes away and faced the man that the Gods had christened as my fate…

*A very angry King*

# CHAPTER 39
# CURSED PROTECTION

After standing there absolutely dumbstruck for a moment, Draven's order penetrated my thoughts. I looked up at him and the sight nearly took my breath away. Even in all his anger, he was simply magnificent. He was masterful, wearing his long black jacket, black jeans and black t-shirt that rippled with his heavy breathing. His intense stare matched his dark attire and I could have easily got lost and trapped forever in the depth of two onyx eyes. He was stunning. And this painfully beautiful man wanted me for a reason I was no longer certain of.

"Keira!" The sound of my name coming from those perfect lips was nearly my undoing. I wanted to throw myself at him just as much as I wanted to run away. I was being torn in two here, not knowing what my future with this man held. From day one he had kept things from me and if this was just the tip of what was to come, then I didn't know if my fragile heart could last without cracking under the pressure.

"You lied to me Draven." I said before I could stop it from spilling out. His frown deepened and his lips were now set in a hard line. He turned just his head from me over to Lucius and snarled at him like the beast he was portrayed in my dreams that night. I saw his knuckles turn white on his olive skin from the fists he held at his sides.

"What have you been telling her?!" He snapped.

"More than you do, it seems. I have told her nothing but the truths in which brings us here now." Lucius stated simply and I thought I saw

Draven flinch. Well if that wasn't a sign of a guilty man then I don't know what was!

"Ah, so this is the game you play! You think to turn her against me with tales of a past, scorned for a second time." Draven said and then began to do something completely out of character. The loud bangs that vibrated the room from the impact of his hands slapping into each other made a sickening clap. Everyone in the room flinched when his hands clapped out in mock amusement and when he finally set his disappointing gaze on me, I felt like crying. He had just made me feel like I was the traitor in this drama playing out underground.

"So this is the truth of it?" He asked me and I couldn't find the words to answer him.

"Answer me Keira! Say the fucking words!" I had to take a step back at the rage he directed at me. He had never sworn at me like this before and it spoke volumes to the amount of fury he was trying to keep on lock down.

"I believe him." I said feeling like every word was dragged across a serrated blade. I saw the second my words hit home and it looked as though his royal world had collapsed.

"Of course you do." He said shaking his head like he was still trying to believe it. I wanted to say something else, I wanted to shout that I still loved him and drag the Draven I knew back to me but I was at a loss to what was happening in his mind. Was this it? Was he now going to walk away and leave me to Lucius? My answer came as soon as I could finish thinking the worst.

"Transfusion! Tomorrow night." He said turning from me and I felt the tears roll down my cheeks at seeing him with his back to me. It looked as if he couldn't look at me anymore and that thought broke my heart.

"And Lucius...if any harm comes to her before then, be warned that a whole race of people won't keep me from killing you, balance be damned!" His deep voice rumbled his threat and I saw Lucius narrow his eyes at him, before shocking me by nodding his head in acceptance of his fate from Draven if he failed.

I saw his figure start to waver and just before it vanished completely, his parting words were nothing short of a threat of my own,

"Tomorrow night, Keira!"

As soon as Draven went out of sight I wiped away my tears with an angry swipe and stormed off back in the direction I had come.

"Keira wait!" Lucius shouted after me but all he got from me was a "GET LOST!" over my shoulder. I saw him coming after me and catch something in the air that Pip had thrown him.

"Get everything ready. We leave within the hour!" Lucius ordered his council as he was still pursuing me through the ups and downs of his stone fortress. I made it back to his room and once there, I spun on my heel to face him, close to spitting venom I was that angry. Whether it was more at him or myself, I wasn't yet sure but I think they were more than likely on equal levels!

"You used me and pushed me into that situation!" I accused furiously.

"Yes!"

"Yes?" Was that it! A simple yes!

"What do you expect me to say, Keira? I kidnapped you for a purpose and now you are fulfilling it, I am not going to be sorry about that!" He said folding his arms across his chest which was another habit the Two Kings had in common.

"Yes, but did you have to goad Draven into thinking I am in bloody league with you!?"

"I didn't ask you to place your faith in me or to make Draven aware of the fact." Lucius stated absurdly making me cough my disbelief.

"What a load of steaming shit! You gave me little choice and practically begged for that outcome! I don't even understand why you would want him to think I put my trust in you over him. After all, your whole plan here is for him to give you the Tip in place of me... why would you care that I know the truth when it could ruin those plans?"

"My plans were never in any danger, Keira and everyone deserves the truth." He said plainly and I looked deep into his eyes to find he was speaking the truth.

"You rubbed it in his face, Lucius."

"Yes well, the bastard needs to learn whose heart lies at the end of the stake he holds and if he is not careful, it will not be mine like he thinks!" My mouth actually dropped open on hearing this. Was he saying what I thought he was saying?

"You're worried I am going to get hurt?" I asked quietly, and I couldn't believe my eyes when I saw him start to blush before turning away from me.

"You're an innocent pawn in this Keira, despite how the Kings on the board use you for their gain." He said this with his back to me and with his head lowered. I felt a lump form in my throat.

"You sound sorry for that." I said and the only response I received was Lucius' large shoulder shrug.

"Lucius?" I said his name but I still got nothing but his back and my mind started to whirl. Something was going on here and it was far greater than just the time I had been here.

"I need you to answer a question." I said and finally he faced me.

"What do you wish to know?" His face reminded me of a picture in a broken frame, he was there but not whole. And it was then that I realised that the meeting with Draven had taken its toll on him.

"You still care for him, don't you?" I asked, turning his lost features into hard steel, starting with his disapproving eyes glaring down at me.

"Is that your question?" And with that one question, he was right back to being the Lucius I knew well.

"No, it isn't."

"Then I suggest you get to it, before my patience runs dry!" I understood that I had gone too far this time and I turned to flop down on the edge of the bed. I rubbed at my temples in a useless attempt at ridding me of a pounding headache but then, a pair of hands stilled me.

"Ask me." Lucius said, this time using a much gentler tone and I looked up to find him on one knee at my level.

"When did you really first hear about me?" The question that had been playing on my mind the whole time I had been here rolled out without thought or barrier. I knew what he told me that night about it being since I was seven, he was holding something back and now was the time to find out. I watched as he was clearly taken back, but I knew he would answer me. It meant too much now, for him to refuse. He had already been portrayed as the only man that would honestly tell me what I needed to know and right now…I needed this

"After I left my place at Draven's side I went in search of Pythia."

"The Oracle?" I said in surprise.

"Ah, so Draven does tell you some things at least?" I frowned at him but he just ignored it and stood up. He moved over to sit next to me on the bed and the way we both sat was like sitting on a swinging bench next to an old friend.

"I never expected she would even see me but when I walked in, it was as if she had known all along that I would come. What she told me not only changed my life but it gave me a greater purpose. Up until that point I had been letting the rage I felt for Draven start to consume me, until the red mist of hate was swamping my senses to think logically."

"What did she say?"

"She told me that my destiny would be complete when the Chosen One entered this life and that she would be the one and only means to obtain the Tip from the King." He spoke as though he could see that day like it was yesterday's events.

"Man, I didn't stand a chance, did I?" I said shaking my head wondering if fate really was on my side or not.

"Not really, no. But as you can imagine I became very interested in you once I heard my time in waiting was coming to an end."

"I bet!" I said sarcastically.

"Well, after hearing this, I was no longer without guidance and I had my orders from the Oracle."

"Orders?" I saw a little smile emerge in the corner of his lips and I found myself happier knowing he was no longer tense.

"Pythia told me two other things of importance before I left but only one of them could I do something about. She told me that if I did not complete my mission from the King and put a stop to the war, then the Chosen One would never even be born and all would be lost before it had even begun." I shot up straight at this and found myself grabbing at his arm.

"What?" He smirked at me before elaborating.

"Your Grandfather was readying himself for the war, I believe." I thought back to my mum's dad who was just coming of age and waiting to be drafted but then the war ended. This, my mum was convinced, was what saved his life and therefore our family was born. My mum, I and Libby, all products of the most profound question to ask… 'What if?'

Well now I knew the answer to that one. So a whole war ended because a young man was born a month too late and missed out on glory for the sake of thirty days. It was mind boggling to think about.

"And just how did you stop the war exactly?" I asked raising one eyebrow, not being able to help my scepticism. I mean come on… Lucius was the one that put a stop to world war two? It just seemed too far from the line to see the truth.

"It was simpler than it sounds Keira, after all, the Demon had invested a lot of time into making it as easy as just taking his place."

"What do you mean…take his place?"

"I would have thought I was making it perfectly obvious. I controlled him. I have had my fair share of experience in battles Keira and although the weapons change, the tactics don't." The thought of Lucius and Draven fighting side by side popped into my head and all clad in leather and steel, it made for a mighty breathtaking sight.

"So you just had to plant a few wrong moves and then…?"

"And then watch as the world did the rest. By this time most that had come into contact with Hitler knew the level his mind had degraded to and so with a few whispered words, Adolf Hitler committed suicide by gunshot on 30 April 1945 in his Führerbunker in Berlin." He stated as calmly as if he was talking about the weather!

"Holy shit!" I shouted and he actually laughed at me!

"You killed Hitler!" Okay, so now he was seriously rolling his eyes?

"I did what I had to do, yes…why is this so shocking to you?"

"Are you friggin' kiddin' me!? You saved thousands, hell, probably millions of lives and your acting like…like…"

"Like?" Okay now he was mocking me.

"Like you're not a hero." I said softy and his smirk turned into a heart-warming smile that reached his eyes, causing crinkles at the sides. The look he gave me was more than that of a handsome rogue, this time, it looked blessed by the Gods and he didn't even know it!

"I am not a hero Keira, far from it but the thoughts coming from a soul such as yours are a blessing I will never forget…thank you." He had lifted my hand to his lips and kissed his thank you over my skin causing me to tremble slightly at the intimate contact.

After a few silent moments he got up and walked over to the bag he had dropped by the entrance. It must have been what Pip had thrown him earlier.

"Get dressed, we leave on the hour and it is cold out there." He continued to speak softly, as though my last words were still lingering just beneath the thick skin that Lucius wore. He dropped the bag on the bed by my side and traced the back of one finger down my cheek before leaving.

"Wait, what about Eva Braun, she was there too, right?" I shouted out remembering my history.

"She had a choice and she decided her fate for herself, a fate I didn't play a part in. She died in the bunker after I left her."

"Oh… cyanide?" I asked knowing this was the side of the story I had heard about.

"I believe so, yes. Be quick Keira!" He said getting me off the subject.

"Wait!" I said once again.

"What is it this time, pet?" Lucius stopped just before going down the steps to leave the room.

"The last thing I wanted to know." I heard him expel a sigh but he didn't face me. Did he already know what I was going to ask?

"You said that the Oracle told you two things of importance, what was the other thing?" I didn't know if he would answer my question and the silence had me torturing my bottom lip in anticipation. Then Lucius surprised me by turning to the side and looking at me like it was the very first time he had ever seen me. I took a deep breath, ready to hear something vitally important here but no amount of air inhaled was going to prepare me for the deeper meaning my life meant to Lucius.

"She told me that I would meet a mortal girl who would show me the light and that this 'Bringer of the Sun' would one day..." He trailed off and I stood up quickly desperate to know.

"What...would one day...what?" I took two steps forward and two soon became enough to bring me next to Lucius. I looked up at him and my hand with a will of its own reached out and cupped the side of his face. With a little pressure I brought his face round to mine and his eyes swirled amber in a grey storm.

"The one that shows me the sun will one day save my life and... my very soul." I gasped and staggered back in shock. He moved to the other side of the room in astonishing speed and just before he left I heard his whispered echo as though it was next to my ear...

*"My freedom"*

# CHAPTER 40
# SHINY BEASTS

After that supernova sized bombshell from Lucius, in the end the hour I had to get ready ended up being fifty minutes of sat on the bed shaking my head and ten minutes getting ready, while stuffing much needed food down my throat. It was only when it hit my stomach and started making noises like someone throwing pebbles down a well, that I realised I hadn't eaten in a long time.

It was also at this moment that I looked down at my body and saw that I had lost quite a bit of weight. It looked as though I was at least a size smaller but instead of jumping for joy I found myself nervously biting my fingertips. What would Draven think...? Well if Vincent's thoughts were anything to go by, then I knew what Draven would think.

I tried not to think about it but as I got dressed it was hard to ignore when the jeans kept edging downwards to bony hips. I definitely needed to get some junk food in me and stat. The image of me like this didn't help with my repressed memories one little bit, as the last time I looked like this, it was after 'the incident'... wow it felt like an age ago since I had referred to it like that!

I shook off the feeling and finished getting ready just in time for Pip to come bouncing into my world like a gothic bath bomb!

"Nice trouser shoes!" I said wondering what the actual correct name would be for what she was wearing. She stopped before she reached me, gave me a cute little grin before skipping the rest of her way to me.

"You like?" She said and we both looked down at her tighter than tight clothing. The trouser shoes started as charcoal grey converse shoes that tied up with dark red ribbons instead of laces. But in true Pip fashion, this wasn't where the strangeness ended. No, instead of your usual converse shoes ending just past the ankle, these ended at her waist! The ties continued all the way up her legs and a bow was finally tied at her crotch.

She twisted one foot in a cutesy girly way that made the white rubber tip squeak against the floor. I continued my gaze up now getting past her strange trousers and focused on the rest of her. She also wore a blazer style jacket that was cut up high under her breasts and showed her flat tattooed stomach and then swept down low at the back into two tails that flicked out over her bum. The material was one I couldn't name but it looked to have been tie-dyed in darker shades of the rainbow. Her green hair was in a cute high ponytail with a massive polka dot, red and white flower bow attached to one side.

"So, you ready to make like a disc?" Pip said leading the way with an outstretched arm and a very confused human trying to decipher Pip code.

"Okay, I have heard of 'make like a banana' but disc...? You've got me on that one Pip." She giggled as we walked back out of the bedroom and turned in a different direction to the way I had been before.

"I don't get that, why split...when you walk away, you don't split, that's just crazy talk right there, now suck...you can suck a banana or bite but you don't do that either when walking away, unless you were on your way to eat somewhere, then I guess it makes sense...or suck, then you could grab hold of a di..."

"LALALA, Pip!" She laughed as always when I did this and it echoed in the next room we were in.

"So, disc?" I reminded her as she continued to lead the way through a small doorway that needed us to be in single file. I followed her through the damp tunnel and instead of producing some over the top, medieval flaming torch, she reached in her back pocket and lit the passageway with the light from her mobile phone screen.

"Disc drive. Make like a disc and drive, we're driving outta here." She said this like it should all be obvious to me. I rolled my eyes behind her back but when she giggled again it was if she had somehow seen me do it.

For the rest of the journey I listened to Pip natter on about

Transfusion and her wardrobe there and I was thankful we arrived just before she could start to explain further into the benefits of the playroom her and Adam had in their apartment. I don't know if LALALA's would have been enough to cut through that conversation.

The walk had been a series of rock tunnels, steps up and down and then one big hallway that was large enough for two double-decker buses to have a drag race down. This was the end of our destination and after walking through one more door, it opened up into a massive cavern that was an underground garage. Now this was like the bloody bat cave!

There were different vehicles parked everywhere I looked and if I thought Draven had an obsession with fast and shiny things he could manhandle, then Lucius took first prize in car mania! It made me wonder out of the two, who started with the obsession first? Of course, this particular line of thought then brought on images of the two talking about cars, just like you would find two regular men doing in any pub in the world. It was weird, but I seemed to have this fascination with the fact that these two powerful and complex men were once great friends. It made them seem almost...normal. Of course, one look up and around made that image melt like a chocolate teapot!

'The Bat Cave' was amazing. One look up had you seeing a world created by thousands of years of natural beauty and one look down had you seeing beauty of a different kind...one man made. There were too many cars to count but each one looked as new as the day they were made and that even included the classic cars.

"It's a friggin' museum!" I said with a gasp and Pip beamed at me. This, I soon found out, was because Lucius and Draven weren't the only ones obsessed with expensive gears and metal.

"You like?" She asked twirling round as we came down the last lot of steps. I think she took my hanging jaw as a yes because this spurred her into 'Car mode Pip' and if I thought the girl hardly took a breath before, then now it was like Pip on Car Crack!

"And over there is the Jaguar D type, which won the 1957 Le Mans by the way, oh, oh and over here is the Dodge Charger and as you can plainly see the super charger sticks out of the bonnet, I think it looks pretty, like metal flowers in a flower box...oh but wait, now this one...come on, keep up!" She waved me on with an excited little bounce and continued with a squeal.

"This baby is the Audi r8, v10, 5.2 litre which can fly to heaven at

199 mph! Oh and see that one, the Ac Cobra of course with 7.0 litre v8 engine and a 485 brake horse power...man all those horses, now that one for its day to reach 185mph is impressive...man where was I in 1965? Anyway, I like it 'cause it's really loud!" I think my head was close to exploding all over these shiny beasts when thankfully I heard voices coming through one of the far tunnels.

"Oh just to give ya the heads up, try not to mention the 'F' word around Luc." I shot her a look, as if to say 'What's the 'F' word'! She rolled her eyes at me but the smile she had plastered on, kind of counteracted that sarcastic motion. She came up closer to me and went on tip toes to my ear and I loved how being around little Pip always made me feel taller.

"There is a serious lack of Ferraris here for a reason...Our Vampy King is a Lamborghini man, while it is well known our other King is a serious Ferrari lover...I mean he does know the family and all, but it has been a rival between the two ever since...well two supercars made in the same town is like two Kings in the same court, if you know what I mean."

On hearing this I couldn't help but laugh. It was such a man thing to rival over and again brought me images of the two arguing over something so...un-supernatural!

"Oh and over there is my car...come see." I felt my long sleeved top being tugged as Pip weaved her way in and around so many cars. I saw Lucius roll his eyes as we passed and Adam just smirked at the sight of his wife's obvious pleasure. She pulled me over to a very 80's looking Lamborghini but I couldn't help the bug eyes seeing her car did to me. It was so...Pip! The only way to describe it was like a baby pink cheese wedge with a serious 80's hang-up! Instead of the holes in Swiss cheese it came with a painted rainbow splashed across and 'My Little Pony' stickers...yes, that's right, My Little Pony stickers, on both doors and one of the whole gang on the bonnet!

"Umm...wow!"

"You like my baby?" She asked rocking on the balls of her feet.

"Umm...just...wow!" It was the only thing I could think of to say.

"Lucius bought it for me for my birthday one year and the next year Adam had it painted like this for me. I love my little Lambony Pony!" She said while stroking it like a cat waiting for the purr.

"Eh...your what now?" I asked, thinking I had never heard that car name before and I know I wasn't exactly a car connoisseur here, but Lambony...really?

"It's my Lamborghini Countach and instead of getting a pink puppy, I got a v12 pony that does 205 mph! It lives longer and I don't have to clean up its shit, that's how Lucius put it anyway." I tried to keep the smirk from my face but it was all in vain as I ended up laughing.

"Shhh! She will hear you!" Pip said before continuing to coo at her car. I was still shaking my head when I felt Lucius come up behind me. I didn't even hear him approach but the electricity it created in the air was enough to raise the hair on my neck.

"Pip! We don't have time for your love affair, Adam is waiting for you." He snapped and with that, she smacked a kiss to her palm and slapped it on one of the My Little Pony's butt. She then spun round, gave me wink and went off running to Adam's waiting arms.

"Nice collection." I said as I didn't know what else to say to the man who came to my side and still hadn't spoken to me. He made a huffing sound, which I didn't understand and then I felt the top of my arm in a vice grip, moving my body along with him.

"Hey!" I objected to the whole, 'me man, you woman' caveman deal but he didn't let me go. He pulled me along the zigzag of cars and I noticed as we went past some really old models, I pulled my arm from his hold.

"YO, grabby McGee, ease up will ya!" I said exasperated at my manhandling. He looked at me rubbing my arm where I could still feel his fingers embedded in my skin and his frown softened slightly. He looked like he was trying to find the right words to say and I doubted it would be the 'sorry' that was the usual response for hurting someone but he looked as if he was struggling on that front, so I cut him a break. I turned round to something that had caught my eye when being tugged around the place.

We were stood next to an old black car that had a long body and soft top, that at the moment was folded back to show the Swastika flag hung over the back seat. It was higher up on a raised platform and it looked like it hadn't been touched in a long time.

"Is that what I think it is?" I asked shaking my head in disbelief.

"That is Hitler's armoured Mercedes Grosser." Lucius said and I looked up at him in wonder.

"It isn't?" I asked like a numpty and his bad boy grin had my heart pounding. He leaned down to my neck and just when I thought he was going to start kissing me there, I felt his lips move up to my ear.

"Well, I needed something to drive away in, after someone's head went bang, bang!" I shuddered at his crude words and the light kiss he gave me under my ear contradicted the murderous actions he was joking about.

"Times a ticking princess and your carriage awaits." I let him turn me around and this time, the grip on my arm was of the gentle variety.

I saw the others gathered around a big black four wheel drive that looked like a black, road legal tank.

"Adam, take the others to the helipad and get things ready, we will meet up with you shortly." Lucius' voice had retracted back into order mode and Adam nodded at his master's command. But my mind was screaming at the word 'helipad' and what was next on my list of horrors! I tried to pull out of his hold again but it was made near impossible when instead of letting me go, he simply repositioned me to stand in front of him and rested his hands at my waist in a possessive hold. Now I had his solid chest at my back and both his hands keeping me from running far away from any word that had 'heli' in it!

"Keira behave, or I will be putting you in that car to join them in that machine you call a death trap!" He growled in my ear after pulling my head back by the long pony tail I had put my hair up in. His fist around my hair sent a shot of something I didn't want to think about straight to my core, one that prevented me from arguing back. I nodded the tiny movement his hold allowed and after a second more of his show of dominance, he let me go.

"Oh man, why does she get to go in it and not me...I have been waiting ever since you got one and you said no one could go in it but you...You lied Luc!" Pip started complaining just as Adam was picking her up and placing her, still moaning, in the truck. Lucius started laughing behind me and I had a really bad feeling about what Pip was referring to.

"My Lord." Adam said before nodding once and followed his wife into the black brute of a car. The door closed on Pip's squeal and Adam's laughter before roaring out of the space. The whole room was centred around a cleared middle stretch, which I gathered to be the road out of here and when I saw a massive metal door roll up, I knew it must have led down the tunnel I had heard about. Then the back car's lights went out of sight, leaving me and Lucius standing here alone.

"I am not getting in another helicopter Lucius! No way, no how!" I said turning to face him now that I had been released.

"I know you're not." He said simply and before I could register his answer I had started arguing my case again.

"And I will throw up on you this time and I won't…wait…what?!" I shook my head quickly as if this would help to make sense of this man.

"Did you hit your head on the ice…I said, I know you're not…so we'd better get going, I am going to have to drive fast as it is."

"Err…come again?" I ask bewildered.

"Did you perchance wake this evening with brain cells dripping from your nose? Just in case, let's make this simpler for you…Come. With. Me. Now." I listened first to the sarcasm and then the demanding order which both combined into clear cut frustration. What the hell he has to be frustrated about I have no idea but I found all these thoughts assaulting me as I was once again being dragged over to another car, only this one had the doors open in waiting.

Okay, so if I was now stood in the Bat Cave, then this thing in front of me was most definitely the Batmobile! Only without the daft tail fins and exaggerated rounded wheel arches. Oh no, there was only one word that could describe this machine and that was… lethal.

The car was more like some winged mythological monster waiting for its prey to willingly get inside its belly to be devoured with ease. Yeah, it looked all sleek, low to the ground and curved into silky lines of its body work but the front and back couldn't fool you with the snap of sharp edges and big black grills that looked bottomless. Like an open mouth needing to consume. Even the colour of dark gun metal grey had it looking more like a weapon than something you would get in and drive.

"Oh, hell no! I am no way getting in that thing!" I said pulling back on his hold to no avail. He gave me a cocked head look, to say 'what is wrong with you now' but of course I was referring to another death trap that stood like a black panther that wanted me to ride on its back…claws and all!

What did he expect? I know it may seem like I was an overreacting, whiney pain in the ass and that may be, but considering the times I had been in the car with a supernatural being, I knew the outcome would be the same with them all. It was this indestructible persona they all wore and well, let's just say, I was so not shopping in the same stores. Heck, I was now stood in the 'very breakable human' aisle and there was a sale on in how to stay alive!

Lucius let go of me and stood with his arms folded as if this would have prompted me into doing as I was told. I mean really…did he not know me yet?

"Keira my dear, there are two ways this is going to play out, one, which is the one I would prefer, is that you get that sweet behind in the car, all by yourself like a good little girl…" His voice was sweet and condescending but then his tone changed with the other option he didn't want to deal with,

"Or two, I put you in the fucking car, screaming if you must, which I can't deny would be fun to hear… now which is it?" His gaze burrowed into mine and I realised I was mimicking his stance by folding my own arms. Okay, so now was the time to think, do I anger the Vamp that could scare the crap out of me when he really hit rage mode or do I face that same Vamp behind the wheel of a man made killing machine? Umm…my choices weren't looking hot right then.

"Time's up, pet!" Lucius said and I found myself being hauled up over his shoulder quicker than I could say shit! I made a girly and pathetic screechy noise before I felt him bend and deposit me, none too gently, into the bucket seat of the car. The door slammed shut downwards, closing me in like I was sitting in the bloody cockpit of some stealth jet fighter! What the hell was this car anyway! I looked to the right and saw the word 'Reventon' embedded into the interior in large letters and couldn't help the hard swallow. I had never heard of this car but even the name sounded as terrifyingly fast as it looked.

I jumped when I heard his side door slam shut and I looked to my left to see him looking at perfect ease behind the controls…I mean Christ, he even looked near giddy as he gripped the wheel like it was an old friend he hadn't seen in a long time.

"Belt up Honey, it's time for a spin." He said slipping back into cocky gear with as much ease as starting the engine in front of us. I jumped as the sound vibrated around us and there was no disputing the raw power that roared off every surface in the cave. Then with an over the top rev he had me clawing at the belt to try and get it clicked into place, as without warning he sped out of there like…well like a bloody bat out of Hell!

He zoomed towards the dark tunnel and the night of my first time in Draven's car hit me when I thought we would hit the stone wall. That one moment in time with Draven had knocked me so far off my world's axle, that after that, there was no way of it ever getting on the straight and narrow again. I looked to my left and for a second the two men blurred into one. Lucius wore a plain navy t-shirt that was tight across the bunched biceps that were controlling the car like it was only travelling at crawling speeds, not the instant death speeds the aggressive engine was screaming we were doing. The sound of it echoing in the tunnel that was lit by the eyes of the metal creature was deafening as it snarled and lashed out with every gear change.

His hair was pushed back and looked as controlled as his physique did at that moment but his eyes almost glowed in the dark and the ease didn't reach his intense gaze. I optimistically put it down to his extreme concentration. It was only when I could see the entrance at the end in a moonlit glow that I felt a little less dizzy.

"I gather by the way you are unnecessarily hanging on for dear life that you are not fond of one of my favourite Lamborghinis?" His voice penetrated my fear at seeing the world zooming past at an unbelievably fast rate. I don't think I could even concentrate enough to form words and wished he would do the same by spending all his brain power on not getting me killed! Okay, so I fully admit that I am a full-blown pansy in this aspect but as someone who has never driven over the speed limit in her life, then this was one of my nightmares. At least when Draven did it I was dating him, so I had the girlfriend's right to shout at him until he drove at a speed where I wouldn't find my fingernails embedded in the fancy upholstery.

"Umm…that would be a no." I whispered, and his laughter filled the small space in the car. When he finally stopped laughing at me, I felt his hand leave the steering wheel and reach for me. He uncurled my hand that was gripping onto the seat in a death grip and placed it on the middle console with careful and slow movements that said he took my fear seriously.

"This is the Lamborghini Reventon, it's a 6.5 litre v12 and does 221 mph…"

"Telling me how fast it goes is not going to help me here." I cut in, looking out of the window into the night blurring past. He chuckled and I flashed him a filthy look, one he ignored. I watched as he changed gears with paddles on the steering wheel and felt the pull of the car as the road opened up in front of us. I must have made a noise as he sped up, so I was surprised when he slowed it down.

"I will make you a deal."

"Does this deal benefit me in any way?" I asked.

"It should do. I will drive at a sensible speed on these roads through the mountains…if…"

"If?" I had a bad feeling about this.

"If you have faith in my ability to control this car and get us there at a decent time without flinching throughout the entire process." Okay, this was too easy.

"Why do I feel a big but coming on?" I said sarcastically.

"Oh there's a but alright, one you won't like, but considering the other options you left me with, I think this one will have the better outcome...for you anyway." He added dryly.

"Can you elaborate on that, please."

"You hate heights, that much has been established. So I could either have had you drugged and flown back to Munich or driven in a very fast car, I picked the latter." As much as I hated to admit it, I preferred his choice.

"But, I will not be going at this speed the entire way Keira, I need to get there quickly and having you screaming in my ear all the way will serve as a distraction, even if it is the car making you scream and not my hands." I nearly choked on my breath.

"Blunt much?" I replied making him laugh once again.

"Always!" He promised with a dark smile directed my way and with the added glow from the console, it was downright sinister.

"So what's the but?" I said getting him back on track and away from dangerous flirting grounds.

"Let's just say I like the Autobahn for one reason." Oh shit, I knew this reason and it made me want to start clawing my way out of the car.

"How fast did you say it could go again?" He swallowed his laugh but his eyes crinkled at the sides and there was no hiding that breathtaking smile from anyone with a pulse.

"Okay, let me try this another way. I have enhanced senses, Keira. That means that if a foolish animal did a kamikaze across the road a mile away in the pitch black, I would see it and I could react far quicker than any human could. This car, in my hands, is just an extension of those senses...In other words, I control the damn car, Keira and I do not intend to waste over two million, when only twenty one were ever made, just to prove the point that IF, by some divine intervention the car crashed, that my first and only priority would be saving you. Besides, I love this car." He finished this little speech and I was left gobsmacked! But his words had hit their mark and I started to relax back and just let him take hold of that control I knew he could own and manipulate so well.

462

After a few minutes of silence I decide to ask some questions as I knew once we got there, this was most likely going to be the last time we had to talk alone and I still had one question my life might depend on...

*"What's the Triple Goddess?"*

# CHAPTER 41
# A FAST WAY TO GET BITTEN

**W**as I seriously getting growled at for asking that question? "And tell me, Keira...how exactly do you know about the Triple Goddess?" His voice had that hard icy edge to it that had me regretting saying anything. Maybe I should have just waited to talk to Pip about it.

"Well I don't know though do I, that's my point and the reason I have asked about it." I snapped back after spinning my worries a full 360° and deciding his hard tone wasn't going to deter me from finding my answers.

"Don't be obtuse Keira, you damn well know what I mean! Now tell me where you heard about it." I rolled my eyes at his attitude just before giving in.

"Right fine, but just so you know, you're not going to like it and I am not sure whether this conversation isn't best left until you're not in control of something with that many zero's." He shot me a sideways glance that would have caused the bravest of men to flinch.

"Start talking Keira or this deal is off and you will find out what it is like to fly around these mountains at those death speeds you fear." Okay, so this time there was no rolling my eyes but more like the look of horror that made him give me a nod of acceptance.

"I went for a walk up to the silent garden and..."

"By yourself?!" He shouted, interrupting me and I could only nod this time.

"You stupid girl!" He yelled and I sunk further into my seat feeling like a naughty kid getting told off for nicking a cookie before tea time!

465

"I...I..." I started but he made a slicing motion with his right hand and I stopped.

"Just continue Keira but know the thought of your recklessness just pisses me off even more!" This time I found my backbone.

"You are the one that said that place was safe!" I shouted but from the looks of things, this was so not the right thing to say. His eyes had all but turned into slits and his knuckles were turning white from his grip on the steering wheel.

"I did not! I think if you recall that night, you would hear me telling PIP to take you to the silent garden, not for you to ever go there alone!" So he might have been right about that but a little information would have been nice!

"Yeah well I .."

"Enough! Explain what happened Keira. Right now!" Once again he cut me up mid-sentence and it was a tone I wasn't about to argue with.

"Fine! I went up there and then two women came out from the woods!"

"FUCK KEIRA! Are you trying to get yourself fucking killed girl?" He shouted and I began to think just how important getting this information really was and if it was worth me getting my head bitten off by a very angry Vampire!

"CALM DOWN WILL YOU!" I shouted at him and then covered my ears with my hands trying to think straight without getting bellowed at.

"Just continue before I self-combust and I am warning you, if you tell me how close you came to being harmed, then I really will spank some sense into you for next time you think about pulling some shit like that again!" His warning was enhanced by the look he gave me and the sight of his biceps tensing under the tight material that looked close to ripping.

"Look, I will never get to explain what happened if you keep bloody snapping at me and saying stupid shit like threatening to spank me like a kid!"

"Oh, it was more than a threat Keira and if you pull that crap again it will be a damn promise, now tell me what happened." He said, thankfully in a more controlled tone.

"Right, well as I said, two women came from the woods and tried to get me to go with them. They called me some weird 'sister triad' thing and went on about me being the Triple Goddess." I said and although I could see he was still tense, his voice remained cooler.

"What else did they say?"

"They spoke about the moon and some Horned God that wants me to complete the cycle. There was also a bit about re-birth of 'his Lord' and then they called me the maiden." When I was finished Lucius looked less than pleased and he dragged a hand over his face in frustration.

"Let me take a wild guess and say one was a beautiful pregnant redhead and the other had a face like an old boot that had been chewed by a dog for ninety years." I couldn't help but laugh a little at his perfect take on the old lady.

"Umm yeah, I would say that is accurate. So what did they mean? Why do they want me and why do they think I am…"

"The maiden. That's because you are." He stated simply and I shuddered.

"You need to explain, Lucius." I all but demanded.

"The Triple Goddess is not just a ritual, it is more of a passageway, a legend written for a God trapped and forbidden to enter this world because of his past. You do not just get rogue Demons and Angels but on occasion… Gods. For Wiccans, the Horned God is the personification of the life force and energy in animals and all things wild but his control of the land is what gives him his power."

"What happened to him?" I whispered.

"He is also known for his increased sexual appetite on the days of the full moon and one day his appetite found the likes of a young maiden, one untouched and forbidden from the hands of men. He fell in love with the maiden and when she rejected him, he cursed the land upon which she walked."

"And I am gathering that was a big no, no?" I said trying to cut some of the tension that had seeped into his story.

"His big no, no, killed thousands in famine. The wells dried up and the land refused to grow grain. Any food that did manage to hold on to their roots rotted before any lips could taste them. His rage upon the land killed all apart from the maiden he loved and only when she committed suicide did the other Gods take notice." He looked over at me to make sure I was still with him on the story and I nodded for him to continue.

"As punishment he was sentenced to carry the souls of the dead to the underworld, the first being that of the maiden. As a suicide, her soul was not welcome in the heavens and it is said, that until another maiden picked by the Gods was born, then no passage would be open for the Horned God to arise again"

"What! And they think it is me?" I shouted, thinking it was all a huge mistake.

"It is you Keira!" It was clearly the truth by the way he said this, the amount of weight behind every word.

"Why?"

"Because there is only one Chosen One and as you have been told enough times, that Chosen One is you. The ritual states that the sisters' triad is made from the Mother, who represents the earth, the Crone who is the underworld and then there is the Chosen, the most powerful, as the maiden represents the heavens. Each has been chosen and each has been waiting." He said gently as though trying not to freak me out any more than I already was but it was taking me a while trying to process all this.

"So Malphas wants me to complete the ritual as this maiden, but why him?" I asked and this made Lucius' face turn to granite.

"Because, whoever completes the ritual and brings all the elements of the Triad together on the Winter Solstice becomes host to the Horned God, binding together the two powers and trust me when I say…that would be a bad thing indeed." Lucius said this last part in an eerie seriousness that brought on my next question.

"And if that happens, can the Gods not just intervene again?"

"Not when the two powers will be combined. Malphas is a President in Hell and has forty legions of demons under his command, which he can call upon at any time. They can be cast back into Hell easy enough but if Malphas were ever to become a God then those Demons would remain on the Earth's plane and no one has an army big enough to destroy that amount of power, not I and not even the King." The picture he painted was one of war and in my case, humans being the collateral damage.

"Could nothing destroy a God?" I asked, making him turn suddenly to me and raise an eyebrow.

"The only thing that can destroy a God Keira, is another God!"

For the rest of the drive his words stayed with me like an itch I couldn't reach to scratch but still had to endure. The thought that I could be that last piece to an ancient puzzle, one that could bring a God here on Earth, had me close to meltdown. It was one thing to be called a Chosen One and hear about a power you didn't yet feel but to know the end result of you being alive could bring about a supernatural war was beyond words of the unbelievable.

Even the sound of the aggressive engine that reminded me more of a formula one car racing round a track, didn't bring me out of my shock. As Lucius promised, he put his foot down when on the German motorway and the reason he loved the Autobahn was frighteningly clear... there was no speed limit.

I couldn't even guess what our top speed was but at one point I was not only thrown back in my seat but the world outside could have been lost in space for all I knew, as I got a taste of what being in a rocket was like. I tried not to think about it and considering all Lucius had told me about The Triple Goddess was enough to prevent me from screaming in fear. Of course, after about ten minutes it became easy to see that Lucius' control over his prized possession was one of pure skill. He was right, the car was just an extension of his body and every muscle flexed was a movement the car would follow.

It didn't take us long at all before I found myself looking up at the club I had been brought to when I was first kidnapped. Lucius drove past it and down a street that dropped down under ground. He turned the car sharply to the right and the road twisted down into an underground garage that was situated directly under the club. I saw a few different cars were already parked and everyone had the same black four-wheel drive that all looked armoured.

"Well, you survived." Lucius said as he cut the engine. He was right, I had but not without that drive taking it out on me mentally and I wasn't referring to his speeding.

It was only when we got out of the car that I had made up my mind. The consequences of what could happen if Malphas ever got his hands on me could be catastrophic. I grabbed Lucius' arm to hold him back from walking away.

"You have to hide me, Lucius!" I said, and his eyebrows pulled together in worry.

"Keira..."

"NO! You have to, I don't care what happens to me, but you can't let him get near to me. I won't let him use me to bring so much destruction to the world...I just can't...I..." At this point Lucius pulled me into him and it was only then did I realise I had tears streaming down my face.

"Keira, listen to me, he cannot take you from here. You are safe.

Your guards are strong and not even I can breach the walls in your mind. You have nothing to fear." He pulled me back and wiped the few tears away that had not soaked into his t-shirt. He lowered his head until he could see into my eyes.

"Alright?" He said and it was only when I nodded did his worried expression fade. He took my hand and led me silently over to a double door that turned out to be an elevator. I got in without argument when I felt his large hand span the base of my back and give me a little push. He didn't remove his hand and I felt an odd comfort in his touch. He pressed a panel hidden in the wall and when it popped open, he entered a code onto the small touch screen. The elevator shot upwards at quite a speed and Lucius shifted to hold on to my waist from behind. His grip only eased when we reached the top.

The doors opened to a large round entrance area that had three doors, one in front of us and one either side. In the middle was a large round table with a statue of a marble woman upon it. Her body was being consumed by a coiled black snake that looked as though it was made from burnt wood and the head of the snake was level with her frightened eyes. Its mouth was open as if getting ready to strike.

"Come!" Lucius said snapping me out of my daze. He walked me to the doors in front of us and told me this was his private apartment. As soon as the doors slammed shut behind me, he left my side and walked straight into the large open plan living space. It had a beautiful masculine elegance, with its dark slate floors and light grey couch facing a glass fireplace. The place was dotted with white furniture. Tables and chairs all with metal legs that matched that of the modern décor. Whitewashed walls held large black and white pictures of lakes, forests and snowy mountains I knew well, considering I had just spent over a week there.

Lucius had walked over to a bar area and poured himself a glass of what looked like Vodka. It was a clear liquid but the bottle was frosted with ice. He shook the glass at me and asked,

"Want one?" I shook my head as a no but said a quiet 'thanks', at which he shrugged his shoulders and downed the lot. He refilled before putting the bottle back. He came over to stand near me and looked at the pictures I was staring at.

"Why did you stay in Germany?" The question just blurted out before I really thought about the personal nature of it.

"I was told to." He replied simply and I no longer found interest in the photographs of his home.

"By Draven?" At this he cocked his head to one side and a smile crept up on one corner.

"No, not by Draven. The Oracle told me about the place at the lake and that it would become my home. Of course even handier was that no-one would be welcome within the mountain without the owner's acceptance. Needless to say that Dom was never on the list." He added smirking.

"And how does that happen exactly?"

"What, more questions? Why Keira, I am surprised." He said, this time dropping smugness for the sarcastic route.

"Oh yeah, I forgot that I was born brimming over with all this supernatural knowledge…how silly of me!" I said fighting sarcasm with sarcasm. The smile I received nearly knocked the breath out of me. Lucius really was a man born to smile and I didn't know whether it made it more potent because it was a rarity to me in the beginning or just the fact that he was far too handsome for his own good.

"Touché little kitten, touché. The only way to describe it is like a gulf stream in Hell. Its core runs parallel with a river in the underworld and therefore no Angelic force can enter it without permission from one of Hell's own. That last one being me of course." He said nudging me in a playful manner.

"Sounds like a good place to keep kidnapped girls held against their will." I commented dryly, making him laugh again.

"As it turned out, yes it was." I huffed in response but when I looked up he wasn't taking any notice of me. He was looking back at the door we used but when I turned to look I didn't see anything. I heard his glass being placed on the table and now I was concerned.

"What's wro…?" I half said and turned round but his intense red gaze stopped me mid-sentence. His eyes were bloody and glowing and to my horror his fangs had lengthened past his lower lip. I tried to step away but he grabbed me by the top of my arms, proving that his strength was too much for my struggles.

"Lucius…what…?"

"Ssshh little dove, don't fret…it will only make it harder for you." Okay, now I wanted to panic big time. His look was completely predatory and utterly unrestrained. He pulled me closer to his chest and I used all my weight to pull back, even though the little good it did me.

"I am sorry Keira, but you are right. I can't leave it to chance that Malphas could take you, so this leaves me no choice." He said coming closer to my neck. I wanted to panic like the little dove he called me and flap like crazy just to get away.

"I can hear your pulse going wild, Keira… calm for me!" Was he insane! How on earth could I calm in the face of those fangs about to sink deep into my skin. Would he really kill me? I thought about what was needed to be done in any hopes of preventing a war no human would ever survive and I find my neck stretching out on its own to one side. My pulse didn't calm but my neck was now at an angle that was more accessible to his impending bite. I knew what needed to be done but my breath still hitched when I felt his teeth graze across my skin. He didn't break the skin and I found myself wishing he would just get it over with. I gave my last thought to the man I loved, despite all the looming odds against us and wished as I always did in the face of death, that I could see him just one last time.

Draven.

But the bite didn't come and I looked down to find my fists embedded in his T-shirt, twisting the material as I waited for the only destiny that would bring peace. But still it didn't come.

"I…I am waiting for your bite, Lucius" I said, surprising myself with my bravery.

"Are you now?" He said along my neck and even though I knew it was coming and more than likely was to be my end, I still felt his touch slide along every nerve in my body. His arm came around my back and pulled me roughly to his chest cutting away any space between us.

"I hope you understand why this has to be done Keira, I really do. You ready?" He asked and I nodded a little but then Lucius grabbed my hair and tugged my neck taut to the side.

"I wasn't talking to you, Keira." He said and I gasped at his meaning. That's when I felt the other person in the room or more importantly, another person at my back. The person must have nodded, because Lucius tightened his hold all over my body and whispered a little sorry against my neck before then moving his head back to make room.

"Wait I…!" I started to say when a flash of green came into my peripheral vision.

"Don't worry, Toots, this will only hurt like a son of a bitch for a little while." And then I felt fangs rip their way into skin and tissue as I stared into the glowing red eyes of someone who clearly wished it was their bloody lips at my neck. I started to slip down into a dark place of pain as my last thoughts drifted me closer to my oblivion.

Pip was right...

*It did hurt like a son of a bitch!*

## CHAPTER 42
# LAST STRAW

I was far too comfortable to be dead. I opened my eyes at the sound of a door closing and found I was lying in a massive black sleigh bed under rich crimson coloured sheets. The reason I could see myself so well was thanks to the mirrored ceiling. Only this wasn't some cheesy porn style that was covered in a tile effect, no, this was more like someone had brought every fancy gilded mirror in the shop and then fixed them to every inch of the ceiling space.

Every shape and size had my reflection staring back at me in shock. All of them had a black lacquered frame and some even overlapped each other but no two were alike in design. I lay frozen, locked like a rabbit in view of myself and with the immense size of the bed I was in, it made me appear tiny and childlike. I shifted and sat up gingerly, still feeling a raw pain in my neck. That's when it all flooded back to me...

Pip had bitten me... but why?

I didn't have the faintest of ideas why but I knew only one way to do so, I needed to find the Imp herself. I was at least glad to see I was still dressed and with a bit of wobbling around, I found my balance and got out of the bed. Now I was stood up I could see the room clearly and if I thought that Lucius' sparse and modern living space would have followed through into his personal room, then how mistaken I would have been.

This place was a Gothic fantasy room and looked like something from the Adams Family! The walls were papered black with black velvet written scroll that looked like it could have been Latin. The bed

I had been in, consisted of the head and foot sides coming up so high they reached past my shoulders and the carved wood had been painted black. Each side curled around the top edge and had a twisted metal bar going across that had chains in the corners hanging in swags. It was quite strange and I didn't understand why the designer would decorate a beautiful natural bed with chains...?

That was, of course, until I walked further round and saw black leather manacles attached to the middle of the chains. I could feel the colour rush to my face at the thought of what Lucius did with them and the idea of seeing my wrists firmly locked inside them, had me biting my lip. I shouldn't have been surprised that Lucius was into the rougher side of sex but being in this room and seeing the King's sex dungeon style bedroom was enough to make any woman blush.

I turned from the bed and pushed all thoughts away of the man who had put me there. I pulled my top round from where it had twisted in my sleep and pulled up my jeans that were now a size too big for me. I let my hair down after finding it lopsided and loose and gathered it all back up again. Although when I walked further in the room, I found I needn't have bothered as I found a note on a small side table next to a lavish Chesterfield couch in cherry red with black buttons. The order was simple...

'Be Ready At 8pm'

I frowned down at the thick cream parchment with the command written in black ink that barely looked dry. I didn't know what Lucius was planning but both he and a certain green haired beauty were going to get an earful for scaring me last night. I looked to the line of arched windows along one wall and through the leaded diamonds I could see the rain battering against the glass in the dark. I wondered what time it was and how much time I had to get ready when a clock chimed seven times. So I only had an hour, well that was fine considering I only needed a quick shower. That was until I turned round and found another table with a tray upon it.

I walked over and found myself a little feast with a bowl of some beefy stew and freshly baked bread. There was a glass of wine along with a small jug of water. Oh wow, there was even dessert in the form of some little white mousse in a tall thin glass. I would like to have said I savoured every last bit but to tell the truth, most of it went down so quickly it didn't touch the sides.

Before I got in the shower, I found a white box tied with a violet blue ribbon sat waiting for me. The box was about a metre long and a foot wide. I found it after I wolfed down my food and did a nosy poke around the room. It was left on a beautiful ornate chair that was black framed and reminiscent of the elegance and sophistication of the regency period. However I doubted the pattern was from that era, not with its printed grey shaded skull upon cream leather upholstery.

I laid the box on the bed and opened it to find it near bursting with layers of lush material. I lifted the dress from the box and held it up at arm's length. It was a stunning deep navy taffeta that shimmered in the light and had thick straps which plunged down into a deep V-neck. One side was wrapped around and secured there at my left side with a black stone brooch the size of my palm. It was like a spiral star with five curled branches and small spikes in the middle, all of which had numerous diamond shaped leaves attached.

The dress itself only went to above the knee but from the tight bodice it then flared out into a layered skirt. The wrap around design at the front extended to the skirt in a split and underneath were layers upon layers of glittering silver lace. It looked so delicate that it could have been spun from a spider but despite its delicacy, its bulk provided body to the skirt and unusually I found myself itching to try it on. Only of course I was running out of time.

I had raced into the lavish bathroom that followed on with the black and red theme, which included a monstrous black clawed tub that, like the bed, went up higher at the back. The shower was a black tiled square that was up on a raised platform with steps. The door was bubbled glass with a red bleed from each bubble giving the effects of a bullet riddle body. I even shuddered when getting in but once the multiple jets hit my body with warmth I couldn't have cared less as to my Gothic surroundings.

I had found everything I needed in another tied box, on a black granite worktop that also dipped into a large sink. I had the world's quickest and most dangerous shave, which inevitably had decorated my legs in little red cuts that looked far worse in the streaming water than the little nicks they were. I just hoped they would stop bleeding before I walked out of here as the last thing I wanted was to walk in to a room full of hungry Vamps, waving a bloody flag!

I had just gotten out of the shower when I heard whistling coming from Lucius' room. Wait…was that 'Over the rainbow' by Eva Cassidy? I walked in there with only a towel round my body and a matching one twisted on my head, when I saw the green eyed monster with a demonic grin!

"If you have come here for the second course then you can just whistle your way out of the door!" I said folding my arms over my chest.

"Aww Toots, don't be like that. And besides I would have classed you more as a dessert than a main." She said with a wink and a shit eating grin that screamed trouble.

"Cut the crap Pip, why are you here?" I said more firmly because if she thought I was just going to forgive her for all but taking a chunk out of me, then she had another thing coming!

"Why, I have come to help you get ready of course." She said swapping her grin to a little smile of reassurance.

"Forgive me if I am not ready to be bessie buds and willing to get close enough for you to sample the goods again."

"Okay, I guess I deserve that but now the time has come to ask you to just trust me and understand that last night was more like a… necessity." She said being serious which again, as it always was with Pip, was hard considering what she was wearing. But one look at her face and I felt all the steam leave me taking all my anger with it.

"I am going to need you to explain this to me, Pip!" I said but she had already started shaking her head before I even finished that sentence.

"Please Keira, you are going to have to trust me and Lucius on this. We didn't do it to hurt you, I swear it." The very fact that she called me Keira only added to the sincerity of her statement. I closed my eyes and nodded without looking at her. My eyes only flew open again when I heard her clap loudly. She was jumping up and down and then threw her arms around my towel clad body.

"Thank you my friend." She whispered in my ear and I tried not to smile…I really did try, but it was like staying angry at a toddler with the biggest eyes you ever saw on a kid!

"Right, but when this is all over you will tell me…alright?" She nodded quickly and then gave me a salute.

"Sir, yes Sir!" She said then giggled, that was until she saw that I was nowhere near ready.

"Come on Toots, time to play Godmother to your Cindy ass." She then proceeded to march me into gear and before I knew it she had completely taken over in getting me ready, giving a different meaning to the type of Cindy she had dubbed me, switching the fairy tale version to one made of plastic and bought in toy stores across the globe.

Sooner than I thought, I found myself standing in front of a mirror dumbstruck at the transformation. The dress fit to perfection and I found myself a little embarrassed about the ample amount of cleavage showing in the V shape neckline. I also had found a pair of shoes and some over the elbow gloves to match, hidden at the bottom of the box. Pip had arranged my hair in a sleek up do that was twisted and then rolled over at the top making it look rather elegant. I also had the sides pinned back, which framed my face nicely. She had also done my makeup in a smoky blue and with a fine line of black liner over the lid and under my long lashes, finishing the look with a sweeping of mascara.

With Pip and I stood next to each, it was like looking at the stormy seas crashing against a jungle island. Pip's dress was incredible and just looked as though she was wearing a thousand butterflies, all green winged with bright pink and electric blue centred swirls and patterns. It looked as though she also wore a skin coloured tight material that separate butterflies were attached to making it look like her bare arms had some that had just landed. They dotted along all the bare parts and the large flowing skirt had them disappearing in flight at the end on fine netted material.

When she turned around she had a pair of wings in the shape of a butterfly made up from even more tiny little wings. It was damn cute and the shape of the dress was very fairy princess, with its tight bodice, loose straps that swathed cross the tops of her arms and a full length skirt that would have looked right on any wedding dress. The fairy tale theme didn't end at just her dress, no, she also had her hair in a loose and whimsical plait to one side, which also had butterflies attached. Her makeup over her eyes, were three stripes of the green, pink and blue along her lids and her lips were green lined with hot pink.

As we walked out of the apartment I complemented her on the way she looked which made her give me a full spin on one pointed toe like something from a magical ballet.

"Why thank you, Miss Hot Stuff." She said causing me to do a red cheeked eye roll. Just then the phone started to ring, so she danced off to the bar area that Lucius had used the night before. I think I could have done with that vodka right about now. She listened for a few moment and then said,

"Wir kommen jetzt" ('We're coming now' in German) and then she clicked 'end' on the handset.

"Good news, your Prince has arrived, wanna go see?" She said and the light in my eyes must have given her my answer because she mirrored my smile. She grabbed my glove covered wrist and pulled me excitedly to another door in the apartment, one that was a hidden panel in the wall. However, with one little press in the right place, the door opened to a room full of monitors and technical equipment. We walked in and each screen showed a different part of the club. There was the main part of Transfusion, the bar area, the dance floor, even the VIP but none of these held my interest. It was the outside street level that I found on one of the monitors to the left and the Limo parked right outside the main doors.

I walked over to stand directly in front of it waiting with bated breath till I could finally catch my first sight of the real Draven. The man I had waited all this time to finally touch without fear of either one of us floating away.

At last the door opened and first to exit were Zagan and Takeshi, both dressed in black, Zagan with his usual hood covering most of his face and Takeshi in a Japanese robed jacket and black suit trousers. Then I felt the very veins in my body start to buzz as I saw the next leg emerge. Draven's long frame exited the Limo with the actions of a jungle cat and I actually gasped at the sight of him. He was purely magnificent and every breathing body stood in the line was as captivated as I.

I wanted to run from this room and get to where he was so badly my limbs were starting to shake. My God I wanted him.

But then all my dreams seemed to shatter into a million pieces and my heart broke all over again. He glanced up at the building as though looking for something and then when he didn't find it, he turned back to the car. I watched as he motioned for someone to come nearer and I winced as Aurora then shifted to the open Limo door. Draven rested one hand on the roof and bent slightly so that he could whisper in her ear.

I felt like throwing up and now, by this point, I should just save myself the pain and look away but I simply couldn't. I was stuck now and with no way to back out I was forced by my own stubborn will to watch as she turned her head to one side and the smile she gave him should have been illegal, it was that dripping in dark sexual promise.

He said something else to her and her features looked serious for a moment until Draven brushed his fingertips down her cheek in a loving caress. At this point I actually had to swallow down the bile that was burning to escape.

She then shook her head slightly and Draven looked relieved but I didn't know why. And then, I just didn't care! I just continued with my torture and watched the rest unfold as Draven gave her one last nod before closing the door. The three men then walked into the club and that was when I finally managed to tear my eyes from the screen.

"Oh Toots...I..." I held up my hand to stop her and shook my head lightly. Right now I didn't need kind words or pitying looks from my friend, no, because right now the only emotion that was going to do me any favours and that was...

*Anger*

# CHAPTER 43
# ANGRY RE-UNIONS

P ip and I made our way into the VIP area and just as I remembered, it was like walking into a supernatural sex club. But this time not even the sight of naked girls laid out like treats of candy on table tops was enough to diminish my burning anger!

I seemed to be stomping my way through the room as though my veins were fuelled with a concoction of rage and revenge. I mean how dare he? The man that was supposed to love me like no other and when the time came to save me and take me back, goes and brings his ex-girlfriend, the bloody woman he most likely cheated on me with...I mean how convoluted was that!

Pip, for once, couldn't seem to keep up with me and it was only when I found her hand on my shoulder that I began to stop my determined march.

"This way speedy, Lucius and the Scooby gang are in another private room." She said and then tilted her head to the right to indicate the way. This time I had no other choice than to follow her. She led me to the back of the sex themed room, to a pair of double doors. We were met by a couple of thick necked wrestler type guards but one look from the little Imp in front and we were being nodded through.

The doors opened into a single open plan room that was the size of half the VIP room. It was decorated to look modern and cool, with its stark white leather wrap-around seating and its blue back lighting. Stainless steel tabletops and black flooring both reflected the calming colours around the room and multiple flat screens were mounted on the walls that showed the activity in the various areas of Transfusion.

Directly in front of us was Mr Cool himself and instead of the usual casual Lucius I was met by one that looked as hard as the steel his drink rested upon. He wore a gun metal coloured suit complete with waistcoat, black shirt with the top button open and a matching tie with the knot low enough to show all his neck. His blonde hair looked darker with it all styled back, showing off his high cheek bones and chiselled features creating a more formidable presence.

He was sat in the middle and as always, acted as though he was the main focal point of any room. Of course, in this case he was, seeing as up until now, he had in fact owned every room I had been in. And of course, being sat in the middle of the room with his council on either side of him was more than enough to prove his dominance but what would happen once Draven entered the room? I was glad to see that Draven hadn't yet made his appearance in this room and I briefly wondered what he was waiting for...surely he would have been up here by now?

"My little Keira girl!" Lucius said, clearly smirking at my obvious rage. I felt like a whistling kettle shaking on the flaming stove, I was so pent up. And it certainly wasn't helping the way Lucius was eyeing me up like I was a giant blood flavoured candybar! He rose from his part of the couch, which I then noticed had a higher back than everyone else's place. He came forward with long legged strides and was stood looking down at me in a heartbeat. He placed a single fingertip under my chin and I had no other option than to be captured by his lust filled eyes.

"You are simply stunning, little doll!" He said in husky tones. His eyes momentarily flashed hot like amber coals before licking his bottom lip. The action was as if he could remember the taste of me and even through my anger I felt the usual flush invade my skin.

"Th...umm...thank you." I said after having to clear my throat. He gave me a head tilted cocky grin before nodding to himself. He then took my hand and pulled me to the empty space next to him. The seating was in a U shape and I found out the seats weren't actually as hard as I thought they were. The leather groaned under my weight and I pulled my legs together as the skirt exposed more of my thigh, so I twisted slightly to the side, unintentionally putting me closer to Lucius.

I saw his lip curve but I was glad he chose not to comment. It was bad enough that I had just seen Draven's little friendly display with a certain Angel I wanted to bitch slap to Birmingham, so the last thing I needed was another royal male super ego pissing me off!

The room was set out so that everyone could see the rest of the VIP as the walls were like a massive one way mirror. For the outside, the rest of the VIP were walking past and enjoying their night like there wasn't about thirty people all staring at them like they were the entertainment. The screens situated on the walls showed them in more detail like some porn movie with others, like the biggest one behind our couch, showed the band that was playing tonight down in the main part of the club. They looked like a heavy rock band and although I couldn't understand what they were singing about, being as it was all in German, they actually sounded good. Their heavy Goth attire matched the thick black elaborate frame that surrounded the huge flat screen TV and it was like watching the Kerrang rock channel in sophisticated style.

"Drink?" Lucius' question brought me back to the situation at hand and it was an answer easily given.

"Hell, yes!" Okay, bad choice of words but finding myself sat here waiting to see Draven was starting to make me bloody nervous and there was only one thing for it. I looked up at a half naked waitress with a shaved head and several facial piercings and said the name of my only cure…

"Tequila, please." She gave me an impressed nod of approval and turned on her high booted heel. I looked to my side to see Lucius had raised an eyebrow my way.

"What?" I asked haughtily.

"Nervous, perchance?" He asked without hiding his amusement.

"Actually I am blinding mad." I said honestly and for once, he looked surprised. He even looked towards Pip, who was situated on her husband's lap like always. She shook her head slightly as if to say 'don't ask' and proceeded to gather up more butterfly covered material and place it over Adam's shoulder. Needless to say, Lucius didn't listen to Pip's warning.

"Is this because of what I had Pip do last night?" As far as guesses went, this wasn't half bad and if I hadn't just witnessed a secret caress between my so called boyfriend and his ex, then yes that would have been reason enough for my anger but right at that moment, even a lifetime of Hilary crap didn't amount to the level of ass kicking I wanted to give Draven!

"Unbelievable as it sounds Lucius, there is someone out there who can piss me off even greater than you!" I snapped but this just made him laugh once before swigging back his beer. I turned to face him about to give him and his happy mischievous eyes an earful when he nodded to the doors in front and said,

"I gather the source of such adorable temper tantrums is about to walk through the door." I actually gasped and my head shot round as though in the hands of a young lad with a slingshot. My aim landed on the living God that had just stormed through the doors making them slam back with the force. Like me, everyone in the club flinched in sync...all of course except Lucius.

The sight of Draven in the flesh caused my body to react in the ways I had forgotten about. My breathing became laboured and I swear the whole club could hear the bass my heart was playing. I could feel the tiny beads of sweat dampen my forehead and I was fisting my hands so tightly that I was no doubt cutting into the skin on my palms. Jesus, was there ever going to be a time when the sight of this man didn't reduce me to a whimpering wet mess that mentally ended up a sticky puddle on the hypothetical floor at his feet!

'You're angry Keira...just remember that and try not to concentrate on how insanely handsome the Adonis in the room is'. I tried to tell myself this but seeing Draven suited and booted ready for a fight and looking like a bloody commando, one swapping black fatigues for an all black suit, was so not helping matters. If anything it looked more like these two warriors were going to battle it out in a boardroom.

Draven was walking towards us with his usual formidable force, eyes dark and intent on one person alone...me. He was being flanked either side by Takeshi and Zagan but one look from this man told you the last thing he needed was any kind of back up. No, this was not a Being that would be calling for help from any man. When that black gaze found my wide eyes staring back at him, then it was only slight, but I was sure I saw his eyes soften for a second. What was that... guilt? I didn't have too long to consider the root of it because now he was stood directly in front of us and I was positive I wasn't the only one that gulped at the sight.

His raven black hair made his eyes look even more intensely fierce and his olive skin now had dark stubble that was more than a day old on the lower half of his face. It made him look harsher, more brutally raw and oh my God but even more damn sexy!

As everyone in the room descended into deathly silence, Draven took his time to take in my form. He scanned every inch of my body and I felt the heat travel up my body with his assessing eyes. He lingered on my bare legs and I now wanted to shift further away from Lucius but I didn't get the chance, when Draven finally spoke.

"Keira, come here!" His order was a controlled deep shout barely kept in check with the aid of fisted hands. When I didn't move he folded his arms making his suit jacket tighten around his biceps... Christ, it looked close to splitting at the seams.

"Come. Here. Now!" He defined every word, giving it a greater depth than just an order, it was now law. But despite the level of intimidation his presence inflicted on me, I still couldn't find myself caving in. I mean how dare he! He just storms the castle for me and demands I come with him while he gets to keep his other wench in the car waiting...and he expected me to just get up and run to his cheating arms like a goddamn puppy! Well he was about to learn an important lesson in his long life of getting whatever the hell it was he wanted...I ain't no fucking door mat!

"NO!" I said loud and clear making everyone but me, Lucius and Draven inhale sharply. I saw a muscle in Draven's jaw twitch and the material around his shoulders stretch to the point of pain. But the most frightening sign of all of his building rage was the flash of purple that fired in his eyes.

It felt like the earth had stopped spinning for the seconds it took this moment to break free of its magnetic pull that Draven controlled. The world was waiting and this showdown was a monumental moment in history as the rest looked on and witnessed the human disobey the mighty supernatural King.

"So this was your plan?" Draven said with surprising calm to Lucius and I whipped my head round when I heard hearty laughter erupt from the man in question.

"On the contrary Dominic, I believe this is your own doing and a case of viridi luscos monstrum" ('Green eyed monster' in Latin) I didn't know what Lucius told him but whatever it was, it made Draven raise one eyebrow in shock.

"We made our deal and I stick by it...that is of course if the girl chooses to leave here with you. If not, then I am sure I can see to her protection." At this point Draven lost all his cool and one minute there was a table in front of us covered in drinks and the next it was being flown backwards as Draven sidestepped to allow it to fly past him and crash into the double doors. The roar that went with it raised every hair on my body to stand to attention.

"I gather that to be a no then?" Lucius said with sarcastic humour.

"Don't play fucking games with me Luc, Keira is MINE and she will always be MINE!" On hearing this I felt all my anger bubble and steam to the top until I realised I was now on my feet shaking with fury. I could feel everyone's eyes snap to me and my taught body, so highly strung someone could have picked me up and used me to play a bloody violin! My vision was misting over as I felt my body begin to tingle. It started in my fingertips and was channelling its way up my arms and into my chest. My very core was getting ready to explode and I heard gasps coming from both sides of me but I couldn't look. My vision was showing me only Draven and for a second I saw him flinch. I felt like I was getting so hot I would self-combust. Hell, I felt like I was glowing like poked embers.

"Keira?" Draven said gently. I tried to calm myself down but I was now panting like a rabid dog and Draven was looking worried.

"Keira, listen to me, I don't... توسط خدايان ...I don't know what's happening to you but you need to calm down and right now...do you hear me?" ('By the Gods' in Persian) I heard the slight panic in his voice but the command at the end was what made me snap. It was like stoking the fire and I felt something in me just bang, pop and smash its way through me.

I was assaulted with images of Draven in bed with Aurora and the same video footage that had tortured me for every minute since being made to watch it. I could see it like it had painfully been scorched to my memory bank and when his hands pinned her wrists to the bed's frame, just below where my picture hung, I finally lost it. I watched with the rest of the room as every TV screen on the walls started to play my exact thoughts. The image I was seeing in my head was playing in exact time as my memory was relaying it and now everyone, including the guilty, could watch his actions with me. I watched his utter astonishment transform his hard features into lines displaying the unbelievable. I watched as the emotions played out as his head flicked to every screen but the only one missing was the one I was counting on to tell me he still loved me...guilt.

At that point I screamed out at the searing pain that ricocheted through my brain and continued on and on until it had me gripping at my head with both hands. I heard things around me smashing and glass raining onto the hard flooring like hailstones. I heard other people screaming in fright and shock but I didn't look, that was until the biggest smash of all.

The sound of the walls shaking brought me from my pain and the immense heat started to subside. I opened my eyes to see that my hands were glowing like a light bulb was beneath my skin but then it started to flicker as my pulse started to slow and the tingling in my body started to fade. I turned around and saw what everyone else was looking at.

The biggest screen of them all that was behind the seating was now smashed as though the hulk had used it as a plaything. The frame was now in black glass splinters on the floor and the screen looked like it had gone a round with an automatic weapon. Sparks flew from inside and I looked round to see the rest of the damage to the room. No screen had survived and there were even some cracks on the walls with now some of the light fittings hanging down like limp dying flowers.

What had I done?!

"Oh, Keira." Draven said and made a move to touch me but I recoiled back.

"DON'T TOUCH ME!" I screamed at him, both afraid of hurting him and of what his touch could do to me. It was the very thing I had craved for so long, having him standing here, so close, close enough to touch was like waving a syringe in front of a drug addict. And Draven was most definitely my grade of poison.

For once Draven listened and not only did he obey but he now looked afraid of what would happen if he didn't. I had to get out of this room and away from all these judging eyes that made it feel as though the walls were closing in on me. Draven looked past me and I felt Lucius' presence at my back.

"Keira girl?" He whispered close to me in concern. I felt his hand barely touch my shoulder before I shrieked out and jumped a mile.

"No! I said don't touch me! I...I...don't know what...what happened...I...No! Please don't." I said again when I saw him reach for me a second time. I was backing away and one of my heels caught on the rubble my outrage had caused. I stumbled a bit and saw Draven about to reach out when I righted myself at the last moment.

"Pplease!" I stammered, thick with emotion, halting him in his tracks.

"I have to get out of here." I said backing up, looking frantically round for my escape. I couldn't understand what had happened to me but whatever it was, it left me feeling like an emotional wreck, shaking like a leaf in a thunder storm. Tears were streaming down my cheeks sending black drops to the evidence of my destruction on the floor.

Thankfully my saviour was found in the only face that wasn't looking at me as though I was someone else. Pip made a whistle to get my attention and then pointed to a small bar area that had a glass door to the side. She winked at me and I ran to the door trying to get away from any sight that reminded me of what I had done. What had happened? Where had that come from and how on earth would I ever stop it from happening again. Was that it now, every time I got angry I would hulk out Demon style and end up killing every TV in a thirty metre radius? Let's just hope nobody ever pissed me off in an electrical store or sparks were going to fly!

I tried to ignore all the frightened glares being sent my way and pushed on the frosted glass doors hoping my touch wouldn't make them shatter. I didn't fancy becoming a grated Keira or being embedded with millions of glass knives any time soon.

I was surprised to find the outside world behind the door as it led onto a metal staircase that twisted up to the roof. The cold air hit me and I welcomed the sensation of it cooling my still heated skin. I walked up to the top and found a contemporary little garden with weathered wooden decking that had turned a greyish shade and a dark slate whirl in the middle of the round courtyard, like a pathway with no destination. It kind of represented the way I was feeling. I felt that level of craziness that I might have just walked it!

The roof was surrounded by a waist high wall that was also overflowing with different plants and shrubs. At the corners the walls were built up into higher pillars and had sculptured topiary on top. At one side was a built in water feature that was a solid piece of white marble that stood like a car upright on its bumper. The water trickled down from the top and cascaded on all sides of its rough edges like it had just fallen from the mountain side. It was beautiful and the sound was soothing in the still air. I walked to the edge and was surrounded by the sparkling lights of the city below and it cast a warm orange glow to the night sky.

"It's a beautiful sight and one I haven't seen in far too long." I shuddered at the deep voice behind me and soon my skin heated once again, only this time for very opposite reasons.

"Draven." I whispered his name as if it held all the answers to every single question that had run through my brain since the time I was taken.

"Munich is beautiful." I said as I didn't know what else to say.

"I wasn't referring to the city, Keira." His words were now right behind me and even though he still hadn't touched me, his presence was like a solid wall at my back waiting to catch me.

I wiped away the last of my tears and I knew my makeup was now half way down my cheeks but I didn't care. Of all the times I had thought about seeing Draven again, being right here, in the personal space of his awaiting arms, this was not the way I ever expected things to have happened and it was killing me.

"Draven, I can't do this." I managed desperately and still keeping his inch of distance between us I felt his breath dance along my neck. I knew why he hadn't yet touched me and at this point I was thankful for it but when he leaned close enough to whisper, "Ssshh" in my ear, it was still like all my nerve endings lit up and his touch came through in other ways.

"Keira, stop." He said firmly when I started to shake my head. I didn't know what I wanted anymore. I was being pulled in two directions and neither one was going to help me from being lost. I wanted Draven to wrap his arms around me and I wanted to drown in the heart of him. I wanted to snuggle down so close that no one would ever be able to get me off him. But in my other mind I wanted to run from him and never look back, in the fear that if I did, he would catch me and never let me get away from the heart-breaking knowledge that he cheated on me.

"I just didn't realise this would happen Keira...I mean...I never thought it possible."

"What are you talking about?" I asked, still without looking at him.

"I am talking about your obvious powers Keira, what else would I be talking about?" Really?! What else...? Was he sodding joking!

"Oh I don't know..." I said just as I turned round to face him, because for what I needed to say I had to witness his reactions to gauge the truth.

"How about the fact that you have been lying to me from the very beginning! The fact that sleeping with me has been changing me into some super human demon half breed that can now destroy rooms...or how about all the stuff you kept from me about why you and Lucius really argued..." I was now getting angrier by the second and was walking him backwards as I continued.

"Or let's get to the real gritty part should we Draven, let's talk about how I saw you and your not so angelic EX having SEX in what was supposed to be OUR bed! So how is THAT 'else' for you Draven?" I had completely snapped now and was angrily once again wiping away at the tears that came along with my fury.

But it was the look on his face that finally stopped me and there was no mistaking the look of complete bewilderment I found instead of the guilt I was counting on.

"What on earth are you talking about?" Draven bellowed at me as it now all sank in. The lines in his face defined his scowl and the trade mark brooding frown was replaced by one of indignation.

"How can you not know Draven, you were there after all?" I said but Draven's eyes focused on mine as if searching for something before realisation hit and from the look of things, it hit hard.

"What was on those screens in there...the images you projected was what you think has actually happened?!" He shouted this last part, but I stood firm. What else could they have been...maybe my worst nightmare, but even my own mind wouldn't have been so cruel. I found though that I couldn't answer him with words, so I just nodded and in return his eyes glowed a deeper reddish purple...oh yeah, he was angry alright.

"And where the fuck did you get that image from?" He growled at me and I couldn't help but flinch when he said the F word at me. I didn't want to tell him as I just knew as soon as I said the name it would only inflame his rapidly growing temper. But when I still hadn't given him a name then he said my name in a warning.

"Keira!"

"It doesn't matter Draven, I just want you to tell me if and when it happened." At the sight of his outburst I think I would have been better saying the bitch's name. He clenched a fist, brought his arm back and embedded his hand into the wall closest to him. The pillar didn't stand a chance and when he whipped his hand back a waterfall of soil came with it. Oh and did I mention the mother of all roars that went with the colossal man paddy.

"IF AND WHEN!? How about FUCKING NEVER!" He screamed at me making me take a few cautious steps back. I was now speechless but that didn't seem to matter to Draven as he was now taking my place and was in full wrath mode.

"Did Lucius set this up? Is this what he had planned all along? He is clearly trying to turn you against me and you are letting him! You are a pawn in his little game and you are letting him win! How could you?" He accused and I cringed before regaining my anger.

"I can only go by what I saw Draven and besides, it wasn't Lucius who showed me and he certainly didn't have anything to do with it!" Ha, I thought as I watched his eyes narrow but then they fly open again.

"And you naively, no doubt, believe his bullshit! That's it I really am going to kill him this time!" He snapped back.

"Yes I do, considering why a man would pull something like that when the thing he wants relies on YOU wanting me back! That and the fact that he bloody defended you!" At this he looked taken aback and for a minute I thought he was going to argue the reasons why, but he must have stopped that train of thought as another realisation hit.

"Oh no, don't tell me Keira...if you confirm what I am thinking then I am going to be beyond furious." He warned and a number of panicked thoughts of the past ten days flickered through my head all in seconds. I knew what was coming and I knew that I was going to have to try my hardest not to react if he guessed right. But then he went and said the name that would always get a reaction from me and no matter how small, Draven noticed it.

"Layla!" He hissed. As soon as he saw the truth of the matter from me he erupted, but this time instead of the wall getting any new additions he was at me in a blink. I jumped as his arms enveloped me and I found myself being crushed to his chest. At the first contact with Draven in all this time my mental damn cracked and all my walls came crashing down into oblivion. I buried myself into his chest and sobbed for every single day we had been apart, for every single minute we'd missed and for every single time I thought of him in the arms of another woman. And all through this he remained a constant strength in front of me, holding me to him and whispering soothing words in my ear.

Finally, once I had finished having my meltdown, Draven held me back slightly so that he could look at me and he held my head with both hands and rubbed his thumbs on my cheeks to take away any stray tears. I looked up at him and I knew instantly he had seen everything I just cried about through my open mind. He knew everything I thought he had done to me, what Lucius did to me and how Layla tried to kill me once again. But where I would have expected Draven to have erupted into a mass of murderous rage he gently leaned down and picked me up like he always did at Afterlife.

493

He didn't say a word as he took me over to a bench seating area that was sheltered by a canopy of ivy over a wooden pergola. He took his seat and instead of placing me down next to him, he sat me so I was nestled on his lap. The feel of his large hands on my body did crazy things to me and I found myself not only comforted but that my body was being awakened to craving the kind of pleasure only this man could give me. He must have felt it too because the next thing I knew I felt a very solid presence of Draven pressing into my thigh and he had buried his face into my neck. He inhaled deeply as if taking in the very essence of me and his length hardened even more.

"By the Gods Keira, how I have missed you." He said against my neck and he kissed his way up my jawline as if too afraid to push for a kiss just yet. As if I was still too fragile and he was right, I needed all my answers before I could let my senses take over just by Draven's touch alone.

"I need to hear you say the words Draven, I am sorry, and I know you might hate me for it, but it is the only way to eradicate the image from my brain...I need this Draven." I said quietly. I felt him stiffen beneath me before releasing a big sigh.

"I know you do and for the record, I could never hate you, not even close." He said placing his forehead to mine and I closed my eyes so that his lips being so close to mine didn't tempt me but the scent of him alone was having a drugging effect on me.

"Keira, listen to me now when I say that I have not shadowed the love I have for you by clouding it in sin. I have not touched another since I first knew of your existence in this world and nor would I again."

"Oh, Draven!" I said, throwing myself at him and clinging to his neck like he was one giant life preserver. I shifted my weight so that I was now straddling his hips and like this it was hard to ignore the weight of his arousal pressing against my core.

"I love you and oh my god, how much I do love you Dominic." At this I heard him inhale sharply as he took in not only my words of love, but the way it was reinforced by me calling him by his first name and for me, this was a sentiment saved for times like this, times when my point needed his full understanding...saying his name always did it.

He once again framed my face with his hands to stare deeply into my eyes. I felt lost in them and the emotions I saw there, emotions he didn't need to say but did all the same.

"And. I. Love. You. Keira." He sounded out each word in tense frustration at holding back. I knew this because then he swore and crushed his lips to mine in a searing first kiss that reunited our bodies back together again at last. It was like every cell in my body hummed and communicated with every cell in his and together they finally found blissful peace.

One of his hands fisted in my hair and the up do that Pip created was happily ruined and fell into his fingers as all the grips dropped to the floor like someone just switched on a high powered magnet. He used his hold to control my head and now it was bent to the side as he plunged in deeper and I felt the pull of his power taking me to a place only he could take me to. I lost myself in him and his incredible taste. I felt his other arm that he had anchored around my waist pull me even closer to his body, eliminating the last inches of space between our bodies.

The kiss felt like not only a kiss but also an act of repossession. As though he was marking himself on me, stating his claim and burning his passion into me for everyone to see. And I gladly let him.

I even found myself disappointed when my air started to run out as I couldn't drag enough in and Draven had to let me go before I passed out. I was amazed to find I was not the only one panting and I did a little mental victory dance in honour of what I could do to him. I was more than happy to see that my effect on Draven hadn't faded in my absence.

"Holy Shit" I said as I couldn't find any other thing to say but that. I was happy to see that I receive a cocky grin, one I had sorely missed.

"Damn straight, Vixen!" He said before pulling me harder onto his arousal making me moan at the contact.

"I would love nothing more than to take you right now and bury myself into your very core. If however, I wasn't on a rooftop belonging to my enemy, one who kidnapped you, I might add." He said as though it pained him to admit that our proper reunion would have to wait. He groaned when I shifted on top of him and I laughed as I got off, but I didn't get far. He grasped my wrist and for a second looked brutally possessive.

"You do not leave my side Keira, do you understand? You go nowhere without my touch." Oh my god, he was being completely serious!

"Draven you can't be..."

"No Keira! You will not fight me on this, end of conversation.

Now come, it is time to take you home." He tried to level his voice but the strain it took told me the idea of me leaving his side again was something he could never allow to happen again. I decided not to argue, there would be no point until he had calmed down and some time had passed. I couldn't believe this was the end, all that time waiting for this moment and now it didn't even seem real, more like a dream. So when that thought hit me I kind of panicked a little and quickly pinched him, extracting a moan from him.

"Hey, what was that for?" He said with his lips quirking at the sides. I smiled as I knew it hadn't hurt, I didn't know what could hurt this man...oh wait, well maybe I do now... me leaving again.

"I just wanted to check I wasn't dreaming."

"You know you have the process of checking for dreaming all wrong, don't you?" He said and I saw that mischievous glint in his eyes that had my heart hammering at the sight. I mean bloody hell, if he got any more handsome I think my heart would literally stop beating. I saw what was coming and tried to dodge his attack but of course against Draven I was too slow. He grabbed me and pinched lightly at my sides making me snort with laughter. I was laughing so hard I could barely take a breath and he laughed with me...or more like at me. I just couldn't believe I was now crying with happiness and if someone had told me this would be in my future for tonight then I would never have believed them.

Once I managed to get composed, Draven lifted me as though I weighed nothing at all and held me there to the right level while he kissed me softly but thoroughly. He left my lips but then by the time he got to my neck he seemed more desperate to have more of me. I felt him fist my dress at the back and I kept thinking any minute now I would hear the ripping of this beautiful fabric.

"Draven, are you prepared to walk me back in there naked?" I quipped and he growled into the juncture where my neck met my shoulder. I felt him then shudder and he raised lust filled eyes to mine making me join him.

"My beauty, I will carry you back there wrapped in my wings if I need to." He said so softly it formed a lump in my throat. I placed my hand to his cheek and he turned his face into it.

"Thank you." I hummed in his ear and I felt him smile before I saw it.

"You never need to thank me for that Keira...ever." I closed my eyes as the love he projected hit me and the overwhelming feeling of being protected once again was so comforting it was beyond all words.

I felt his hand finally relax and I was lowered to the ground slowly feeling the hard length of him all the way down. He then took my hand and pulled me gently to the door I came through. We were just there when I pulled back as I remembered what I wanted to ask him.

"Did you give Lucius the spear tip?" He looked at me quizzically for a second before shaking his head.

"No, the deal changed."

"Changed? But how…who said…?" I asked shocked that Lucius had let me go without gaining possession of what he so desperately needed for over two thousand years.

"Keira, I will explain soon but later, when I have you safe and…" He stopped mid-sentence as absolute horror and sheer terror transformed his handsome face. He was looking at me as though I was a ghost, as though he had never seen me before.

"Draven? Draven…what's wrong?" I asked him not even trying to keep the panic from pitching my voice higher. I watched him raise our entwined hands and I finally saw what he was seeing.

"No…this can't be happening…this, it can't…I am not asleep… I…" I stammered as I looked up at Draven and saw his own panic. I watched as his hand got tighter but my fingers didn't feel it. How was this happening?

"Draven…? Draven! NO!" I shouted as it travelled up my arm and soon more of me was invisible and fading away just like I always did before.

"How is this happening?" I shouted and this was when Draven lost it and thundered in a demonic growl that ignited his whole body into his other self.

But it was too late and the last thing I heard before my whole body faded away was my name being screamed by the man I loved…

*My dark Angel*

# CHAPTER 44
# SAY HELLO TO MY LITTLE FRIEND

I woke up with a start, mainly because I wanted to be sick and before I could look round for a suitable place, I vomited over the side of what I assumed to be a bed. For the moment nothing else mattered than the acid taste I needed to get out of my body and I heaved until nothing was left but burning nostrils and a raw throat.

Where the hell I was I didn't know but one thing became very apparent…I was in a cell. Unless it was the worst B&B in history, I didn't think there was any other thing to call the small stone room that had bars on the door and window. So with that one thing became clear, I doubted I would be checking out of here anytime soon.

There was a small fold out cot bed pushed against the wall that I was sat up on and the other side had a little table with a bowl of water and a tin cup next to it. In the far corner was the only other item in the room and it made me say out loud, "Ahh, hell no!" There was absolutely no way I was using that dirty bucket to pee in!

I tried not to panic as I knew in cases like this, unfortunately from past experiences, that panicking never helped. But it was taking all my strength not to. I wanted to scream out at how entirely unfair this was, for me to have finally got Draven back in my life to then be once again cruelly snatched away was enough to bring on watery eyes. I didn't want to cry, not again, so I rubbed my eyes to try and stop myself from making a crappy situation worse.

So, instead, I walked over to the small table and was at least thankful that the water in the bowl looked clear. I dipped my cup in it and took a long swig of water to try and eliminate the taste of bile in my mouth. I decided not to overdo it on the water as the very last thing I wanted to do was to try out my first class toilet facilities.

After doing the obvious things like checking the door was actually locked and that the bars on the windows wouldn't budge I did the only other thing I could do, I sat gingerly on the bed as I didn't feel like making things worse but becoming a bed burrito by having the sides snap up and swallow me…it happened once and now I hate the things.

It felt like hours later and by the way the sunlight was shifting in my little window I knew it had been. I did the math in my head and knew it must be getting on for at least four o'clock as I had gathered that when I did my disappearing act, it was already getting late. I must have been drugged to have slept through the night, which would explain the throw up session this morning. I had tried to understand how this happened but even with hours to stew on it I was still coming up with nada!

The list of suspects was at least narrowed down to two people and as time went by I knew more than likely my captor was going to be Malphas. If it had been Layla I doubted she would have let me sleep the night away before slitting my throat. So now I was left with my only other option, I was left to wait it out and hope like holy hell that someone would be coming to rescue me pretty soon.

The very thought of what Draven must be going through at losing me for the second time made me wonder how many rooms would be destroyed from his wrath this time. Well, I hoped when he found me then he could put that wrath to good use and kick some demon butt! I think at this point I must have lost it slightly as I started laughing but then it turned to tears and it took me a while to get myself back in control. I would like to say that it was the lowest point of my lovely day out at this rustic, exclusive health spa but unfortunately, I would be lying as I quickly found myself so desperate for the toilet, I had no other option than to use the bloody bucket.

Well at least there was toilet roll, even though I had to expel the outside layers until there was hardly anything left, as the disgusting filth of the room had seeped into the roll until it looked mouldy. I had to keep swallowing to hold down the last of my bile but I managed to until I had finished.

When I finally heard footsteps for the first time I shot up and faced the door. I wanted to grab something as a weapon but I didn't think a tin cup was going to cut it against a Demon so I decided to hold onto my dignity instead. I started trembling but not in fear more in anticipation of what was to come. Of course it didn't help that I was still in my little dress and it was freezing in this damn stone cell.

I looked through the little bars at the very top of the door but it was too high to see anything so when the door finally opened I didn't know what to expect. There was only three things I could tell about the figure in front of me, one was he was definitely male, two that he was definitely a demon and the third...given the tray he was carrying...he was definitely a lackey minion. He was covered from head to toe in a black cloak and the hood covered every inch of his face.

He was also huge, with a massive frame that barely fit through the door. His legs were encased in leather and strapped to them were numerous weapons in the form of curved blades, throwing stars and even some strange silver discs that looked to have razor sharp edging. It also looked like he was wearing some strange metal plating on his chest that was grooved to show the contours of his muscled frame. This was most definitely armour of some kind and it was engraved with symbols I had never seen before.

Gloved hands held the tray as he entered the room and I stepped back enough to bump into the wall behind me. My palms found damp wall to grip onto and I felt my nails scratch at the stone blocks. One look at that tray had me close to hyperventilating and the syringe that lay next to a little medical vial didn't take a genius to figure things out.

"Oh no you don't...you and your creepy ass are not drugging me again!" I said bravely, making him cock his head to one side as if he didn't understand a word I was saying but then it didn't matter too much, as in the next second the lackey made a strangled gargle and then dropped to the floor as if he'd been hit by an 'acme' anvil. He fell forward and the tray went smashing to the ground, happily breaking its contents. I watched with my mouth hanging open as I took in the cause.

"PIP!" I shouted in disbelief at the sight of my favourite Imp stood in the doorway, looking like Rambo with a massive knife in hand. She gave me a beaming smile, which I promptly knocked off her when I launched myself at her.

"Whoa! Nice to see ya too, Tooty cake." She said as I gripped onto her for dear life, never being so happy to see my green haired friend here to rescue me. She had to drop the knife to pry my arms off her and when I let go and looked at her, she was grinning at me like a mad woman!

"Happy to see me, I take it." She said stating the obvious and it made me want to cry with happiness.

"Oh God, yes!" I replied making her giggle.

"Well I'm not a god yet darling but given the amount of times I end up saving your skinny butt then I might become one soon. So... this is a nice place you got here."

"Oh you like it? Good, 'cause my rent's up and it was a bargain but I really think we should leave before any more rats come to investigate." I said giving a nod to the dead guy on the floor. She giggled again and then picked up her weapon before she wiped her blade along one of his trouser legs.

"Mmm, yeah I see what you mean, but unfortunately there are also more big ass rats out there too...oh but don't worry Toots, of course I have a plan." She gave me a cute wink and with her army combat gear you would have thought the two would have been polar opposites but the combat print kind of defeated the object when it was black and pink camouflage with rhinestone edges. Where would she be camouflaged...a gay club on drag queen night?! It was funny but the only part of her that would have been camouflaged in the usual green surroundings would have been her hair, which was currently hidden under a military style floppy cap in the same crazy pattern.

"So, what is this amazing plan?" I said without bothering to keep the hopefulness from my voice.

"It's a good one but we need to get to the roof, so it's time to haul ass and jump ship." She stepped over the big mass of body parts that was the dead man and motioned for me to do the same. We got out of the door and I flinched as I saw that there was also another dead guy thanks to my little friend. She continued to pull me down the stone corridor towards a door at the end and we had to step over another dead body. Jesus, just how many guys had Pip killed in her time here anyway?

"Who are these guys?" I whispered but she gave me a toothy grin when she corrected me.

"Don't you mean who 'were' these guys? But in answer to your question, these square dudes are pretty much soldiers of Hell."

"What!" I yelled way too loudly for our situation but Pip didn't look worried, which told me she had eliminated any chance of us coming across unwelcomed visitors.

"Okay, here's the skinny on our situation Toots, as you have no doubt gathered by now, the big cheese in this picture is our bad old boy Malphas and see, he is like a President of Hell. This comes with certain perks, those being like a whole heard of demon soldiers all ready and waiting for the whistle blower, which yesterday… he blew…hence demon square dudes that can't dress for a shit date." As I took all this in, Pip was leading us through the door which I noticed had the lock kicked in. I looked down at her booted feet and saw the heavy metal soles and steel tips…yep, that would do it.

"Okay, I think I am pretty much getting a clear picture now thanks, but there is one more thing you could tell me." I said as she held the door open for me.

"Well I am on a roll here, so why the hell not. Fire the cannon."

"Err… what now?"

"I mean ask your question." She said translating herself.

"Okay well… how did you even find me?"

"Ah, now this is the good stuff and the real genius part. Luc was concerned something like this would happen so he took precautions in case. And well, I didn't mind, you actually have a very aromatic flavour and also taste a little like Turkish Delight." Okay, at this my mouth made that trade mark O shape when being around Pip.

"Lucius made you bite me that night so that you could find me again?"

"Yep…bit like a beacon to my homing pigeon self. Anyway, that neat little trick I do when I send you packing in your sleep, well it's a bit like that, only instead of just my soul going on a trip, well with me, my body can tag along for the ride…so here I am." She did a little twirl round when announcing the 'here I am' bit and I was stunned. She could actually do that?

"So it's a bit like 'beam me up Scotty' type thing?" At this she laughed so much, she had to stop and bend over to grasp her stomach, she found it that funny.

"Kind of, only without the Scotty…Man you're funny! Anyway what was I going to say…Ah yes, well I would have been here sooner but it takes so much juice out of me I have to wait for the sun to rise. I am a bit like a solar panel in that way. Plus we needed to make a plan of action and pull forces, gather the troops, that type of thing." This I was happy to hear about and it instantly made me wonder if Draven and Lucius were finally working together again.

I didn't have much chance to give it more thought as we made our way up a spiral staircase, which I gathered led to the roof.

"So how is this going to work, how do we get in contact with them and why do we need to be on the roof?" I knew this must have been really annoying as it was an irritating trait of mine but I couldn't help all the questions. But one of the best things about Pip, was that it never seemed to bother her and she rooted into one of the pockets on her combat trousers, lifting up a glittery flap before digging in deep. She then pulled out her blackberry phone and said,

"I need a signal." I couldn't believe this was part of our mission. I mean she beamed in here like something out of nearly every sci fi movie I have ever seen and then used a simple mobile phone to call the cavalry. She then held it up to wait for the bars to flash and indicate she could call as we walked the rest of the way up. I finally saw a door and wondered how high up we had come as it felt like I had climbed for a small eternity and my legs felt like lumpy custard had been injected to replace my bones.

I was just about to ask what would happen once she rang as she opened the door but her gasp stopped me. I ran up the last few steps, feeling even more wobbly doing so but when I got next to her and the blinding sun allowed my eyes to see things properly we both said the same thing at the same time, although as usual Pip embellished her version.

"Oh Shit!"

"Oh Shitio!"

"Tell me your plan involves them?" I asked at the sight of an army of 'big square dudes' as Pip called them, all stood there waiting for us. We both looked at each other and Pip did something that I would normally be doing right about now, she bit into her bottom lip before answering me.

"Umm, that would be a no." She answered what I was expecting her to say and turned back to the twenty cloaked bodies all of which were holding blades of some kind. Pip moved me behind her slightly and then reached her back to the handle of the blade she had strapped there.

"Pip." I whispered praying she wasn't going to do what I thought she was going to do.

"Go back through the door Keira, do it now!" The sound of Pip being serious and calling me Keira was as frightening as Draven's rage. It was still something I wasn't used to hearing which went the same for seeing Pip like this.

"Tell me you're not going to fight them all!" I said in panic.

"GO!" She shouted before running full speed right in the centre of where they were all gathered, waiting.

"PIP NO!" I shouted afraid for my friend's life. I didn't know what to do, but I knew that I would never just leave her! If only I could get that mojo back like I did before and destroy these guys the way I did with TV's. I tried to concentrate hard but nothing was happening and I had to watch in horror as Pip engaged in battle on her own.

She was aiming for one of the men with her blade held high and the soldier was doing the same. I tensed all over as I waited for the sound of clashing blades and the fear for Pip had me shaking. But then just seconds before the blades would first connect, she dropped down to her knees and skidded before whipping her blade round at such a speed that I saw the man fall before I saw why. But then other men around her fell in the same way as she spun her weapon that fast that no one could get near her. It was like the blade had grown longer than herself and she was using it like the blades on a helicopter. With five guys all now on the ground around her the others started to take a different approach.

I watched two join forces and use each other's weight to swing around and I cried out when the legs of one hit her, knocking her down. But she was soon on her feet again and with a running jump, she launched herself at the two. She practically ran up the large body and flipped over but upon righting her frame she sliced upwards, taking the blade through the middle of the man's chest, splitting him nearly in two pieces. I expected a fountain of blood but there was only vapour powder that came floating out of his centre.

She then spun again and with an aim to the side she sliced diagonally across another body. Considering it was one against twenty, Pip was kicking ass...or more like slicing her way through it. I watched as she was then ganged up on from three sides and she decided to take another approach. She ran for the side of the roof and was followed all the way but at the last minute she jumped over the side and I gasped as she hung on with one hand to haul herself back up behind them so quickly they didn't know what had happened. She managed to slice her way through another two at their backs.

Now with only eleven left I felt like jumping up and down and cheering her on, as I was close to doing backflips. Watching her work her way through these guys was just incredible, she was a force to be reckoned with as she glided fluidly around the space, slicing as she went. Now she was once again using the momentum she got from

505

running and using her body weight and the laws of physics as another weapon. She headed for another guy and used her blade as a pole vault to propel her forward landing with her feet in the guy's chest. He staggered back and Pip didn't give him much chance for balance as she stabbed him deeply.

I still couldn't believe that in the matter of minutes Pip had killed ten men and I was unable to take my eyes off her or keep the look of awe from my face. She hadn't even made a sound, a grunt or anything! But then, just as she had got rid of two more standing in her way, everything suddenly changed. The air seems to crackle like an electrical current had just charged the atmosphere and the rest of the men dropped quickly to one knee, holding their weapons pointed upwards. Pip staggered back a bit and I noticed even from where I was stood, she tensed and then turned to me and screamed,

"KEIRA RUN!" And this time I did as I was told. I turned around and made a grab for the door, only for it to be opened by someone else...

*Malphas.*

# CHAPTER 45
# MAIDEN RE-MADE

I realised that I much preferred getting drugged as opposed to the mother of headaches I now had thanks to being knocked out by the butt of someone's blade. After opening the door to Malphas I was quickly seized from behind and then the next thing I knew there was pain before blackness overtook all my senses. And now, I just hurt.

Opening my eyes was no better but I knew it needed to be done. As predicted it just added to the pain and I tried to move my arms to cradle my head, only I soon found that I couldn't move. I tried again but only heard a rattling and something heavy banging against the bones in my wrists. I knew what I would find but I looked anyway to where my arms were locked. They were pulled taut above my head and my wrists were bound together by double shackles that looked barbaric and crudely made.

My eyes followed the thick chain links all the way to the iron ring they were attached to and the white marble the ring was embedded in. The same marble slab I seemed to be lying on. Oh dear...this so did not look good for me right now!

"Oh goodie, you're awake." I heard Pip say and my head shot up as far as it was allowed and I frantically looked round. Only when I found her I wanted to cry. Pip was now strung up by her arms dangling down from a massive pillar by the chain that had been wound all the way down the top half of her body as well as her wrists. It looked painful and it also looked like she had received a bit of a beating as well.

"Oh Pip." I said gently, referring to the busted lip, black eye and nasty bloody gash on the bottom of her chin which covered her neck in dried blood.

"What this...Ha, the bastards could barely touch me and they ended up needing their old fart of a master to gain the upper hand... don't worry Toots, this is nothing." She said laughing like this was all a big game and the most fun she'd had in years.

"Anyway, it's you I am worried about, even if the dress does look good on you, I doubt it is a good sign...though it does look like a Gucci." She said on a giggle and I looked down to see I was in fact wearing a new dress. It was stark white, fitted tight to my body like a second skin and was almost see through. It was a light material and fell in between my legs making them look like milk. Unfortunately my legs were also chained and it worried me to see them slightly apart and secured to two metal rings at the bottom of the marble.

It was hard to tell the difference between the marble I was lay on and the silk I wore and even though it was low cut to my chest it was longer on my arms, reminding me of one of Pip's medieval dresses. I felt a bit like lady Guinevere being readied for the slaughter or in this case, the sacrifice. My hair was loose and cascaded down my sides to my waist in blonde waves that looked golden in the many huge candelabras that hung down from the vastness of the high ceilings.

When I started to look round and take in my surroundings at greater depth, it looked like we were in some kind of grand hall and I was sure I had seen something similar. Until then it hit me, I had been in something similar and if I remembered correctly, that night didn't exactly go so well for me then either. I looked back at Pip and unbelievably she winked at me. I followed that pillar to the next and then on as far as I could see. I looked up and saw the domed roof and the same symbols that decorated the soldiers' breast plates, also decorated the Temple I was lay in.

"So I am going to take a wild stab at the obvious and say that this doesn't bode well for us...does it?" I asked, rattling my chains to add emphasis.

"Don't worry sexy Toot, I will 'hang' around." I couldn't believe she could joke at a time like this!

"Ha, ha Pip, way to go on making light of things."

"Hey, I am just glad I got the chance to 'hang out' with ya before you went and left me with his highness, lover King." At this point I just couldn't help but laugh and I think if there was ever a girl that knew how to help me keep my sanity it would forever be my crazy friend Pip!

"So what are we going to do now, I gather this was NOT in the escape plan?"

"Err that would be a no again, rather that or I missed a biggy in the brief of operation 'save skinny arse'...maybe I was in the loo." She winked at me again and I couldn't believe I actually laughed again.

"I bet Draven was mad." I said thinking that if Draven could see me here laughing about this then he would want to shake some rational thoughts into me.

"Yeah, well that is a bit of an understatement considering he destroyed Luc's pretty rooftop garden." I coughed, although I shouldn't have been surprised, I did think he would have destroyed something.

"I am glad that was all he destroyed."

"Oh, I didn't say that was all, but that was where he started. What was surprising is that Lucius was the only one who managed to calm him down enough to get him to see reason and then we formed a plan. Only that kind of went to shit when we walked into the fan."

"Yeah, you can say that again." I then shook my head and said a pleaded 'don't' when she began to repeat herself.

"So...is there a new plan?" I asked, being hopeful.

"Umm, I can't say for sure, considering I am not there and all, but I did manage to smash my phone so that should help." I almost refrained from asking, as I was dreading the answer to that one but, it's me, so of course I did.

"And how will that help, Pip?" I asked not helping to keep the exasperation from my question.

"Ah, have faith dear Tootie sweet, for I came prepared." Okay, I so didn't have the time or the patience for Pip code.

"Please elaborate my friend." I said feeling that I could so use a frustrated eye rub right about now.

"Aw, you're no fun at guessing games. Okay well, my phone has a tracking device in it so now that it's down they will not only know where we are but that we are also in a spot of bother." She said the last part in a posh English accent you would likely hear in Harrods, London.

"Oh my god, that's great news...so they should be here any minute then...right?" This time she didn't look so positive.

"In theory yes...I just hope they locked onto my signal quick enough, I didn't know where you were until I got here myself and there would have been no signal until we got on the roof, so I don't know…but fingers crossed eh?" Fingers crossed…! Was she kidding?

"I think we are going to need a little more than just a few crossed fingers here Pip." I said, being negative and not being able to help myself but I mean who could really blame me, this month wasn't exactly one of my luckiest so far.

"Is someone being a negative nelly… um?" I rolled my eyes and decided to keep quiet on that one, but with my silence came the sound of enormous doors being opened. I turned my head to the side and regretted it instantly. Malphas was cutting the distance between us with long strides and the sound of his heeled shoes tapping on the marble floor was like a ticking clock. He was being followed by the two women I saw in the woods that day and the face of the old Crone was enough to make me want to gag.

She wore a long black robe that I was sad to say didn't hide her hideous face. The pregnant woman wore a long red velvet dress that was tight to her swollen belly and was in the same style as the medieval dress I had been put in. It matched her hair that was plaited to one side and was as long as mine, reaching to her waist. It was strange to see but it looked as though we could have all been related, seeing as my own sister was a red headed beauty and if the old bird hadn't been about a million years old, she too could have been a descendent, given that her hair was also the same as ours, only now it was a dirty grey colour with strands of startling white.

As they came closer I also saw a small army of the same soldiers that had been on the rooftop all marching behind their leader. Pip made a snarling sound, which was ignored as they made their way to the end of the Temple room. Malphas then made a gesture with his arms spread wide and this was the cue for the soldiers to separate and two rows of three men came to rest along the Temple walls, situated behind the massive pillars that spanned the full circumference of the room.

"Silence Imp!" Malphas hissed as he passed the growling Pip and I tensed at the anger that I was mentally directing at Malphas for hurting my friend. I pulled against my restraints bring his attention back round to me and the evil grin I received at the sight of my struggles only told me that it was a pointless act and one he enjoyed watching. I turned away from him and directed my sight at the domed roof that had a large section painted gold at the very top and I was stunned to see it moving like trapped liquid beneath a curved glass panel.

I jumped when I felt a cold finger travel the length of my cheek.

"So soft and so obviously touched by the Gods. You will be my heaven on earth tonight child but first, I must make you pure once again. For to be my Maiden, we need to restore your innocence." I looked up into a pair of cloudy eyes that reminded me of someone with icy cataracts. The tiny black dot in the middle made me shiver under his touch as they scanned the length of my body.

His frost white hair hung down straight as a pin and his high forehead and pointed features gave him an elf like quality, with his beady eyes looking down his beak nose. His skin had a bluish hue and appeared almost transparent across his slender frame. He wore a half cloak that covered his shoulders and half of his chest but finished in an arch that went longer at the back to the floor. His pointed hood was pushed back and the material of the cloak was thick black brocade with patterns of thorns and the different moon cycles in a darker satin finish. Underneath it all he wore a pair of wide legged trousers that had a large wrap around flap of material that tied to his side making it look like a skirt. To this was added a tight black top which, like his soldiers, was covering his chest in a metal breast plate.

He moved slightly back and turned to motion his female companions forward. He definitely looked like he was ready for a ritual and my anxiety doubled when I saw both women coming closer each of them holding a tray.

"I told you my dear, that I would be seeing you again and how much I was looking forward to it but first, let's see how well you co-operate." He took a wicked looking knife with a curved tip, off the tray the old woman was holding and brought it to him as he approached me.

"I want you to offer your blood to me." He said in a hoarse voice and I took one look at the blade in his hand that had a golden bird's foot around the base and started to shake my head.

"I am not going to do that." I said bravely and I surprised myself with how strong and steady my voice sounded. He smiled at me as if he knew this was coming and nodded his head at some of his soldiers.

"I thought that is what you might say, so it is lucky for me then that I have a bargaining tool." He looked over at Pip and even though I knew what I might find, I still looked towards her. She was now faced with a colossal axe's blade held firmly to her neck and I could see the bloody line it was forming.

"NO!" I screamed out and Malphas motioned for the blade to be lowered.

"Toots don't listen to him, he can't kill me...he can't..." She was then silenced by one of the men with a punch to the face. Her head cracked to the side and a spatter of blood hit the floor.

"NO STOP IT! PIP!" I screamed, pulling madly against my chains.

Malphas leaned down putting his lips at my ear.

"Do you know there is only one way to kill an Imp?" He whispered and my eyes desperately sought out for any sign of life from the lively crackerjack Pip I knew so well. She was hanging limp with blood oozing in a long drip from her open mouth and I felt the tears start to mist my eyes.

"You have to tear off their head or in this case an axe will do the job quite nicely." I screamed and started to shake with the thought. I couldn't let that happen, not to my friend. So with tears now streaming down the sides to my hairline I turned to face the bastard that was holding all the power and said with gritted teeth,

"I offer my blood to you." As soon as I said the words I heard a mighty scream from Pip and just before I turned towards her, I saw Malphas' sadistic grin.

"Good girl." He praised and I couldn't help snapping back at him,

"I didn't do it for you!" But he just laughed before swiftly bringing the knife to my flesh.

"I think we will start somewhere already tainted." He said as he moved the blade from the top of my breast to my scarred arms. I tensed and then cried out as I felt the searing pain slice into my skin. I tried not to look but failed when I felt him moving something under my arm. He placed a small copper bowl underneath the open skin and used it to collect my blood. He then removed it and held it over his shoulder without letting go of my arm. It was then taken from him by the redhead and she backed away, bowing her head as she went.

"Now it is time to see if Draven's essence is strong in you." Malphas then dipped his face to my cut and started to lick the blood trickling down like crimson rain. He then made a humming noise before letting me go.

"Ah, I see he has used your body well... his power is strong and well rooted inside your blood stream, the cleansing should take well." I didn't know about any cleansing but I wished that Draven's power would show up so I could crack some heads like I did flat screens.

Malphas moved away from me and walked over to the waiting

redhead and made quick work of slicing her arm as well. I couldn't believe my ears when I heard her hum in pleasure. I didn't think I had received the same treatment as her, I thought dryly.

He did the same thing as with me and collected up her blood in the same bowl before kissing her deeply on the lips. I shivered in repulsion at the sight and thought about kissing those sadistic thin lips.

"With the mothering full moon's blood mixed with Heaven's essence of the waxing moon, my Holy Maiden will be born into virtuous rebirth and will become my innocent sent from the Gods to complete the ritual." Malphas' hoarse voice boomed out and echoed around the Temple before he came to my side once more. He swirled the blood around the bowl with one hand, which flashed me back to that night he did the same to the brandy glass in the back of his Limo.

With his free hand he then gave me a startled scream by ripping up the skirt of my dress and exposing my naked legs and womanly core.

"GET OFF ME!" I screamed at him but this just extracted another grin from the evil bastard. He ran his fingers up my legs and I started to thrash about on the hard marble slab just to get away from him. Then just before he reached the junction of my thighs he stopped and moved the bowl over me.

"To the rebirth of the Horned God's true Maiden!" He saluted the bowl in the air before he poured the blood over my lower stomach. I screamed as I felt the cold blood drip down my body as if alive and looked down in horror as I watched it congeal together in one big mass and then it made its way like a blood snake to my private place.

"Aahhh!" I moaned as I felt it turn hot and then back to cold again before reaching the most sensitive parts of me. It slithered down my core and out of sight, until it then had me screaming as it entered me.

"Get it out, get it out!" I screamed as I thrashed harder, feeling the pain it caused as the heavy metal rubbed and banged against my wrists and ankles. Malphas looked down at me with satisfaction and nodded once before leaving me to aimlessly fight against the intrusion to my body. I could feel it inside me twisting and turning as if trying to coat every last part of my channel. It didn't hurt but was definitely uncomfortable.

"If you relax, you might even enjoy it." Malphas said over his shoulder at me before reaching the redhead, the one he called the full moon. I snarled at him but he ignored it and continued to let me fight against something I couldn't see.

"Now to complete the next stage of the ritual." He said opening his arms wide and this was a cue for the crusty old hag to help him. She started by pulling his hood over his face and then she untied the flap of material across the front of his pants. There was also one on the other side and once she had untied the last one, she opened it so that it now displayed his naked manhood. His erection was at the ready and I inhaled sharply as I saw what he was about to do with it. The redhead had bent over another marble slab like mine that had symbols of the full moon carved into it. She lifted up the skirt of her dress and waited for Malphas to mount her from behind.

The old woman stood by to hold the hands of the redhead over the side as they both start to chant in a different language. I tore my head away when I saw him thrust into her to the hilt and I heard her cry out in rapture. I closed my eyes tight to the sounds of rough sex, the slapping of skin on skin contact and the grunts and moans of pleasure being given and received. It became a background tempo to the feelings the moving below caused me and I tried to fight against the growing of my own desires but it was hard to ignore when it started to tingle and vibrate.

"Let it go my child." I heard Malphas say and I didn't know whether it was to me or to the redhead he was pounding into. I felt the building in the base of my spine and then without warning, I cried out as the sensations became too much and the whole centre of me became a burning centre. That's when the cries of release filled the Temple from the three of us. But my own waves soon turned from ones of wronged bliss to fires of regret and torture. The thing inside me started to pulsate and it gripped at my insides like thousands of little tentacles were growing and building something together with my flesh. Like it was trying to re-fuse pieces of me back together and I was screaming in the sheer agony of it.

"Keira!" I heard Pip screaming my name in the bedlam of it all and I tried to wrench free from my restraints again just to get the thing out of me.

"Keira, listen to my voice…hear me Keira…hear only my voice." Pip said desperately and when I started to concentrate I felt the excruciating pain start to subside. I started to relax my body as I finally felt the thing inside me start to leave and I was left with a cooling sensation in its absence.

I looked to the side, once I had finished panting and dragging the much needed air back into my lungs, to see Malphas had finished with the redhead and was now at the ready once again with knife in hand. I felt like both sobbing uncontrollably and getting a hold of his head and ramming it into the marble slab he just found his jollies on!

"And now with my seed planted firmly in the womb of the Mother goddess it is time for the blood of the underworld's Crone and the Maiden of the earth on this Winter Solstice so as the Horned God will finally be reborn and we will become one." Malphas said before he pressed his palm to a raised part of the stone on the side of the marble block. I felt the stone beneath me start to shift and the part below my back started to concave down so that my back was suspended by the sides. I saw him bend down to my side of the marble but I couldn't see beyond that.

At this point Pip started going crazy on her chains, calling Malphas every name under the sun to try and get his attention. I gathered her plan was to try and stop what he was doing, which told me that what he had in mind was not a good sign.

Finally she must have said something in a different language that hit home because he growled low in his throat before straightening up to his full height and storming over to where Pip hung.

"That's it asshole, come and use me as your sacrifice, I would just love to see my God come in here and kick your pale ass!" Pip spat at him when he reached her and when the bloody saliva hit him on the side of the cheek he lashed out and hit her hard in the stomach.

"NO!" I yelled but it was no use. She pulled her legs up and was now swinging back and to in a protective ball and when I saw her shaking, my first thought was that she was crying in pain.

But I was wrong.

I shrieked out like everyone else did when the walls around us started to shake and the vibrations of the loudest roar I had ever heard echoed throughout the Temple making it rain with debris from the ceiling. I felt the sound through the floor and the marble even trembled under me. Everyone in the room staggered when the earthquake hit and great cracks travelled the length from the door of the far end, like forks from lightening.

Then the booming noise of a creature so big, it must have been bigger than the Temple's castle doors, because it caused a crashing sound of splitting wood to fill the vast space.

I looked back to Pip and saw her still shaking but that was when I first realised it wasn't from fear or pain. No, it was from gut wrenching laughter. She then stopped and looked Malphas straight in the eye and with a deep smirk, she said in calm tones,

"Malphas, I don't believe you have met my darling…" She waited until the doors at the end burst into splinters the size of your hand and stared lovingly at the beast roaring at its opening before continuing,

*"Abaddon, my husband!"*

# CHAPTER 46
# HELL BREAKS LOOSE...
# FOR REAL

After the doors were smashed open, the beast that entered the Temple was a house sized monster that was a breathing entity of pure untamed and uncontrollable rage. This creature was not just the stuff of nightmares, it was also the only being that the very Devil himself feared and finally seeing the beast himself, I could certainly understand why.

Standing before the Temple was no longer the man I knew as calm and collected Adam but the frenzied Hell's beast that no God could destroy. And right now he was trying to find the only person in the world that could control him and when he saw her hanging from a chain with blood dripping down her body...that was when the Heavens and Hell could hear the blood curdling, ear splitting roar of maddening wrath being released.

Abaddon was the size of a building and he resembled nothing I had ever seen before. His very skin seemed to be made from the bones of victims, as though he had been swallowing heads and the decayed skulls were showing through from the inside. He had no neck but his massive head was situated closer to his shoulders and was mainly made up from just a forehead and mouth. Twisted horns came from what looked like slits for nostrils as he has no nose to speak of. They reached up and outwards tipped blood red on grey bone and his mouth was a snarling mass of small fangs in rows down his throat. His high cheek bones touched his low forehead, which made his eyes into thin strips that could hardly be seen. His skin was like that of a rhino with massive lumps underneath that were like moving souls trying to escape.

He ran into the room and smashed his way to Pip causing a path of destruction on a monumental scale. Arms that reached the floor took out about forty soldiers with barely a movement and I felt the earth shudder beneath me with each immense step. I watched Malphas take stock of what was happening and he quickly used his power to run, jump and skid his way from the falling rubble to get out of the beast's way. He was then at my side and freeing me from my chains.

"Time to go!" He said lifting me and when I tried to struggle he threw me to the two women to hold me still. I felt the long dirty nails from the old witch cut into me and with a cry I tried to break free.

"PIP, TAKE CARE OF HIM BEFORE HE DESTROYS EVERYTHING!" I heard Lucius' voice shout amongst the devastation continuing on around me and then I saw Pip start whistling and waving her hands to get the beast's attention.

"Oi, sweetheart, get your big heinie over here!" As soon as he heard her, he dropped the pillar he had smashed free, that looked more like a baseball bat in his hand! He then crashed his way to her and I thought for a second she would get crushed by accident. However he stopped in time and it was the first time since being in here that he seemed to calm slightly.

"Hey big guy," Pip said softly and I couldn't believe it when I heard a high pitched moan coming from him that sounded like pained happiness. It hurt my ears but I couldn't tear my gaze away from the sight of him trying to nuzzle her so gently that all she was doing was swaying back and to on the chain. She must have made a sign of pain because then he roared, smashed his fisted claws into the solid floor that crumbled like pastry and ripped the pillar that held her chains from the floor like a twig.

I screamed out, worried for her safety but there was no need. He had grabbed the chain, tugged it free, and was now pulling it from her body with as much care as a monster his size could accomplish. Once she was free he drooled on her before a massive tongue came out from the danger of his teeth and he licked her clean from blood. Soon she was dripping wet but amazingly he was purring like a fifty ton cat!

"Okay, okay, I am here baby." She cooed and I was gobsmacked that he seemed to understand her. He then pulled her close to his body and cradled her to him as he ran and smashed his way out of the

Temple with his car sized shoulder, making the last of the walls supporting the roof start to cave in.

"KEIRA!" I heard Draven scream my name at the sight of the Temple's pillars coming crashing down but it was too late. Malphas hauled me to him and the redhead and the crone held onto his back as everything around us faded like it did that night on the balcony.

"DRAVEN!" I screamed and was still screaming his name when we re-emerged in another room. I tried to pull away from Malphas but he grabbed me by the top of my arm and swung me round before pushing me back onto another stone altar.

"NO! GET OFF ME...DRAVEN!" I shouted out until my voice was cracked and sore but I couldn't stop. He had to hear me and even when I was backhanded by Malphas to keep quiet, I still carried on.

"Gag her!" He snapped and the old hag came at me smiling. Malphas wrenched my hands up and I tried to fight him but he was too strong. I found myself being tied by all three of them and then a left over piece of rope was forced in my mouth and tied behind my head.

"We don't have long before they find us. Get the ritual started while I summon more of my legions here!" He barked out an order and I watched him walk over to a pool of water that ran down the centre of the room in a long rectangle. I took this opportunity to look around to see where we were this time.

It looked like some long grand ballroom that had high ceilings which were all made from rust coloured bricks with glass panels at the top and they curved round slightly where they met the flat glass roof. Four massive chandeliers hung down in different sections of the room, each being made up from three tiers that were gradual wrought iron rings that cupped church pillar candles around each edge. The same style lamps were on the walls and the room glowed thanks to the reflection from all the glass above.

The long room had arched church doors at each end and the altar, I was now once again tied to, was cast sideways on a raised dais acting like a large bridge over the pool running down the room. I looked to my left and saw two other altars like mine in a row so there were three all side by side. The two women stood next to their own altar and I noticed the different moon cycles carved into them. They then each dropped their clothes to pool around their feet and climbed on to lay down on their stone slabs. I shuddered at the sight of the old hag's wrinkled body that was more fold after fold of baggy skin than that of a human body. It looked as though her skin was about to drop off her as if weighing too much to stay attached to her flesh and bones.

I looked to my right and saw Malphas stood in the body of water and he was chanting in a demonic voice that made the chandeliers shake. Wax dripped down and made a sizzle when the red hot drips landed in the water. I then felt the air change as if a storm was coming. I saw the water start to mist and then it turned to dirty grey then to tar black. It started to bubble and pop as though boiling as it turned to thick black goo. As one more word was spoken out like a command, heads started to emerge from the liquid in every available space the pool had and soon there were over fifty tar covered figures rising from the pool like a new race of soldiers from the depths of Hell.

I watched in horror as the black tar substance started to seep into their skin and morphed them into lava skinned men with smoothed rock masks and the same rock armoured plating covering all their vital body parts. Their faces were hidden under the cooling lava rock that was still steaming and it was as though the two halves the masks made up met in the middle and formed a large point like a tusk coming from the centre of their faces. The eyes were only seen as two points of fire and the rock around them glowed red as though flaming hot from contact.

The new born soldiers to this world stepped out of the pool and as soon as the last ones left the black goo, the pool instantly turned back to pure water that splashed down in a little wave, like the whole thing had never happened. Each man was now stood to attention, waiting for their master to command them. Malphas left them to wait and walked back over to the three of us to continue with his plans.

I knew what it would mean for the world if he completed the ritual and I knew that deep down I must do anything I could to stop that from happening. I was suddenly transported back to my past and I was once again sat in my basement cell looking at my only option to put an end to a situation that could result in my family's death in the form of a mirror. My reflection said it all as my tears fell onto the glass and I found myself gripping it tighter, waiting to hear the devil of my dreams. The sound of him entering the house was a starter gun firing and I dug the sharp edge into my flesh. I did it then and I can do it now. And like then…I had no other choice.

I frantically started rubbing my head and cheek on the side of the stone to get the gag to loosen and when it finally slipped out of my mouth I was thankful for the old woman's obvious arthritic bent fingers that did a lousy job in tying the knot at the back of my head. I spat the rope to one side and quickly got to work with my plan.

"Hey, asshole!" I called out trying to get his attention. I knew he was carrying a blade on him, so if I could somehow manage to get him over here close enough, maybe if I made him seething mad, then I could get him here to then thrust myself against it. I didn't know if it would work but I gathered the only reason he hadn't yet killed me was that he needed me alive.

He turned round and sneered at me and I knew I was going to have to try harder. I lifted myself up to test how much leeway I had and I found, thankfully, I wasn't tied down as tightly as before.

"Hey limp dick! I am talking to you!" I said hoping even Demons got pissy about the insinuation of a small penis. And from the looks of things I had hit my mark.

"Yeah, I saw you trying to give it to that slut bag but I was surprised she could even feel it with it being so small! Hey, are you sure this ritual is even going to work...'cause, I don't think your packing enough!" Oh shit, yeah, that did it. He looked barking mad now and stormed his way over to me. I watched as he pulled something strapped to the side of his leg and I didn't notice it before as it was black and camouflaged. I thought it would have been another blade but as he got closer I could make out what I was seeing.

"I know what you are trying to do and it won't work. But let me give you a little something to think about." He held up something that looked like a twisted dagger only it was charred black and made from wood not steel. I could tell someone had this carved from a thick branch and then mounted to the tarnished silver handle.

He held it up for me to see and his pale fingers looked like tissue paper against the smooth black wood.

"Do you know what this is?" He asked me and I didn't need to answer as my face said it all. Now he was the one smiling.

"This was made from the rubble left from a burning tree. I must say, he did do a very good job destroying the only substance strong enough to kill a Vampire King" I gasped as realisation hit.

"That was made from the tree Judas hung himself on?" I asked already knowing the truth. I remembered Draven telling me the story of how the only thing that could truly kill Lucius was being pierced in the heart by wood from the very tree he was tortured on.

"Ah, now this has certainly got your attention. I knew that night I came to Lucius' stronghold on the lake, of his affection for you but what I did not count on was your own affection for him. The way you drew comfort in his touch was a nice surprise and it means I will take even greater pleasure seeing your pain when I plunge this deep into his heart. I will be a God standing over his rotting corpse and you will be at my side as my Goddess."

"I would rather die!" I screamed at him but he just laughed.

"You will be by my side that is unless you want your lover dead!" I cried out at the thought.

"NO! You can't do that, no one can kill Draven."

"Ha, is that what you think? Then you are more foolish than I gave you credit for. I will be a GOD! There will be nothing I can't do." He finished, calmly walking back over to the old crone.

I hadn't had a chance at his dagger, he never even got close enough and now I was faced with Draven's life in the balance and me to be Malphas' bargaining tool in exchange. That thought alone was enough to have me frantically thinking of other ways to end my life. I couldn't let myself be used to bring on so much destruction. Too many lives were at stake and my life for the ones I loved and more was a small sacrifice to be made. I knew Draven would disagree but at this point saving everyone from the aftermath of some Demon on a big ass power trip to God status was more important than one human life.

I watched as he drew the blade from his back and it was the same one he'd used on me and the redhead earlier. He stood over the old naked baggy woman and held the knife high over her chest.

"I call forth the power of Hecate, represented in this body as the Old Crone and this side of the waning moon. Bring forth your wisdom, repose, death and the power of the underworld for with your blood becomes my own and the first key in freeing the Horned God is opened with this holy blade. I communicate with thee!" As soon as he had finished he held the blade to his lips, kissed it quick and then plunged it down into the old woman's throat releasing a blue glow before spilling her blood onto the altar. I watched as it drained down the sides and followed the groove of the waning moon symbol until it reached the bottom and then started to flow into the pool beneath her.

He then moved over to the redhead and lent down to smooth her hair back from her face before dropping his lips to hers. I bet the old lady would have been gutted if she'd seen she hadn't received the same treatment, I wanted to comment sarcastically but refrained.

"I call forth the power of Selene, represented in this body of the Mother and the ripeness of the full moon. Bring forth your fertility, sexuality, fulfilment, stability, power and life of the earth, for my seed planted in your womb will combine us as one and with your new blood life becomes the second key in freeing the Horned God with this holy blade. For this is our survival!" He then kissed the bloody blade again and plunged it down deep into her genitals, this time releasing a red glow. The sound of her howls echoed as the blood seeped away from her body into the grooves of the full circle representing the moon. As it did with the old crone, the blood flowed down the symbol until it reached the pool underneath.

Of course now I knew what was coming next as he left the dying Mother and came round to my side of the altar.

"And now it is time to bring the beating heart to our God and give him back his lost Maiden." He said, thick with emotion. He pushed my hair back but thankfully didn't kiss me like he did the redhead. Instead he closed his eyes and looked up to the full moon that was now high in the night sky and shining down at us through the glass roof. It looked like it was ringed with a yellow glow and I didn't know how but I felt it in my bones that this represented the power in this night.

"I thought you weren't going to kill me?" I asked both stalling for time and readying myself for the end.

"The mighty Horned God will take your heart and mend it like he could not do with his own Maiden. When she plunged this very knife into her heart she sealed his fate, now it is time for you to undo that fate and for him to heal that heart." He said proudly and then added quietly,

"We have waited a long time for you." And then he leant down to take in my scent before starting the very words I knew meant the end of not only my life but of every life. How could this be happening, why didn't the Gods put a stop to this! Was this how it was supposed to happen? Was this what the prophecy meant, when my death would mean the end of the world?! I did the only thing I had left, I screamed out the last name I ever wanted to utter past my lips.

"Draven!"

"I call forth the power of Artemis, represented in this body of the Maiden and the new beginning of the waxing moon."

"Draven!" I screamed again but my interruptions don't stop him.

"Bring forth your enchantment, inception, birth and youthful enthusiasm for your heart holds the power of the Heavens."

"Draven please!" I kept screaming his name but he didn't come... he had to come. He just had to!

"For with your blood becomes the third and final key in freeing the Horned God with this holy blade. Let it be used once more as it was that day to bring back life and take back the death. This, my mighty Lord, is for your love!"

"DRAVEN, I LOVE YOU!" I screamed out so loud before seeing the blade kissed for a last time and held above the heart that only one man would ever own. I waited like time was standing still for the pain and death to take me to a new place when something finally happened.

I heard the sound of screaming and this time it wasn't by me. I looked to the side and with blurry vision I saw soldiers moving quickly around like black flies in the mist of heated desert sands. And in the centre of it all I saw,

My dark hero...Draven.

He came for me.

He had finally found me and just before Malphas could finish the ritual, the blade was flying from his hand and blood was being sprayed over me from the stump that was now being cradled to Malphas' chest.

I looked up once my vision had cleared and I realised as I blinked rapidly that from the tears rolling down my cheeks, I had been crying as I waited for my death. Malphas staggered back and I turned my head to where the flying weapon had come from. I couldn't believe it when I saw Lucius stood up on the edge of the pool at the right height for his target and with his arm still held out on a throw.

Once Malphas had retreated further, Lucius finally looked at me and gave me a wink in his usual cocky manner. It made me feel like crying all over again, only this time in happiness. He then turned to engage in a fight with two soldiers that had run at him. I tried to follow the swiftness of his movements but it was too difficult given the sheer speed he was fighting. One minute there were two black bodies and the next they were on the ground melting back into the earth to the Hell they came from.

I looked around and saw the battle going on and the extreme chaos of it all. My breath caught when I saw Draven cutting his way through his enemies to get to me but his movements were more precise than Lucius' style of fighting. Where Lucius seemed to be more of a dirty fighter, Draven's movements were fluid. And, as if proving my point further, I watched as Lucius grabbed one body and rammed his forehead deep into the man's face, cracking his rock armour in two, revealing the hideousness underneath.

They had, without a doubt, been made from the pits of Hell and the power was still flowing freely through their veins. They looked like their skin had been ripped away to just show the tight muscle underneath that was still steaming like cooked flesh, both charred and burning, with hot coals for slanted eyes. Their lower jaws came up over their top lip with two fangs curved round back into their mouths.

This particular one spat what looked like lava at Lucius' head in a snarl but he dodged the stuff and pulled a throwing knife from his back and he threw it straight and true, hitting the soldier in the centre of its sickening face. It howled in pain but Lucius didn't give it much chance for revenge as he drew a sword and sliced him in two with a quick spin of his body.

After I could finally tear my eyes away from Draven and Lucius, who strangely, looked to be working as a pair, I could then see who else was here fighting. I was shocked to see Sophia, fighting her way through the hoard dressed in black leather trousers that had guns strapped to her thighs and a little cropped leather jacket that was crisscrossed with straps that held ammo and smaller blades. Her hair was loose and curls flew around her head like a halo as she spun round a heeled boot and did a round house kick before landing with one knee bent and the other length extended out. The reason for split legged landing became apparent when she used her curved blade to stab right up into one of the soldier's groin, who was approaching her from behind.

I then saw her nod to another Angel in my life and my heart stopped slightly at the sight. Vincent nodded back and I heard Sophia shouting,

"Catch!" to her brother before laughing heartily, when grabbing a soldier by the arm that had thrust his blade at her. She side stepped and used her strength to propel him towards Vincent. I couldn't believe he actually rolled his eyes before using his weapons to cut the man in four pieces with one rapid movement, bringing down his strange double edged swords in a V shape. His weapons were like two samurai swords connected side on together and instead of the handle being at the end, it was in the middle. So in effect he had four swords to play with and boy, did that man know how to use them.

I would have thought that Vincent's style of fighting would have been overshadowed by that of his brother but in this case I would have been wrong. Vincent was a pure killing machine and he made it look like there was no effort put in his incredible actions at all. Six soldiers all surrounded him and holding one of his double swords to span the length of his arm, he defended his body from three swords while bending backwards. He then slashed round with the flick of his wrist and slit the throats of three guys at his back before then coming back round to do the same with the front three. He then calmly stepped over bubbling dead bodies as they sank back into the ground and he walked away from the six guys he killed in less than ten seconds.

"Show off!" Sophia said to him before shooting one in the face up close and slicing down another with the sword she had in her other hand. Vincent started laughing whilst fighting another set of soldiers that were quickly left in pieces and found their way back to Hell.

"Brat!" Vincent said in retaliation and she gave him a pout before ramming her blade backwards into someone's gut, without giving the guy a glance.

"But you're a beautiful brat, my darling." Zagan said in a deep accented voice from behind her and then stood on the guy's upper body so that she could pull her blade from his chest cavity before then wrapping his arm round her waist and yanking her to his lips for a full, deep kiss. She pulled back, smiled and then shot another man in the head over his shoulder who was trying to creep up behind him.

"Thanks, sweet pea." He said before spinning round to run and, whipping his two scythes in a crossed motion took four guys down leaving them now without arms.

"Will you guys please stop killing loads at once, pretty soon there won't be anything left for me to play with!" Sophia said making Vincent roll his eyes and Zagan laugh before throwing one guy her way.

"A gift for you, my love." She grabbed his arm and swung round sending him off towards Vincent, who then dealt with him in a cutting manner.

"Hey, this is fun, like pass the parcel of body parts." She said but then Liessa appeared and pointed my way.

"Then I hope you enjoy your games because here comes another round to play with." I looked to my side and saw that now Malphas was stood in the pool being protected by his minions while he summoned more of Hell's soldiers, only this time, when heads start popping up, they didn't stop coming.

I arched up to watch as everyone finished with the last of the soldiers before coming to stand together. I could now see everyone stood waiting and watching as the army grew and grew. Liessa, Caspian and Ruto all stood together at the back, with Hakan and

Takeshi speaking with each other. Then there was Zagan, Sophia and Vincent stood in front of them. But there was no mistaking the two in charge, as Draven and Lucius stood side by side with their arms crossed over their large chests.

I counted ten against the hundreds that were growing and rising up, as if from a crypt, but not one of them looked worried, in fact, most looked excited. Sophia especially as she started to roll her neck as if getting ready for the gun fight...hers being the only gun.

"So which is it Luc, Budapest or Scotland?" Draven asked Lucius in a dry unimpressed tone and Lucius laughed.

"Forget Scotland Dom, that almost lost me a limb and your aim is shite, let's go with an old favourite and stick to Persia." Draven just nodded his agreement and it left me wondering what on earth they could mean.

"Ready?" Draven turned to the rest of them and everyone bowed except Sophia who instead shouted out,

"Oh Hell, yeah!" And I couldn't believe how calm everyone was in the face of such odds. Then I soon found out why.

"Now!" Draven and Lucius shouted at the same time and every one of my friends turned into their other forms and now the 'great army' didn't look so great.

Draven and Lucius were now a mass of glowing, pulsating power but they couldn't have looked further apart. Draven was stood with the essence of Heaven and Hell singing in his veins and his wings outstretched made him look like a dark Angel of Death waiting for the chance to steal souls. Lucius was now once again his right hand man and his direct line to the Devil himself. The skin stretched over the bones in his wings shook as if readying themselves for flight and his horned back turned round to face over his head as another weapon.

"Once you come up again, get to Keira and get her out of here." Draven said in his Demonic overlord voice that boomed over the noise of soldiers getting in their ranks. Lucius nodded then he stepped past Draven and looked back over his shoulder at him.

"Try to keep up old man." Lucius said to Draven before launching himself up in the air and as he was going up, Draven growled at his comment and started pounding into the ground until it opened from a mighty crack resembling the result of an earthquake more than from the hands of someone Draven's size.

I watched on in astonishment as the crack started to reveal Hell itself and Draven roared in the air like a wild beast before pounding down one last time, making it even bigger. Meanwhile Lucius was still hovering in the air above the chaos waiting for his cue and when he got it he took a nose dive straight into the abyss of Hell's fire. I couldn't help scream out when Draven sealed it closed and the two fighting forces all ran to meet each other in the middle.

I tried to make some sense of what just happened and why Lucius had just taken a trip back home to Hell, when the clashing of weapons and the shrieks of death cries pierced the air and stole my focus. I watched Ruto shoot up into the air with his metal wings and send a raining hail of small daggers into the rock clad bodies below and some found home enough for the first of the bodies to start dropping.

Liessa was leaking from every pore in her body a deadly ink that meant every touch she received sent men dying at her feet. She had no weapons herself so when any blades were pointed her way, she simply shot that ink from her neck and she watched as her enemies fell.

Hakan stormed past her like some masked villain and was unravelling the wire from his body. It started to glow like a heated coil element on a stove. He tested it in his hand and when steam rose from his palm he seemed happy. He used it as a whip and snapped it out, cutting a whole line of soldiers clean in half and their armour was still smoking from the contact. It flew back at him with a little flick and curled back round him like a snake before Hakan stepped aside to let Caspian come barrelling through now in his other form.

I couldn't believe what I was actually seeing and even though I was surrounded by the impossible, as I lay witness to this supernatural battle, I still found enough shock left to see Caspian had now turned into a bloody Minotaur! He put his head down and started knocking down the soldiers like pins from a bowling ball. He butted his head from side to side and his massive bull's head sent a few flying thanks to gigantic horns.

Just when I thought it wasn't possible to witness any more power, the earth beneath the room started to tremble and this time I actually thought it was an earthquake that had hit us.

"I am waiting, Luc!" Draven shouted as if he was getting bored and I wondered what he was waiting for. Then the sound of pounding was reversed and the world seemed to split upwards coming from only one place...Hell.

"Hey Bro, sounds like Hell's a'knocking." Sophia said as she came up next to Draven in her other form also. The sight of Sophia as the Demon she is, was always a shocker but this time I got to see her in action and soon one thing became very clear…Sophia made one kick ass Demon!

As her other self, Sophia looked like she had been taken over by a desert storm and frozen in time as a baked sand girl. Her lips were cut high up her cheek bones and even now her sadistic grin gave me shivers. But the power that came from her was a sight to see. She stood in front of the others and created a sand tunnel from her body and then sent it crashing into the centre, forcing the ranks to split ready for an eruption from below.

Lucius then burst through the floor and left an opening the same length as the pool and just as wide. Each side was now packed with soldiers all crushed tightly together and Draven used this to his advantage.

"Enough! Vincent, its time you and I send these bastards packing." Draven said motioning for his brother to come forward. The sight of Vincent in all his Angelic glory was almost too painful it was so beautiful. Almost like looking into Heaven itself. He was glowing white and his full wings were so white and pure they looked like they were hand woven by a Goddess. Holy shit, he was pure perfection and utterly stunning to watch.

"I hope Luc's not right and your aim hasn't gone to shit brother." Vincent commented making Draven growl at him. Vincent just laughed it off and slapped him on the back in jest.

"We shall see won't we…? Ready?" Draven said in a voice like gravel.

"Always!" Vincent replied and they both separated to stand ahead of the struggling soldiers while the rest of the gang kept them from spilling forward.

They both looked up to the Heavens and held out their arms and wings waiting for something to happen. Then the sky above lit up the night and the storm hit with the mighty force of the Gods. The lightening travelled down and I screamed as it hit each of them and the electrical current was now being manipulated by the bodies they had entered. They both nodded once to each other and then let go of their new power, letting off streams of lightening towards their side of the soldiers. At the last second the others moved out of their way and it shot forward at such a rate that it was like a flash bomb going off blinding me for a few seconds. Once I opened my eyes again I was expecting to see hundreds of charred bodies but what I saw took me a while to comprehend.

The newly released energy had caused two walls being fed from the hands of two men I loved. Vincent's face was an impassive blank wall that looked like he could take or leave what was happening. Draven was frowning but definitely not from over exertion, more from annoyance at having to deal with this inconvenience.

"My army is waiting, my Lord." Lucius said, coming down in the middle of Vincent and Draven from flying to keep out of their way.

"Good to know." Draven said and then looked to his brother.

"You heard him, Brother." Draven waited for Vincent to acknowledge him and when they both nodded twice, the electrical walls started to close in on the soldiering hoard. It pushed them all together and they ended up with nowhere to go but into the deep crater with one destination. As the first line started going in, hands made of lava started to grab the soldiers by any means and some fought to scrabble away but it was useless.

As soon as the last man was back in Hell, the gateway to the underworld started to close with hands still making desperate grabs at the air hoping for some more limbs to find and drag back down with them.

"That should keep most of them busy so that they cannot be re-summoned. If Malphas keeps his legions coming at least my own army will slow him down as the fight continues beneath us." Lucius said to Draven.

"You've done well. Get to Keira and get her out of here while I deal with Malphas. I don't want her to see what I have in store for him." Draven replied and looked at me. Once he had scanned my body, he seemed to calm. I gathered that he was checking me for injuries and was satisfied when he found me in one piece. I whispered his name and he nodded to me in silent communication that he'd heard me.

"You need to drop your shields around her for me to get through, Dom." At that Draven looked around me and concentrated like he was trying to pull some unseen force back to him. Once the frown line disappeared from his forehead, he turned to Lucius and said,

"It is done. Go." Lucius made to leave but Draven grabbed him back by the arm and stopped him in his tracks.

"Be careful where you touch her Lucius... never forget that she is MINE." Draven growled out the word 'mine' in his demonic voice and I jolted at the sound of its echo. Lucius looked down at the arm holding him and snarled. Oh no, that's last thing I wanted now was these two fighting when they had just been working together for the first time in over sixty years.

Draven let him go and Lucius shrugged his tight leather jacket back straight before striding over to me still lying on this bloody altar like a slab of meat in a butchers shop!

"Hey little Keira girl, nice dress." He commented with glowing red eyes and now I was growling at him.

"That's cute doll, but it's time for me and you to blow this joint, I would opt for dancing at my club but your boyfriend kind of trashed the place." He said making my mouth drop...he trashed it?

Lucius gave me a cocky grin before whipping out a blade from behind his back and proceeded to cut through the ropes with little effort. I lowered my arms and moaned as my muscles protested making Lucius tut at me.

"You need to get more kinky action in the bedroom if you're just moaning after that...what's wrong, Draven not cutting it in the bedroom department?" Lucius said with a wink and I shook my head at him.

"Well, I am out of practice as I have been holed up with right wanker for the last ten days...you might know him, massive ego... kind of alright with a blade." He laughed before he pulled me up to a sitting position and lifted me down from the altar.

"Last I heard, this ego saved your life I don't know how many times, isn't that right?"

"Umm, he might have, but it's all a little fuzzy round the edges, you might have to ask me when I haven't just been nearly sacrificed... call me crazy but a girl needs a cuppa after shit like that." This time he threw his head back and laughed harder. I couldn't believe that after everything that had just happened I was now stood here, while the battle carried on and was laughing and joking with Lucius like best mates do.

"Hold on sweetheart, time to take you for a test drive." He said referring to his wings and I was amazed that even with Lucius in his other form he didn't scare me anymore and like this it was still easy to see the Lucius underneath the mask Hell had knighted him with.

Lucius turned round and motioned for me to climb on his back but I saw something flash quickly in the corner of my eye. I turned to face it and then everything happened so fast it was hard to think through the actions before instinct took over. Malphas had jumped onto the next altar and was stood over the redhead's body and just as I screamed

Lucius' name I was too late to stop what was happening any other way.

Malphas leapt in the air above us and was crashing down just as Lucius was turning to face him. I saw what was in his hand and knew I had to stop him. Without thinking I pushed Lucius with all my might and jumped in his place to take the end of the weapon Malphas had pointing down.

"KEIRA, NO!" I heard Draven's call before I felt the pain and I looked down in shock as I saw the reason for his cry. I fell forward over the stone altar and looked up to watch as my blood gushed from my pumping heart. The sight of the wooden dagger protruding from my chest was enough to realise my sacrifice had been enough to save the life of my Vampire friend but not the rest of the world. I slumped down off the stone to the floor and watched in horror as my blood made the same journey as the other two and it slipped down either side of the waxing moon and dripped into the bloody pool below three dying bodies. My last thought before I let the pain take me to unconsciousness was...

*What had I done?*

# CHAPTER 47

# THE GOD'S WRATH

I opened my eyes and saw myself as I had once before. I stood on the side lines of a Temple wall, all white marble, glass and stone. I looked around and saw the faces that I now knew to be my friends. They were all dressed in combat gear and ready for the battle to come. But something was wrong in this dream, it wasn't like before. Last time I was here I was stood in the middle of the room dressed in white and bleeding from my chest. I started walking down the centre and I was screaming at myself to stop but this time was different, this time… I was dead.

I looked down at myself and saw I was wearing the same pyjamas and with my hair plaited to one side as I did that night. It was just after I had found out from Draven when he first knew about me, the night I was born when Pythia the Oracle told him his time to claim the Chosen was coming.

I saw the utter horror on everyone's faces and for the first time I saw Sophia crying. She had her face buried in Zagan's shoulder and was sobbing but apart from her, no one else was making a noise. I looked and found an army at a standstill as if waiting for something to happen. Then I followed every gaze and I knew what I would see. There I was in my white dress that was now soaked crimson, with a knife only intended for Lucius, protruding from my heart.

I cried out but I was the only one who heard my haunting echoes. So this was it then, I was now dead and this was where my Afterlife began. I didn't try and stop my feet as I walked toward myself at the stone altar that was now glowing green and as I neared, I knew it was coming from my heart's Chakra. I don't know how I knew this but I was just bombarded with the knowledge that I had never known before. I also now knew it was the same powerful Chakras that had come from the other two deaths. Blue communication from the age of the world, red survival from the mother of the earth, yellow power from the moon's Heaven and now my green for the love in my heart. The ritual was complete and now the Horned God would come.

I made my way up to the altar and then the sound hit me as if someone had flicked a switch. Draven was speaking to me softly in another language and Lucius had bloody tears streaming down his face as he swore and cursed me for saving his own life. Then Draven gathered me up in his arms and laid me down so gently on the altar, it was as though I was made from thin sheets of ice, I looked so pale.

"Keira...Keira, hear me, you will not leave me, do you hear me?!" He spoke over me but it was clear as my skin that I was not there anymore. I cried out for him in desperation but no one heard me...of course they didn't. I was dead.

"Keira, come now, wake up...you...you're not gone Keira, you're still with me...stay with me." His voice was so fraught with pain I couldn't bear to hear him like this.

"Sweetheart..." He whispered and I heard Lucius swear behind me.

"DOM, listen to me! We need to do something and NOW!" Lucius was frantic and I turned to see him pummel his fist into the side of one of the altars and half of it crumbled into the pool below letting the redheaded corpse's legs dangle down.

"Keira wake up my darling...Keira pleaseee!" He lay his head to my forehead but there was no movement from me at all. I then turned to see that Malphas' body was floating on top of the bloody water with his own heart missing. I looked to Draven's hand and saw it bloody up to his forearm, so it didn't take a whole lot of thought process to know what had happened, especially with the discarded heart that had been smashed to the floor.

"DRAVEN!" Lucius screamed and then Draven looked up from my face and started to glow once more, only this time there wasn't an inch of him that was purple, it was now just red and being fuelled from Hell.

"KEIRA WAKE UP! YOU WILL NOT LEAVE ME! EVER...DO YOU HEAR ME...EVER!" He reared his head up and roared causing the room to shake but just before his fury could get out of hand he was pushed away from me by Vincent, who I hadn't seen emerge. He looked down at me and from this angle I saw a single stray tear roll down and land on my lips. I inhaled sharply as I felt it touch me like a kiss from Heaven but it didn't make any difference to the lifeless me that was as still as the stone I lay on.

"She is holding on brother but there is little time before the pull of Heaven calls her. I have bought you some more but you must hurry. She needs the blood of royal blood and it cannot be mine and yours for we are related and yours alone will not be strong enough."

"Then what?" Draven screamed at his brother but Vincent wasn't looking at him, he was looking at Lucius.

"Come here son of Lucifer and kneel before your King, for he has a gift to bestow on you." Vincent said and motioned to Draven, who looked stunned.

"What!?"

"What!?" Both Draven and Lucius said at the same time but Vincent just crossed his arms over his chest and his wings erupted into blinding white light.

"NOW!" Vincent shouted and it was the first time in my life that I had seen him lose his cool. But it worked and now Lucius walked over to Draven and dropped to his knees to then bow his head.

"My Lord." I knew at this point that what I was seeing was something as old as Lucius' time as a Vampire. This was the very first act of loyalty that had happened all those years ago. Draven placed his hand on top of his head and said in a commanding voice,

"Do you give your life to me as you once did?"

"Yes My Lord, take my life and use it as you will, for the good of mankind and the balance in which we keep. My blood is yours." Lucius said and I saw another blood tear drop from Lucius as Draven inhaled sharply.

"Then be my brother once more and rise to accept your rightful place." Lucius rose from his knees in a graceful manner and waited before his King.

"Time is not on our side but what I am about to do is for the woman I love. Do not fail me with this added power, Lucius."

"No, My Lord." Lucius looked as if he didn't have a clue what would happen and Draven then surprised everyone except Vincent as he spun Lucius round violently and pushed him to his knees.

"Draven?" Lucius said uncertainly.

"Shut up Luc and take it like the Gods have chosen you to!" Then Draven reached behind his back and at the top of his spine, hidden under the feathers of his wings, he dug deep, winced and made a hissing noise before producing a bloody metal triangle in his hands. Lucius couldn't see what he was doing but he was shaking in anticipation. Did he think he was going to receive his punishment from his executioner or did he understand that Draven now held the tip that pierced the side of Jesus Christ. I could see it glowing in Draven's hand and then with his free hand on Lucius' shoulder to keep him steady, he plunged the tip deep into his back in the same place Draven had had it hidden.

Lucius cried out and Draven held him steady and wrapped his arm around his neck in a choking hold. He rested his head on Lucius' shoulder and then turned to his ear and said,

"How's my aim this time, asshole!" Vincent started laughing behind me and I turned to see him watching this play out like he knew all along this was the way things were going to happen. Then Lucius started to violently shake and Draven held him tighter to his chest.

"Easy, just let it happen Luc, take control of it and let it happen…I need you in this." He whispered soothingly and I watched as Draven held him steady as he started to convulse beneath his arms.

"He is near, Dom." Vincent warned and I held my breath as I witnessed the transformation in Lucius.

"NOW!" Vincent called out suddenly and Draven let go and flew backwards just as Lucius erupted up from his knees and into the air as if being held there by some unseen force. His body went taut as a bow and all his muscles turned so tense they looked as if they would burst the skin. His wings started shaking in quick vibrations. Then something started to change and the air around him became lighter and lighter until it started to seep into him and glow within his very veins like Draven's did. The brightness dimmed slightly as his body took on the last of it into him and it warped his blood into pumping a new kind of energy. I watched as it made its journey around his body and when it reached his back, he screamed out in pain. His wings stopped suddenly and then the most incredible thing happened.

I watched in utter amazement as feathers started to emerge from the skin over his long boned fingers that connected his wings together. The first wave of feathers were white tipped and they flowed to the ends as the first lot found home, then as the waves continued they began to change in colour. They became pale yellow to rust and then in the centre of his back the last of the feathers emerged as blood red and he reminded me of a giant phoenix, the fire bird rising from the ashes.

"Keira...our child...come home, find your way." I heard the voice in my head but something told me to ignore it and I even batted around my head as though it could touch me. I looked back to Lucius and tried to phase out the voices by concentrating back on what was happening.

As soon as the last of his new feathers had come through he shook like a ruffled bird and then came back down to the ground. He rolled his shoulders and I noticed the flash of his horns were now more gleaming white and tipped at the edges with gold. His muscular frame looked slightly bigger, putting him at the same size as Draven. His hair had gone from looking sandy to a more golden colour, lighter like Vincent's and his eyes were still red but now they were deeper with swirls of yellow ochre at the centres, making it seem as if looking into flames and glowing embers. They were wholly mesmerising.

"I am ready, my King!" Lucius' voice had also gone a tone deeper and the natural dominance in his voice had gone one step further.

"Yes, and now you are my King of great alliance." Draven replied and then looked toward Vincent who had not moved from my bloody body.

"The time is now or never, Dom. The Heavens are starting to reach out to her." Draven's and Lucius' heads shot round to my body at the same time and both were at my side in a heartbeat...well for them not me. Wow, even dead I managed to keep my sense of humour, I thought weakly.

"Do you have any idea what will happen to her if we do this?" Lucius asked but Draven growled.

"I don't care as long as it brings her back to me! On three, Luc." They each grabbed the other's arm and held them connected over my open chest. Draven ripped the wooden blade from my chest and threw it away angrily. Then he motioned to Vincent who drew a large sword from his feathers and it gleamed like Excalibur. It looked to be made from solid silver and the handle from solid gold and in the hands of this Heavenly Angel it looked the most fitting weapon for him. He didn't look up or take his eyes from my face as he leant over, kissed my forehead and then said in a voice heavy with an emotional turmoil I was shocked to hear,

"Bring her back to us, Brothers!"

"One, two, three!" And then on Draven's three, Vincent slit across their joined arms in one single swift motion that left them bleeding into the hole in my chest. As soon as the first drop of their combined blood hit my organ, I doubled over and grabbed my chest as a pain shot through the centre of me like someone lighting me up from the inside. Then I looked down and saw my body start to flicker just like it did all those times I was sent back to Draven in my dreams.

"It's not working!" Draven cried out and looked to Vincent for guidance.

"Give it time." Vincent said and once more opened up the veins with a slice of his sword. I winced as the healing skin on their forearms was reopened and then I felt the pain again shoot through me at a greater force this time.

"Time is not something we have left gentlemen...look." Lucius said and nodded to where Malphas' body was floating on the surface. My hands flew to my mouth when I saw his eyes flicker open and what was once a white mist was now consumed with darkness as black as the bloody water had turned. He rose out of the water with his back still straight and his arms still at his sides. It was as though invisible hands had lifted him and when he was upright, he looked straight to Draven.

"YOU DARE TRY TO DEFEAT A GOD!" The voice that came from him flew out with a great gust of wind that knocked the three winged men from my body and sent them crashing into the other side of the room. The walls cracked under them and each groaned as they got up. Lucius shook his head to displace the stone from his horns and Vincent ruffled his feathers from the debris. Draven was the only one who had been harder to knock down as he now stood at the ready.

I looked back at the source of such power and I was no longer met with the picture of a pale slim Malphas, no, now he was changing... now he was becoming a... God.

"NO!" I screamed but no one could see me, let alone hear me. I ran over to my still body on the altar and took hold of my shoulders and started to shake myself in desperation.

"DO SOMETHING! WAKE UP AND STOP THIS!" I screamed at myself. I didn't know if I could stop this but I had to try. I knew I had to do something to put an end to the madness I had helped create. I slapped myself hard on the face and felt the effect of it as my head whipped to the side. So I could feel but my body couldn't. I needed to join the two, I needed to find my way back somehow!

"DAMN IT! PLEASE...I DON'T KNOW WHAT TO DO! I don't...I don't know what to do anymore!" I started sobbing onto my bloody chest as I heard the chaos of the battle around me. I heard Draven shouting orders and I looked to the side to see Vincent calling forth his armies from the Heaven. I saw the earth splitting in two and Lucius trying to command his armies in Hell to stop the legions coming through the black swirl of a portal. I saw the world as I knew it falling to the ground and coming to an end. I had to stop this...I just had to!

"I am praying for you to hear my pleas for help, take my life, I give it to the Gods freely but before you do, please give me the power to stop this! I beg of the Gods! I pray to the Gods! I give my life to the GODS!" I screamed to the Heavens and with one last cry out, I let my tears drip down and when one single drop landed on my still heart I felt my answer in an explosion from the Gods!

I looked up and saw the brightest light that was a tranquillity hidden behind a blinding glow. I looked down at my body that had turned grey and knew my time here had come to an end. I got up and started to run as fast as I knew how towards the light at the end of the room. I ran past the sight of soldiers falling, the piercing battle cries of Angels and Demons fighting for the earth... and I ran until my last breath was taken as the sight of Heaven took me into its arms and swallowed me whole.


HEAVEN


I opened my eyes and looked down at myself to see I was back in my body but this time I wasn't alone.

"Fear not my child, as we become one." I heard a voice in my head and it sang and floated like a musical echo in my mind. It made my body tingle and the sight of myself like this was like being reborn into a new body but taking with me my old soul.

"Who are you?" I said out loud but I realised I was wrong before. Her voice wasn't in my head, my voice was now in hers! She was the one in control of this body and I was just along for the ride.

"I am the Goddess in you, awakened by the blood of those who love you." She said sweetly and the comfort she brought was like a mother's kiss. Then my body sat up and it was a covered in a radiant luminosity that shimmered with every movement. I moved my arm, although it wasn't me in control, a stream of blue energy was left in its place and stayed in the air until it dispersed like smoke.

"How is this happening?" I asked and I felt the Goddess inside me smile.

"The power of the two Kings and royal bloodline brought me forth to heal you but I think I can do more than that while I am here." We got up from the altar as one and I heard Draven scream out my name in disbelief. I tried to turn towards him but she wouldn't let me.

"I want to go to him!" I shouted, but she just laughed sweetly.

"In time Electus, in time, but first let us put an end to this stolen power." She said after turning to let me see Draven fighting the masses of soldiers trying to force their way out of Hell to aid their master. She turned us back round to see the Horned God had now completed his transformation and there was very little left of Malphas to see.

The Horned God stood at about ten feet tall and was about the size of five Ragnar's put together. His bare muscled chest and arms were metres wide and his thick skin was like tree bark with slashes cut into the folds of his arms and cut of his muscles. His chest cavity was open and bones were broken outwards with a gaping hole that suggested no heart lay there. In one hand he wore a man's skull as a boned glove and the other was fused to a hammer weapon that was spiked wood coated in a sticky substance like tree sap. It glistened and when he forced it down to the ground the crack to Hell widened and allowed more men to come flowing over the edges like a wave of black insects the size of men.

His legs were hidden under a leather skirt made from skinned bodies sewn together and held in place by a massive horned skull that matched his repulsive face. His head was all bone, like that of a sun bleached desert skull, sand blasted and smoothed until it reached to two ridged, winged bones that framed each side of his head. These connected to the three pointed horns that nearly met high above his head. The hollow of his eyes looked like black pits of eternity and in his open snarling mouth only a top row of teeth remained, like enlarged human ones only without the protection of gums.

As soon as we approached, his head shot up like someone blew a whistle at him. I shuddered in fear hidden deep within my body but the Goddess remained strong and soothed my fears from the inside.

"Have no fear my young one, for I am with you." I felt the warmth arise in me as our entwined body erupted into blue flames sent straight from the powers of Heaven. The Horned God saw this and brought his chest forward and his arms back as he roared at the night sky before knocking three bodies back with his hammer. I screamed as I saw Ruto, Hakan and Caspian go flying backwards into the wall. On a scream the raging God stood on the other side of the pool waiting for my tiny self to attack. I knew I should have faith in the Goddess in me but given the size difference it was hard to see what strength we had against such a being.

"Faith is always the mightiest of weapons, child." She said with certainty and I knew she was right. I had called for the help of Heaven because I believed they could help and now I needed to reinforce that faith and in essence that power.

"Let's kick ass!" I said to her and she started laughing before she nodded our head.

"Let's protect those that you love first before I unleash Heaven's will on the beast of my brothers and sisters." She turned from the God and held out our arms to the fighting forces of good and evil. She then clapped our hands together in a straight line in front of us and then started to part them slowly, forcing the fight to stop and the bodies of those I cared about to part. They were then pushed back to the walls, which unbelievably were still standing, and held them captive so that they couldn't move.

"KEIRA!" Draven called as he watched immobilised and helpless to get to me, as he had been trying to.

"I ask for assistance in protecting thy soldiers of the Kings' balance and aid in keeping them safe." She looked up to the Heavens and the sky lit up with shimmering Aurora Borealis before floating down through the glass and building a wall of protection in between the ten bodies that had fought Hell's escaped hoards.

"Thank you my sisters." We turned back around and found the Horned God had been raising Hell's warriors all armed and ready to fight but they couldn't get past the protective wall and I let out a sigh of relief.

"You are not welcome in this realm. You were cast down and punished where you have become lost in the abyss of grief. The world you knew is not yours to control anymore."

"YOU WILL NOT STOP ME!" It roared in response and then lifted his hands upwards to start raising the deep buried earth upwards through the ruined marble floor. Flaming tree roots burst out and came stretching out towards us in an attempt to capture us in a scorching hold. But the goddess hardly moved and with little effort held out her hand that froze the roots mid-flight and doused their flames into ice that travelled down their lengths until it reached the source of the tree and it then exploded like glass. When the shards hit the floor, they became puddled water that sank back into the exposed earth.

"The earth you control has turned against you, now release your dying host and go back to the prison from which you came."

"NEVER!" It thundered and with a resounding nod the Goddess whispered a,

"Very well," before she jumped us down from the bridged altars and landed into the black pool that was moving around like sea serpents. She placed our hands in the pool and I screeched out as I felt it singe my skin.

"In nomine Patris et Filii et Spiritus Sancti. Emitte Spiritum tuum et creabuntur et benedic Deo aquam manibus. Amen." ('In the name of the father, and the Son, and the Holy Spirit. Send forth thy Spirit and they shall be created and bless this water by God's hands. Amen.' In Latin) As soon as the last word of the prayer had been uttered, the water started to bubble cool around us before turning the water crystal clear. Then she stood us upright and the blessed water lapped at our bare legs as if getting ready. She then faced the holy beast, raised up our arms and pounded our fisted hands together at the sides.

"I INVOKE THY PUNISHMENT ON TO YOU AND ASK THE MIGHTY GODS ABOVE TO BLESS MY JUDGEMENT IN CASTING YOU BACK TO THE UNDERWORLD, FOR YOUR PRISON AWAITS YOU ONCE MORE!" The voice that came out of me didn't belong to the sing song voice of a sweet Goddess but now that of a thundering God in all its holy wrath. The room shook like never before and the glass panels above and around smashed all at once like a holy bomb had detonated. The glass rained down and the walls crumbled outwards. I felt myself flinch inside but the deity that held my body captive didn't move a muscle as the glass came to an impossible stop above our heads.

Then a voice entered my head as if the Goddess knew I needed to be reassured. It was the voice of Lucius and I couldn't help but find comfort in it.

"The only thing that can destroy a God, Keira... is another God." I held onto those words and heard the Goddess inside me praise my decision to hold such faith in her and I believed this was what made her greater power possible. She needed my belief in her for her to really cast the God back to the depths of where he belonged.

"Then it will be Electus, my daughter." She said softly before she held one hand up to waist height and then brought it up in a great whoosh making the pool of water between us and the Horned God fly upwards like a gravity defying waterfall. The wall of water served a greater purpose as every single shard of glass shot forward through the great mass of holy water before getting to the other side and finding home inside the beast.

The raging God boomed his cries of pain and the water dropped around us, soaking me and my Goddess friend. I looked towards the bellowing of pain as the God fought with the smoking glass that was burrowing its way into his body and the bright lights shone from the gaps every piece left behind. It looked as if the light was filling him to the brim and his body could not contain it for long. The skull on his waist cracked at the same time as that of his head and with one last cry the body burst sending pieces of him around the broken room.

With their leader destroyed the legions of Malphas had no one to lead them, so they all halted and stood to attention awaiting their new master to come forth. The protective wall sheltering the good side was dropped and I saw Draven flying over to me in a panicked speed.

"KEIRA!"

"Draven" I said only it didn't reach my lips. The Goddess held out our arm to stop him as he landed and when he didn't heed her warning he dropped to his knees and couldn't move.

"Leave her body!" He demanded and I couldn't believe he was speaking to a God this way!

"She gave her body as a sacrifice for the Gods to intervene, she is ours to do with as we please, Son of mine." Holy shit! Was this for real, was she really who I thought she was?

"Mother, please...I..."

"Silence my child. As I said, she is ours to do with as we please and what would please me, is for my own flesh to be her guardian as was always intended to be. She belongs to you my son and such are my reasons for coming myself, so that it would be ensured. Take good care of her, blood of mine." Draven bowed his head in deep respect and kissed his palms before holding them out to the Goddess, which just so happened to be his mother!

"With all my heart and every breath I take, it is done." She nodded our head, kissed our own palms and then placed them in Draven's hands. As soon as our skin made contact, I felt her leave me on a parting message that soothed my soul to its core. I felt every last drop of energy leave me with a bang and I fell forward into the arms of Draven...

*The only place I ever wanted to be.*

# CHAPTER 48
# COMMANDING THE LEGIONS

"Take care of his heart, for my son will protect yours with every beat of his." Her voice echoed in my mind and when I felt it fade, I knew she had left me. Well that was one thing in this relationship I never thought I would receive and that was the blessing of Draven's mother.

"Keira! Keira open your eyes baby, come on now." Draven's voice surrounded me in the nicest way possible and it felt as comforting as my own heartbeat, which I was happy to report, was beating just fine.

"Draven!" I croaked and heard him inhale a sharp breath before I felt his arms crush me to him. I felt cold and wet but I wouldn't have cared as long as I had Draven with me, I couldn't have given a damn about my discomfort.

"Oh Thank the Gods!" He said into my hair and I couldn't stop my little laugh. I pulled back and looked up into his battle fought handsome face and said,

"Don't you mean 'Thank your Mother'?" The smile he gave me warmed me from the inside and I found I was no longer cold.

"Yes, I guess I do. Oh Keira, don't ever do that to me again! Do you realise what nearly happened! You nearly left me...me! How could you, I won't let that happen, not ever again do you hear me! I..."

"Hey, Stop. I would not be the person you loved, if I let my friend die." I interrupted him and he looked like he wanted to argue more when one of my words hit him.

"Friend?"

"Yes. I am sorry Draven but yes, Lucius is my friend and he saved my life. I would never have let him die if I could have prevented it... not again." I added quietly referring to the first time he died and before Draven thought to fly into a rage something in his head must have clicked and he let my comments slide. He simply nodded before burying his head in my neck and kissing me there. I hummed in pleasure and just as he was about to say something else, I could wait no longer. I grabbed his face and pulled his lips to mine in a searing kiss, deep enough to burn the memory of him to me.

My lips moulded to his and after the initial shock, he then took control and grabbed my face to hold me to him. He tilted my head and took the kiss to a deeper level still. I felt his taste mix with mine and my blood lit up and I didn't mean figuratively. I was now glowing a very faint blue colour and I looked like a dimmer version of the Goddess that took control of my body, in this case, Draven's mother... how weird was that!

I pulled back and he growled at me which I ignored due to my new state.

"Draven, I am glowing!" I held up my hands and he took them in his larger ones, engulfing my daintier ones.

"It will fade in time my love, don't fret."

"I'm not fretting, I think this is so cool! I look like a living nightlight! I will never trip up again on the way to the bathroom in the dark!" I said and with Draven staring at me like I had lost my marbles, I heard Vincent and Lucius start laughing over Draven's shoulder. He turned his head and started growling at them, making Lucius hold up his hands in defeat, while Vincent just smirked and then winked at me, making me blush.

Draven shifted his hold on me and then lifted me out of the pool I didn't realise we were still sat in. No wonder I was bloody cold.

"Keira!" I heard my name being called frantically and I smiled at the sound.

"Let her down so I can drown her again!" Sophia was barking mad and I frowned down at her. But her anger subsided as soon as it had arisen and she threw her arms around us both, splashing in the water as she did it. Draven grunted and I just giggled.

"Hi Sophia, did you miss me?"

"Don't you ever scare me like that again! I dread to think what could have happened if mum hadn't come and saved the day!" She said looking at Draven and Vincent in turn. Only she must have seen something in Vincent's face because she blurted out,

"You knew!" He just shrugged his shoulders at her and then said,

"If you talked to her more often then maybe you would have known she was watching out for these two." I gaped at him and I felt Draven tense around me.

"Yeah, but she just nags at me lately." Sophia moaned and Vincent huffed but then went to put his arm around her shoulders, dwarfing her with his size.

"You, my little sister, have been saying that for the last millennia." Then she huffed and elbowed him in the ribs.

"So, what are we going to do about these guys, 'cause I don't think I have enough bullets on me" We all look around to find the legions of Malphas' army all stood awaiting their new leader to well... lead.

"Dom, it must be done." Vincent said softly placing his hand on his shoulder and I soon found out why he was walking on eggshells.

"NO! She has endured too much, I will not put her through anymore and that is final!" Draven shouted and I saw a few people flinch.

"Wait! What do you mean, what do I need to do?" I asked, but Draven roared in fury and started to take me from the room. He jumped down effortlessly from the altars and landed amongst the rubble with an angry boom, causing the dust and debris to float around us in a cloud. I coughed it back and Draven had the decency to look sorry about letting his anger get the better of him.

"Draven put me down." I asked softly but he ignored me and was striding towards the broken exit.

"Draven," I warned but I was rewarded with a simple snarl.

"DOMINIC PUT ME DOWN RIGHT NOW!" I screamed making him come to an abrupt stop. He let go of my legs, letting half my body slip from his hold and I slid down his front.

"I don't want you doing this." He said but I just shook my head at him.

"I know," I whispered and then hugged him to me. I then took his hand and turned to pull him back to where Vincent and the rest of them stood, Draven in tow. I heard him grumble about stubborn women once or twice before we reached Vincent, who was looking amused. With his arms crossed over his large chest and wearing a plain white T-shirt, wings still out and set back slightly in a relaxed position, he looked like every image I ever thought an Angel Warrior would have looked...of course that was minus the ripped, stone washed Levis, he seemed to favour.

"What do I need to do?" I asked Vincent and I felt Draven's chest come to my back like a wall of muscle and looking at the two, it was like night and day. Vincent's easy going white light to Draven's black combat gear, dark features and scowling eyes, the two couldn't have been further apart.

Draven wrapped his arms around me and held me to him as if he needed the contact just as much as I did and I hummed at the pleasure of the feel of him. Vincent nodded towards the awaiting army and I felt Draven tense.

"As the Being that destroyed their leader and now, thanks to the royal blood that courses through your veins, they await for your command."

"WHAT!" I couldn't help shouting out and Draven's arms tightened.

"You don't have to do this Keira...she doesn't have to do this Vincent!" He first whispered to me gently and then shot his brother the same thing in a sterner voice.

"I am afraid there is little choice in the matter, she must either lead her army or she must bestow the command to someone else."

"Oooh, I opt for that one." I said, thinking I very much doubted it was going to be as easy as posting an ad on Gumtree. I turned my head up to Draven and gave him what I thought was my most dazzling smile but was most probably just a cheeky grin. He looked down at me and raised one eyebrow which had me raking in a breath as to how bloody sexy he was doing it.

"I know where your thoughts are headed love, but it cannot be me." I must have looked shocked because he frowned in usual Draven fashion.

"Why not?"

"Because it must be a person born from a Royal bloodline and seeing as your body is already host to my brother's blood, it will not accept him, or Lucius for that matter." My answer came from Vincent and when I turned back round, I found him closer to me looking down. It felt like being in a Draven sandwich and I quickly tried to bury that thought but my blush must have given me away because Vincent and Draven looked at each other and smirked.

"And you...? Don't you fancy a little army of your own?" I said as if trying to sell a second hand car with a clutch problem. One side of his lips curved in a mischievous little grin.

"Thank you for the thought Sugar, but not only do I have my own armies to command but I cannot lead those of the underworld." Ah, but of course he couldn't...I felt like smacking my head and shouting 'Well Durr!' He was an Angel and this army right here was straight from the realms of Hell.

"So who then?" I asked thinking this would have been so much easier if I could just go up to them and ask if they fancied taking early retirement but something told me they didn't have that option in Hell.

"My Lord, I would be honoured to join my own legions to those of the Queen's new army." Zagan came forward and knelt down to bow respectfully, causing his hood to cover more of his face.

"Hold up...the Queen's? Who is the...?"

"Good. Then it is done." Draven interrupted me and I knew it was on purpose.

"Keira, to do this you have to first address your men and then present them with your replacement before handing over the power to Zagan. Can you do this?" Vincent asked and I felt Draven harden behind me once again.

"I...I guess so." I said timidly not really relishing the idea of walking up to the mean looking bastards and saying 'hi', let along commanding them to accept a new master...email was so much easier I thought dryly as Vincent held out his hand for me to take.

At first I didn't think Draven was going to let me go and wondered why he wasn't the one taking me to them.

"She will be fine Dom, and you will be right here watching. I have her." Vincent said reassuringly and after another snarl from Draven he finally let me go and I felt cold walking away from him.

"Why isn't he coming?" I asked, once I had taken his hand and let him lead me away.

"Because he knows his presence at your side won't be recognised and they will see it as a threat to their leader." I shuddered at the thought of all these soldiers attacking Draven, although seeing the power in him and the way he fought was enough to know fighting Draven was never going to be an easy feat.

"Vincent, how did...?"

"I know you have questions Keira, you always do, but I promise I will explain soon. But right now I fear if I don't get you back to my brother soon, then this army will not survive his wrath... his patience will only stretch so far and I doubt even I could calm him this time." Vincent added, and I turned to see not only Zagan following behind but Draven looking so tense someone could have used him to prop up the roof!

I watched as the army of over fifty soldiers were stood to attention and I noticed that the portal to Hell had not yet been closed. The crater at the end of the room was wide open like a giant tear in the Earth's crust and as I neared, I couldn't believe what I was seeing. Was it possible?

"Vin...Vincent, that...that isn't what I think it is...is it?"

"Don't be afraid, this will most certainly be the last time that you see Hell and that of the Legions down there that are yours for the moment." I felt his hand go to my shoulder but as soon as he did the army ahead all raised their weapons at once and looked ready to attack. He dropped his hand immediately and they relaxed their weapons. I was starting to understand what he was saying.

"This is as far as I can go but when you are ready and have addressed them all, you can then hand over your control over to Zagan, he will tell you what needs to be done. Just call him when it is time."

"But what do I say to them?" I looked nervously to the dark force that was crazily now mine to control.

"Whatever you want to."

"So what, if I asked them all to drop their weapons and start doing the funky chicken dance they would do?" Vincent laughed along with a few others that could hear what I was saying...I think even Ruto was one of them.

"That would be a sight indeed, but I doubt you are cruel enough to inflict that torture on anyone...besides, I can't imagine they even know what that is... Hell, I don't even know." He said on a laugh and I joined him when I heard Sophia shout over,

"I can teach you!" He groaned and then winked at me before leaving me to face my army?

"I think I will pass." I heard Vincent comment dryly as he made his way back to his sister.

So now, here I was, stood at the edge of Hell and not only faced with the black clad men with horned masks carrying all sorts of deadly devices but I also had a bloody swarm of Hell's creatures all waiting below for me to jump. I could barely believe I was staring straight into Hell itself. It was like looking into the belly of a volcano and seeing wave after wave of soldiers glowing under the flames. I wondered just

550

how many men were in these legions because right now, it looked like thousands!

"Go on my Lady, say something to them." Zagan's voice brought me back from the fear and the only thing I could do was try and clear my throat.

"Em...umm...Hello all." I said and I whipped my head round when I heard a few sniggers.

"Silence!" Draven commanded and all noise ceased. He then nodded to me to continue and I gingerly looked back to the Demon hoard.

"Okay...let's try this, just to make sure someone has got this wrong and then the shit really does hit the fan...Army, place your weapons on the ground!" I shouted and like well-choreographed extras in a movie they all lowered their weapons and then stood back to attention awaiting their next order.

"How friggin cool is this!" I shouted in excitement. Okay, there was just one thing that I must do before handing them all over to Zagan and I knew I was nuts but really...who could resist.

"Okay...Army, I want you all to copy me and do this symbol in the air." I tried not to laugh but it would have been the hardest thing in the world to accomplish when I was now looking at row after row of a demon army all with their arms in the air doing the peace sign...and I didn't even need to say Simon says! Brilliant! Everyone laughed and when I looked round even Draven couldn't contain a grin. It was such a heart-warming moment and one that needed to be cherished. Every one of these Angels and Demons had combated and fought for not only their Kings but also in saving my life. And now, all dirtied and battled scarred, they were celebrating their victory the right way.

Liessa had her arms draped round her serious husband Caspian, who for once wasn't scowling, Ruto had lit up a cigarette and was passing it to Hakan for a drag, both were smiling. Takeshi had his hands hidden in the wide sleeves of his Japanese robe and his eyes twinkled in amusement. Vincent had his arm round Sophia and was ruffling her hair playfully after she had just stomped on his foot.

And then there were the two Kings. The heroes that once fought against each other but had now found an alliance once again. But that wasn't only it. I saw Lucius slap Draven on the back in a manly acceptance and both men were staring at me like I was the source of their renewed friendship...And after everything that had just happened, I gathered that I was. Draven gave me a head nod and a smile to say that he approved of my little joke and the smile I gave him back said my 'thank you'.

"Right time to get this over with...oh, you may put down your arms now." I jumped at the sound of everyone moving at once and then whispered a little 'right, okay then' before standing straight and looking serious.

"Army, as your leader I have decided to pass on my command to one worthy of your service. This is your new leader...umm... Commander Zagan?" I tested the name and heard him chuckle as he approached.

"I am actually a Prince of Hell, but commander will do fine, thank you my Lady." I blushed and he smiled down at me before shocking me and revealing his full face for the first time.

His trademark black hood was now hanging down his back and I gasped at the raw, twisted beauty of him. It was like he was made by light itself and his long, straight white hair hung down like silk. His eyes were like polished white quartz crystals with a thin black ring around both the iris and the pupil. They were the most incredible eyes I had ever seen other than Draven's purple ones and combined with his pale skin, he looked more like an Angel than a Demon. The startling contrast to the angry red scar that ran down one side of his face was even more prominent against his milk white skin and was only hidden slightly by the swirls and points of his tribal tattoo that ran the full length of his face and neck. No wonder Sophia fell hard for him...he was stunning!

He started talking in a different language and I remember hearing Draven speaking it occasionally which made me wonder if it was Persian as they were both from the same place. Once he had finished he then turned to English and I wondered if this was just for my benefit?

"I am Zāl, son of Sām and the grandson of Nariman, both of Royal blood and heroes of ancient Persia. I was reborn into this world as Zagan, Prince and President of Hell and command thirty-three legions within its depths. I take each and every one of you into my power and will accept your allegiance till your death." He then turned to me and gave me a sweet smile.

"My Lady, please give me your hands and release your hold of this army." I leaned in close and whispered,

"And how do I do that exactly?" He grinned at me and like Vincent often did, he winked at me.

"Trust me, I will do most of the work for you."

"Oh…okay then. I give you this army." I said loudly and placed my palms in his hands. He nodded his thanks and then his fingers curled round mine. He closed his incredible eyes and it began. I started glowing like someone had just plugged me in and I felt a tugging deep down inside of me. It was as if my energy was being sucked out and I watched as my blue glow travelled down my bare arms to my scarred wrists and through my hands that held on tightly to Zagan's paler ones.

"ENOUGH!" Just when I thought I would be passing out from the energy zap, I felt Draven come up behind us and he swiftly pulled Zagan from me, losing our connection and leaving me feeling like a drunk at the end of the night. He grabbed me to him and I could feel his tension seep away upon the contact.

"I have waited enough and it is time they went back to where they came from!" Draven shouted and his next action blew me away. He reached out his arm and with a simple movement he sent every last soldier crashing into the hole like ants. I saw them scrabbling to get out and readying themselves for the fight but before they got that chance Zagan was there giving them his orders and closing the entrance to Hell. It looked like some giant with a colossal needle and thread was sewing up the ground and pulling it tighter and tighter until it was sealed.

"Draven!" I called his name as I felt myself being hoisted up over his shoulder and my wet dress clung to his T-shirt.

"Ssshh, now it is my turn." He said and with a renewed determination walked us both to the entrance at the end, leaving the rubble behind us…

*Where it always belonged.*

# CHAPTER 49
# MOTHER OF OUR SINS

I must have fallen asleep on Draven at some point because when I woke up I was on a very comfy bed. I kept my eyes closed as I stretched out and as soon as I felt my naked body under a thick warm quilt my eyes flashed open.

"You're safe." Draven's voice cut through my surprise and I looked in the direction his voice had come from. I found him sat on a lounger seat in grey suede, with his body relaxed, leaning back and a hand covering the lower part of his face with his elbow resting on the armrest. He was looking at me with a fierce intensity and of course, I started to bite my lip.

"Are you okay?" I asked shyly, wondering why he was looking at me like he was going to take a bite right out of me. His finger tapped on his lips for quite a few seconds before he moved...and boy did he move. One minute he was in the chair and the next he was looming over me with my wrists pinned above me.

"I am now." He said before taking my lips in a brutal kiss. Was he trying to devour me? Well if not then he was doing a bloody good job pretending to...Jesus! With my heart pounding and my palms getting clammy from the fingers pressing into them, I was ready to start panting in his mouth. His tongue duelled with mine for dominance and I thought now this was my type of battle! His soft lips were definitely in charge as they kissed sucked and teased my senses into oblivion. He groaned in my mouth and then let my lip roll between his teeth and my toes actually curled.

"Fuck me, how I have missed that!" I gave him a cheeky grin and then bit at him which he dodged.

"Since when do you swear around me?" I teased.

"Since some bastard stole my girlfriend and took this delicious body away from me. N.E.V.E.R. A.G.A.I.N!" He bit his broken words down my neck, collar bone and to my breasts with little kisses and sucks in between.

"Oh God!" I moaned as my head arched back into the pillow. He chuckled around my flesh and then looked up at me making my breath catch. He looked pure primal.

"No, not God Keira, you don't want to see me jealous, now do you?" He said and I bit my lip again making him drag himself up to me suddenly.

"I believe that is mine." He growled and took my lip from me and started biting on it for himself.

"I am going to self- combust." I moaned again, closing my eyes at the feel of his hands sliding over my breasts as if trying to draw the life from me.

"Don't worry baby, I won't let you...not yet anyway." And as if to prove his point he dove down and took a hardened nipple into his mouth and worked me into a near frenzy. Just the power of this massive muscular mountain of a man over me like this was enough to make me want to explode and he hadn't even touched me down there yet.

"Draven." I hummed as his hands flowed down further and when they hit my rib cage his head whipped up and his eyes flashed purple. Oh shit, that was not a happy man, 'I'm feelin' the love purple', no, that was 'I am seething mad purple'...what had I done wrong this time?

"What the Hell is this!?" He shouted down at me before ripping the covers from me making me shriek out.

"Draven what are you doing!?"

"Silence!" He snapped back and I recoiled at his outrage until I saw his head lower to what he was looking at. Oops...I guess he didn't like the look of skinny Keira. His hands ran along my ribs that were now slightly sticking out and then down to a waist where there used to be a bit more padding...okay so a lot more padding. He inhaled sharply when he saw my pelvic bones raised and his fingertip gently tickled the bone unintentionally. I giggled and he snarled at me.

"This isn't fucking funny!" He snapped and I frowned.

"Well here's an idea caveman, don't bloody tickle me and you won't get an F'ing giggle!" I snapped back.

"Why the hell didn't you eat? You look half starved for God's sake!" He rolled off me and was quickly stood by the bed staring down at me as if he was looking at me for the first time. I angrily grabbed the covers and felt my cheeks go red at the embarrassment. This was not how I thought our first time together in a bedroom was going to go.

"Oh I am sorry, I kind of had other stuff on my mind, like watching Ragnar nearly getting killed, then watching Karmun getting killed, being kidnapped, getting pummelled in the face by some goon named Klaus, watching said goon getting himself killed by Lucius' command, going on a helicopter ride from Hell!..." I hadn't finished as I was now on my knees, naked on the bed poking him in the chest with every point and even though his face should have told me to stop, my filter wouldn't engage and I kept going.

"Nearly getting the life sucked out of me by some mountain mud monster, watching a bloody Video in HD for Christ sake, of my boyfriend giving it the big one to his ex..." I nodded to his manhood that, after this rant, was not stood to attention any longer but I still couldn't stop.

"Nearly getting kidnapped again by some ugly ass old bird and Miss redheaded preggers, and then being slashed at again by good old Layla that just can't help the shits and giggles it gives her by trying to kill me, nearly drowning in a God damn frozen lake, taken on a death ride in some ridiculously fast Lamborghini, what the Hell is it with you Royal asses and speed anyway?!" I didn't stop for my answer.

"Then being bitten by a sodding Imp before lighting up the VIP with my new aversion to flat screens and then after one of the best kisses of my life being...and I can't believe it, I really can't... kidnapped yet again and nearly sacrificed to resurrect a real life God, with not one ounce of dress sense and then, last but not least, after being stabbed dead, having my body taken over by none other than your Goddess mother! I mean Draven, can you imagine how embarrassing it is meeting someone who could one day become my mother-in-law that way! But oh no...wait, cause here comes the biggy...I didn't eat enough bacon butties, cream cakes or fat filled pasties! So please YELL AT ME SOME MORE!" Okay so I was panting like a mad woman and it was officially the longest speech of my life but man did it feel good getting it all off my chest!

For the longest time we both seemed to be staring at each like wild animals waiting for the other one to make the first move. Draven was no doubt processing all I said and I was quickly regretting every last word. Then just as it looked as though Draven was about to burst a blood vessel he thundered out a roar making the whole room shake and alarms went off and a red light started to flash. Oh shit, what the hell was happening and what was the hotel manager going to think when one temper tantrum could bring down the building!

"I AM GOING TO KILL HIM!" Draven boomed and then ripped off the bedroom door and stormed out...oh no! On impulse I got up and ran after him in my birthday suit. I could see him just ahead and his body was glowing with unchecked fury.

"My Lord?"

"Dom?"

"Brother?" Everyone said at once but Lucius was the only one he was fixated on and one look from Draven gave him his reason why. He stood quickly and got ready to defend himself when I did the only thing I could think of to stop him from ripping Lucius' head off. I cut the rest of the distance between us and took a running leap right onto his back. I tightened my hold in a death grip and everyone's eyes looked to me in utter shock. I must have looked like a naked, furless monkey hung on like this and it began to sink in that I was here, in this room, which was still shaking, in front of everyone....and I mean everyone!

"Hey Toots, looking good." Pip said giving me a wink and then was quickly shut up by Adam's hand clasped firmly over her mouth.

Draven had at least frozen his attempts at murder and I think Lucius looked relieved. I felt him trembling beneath me at his concentration on holding back and I squeezed his waist more to gain grip to pull myself up to his ear.

"I am naked." I whispered shyly.

"I am aware." He said shortly.

"So if you kill him you will drop me, bruise my skinny bum and flash me to everyone...even the men." I added knowing this was the clincher of the deal. When I heard him groan I knew I had him and I smiled into his neck.

"Don't smile Keira, you will just piss me off more." He warned but I pushed it and bit his shoulder before saying,

"Yes Sir...No sir." And giggled a little making him groan again. He released a big sigh and then snapped out an order.

"Close your eyes!" He told everyone and then as quick as a switch he had me latched onto his front, holding me by my bum and facing the open door I flew through.

"Sort out my plane before I have to fly it...NOW!" He shouted when no-one moved and now I was the one shaking...I was on a plane and it was bouncing all over the place! I felt him rub my back reassuringly and telling me to 'Ssshh' all the way back to the cabin I burst from.

"It will stop soon."

"What...what... if it goes down...oh shit, ARHHH." I screamed as it seemed to drop a few times all at once. I clung onto him and even when he tried to put me down on the bed I still wouldn't let go. He groaned and then decided trying to force me off him right then was not the best option. So he stood back up and grabbed the covers off the bed with one effortless yank. Then he sat back into one of the matching suede sofas in the room and covered us both in the quilt. He shifted my legs from around his waist and draped them over his legs so that I was now cocooned on his lap and as close to his body as I could get....well without him being naked that was.

"Do me a favour, the next time we're on a plane, please don't fly into a rage...okay?" I asked him with my head still on his chest.

"Then maybe next time, don't send me into one and we should be fine." He replied sternly and made a huff sound.

"I thought we were in a bloody hotel, Draven! And besides...no girl takes rejection well." I added on an embarrassed whisper.

"You thought that was rejection? Oh you silly girl!" He scorned and I lifted my head to frown at him.

"Don't call my feelings silly!" I said and then made a move to get off him but there was no way that was happening and secretly I was glad.

"You're not going anywhere, so stop struggling. I stupidly let you go once before and look what happened...never, ever again! And as far as your feelings were being referred to as silly, well they are when you think I would EVER reject you!" He said angrily before continuing,

"And while we are at this, if you ever walk out naked in front another male I will not be held accountable for my actions or their new blind status...do I make myself clear?"

"ARRRH!" I growled out and then twisted my body so that I was straddling his hips and sitting on his lap facing him. I whacked him on the shoulder and glared at him, which I received right back.

"You…You…"

"What?!" He snapped back and it just made my blood boil even more.

"YOU BARBARIAN! I didn't know you had every Tom, Dick and their mother out there or did you think in the time away I have filled my time with becoming an exhibitionist!"

"Keira, unless you like turbulence, I suggest you refrain from speaking that way." He warned and I couldn't help but slap him in the chest again.

"You stubborn old fart!"

"Did you seriously just call me an 'old fart'?" He asked in shock and I did a mental Ooopsie, my bad.

"Umm nooo… I called you an old cat." Okay, so I knew it was a long shot and when one of Draven's eyebrows raised I knew he did too. He was about to say something when I butted in but in the best way ever.

"Oh shut up, you old fart!" I shouted before flinging myself at him and taking possession of his lips. He stilled and then started to kiss me with a renewed desperation that soon had me on my back and him pinning my body underneath him.

"Stubborn beautiful, Vixen." He said into my neck and then took my lips again. Kissing Draven was like coming home for every molecule in my body and the way my body arched up to his every touch, I would say he knew it too.

"I love you." I said when he was kissing his way down my body and he stopped with his lips still at my side. I bit my lip and waited… why had he stilled? Oh no…maybe he felt differently…I mean we hadn't really talked about Aurora, only to tell me the Video was a fake but how about all the other times…Oh God!

"I didn't mean to say that." I quickly got out feeling suddenly ashamed. His head shot up and the black eyes I received told me the last thing I said was not a good idea.

"You just ruined one of the best things I ever heard after all this time apart" He said in a tone like steel.

"I didn't mean it." I whispered feeling so utterly guilty now.

"Which part? And be very careful with your words this time." He warned tensing his body over me.

"I just thought when you froze that it wasn't something you

wanted to hear anymore." I flinched when I saw the pain in his eyes and again felt like shit about it.

"And what completely ridiculous reason would that be exactly?"

"Umm…it will make you angry." I said wishing I would have just let his lips continue their incredible journey, I definitely would have been in a better place right now if I had kept my big, stupid, self-conscious mouth shut!

"I am already angry, fuming really, so spit it out, Keira." I felt trapped under him and with his head now looming over me it looked as if he was trying to burrow the answers out of me.

"Aurora." I whispered, making him snarl and his eyes flash their trademark angry purple.

"I thought we had cleared this up but it seems you have more to say on the matter." He responded looking mighty hacked off.

"Let me up." I demanded, but he just shook his head.

"No, I think not. You will stay there and answer my questions."

"What?!" I said in disbelief. This was supposed to be my interrogation not his!

"You heard. Now answer me this…you trusted me when I said the footage you saw was a fake…yes?" He lowered his head as if to draw a yes out of me, which he did.

"Yes."

"Right answer my girl. Alright, what else could it be…?" He tapped his chin and gave me a thoughtful look but as I was sick of playing this game, it was just making me angry, I tried to shift from him. His hand flashed from my side and shackled my wrists into the sofa's armrest and then he just tutted down at me.

"Ah, I know…you were watching when I arrived at Transfusion. That is it, well let me enlighten you my dear. Aurora has certain gifts…"

"I just bet she does!" I snapped sarcastically, making him bite my neck in retaliation.

"Behave." He cautioned holding my skin in his teeth like some controlling Lion with his unruly mate.

"Where was I before I was rudely interrupted…ah, yes my irrational need to explain something where trust should be playing the lead part. Well considering all my very obvious infidelities in the past I must put your mind at rest."

"Sarcasm doesn't suit you, Draven."

"Right back at you my love. Aurora is a sensor for our kind and can detect Angels and Demons by the different signals of power they emit. I had her with me before I entered as I wanted to know what I was up against. Lucius told me what happened with Layla." He snarled her name, tensed his hold on me before continuing.

"And how Malphas had plans for you and he feared for your life. A deal was made but that is getting off the subject that seems to matter the most to you. Aurora was scouting the place for the presence of Layla or Malphas, that is what you saw." He finished angrily making me huff.

"Well she did a lousy job considering Malphas made me do a Houdini on the roof top." I blurted out and I recoiled because hearing it back I did sound bitter and petty,

"Ah, well that, my jealous girl, was actually your doing."

"WHAT!" I shouted in disbelief.

"I don't know what Malphas was planning but when your defensive walls came crashing down around your mind, you made it easy enough for him to get to you and that, Aurora couldn't predict." I hated the way he was defending her and the fact that what he was saying was right, it still hurt and felt like being stabbed in the back.

"Alright then, but while you're in an answering mood…"

"Hardly." He commented dryly which I ignored and carried on.

"Why, when Pip sent me back to see you, did I open the door to our bedroom and find you in each other's arms just after telling her about your feelings!?" I shouted at him and for a moment he looked dumbstruck. I gathered his siblings had kept that little bit of info from him as he continued to stare at me in disbelief. Then he shouted out in another language, which I gathered was the F word and flew away from me. I grabbed for the covers and wished I was dressed so that I wasn't having this argument, a mile in the air naked.

"Unbelievable! I have waited my entire life for the Gods to grant me the love of my long life, the Chosen One by their very hands and they pick the most stubborn, self-conscious, untrusting mortal they could find! Bloody marvellous!" He ranted, throwing his hands up in the air making me fist my hands in the quilt in anger. I got up, wrapped the cover round me and stormed to the only door I could see, which was the way out. I didn't care if anyone saw me this time, I just needed to get away from him! Which was completely ironic considering the amount of time I had spent just wishing I could see him again.

"And where do you think you are going?!" He barked and I ignored him as I grabbed the broken door and pushed it out of my way.

"Oh I don't think so!" And then I was grabbed from behind and hauled to his chest.

"Let go!" I shouted to no avail.

"Oh no Keira, I warned you that you would NEVER be leaving me again and I was damn serious! So sit your behind in that chair and listen to the truth of my words!" He lifted me up high in the air like I was nothing but a basketball and plonked me none too gently into the chair he was sat in when I first woke. He then trapped me in by bending his knees and leaning right into me.

"Now, listen up you insufferable love of my life! I don't know what you heard but it obviously wasn't the whole of it, so let me enlighten you with the rest. That night I was in such a rage that I destroyed three rooms in my home and was about to do even more damage to the rightfully called 'our room'. That was until Aurora came to me to try and calm me down. It didn't work so well until I heard her ask me if I really did love you? That made every memory of you I had burned to my thoughts come hitting me in my mind like the hammer of God! I lost all my will to destroy and instead found myself crumbling to the floor in hopeless defeat. My worst fears had happened and you were taken from me due to my arrogance at believing myself powerful enough to keep you safe." He started to shake his head as he carried on,

"I had never felt self-loathing like that in my life and you can imagine the amount of time we are talking about here." He got up and raked his hands through his raven hair in frustration and the memory of what I was making him relive.

"I told her of my deep love for you and that no matter of our past it didn't change one single shred of the unbreakable feelings I had for you. No woman could seize hold of my heart and keep it for hers to own like you do. When she started to cry I told her that 'I am not afraid of speaking my feelings Aurora, not when those feelings are of love' which was making myself clear. I then continued to explain that I didn't regret my time with her as every day of my history only brought me closer to you. I explained how she could not find this shocking, given the evidence before her very eyes, my obvious displays of deep affection for you and the rage in which I so freely displayed upon having you taken from me." I was crying now and he leaned back down to wipe my tears from my cheeks with two gentle swipes of his thumbs.

"When she spoke of what I needed from her and hugged me, she whispered the answer we both knew in my ear to be the only way, which was exactly the only thing I needed from her...she was letting me go, Keira." I cried out and flung myself in his arms and he landed backwards on his back with me sprawled on top of him naked. I was hugging him and kissing him all over in between saying,

"I'm sorry, I'm so, so sorry...I should have trusted you...I'm sorry...I love you, I love you." I repeated over and over again into his skin.

"Good to hear as I also love you, more than you could ever truly know my Vixen." He sat up and lifted us both so that now we were facing each other lying down on the bed with both of us under the covers.

"You will never think those things of me again...do you hear me?" He said harshly but I ignored his tone, just being too overjoyed that all this time I had it wrong, he didn't love her...he loved me!

"I won't, but in my defence what would you have thought if you saw me naked and doing the oldest dance in the world with another man?" I saw his dark eyes swirl purple and wanted to mentally slap myself...again! And then I thought about how many kisses Lucius had given me and felt like tearing my heart out to him as an offering. I knew I had no choice but to tell him but what would happen? Would he kill Lucius...? Probably and was that wise when we were in a plane?

"I can hear your heart pounding and see your mind working ten to the dozen sweetheart... something on your mind?" OH SHIT! What was I going to say now, I was a lousy liar and Draven knew it, hell, he was probably bloody counting on it!

"I...I can't tell you!" I blurted out. How that would help, I didn't know! He smiled at me which I knew wouldn't be lasting for long.

"I am going to take a wild stab in the dark here and say it has something to do with a certain Vamp who had my girlfriend captive and knows how to piss me off like no other." I was amazed at how calm he sounded.

"And that combined with the utterly but adorable cute, guilty look on your face I would put the two and two together." Oh shit, oh shit, oh God, oh God!

"Please don't kill us all in a rage, I am terrified of heights, hate flying but hate dying more and don't fancy making the news tonight." He actually laughed.

"I am not about to destroy something I paid over $350 million for and seeing as I had this Boeing 747-8I VIP especially made for me, I really don't fancy seeing it on the news either. As for you worrying about plummeting to your death, you do realise I have wings right? Besides, I knew about Lucius kissing you before and I haven't yet killed him for it."

"What! You knew…when?! How?" And also was he kidding… $350 million?!

"I saw everything in your mind that night on the roof top and as much as I wanted to kill him for it…still do in fact…I also knew that it was part of his destiny along with yours and seeing, as it stands, I can't yet kill the fates that are bestowed on us, I have no other option to just live with it and ensure it never happens again." At this I felt so terrible and my heart broke with what seeing it must have done to him and considering he had never once cheated on me, it made it ten times worse!

"I'm so, so sorry." I said pathetically knowing that was never going to be enough.

"I know you are, my heart, and trust me when I say it helps, but I know it wasn't your fault and can definitely understand the lure you hold on the male population…even if you don't see it yourself." He added when I screwed my face up. I still couldn't believe how cool he was being about all this.

"But wait, so you don't try to kill him for kissing me but you do, for not feeding me right?" I said with scepticism.

"I never said I didn't try to kill him for kissing you and once he made me see his fate, one predicted by the Oracle herself, I knew I had to let go of his throat… even if it did pain me to let him take a breath… but nowhere in that fate did it state it was alright to let you half starve to death, I mean Keira, you are skin and bones! Which reminds me" He said getting up and leaving me alone in the bed while he walked over to a control pad on a small table next to the cluster of comfy chairs.

I just couldn't believe we were in a plane…this room was huge!

"Bring us some food immediately…wait a moment!" He clicked a button I gathered was hold and turned back to me to ask…

"What's a bacon butty?"

*I fell back on the bed laughing.*

# CHAPTER 50
# BODILY CHANGES AND IMPISH REASONS

After I explained that a 'bacon butty' was actually a bacon sandwich and that I was being a sarcastic cow by mentioning a 'fat filled pasty', which thankfully wasn't brought with the food…'cause Yuck… we ate and acted more like the couple we still were. For me it was like a huge weight had been lifted from my shoulders and now I could finally see the future ahead of us. I decided that I was never again going to be irrationally jealous and after everything Draven had gone through to get to me, then really… shouldn't I have had faith in him to begin with. It sounded so obvious that the footage was a hoax now but at the time, with where my head was at, then I guess my insecurities just overtook logic.

After he had made sure I ate every last morsel on my plate, he then led me to an ensuite bathroom and I was like a tourist getting excited about the fact I was about to have a shower a mile up…was there a secret 'shower mile high club' that only the rich and famous got to do?

After Draven kept assuring me we weren't going to have a plane crash and I would be in the shower as the plane went down I finally relaxed enough. And it helped when he told me he could fly the plane himself if the pilot had a heart attack, which was my next worry. He had laughed at that one while walking out the door.

When I was done with a much needed shower I found fresh clothes, my own this time, on the bed waiting for me. When I had smelled my armpits in the shower I had almost gagged and then shame fell over me wondering what his mother must have thought taking over the body of such a smelly girl. I decided not to disclose my feelings on this matter to Draven as I was embarrassed enough as it was.

It felt like a little slice of Heaven finally putting on my own stuff and with my softest, much-loved pair of worn to blazes jeans, I added a long sleeved black top, with my favourite thumb holes. It had a wide neck across my shoulders and was made from a clingy, stretchy material, so I added a zip up hoodie that was a nice grape colour and had a soft fleece lining. I didn't want to start complaining but I didn't think the supernatural could feel the cold like us mortals, so I zipped it up a bit to add more warmth.

I was just about to walk out to see everyone when the 'repaired' door opened and Draven stood there filling its frame with his impressive physique. I dragged in a breath at what the sight of this man did to me. I wished earlier I hadn't just been subjected to eating, kissing and playful touching. I really wanted Draven to ravish me but every time the subject had come up, it was brushed off with the need to rest, to eat more or finally the need to shower and after smelling myself I wasn't surprised. But now, at the sight of him, I was hoping he would like to see what clean Keira really smelled like... everywhere! I was just about to jump on him again when a green haired Imp popped her head round his frame making her look like a child hiding behind a giant.

"Tootie Pop!" She said excitedly and Draven saw my reaction and couldn't hold back his own smile at the sight of me beaming.

"Squeak!" I squealed back and she actually pushed Draven out of the way and ran to me so fast I had to actually catch her as she threw herself at me. Draven rumbled at being man handled by a little thing like Pip, who believe me, was not as weak or fragile as she looked. She hugged onto me and squeezed me tight.

"You silly skinny butt! Toots really, don't you know nothing can kill an Imp like me. That axe would have just shattered if it touched my bones and then I could just heal myself, so next time just let the bastard try!" She said and I laughed.

"Umm, I think I will opt out of anymore adventures Pip, so next time how about we just go for cocktails...deal?" At this she clapped and bounced off me. I looked up to find Draven's hand on her shoulder that stilled her instantly and she bowed her head in respect.

"Calm yourself Imp." I frowned at his name for her and cleared my throat.

"Not getting any, eh?" I frowned but she just held up her hands and giggled.

"Hey I know the look…Adam cut me off once when I might have accidently on purpose bought a sex club and surprised him with a pole dance in front of a few of Hell's officials…but hey, it was for his birthday but go figure, he doesn't like to share." She shrugged her shoulders at me shaking my head.

"You're a class act, Pip."

"Yeah, well he didn't think so that night… I had to go a whole day without sex! Do you know what that's like for an Imp?!"

"Oh poor you, my heart bleeds for your one day in…what, how many years?"

"Okay, so you have a point but do you want to know why royal lover boy, hottie bad wings, won't put out?" She said raising her eyebrows and I rolled mine in return.

"No why? 'Cause I smelled like I hadn't showered since I left Afterlife?"

"No, I think if someone had rolled you in year old cheese that had been baking in the sun, that boy would still find his boner, so no, that is not the reason."

"Then what is it, sex educated Professor Pip?" I asked folding my arms across my chest but the answer didn't come from Pip, it came from the door way.

"Because you're now a virgin again!"

I was just so happy that answer didn't come from the Draven I was sleeping with or the one that winked at me and made me blush like a… well, like a virgin!

Sophia had walked into the room and like a group of teenage girls we all jumped up and hugged each other and soon the room was filled with girly chats and it was a real eye opener when I stopped and thought, well here I was sat on a bed in a $350million private plane the size of a jumbo, with the most stunning Demon and a Green haired, tattooed and pierced Imp chatting about boys, clothes and when we could all go shopping together...and this was now my norm in life… wow life had most certainly changed alright and I could never call it boring again, well, not like I ever did!

As it turned out Pip and Sophia were great friends and when the feud had happened with Draven and Lucius, they had no choice than to say goodbye to one another. Looking at them now I could see why Sophia and Pip made such good friends. I mean they were both mischievous as hell and I bet got into loads of wicked trouble when they were together. They both loved fashion, although looking at Sophia's designer red winter, woollen dress with thick tights and soft knee high leather boots to die for, she couldn't have been more opposite to Pip.

My little friend was dressed in skin tight PVC leggings that had two great slits up the front held together by safety pins the full length and a fake blood spattered top with BIO HAZARD written across in yellow writing and on the back a spray painted warning saying 'My Zombie killin' top, mother F...' and you can guess the rest! So you can see that these two best buddies couldn't have been further apart but to watch them you could tell they had been friends for years and with the way I felt about the both of them, I could not have been happier.

"Okay, now does somebody want to explain the pink elephant in the room and tell me what you mean about me now being a virgin again?" I said once we had gotten past the girly essentials and the plane had landed.

"It's true, for the ritual Malphas needed the Maiden to be...well a maiden. So he used Draven's healing blood in you and the blood of the Mother Goddess, the 'randy redhead' to you, to rebuild that part...you know...the flappy bit."

"Eww, Pip...a little bit gross and I don't know how many friend lines you just crossed with that one." I teased but still not being able to believe the fact that I was now a born again virgin...a real one!

"So that is why Draven won't touch me?" I asked and thankfully it was the more diplomatic Sophia that answered me.

"Can you blame him, after everything you've been through. Give it time, he just doesn't want to hurt you." She said softly and then Pip nudged her.

"Hey, can you imagine, I mean your Kingy Bro must have some real restraints...finding a virgin we can sex it up with, for our kind is like the holy grail for a mortal...bottoms up!"

"Thanks Squeak...discreet as always." Sophia added.

"She's joking though, right?!" I said shocked Draven would consider my virginity as such.

"Actually she isn't and I can't imagine my brother is having an easy time with it. Talk about being torn between a rock and a hard place." Sophia said shaking her head but Pip burst into a fit of laughter.

"Torn! Ha that's a good one, like as in torn hymen!" She shouted excitedly and I groaned at the thought.

"I am glad you're excited Pip, jeez...I am glad you weren't around the first time, I would have crapped myself."

"Was the first time any good?" Sophia asked and I started playing with my sleeves nervously.

"Well no, not really...you know how it is...couple of drunken teenagers fumbling around and trying to find the right way...well I guess you guys don't." I said looking up and seeing the amazement on their faces.

"Well there you go then! At least your next first time will be better...I mean, mmm... Draven." Pip said and I laughed at Sophia's face.

"Eww Pip, brother remember." I laughed at them both and the rest of the conversation continued as such.

We were soon speeding down another runway and I had no idea where we had just stopped off but considering the size of the plane I doubted it was to refuel. I asked Pip and Sophia but neither wanted to answer and they ended up skirting round the subject with other supernatural gossip about people I didn't know. As time went on I got the distinct impression that two things were going on. One, that I was being kept in my room with the help of two girly conspirators and two, their mission was to keep my mind from leaving the room and thinking about Draven...neither of which were working.

"So, why are you two keeping me hostage then?" I blurted out halting their conversation about the benefit of sex swings, something I really couldn't contribute to.

"Umm, what do you mean?" Sophia said unconvincingly, and Pip started nervously playing with her lip ring and tongue piercing, which today's choice was a pentagram. I rolled my eyes at them both.

"I am a bit of a pro at this subject guys, I could write a book on being held against my will, now fess up...why doesn't he want me leaving this room?"

"Lucius!" Pip yelled and then slapped her hands over her mouth.

"PIP!" Sophia yelled back.

"What? I cracked under the pressure!" Sophia rolled her eyes.

"Really Pip, it's not like our Keira is in the Gestapo or the Spanish inquisition, you didn't even need to lie, you could just have not said his name!" Sophia argued and just before Pip responded I put my hands up, playing peace maker.

"Guys, it's a little late for shoulda, woulda, coulda...so he doesn't want me leaving here because he doesn't want me seeing Lucius?" I shook my head at the obvious reasons from my control freakishly handsome boyfriend that had some major issues with jealously but considering why I knew I needed to cut him some slack. So, I started laughing.

"I am glad you find it so funny." Draven's voice cut through my laughter and I gulped before I turned around to face my man standing in the doorway for I don't know how long.

"Umm, I think this might be our cue to leave, Pip." Sophia said with humour and I would have whispered 'Judas' if that hadn't been the other name to the man Draven was angry about.

"Mmmm...oh yeah, right...damn I could use some popcorn...hey did you ever watch that Transformer movie? But not the Hollywood one, that was pants, I'm talking about the real emotional one, the one where Optimus Prime dies and then..." I heard Pip saying to Sophia as they walked out of the door.

Draven closed the door without turning from me and I didn't know what else to say but,

"She's right it was really emotional when he died."

"Excuse me?" Draven said not following me.

"Optimus Prime, he...urrr...dies in this movie and well...umm..." It was hard to talk when Draven was stalking me like I was topped with trimmings and garnish on the side. He came over to me with long strides of his dark denim clad legs and his own long sleeved T-shirt that clung to every muscle like black liquid. Man, pretty soon I would be fanning myself it was getting that hot in here.

"You were saying?" He hummed over me as I fell backwards thanks to his body coming over me on the bed I was still sat on. He crawled over me and I felt every inch...and I mean EVERY inch, of him rest against me and I thought I was going to forget how to breathe.

"I don't remember." I said without the air to back it up.

"Is something wrong, Keira?" He asked seductively and I noticed his bad boy, cocky grin was back in full force.

"Not anymore, no." I said, smiling up at him before reaching up to run my hands through his feather soft hair. He closed his eyes and groaned when I used my nails to scratch his scalp. I felt him arch off me a little and I knew I was witnessing a real sensitive spot on my bad boy Draven. Ooh, I might be able to use this to my advantage. I did it again and when I got the same response I smiled.

be some hillbilly wood cutter for all I cared and with those arms then, man you could really go at it all day." He laughed again and the way his eyes lit up was like someone turning me to the 'warm and gooey' setting in my heart.

"I know you don't care for my money Keira, if anything I would think you would prefer me without it."

"Ah, now you're catching on." I said into his neck I was now nuzzling.

"I have a lot of money Keira, but the most precious thing to me in the world I hold in my hands. That will never change, no matter my extreme wealth. But I must confess…I do enjoy the notion of taking you against one of my Ferraris or on the sands of my private island."

"You're joking of course…you do not own an island…right?" I looked up at him and was surprised that he was now biting his lip playfully before winking at me and saying,

"Maybe." I closed my eyes and dramatically dropped my head to his neck to groan,

"Oh, Good Lord." I moaned again making him laugh before kissing me on the side of my head and whispering,

"I am trying to be." He felt me smile against him.

"I wish you wouldn't be." I complained.

"Keira, we have been through this, there is a time and a place and I am definitely not about to take your maidenhood in a damn car!"

"Maidenhood…you're showing your age with that one." I commented on a laugh and he snapped his teeth at me in retaliation but even that act had me getting damp, as I would have liked nothing more than the raging beast version of Draven ravishing me.

"Anyway, you do realise that losing your virginity in the back of a car is a teenage pastime for most, right?" He raised an eyebrow at me and smirked.

"That would certainly make it authentic or there is always the losing it on your parents bed, which I think we are a little far from and plus…gross." He laughed, gave me a look I couldn't decipher and then turned very serious at the click of a thought, one I knew was coming given the subject choice.

"Which one was it for you then?" I smiled and then tried to smooth out the deep ridge of a frown line with my thumb.

"It was neither actually…it was in a tent after a bottle of Lambrini."

"WHAT!" He shouted making me flinch at his outburst but he held me tighter to him and made soothing circles on my back even though he was clearly angry.

"Well you did ask." I reminded him.

"Yes, but I did not expect you to tell me it was after some cheap foul wine in a cold damp tent in the middle of nowhere! How irresponsible." He muttered and I couldn't help but find the funny side in that statement.

"Yes well, seventeen year olds are not really expecting the Hilton on a bed of roses and room service the next day...hormones and all, kind of negate the need for such luxury and besides, I liked the wine, it was summer and it was on a camping trip very near to a lodge full of very responsible people...is that better?"

"No, not at all but it soon will be and even with you grinding on me like that, it will not be in the back of a car either!"

"You do know it is not really my first time...I have played this game before." I whispered in his ear before biting the lobe and being playfully brave. I smiled when he groaned.

"Keira please, just give me this. It is a gift to me that now I will be the only one to have taken something that was my birth right. It should never have been anyone else and as I said to you before, if I had known where you were beforehand I would have been your first."

"And now you will be." I added feeling touched he felt that strongly about it.

"Yes and it will be more honourable when I do."

"Okay, I won't tease you any more, let me off." When his hands didn't move I said his name in warning.

"Draven."

"I did not state in this deal that I would not touch you." He stated seriously.

"Ah, but will this not just make things harder for us both?" I looked down to our bodies that had fit together with only our clothes in between us....that and Draven's new vow of chastity.

"I believe it is also customary for first time lovers to 'make out' before hitting all the bases, I think we need to practice before the big game." He said running his fingers into my ponytail and pulling my head forward abruptly for a Supernatural King's version of a 'make out' session...

It turned out to be the best car ride of my life.

Draven wouldn't tell me where we were going and as it was night outside and he was keeping me very entertained in all lovely and delicious manner of ways, I gathered we were making our way back to Afterlife. Although the plane ride seemed to be very short I didn't know how long as I had slept through it on the first leg of the trip but the second half was only a few hours.

I was looking forward to getting back to the place I knew to be my home and if Draven would have let me, I would have been bouncing up and down like an excited kid at Christmas, which reminded me was coming up very soon. That thought had me feeling guilty as hell that I wouldn't be seeing my family and then it hit me, what had Draven told my parents about my absence? I was just about to ask when Draven pulled from sucking and nibbling on my neck to announce,

"We are here." I went to look around but then the windows steamed over and the fog stayed as if glued to the glass.

"Draven?"

"I want it to be a surprise, so you can't look." I gave him a 'what are you up to' look and he simply shrugged his shoulders trying to play it down. We came to a stop and the door was opened by the driver, once I promised Draven not to open my eyes. I hoped he hadn't done something ridiculously expensive like traded my big blue in for some little sporty thing that had a temperamental accelerator. He helped me out and sounding more excited than I had ever heard him, he said,

"No peeking, not yet" I found his mood seeping into mine and soon I was nearly a giddy mess of excitement and nerves.

"I wanna see." I complained and he laughed. I felt him come up behind me, tug the jacket he insisted on me wearing closer together, and then wrapped his arms around me in a tight hug before saying,

"Okay, open your eyes." I did as I was told and I couldn't believe what I was looking at. I was now stood in front of my childhood home, that I'd spent more years in than not and it took my breath away! It was like most of the other four bedroom houses in the cul de sac, red brick, with a red painted door and garage to match. It had fairy lights hanging from the hooks hanging baskets normally were hung from in summer. It had a little Christmas tree outside with a mishmash of lights, where some worked and others didn't and every year my dad would just buy a new set and combine them with the old ones. I smiled at the thought of my mum complaining that it looked cheap. My dad would answer the same way I always remembered...nothing Christmassy ever looks cheap.

The lights were on and I could hear the music and the excitable shouting as some game was being played, from down here on the drive.

"Merry Christmas, baby!" Draven said from behind me and I spun round in his hold and squeezed him to me.

"How, when…did you?" He beamed down at me and it no doubt matched my beaming smile up at him.

"After it happened I made them believe that while waiting for your next flight you came down with a terrible virus and you were too ill to travel but I assured them you were being well looked after and gave them daily updates…well you did actually."

"And how did I do that?" I asked seeing his bad boy glint spark up in his eyes.

"Celina is very good with different voices."

"Ah, I get it, so my family bought it but how come they're here not in Cornwall?" I asked seeing my family home on the outskirts of Liverpool where we had always lived.

"They decided it was better for your grandparents to come to them, something about your mother hating their stove and lumpy mattresses that they refuse to replace." I smiled at the thought of poor Draven having to listen to all these little dramas of my mother's whilst trying to deal with more pressing issues, like my kidnapping.

"They don't know I have surprised you but us being here is their surprise." He added.

"They don't know?!" He shook his head and my grin could not get any bigger. They were going to seriously freak out with happiness!

"Don't worry if they don't have the room, then I have a suite held for us in the city." Of course he did.

"Oh it's not that, I am just wondering who will cry first, my mum or Libby." He laughed and then came round to take my hand.

"Come then, it is too cold for you and besides, I think they have waited long enough." He pulled me up the driveway and looked back to see the Limo only just fit but if Mr and Mrs Sutton wanted to go anywhere tonight, then he would have to move.

"Keira, you're shaking."

"I'm just so excited, I didn't think…"He pulled me to him, wiped away a stray tear and kissed my nose before saying,

"I know sweetheart, I know." Then before I could think anymore into it, he reached out behind him and knocked firmly on the door. I could hear my mum behind my dad's frame asking 'who it could be?' My dad in his usual dry humour replied,

"Well it's too early for Santa but if he's come with a new drill, then he can stay for a brandy." I was still laughing when he opened the door and my parents were both stood there dumbfounded and speechless… which hardly ever happens to my mum!

"OH MY GOD!" My mum shouted

"HOLY SHIT!" My dad shouted.

"Language!" My mum shouted before she launched herself at me, barging my dad clean out of the doorway.

"MY BABY!" She screamed kissing me all over.

"Hi mum, hi dad." I said round my mum's mass of curls that Libby had inherited.

"Oh honey, I am so glad you are better and I could…oh Eric…our baby…"

"Oh mum, don't cry, you will set me off." But it was too late and now I heard reinforcements coming down the hallway who would no doubt be adding to those tears.

"Mum, who is it, you're letting all the heating out and…Holy shit!" Libby screamed and then ran towards me and my poor dad was once again being pushed out of the way muttering,

"That's what I said."

"Language!"

"And that's what she said." My dad added smiling as Libby threw herself, baby bump and all at me.

"KAZZY!"

"Hey Libs." I said feeling the emotions bubbling up.

"We were so worried! But I knew someone would be taking care of you." She winked at me and then I looked behind me to realise Draven had stood back out of sight, while my family took in the shock before showing himself. He stepped into sight and my mum actually gasped and then the unbelievable happened,

"Holy Shit!" My mum blurted out and then slapped her hands to her mouth in shock at her blunder. We all laughed, including my dad.

"Mum, dad, this is my boyfriend…Dra Dominic Draven." I said ushering him inside and closing the door behind him.

"Oh my." I heard my mum utter and my sister whispered in her ear,

"I told you so." I smiled as Draven tried to ignore the blatant drooling from my female family members and it was left up to my dad to take the lead for once.

"Y'alright, mate, come on in and meet the rest of the nutters, seeing as you've already met me wife. Come and meet the in laws... that should be interesting but do us a favour lad, try not to give the owd lady (old lady) a stroke and watch for those wandering hands of hers, she's got a mean ass pinch." I burst out laughing at my father's northern humour and easy acceptance of any man in my life. Draven gave me a massive grin and I thought I heard my mum swooning behind me.

"Oh my god Kaz, that man gets finer every time I see him!" Lib said and my mum started nodding like a goofy love struck teenager.

"Oh my!" It seemed to be the only thing my mum could say at the moment.

"So, happy to see me then?" I asked and they both threw their arms around me and we did a happy little family hug dance in the entrance way.

"Oh lovey, you really must have been ill, you have lost so much weight, too much...far too much, we need to fatten you up this Christmas and now we will be a proper family...oh, my girls."

"Great, here she goes again...you know she hasn't stopped blubbering since she thought you were going to miss it." Libby informed me and I pulled my mum to me for another hug, as we walked in the living room to find Draven and Frank shaking hands.

"Oh mum, the Gods couldn't even keep me away." I said sending Draven a wink and he looked momentarily like he'd swallowed a bug. I laughed and let my mum go readying myself for the brotherly Keira bear hug I always received from Frank.

"Here she is, our little Kazzy!" Frank said leaving Draven's side and coming over enthusiastically to pick me up for a Frank squeeze and I moaned when my ribs protested. Draven tensed as if hating every second of it. Then I spotted my grandparents sat in the same chairs they always did when coming here.

"Nan! Granddad!" I shouted and ran over to them giving each of them a hug, making sure my Nan didn't get up as she had a bad hip.

"Hello petal... oh Reg isn't it good to see her... Reg, Reg fetch my glasses, no they're for reading, the other ones...yes, yes in the blue case...now let's have a look at you." She said taking her glasses and slipping them on making her eyes double in size.

"Still wearing those jam jar bottoms, Nan?" I said and my Granddad laughed as I said the same thing every time I saw them.

"Oh dearie...Joyce! Joyce!"

"Yes mother." My mum came up to me and started taking my jacket off and then turned to Draven in case he was wearing one.

"Joyce, what are you feeding her, carrots and celery? You need some chocolates deary, here...Olivia bring out some of those Quality Street for a nibble." She said pointing to the tin and I smiled.

"Nan, this is my boyfriend, Dominic Draven." I said pulling him closer to me so that my Nan could see him.

"Pardon, sweetheart?" My mum came up behind her chair and whispered 'Boyfriend' and hearing that title snapped her head up...and up...and up at Draven. Her eyes got wide and then she smiled like my mum had.

"Oh my!" She said a bit breathlessly and then patted the underneath of her tightly curled bob.

"I am pleased to meet you, Edna." Draven said and I shouldn't have been shocked that he knew her name already....was there anything this man didn't know about me?

"Oh Joyce, he looks like that superman fellow, what was that actor's name, when he was younger...?Clark Kent....was that it? Oh, he was so handsome."

"Mum, he can hear you and it was Christopher Reeves." She said smirking at Draven.

"I am Joyce Williams, its lovely to meet you Mr Draven." My mum said sweetly and I could already see a soft spot forming.

"Dominic please, and it is my pleasure. Keira speaks about all her family often and I am just happy she is better so that we could come to your lovely home." Oh my god, now that was it! Not only did he look and sound as delicious as he did but calling my mother's home lovely was the deal clincher. My mother could have made being house proud an Olympic sport! Was she actually blushing...oh my, was certainly right!

Then I could not believe what he did next, he took my mum's offered hand and pulled her toward him to kiss her on the cheek, then doing the same to my sister and then my little Nan who couldn't catch her breath after it. He then turned to me and whispered he would be back in a moment as he left to talk to my dad and Granddad, who were now getting his hand shake treatment, leaving four women all swooning and in need of smelling salts and fans.

"Mum, do you have room for us to stay?" I asked pulling her from her droolfest and it looked as if she had to drag her eyes away from the sight of Draven in dark denim and a body that filled every fibre of his clothes with solid cut muscles. What was my question again?

"Mmm, sorry what dear?"

"Of course we have room, don't we mum?" Libby saved me and she winked at me...on no, what was she up to?

"Yes of course."

"But what about me and Dra...."

"Oh mum, you're not going to make him sleep on the couch are you?" Libby interjected and my mum finally looked round at us both.

"Most certainly not, for starters a lad that big would never fit, but that is beside the point, he is a guest." She said sternly and I knew where Libby was going with this one.

"But Keira can't sleep on the couch, not with her just getting over being ill, so what are we going to do?" Libby faked the innocent question and my mum's eyes narrowed.

"I know what you are up to Olivia and there is no need. Kazzy is a grown up now and besides..." She looked back at Draven and then whispered,

"I won't be so cruel denying you something that delicious to sleep with Kazzy." We both burst out laughing and from the looks on Draven's face, he had heard every word.

After my family's trade mark rite of passage cup of tea ritual, complete with posh tinned biscuits, Draven retrieved our bags before sending the Limo away. Of course before this happened, my dad and Frank had to go out and see the thing in all its luxury before it was allowed to leave and even John our neighbour came out in his slippers to see it. I think Draven was a little embarrassed over all the attention and with my mother's cooing, but beamed at the point when she said he was spoiling me. He then firmly told her, that was only the very least I deserved and he would never change that, which she loved hearing and gained Draven about ten new brownie points.

"Kazzy, do you want to show Dominic where to put your bags?" And here it was, the moment of truth, I thought as we made our way up the stairs to my old childhood bedroom, that I never in a million years thought I would be showing a man like Draven. I felt him behind me and his head staring at my door over my head as I was over a foot lower. His arm reached out around me and he started tracing the colourful wooden letters that spelled out my name on my door.

# CHAPTER 52

# CHILDHOOD, KEIRA STYLE

M y room was exactly the way I had left it when I had closed the door that morning before getting in a car, driving to the airport and getting on a plane to start my new life. And now here I was, with Draven at my side, well more like peeking over my shoulder, in my childhood room surrounded with memories good, bad and truly ugly. But none of that mattered when I turned around and found the love of my life sharing everything with me.

"Well, as you can see, this is my room." I said lamely not really knowing what else to say about this small square space filled to the brim with colour and mad style sense. The walls were painted two different shades of purple but most of the space was covered in posters, paintings, pictures or shelves overflowing with knick knacks, books and little crystal figurines, I went through a stage of collecting.

My double bed was covered in tie dye bedding that I did for a project in high school textiles and had six different sized cushions that didn't match but Draven picked up the one with the peace sign embroidered in sparkly sequins on it.

"I seem to remember this symbol from somewhere." He said smirking and I blushed.

"I just couldn't resist." I replied, wondering if that sign was taking off in Hell at the moment as the latest craze…I couldn't see it somehow. He then walked over to a big pin up board I had painted butterflies in the corners that was covered in pictures of school days, my Uni acceptance letter, and old doctor's appointment for…eeeek a smear test! I ran over to him and stood in front of him trying to get him to move from my desk where my board was hung over.

"There's nothing important to see here." I said trying to pull on his arm but he wasn't yet finished noting down every last bit of personal info he was getting from this time in my room.

"I have a doctorate Keira and have a full understanding of the female reproductive system…was this taken in school?" He asked abruptly changing the subject of my girly parts and pointing to my last day of school where I was holding up my signed school shirt with wet hair as me and some other friends had been pushed in the pool by some boys we fancied. I looked so different with my long hair all wild and free and wet around my face. I was wearing a tight little vest that didn't leave much to the imagination and little denim cut offs, with a pair of sunglasses hanging from one pocket.

"I was a bit different back then, eh?" I said because really I didn't know what else to say.

"Very carefree, if not a little too…exposed. I must say I like you with layers when around so many eyes, this tempting body is for my eyes only." He said turning quickly and grabbing said body.

"It sure is." I confirmed making him groan on top of my lips.

"Are you happy to be home?" He asked me once he kissed me, making my thought process stammer.

"Sorry?" I hummed dreamily. He laughed and then said,

"I will take that incoherence as a good sign and I gather that yes, you are happy, if not a little turned on."

"A little? Bloody hell Draven if you said the word Sex I would find my legs stopped working…so are you going to do something about it?" I asked lowering my eyes and blushing at my boldness. He placed a single finger under my chin and raised my face till our eyes met.

"I would love to but I doubt your mother would approve." I was just about to speak when the door opened and Draven was magically on the other side of the room, with one of our suitcases on the bed. I was still left wobbly legged and trying to find the right words.

"I just wanted to check you two had everything…extra towels… Keira I washed your favourite bedding that you made." I looked at Draven, who was still trying not to look like he was concentrating as he lifted clothes out but when he heard the part about the bedding I saw him pick up a bit and rub it between his fingers and thumb…It was a very sweet gesture.

"Also, as I am sure you have noticed, your father made me go back up into the loft and get down all your paintings to put them back up...I hope you don't mind...but we thought...well, enough of that." She was, of course, referring to the night I came back from hospital and in a rage tore every last painting from the walls in the house that I had painted and threw them out of my window. It hadn't been my best day.

I looked to Draven and saw him fist the suitcase until it ripped the expensive silk lining and I knew that the memory of that day had just seeped in, not by me but by my mother's open mind.

"Mum, its fine and I already knew dad wouldn't let me throw them away. I saw one in the kitchen earlier." She blushed and then came over to me, gave the tops of my arms a squeeze and then kissed me before telling me dinner was in ten minutes. She smiled at Draven before she left and as soon as the door closed I squealed as I was picked up and thrown on the bed and then covered by Draven kissing me like he was trying to take the memory away from me...it worked.

Later that evening I found a very surreal moment when we were all sat around the dinner table eating chicken casserole with my mum complaining that if she had known a guest such as Draven would be 'dining' with them she would have made something more extravagant. Draven had assured that he was just happy to be here with us all and that any extra effort on his part wasn't necessary. My mum had ignored him and got out the fine china and silverware anyway and Draven made her year by telling her how lovely the table looked and how good the food was. I think if at that moment Draven would have proposed to me, my mother would have wept with joy.

While we were waiting to be seated I had to move Draven from an assault from my Nan just saving him in time before he got a grope from an OAP with a good grip for her age. He had truly looked scared for a moment and I couldn't help but laugh when my Nan winked at me. I laughed again when I did as she motioned for me to do and I pinched it myself...Draven jumped a mile thinking it was my Nan and the relief of his face was priceless.

"Ya gotta watch out for that one, she is stronger than she looks." Frank whispered to Draven having witnessed the whole thing.

"Thanks for the heads up, I gather you were the backside menu choice until I arrived." He responded coolly and Frank laughed before slapping him on the back in jest,

"Sure was bud, so remind me to buy you a cold one when we get chance, you've earned it with this family." He nodded to me and then said,

"We can't thank you enough." And then chinked the neck of his beer to Draven's before going to hug Libby, leaving me with another lump in my throat. Draven wrapped his arm round me and then said,

"I really like that human!" I smiled and then went on my tip toes to whisper in his ear, thankfully he met me half way or I would never have made it all the way up there.

"And the Demon in the corner, with her perverse obsession with a fine butt?" He laughed and then whispered back,

"Yes, her as well. I like all of your family Keira but do you know what I like the most about them?" I shook my head and waited for his answer.

"I like the way they love you."

After dinner, Draven and I escaped embarrassing Keira growing up stories, and we were in my room where I was being bombarded with questions. He wanted to know about past boyfriends, things I used to love doing, first time I drank and my hobbies, which included a scrapbooking phase that he made me show him. He flicked through all six books of my life in paper format and would linger on every picture of me as though he was trying to live it with me all over again.

"Is it weird?" I asked after he had been silently staring at a picture of me with Libby at a family BBQ.

"Is what weird?"

"Being so immersed in human life?" He finally looked up from a younger me and a little smile crept up on one side of his lips.

"I am immersed in my little human girlfriend, who I just so happen to love intensely, so I know that other humans come with that package deal but I must confess, I am a little fascinated." I gave him a daft grin.

"I can tell." I said nodding to the book he had scanned for the third time.

"Have you ever noticed before, how every picture of you seems to glow with light, like this one, look at the brightness behind you, yet the sun is behind the clouds." I looked down and saw he was right. I turned a few more pages and noticed the same thing on every one.

"I…I never noticed before, what does it mean?" I asked knowing he would have the answers.

"It means you were being watched by the Gods, which angers me."

"Why?" I was shocked, why would something like that anger him?

"Because they knew where you were all that time and nobody told me. This life…"He motioned to the book on his lap,

"Your life, I could have watched, I could have been with you behind the scenes and I would have had the pleasure of every laugh, every happy thought and every smile." He said tracing my lips gently with his fingertip.

"And every tear, every kiss with another boy, every frightful moment, I saw one of your kind or tossed and turned with my nightmares…Draven my life was not all like it seems in this book, I have others filled with sketches of your kind my nights showed me."

"Hey!" He said lifting my face to his.

"I could have helped you know."

"And how could you have helped when I cried over a boy I fancied or fell out with my mum because she wouldn't let me buy a dress that was too short?"

"I knew I liked your mum." I tried not to laugh and gave him a serious pout.

"Well for a start I would have had the boy removed from your sight."

"Which wouldn't have helped me." I informed him but he gave me a devilish smile.

"No, but it would have helped me greatly." He winked and I smirked back.

"Yeah, tell me about it! If it had been left up to you, I would have been having my first kiss at twenty three." I commented and rolling my eyes when he said,

"And?" He said with a frown.

"And what a lovely first kiss it would have been." I said changing my tune and making him nod.

"That's better." I then, feeling playful, grabbed the book from him and jumped on him again, in I don't know how many times in the last few days.

"Did I just say lovely…what I meant to say was, amazing, fantastic, mind blowing, earth shattering…"

"I think I get the picture, my dear." He said trying not to laugh as I attacked him with little kisses. Then when I got lower he started to get turned on and to stop me from manhandling him he grabbed my waist, flipped me over and started tickling me until I was snorting and pleading with him to stop.

"What a truly adorable sound, how does the children's rhyme go… this little piggy…"

"Oi!" I said slapping him on his granite bicep that was still tensed from holding me down.

"No, no, Keira , it's Oink not Oi but let's hear it again, just to be sure." And once again he was tickling me into a merciless laughter which even added some new animal noises to the mix, I think Draven liked the donkey best as that one made him laugh the hardest.

"You do realise we have a small audience outside your room listening to you laughing like this, that was until your father told them off for spying." I laughed again and this time he just hugged me to him and rolled us over so that now I was on top.

"Are you having fun?"

"I am having more than fun Keira, I am the happiest I have ever been. I am here, with you in my arms, where you will remain for the rest of my days and I am bringing tears to your incredible eyes with my ministrations...I am beyond happy." He said kissing me softly. I was just about to get carried away when something he said made my head snap up.

"In the hopes of not ruining our perfect day, can I ask you some questions?" He raised one eyebrow and I ran my fingertip over its perfect dark arch.

"I was wondering how long it would take you and without any other means to distract you from your busy mind, I will comply, my adorable little piggy."

"Oh no! Don't you dare start calling me that! I think I prefer Vixen or even little rabbit but nothing that includes something smelly and eats like, well like a pig!"

"I wish you would, I need my lush curves to pay me a visit, I feel as though I will break you, being so thin." I pouted and he bit my lip in response.

"Anyway, if you have stopped being silly, then about my questions...are you going to get mad?" I asked this time biting my own lip.

"I don't know... am I going to get angry Keira?" He said with enough humour that I decided to go for it.

"I would like you to explain to me about what your...umm...stuff does to me exactly?"

"My stuff?" He looked left and right and then whispered behind his hand,

"Do you mean my sperm, Keira...or you would like me to call it my man juice?" He mocked, and I slapped him on the arm.

"Behave! Alright Draven, you asked for it!" I dragged myself up him and positioned myself over his lips and said seductively,

"Why Draven, pray tell, what does your come do to me once it erupts deep inside me?" He closed his eyes and arched his head back into my colourful pillows and then shook his head slightly.

"Gods woman, you don't play fair at all." He said in a strained voice that added to the bulging vein in his corded neck.

"Right back at ya buddy!" I said smiling to myself.

"Alright sweetness, you win this round but remember once I get my wicked way with you, then it will be pay back and baby, then I don't play fair!" He warned and flashed me his purple lust making my insides turn to wet tissue. If there was one thing that Draven was a master at, it was manipulating my body into anything he wanted and the idea of making love to Draven's other self was a mouth-watering thought indeed.

"Does it have anything to do with ravishing me?"

"Oh sweetheart, with what I have in mind means you will need a week to recover and then, I may just do it all over again or never stop…I haven't decided yet, but one thing you can be certain of."

"Wh…what's that?" He could hear the waver in my voice and he smirked knowing how he was affecting me.

"You won't be walking away from my bed any time soon."

"I… don't doubt it for…for a second stud." I said trying to be as cocky as he was but given the stammer in my voice, it was hard to be convincing and with that grin I was getting, man did he know it!

"Ask your questions sweetheart before I embarrass myself and act like an adolescent teenager in his girlfriend's bedroom."

"Is that so?" I asked shocked that I could do that to him.

"It's hard enough given the ideal setting for this fantasy and knowing your new virginal sexual status." Okay, so I was teasing him as I could feel an erection that could have hammered nails into concrete.

"Then why are we doing this to ourselves, Draven?"

"Because if there was ever a time that I would have to not give into my sexual urges and show restraint with the love of my life then it will be for this reason and this reason only. I don't have reasons not to touch you Keira but this one." I finally gave in and resigned myself to the fact that I would not be getting any from Draven until he was ready and I knew it wasn't going to be in my childhood bedroom on a rainbow quilt with a picture of my smiling family on my bedside.

"Okay, so back to my question, explain what happens."

"Alright but please know, I didn't keep it from you out of deceit. It was… well, I was arrogant in believing that you were mine and was not allowed a choice in the matter, which you are still not by the way but you do at least deserve to understand it better."

"Oh jeez thanks." I said sarcastically.

"Well, do you want to leave me at any point?"

"NO!" The thought was actually a painful one to think about.

"Well then, it is a moot point. But the basics of it are relatively simple. I make love to you and my essence gets transferred every time and not only passes on my regenerative cells but also, as it would seem from what happened at Transfusion, some of my powers also and that part was unexpected indeed."

"Okay, just so that we're clear, or more like I am clear, I won't grow old, get wrinkles and start to forget my friend Betty down the road?"

"You have a friend Betty?"

"Hypothetical friend. So am I correct?" He smiled at my attempt at making a serious conversation humorous.

"Yes, you won't forget 'Betty' or anyone else for that matter. You won't age any more than I do and considering I have had this body for a very long time, I would be correct in assuming my blood will have the same effect on your body also. As for the powers, I am in the dark on that one. But I will be with you every step of the way and from what I gather it only occurs when you are extremely pissed off…I won't be making that mistake again around my games room or my garage for that matter." I could just imagine the amount of leverage this gave me, especially as it would come in handy no doubt when he was driving too fast….oh the power, I thought in an evil baddie mode.

"Okay, so next question."

"Am I right in saying this is the one you think I will fly into an uncontrollable fit of rage at?"

"I thought I would start you off easy and ease into it."

"Please give me some credit, Keira."

"Ha, coming from the man who nearly caused a $350 million plane to crash so that he could kill someone in a rage because you found me a bit skinnier than before…sorry Mr Credit, but I need a deposit on that one before I give you that amount of trust in your trademark raging!" I smiled at my clever argument before continuing,

"And don't frown at me 'cause you know I am right." I said flicking him on the nose.

"I think I preferred it when I intimidated you, you were more compliant back then." He added dryly and I huffed.

"Ask your question Keira."

"Fine, but no raging allowed!" He held out his hand and motioned for me to continue.

"Why was it that you never told Lucius you had the Tip of the Spear all along and why couldn't you give it to him, but did when... well...when what happened to me in the Temple room?" To give him his credit, he didn't fly into a rage and the only noticeable anger was when he closed his eyes and his whole body went ridged underneath me. He moved slowly sitting me up and placing me opposite him ready to hear his reasons.

"Keira, do you trust me?"

"You know I do."

"But you didn't, back when you were in Lucius' cave room." He reminded me and I lowered my head shamefully.

"Well, I was angry at you, it was like I was just another object to be bargained with and I did kind of think you were having your cake and eating it too." I confessed feeling even more like shit knowing what actually had happened.

"Keira, look at me." When I didn't he said more sternly,

"Look. At. Me. Keira!" I did as I was told and was granted with the back of his fingers on my cheek in a caress.

"Good girl. Now I want you to listen to me when I say that you don't need to feel guilty, I can very well imagine where your confused mind was at and I would never blame you, never. But in this, I need your trust." I nodded and he continued.

"Very well. That day as you know, I was at the Crucifixion and I know I lied but it was for your own good as at that time I could not go into the reason why I was there. For this you must forgive me but as I have said, it was unavoidable. I found out the only interference I was allowed to partake in was to retrieve the Tip and leave. I know it is hard to understand but even I must sometimes obey and do as the Gods ask of me." He was right, it was hard to see indeed. Draven lived and breathed leadership and dominance that seeped from every pore, so this did make it a difficult thing to see indeed.

"I was told that a re-born Vampire like no other was to become King to all creatures of his kind and he was to come to me and swear his life and loyalty. For years Lucius and I were not just companions with the same goal but also we were friends. But the one thing that I was sworn by the Gods to do was to keep the Tip from him until his time came, along with mine."

"I don't understand, what do you mean his time, along with yours?" I shook my head making him take hold of me and kiss me sweetly before explaining the impossible.

"His destiny told him of the Tip and that he would only get it back when the Chosen One was found and added to this was a mortal girl that would show him the sun and save his life."

"I know this, he told me but I never thought it..." I couldn't carry on, it was just too mind blowing to piece together but then Draven delivered the biggest shocker of all.

"I know this is hard for you to trust in, but everything told has come to pass"

"And what of your time then, what was predicted for you?"

"Oh Keira, I was always told that by keeping the Tip from Lucius, that it would one day aid in saving the life of the Chosen One and for that, I would have done anything ...

*"Anything."*

"Yes I gathered, thank you." He replied frowning and I couldn't help but smile around my mouthful of bun and burger. When he still hadn't opened it I dropped my burger and said,

"Oh for heaven's sake...here, I do this." I opened it up and poured his fries into the other side of the lid and then even added a squeeze of ketchup and mayo in little mounds at the corners. Then I lifted one of his fries and dipped it in his mayo and popped it in my mouth. He stared at me like I was a recently escaped mental patient.

"Yum, here, try it." I said doing the same for him and I saw him reluctantly open his mouth for me to plonk in a fry. I saw him chew as if I had just fed him a slice of lemon and I laughed.

"Bloody hell Draven, it's only a potato not poison!"

"That's debatable. Keira this food looks like stepped on rubber and you shouldn't be filling my delectable body with it."

"Bighead!" I said causing him to scowl.

"I was, of course, referring to your delectable body, the one that belongs to me." I dropped a fry and then looked down.

"Oh!" My cheeks flamed and I took a long swig of my diet coke to cool it down.

"No wonder it was so cheap, what meat is this ...dog?" Draven said flicking his bun lid off in disgust.

"Draven, don't be daft. I know it's not exactly a la carte but I do love a whopper." His head snapped up.

"You have eaten this shit before and yet you still come back?" He was shocked.

"I happen to like this shit, thank you very much, so you can sit there and sulk for all I care, I am enjoying my meal." I said and I could see the cogs working and trying to come up with a payback of his own. He hadn't mentioned the shower incident but he must have known it was me, thanks to the massive smirk he was welcomed with when he got out of the shower.

Once I was finished and Draven didn't eat any more than the one fry I forced on him, we went back to shopping. I rubbed my belly through my warm coat and said,

"Mmm, nice and full!"

"Must have been all those lovely preservatives, incomprehensible cuts of some form of meat and watery veg that had not one single shred of nutrients left." I laughed at his usual moody tone when not getting his own way and replied,

"Yep, sure was filling and delicious I might add...tell me, are you hungry?"

"Funny, little rabbit but just so you know, this is all being noted and added to the list of punishments I will be dishing out when I get you back to our home."

"Umm...mm, whatever you say there Mr Moody Pants, now let's get this finished." I said putting an arm in his to tackle the rest of the shops. This time I had no choice in the matter as it was Draven's turn to play it his way of shopping. He took me into the Metquarter where all the designer shops were situated and he even complained that these weren't even expensive enough for what he had in mind. We walked around and now instead of just everyday ordinary women to contend with drooling after Draven, here I had the city's elite and females dripping in designer clothes. But for once I didn't care and was just basking in the glow of what having Draven's arm around me did to my insides, along with my self-confidence. Well at least he looked more at ease inside this expensive cocoon.

The rest of the day was filled with Draven having the car brought around to load our bags into and then off we would go again. I refused absolutely everything Draven tried to buy for me, including a gorgeous red dress that I stared at in awe for a while.

"That would be a beautiful colour on you." He hummed in my ear from behind but I just shook it off and wrapped my arms round his neck, telling him that the effect of him kissing me would be an even better colour on me...he had to agree.

The one thing I did see that I wanted to buy without Draven knowing about was something in a window we passed on the high street earlier but I had to wait until I was in the ladies bathroom to ring Sophia. Luckily I found my mobile in my luggage and quickly rang her to ask for her help. She laughed and told me it wouldn't be a problem. She swore her secrecy to me like last time I had bought sexy lingerie and when I said the name Ann Summers she whistled and said,

"I would offer to buy some other toys for you but I think Dom would have my head if anything but him was to satisfy you." This made me nearly trip up on the way out of the ladies getting me a few snooty looks. When I said goodbye to Sophia before Draven could see, I found one lady asking him the time, although it was obvious she was wearing a watch and then there was another group of girls staring at him as though he was the elixir of life...which I guess for me he was!

As soon as he saw me he beamed above the beautiful girl's head and she turned to see where his gaze was concentrated. When she saw it was just plain old me, not a supermodel she smiled and then turned back to him to touch his arm and whisper in his ear.

"Excuse me madam, but that is highly inappropriate and disrespectful of the woman I love. I suggest you take your hand off me and run along now to your husband while I indulge myself in a real woman…my real woman! Now excuse me!" Draven snapped cutting her down with a lethal look, shocking not only the woman but also everyone that had heard his booming voice. He shamelessly removed her hand like it was dripping in filth and came over to me and kissed me deeply making some women gasp at the intensity, me included. I looked up when Draven had finished with me and saw the woman storm past us to the ladies room wiping angry tears from her eyes.

"What did she say to you?" His eyes flashed purple at the memory and then cooled when they looked down at me.

"It is not worth repeating but know this, no-one and I mean NO-ONE disrespects you. She deserved far worse than my harsh words."

"Hey, it's okay. It can't have been that bad." He softened as I touched his face and turned it from the toilet door that was getting the death look.

"It was not nice. Come on, I want to spoil you, it is the only way to clear my sour mood." I rolled my eyes but let him have his way.

Once we finished shopping, the day then consisted of me sat on the floor of my room, wrapping presents with Draven assisting in holding the paper down when I needed a strong finger. My favourite Christmas movie, National Lampoons Christmas Vacation, played in the background on my little TV screen and I would giggle every now and again at the bits I found the funniest. Draven had complained in the car ride home because I wouldn't let him pay to get them professionally wrapped but I told him it was all part of the fun, and now, watching me grinning, I think he was getting the point.

My mum came up later with white chocolate and raspberry cookies that I love, from a bakery near the butchers she picked the turkey up from this morning, with a pint of milk. Draven looked at me in fascination as I ran to the door and shouted the trade mark 'don't come in' whenever one is wrapping presents. The rest of the night consisted of him keep telling me how adorable I was, especially with a milk moustache that I kept teasing him with…very virginal and all and I noticed him adjust his jeans more than once.

I ended the night by asking him if he enjoyed his shower that morning and if it would help with his problem, nodding to his pants. That just got me a firm,

"Right, you asked for it!" and then a punishing tickle round on the floor, which ended in kissing in the middle of ribbon, tape and Christmas wrapping paper that didn't survive Draven's stealth attack.

Christmas day came and went in a flurry of activity of mad family traditions that Draven was still trying to get his head round. Like the fact that my dad still left out a brandy and a carrot for 'Father Christmas' even though it had been quite a few years since Libby and I had believed. I explained to Draven it was because my dad liked the excuse for a brandy before bed. This then ended up one of the reasons for Draven's gift to my father. He gave him a very expensive bottle of something called Hennessy Richard Extra Cognac that came in a handmade glass decanter that my mother cooed over. I asked how much but Draven refused to tell me and reminded me that I really didn't want to know.

All gifts from Draven, that I knew nothing about, were along the same lines, all very expensive but also personal to what each member of my family would like. For example, he noticed my mother liked the colour green, so he gave her a Jade coloured scarf from a designer none of us had heard of but was no doubt one of a kind. My sister received the same treatment with a cherry red Louis Vuitton handbag, because her favourite colour was red. Even my Grandparents got a gift in the form of a mini cruise that already had my Nan on the phone to her neighbour boasting about.

Frank was soon jumping around like a mad man when Draven presented him with a driving experience like no other, which turned out to be a trip for the family to one of his holiday homes near his personal race track. The Spa nearby was also booked for full treatments for my mum and Libby for anytime his guests were to be staying...after the baby was born of course.

My family all came through and got Draven gifts in the form of a scarf set knitted by my Nan, some aftershave from my folks, that I would never let him use...but they didn't need to know that and what I thought was his favourite gift, Libby and Frank had got him a personalised Ferrari gun metal phone case for his expensive smartphone and they told him I had mentioned how he likes Ferraris. He ran his finger over his name engraved at the back and seemed genuinely touched by not only my family's gifts but also their easy acceptance of him.

I felt like a big kid again when giving and receiving my gifts and Draven watched with a constant grin every time I tore into one of my brightly wrapped presents. I soon had everyone laughing at me when I did my ritual of trying to get on everything at once but found it too hard to open my next gift with mittens on. So I took off my hat, headband, two pairs of gloves, a new jumper, woolly sock slippers, sequined belt and rubbed the hand cream lump Libby had added to my nose, to carry on opening my new things. Draven had laughed the whole time.

Later on when dinner was finished, crackers had been pulled, silly hats worn and all bad jokes told, Draven and I both declined Christmas pudding until later, as most people do after the biggest meal of the year and left to go up to my room, to be alone. There were just two gifts left that we wanted to open in private and I was very nervous about what Draven would make of my gift to him.

"This is the reason we stopped at Switzerland." He said, surprising me.

"I didn't know where we stopped." I replied and let him hand me a beautifully gift wrapped box, in swirled black paper and a thick purple ribbon which was Draven's colour of choice.

"Yes well, I wanted this to be a surprise and I have been planning to give it to you since we first met, but Sophia advised I waited until the time was right." I smiled up at him after playing with the satin ribbon that I was going to keep, just like the one that had been tied to the rose he left me on my pillow.

"The ribbon is nice Keira, but it isn't your gift." He said bringing me out of my happy place and putting me in a different one entirely with the handsome look he gave me. I took a deep breath and carefully this time opened the gift so that the paper didn't tear. I gasped when I took the box lid off and found a blue velvet jewellery box. Draven looked over and saw that I was only at the next box stage and when I wouldn't open it, he sighed and took it from me.

"You're not very good at putting me out of my misery Keira, here allow me." He said and then he opened the lid back and my hands flew to my mouth. After giving me enough time to process the beauty before me, I still hadn't said anything.

"Say something Keira. Do you not like it?" His voice sounded so vulnerable and when I looked up I found the uncertainty in his eyes.

"It's…it's utterly breathtaking Dominic." I said and I think at this minute I was witnessing the biggest grin I had ever seen to date on Draven.

"Thank you Catherine, you have made me incredible happy to hear you say that." He looked so relieved and I felt guilty saying the next words out of my mouth.

"But Draven, I can't…this is too much…I…" Thankfully he was still smiling.

"This has been waiting for you for a very long time, sweetheart, and has never been worn by another living person on earth."

"Oh God, you didn't get it from a dead guy did you?" I asked tactlessly but Draven just threw his head back to laugh out load.

"No, in fact I found this stone at a very important point in my life and I had it made into this necklace by a master craftsman. It was always intended to be for you." I had tears forming in my eyes at the thought.

"Oh Draven!"

"Can I put it on you? I have been waiting a small forever for this day…along with another day I will be experiencing soon." He added and I flushed, knowing what he was referring too.

"Please." I said lifting my loose hair to one side. He got off my bed and came to stand behind me. He then raised the necklace before me and then stopped before placing it on me.

"I have another request" I waited for him to continue and I heard him exhale.

"Do have any objections to wearing this all the time?" I looked in the mirror on my wall that was positioned just right to show me both our reflections and Draven, unbelievably, looked as nervous as hell. It was obvious how much this meant to him and in turn, it meant a lot to me.

"None whatsoever." I answered on a whisper and he closed his eyes as if every wish he ever asked for had all come true.

"By the Gods, you make me so happy, Keira!" He said before lowering it to my skin and then he tied the black silk cord behind my neck that was so incredibly soft against my skin.

"Then let it be, it has been fused together and only one force alive can ever remove it from your body." I gasped in surprise.

"It can't be taken off?" I asked in awe.

"No, not by another's hands and only by yours in the right or I should say, the wrong frame of mind."

"Which is?" I asked touching it for the first time and feeling a raw power being drawn from it.

"If your love for its heart's owner ever falters." He said with heavy lidded emotion and I touched his cheek before saying,

"Well if that means you, then that will never happen…you know that, right?"

"Keira, if I ever see the day that necklace is not on your body, then that will be the time I truly feel my heart break for the first time in my life." I leaned in, rested my forehead to his and then said over his lips,

"Then I am happy that day will never come. Thank you Dominic, it is now a part of me as you are. I love it, as I love you." As soon as I finished speaking the last word he held my face quickly and brought my lips to his for one of the most memorable kisses of my life.

Once he let me go I got up and looked at the new adornment to my body and I was mesmerised at how stunning it was. It wasn't some plum sized diamond or covered in a sparkling array of precious gems like something Kate Winslet wore in the film Titanic. No, this was unlike anything I had ever seen before.

It was a deep purple stone that had been carved into an intricate heart that fell in a tear drop shape the size of a strawberry. A tiny slit had been carved in its centre where a fixed blood red gem was placed to make it like a bleeding purple heart, embellished with a swirly design making it delicate and pretty. It then hung unusually on a twisted black cord in an Asian fashion. I had never loved the look of a piece of jewellery so much before.

"It's a very rare piece of purple jadeite and it symbolises royalty, sophistication, and spirituality. It is also said that it can help to evoke imagination, inspiration and peace of mind, which is quite fitting for my little artist, don't you think?" He said coming to stand behind me and he placed his hand over mine where I was holding it.

"I can feel it, as though it's calling to me or something… does that make sense?" I asked feeling a pull, like it was connecting with me, body, mind and soul.

"But of course. It holds a piece of me with it and it can sense my essence in you, we call it '唱歌給你的愛人血' which means 'to sing to your lover's blood'. The teardrop coming from its centre is just as rare as the jadeite being that of a red diamond. I had it carved to represent the only one that would ever wear it… the only woman that would ever be able to make my heart bleed." Oh god I could barely breathe. This felt so much more than just a gift, it felt like he was giving me a piece of himself and in a way I guess, he was.

"I don't know what to say…it's the most stunning thing I have ever seen Draven…but please, never tell me the price." He laughed and kissed my neck by the soft cord.

"It is like its new owner Keira, utterly priceless." At this point I couldn't stop from turning and having him the way I wanted. I jumped up and he caught my behind in his large hands, putting me at the right height to kiss him madly.

"What about my gift?" He said against my lips and my heart plummeted. I could never and no way give him mine now, not after this.

"I can't…I'm sorry, I will get you something else but I can't give it to you now." I said touching my purple heart. He noted where my fingers were and then he frowned.

"So, you think the only thing I could ever accept from you has to be of great monetary value, you believe me to be that shallow… yes?" Okay, when he put it like that it was a little insulting.

"No, it's not that at all…it's…."

"Good, I am glad to hear it. Go on and fetch it then, as I am excited." He said dropping me and giving my behind a little pat. Oh God, this was going to be so embarrassing. I got on my bed and leant over the side and pulled it from under my bed where I had hidden it.

"I must say, I am enjoying it already." He said cheekily and when I lifted my head up, I saw him staring at my bum. I rolled my eyes at him and then came back up with a white papered bundle also tied with a purple ribbon.

"Ah, great minds." He said holding the ribbon in between his finger and thumb.

"The ribbon is nice Draven, but it isn't your gift." I said mocking his words earlier and he raised his eyebrows at me.

"Oh, you do play the game well." He said before opening it with a care that surprised me from such long thick fingers. He was just about to reveal what it was when I stilled his hands.

"Wait, let me first explain."

"Is that customary?" He mocked back but I ignored him.

"I have something else for you to open but it's at home and if you don't like it…well, you might not like it…I mean, you might find it… umm… look I'm not saying this right…"

"Hey, Keira look at me." I did and his eyes softened as he ran a thumb over my bitten lip.

"Trust me, anything you think in your heart to give me will be accepted with nothing but loving gratitude and a fierce protectiveness. I treasure anything you give, especially the memories you give me." I swallowed the hard lump and took a deep breath.

"I am glad you said that because if that is the case, then I think you will like this gift." I let go of his hands and he pulled back the last bit of paper, letting every one of my scrapbooks to come tumbling out. I watched the shock transform his excited features and it was the look of utter disbelief and wonderment.

"I didn't know what else you could want, I mean what do you buy for a man that can buy anything he wants, so I gave you the only thing I knew you wanted but couldn't possibly pay for...my childhood." I must have gone bright red with waiting for his response. Would he find it silly?

"This one here is empty, I bought it today in hopes...umm, maybe, you know...like the next chapter of my life...with you in it." At this he finally looked up at me and now it was my time for my utter shock...he had tears misting his eyes!

"I hope that means you like it and don't think its lame?" I said and in a millisecond he grabbed me and had crushed me to his body in an unmoving embrace. I heard him saying things into my hair that I didn't understand and I felt the pull of the necklace with our closeness. He was right, it was singing to him. I let him hold me for as long as he needed, being completely taken aback by his response and then when his whispering stopped he pulled me back. His eyes were damp and brimming over with deep seated emotions I knew he wasn't used to feeling.

"I love you and this gift you have given me means the world to me, more in fact, as now I have the two most treasured things that I own in my life and they both contain you. I am honoured Catherine, beyond the strength of these words and more, I am forever honoured." He said taking both my hands and kissing them both on the palms.

"I..I...am so...glad, oh Draven, I love you so much!" I said and the next kiss was the second of the day that I would never ever forget, not if I lived for an eternity.

And with Draven's love...

*...it was now possible.*

# CHAPTER 54
# RED GIRL WALKING

W e stayed at my parents' house until we had to fly back for the Annual Afterlife New Year's Eve party. Draven told me that they didn't really celebrate at Christmas so being a part of humans' traditions had been an experience. Although he did point out that Sophia still made him buy her a new car every year, this year it was a Mercedes SLK Roadster.

He also explained that the New Year's Party was their biggest celebration as it represented more to them than just the passing of a new year, it was to celebrate the Roman God Janus, who the month of January was named after. He is a God with two faces, one facing front and the other facing back and is the God of doors and gates. Draven also explained that he is the God that controls all beginnings and transitions and more importantly, doorways to these beginnings, endings and all time. In other words he is the father of Pythia the Oracle and controller of the future that she foresees and also the past.

I was utterly fascinated when he told me the story in bed one night but his whispering in my ear of stories of the real mythology in that hypnotic tone soon had me falling asleep with a mind full of the Gods, in Draven's arms.

After a tearful farewell to my parents and promising Libby I would be seeing them soon when they were back in the new year, we were soon on our way back to the States just in time for this monumental occasion that I was actually getting nervous about. I asked Draven lots of questions and each time he laughed at me before answering with a soothing voice, one I couldn't be angry at for making fun of me. The rest of the 'gang' had gone back to Afterlife already and he told me it was one of Sophia's favourite things to plan and getting it all ready for the big night was like her version of me at Christmas.

We were now on another one of Draven's private jets, this time a lot smaller but just as luxurious and he lifted me into a massive leather seat that engulfed my small frame. Draven had been delighted with my mother's efforts in putting weight on me and after nearly a week of gorging myself on Pringles, cheese puffs, After eights, Christmas cake…with the crunchy icing of course, and buffet food that included my favourite duck spring rolls and leftover turkey sandwiches I had gained back my weight and no longer had to keep pulling up my jeans so as not to flash my new Mr Men knickers from Libby. Draven had even made me put on Miss Giggles and gave me a real reason for the name, which ended up in me doing an assortment of farm animal noises.

"Do you need anything, drinks, food or I did request one of those Christmas movies you love so much? Just ask the stewardess for anything you need." I looked up at him leaning over the back of my chair and playing with a shorter strand of my hair at the front.

"Why, where will you be…do you have work to do?" I asked wondering just how many businesses a man like Draven had to deal with.

"I do indeed." He leaned in close, brushed back the hair he had been playing with and whispered in my ear,

"I will be flying the plane!" At this, it was as if someone had just jack hammered a steel rod down my spine. I tensed and if Draven hadn't been over me I would have shot from my chair.

"Easy, love."

"But Draven, no…why can't you get one of the pilots to fly, I mean…I…"

"I think I have been flying a lot longer than any mortal pilots, don't you? Trust me Keira, I won't let anything happen to you or my plane." And with that he kissed me lightly on the cheek before turning to speak to a stewardess in hushed tones. No doubt warning her about his temperamental and irrational girlfriend who hates to fly, even when the pilots himself has wings!

As it turned out Draven had recommend that the stewardess pretty much made it her mission to get me tanked up on champagne which was surprisingly good at taking the edge off flying and that, combined with popcorn, Santa Claus the Movie and an endless stream of the good stuff, I hardly noticed we were even on a plane…that was until I heard Draven's deep commanding voice over the intercom for me to be shown to the cockpit. I tried to refuse but then his voice came over us again,

"You don't want me to come back there do you, Keira?" At this I was up like a shot and storming into the little control room to find Draven's booming laughter.

"Good girl, now won't you take a seat?" I think I actually growled at him.

"And if I don't?" I tested but he just gave me a sideways glance and I saw his grin twitch as he tried not to laugh.

"Then I could get up, fly the plane with my mind and see what Little Miss panties you are wearing today…although given your scowl I don't think I find them to be 'Happy' but what about 'Naughty'…? Oh I do hope for 'Naughty', now come here!" He added and crooked his finger at me. I complied, of course I did, especially with that voice!

"Sit!" A simple order which I did, because I really didn't want to think of Draven ever controlling a plane with his mind, not if it had to be shared with kinky thoughts. So I did as I was told and was crapping myself the whole time.

"Trust." He reminded me and then with a cheeky grin he said,

"You can be my co-pilot."

"No, I bloody well can't! I am not touching a single thing!" I said looking at all the switches, buttons, lights, levers and most scary of all, a window to the most beautiful view of sky I had ever seen.

"Oh wow!" I said breathlessly.

"Stunning isn't it, that's why I wanted you to see it and I could never fly you this high by myself, I think you would have a heart attack." He chuckled and I smacked his arm without looking at him.

"Ssshh, don't ruin it with crazy talk." I joked and he laughed. I eyed him out the corner of my eye and saw how happy he looked, so laid back and easy it made my insides tingle at the sight.

"You know the real view is out there, right?" He commented, when I must have turned to stare at him in open wonder….was he blushing, no…never!

"Oh, my god! You're blushing!" I blurted out and he frowned.

"Don't be ridiculous, of course not, for starters it's in the King's handbook, that absolutely, none what so ever, die by one's own sword, to ever blush in front of a beautiful woman staring at him with obvious open lust." He said teasing and I laughed.

"Well, it's your fault for being so ridiculously stunning." I said this time without humour.

"Why Keira, do you think me handsome?" He said light heartedly.

"You know I do and you know full well the effect your gorgeous looks have on the female population." I replied and at this he just shrugged his shoulders.

"As long as you like the way I look, then I am happy with the way I look. I couldn't give a damn what the rest of the population thinks of me. This body was only ever meant for the temptation of one person and if you say it works, then it has done its job." I couldn't believe the seriousness of his statement. Surely, he didn't feel this way.

"Oh my God Draven, you can't be serious."

"Deadly. Keira my body is yours and yours is mine. This is a pointless argument unless you are not happy with the Gods' selection of host for me?" He turned to me and I couldn't believe he was talking about his body like it was something he could just change like picking a new outfit.

"God, no! I love the way you look, every last inch in fact! You must know this, I mean is it not obvious…? I turn to jelly at just the sight of you and if you ever want to render me speechless all you have to do is take off your shirt." Once I had finished he beamed at me.

"Then all is well, and yes Keira, I know now." He said, and I couldn't believe he didn't know before, he must have…surely or had I just taken it for granted that he would know. I would have assumed a man like Draven would have just had to look in the mirror and seen every pore oozing with charm and breathtaking good looks but maybe I was wrong.

By the time we had stopped to refuel and I had thankfully not been made to sit in the cockpit while landing, Draven had finally got another pilot to fly the rest of the way so that he could be with me. We spent the rest of the journey playfully kissing and Draven trying very hard to find out what today's knickers selection was.

I must have fallen asleep at one point because the next thing I knew we were in a car and I was waking up from resting my head on Draven's lap curled in the seat next to him like a big cat. The soothing strokes on the side of my head were down to Draven's big hand and I almost purred. I stretched out, yawned and then sat up.

"What time is it?" I said rubbing the sleep out of my eyes.

"It's early and we're not far now, why don't you get some more sleep. The party is later tonight and that will take it out of you." I looked up at him and then down on his tempting lap and decided to give into the temptation. I was back asleep within minutes of Draven's stroking hand and soothing words.

The next time I woke was when I opened my eyes to see Draven carrying me up a staircase, but my exhaustion wouldn't allow me to move other than to burrow closer to Draven's heat. I felt him kiss the top of my head that was nestled deep into his jacket and then the last thing I felt was being lowered onto a familiar bed and I fell back to sleep with a smile on my face, thanks to the surprising thought that this bed still smelled of me.

I woke for the last time to Draven's lips at my neck and the sight of his tousled hair, morning stubble and lazy eyes was the nicest thing in the world to open my eyes to and the fact we were back in our bed was the cherry on top.

"Morning little Miss Sleepy or should I say... little Miss Sunshine?" He said playfully and I lifted the covers to see, yes I was naked all except my little Miss Sunshine knickers.

"You don't play fair." I said making him laugh.

"Well, I am half Demon so really Keira, what did you expect? An unconscious beauty in my arms was just too much temptation to resist."

"So were you disappointed to find they weren't in fact little Miss Naughty?" He sucked on my neck and then held it in between his teeth before smiling at my loud moan.

"Not at all, I think there is enough 'naughty' in this relationship than to add more..."

"Oh?"

"I have very naughty thoughts about you Keira and later I finally get to show you." He said in a thick hoarse voice that flooded my senses.

"Now it's up you, Sophia and Pip are waiting to play with my favourite dolly." He said in my ear and then laughed when I rolled over, buried my head in the pillow and cried out a muffled,

"Oh God, No!"

The next few hours were exactly as Draven had described to me...I had become a living doll to the two people in the world who loved nothing more than to play 'dress human dolly'. I found myself once again transported back in time to Sophia's bedroom and swiftly stripped of my clothes and pushed into a bath, big enough for an elephant.

"You two really need to learn some boundaries." I advised or threatened...whichever way to a Demon and an Imp it came across....my gut instincts told me they ignored both.

Thankfully, I had been left to shave and wash myself alone, after getting them both to leave or I threatened to sit there and prune all day, I got up feeling refreshed. I think I had almost fallen asleep at one point but I put it down to the jasmine scent in the water and the soft luscious bubbles that were surrounding my body. I was just thankful that my period was a short one as I had come off yesterday so I was hoping, given Draven's earlier comment, that tonight was finally 'the night'. When I got out of the bath I found my suspicions to be confirmed.

"That isn't the set from Ann Summers!" I said staring down at Sophia's bed where a stunning underwear set lay in waiting for my body to fill it.

"Do you like it?" Pip asked all excited while Sophia just grinned. I think they could tell from my face that I liked it alright.

"I still got you the one from Ann Summers, but for tonight my dear, I had my orders." My head snapped up to Sophia.

"What do you mean?"

"Dom just said one word and your choice was anything but." I rolled my eyes and said,

"Say the word Pip." I said turning to the excitable bouncing bubble of colour that couldn't keep still.

"Virginal!" They both laughed when I fell onto the bed dramatically and groaned.

At the end of a very long day of being primped and pampered I was now scrubbed, buffed, moisturised, smoothed, shined and brushed ready for the dress I hadn't been allowed to see and had make up applied that I wasn't allowed to touch. Everything had been a flurry of excitement for my two friends and I hated to admit it, but it had been nice to be so fussed over. Talk about personality re-wire or what!

They even helped me first get into my underwear and then a very heavy dress. I felt like Cinderella with two very unlikely fairy Godmothers buzzing around me, moving me this way and that after the tugging started at my back.

The underwear that had been picked by Sophia was a stunning

corset with a sweetheart neck line in ivory satin. It had metal hook and eye clasps up the front and a ribbon tied at the back that was, at this moment, being tugged into an hour glass shape. The front was very low and barely covered my breasts but at least it kept them pulled in tight thanks to the strong boning, causing quite an eyeful of cleavage. I was surprised with Sophia, as it was quite a plain material but the skirt part it had attached was a gorgeously graceful, see-through soft organza in the same colour. It moved like liquid the full length of me and it made you want to do the whole girly spinning around thing, but with my designer captors behind me I had to remain still.

"Is that it?" I said when Sophia had all but broke my ribs but she just clapped her hands and said,

"Now it's time for the fun part." Before I had chance to ask her what she meant with a cautious voice, she had Pip coming at us with arms full of thick ivory ribbons.

"Now it's time to wrap a gift fit for a King." Sophia said and before I could voice my objection, her and Pip had both started to wrap my corseted top half in metres of lush ribbon. They worked like I was a human Totem pole and soon I looked like exactly what they were trying to achieve…an ivory gift.

"Now the final seal." Sophia said coming to my front and tying the two long ends into a bow under my breasts. Then with closed eyes, she ran her hands over my sides and the looser parts that didn't lie flush with the corset, pulled in suddenly and sealed themselves to the rest of the material. Even the bow at the front glued down so it didn't add to any extra bulk under the dress I was to be wearing. It now looked like the corset had been made like this and soon the realisation hit me, that without Draven's help, there was no way I could get out of the thing.

"Is this wise?" I said after Sophia had finished but she just gave me a sly smile as if to say 'Oh yes' then I was swiftly put in my dress demanding I close my eyes the whole time.

"Okay, now open!" Pip shouted clapping like an excited seal.

I opened my eyes to the biggest dress I have ever worn and I would have felt my heart pounding if there had have been room but thanks to my corset, it kept it from leaping from my chest.

"Oh God!" I said making the girls giggle.

"I don't think I can do this." I said but when the girls saw the panic on my face they quickly came to my aid in the form of champagne and turning me from the mirror and even more champagne.

Don't get me wrong, the dress was spectacular and exquisite and I felt like a bloody princess in it but knowing Draven would be seeing me in it, along with everyone else I knew, had my cheeks matching the colour of the dress. It was the exact colour of the dress I had seen at the shopping mall on Christmas Eve but oh so very different.

The dress was unlike anything I had ever seen before and looking at Sophia's beaming face, I just knew it was one of a kind and wasn't bought from any store. The top part was incredible and consisted of a scattering of black velvet flowers raised on top of skin coloured organza so it just looked like someone had painted them straight onto my skin. They started thicker, with bigger roses near my waist and up over my breasts then they fanned out into smaller ones over my shoulders and down my arms. The neck was cut into a deep V shape that showcased the necklace Draven had given me and the red diamond matched the scarlet coloured skirt.

I spun round and saw the mirror image of the top on the back and my shoulder blades each had a sprinkling of flowers that also grew thicker at the back. Amongst the flowers were also vines and thorns making it look as though my naked torso had been taken over by some demonic velvet plant. The dress continued down into a thick black sash high around the waist in the same material as the skirt, which was a thick shimmering taffeta. It was floor length but one side of the scarlet taffeta was brunched up and secured at my hip height, showing the floaty material underneath that was pure silk.

To this was added simple high heeled shoes in the same colour that couldn't be seen underneath the long layers of the dress. I didn't even need gloves as the flowers on the sleeves were placed in such a way that they covered every one of my scars. Sophia had told me the top part of the dress was something called devore velvet and the underskirt was made from the finest silk, then Pip went on to talk about silk worms and if that would be like eating material. Sophia and I both shook our heads and laughed.

My makeup had been done in a very natural way being another Draven request, promptly telling his sister that I didn't need it. But I still found myself with a sweep of mascara, a natural shade over my eyes but the most startling change was deep red lipstick that made them look permanently wet and glossy. My hair had been curled into a whimsical fairytale style that was all held up with one strong clip. It had a big black silk rose on the side to match the design of the dress and my new big curls overflowed down my back into a V shape that matched the back of the dress.

"And the princess is ready for the ball." Sophia said, and Pip added her,

"Oh, hell yeah she is, you go and rock that room, Tootie doll! The King is going to bust a vein when he sees ya!" This made me down the full glass of champagne I had just been poured.

After I was done and was ready, I was finally allowed to sit down and wait for the other two, who both took about five minutes each thanks to a very handy supernatural click of the fingers. Sophia had this gift and although Pip didn't, she still didn't take long due to her, 'I just throw clothes up in the air, and what I catch, I wear' approach.

Sophia came out of her dressing room wearing a beautiful strapless fitted, white ruffled dress that was long and was an A-line shape with the bodice cut straight across her chest. She then had a thick black satin sash, with a big tied bow hanging down under her bust. Her ringlet curls had been straightened into a sleek twist and held high to her head with a diamond encrusted clip running the full height of her head and tucked into her hair. She had on a choker, teardrop earrings and thick bracelet to match.

Pip sauntered out next all dressed in black and it looked like someone had made a kinky ball gown out of PVC and feathers! The top was a PVC long sleeved top that looked like she had been dipped in black ink, high up to the neck and under her little breasts was a tight half corset that went lower at the back and curved down over her bum. Then the skirt part flared out in a fish tail design that was all made up of thousands of big black plume feathers that swished when she walked. The back had a long train and the front came up high to the top of her thighs to show off her over the knee boots with spiked white heels.

It was the first time I had seen Pip all in one colour and even her hair had been hidden under a full sized velvet top hat just showing one big green curl at the side. Even her lips were black with bright white liner and white painted eyelashes making it look as if she had been out in the snow that was still coming down around these parts.

"Okay ladies, time to make our entrance." Sophia announced and then held up her glass for us to do the same. We each stood like a material layered triangle and raised our glasses.

"To best friends!" I said.

"To the best night with best friends!" Sophia said.

"To our best friend losing her virginity!" Pip said and I groaned.

We chinked glasses and thanks to Pip's toast, I downed my fifth glass in one gulp.

When making our way down to the party I had thought that it was going to be in the club part of Afterlife but I soon found out I was wrong when we started towards the Temple. It turned out that the party was thrown here every year and if any of their kind wanted to get married then this was the only date it was done on, to be blessed by the God Janus to ensure a happy future. However, Sophia informed me there was no wedding tonight. They both looked disappointed by this fact. I just gathered it was because they both were suckers for crying at weddings, so I didn't enquire further.

We came into the Temple from another angle but the door we reached still needed Sophia to open it with her blood. She didn't even flinch when something in the hole she placed her hand in cut her palm deep but by the time we were through the door, the slice was closing up. She flexed her fingers as she walked us through the maze of rooms and statues of God, Goddesses and pretty much every mythological creature you could wave a stick at.

Finally, at the end of the long pillared walkway that was all carved sandstone, the great doors at the end opened up by two dressed guards on either side. The light flooded all three of us as the gap got bigger and bigger and when my eyes blinked back the brightness, I gasped at the sight. The largest part of the Temple had been transformed into a black and white wonderland of elegance and splendour. The pillars that spanned the domed ballroom were covered in full length entwined black and white silks making it look like sails on a ship.

The room was aglow with lit church candles in black lacquer holders up to your knees and four branched candelabras in the same style sat in little alcoves or on the white clothed tables set around the edges. Giant wine glasses were filled with black beads that looked like sweets and others had clouded white liquid that was being served in long stemmed glasses.

The whole place looked magical and everyone was dressed in glorious ball gowns and tuxedo suits...but wait... I turned round to Sophia after taking in the whole room and stared at her with an open mouth.

"Sophia...why is everything and everyone in black and white?" I asked just as every eye in the room turned our way, creating a wave of movement that was hard to miss. Only they weren't all looking at

Sophia or the naughty looking Imp stood on my other side who was dressed with one thing clearly on the brain...oh no, not even sexy clad Pip could draw the attention from the only person in the room standing out in a sea of black and white. The only girl at the party...

*Wearing blood red!*

# CHAPTER 55

# 'AT LAST'

"Sophia?!" I said in a stern whisper.

"Ooops!" She said sweetly taking a glass from a waiter and then smirked over the rim at me.

"OOOPS?!" I said a fraction louder.

"At least you will stand out, Toots." Pip said and I wanted to rattle her and scream in her face but that would have just made my skin match the dress I was wearing.

"I think that's her problem, Squeak." Sophia said trying not to laugh. I turned to face her and was about to demand why she set me up like this but she nodded behind me and simply said,

"I am afraid giving me the death ray look won't detract from the fact that I was under orders."

"By who?" I said, not caring if people could hear me anymore.

"By me." A voice said from behind me, a voice that would forever turn my insides to liquid.

"Draven?" I whispered before I turned around and faced a staggering sight...

Dominic Draven was wearing a tuxedo.

"Holy shit!" I blurted out, like the rest of my female family members did at seeing the sexiest damn sight I ever had in my life. He was heart stopping, earth quaking beneath my unsteady legs, drop dead right now with my last breath still stuck, gorgeous! I mean a picture of this man should be in the dictionary next to the world Heavenly.

I started at his high polished dress shoes, following black encased legs up to a matching black tailored suit jacket that hugged his V-shaped frame. His lapels of black satin framed the white shirt and matched his perfectly tied bow tie and I could just see the folded cuffs of his shirt from his long strong arms to the wrist and the glint of his onyx cufflinks. His hair had been styled back from his face and curled just over his suit collar and his face was smooth and freshly shaved.

We were both in some sort of lust induced daze that everyone in the room was witnessing but I didn't care...for once, I really just didn't care. His eyes were doing exactly the same thing as mine and when we both made the luscious journey and drank our fill of each other, our eyes finally met. The silence in the room was deafening to our private show but Draven looked completely unaffected by our audience.

"My Goddess mozzafiato!" ('My stunning Goddess' In Italian) He said loud enough for every single ear to hear and then held out his hand for me to take. As soon as my hand touched his he gripped on tight, striking like a cobra and pulled me into him, where he dipped me over his arm and kissed me until all logical words fled my brain. Once he had finished with me I was placed upright, tucked close to his side and walked through the parted sea of black and white. Now I knew my skin was the same colour as my dress!

He walked us up to a raised platform with a few steps and behind a long table to the two largest seats in the room. Oh god, it was like we were at court and we were the royals of this picture, which for Draven was just fine and dandy, but me...I was just a little Liverpudlian girl way, way out of my league!

The whole room bowed down on one knee as we approached our seats and Draven let me sit first, as he always did. The rest of his council were spread out along the table and Sophia was next to me as in the VIP. Draven then sat and the rest followed suit. Their King called out a command and everyone in the room returned to their activities from before we entered the room. My face was burning the whole time.

"Your beauty knows no limits Keira, you are stunning and I was right, that colour suits you very well indeed...good enough to eat in fact." He said turning his whole body to face me and looked at me with open desire that shone a deep and dangerous purple. He then turned to a server and motioned him forward with the flick of two fingers. The action had me curling my toes in my shoes.

"Bring us some strawberries, I am in the mood for something red, delicious and sweet." The server nodded and walked away, leaving me gaping at Draven.

"I can't believe you did that!" I said in astonishment.

"Ah, so my beauty speaks, good I was worried for a moment there." He pulled me close by placing a firm grip at the back of my neck.

"I could have added soft," he said running a fingertip down my cheek and down my neck,

"Or blushing," he said running it lower over the rise of my flower encased breasts,

"Or ripe," he said openly following the curvature of my heaving chest until he travelled further still to my stomach,

"Juicy and oh, my favourite," he said finally getting to my core which was protected by yards of red,

"Wet. Tell me my Vixen...are you wet for me?" As soon as he said it I sat up straight and grabbed Sophia's glass to gulp down what she was drinking making Draven laugh heartily next to me, but he refused to move his hand from the top of my thigh, even when he turned to speak to his brother.

"You don't play fair." I complained to myself but of course he heard my private thoughts. He looked over his shoulder at me and responded coolly,

"I never said I did, but looking as exquisite as you do, did you really expect anything less?" I scowled at him making him laugh and give my leg an affectionate squeeze before resuming his conversation with his brother.

I looked around the room and saw the largest space in the middle had groups of people all chatting and some I recognised from being earlier regulars from the days I worked in the VIP area. But there was a lot of faces I had never seen before and I couldn't help wonder if these were all of the people Draven delegated to help run the different areas of the world to help in maintaining 'Balance and Order' as Draven puts it.

I then looked down the table and when I saw Lucius sat at the very end I inhaled sharply. I just couldn't help it. The man even knew how to look roguish in a black suit at a formal gathering. He was talking with Adam who was stood at his side with a happy looking Pip on his arm. I had to smile at the sight of Adam dressed in a white suit, black shirt and tie, with a big feather being teased around his head from a naughty Pip who wouldn't ever leave him alone. Even when he kept snapping his fangs at her she would just giggle and then attack him again, only then doubling her efforts.

"And might I enquire as to what you find funny?" Draven asked and I turned to say one name,

"Pip" He looked relieved for a moment before taking up his glass and drinking it dry. I looked back and saw that Lucius was looking at me and he raised his glass my way before taking a large sip. Draven growled.

"I don't think that is necessary, I think you made it quite obvious who I belong to when I first entered." I said with humour turning away from the flirtatious bad boy at the end.

"And so I should as it is my right."

"I agree." I simply answered making him lose the jealously and grin.

"Draven why did you have me wear this massive red dress when it is clearly a black and white night? I stick out like a sore and bloody thumb!" I complained wondering if, A- there would be a time tonight when people didn't stare at me and B- if my flushed cheeks would ever go down.

"Keira, everyone is staring at you simply because you are the most beautiful and remarkable creature in this room, along with any room for that matter...and you're all mine." He ended possessively and I shuddered at the bite in his words.

"Draven, this is hard enough as it is for me but making me stand out like this...it's..." I was trying to find the right words but he cut me off by turning my chair to face him.

"Hey, it's my rules remember...this is my party, this is my game and more importantly this..." He motioned up and down the length of me,

"...is my body, my canvas to paint as I see fit, and tonight I wanted to see you, and only you, painted the same colour as the vibrant love that you make me feel. You make me happy Keira and seeing you like this makes me happy, so you should feel proud not embarrassed that you have done this for me...I am very happy indeed." He said and then kissed me deeply making me truly forget my discomfort. Damn him and his wonderful way with words!

"Better?" He asked dipping his head to capture my eyes. I nodded and he grabbed a white cloth napkin from near his glass and he placed his thumb underneath it to then smear across my lips in a sensual swipe.

"Beautiful, but this I am afraid will get in my way for the need to kiss you more deeply and besides..." He leaned in closer and then whispered,

"I don't think this colour suits me as it does you." I laughed as I turned to see him wipe off the lipstick I had left on his perfect lips.

"Oh I don't know, I could do you up like a dolly one day, you know, some painted toe nails... a bit of blush... as you're not allowed to naturally, due to the handbook and all." I said smirking into my glass.

"You're not that cruel, Vixen." He responded playfully.

"Oh no? Just you wait, I could be."

"Never." He hummed on my neck and I shivered under his lips.

"But just in case I have underestimated my little red rabbit, let me once again gain the upper hand." He said and then he shocked me by standing up and signalling for silence.

"Draven...what are you doing?" I whispered nervously squirming in my seat.

"My friends, guests and loyal subjects, let me bless this night on the Eve of the birth of Janus and let us walk into the New Year never forgetting the steps we have taken behind us, for they are the map we leave for others to follow. So raise your glasses and let us not say goodbye to another year but to the beginning of another important step we take...To the leaders of the balance and all who follow our map!" Draven said in his commanding voice that stole the room of its essence and poured it back out in a powerful and accepting speech of a master and King addressing his people.

Everyone in the room cheered and drank to their King's words, myself included and I was just about to tell him what a good speech that was, and if he thought of a career in public speaking when he continued, adding to an even greater reason for me to get stared at and for my cheeks to melt off.

"And now to start off the evening, I will be taking the floor this year in our first dance...Keira, if you will be so kind and give me the pleasure of your hand as we start with the ceremonial first dance." The look he gave me was one trying to be serious but deep inside was laughing their ass off at the look of sheer horror on my face. I looked at his hand as though it would turn into a snapping turtle and just then the band that was situated further back in a little alcove, started to fill the room with beautiful notes.

"Draven, I'm too short for you... I can't dance..."

"No, but I can, so come on sweetheart, don't break my heart now." He said smiling and I had no other option than to place my shaking hand in his.

"That's my girl!" He said proudly as he pulled me from my chair and took me into the centre of the Temple, where people had formed a large circle of bodies all waiting to watch the show. Well what they would get was me no doubt tripping up their King with a few toe stepping in between.

"Don't look so frightened, I have you." He said softly before taking his stance, with one hand at my lower back. He gently placed my hand at his shoulder and then joined our free hands ready for the right moment to start moving around the open space.

"Ready my darling?" He said sweetly and then the words 'At Last' filled the room shocking me into disbelief.

"At Last by Etta James?" I said knowing the song well as it was the song played for Libby and Frank's first dance as it was at my parents' wedding. My mother had been telling Draven about it when my father had it playing and then grabbed my mum up to dance in the living room as he did every Christmas night. The same night he proposed to my mum, broken down at the side of the road when it started snowing. This song was a family favourite for that reason and Draven had listened intently to the words, nodded once and then said to me, 'very fitting' but didn't elaborate at the time.

"What else?" He said before picking me up by a solid arm banded at my waist, putting me at the right height and then he started to move us around the room in perfect timing with the most perfect song echoing around the most perfect setting, making it one of the most perfect moments in my life...

Dancing in Draven's arms.

"The words in this song are perfect for me in the way I feel about you Keira. My stars are blue for you, my heart wrapped in clover the time I looked at you and Keira, you will always be my dream." He whispered and my eyes glistened over with tears as he put the words of the song to his feelings. And then with another circle of the room with me still being held by one of the strongest arms I have ever known, the song came to an end with the most fitting lyrics that Draven sang back to me in lush deep tones...

Words I completely agreed with...

*"For you are mine at last."*

# CHAPTER 56

# IT'S NOT A PARTY WITHOUT A RAGNAR

A fter our first dance the rest of the couples came and joined us and we had a few more dances, where throughout Draven still hadn't put me down. So when he finally did to walk me back to our seats, I wobbled a bit but Draven just smirked down at me and said,

"Does that mean it was as good for you too?" I winked at him and laughed when I heard him groan behind me.

"Vixen." Was soon whispered in my ear, as I walked ahead of him back to the table.

"Oh that was so beautiful, you two." Sophia said and it was clear to see that our first dance had made her all emotional. So I did the only thing in my heart that felt right, I leant down to put my arms round her and hugged her from behind then softly spoke in her ear,

"Thank you my friend…for everything." She then turned abruptly and took me in her arms and whispered back,

"He has waited so long, Keira…so thank you." She said putting the emphasis on her 'thank you'.

With the night in full swing I turned to Draven and asked the question that I kept asking since being back here and every time I found myself being brushed off in some way, so now I was on a mission.

"Draven, can you please explain to me where Ragnar is and why I haven't yet seen him?" With one look at me and seeing how serious I was, he placed his glass back down and gave me a quick look of concern before standing up.

"Come with me, Keira." He said a bit dejected and I placed my hand in his for him to lead me away. I let him take me from the Temple's main room before I asked,

"Where are we going?" He didn't look at me when he answered.

"I am taking you to him." His voiced sounded so lost I wanted to comfort him but I didn't know how. So with the worry of saying something lame I remained silent until it was clear we were getting near. We had walked through a different section of the Temple and this time we seemed to be heading further underground as the last door to go through was after a series of tunnelled steps Draven helped me step down.

It wasn't far, only five minutes really and easy to get to but the door that stood in our way was made from solid hardwood and crisscrossed with iron strips fastened there by big wrought iron studs. A small metal disc was below what looked to be the locking mechanism and I remember seeing this before when I had found my way into the prison part of the Temple.

I watched as Draven pulled back his cuff and raised his palm to his teeth. One fang grew longer than the rest and I saw his eyes glow in the dimly lit tunnel as the power of the Demon came through. With one quick and efficient swipe, he sliced into his palm making me jump at the sight. I hated ever seeing Draven doing anything that might hurt him but from the triviality on his face it looked like he could have just been cutting his nails for the feeling it caused. He then fisted his bloody hand over the little bowl making an overflow of miniature scarlet rivers come escaping from the confines of his tight bent fingers. The noise of heavy bolts moving back and cogs turning echoed in the space.

"Draven?" I said taking his hand and turning it over to peel back his bloodied fingers. I bent to pick up the corner of my dress then Draven's free hand stopped me.

"No, I will not have you ruin that pretty dress, here take this if you insist." He said passing me a black satin folded bit of material from his breast pocket. I took it and gently wiped the blood away and watched as the cut started to heal instantly. I then lifted his palm to my lips and kissed him there, tasting the smears of blood left behind. I felt his knuckles on his free hand caress my cheek and then he kissed me there saying,

"You are so very sweet to me, Keira." He took hold of my hand and pushed open the door to reveal a gasp from me.

632

I walked past him and wanted to burst into tears at what I was seeing.

"WHY?" I shouted running to the glass cage that was etched with hundreds of symbols that looked like they had been scratched crudely with a set of claws.

"I wanted to wait until after tonight, but I could see I could put it off no longer. I didn't want to upset you." Draven spoke behind me from afar, in a voice so distant it had nothing to do with the space between us. This was what Draven sounded like when he was upset and considering what I was seeing, I could understand why.

"What's wrong with him?" I asked quietly looking at the Demon form of my giant Viking protector who looked lost to the world he once knew. He was situated in the centre of this glass square by chains that attached to numerous heavy metal cuffs. His head held in place by some of these cuffs secured around the great horns that covered his face like a boned helmet.

They were twisted and came from deep within his back but entwined at the point of his chin into a solid beard. His massive shoulders were raised higher than his neck and his clothes were torn and hanging in shreds like limp tails where his size had more than doubled. The most heart breaking thing was this was exactly the same way I remembered seeing him that day on the tarmac.

"He has been like this ever since you were taken." Draven's empty voice explained.

"Why is he in there?"

"I put him there." And just like that I snapped round and said accusingly,

"WHY?!"

"Keira, try to understand. He is an incredibly powerful demon, one intent on destroying everything in his path. When I found him finally woken, we fought and I had to imprison him in here where these runes and scriptures hold his power in check and keep him from killing. But without them he would be too powerful to let loose." He finished explaining and I reached out to the glass to place my palm flat against the cool surface. He didn't move once. He just hung there on his chains and I felt more tears fall.

"What is it I can do?" I asked knowing I would do anything I could to save the life of this man as he was willing to give his own for mine.

"Oh Keira, there is nothing you or I can do…I…I wish I didn't have to do this, but Keira…I brought you down here to say…

633

goodbye." His voice didn't waver but I could hear how hard it was for him to tell me this and how it was even harder to hear me cry out before falling to my knees.

"Keira!" He called my name and then he was there, holding me from behind and trying to give me his strength but it wasn't enough... it would never have been enough to say...

Goodbye.

Draven led me away at the point I couldn't find the energy to cry anymore. I turned one last time to see my friend and saw my handprint on the glass disappear as though being sucked in by the power of the cell and the last thing I thought I saw was Ragnar's chains move. I wanted to go back but I found the door being shut firmly behind me and Draven took my hand to pull me from this place.

I couldn't bring myself to say goodbye and by the time we got back to the Temple doors I had formed a plan. There was no way I could stand back do nothing and if what I saw was true, then maybe there was still hope. But the trick was getting Draven to let me go.

"We don't have to go back in there if you would prefer." He asked but after a quick sniff and snuffle of my nose and a wipe under my eyes, I looked up to his concerned face and said,

"I will be fine... I think I just need to use the bathroom though."

"Certainly, let me take you." Draven said pointing to the direction we should go but I decided it was now or never.

"That's alright, I can manage, but do you think you could get Pip for me...you know, girly stuff." I said and Draven seemed to ease. It was as though being able to do something for me would help ease a guilt that wasn't founded. I knew Draven was just as upset about Ragnar as I was but he just showed it in other ways. But the fact of the matter remained, Ragnar was uncontrollable and by the law of the King, being Draven himself, any Demon or Angel deemed unfit to remain on earth's plane had no choice than to be sent away from it, to their underworld. And that was the last place either one of us wanted to see our friend go.

"Of course, I understand you will want to see your friend. Wait here and I will send her out to you. I will be a moment informing people of our plans but you will find me here waiting for you by the time you have finished...take your time my love." He said giving me a light kiss.

"Hey Toots, what's up, the big man said you needed the pleasure of my Impy charms." I laughed at Pip's graceful approach.

"Oh Pip, you're the only Imp for the job." I said grabbing her hand and tugging her the way Draven and I had just come. She frowned at me and said,

"Hey, unless this is a massive detour, the bogs are that way, Tootie bean."

"I know, but I wanted to show you something first." I said and I knew it was cruel but needs must when my friend's life was literally hanging in the balance. She seemed to accept my deception making my guilt double but now I was at the door there was no going back.

"Umm, I think you made a wrong turn or something here Toots, 'cause this door says we're at a big NO, NO." Oh poor Pip, I just hoped she forgave me after this.

"Oh, you might be right...oh would you look at them, wow Pip you really out did yourself with these nails this time, let me look." I said and she smiled at my compliment, gladly showing me her black and white chess piece nails that as always were razor sharp points. I grabbed her little hand and bent the nail as if to look more closely before slicing it directly across my palm with a hiss.

"Ooops, look what I did?" I said and Pip's face drained of colour.

"Oh Toots, I am so sorry! I should have warned you...give it to me I will heal it for you." She said but I put it behind my back and felt for the little dish hoping Draven's blood was still strong enough inside me.

"Nah, its fine...a tiny scratch plus we should really get back before Draven worries." She shrugged her shoulders and bought my lie before the door clicked open.

"I'm so sorry Pip, I really am." I said before getting in the door quick enough before she could react to my deceit. I slammed the door shut just as I heard her asking 'why?'.

"Sorry Pip, but I had no other choice...tell Draven I tricked you!" I shouted through the door hoping she heard me. When the banging started I knew she had and I had to smile at the blue language she was using.

"Jesus Pip, you would make a sailor blush." I said and when I heard her scream,

"Jesus won't help you when I get my hands on you!" And then with one last bang I knew I didn't have much time before Draven came to the rescue. I just hoped that I didn't need it, I thought on a gulp.

I turned to the glass cage and after a deep breath I did what I knew needed to be done. Draven had explained in my depressed haze that he thought the reasons behind Ragnar's meltdown was due to his past, the feeling of failing his daughter for the second time. With this information, combined with the twitch of chains I saw, gave me enough hope to believe the sight that he didn't fail and that I was still alive, no matter the amount Draven had tried to convince him of this, would be enough to bring him from the depths of himself.

I ran over to the glass door and when I didn't see a little dish or anywhere else to put my bleeding hand to, I just did the last thing I could think of. I slapped it hard to the glass and waited for something to happen. I waited with baited breath and finally just before all my hope was lost, I saw my blood being drawn into the symbols and as it sank further in the cell the glass formed a clear door, void of its capturing magic.

I pushed and walked inside quickly, too scared that Draven would be bursting through that door any minute.

"Hey big guy, it's me…its Keira." I said moving slightly closer.

"Oh come on, you remember me, big pain in the ass that keeps you on your toes." I said trying to keep my distance in case he snapped awake and fancied a snack but when I got nothing, I decided I was not going to pass up on his last chance and mine.

"Okay look, we are pressed for time here so listen up big man, you are my guardian, I offered you hot chocolate that was far too hot, I fell going up the stairs being too loaded down with shopping bags and you healed my bleeding knee, you saved me from the wall of hands, when I was about to get my face bitten off…come on, you know me!" I said but still nothing, so I did the last thing I could think of, which just so happened to be the most stupid!

I took that last step out of the safe zone and raised my hand up as far as I could to touch his horned face.

"Ragnar, come back." I said softly, as a tear escaped. Then like a thunder bolt hitting me from a clear sky, his hand yanked the chain from the floor, giving him just enough room to encircle his hand around my throat and lift me up to his face. The hold wasn't choking but it was still scary as hell and made me scratch at his hand to let go.

"KEIRA!" Draven's panicked voice screamed behind me but I raised my hand up to stop him.

"Draven ssshh, it's fine, he isn't hurting me." I said as I knew it was like showing fear in front of a feral animal.

"FUCK KEIRA!" Draven bellowed and he must have made his move because Ragnar roared at him.

"LET HER GO!" Draven roared back making Ragnar's chains shake.

"DRAVEN STOP…just stop for a second." I said trying to calm it down.

"Ragnar, you know me, but you're lost, you need to come back and protect me, I am in danger if you don't and you would have failed in protecting me…you don't want that do you?" I said making the beast's side of him whine like being wounded. His other chain snapped making me flinch and his other hand came to hold me more gently around the waist.

"That's it, that's better now isn't it…I feel safer but Ragnar I need you to lose the horns and scary shit so that I know it's really you…can you do that?" I said softly making his face come towards me and give me a sniff with an unseen nose.

"KEIRA, PLEASE…Oh, by the Gods, don't do this, don't take her from me!" Draven was losing it behind me and I said the only thing I could in hopes for him to calm. It was like trying to tame two beasts not one!

"Okay, last try big guy, let's see if you have heard this one…Why couldn't the skeleton go to the Christmas party?" I said making sure he got where I was going with this and that the memory of that car journey helped in bringing him back.

"You've got to be fucking kidding me, Keira!" Draven said harshly and I just knew that if Ragnar didn't kill me then after this stunt Draven would!

"Quiet! You will ruin my joke! Come on you big oaf, any guesses….no, Well of course the answer is because he had no body to go with." I said and I waited for it to sink in and couldn't believe it when my body started to shake as a result of the laughter coming from the beast holding me. It took a few minutes of constant rumbling but little by little his size decreased and then the horns retracted from his face. I concentrated in my mind on blocking out the Demon within him and soon I was faced with a very confused looking Viking holding me round the waist.

"Keira?" He said in his usual deep baritone voice and I cried out his name before throwing my arms as far round as I could get them.

"Oh Ragnar! I am so happy you're back!" I said crying into his chest.

"My Lord...is she unwell?" He spoke over my head and I laughed, combined with a little hiccup. I felt Draven come up behind me and gently extract me from him.

"She is more than well now you are back, my old friend." He said softly, placing his hand on his shoulder.

"I fear I am too confused to understand where I am or why...did something happen?" He asked and Draven quickly regained his authority, turned to me and with cold and very pissed off eyes that frightened me, he spoke,

"Leave us!" He snapped making me flinch. In my own anger at being treated like this for saving a life, I childishly let out a frustrated "Arrrh!" I flung my arms up in the air and stormed out of the open door slamming it shut behind me with a force I didn't know I had. The frame work actually cracked!

"You used me?" Pip's little voice said and upon hearing it my anger evaporated.

"Oh Pip, I am so sorry, I had no other choice...I..." I said feeling terrible involving her but knowing I had no choice. Draven wouldn't have let me go to the toilets on my own and Pip was the only one I knew who wouldn't have asked lots of questions.

"Save it, Toots!" She snapped out and then turned on her heel and stormed off leaving me feeling like the biggest shit in this supernatural world.

"You just can't help pissing people off can you?" Draven's voice was like ice and I shivered before turning round to look at him. Oh yeah, he was furious alright!

"I guess not, no, but you know what, I don't regret one single second of it, whether I pissed off Pip or not, I just don't care because I saved a friend's life and if you think that makes me a bad person then I guess I ain't the girl you thought I was!" I said and then I turned on my heel and stormed off following in Pip's footsteps. I heard a mighty growl behind me and then I was roughly grabbed and spun around to face one furious Draven.

"Let me go!" I screamed trying to get free of his unyielding hold.

"NEVER!" He bellowed in my face, making me pull back.

"You act like a selfish, spoilt, insolent child! How dare you do that to me!" Oh shit, now this was mad and in my crazy mind I decided screaming back at him was going to help.

"How dare I?! How dare I what exactly?! Save someone's life! You are one crazy asshole...do you know that! You call me selfish, like saving someone's life by putting my own on the line warrants the word!"

"Ah finally she gets it! Yes, you are indeed selfish! Tell me Keira, did you not stop for one single second in time to think? To use that beautiful head of yours to fully understand what you were doing!?" I tried to move but he decided to put a full stop on that idea and grabbed my wrists in a brutal hold. He held them high above my head and leaned down getting right into my face.

"So you're mad, I get that." I said losing some of my steam.

"Oh I am not mad, Keira..." He came inches from touching me and his eyes burned into me as he said,

"I am seething!"

"Well get over it!" I shouted back, feeling my rage boiling back up.

"Get over it? You want me to get over the fact that you keep coming so close to death you practically beg for it! Is that it, is that the only way you think to leave me because I will tell you this now Keira, if anything happens to you, then they will have me at the gates of Heaven with a GOD DAMN army from Hell at my back! I will drag you back to this earth's plane and lock you away if needs be, but you will remember one thing, you are MINE! In this life or the next, you always will be!" Jesus he was really losing the plot!

"Have you finished?" I asked feeling myself shaking after his threats of the ultimate possession.

"Oh sweetheart, I am not even fully started!" He warned and that was when my limit snapped. I took a deep breath and raised my knee with all my might, hitting him in a place that no matter how Godly you are that will hurt any man. His hands released me and he staggered back a bit in utter shock but I was impressed to see his hands didn't automatically go to the royal baby makers!

"Now it's my turn. I chose you Draven, not because you're some bloody rich ass king that is used to pulling rank and getting his orders obeyed! I am NOT a subject or the crown jewels and this is the life I choose to live, not because you tell me to or not! MY LIFE IS MY OWN! And if I choose to use it for good and in what I believe in, then it is because I was made this way. So this is the moment Draven, you either live with it or live without it, because I am telling you now, if a little girl was ever crossing the road and some idiot that drives too fast was going to hit her, then I would, without one single doubt in my selfish brain, do everything in my power to save her life, even if it meant taking my own!" I was shaking and also lit up like an electrical current was being passed through me.

Draven looked stunned and his eyes scanned my body resting on my fists that were curled tight. But this wasn't what made them even the tiniest bit threatening to Draven, no but what did, was the flickering blue flames that were flowing round them like liquid fire.

"Oh shit!" I said and then looked back to Draven in panic.

"Do something!" I said as I started to wave them around like trying to put out real flames. I couldn't believe how it didn't hurt, hell it wasn't even hot...it was a mad sensation looking at something every single memory of seeing flames screamed a warning of burning heat but to actually feel the cold was the biggest mind trip!

Then in an unbelievable act from Draven, he took one large step towards me and grabbed my face to pull me for a devastating kiss. This kiss was one made of pure and raw carnage, one meant to deliver a message and one of utter ownership, and by the end of the this kiss, I realised it wasn't just him stamping his mark but it was me also.

I felt the negative energy seep out of me and be replaced by one of dark desire. Soon we were like two uncontrollable forces fighting for dominance, duelling for a fight long forgotten but leaving a slipstream of fresh abandoned power behind us. I felt our tense, tight bodies clash together as our hard lust tried to get to grips with the new situation. I felt like I turned into some wild beast trying to claw my way to his body...I needed skin, I needed to feel his body on mine, with no barriers allowed between us.

"Draven I need..." I said over his lips with my hands knotted tightly in his hair, keeping my drug so close.

"Keira, so help me my girl if you pull another stunt like that then..."

"Oh shut up and just don't stop kissing me!" I said tightening my grip, making him growl before giving me what I wanted.

"Oh God, Draven please...please give me what I want...what I need." I begged and he growled again.

"Keira, I will but you have to promise me things." He said pulling my hands from his hair and letting my body slide down from the height he had pinned me at.

"Anything...Draven please...don't torture me." I was shamelessly begging now having upped it a notch. And when I saw Draven's grin he knew exactly what his new leverage was in playing this game, its name...desperation...my desperation!

"You want me to take you don't you? Tell me, speak the words to me!" He commanded and then both his hands ran from my neck, palms flat down to cup my breasts and a sharp inhale told him of my combustible desire.

"Yes...yes...please, I want you...Draven please take me." I said in utter unrestrained hunger. I felt his smile at my neck and damn him but he knew the scales had flipped, putting him back in the powerful driving seat!

"And I will Keira...oh I really will but first you must comply with what I tell you...can you do that?" He said seductively and when I didn't answer, one hand slipped down to cup my sex.

"Oh God! Yes, yes I can...pleeease." I said hearing my own mind beg as well as the words that it produced to ensure Draven fulfilled his promise.

"There's my good girl back. You're doing good Keira, now first tell me...to whom do you belong?" He asked in my ear and just as I was about to defy him and tell him I don't want to play this cruel game, his hand bunched up handful after handful of my skirt until soon he was at my naked core. He touched me once and I shouted,

"YOURS...I AM YOURS!" He actually chuckled, the bastard.

"Yes... YES YOU ARE!" He added on a shout himself and then his fingers stroked through the most sensitive part of my nerves and it felt like he communicated with a deeper part of me.

"Draven." I said his name like I was searching for a lighthouse in the storm, one he himself was creating.

"I know, love and you are doing well...we are nearly there." One more stroke and I moaned at his control...his beautiful and completely irrational control.

"So if you are mine, which we have clearly established you are... then of course this body is also mine...nod your head if you can't speak Keira." He ordered and I complied before receiving another stroke.

"Ohhh...ahh" I moaned but I was so close now, I just needed a little more pressure...just a little bit more, one more stroke...just one.

"Pleeease Draven, give me more...I need..."

"I know what you need Keira, I will always know...so just one more question and this time sweetheart, the last right answer you give me, will get you your reward...and Keira..." He bent his knees slightly to get to my ear before whispering my salvation,

"I will make it a good one!" I almost came apart at those words alone and I think I would have done if not for this crazy man's control over me. My moan was my only telling noise to say I understood.

"Good, you please me greatly. Now for my last question Keira, are you ready?" He cruelly held his palm flat against me and the heat he was passing through my entire sex was ready to burst into blissful deliverance.

"Say the words my love, let me hear you, loud and clear now."

"I AM READY!" I shouted in anger, frustration and a fierce need that was consuming me.

"You are mine, your body is mine, your soul is mine and your life is…?"

"YOURS!" I shouted and then Draven said over my face,

"You're GOD DAMN RIGHT IT IS! And if you ever, ever put it in danger again the punishment will be far worse than this unbearable need I control! I will tie you to my bed and do this to you for hours, for days and I will only let you find release when I say so, do you understand me!?" He shouted out losing his cool for the last time.

"YES!" I screamed at him making him give me an evil grin.

"I see you finally understand the way of things. This is how it is Keira and how it will only ever be. You have done well and I am proud of you." His hand moved slowly and I moaned out as the excruciating build up it created.

"Now open your eyes Keira and COME for me!" He said placing his forehead to mine and his wish became my command! His fingers flexed and applied that delicious pressure I needed to take me hurtling over the edge in to an abyss of mind consuming ecstasy.

"AHHHH…AHH…Ahhhh…hhhh" I screamed as I convulsed under his hand that was still mercilessly taking me higher and higher until I came for the second time. This time he swallowed my screams of rapture with his lips locked to mine and the beautiful wave of euphoria washed over my body, leaving a jellified version of myself in the arms of the one man I loved.

"And I belong to you in the very same way, Keira." He said as he picked my limp body up in his arms and carried me off leaving the plain stone doorway a very memorable place indeed.

"Where are we going?" I asked, really hoping he didn't expect me to be able to dance.

"To a place where I can take what I have wanted to do since finally getting you back to me." His hoarse hard voice told me he was holding on by a single thread of tension wire, one easily broken by this God of a man.

"And that is?" I asked already knowing the answer but needing to hear it with the same amount of tension built.

*"A virginity that was always going to be mine to take."*

# CHAPTER 57
# VIRGINAL DESIRES

Draven hardly spoke as he transported us both through first the tunnels of the Temple and then to the roof of his vast home. He was a man on a mission, that much was clear and as for me, I couldn't wait for him to get there and fulfil it. I even groaned out loud every time we passed a couch, table and then cruelly a bed, just needing any surface for him to throw me down on and take what was clearly always his for the taking.

I had to smile when I found us eventually on the roof top where this all started, our first terrifying kiss that would then set the scene for our heated relationship. See, I had come to the conclusion that no matter how much we argued, no matter how we took the strange world we both had thrust on each other, we still had the one thing that would always keep us tighter together than if we had been fused...

Love.

An undeniable, unbreakable, untouchable love that was set so deep within our minds, within our bodies that we could never dig it out, even if we wanted to. The realisation that this went so far beyond the normal wasn't surprising really, given which two forces had put us together, but the fear of it ever been ripped away was one so terrifying, I clung onto him tighter as the tears formed at the thought. I didn't let Draven know but as he held me tighter to him I knew he had heard.

"Don't be frightened, Keira." He said and that was the only warning I received before he erupted into his demon form and his wings ruffled once, outstretched back as if getting ready and then we took off to the winter sky to Draven's secret place.

645

"How am I not cold?" I asked feeling like I was sat by a fire all cosy, snug and warm.

"Did you really think I would ever let you get cold?" He said looking down at me.

"Don't look away, eyes front!" I said urgently making him finally laugh since our argument.

"Keira, there is nothing up here, what do you expect I am going to hit?" He mocked.

"I don't know…a bird or something." I answered lamely.

"Trust me Keira, if a bird saw me coming, then it would undoubtedly get out of my way." I didn't have a hard time picturing that, as I could just imagine seeing something as large as Draven flying its way, might cause a few little heart attacks to happen.

"You don't seem as fearful flying with me like this, is the reason a good one?" He asked playfully and I felt better hearing it.

"Well, for someone that flips his lid whenever I am in a dangerous situation, then I gathered you would be the last person to ever let me fall." On hearing this, the playful sound of Draven didn't last so long.

"Flips his lid?! Keira if my heart wasn't a strong one then it would have burst long ago at seeing how many times you put yourself in danger. If it wasn't considered cruel and piss you off, then I would have had you a cotton wool dress made to wear and locked you away in my tower!"

"You're not serious!" I said feeling like this might be a crossing fingers moment.

"No… I would have kept you naked in my tower." He said sounding even more serious.

"You do not have a tower." I decided and once again this made him laugh.

"If you like to think so Keira, but if you keep behaving as reckless as you do, you will be seeing it sooner than you may think!" I heard the threat in this, no matter how light-hearted it was meant, as it was obvious just how long Draven had been trying to do just that. The threat of a tower was not something new and it was a warning I received whenever he thought something might take me from him. On some scale you had to love how protective and dominating Draven was and these thoughts had me wishing we would just get there already!

I knew we were flying over the mountains of the national park but with only the moon's faint glow and Draven's powerful essence as our only light source, it was hard to see anything but the shadows of Draven's colossal wing span moving to catch and manipulate the night's air. His wings fascinated me, being an extension of his personality and moving in different ways depending on his mood. The most profound was when he made love to me in this form and seeing how it affected his wings, the way they would tense up, out and backwards. The point they would ruffle after his release before they relaxed close to his body and the way they vibrated under my fingertips when I was brave enough to touch them. This was something I was really hoping to see tonight.

We came in to land and my nerves plummeted with our descent. Draven held me tighter as I couldn't help my fingertips bite into his suit jacket and on instinct I shut my eyes to hide my fear. I felt us come down as Draven's body straightened up and he took a couple of steps to walk into his steady landing.

"Keira." He said my name as a caress and at that moment I would have loved to have known his thoughts on the flight here. I opened my eyes but saw it was so dark that at the moment it was just a black cave buried deep within the cliff side.

"Ah, we have company." He said and I tensed up, wondering up here, who on earth could it be.

"Calm my pet." He said soothingly and up until he filled the cave with a warming firelight, that magically ignited one by one until all along the rough walls were aglow, I thought he was talking to me.

"AVA!" I shouted and Draven let me go so that I could see her. Draven's pet bird was slightly larger than a golden eagle but had the same look, although her feathers were raven black and very much like her master's primary flight ones.

She was nestled into a round bed of twigs and until she saw me she looked quite comfy. But then she got up, ruffled herself and with an elegant stretch, she swooped low and flew behind me. I turned to see her situated on Draven's arm and the smile it brought to his handsome face was infectious.

"Hello my Avis, hush now...calm my pet, she is coming." He said motioning for me to come to him and I did without question, unlike the first time I met her. I looked up at her beautiful face and I lifted my hand up to where she was at her happiest, perched on Draven's arm. When I got close enough, she nudged at my hand with the curve of her beak. So I did as I was requested and stroked down her head to the back of her body. She made a weird pleased sound and Draven laughed when she did as she usually did and that was, show off.

"You know what she wants." I said and he looked down at me with amused bright eyes that reflected the orange flames coming from the twisted wrought iron bolted into the rock.

"I know what she wants but has she deserved it hiding here being a miserable and inconsolable old woman?" He said teasingly making her squawk in his face. He gripped hold of her beak, closing it and giving it an affectionate little shake.

"Well, have you not?" He asked and Ava responded by giving him another little squawk, only this time following it up with a cute little butt on his hand.

"Fine then, you win as usual but I want you to know you are spoilt." He said pretending to be displeased, only boy did she know it as she stretched out her wings and ruffled closer to him making him laugh.

"Alright...alright! Hell's fool is what I am for giving into you every time, here you go my friend...ready yourself now, for it will go far tonight." He warned and then walked over to the edge to lower her down before turning to reach for I gathered was a secret stash of her favourite bird's feet. He pulled back his arm and pretended to throw it and when she was about to go, he tutted.

"No cheating now...alright NOW GO GET IT GIRL!" He shouted and threw it out into the night. I did an excited little noise at seeing her take off at such a speed.

"She is so beautiful." I said looking out for her as long as I could see.

"That she is, but not as breathtaking to watch as another pet of mine." He said only half in jest.

"I wouldn't let her hear you say that, not with those claws." I joked back. He came to stand before me and I had to look right back as always to see his face. I felt his fingertip travel against my cheek, neck and come to a stop at one of the thicker black roses covering my breast from sight. He circled around it, tracing its petals softly, making me bite my lip to keep in the moan I felt coming.

"She knows there is only one bird of paradise in my life... everyone does, don't they my little humming bird?" He stated then nodded slowly himself, making me copy his motions with my compliance.

"Good, then let us see if we cannot make you hum for me." He said in something very close to his demonic voice and I shuddered at the sheer dominance and control being emitted into the air. He grabbed me roughly to him and I felt my body being hauled against his hard chest willingly.

"You are painfully beautiful, Keira." He whispered and I bravely spoke.

"Are you in pain now?" He kissed my neck before answering and then held me captive with his teeth before soothing the slight sting that shot desire straight to my erotic senses.

"Yes, I am indeed and with only one way to ease my suffering I fear it might be taxing on your energy supply…but you will try, won't you Keira?" He whispered and I found my head roll back into the hand he had at the ready. He curled his fingers possessively around my neck when I asked on a breath,

"Try…to?"

"Take it!" He said before gripping my hair and pulling my head back further to take my lips in a conquering kiss. He tasted every last bit of me and more. He pulled away long enough to utter different words of confirmation as to what was happening, what would be happening…his certainty was a warning of such and one I would never heed!

"I am going to consume you, Keira…" He kissed me again, and again he pulled back,

"I am going to keep you here breathless under me until I have to help you breathe again…" Another kiss and another promise,

"I am going to hold you down and make you live and shudder through the intensity I will inflict on you, on what I force upon you…" This time a longer kiss and then his last words were being spoken in a ferocious inevitability of things to come… words spoken just over my lips before sealing his last promise with the last kiss,

"And only then am I going to bury myself inside of you and speak to your very soul, finding my Heaven on earth deep within the home of this body I own and then Keira…" I waited with laboured breaths, knowing that I would soon find my next release with his words alone. I opened eyes bliss had forced closed and found him with elongated fangs and purple flamed eyes with a deadly grin I actually found fear in seeing, a fear that mixed heavily with killer sexual need!

"I will do it all over again!" He roared and then with a quick a twist of his wrist, he yanked my head to the side and bit into my neck making me scream out at one of the most powerful orgasm I had ever known could come from without being sexually touched.

I felt his pull on my blood that mirrored every pull of tremors that kept my orgasm alive for the longest time. Every suck rippled through me as I shook in his arms.

"Draven! Oh, ohh...Draven please!" I called out his name when I couldn't hold onto the intensity of it any longer and when I felt his lips spread into a grin, he released me and licked my escaping blood from my neck in one long and lazy stroke. He held me close and smoothed back the shorts bits of hair that had come loose.

"Ssshh, just breathe sweetheart, I have you now." He said softly as he must have been able to hear my pounding heart. Then I felt his fingertip at the puncture marks he left and soon a tingling crept up on my skin around the area and I knew he had just been sealing his bite shut.

"You should have left it open for the world to know I am yours." I said my thoughts out loud without thinking and I quickly found Draven holding me back at length looking so utterly shocked.

"You just told me your thoughts?" He asked thick with disbelief.

"I...I guess I did." I said shyly, which seemed silly considering what he'd just done to me.

"Did you mean it?" He asked on a held breath and the vulnerability I saw in his eyes was as beautiful as it was astounding.

"I did." I answered simply and his astonishment turned into a level of happiness that made my heart stutter. He then crushed me to his body and held my head to his chest with his hand cradling my neck.

"You make me very happy to hear that Keira and although I would never mark this flawlessly tasting cream that is your skin, for all the world to see, it sends a current of harmony down my spine to hear you say that you would mark it yourself for me. Turn around." The declaration was said in a hum of soft tone and was the complete contrast to the lustful direction he added at the end.

I did as I was clearly instructed and soon the build-up in my core started to climb once again and was readying itself for the next round. As I presented Draven with my back he actually took a step from me and before I could protest his hands came to rest on my shoulders. He drummed his fingers along my collar bone for a moment and it was like he was deliberating what to do with my body first. It was building the tension inside me like a metal coil, getting smaller and smaller, tighter and tighter until finally I couldn't cope.

"Draven?" I questioned with just his name but he just tightened his fingertips and leaned in without taking a step closer.

"Patience is required when taking such pleasure from such a temptress Keira..." He kissed me softly below the ear and then whispered the rest,

"And I plan on draining you dry and drinking in my fill!" The bite in his words brought forth the long moan that no amount of lip biting would keep at bay.

He must have decided what to do to me first as both his hands left my shoulders and quickly he started to take down my hair with deft fingers. Soon the only sound to circulate the cave was that of the crackling of flames in their holders and the sound of pins dropping from steady fingers as my curls cascaded down into the large hands that caught them. Then he gathered them all up and cupped them to his face to inhale the scent of me.

"Les portes d'or à ciel n'ont jamais senti aussi bon" ('The golden gates to heaven have never smelled so sweet' In French) He spoke clear and proud before dropping the curls and sweeping them away to one side over my shoulder. Then I felt his fingers trace my spine down from my neck until he came to the fastening of the skirt of the massive layered dress. I felt him pull the zipper down at an excruciatingly slow rate and if I had been facing him, I just knew I would find him grinning at making me wait. Then his next words made my jelly bones solidify as my whole body tensed causing him to chuckle.

"Excuse me?" I asked just in case I hadn't heard him right.

"You heard me correctly my beauty...Now strip!" He said it again and my heart rate nearly took off and left me. I felt him step away from me and I turned to see him walk further into the room.

It was the first time that I finally had the mental capability to take in the rest of my surroundings. The rock cave was like a secret lair for a giant bird and one look at Draven's purple stare of dangerous demand for my body, it was obviously a bird of prey. The rest of the large space consisted of very little but what there was, screamed out the reason I was brought here. The huge bed was the focal point in the room and dominated its centre. It was round just like Ava's nest and was covered in black sheets. It was so very low to the ground but rested upon numerous scattered black rugs that looked like some type of fur.

I watched as he lowered himself casually on a crudely carved boulder that was cut into a shape of a low backed chair, one that allowed room for his wings to stretch out at the back of him. He undid the single button to his tux jacket as he sat and then I caught my breath as he unravelled his bow tie and undid few shirt buttons, revealing a tanned corded neck straining with the iron will of his control.

"I am waiting, Keira." He said bringing me from my near drooling state and back to his sharp command. He was sat with his legs apart, one hand positioned on his leg, leaning slightly forward with other forearm resting on his thigh and my gaze noted the fisting and flexing of his free hand at the end. This was Draven's control and... it was slipping.

I took a deep breath and walked over to stand before him, only stopping when he motioned me to, about two metres away.

"Take it off!" He ground out between clenched teeth. I would have been smiling at the power I had over his senses if the look on his face told me I daren't. I reached down and gathered up as much of the material as I could and pulled it up and over, taking the clingy top with it. I felt my hair cascade down my back and with the effort combined with the blatant lust coming like steam from Draven, I was breathing heavy.

"Lose it!" He snapped and I threw the dress to the rough ground like it was no more than a rag and Draven's eyes grew hotter in approval. It made me stand a little prouder and with a deliberate cock to my hip and a not so innocent suck on my bottom lip, my single audience growled.

This time it was as if he couldn't find the strength to speak so instead he held up his fisted hand, keeping his elbow resting on his leg and held up a single finger. I watched his command in the form of a circular motion indicating I should turn round for him and with a quick breath and close of my eyes, I did as he wished.

I turned round on my heels and felt the floaty material of the underskirt lap at my smooth legs like cool water on a warm day in August. Hell, under his eyes my skin was scorching hot and even the winter night next to us couldn't ease the burning Draven put there. As soon I came back round to face him, the same commanding finger twitched for me to come closer. As it stood I mustn't have been close enough because on a quick growl he snatched out and took me by the waist, yanking me hard into position.

Once there his hand spanned out against my waist and he ran his palms up my sides with a slow intake of breath. My neck felt like it would no longer hold my head up as it started to fall backwards on a roll.

"Look at me, Keira!" He said, his voice broken with his Demon seeping through the cracks. My head whipped up and my eyes widened at the intensity I saw. I had never seen Draven so controlled yet so in pain by the very fact.

"I want to look into your eyes as I finally get to unwrap my gift from the Gods." He said before raising himself up and soon I was being overwhelmed by one suited Demon blooded male that was tensed to a finely tuned cord. I then quickly found myself looking to the caves ceiling as I heard the sound of rock and metal moving against each other. I could see something in the shadows coming closer as though on an invisible track and then I saw it as it stopped over me. I looked straight up and audibly gulped.

"Draven?" I whispered but his only answer came like a possessed animal. He caught my neck in his hold to still my obvious trembling with his teeth and once it had forced me to stop, he spoke against the bitten skin.

"Don't question me on this, Keira!" It wasn't a tone I was stupid enough to argue with, even when his next order was spoken.

"Raise your arms for me." I took a brave breath and raised them up until they could go no further.

"Good. Now hold onto the chain and don't let go until I tell you to." I nodded, let him place my grip around the cold metal links and then lowered my head. I felt his fingertip tap my chin once,

"Eyes on me, sweetheart." I remembered my place, lifted my head up and his endearment touched me as if his own fingers had stroked down the length of me. Then his hands stopped their repeated motions at my sides and he came to the tied bow of the ribbon encased corset I had been wrapped in.

"What a gift!" He whispered to himself and then, with a little tug at the ends, he unravelled the bow and started to rid my body of thick ivory satin ribbon. He continued to work in a crisscrossed pattern and with my arms suspended above me by my own free will it made it easier for him to gain access to all areas of my body. Soon there was a little mountain of satin on the floor by my feet and the plain boned corset was on display. He ran his hands over every last bit of it and soon the chains rattled as I trembled with the strain of desire pulling at me for another release.

"I think I have put you through enough for my entertainment for

---

take you...

have waited...

properly." Oh no,...

"Draven, please y...
other time he had kissed...
barrier of a triangle piece of the...
the amount of bliss it brought me, I...
it again. I wasn't a prude by any means...
one sexual act that until Draven, no boy had...
the utter vulnerability I felt being that open for...
frightening to me.

"You're not about to tell me what I can't do with this t...
are you Keira...because I warn you, that would be unwise." I...
seriously and when he saw my rising panic at the one thing I had ne...
experienced completely, he came over and softly soothed my fears.

"Hey, look at me...I would never do anything to you that your body would say your body agrees, now it is just time for your mind to catch up...don't be frightened my pet, I take good care of my gifts."
He said and then kissed his way down my body so gently it could have been done by his feathers.

"This, however lovely, is in my way to something lovelier." He stated and then ripped my underskirt into two strips all the way up to reveal my naked sex.

"That is much better." He commented looking down at me and I tightened my legs in a reflex of my embarrassment.

"Keira!" He warned and then tapped the top of my tense thighs until I opened up from him. I took a few deep breaths and with my teeth embedded firmly in my bottom lip, I opened myself up for him for the first time. The sharp intake of breath from him had my cheeks burning into molten flesh.

"By the Gods you're beautiful!" He said and then gently ran a finger along first once side of the triangle of trim blonde curls and then along the other side, making me moan each time. Then he ran a single fingertip back to the top and this time ran it the full length down in the middle, parting me as he went.

"Ohhh...ummhh!" I moaned louder, longer and in even more indistinguishable noises.

"Do you feel that Keira...that tingling heat that is travelling from

655

now." He said running his hands up my arms and uncurling my fin
from the chain. He pulled them gently down and rubbed them
until the tingling faded.

"You please me greatly, with not only your exquisite bo?
your utter compliance. Now lose the shoes and go lay c
wait for your reward." I noticed the way he said 'c
warmed me from the inside along with the soun?
stamped into every demand.

I stepped out from not only my shoes but als
walked on unsteady legs to 'our' bed. I did ?
was finally here, I found my nerves co
building need heightened every sense in ?
live wire being played with...toyed wit?
power to light me up. One look to D
quaked with another wave of emit?

"Lie back." His voice broug?
sat up and staring at him wit?
flash of a dangerous grin b?
did as I was told and lay?
than anything I had ever fe?.
stop myself from touching myse.
I heard heavy breathing over me I o?.
over me like an impending force that w?
the inside out. The size of him looked increa?.
outstretched and it was like a Dark Angel of me?.
find me waiting and wanting the way I most certainly ?

"Virginal indeed and all mine for the taking." He
getting down on one knee. He came over me and I was abou?
him in an embrace when he captured my wrists suddenly.

"My game first." He said across my waiting lips. Then he pushe?
my arms back up and before I could stop him he had tied my hands
together with the satin ribbon and secured me to something I couldn't
see.

"Your smooth skin looked incredible next to the hard links of iron
and if I could find something soft enough then I would have your
whole body wrapped up in chains but for now, this will do." He said
and kissed me softly on the lips and then laughed when I tried to yank
my arms down.

"Draven, what are you doing?" I finally found a steady enough
voice to speak, although it was shaky at best.

my finger to you and right back again. That is the oldest language in
the world. That is my body communicating with yours on such a deep
level that the only part translated into understanding is a simple
word...connected. I will always be able to talk to your body Keira,
with a simple touch. But tonight I want more...I want to taste the very
words your body speaks to me Keira and this time...I am going to
SWALLOW YOU WHOLE!" He shouted out the last part and with his
hands at the ready he pushed my thighs apart as far as they would go
and held me immobilised as he began to devour me whole.

I screamed out as soon as his tongue grazed my small bundle of
nerves and soon he was lapping up my release like a starved man. I
soon found I couldn't have cared for my embarrassment at him
discovering the very last inch of me unexplored. I couldn't concentrate
on anything but the sensations he was forcing upon me and if I thought
after an orgasm he would be finished, I was oh so wrong. No, after he
had licked his fill, he just went right back to stroking, teasing and
sucking hard on making me give him another one.

It soon became an erotic dance with us moving to the music of my
screams. I would beg...beg for him to stop, beg for him to carry on,
beg for him to take me further, higher, longer and faster than I have
ever been. I was in blissful delirium. I was being consumed by wave
after wave, providing feast after feast for this raging beast to gorge
on... And boy did he gorge!

After I had lost count and was fading fast he must have felt my
body being rung dry as he made this his last meal of me. I felt
wonderfully abused and as the pressure unbelievably rebuilt.

"Keira, open your eyes for me, my sweet girl." I did but it felt like
trying to pry them open after someone had glued them shut. Draven
was met by lustful half lidded eyes that watered thanks to the
overwhelming drugging overdose on orgasms.

"I am sorry my darling, I got carried away and took too much out
of you...here drink this." He said and through my blurred vision I tried
to feel for the rim of a glass only to find a wrist.

"Draven?"

"Ssshh, it will help, just drink and gain strength from me...I am
selfishly not finished yet...not by far." He said and then placed his
wrist to me and I felt the warm thick liquid touch my lips.

"Draven, no!" I tried to push him away but he just chuckled and
forced his blood upon me. Once I swallowed that first drop, it was too

hard to stop. It wasn't as gross as you would expect drinking blood to be but felt more like drinking a Red bull when you needed the energy kick. The taste of blood didn't really even register as his essence filled me full of a warming glow that I couldn't fully explain. I think in terms of cars then this would be my equivalent to going to the fuel station and getting treated to premium.

He eased his wrist away from me and I felt a swipe of his thumb wipe away any excess blood from my lips.

"I perversely get a sexual high watching you suckle on me like that." He said after clearing his throat from its hoarseness. I smiled while still keeping my eyes closed and purposely made a meal out of licking my lips and smiled when I heard his frustrated groan.

"Do you feel better? By the Gods tell me you do because you are killing me here waiting for my home-coming." He said with such intensity that I felt my new energy zing to life on the other side of my skin, like his blood was making every cell to scream out at him. I raised myself up as much as I could and then whispered in what I knew would be just as husky as his own tones,

"Then come and get it, Dominic!" Then everything exploded.

I watched in amazement as Draven erupted into more of a brighter light like Vincent and the ends of his twitching feathers turned a blazing white. His expensive suit burnt away from him like a melting negative film strip and soon my eyes were drinking in the most Angelic form of Draven I had ever seen.

He tore open my corset like the metal hooks weren't even there and the material was even ripped from its constricting steel bones. Then he snatched out and snapped the ribbons holding me down and brought up my bound hands up and over his head, locking me as close to his body as I could get. Then with a twist of hips he was ready and positioned at the place he called his home, the entrance to my body and the doorway to touching my soul.

"Say it with me Keira, say the words together as I take the very last step in merging your soul to me...SAY THE WORDS!" This time the voice I heard didn't belong to his Demon side but the booming power of Heaven, making me gasp and with one driving force and the only words that ever mattered, we both shouted together...

"I LOVE YOU!"

"I LOVE YOU!" Then he drove all the way home and destroyed anything in his path as he arrived at my door to the hilt and I was screaming another release and rippling around every last inch of him.

"GODS!" He roared over me, then placed his forehead to mine to wait intimately for my mortal body to adjust.

"By the Heavens above Keira you are so deliciously tight, I must be hurting you?" The intense look he gave me was so full to the brim of emotions I couldn't have named them all.

"You could never hurt me, Dominic." I said and upon saying his name in sweet undertones on the shore of paradise he created, the wave hit and he kissed me with complete ravishment. Once he let my lips slide from his teeth in slow capture, he manage to finally speak,

"Ready?" The one worded question was not only crushed through clenched teeth but it also looked to be the only word he could manage. His face was tense and I knew it was taking all his heavenly strength to hold back for me and when I smiled up at him and cruelly raked my nails down his scalp with tied hands, he growled.

"Oh sweetheart...you really shouldn't have done that!" He said before his movements had me screaming beneath him in intoxicating rapture. He pounded into me, circling his hips to hit the same sweet spot every time and instead of letting my pressure build to bursting and then halting the process so that I could endure more, like he usually did, this time he just let me explode. And explode. And explode. And explode again and again, all the time keeping his own release locked on the pinnacle edge until I was crying out that I could take no more.

"Draven! Draven, Draven! I can't...I...Ohohoh, God! Draven... pleeease!" I begged, hitting the very point where I couldn't take any more orgasms that he kept sending crashing my way. With his hands everywhere he could get to and with every different angle and nerve his hard length could touch I felt myself coming apart once again.

"Draven...pleeease" I begged again feeling the delicious build up that would no doubt this time be my undoing.

"Alright my love, this one last time I promise, now open your eyes and come with me...NOW!" He thundered out as he tensed before finally joining me in my life shattering release.

"DRAVEN...AHHHHHH!" I let go of my cataclysmic scream.

"GODS KEIRA! AHHH...HHH!" He screamed his own devastating shout of pleasure as he pulsated inside me and I gripped on tighter and tighter until he was screaming again as any normal time for the waves of bursting before euphoria hit, was tripled in Draven and it meant taking my own waves along for the ride. And then I felt it, the whole room had started to shake as if an earthquake was vibrating up through the mountains.

I screamed in fright as I saw some cracks form in the ceiling but before I could try to act, Draven's wings were thrust outwards covering us both in a glowing canopy of feathers as Draven continued his immense release, despite the obvious devastation it was causing to the surrounding environment. Or the raining of rock and debris hitting his wings that were still shuddering as he pumped himself deep within me, drawing out the last of his true essence and then I realised what he said was never going to be more true than in this moment...

*He really had communicated with my very soul.*

# CHAPTER 58
# MISSING FATES

After that moment of devastating and most perfect experience of reuniting our bodies, we both passed out still entwined in the most intimate way. I awoke to find my arms still tied behind his neck, my body completely encased in not only his arms but also his wings and the most delicious of all, with his manhood still firmly seated inside me.

When I shifted a little, his length twitched inside of me in protest, his arms tightened me closer and his wings curled round creating a firmer seal around our bodies. Then I saw dreamy eyes open slowly and it was sweet to see him as he took a moment to assess our situation. Once he did a lazy smile erupted and the memory of last night was no doubt what brought on a deep grin.

Waking up this way was the most amazing start to an epic day. We actually spent the rest of our time locked away in his private cave and when we weren't cuddled up talking, we were recreating some of the same blissful moments of last night. I watched as Draven laughed at the state of his cave after his erupting emotions and then he began to fix the rock as though it was a very natural thing to be done after such a literal earth shattering sexual encounter.

Of course, I soon found out why it was so natural as we discovered round four with me being once again tied to the bed. I think in fact I may have found a little fetish of Draven's and when I teased him about it, he simply answered that 'it must be down to him never before encountering a primal need to keep my body in a position ready for his taking'. I had shuddered before we found round five with me taking lead on top.

But after that most exquisite day in Draven's nest, life found a sort of normality that before had been in disarray. The New Year brought along new possibilities and for the first time nothing stood in our way for the only thing we wanted and that was, of course, to be together. Lucius and Draven now had a sort of alliance and although it wasn't as strong as it had once been, the very fact that Draven no longer wanted to kill him was a big plus.

But just before they were all leaving to go back to Germany, Draven nearly lost his control when I asked to say goodbye...privately. After one of our big arguments that wonderfully ending in lots of make-up sex he finally agreed. I hadn't yet really spoken to Lucius since 'The Triple Goddess' incident and my growing need to see him was about the same level of effort Draven was putting in keeping us apart.

I could understand why and my first sight of Aurora had me feeling the same way but every time the subject came up we would ended up fighting our battle in the healthiest way...in the bedroom.

So now here I was, waiting for Lucius to walk back into my life, ready to say goodbye. I found my confusing thoughts brought on both nerves and apprehension. I didn't know when exactly it happened, when Lucius went from being my captor, to my friend to then lastly my saviour, before I became his. But all I knew was that it had happened and as much as I would never admit so to Draven, I knew that I would miss him.

I waited in a small sitting room that I hadn't been in before and for Draven it was the best choice as I knew he was near. It was decorated with lush reds and burnt oranges of the Middle East and the cherry wood timber furniture shone to a high polish. A comfortable looking sofa to match was where my jittery body waited and when I heard the door, I shot up.

Lucius let himself in and closed the door behind him which made me jump.

"Nervous, Sugar?" He said amused and my heart stuttered at the sight of him. He was in usual Lucius fashion, dressed casually in a pair of charcoal grey jeans and a tight black long sleeved t-shirt with the sleeves pushed back to reveal strong forearms. His hair was a disarray mess that always seemed styled that way. His steel grey eyes had flecks of ice blue and the easy smile he wore was cocked to one side with an added playful and roguish charm that gave him the title of 'ultimate bad boy'. And with one look I didn't know what came over me but I ran over to him and threw a massive hug his way making him sound out an "umff!" before chuckling.

"I guess not nervous then…. call me crazy but I definitely detect a certain level of Vamp withdrawal… by any chance did you miss me my pretty doll?" He mocked and I laughed once before giving him a quick jab in the ribs.

"Not at all!" I said smiling and then stepped away to motion for us to sit on the couch. He nodded and we walked over to sit side on so we could talk facing each other.

"I have to ask you something, Keira." Lucius said his face turning serious and brooding.

"Go ahead." I said knowing there was only one thing he could possibly want to know, so I wasn't surprised when I heard only one word come from him,

"Why?" His voice sounded strained and he was now fisting his hands as if trying not to reach out and shake the answer from me.

"I could never have let you die Lucius, even if you can be the biggest asshole in Germany." I said smiling, making him roll his eyes.

"I never wanted that from you Keira…your life. I was always meant to protect it, once I found out who 'else' you were."

"You mean because of what I show you?" I asked feeling my cheeks heat as though I was showing him the sun all over again.

"Yes, but now I know it means so much more." He said raking a frustrated hand through his hair.

"What do you mean?" I asked cautiously.

"Don't you see, it wasn't just the sun, it was my sun, my past and my resentment of the Gods that was a grudge held for over two thousand years. You didn't just show me the last sight I saw in my death Keira, but you showed me the last sight before my forgiveness, which was my rebirth." He got up and then came to stand before me and kneel at my feet, putting us at eye level.

"I…don't…"

"Draven hasn't told you. Keira, I am now like Dom, I now have two forces fused inside me. I thought having the rest of the spear would make me a more powerful Demon and maybe if what happened hadn't, then it could have done, but it was you…you gave me my faith back, you set me free!" He then leant his head down and kissed my hands that had started to twist the bottom of my sleeves anxiously.

"But how?"

"You saved my life, the Fates predicted the one that showed me the sun, the light, would save me and not just my way of life. For a mortal being to take a death that was meant to be mine was enough for the decision to be made that if a child of the Gods could see the good in me then that was to be my second chance. I am now a Vampire Demon and an Angel of God which was promised to me all those years ago." I couldn't believe it, now Lucius was like Draven! This was too much information to take in.

"What happened to you, the reason Draven gave you the tip, he knew what you would become, and he knew it would take you both to bring me back…didn't he?"

"It was all prophesied, yes. It was the very reason he kept it from me all these years but that I am sure you already know." I did and the smile I gave him just confirmed it.

"So, what will it be now, should I start calling you Judas or are you bad ass, cocky Lucius forever?" I teased.

"Umm, I am quite partial to Lucius as it is and besides, I don't think Judas would have quite the same effect with the ladies." I laughed taking him with me in the teasing mode and soon the conversation drew to an end.

"I have to ask Lucius, why were you willing to give me back to Draven without hopes of getting the spear tip back?" He got up and I joined him at the door.

"Because someone once told me a truth I didn't see until the sun shone on her beautiful face." I gulped down the lump that was like a massive ball bearing and asked the question I would always regret if I didn't, knowing I might never see him again.

"And what was that?"

"That power won't ever love me back and she was right, power was only ever gained in loving her!" I gasped at the words I knew and before I could say another word, he lifted my hand to his and kissed the back, never taking his eyes from mine and then said the words that had a tear escaping,

"Good bye, My Little Keira Girl."

After that very door opened, another great friend came ploughing in and soon I was in tears at having to say another goodbye I really wasn't ready for.

"I love you, keeper of my heart."

As the weeks went on I couldn't tell if things got easier or harder. It felt like the first time I came here and I didn't know what to do with myself. I kind of just bumbled around like a lost soul searching for something I couldn't see but knew was still there. It was like trying to find my feet in a new life all over again.

The only times that eased the pain I felt was when I spent time with my sister or my friends. Jack was his usual charming self and we would go to the horrible diner a few times just for a laugh and RJ would complain that we were both clearly insane. We spent a lot of time together and even though I was asked why Afterlife had closed for this length of time I never really had the heart to find an answer. As to Draven, well my phone would go enough times to know that we were still a couple, that was until the end of the month, just before Libby's due date.

I would stare at my phone for hours just trying to will it to ring and then I would give in and ring him, only one day he never answered it. I knew from that moment in time something had changed in the world, so devastating and horrific but I had no idea what. It was only after a whole forty eight hours of constant ringing everyone I knew on his side that my answer came.

The doorbell went one day and I couldn't believe who was on the other side.

"Leivic!" I shouted when I saw one of Draven's best friends at my door. Only something wasn't right, the smile he gave me was all wrong and my heart plummeted at the sight.

"Leivic, what is it...what's happened?" I said reaching out to him but he moved out of my way. He looked down as if what he was about to do he couldn't bear to see my eyes when he did it.

"Please, you're scaring me." I said feeling the tears already forming.

"I am so sorry Keira, I didn't want to do this but this is my debt to Draven that after all these years is now finally done and believe me when I tell you it is the hardest thing I have ever had to do." My hands flew to my mouth and I shook my head in denial.

"No, no, no...he can't! He's leaving me?" I shouted and when I saw a single tear fall from his eye I knew it was worse than that...

"No Keira...I am so sorry but..."

"Just say it!" I shouted making him flinch back and then as soon as the words came, my world collapsed, and I found the broken ground in tear fogged eyes, which would be the end of my days...

*"He's dead, Keira!"*

To Be Continued...

# ABOUT THE AUTHOR

Stephanie Hudson has dreamed of being a writer ever since her obsession with reading books at an early age. What first became a quest to overcome the boundaries set against her in the form of dyslexia has turned into a life's dream. She first started writing in the form of poetry and soon found a taste for horror and romance. Afterlife is her first book in the series of twelve, with the story of Keira and Draven becoming ever more complicated in a world that sets them miles apart.

When not writing, Stephanie enjoys spending time with her loving family and friends, chatting for hours with her biggest fan, her sister Cathy who is utterly obsessed with one gorgeous Dominic Draven. And of course, spending as much time with her supportive partner and personal muse, Blake who is there for her no matter what.

### Author's words.

My love and devotion is to all my wonderful fans that keep me going into the wee hours of the night but foremost to my wonderful daughter Ava...who yes, is named after a cool, kick-ass, Demonic bird and my sons, Jack, who is a little hero and Baby Halen, who yes, keeps me up at night but it's okay because he is named after a Guitar legend!

### Keep updated with all new release news & more on my website
www.afterlifesaga.com
Never miss out, sign up to the
mailing list at the website.

Also, please feel free to join myself and other Dravenites on my
Facebook group
Afterlife Saga Official Fan
Interact with me and other fans. Can't wait to see you there!

facebook.com/AfterlifeSaga

twitter.com/afterlifesaga

instagram.com/theafterlifesaga

# Acknowledgments

Dear Dravenites,

You will always be the first people I thank as each and every one of you have made this wonderful dream possible and turned what was a hobby I loved into a job I love! You will always have a special place in my heart and I will forever be indebted to you for having faith in me and in the Afterlife Saga.

And just remember I am your fan!

My next thanks goes to my eccentric fun family who have taught me that life is about the chances you take and enjoying the journey they lead you to. My wonderful mum, who has dedicated endless hours of dealing with my quirky spelling mistakes and giggling over a few of them too. You may even thank her for getting the chance to read Afterlife as it was down to her convincing me it was good enough to publish, so flowers can be posted to...Just kidding!

We can all thank the amazing and very 'eye' catching front covers to my extremely talented sister Cathy, who puts her heart and soul into every pixel created. You make Afterlife shine and now thanks to you, hundreds of people are saying,

"We Crave the Drave"

As always there are lots of bands I listen to while writing this book but instead of trying to name them all I will suggest just one song to be listen to and that is 'At Last' by Etta James as Draven and Keira's first dance needs to be read in only one way...with a glass of wine, comfy sofa, a few tears and the music blasting! So give it a try as it is how I wrote it

Also, in the mix are the incredible men in my life. As you will find that behind every great loving and caring man in Afterlife is a result of my Dad and my fiancée who has made working each day a pleasure I wake up to. The support my husband gives me in writing this saga is immeasurable and mirrors my own enthusiasm when giving life to my stories. He is my anchor in the storm that is my imagination and keeps me floating along the waves of discovery.

I love you my rock

Another personal thank you goes to my dear friend Caroline Fairbairn and her wonderful family that have embraced my brand of crazy into their lives and given it a hug when most needed.

For their friendship I will forever be eternally grateful.

I would also like to mention Claire Boyle my wonderful PA, who without a doubt, keeps me sane and constantly smiling through all the chaos which is my life ;) And a loving mention goes to Lisa Jane for always giving me a giggle and scaring me to death with all her count down pictures lol ;)

So, I will now say goodbye until the next book and with your help we can one day see the fruits of our labour from the supernatural seeds we planted and get the Afterlife saga to go mainstream! To join our Afterlife revolution, please check out the facebook pages and twitter, along with joining my mailing list for sneak peeks and free chapters.

Happy Reading everyone!

# ALSO BY STEPHANIE HUDSON

Afterlife Saga

*Afterlife*

*The Two Kings*

*The Triple Goddess*

*The Quarter Moon*

*The Pentagram Child /Part 1*

*The Pentagram Child /Part 2*

*The Cult of the Hexad*

*Sacrifice of the Septimus /Part 1*

*Sacrifice of the Septimus /Part 2*

*Blood of the Infinity War*

*Happy Ever Afterlife /Part 1*

*Happy Ever Afterlife / Part 2*

*The Forbidden Chapters*

\*

Transfusion Saga

*Transfusion*

*Venom of God*

*Blood of Kings*

*Rise of Ashes*

*Map of Sorrows*

*Tree of Souls*

*Kingdoms of Hell*

*Eyes of Crimson*

*Roots of Rage*

*Heart of Darkness*

*Wraith of Fire*

# OTHER WORKS FROM HUDSON INDIE INK

## Paranormal Romance/Urban Fantasy

Sloane Murphy

Xen Randell

C. L. Monaghan

## Sci-fi/Fantasy

Devin Hanson

## Crime/Action

Blake Hudson

Mike Gomes

## Contemporary Romance

Gemma Weir

Printed in the USA
CPSIA information can be obtained
at www.ICGtesting.com
CBHW020815190724
11837CB00007B/20